# THE ODIUM TRILOGY

THE UNIVERSITY OF ODIUM
RETURN TO ODIUM
THE END OF ODIUM

"The novel that simply cries out to be a TV mini-series ... the *House of Cards* of the modern British university ... a thrilling satirical exposure of the witless evils of today's academy."

"Clockman has done it again! It's all here: the obloquy which taints all who choose to serve in today's university; the tyranny of social media; Brexit; the banal realities of modern anti-terrorism; even a zombie and ripe evidence that the #MeToo movement is an understatement. I laughed all the way through then wrote my resignation letter."

"At last Clockman's great comic trilogy is concluded. Quentin Tarantino meets the campus novel in an ecstatic renovation of the genre. Gone is all the humanistic twaddle and intellectual imposture which have beset the depiction of universities in fiction since day one. In their place we get the modern institution in all its cold-blooded malice, mean-spirited calculation, narrow-minded prejudice and, ultimately, maniacal self-destructiveness."

J. D. Clockman

---

# THE
# ODIUM
# TRILOGY

THE UNIVERSITY OF ODIUM
RETURN TO ODIUM
THE END OF ODIUM

London
**Jet**stone
2021

A *Jetstone* paperback original.

ISBN 9781910858189

Cover design by The Ever-Shifting Subject.

# CONTENTS

FOR JAMES BINNS

# THE UNIVERSITY OF ODIUM

This is a fiction. The events it depicts
are entirely imaginary. None of its
characters, thankfully, has
any real-world
equivalent,
living or
dead.

## Chapter One (20 September)

Two men stood facing each other in post-handshake awkwardness.

The one who had introduced himself as the Registrar said with professional breeziness, "You have me at a disadvantage, Professor. I've just moved back into this office after summer redecoration and it's taking me a while to unpack things." He gestured with a handsweep to the cheap wooden crates littering the expensively wooded room.

The other man, who was in his early sixties, seemed to know that the Registrar, who was in his late fifties, was wondering how his secretaries had been bypassed. This other had introduced himself as the Professor when the first man had introduced himself as the Registrar. Now he said, "Buckrack."

The word sounded, to the Registrar, like some kind of insult.

"I beg your pardon?" said the Registrar.

"Professor Buckrack," said Professor Buckrack.

"Oh!" the Registrar chortled. "Of course. I am Dr Asterisk. But I prefer it if senior members of the academic staff call me Nigel. Some of them insist on calling me the Registrar, which seems a little over-formal."

Buckrack allowed nothing to be said for an interval. Once the interval had become uncomfortable for Asterisk, he replied, still standing, and with a look at the boxes on the floor, "So, Asterisk, you mean it's taking a while for you to get someone to unpack the stuff for you?"

Furrows appeared on Asterisk's disconcerted brow.

Buckrack continued, "I went into your main office before I came in here, the large open plan one next door, where all your support staff work. Their packing cases were all being removed. They finished emptying them yesterday. Of course, they unpacked themselves."

In an English accent, suffused with some vague historical right to moralism, these observations might have been taken as an affront. In Buckrack's broad Californian, infused with an edgy Bogartian menace, they prompted guardedness rather than retaliation. Asterisk smiled. The excessiveness of the smile gave the appearance of unctuousness, behind which the reality was possibly little different. So Buckrack mused while Asterisk stepped over the crack in the conversation.

"I simply meant I did not have the relevant paperwork concerning you to hand," he explained. "Of course the Vice Chancellor did mention to me that you would be arriving, I knew that. Usually, though, you would see him rather than me. That's why you find me a little unprepared."

Buckrack grunted. "Yeah, Covet's not in town," he said routinely.

Asterisk evenly replied, "Sir Evan … The Vice Chancellor, yes, that's right."

"Where is he?" asked Buckrack sharply.

Asterisk looked puzzled. "I'm unsure, to be honest. It doesn't seem to matter much these days. International calls are so cheap, one is always connected, one's Blackberry is always on, there is little reason to ask."

Before Asterisk had concluded Buckrack had taken out an iPhone and speed dialled. It was at his ear by the time Asterisk had finished. "Or to tell," Buckrack said, as the number he had called started to ring. Asterisk watched, fascinated by the man's astringency with words, and what seemed his unprofessorial directness.

"Hey, Covet," Buckrack hollered into the phone. "Where are you?"

At this Asterisk's eyes widened.

"What's happening, you ask?" Buckrack waxed on, turning his back on Asterisk, stepping fluidly across the crate-strewn floor, and taking a seat on an ornamental *chaise longue*, from which vantage point he stared out of the window across the quadrangle, his face three quarters hidden from Asterisk.

Asterisk hissed with concern, "I think he's in the States!" and was ignored. "It's the middle of the night there!" Still he got no reaction.

"Singapore, huh?" Buckrack turned briefly and looked sideways at Asterisk. "There's a place called The Swastika Hotel not far from the airport. Never been in it, but when I see it *en route* I always think of you, you being so Buddhistic and all."

4

Asterisk, upon whom a feeling was dawning that he had entered the ring as a boxer only to discover that he was actually the referee, noted that this was said without the obvious traces of humour that might allow one to detect that it was mere joshing. The Vice Chancellor was a Presbyterian and did not much indulge in irony of the kind that must have been intended in Buckrack's last remark. Asterisk continued to listen, with increasing curiosity and decreasing self-confidence.

"Yeah, never mind. Listen, Covet, your man Asterix here, he seems not to have been briefed. You won't mind filling him in."

To Asterisk's consternation, Buckrack proffered the phone with his left hand over his left shoulder, all the while continuing to look away, his face turned to the window. Asterisk crossed the room gingerly and took the phone. Buckrack stayed where he was. Asterisk retreated to his previous position and, perplexed by the body language of Buckrack, turned half away and supported himself lightly on his buttocks on the edge of his substantial escritoire, which occupied the area of a ping pong table, but was ten times the mass and fifty times the density. He cleared his throat.

"Vice Chancellor," he warmed. "My apologies, I thought you might be at the meeting in Chicago."

A second later, Asterisk hauled himself off the desk, almost to attention. "Yes, Vice Chancellor!" he affirmed. Then he smelled something acrid. He turned his head and, to his astonishment, saw that Buckrack had lit a cigarette. The American continued to face the quadrangle, his demeanour unreadable.

The trebly squeak of a raised voice in the earpiece of the phone reached even Buckrack's ears, although he could not make out the individual words. Asterisk stood even more erect, yet the stiffened stance had the curious effect, Buckrack saw, as he watched the reflection in the window pane, of making him appear more, not less, discomposed.

"Of course, Vice Chancellor," repeated Asterisk, but with no joviality this time. "Go ahead. Do you mind if I make notes?"

There was another harsh squawk from the phone.

"I see, nothing in writing. Understood. Do go on, Vice Chancellor."

Buckrack counted sixteen *sotto voce* expressions in the side of the conversation on which he then eavesdropped. There were two *indeed*s, four *of course*s, one *naturally*, a further *understood*, a pair of *I see*s, a *really*, two *I shall*s, one *without fail*, one *I'll take care of it*, and one final *golly*.

The first non-phatic thing Asterisk said was some time after Buckrack had dropped his cigarette into the dregs of a convenient coffee cup he had been using as an ashtray. The utterance signalled the end of the monologue from Asterisk's interlocutor, and seemed a gloss on what Asterisk had heard. It was said in a titter that implied a humorous attempt to show understanding and complicity with shady matter: "A covert ops kind of thing, then."

This provoked a high pitched, unmistakably berating rasp from the phone which was, like the others, indecipherable.

"Oh no, Vice Chancellor, I'm not taking it *too* seriously," Asterisk reassured. "But I know that I should take it *somewhat* seriously."

This was said as if to demonstrate that a profound nostrum had been learned and was now engrained. Then, as if to fill up a silence, Asterisk went on, "Vice Chancellor, you know that I shall – ". But there he stopped and fumbled for a button. The silence evidently meant that the call had been unritualistically terminated on the other end.

There was a longish pause. Buckrack did not stir. Asterisk moved the phone in his hand pensively a few times. He was breathing deeply. He was striving for grace under pressure, a pose he liked, and a phrase he used a good deal. The effort made him forget Buckrack for a moment. He put the phone on the desk.

"That's not yours," said Buckrack almost instantly, still facing the window. At last he turned. It seemed an invitation to Asterisk to take a seat beside him on his own *chaise*. Asterisk slowly acquiesced, but had to stop halfway across the room and turn around to retrieve the phone, which he then held out to Buckrack. The American took the phone, examined it, and pressed a button on it.

"I am sorry, I thought I had hung up," said Asterisk, sitting down and leaning too far back. He propped himself correctively forward.

"You did," Buckrack replied.

Asterisk took another deep breath, which helped him rally.

"Well," he said. "Professor Buckrack."

Buckrack said nothing.

Asterisk waved his arm in the air gallantly. "Everything seems to be in order," he said. "The paperwork is all taken care of, I understand, and I am told you don't need the customary tour, or the usual round of introductions. The Vice Chancellor looks forward to seeing you when he returns, and you report directly to him."

6

"That's right," said Buckrack. "It was you who needed to be briefed, not me. But I might need to talk to you again, given that Covet won't be back for a while."

"Oh." Asterisk bobbed slightly on the seat. "You know when he's returning?"

"Yes," said Buckrack. But he did not enlighten Asterisk as to when.

Asterisk smiled apologetically. "Yes." He pressed his hands together. "I must apologise. I was unaware."

Buckrack put his phone in the top pocket of his jacket. "Of what?" he said.

"Of the terms of your appointment. I thought you were the usual kind of Professor."

"I see."

A pause lengthened into another silence with which Buckrack seemed at ease but in which Asterisk appeared agitated.

"Universities these days are places where one should not simply assume things," he said. "I should have asked before the Vice Chancellor left. I made the mistake of assuming."

Buckrack still said nothing.

Asterisk added, "But everything's cleared up now."

Buckrack arose. Asterisk stayed where he was. Looking up, eyes necessarily widened, with a little bit of visionary inspiration suddenly appearing in them, he said warmly, "Actually, it's one of the challenging things about the job today. Everything used to be predictable and, I'll be honest, a little dull. But nowadays something unexpected – something you'd never imagine in a traditional English university – happens quite frequently."

"You betcha," said Buckrack, looking at the door.

"But then everything has changed so much," Asterisk continued. "Did you know, for example, that we now have a campus in China and another in India?"

Buckrack did not reply but gazed at Asterisk unblinkingly.

Asterisk gathered himself and stood. "Before you go, if you wouldn't mind, could I ask you something?"

"Go ahead."

Asterisk looked a little embarrassed, but the embarrassment seemed to hold the promise of an enquiry he hoped would be annealing, soothing, more conciliatory than the discourse had felt so far.

"Have you seen *The West Wing*?" he asked.

Buckrack paused impatiently. "Isn't that exactly where we are? I think I even saw a sign."

"Oh," said Asterisk, "of course, this *is* the west wing of this particular building. But I was referring to the American TV series. You know, Martin Sheen, President Bartlet, all that. Do you know it?"

"Sort of," Buckrack said, and decided to reach for another cigarette.

"The Vice Chancellor gave everyone on our Management Board a box set of all seven series, so we're all entirely fanatical about it."

"Let me guess," said Buckrack. "Covet thinks there's a lot you all can learn about running a university from watching a bunch of actors pretend to run the White House?"

Asterisk smiled affirmatively. "And he's right, you know! He's right. The situations are so similar. The dilemmas. The human drama. The characters! And that's what I was wondering. After I finished speaking to the Vice Chancellor, I was wondering which character you were."

Buckrack's eyes narrowed. "Which character am I? Which *West Wing* wannabe am I? Well, tell me – it might help me decide – which character are *you*?"

"Well," Asterisk essayed, with a look in his eyes suggestive of attempted but failed modesty, "as the Vice Chancellor is evidently the President ... "

"Evidently," agreed Buckrack.

"And he is a lawyer, so ... "

"Evidentially," agreed Buckrack.

"Well, I must be Leo McGarry."

"*Really*?" Buckrack whistled softly. "The White House Chief of Staff, huh? Well, who would have guessed? Is that who you are?"

Asterisk nodded enthusiastically. "I think so."

"Well, tell you what," Buckrack smiled, "we'll have a drink some time and talk more about it. But tell me before I go, have you ever seen *24*?"

Asterisk bit his lip slightly and put his head to one side. "I have heard of it. But I can't say I've ever watched an episode."

Buckrack flipped a cigarette between his lips. "Then you don't know who I am." And with that he left the Registrar's study, a cloud of silver tobacco smoke and yellow nicotine dust mushrooming up towards the high ceiling as the pure oak door swung heavily shut.

"Ladies," was Buckrack's terse valediction as he exited through the adjoining secretaries' office. Alison Stilt and Rachel Brace stared at him in the wonderment that comes from realising *no, one hasn't, after all, seen everything,* and then at each other in the same mode through the trailing grey exhaust he left behind, and then yet again with the same sense of novelty in mind at the closed door of Dr Asterisk's chamber. But the door did not remain, as it often did, inscrutably closed. Instead, Asterisk appeared, looking heavy-browed and menacing, in the mode of a boy who has been bullied and wishes to revisit the punishment on someone weaker.

"Rachel," he said, levelly, "please come into my office."

Buckrack carried the quarter-smoked cigarette in his hand along the empty ground floor corridor until he exited by swing doors into the quadrangle, where he threw it in the nearest flower tub: salvias, he reckoned, if their height was anything to go by. He removed a small bottle of Listerine from his left coat pocket and swigged from it, washing his mouth out so thoroughly that the trilling echoes of the vigorous gargling could be heard ricocheting from the walls of the small flagstoned yard. It was not exactly, he reflected as he swilled, an Oxford or Cambridge cloister. In flat white limestone, with hardly a hint of ornateness in the masonry, and an angular, unimposing gilded clock tower, the building which enclosed it seemed, if anything, a somewhat shrunken, cake-top rendering of London's Senate House, which was the inspiration, he seemed to remember, for one of the Ministries, though he could not recall which, in Orwell's *Nineteen Eighty-Four.*

A jet of corrupted mouthwash landed in the flower tub and made the still live cigarette go *phut* and expire. Buckrack took out his iPhone and started up the voice recorder app. As he listened cursorily to the preliminary exchange between himself and Covet he marvelled, not for the first time, that the effects of mobile Listerine were almost as convenient as those of the mobile phone. His tonsils and tongue tingled anew with the chemical tang. The disgustingness of the tobacco was almost instantly obliterated. Menthol floated lightly past his adenoidal cavity into the nose, and he was reminded how, for all that England's culture was pathetic and its citizenry pitiable, even in its unimpressive pockets one could find air of clarity and sweetness that seemed undiscoverable on his side of the pond. And it was true enough. The early autumn ventilation up here on University Hill was a hundred times fresher than in LA. Odium might be a crappy little provincial town, but there were still some things here, like that slant of jaundiced morning light tilting through the archway on the left, falling cold and weak and beautiful on the white paving, you could only dream of in California. He allowed this reverie to captivate him for the few seconds until he heard the exchange between Covet and Asterisk commence:

> ASTERISK: Vice Chancellor, my apologies, I thought you might be at the meeting in Chicago.
>
> COVET: Oh shut up, Nigel. I'm in bloody Singapore. Stop thinking and pay attention.
>
> ASTERISK: Yes, Vice Chancellor!
>
> COVET: Listen very carefully, Nigel. I don't want any screw ups.
>
> ASTERISK: Of course, Vice Chancellor. Go ahead. Do you mind if I make notes?
>
> COVET: Of course I bloody well mind. You know the drill, Nigel.
>
> ASTERISK: I see, nothing in writing. Understood. Do go on, Vice Chancellor.
>
> COVET: Buckrack has appeared on the scene.
>
> ASTERISK: Indeed.
>
> COVET: He should give every sign of being a grade A bastard.
>
> ASTERISK: Indeed.
>
> COVET: That's because he *is* a grade A bastard. Bastard *summa cum laude*. There's very little else you need to know.
>
> ASTERISK: Of course.
>
> COVET: He has a one-year research contract, and no affiliation to any particular School or Department. There's a reason for that.
>
> ASTERISK: Of course.
>
> COVET: It means he's not accountable to any of the usual peasant mob of Deans, Pro-Vice Chancellors or Professors. In fact, they don't even know about him.
>
> ASTERISK: Of course.
>
> COVET: He has no office, so no one can locate him. He has no University email address, so he leaves no written traces anyone can request under DPA or FOI. He answers only to me.
>
> ASTERISK: Of course.
>
> COVET: Don't pry. Don't get yourself in any way between him and me unless I deliberately put you there.

ASTERISK: Naturally.

COVET: Otherwise you'll only get crushed.

ASTERISK: Understood.

COVET: Give him whatever he asks for.

ASTERISK: I see.

COVET: You can check with me first if you are uncertain about the, er, legality.

ASTERISK: I see.

COVET: He might make some unusual requests.

ASTERISK: Really?

COVET: Don't query them. Just meet them.

ASTERISK: I shall.

COVET: If they seem wildly beyond reason or budget you just tell him you need my authorisation and call me immediately.

ASTERISK: I shall.

COVET: Nigel, I need you to follow these simple instructions *to the letter*.

ASTERISK: Without fail.

COVET: The man is going to sort out a lot of our problems. We'd better give him a codename. Let's call him *Avenger*. It's best you ingratiate yourself with him. Ensure he's comfortable in his house. Check with Butcher in Estates.

ASTERISK: I'll take care of it.

COVET: The reason I am telling you to keep your nose out of things is that he has special, shall we say, talents. But he's also, er, *dangerous*. Gelignite in the wrong hands.

ASTERISK: Golly.

COVET: That's why everything must be under the usual radar.

ASTERISK: A covert ops kind of thing, then.

COVET: Oh for Christ's sake, Nigel, shut up! Sometimes I think you take my odd White House analogy too seriously.

ASTERISK: Oh no, Vice Chancellor, I'm not taking it *too* seriously. But I know that I should take it *somewhat* seriously. [*Pause*] Vice Chancellor [*Covet hangs up*], you know that I shall –

Buckrack put the phone away, tucked his hands into the pockets of his coat, took in a gulp of cool late September air, and stepped out into the quadrangle. He decided to go for a morning walk.

11

**Chapter Two (20 September)**

At around the same time as Buckrack was shaking hands with Asterisk, had a TV or movie camera been panning across the front bay window of a house in Baltimore Street in Bigton – a small satellite town about a mile from the west entrance of the University of Odium – it would have shown us a middle-aged man sitting in an armchair beside a zimmer frame in a dressing gown and exhibiting all the other relevant cinematic or televisual signs of terminal illness. As the camera moved it would reveal to us two other people: the back of a young woman in recognisably nurse-like garb retreating into the kitchen beyond the living room, having put two mugs of tea on a table in front of the evidently dying man; and the profile of another man, preparing to consume the second cup, whose age was between that of the nurse and the soon-to-be-corpse. We would gather enough, knowing viewers that we are, of the general situation without any audio, for it would be skilfully done, with years of *mise-en-scène* know-how and more-than-a-BBC budget behind it. There would of course (ah, verisimilitude!) be something to hear anyway: birds twittering, cars in the street, that kind of thing. But for the details of the particular narrative circumstances spoken language would have to kick in. That would not be a problem, because if there were a camera outside the house there would also be conveniently hidden microphones in the room, which would miraculously allow us to hear what was being said for a few seconds even before the camera point of view switched seamlessly to the interior of the comfortable, spacious lounge where we could, without the apparent knowledge of either Cartwright Miller or James Redman, eavesdrop on their hi-fidelity, hi-definition, Dolby 5.1 surround sound conversation (in which the birds and the cars would now sound from behind our heads while their voices would manifest themselves from a position before us).

Miller seemed to be in very good cheer for a man who will be mouldering in the grave by the fifth chapter of this tale. The conversation was clearly just getting going.

"You know," Miller was saying, "I had a call from an academic acquaintance the other day who actually thought that Macmillan nurses were something one in three British people should be grateful to *Harold* Macmillan for? I had to put him right and tell him, no, that old dipshit and his heirs simply made a profit out of publishing your books, my friend. What next, I asked him, eh? Did he think we were going to have Thatcher Alzheimer Clinics? A blasted Heath Healthcare Foundation? How far might his delusions of ex-Conservative Prime Ministerial charity stretch?"

Redman smiled, but seemed cautious about levity combined with cancer. "You seem, well … "

"Well?" retorted Miller. "I'm not at all well. But I am euphoric at the outcome! I've waited three months for this. It's been agonising! So you can imagine."

"Yes, I meant, well, you seem in good spirits, yes."

"It's probably the morphine," Miller rejoined. "Kylie there helped me shoot up ten minutes before you arrived. You know, it's actually quite fun, being a junkie, knowing there are no consequences. No problem chasing the dragon when there is an atom bomb heading straight towards your head, is there?"

Redman inclined his own as yet untargeted head non-committally.

"I'm sorry," said Miller. "I am making you uneasy. Gallows humour is not so funny if you're a healthy sympathetic onlooker. Look, old chap, you've done a fine job on my behalf. Please tell me all about it."

"About my meeting with Asterisk?"

"Yes, and spare me no detail."

Redman addressed his teacup and then sat back, occasionally referring to a file folder on his lap. "Okay. I called him, as I told you when we spoke on the phone briefly last night, around 4pm. He was not keen to have a meeting with me personally. Said he would rather wait until the hearing this morning. Eventually he caved in and offered me an audience at 5.15. I did see Rachel Brace on the way in and there was a meaningful exchange of looks between us, but nothing more. Asterisk was haughty and gave the impression of bearing my presence as some immense favour. There was a little small talk about the Performance Review and pay negotiations while Rachel brought in coffee and said she was leaving. Then he told me he was surprised that I thought there was anything to discuss about what seemed to him a straightforward case, and he asked me to come to the point.

"I enjoyed a few preliminary remarks, made it clear that I was speaking to him with your full knowledge and that I had your permission to speak on your behalf as your Union representative, given that you were medically incapacitated. He did ask how you were, but I

13

don't think he really listened to the answer, though his head made the appropriate movements and his eyes were fitly downcast for a second or two. I then summarised the case a little, recapping how the meeting scheduled for this morning essentially concerned your grievance to the effect that you were prevented from assuming the Directorship of Information Services, a post to which you had been fairly appointed, for which you had been offered a draft contract as yet unsigned by either party, and which you were due to commence at the beginning of August. I told him we considered that there was no defensible reason for their decision not to appoint you but they had so acted because they had discovered that you were terminally ill. I said that the case would be made from your side that they were not prepared to countenance paying you at the Director's rate through an illness of indeterminate length from which you would not return to service, and that instead they decided to leave you, illegally, as Deputy Director. I made the point that this was detrimental to your likely death-in-service benefits or, if you survived, your pension entitlement upon ill-health retirement."

"And how was he through all of that?" asked Miller.

"He seemed bored. He said that he knew all this from the paperwork but that he could absolutely assure me that the grievance was groundless because the assumption on which it rested was false. He indulged in a long windy circumlocution about how valued a colleague you were and how, even had they discovered that you were terminally ill, they would never have dreamed of altering the terms of appointment for the alleged reason. The plain fact of the matter was that they had not known of your condition when they made the decision and that this could be satisfactorily demonstrated. They had simply decided, in the light of recent administrative and funding developments, which he was of course not at liberty to divulge, that there had to be an unexpected restructuring of the management system in Information Services and that your appointment had of necessity to be reconsidered pending the result of that restructuring. They had expected, he claimed, to appoint you to the corresponding post in the new structure, although he could not vouchsafe a date when that might be agreed upon. He regretted that it had come to a grievance hearing. He felt positively sad that you trust the University so little that you can suspect that it would even contemplate such a dirty trick, never mind go through with it, for the reasons alleged. He urged me to ask you to reconsider a course of action he thought you had taken in a state of clouded judgment."

"Did he seem convincing?"

"With what I had in my hand he could hardly have sounded convincing to me. But I think he was convincing to himself. I asked him to confirm that the decision to rescind the offer of contractual employment was taken at the Management Board of 21 July. I then referred to the University's response to your grievance, which carried his signature, and which stated that the institution had no knowledge of your illness until a communication from you of 23 July. He corroborated both dates. At that point I looked him straight in the eye and asked him to reconsider the claim that he knew nothing about it before 23 July. He smiled back at me and said he had no doubt whatsoever. How could he know before you divulged the fact? He opened his palms in a gesture of accused innocence. I thanked him and fell silent."

"How good a liar is he?"

"He's an excellent liar. Not a blush, not a facial tic, full eye contact, sincerity personified."

Miller smiled. "I love it. So, after the silence?"

"The silence lasted a good five seconds. It seemed to puzzle him. He started to look at me as if I were a little unbalanced. He said, 'Is that it? You asked to meet me just to check facts which, as I have said, are already stated in the papers?' I said no, that I had come to show him a piece of paper we had withheld so far because of its sensitivity. And then I put it on his desk in front of him. He picked it up with exasperated patience and began to read it with histrionic tolerance. It would be about three lines in that I swear I saw the hairs begin to stand up on his head, as he realised what he was looking at."

Miller was almost biting his nails. "Christ, I wish I could have been there!" he hissed.

"I admit it was enjoyable," said Redman. "I said to him, 'Dr Asterisk, that is a word-accurate transcript of part of a telephone conversation you had with the Vice Chancellor about Mr Miller on 19 July. I draw particular attention to your words, *the doc says the sad loser is on his way out,* and the Vice Chancellor's reply, *then put the brakes on the dying fucker.* The entire exchange makes it clear that you both had explicit knowledge of Mr Miller's condition from a named source in the Medical School, and that you were deciding to withdraw the offer of promotion to Director from him on those exact grounds.'"

15

"Said the spider to the fly!" rejoiced Miller, and then coughed phlegmily, and waved at Redman to go on.

"Of course he looked horrified, but was trying to keep this from seeming too obvious. If his head and brain had been made of glass I am sure I would have seen a lightning storm of electrical impulses flashing from synapse to synapse. But all he could think to say, in a tone of insincere moral outrage, was: 'This is *monstrous*! Where did you get this?'

"I said, 'The recording is now in the Union's possession. It was made by you yourself on your own mobile phone.'

"He threw the paper on the desk. 'Rubbish!' he said. 'Even if that were true, how could you possibly know that or obtain it? This is a fabrication. Why would I do that?'

"I replied, 'I can only guess, but knowing this University as I do, I imagine it's one of a number of illegal and/or immoral acts the Vice Chancellor has asked you to commit and that you were recording the conversation surreptitiously as a kind of insurance for yourself in the event of being found out. It would prove that you were simply acting on his orders. Unwittingly, that's exactly what the recording does allow us, the Union, to prove, as well as demonstrating that a University Hospital consultant breached doctor-patient confidentiality to you personally. Your signature on the response to the grievance proves that you lied about the date on which you learned of Mr Miller's illness.'

"He was goggle-eyed by now. 'But it's useless. You cannot use illegally obtained voice recordings in a court or an employment tribunal!'

"I told him that only he and the Vice Chancellor and the doctor had done anything illegal, or immoral, or unprofessional, or all three. The recording was legally obtained and the Union was not intending to use it in a legal setting.

"'How did you get it?' he asked.

"I told him straight: 'It was copied from the memory card in your phone.'

"By this point he was bewildered. 'You stole my phone?'

"I said, 'No one stole your phone.'

"More bemusement. 'But how?'

"I said, 'You will have to work that out for yourself, Dr Asterisk. I assure you no one stole your phone or hacked into it or did anything illegal in respect of it. I acknowledge that there was arguably a breach of privacy but then, as the phone is actually University property, and the content of the call records illegal intent, I don't think anyone is going to think there was not good reason for that. And I very much doubt if it needs an employment tribunal to make the evidence effective. We were thinking more of what would happen if its contents were revealed by the media. You will consider the consequences of that – for you, for the Vice Chancellor, for the member of staff in the Medical School, for the University's public reputation.'

"I suppose by this time his subjective state was rather like someone who has been in a car crash and comes round finding himself trapped in his seat with flames and smoke visible in the rear-view mirror. There was a long, shocked pause. And then he said – "

"No!" Miller interrupted. "Let me guess. He flung his arms out and said, 'What do you want from me?' That's what they all do on the TV."

Redman smiled. "No. He put his head in his hands and said, 'Oh, crap!', which was a much better line. Then he did pretty much ask what I was after. So I told him that we wanted to prevent the grievance hearing from taking place today, or else I would have no choice but to table the evidence at that meeting. The easiest solution to the entire matter would be to honour the original decision to promote you so that you were in post, with the Director's salary, at the point of your decease or ill-health retirement. He said he couldn't see how that was possible. Such a decision would have to go through Management Board and the contents of the phone call could never be explained to members of MB and, in any case, if he let the Vice Chancellor know that he had recorded the call that was being used as evidence, all hell would break loose, he would virtually be committing career suicide. He said I was holding a gun to his head. I said that was true but that he had given me the gun, loaded it, and taken off the safety catch. Then I told him I had to leave. I gave him my card with my personal number and said he could call me that evening if he came up with a solution, otherwise I would see him in the morning at the hearing. Suddenly he wanted me to stay and talk but I left. He called me about two hours later. He said he had spoken to the University's lawyers and that he would be able to make a Compromise Agreement with you at the earliest possible opportunity. If we could postpone the grievance hearing he would negotiate the agreement with us before the end of the week. Employers use these agreements to sweep their dirty deeds under the carpet. They pay employees sums of money, often large sums of money, in return for their agreement to take no legal action against the employer for their employment hitherto and to keep all details of their prior employment confidential."

"You didn't say on the phone how much he agreed to pay," said Miller.

"That's still to be negotiated. And we need our lawyers to vet the draft agreement. But I told him that if he was considering a sum less than six figures then he could forget it. He said okay after a bit of a gulp. This process must be one he has some control over without referring to Covet, or if not he thinks he can finesse it somehow. Who cares? Hence why I am here now and not at the scheduled meeting. I am seeing him later this morning to get the ball rolling on the draft agreement."

"Good golly gosh, old boy!" Miller cried. "Spiffing! Christ, you fucked him ten times over!"

"Technically," said Redman, "it was Rachel Brace who did that. If she hadn't given me the recording from his phone ... "

"Ahem," said Miller, altering his sitting position into one that seemed morally less comfortable. "Yes, Rachel. I'm afraid that on that score I have a bit of a confession to make. You see, I persuaded Rachel to give you the recording. She is retiring in a month, detests Asterisk utterly, is seething for revenge upon him, and there is nothing he can do any longer, even if he can prove her involvement, to harm her. He will suspect her, of course, because he gives her his phone all the time. He doesn't know how to install applications or updates and has her do it for him. But, ahem again, I'm afraid I lied to you a little. Rachel does not listen to his voice recordings and didn't know about this one. It was me who told her about it, who gave her the copy of it, and asked her to give it to you."

Redman was baffled. "I see. But how did you know about it?"

"James," Miller confessed, "I'm the Deputy Director of Information Services. I was the Director Elect. I have theoretical access to every piece of information on any piece of University hardware, mobile phones included. I can, technically speaking at least, read any email and listen to any call. It's largely not even legally dubious: in law, all this data is University property and I have licensed authority to control it. In the case of Asterisk and Covet, I know that they never put anything incriminating in writing. It's all done by phone. I simply installed a bit of software in the telephony system that recorded every conversation made from each of their mobiles and landlines. We have security in place to detect such snooping but, being who I am, I was able to disable that."

"You had a *wiretap* up on their phones?" exclaimed Redman.

Miller shrugged. "I had been diagnosed with the big pancreatic C a fortnight before. When you know you are dying and are beyond the law you find yourself curiously free to do things you would never otherwise dream of doing. What can I say? I caught them in the act. I somehow thought they might do the dirty on me. But I wanted to ensure that they did not find out how I knew. That's where Rachel Brace comes in. If push comes to shove, she's prepared to take the rap. She too has nothing to lose and in some ways I think she'd like him to know she shafted him. They will think she simply took it off his phone and hopefully look no further. And, again hopefully, they will continue in the same vein, unawares, to record their dark secrets by phone."

"I see," said Redman. "Why *hopefully*?"

"Why, so that someone else can stop them, or nail them." Miller fished inside his dressing gown pocket. "I am hardly the only one they do this sort of thing to. You know that better than anyone. And you have been so good to me, James, so conscientious, so brave and resolute in many ways. It takes guts to do what you do. I was trying to think of some way to say thank you."

"Don't thank me. It's the Union, really. That's what gives me the authority."

"Well, the Union, then." Miller held up a USB thumb drive. "On this device are MP3s of all the recordings of conversations between Covet and Asterisk since early July: nearly three months of material. I don't understand it all, but you might. A lot of the personal references seem to be in code. For example, they always refer to me as *Loser*. But Asterisk screwed up in that call to Covet because he quoted the doctor using my real name. So I got what I needed from that one call. I didn't pay too much attention to the rest as I was too tired and none of it seemed pertinent and a lot of it I didn't understand. The executable file on this drive is the programme I used to make the recordings. It's configured so that, if it's installed on any University PC, the snooping cannot be detected by our internal data security. The calls are auto-recorded and downloaded to a secure off-site external server. You just choose your login details for that server and away you go. You are notified by email whenever a call has been recorded. Obviously you should not use your University email address for that. No traces are left on the hard disk of the machine itself on which the software is installed. It just acts as a transit point."

"Let me get this right," Redman asked incredulously. "You mean you are offering to let me *take over your wiretap*?"

"Not you. The Union, really. It may not be Watergate, old boy, but still, it could be one hell of a ride!"

## Chapter Three (20 September)

Most professional workplaces are, in essence, the sum of their conversations. Actions taken are often outnumbered by words spoken by hundreds of thousands to one. In a twenty-first century university, this ratio is more extreme than almost anywhere else, especially in view of the fact that the actions taken there often consist of little more than going and speaking, or sometimes writing, even more words to other, more people. This is exaggeratedly the case in faculties of Arts and Humanities, in which hardly any non-linguistic actions are ever taken at all. The denizens of these university corridors are primarily engaged in activities to be located somewhere within an algebraic continuum in which $q$ speaks to $r$ to entreat her to persuade $s$ to have a word with $t$ about an overlooked document written by $u$ that should have been revised by $v$ with subsequent approval by $w$ (and is so approved after $w$ has emailed $v$ a reminder about it), who then forwards it to $x$, who will review and further endorse it (after having spoken testily on the telephone to $w$ about $v$'s tardiness and affectionately over coffee to $u$ to inform her that she will ignore $w$'s approval of $v$'s incompetent revisions), letting $y$ know, who will confirm to $z$ that he can report the approval to $q$ who makes $p$ aware of the outcome; $p$ then complains to $o$ about how long all this has taken and the fact that the final approved document is not really what she was hoping for, namely $v$'s revised text that $w$ was kind enough to have shown her recently and said he had approved; $o$ then tells $n$ that $p$ is complaining in her usual way, as she does about everything, and $n$ reports confidentially to $p$ that $o$ is having a dig at her again, as she does at every opportunity. And so on.

At exactly the moment Buckrack finished delivering his valedictory and half minatory "Then you don't know who I am" to Asterisk, and Redman was staring in disbelief at the USB stick in Miller's outreaching hand, which he thought may already be a criminal item but knew would certainly become one if he took it and used it, the conversational baton was in danger of flying through a silent lapse of wordless air. But it was immediately caught and carried forward by Avril Poon, Associate Professor in the Department of Cultural Studies, and Sergei Krokoff, an improbably Ukrainian Professor in the School of English Studies. They had convened by appointment in the cramped space of room D4(b), which was Poon's office, and was in the same west wing of the Trump Building as Asterisk's more commodious quarters, but three floors higher up.

"This needs to be a conversation private," Krokoff began. "I would not want colleagues to know of. Not anyways right now."

"Okay," said Poon.

"I have problem," Krokoff went on. "With female graduate student."

Poon's deep brown eyes revealed themselves to him across the top rim of her glasses. "You don't say, Sergei," she said. "Would it be the first time?"

"Hah!" Krokoff exclaimed. "Is nothing improper. I think you think is hanky-panky or something. No. She is not nice girl, not Krokoff's type at all."

"I see," said Poon, but her eyes did not retreat behind her spectacles. "And if she *were* your type, Sergei?"

"No, she is not. Is dog. I mean, she is harmless puppy. You would know if you saw her."

"I wasn't asking *why* she is not your type, Sergei. I was asking *what if* she were your type?"

"Avril!" This was said with a long extension of the opening vowel: *Aaaavril*. The tone was one of wounded innocence. "You are going all feministical on poor Krokoff. I understand. Is not necessary. I am not here because you are President of Union and I have got myself in hot bath. Is academic matter."

Poon reclined a little in her chair and put her eyes back behind glass. "Okay. Go on."

"But has bit of embarrassing confession in it. That's why just between you and me."

"I understand, Sergei. Do please explain."

"Okay." Krokoff hunched forward and put his fingertips together. "Let us call this student Jane."

"Does she not have a name of her own?"

Krokoff knotted his brows. "Yes, is Jane. I said just now."

Poon sighed. "Okay!"

"Something is wrong with name Jane?"

"No! For goodness sake, Krokoff, get on with it!"

"Okay. Now this student, name Jane, she comes here from America with good, effective, first notch B.A., so good she win research scholarship, Vice Chancellor's Award, not even any need for Masters. Her Ph.D. proposal is right up my road, on the importance of 'things not said' in English novel. Narratology, very much a bag of mine. The proposal mostly about the Brontës but it also has legs, can spread. So like me you are thinking *Wuthering Heights*, how whole plot of book in fact cannot happen unless characters fail importantly to tell other people things crucial you or I would tell each other in real world most probable. So like Nelly Dean, who readers think insignificant character, just housekeeper, she is always choosing not to tell – "

"Sergei!" Poon intervened impatiently. "I get it. She had a research topic for which you were the appropriate supervisor. So?"

"Righto it is. So she arrives in January this year. We talk. Her initial idea is that her first chapter needs to be about 'things not said' generally before she gets to 'things not said' particular. She wants to write chapter about 'things not said' and their whole big cultural and social importance kind of thing. Even says fantastical-like that she is reaching for an overreaching philosophical 'theory-of-the-not-said'. I encourage her, thinking can always bring her down the line later, and the time was good for me besides as I was only half-way through *Villette* anyways myself, looking for the not said things."

"You are sure she said this to you, Sergei? Are you sure she didn't *not* say it to you?"

Krokoff closed one eye a little and cocked his head. "You joke me, right? You said say-not-say joke at me, right?"

Poon smiled patiently. "I did. Forgive me."

"I will. But is true there was thing she should have said she did not say which is what has caused me all my mad grief I am about to spill."

He paused. Poon rested her cheek on her right fist.

22

"Student name Jane watches TV," said Krokoff.

"TV?" Poon repeated. "She watches TV?"

"No! I mean, what does Krokoff care, what does anyone give a damn if she watches TV in private, even if she is addict of thing? As long as she keeps it to herself, righto it is?"

Poon rubbed her brow with two fingertips. "Sergei, you are speaking to a member of the Cultural Studies department. Do you expect me to agree with some narrow-minded, old fashioned literary critical view that television is an entirely negligible object of study? From what you say it sounds like she came back and wanted to do something with TV? Is that it?"

"Big time, massive time! When she came back after Easter all theory-talk had been chucked out of window into trash area. The Brontës had been lined up against media studies wall and shot through head with one bullet fired from the side, probably Anne first, bullet travelling so fast it went through all the Brontë skulls one after the other, not even the dignity of any ammo wasted on them individual-like, just a kind of instant economy genocide of the Brontës situation." Krokoff leaned forward and patted the palm of his hand on the desk for every word of his next sentence. "The - girl - had - got - *Lost*!"

There was a silence.

Buckrack was strolling around the campus grounds.

Redman was driving back from Miller's.

"Lost?" Poon said. "Lost in what? Lost where?"

"No, *Lost*!" cried Krokoff. "By her own confession, her bloody girlfriend turned her on. I think she must be a bit like you are, Sapphisticated, to be honest, and forgive me for throwing it up. The girlfriend introduced it into her. She had been missing supervisions with me to watch with girlfriend the whole six seasons of the goddamnit thing."

"*Lost*? You mean the American TV series?"

"Yes, and you can guess the next episode. Oh, oh, *Lost* had more things not said that should have been said than the dead, killed Brontës had to not say, it did, didn't it? One hundred and fifty chapters full of, or maybe I think empty with, things people should have told people but stupidly failed to do. Every singular character a Nelly Dean on steroidals. A far more fertile enquiry bucket than the three assassinated sisters, oh yes, and theory, oh, oh, that went swilling down the toilet

23

soup bowl right after they did too, of course it did, did it not? Her entire Ph.D. thesis was now wanted to be about *Lost!*"

Poon contained herself. "And?"

"Well, what had she done, right? She had torrent-bitted the whole thing and she reached in her bag and put on my desk a USB finger drive with the entire nest of illegal data vipers on it and said I'd need to watch it."

"And you did what?"

"I looked at it. Flash drive gave me flashback. My first night in Budapest, I am walking along main street to my hotel when pretty girl, very pretty girl in tweedies and Sherlock Holmes deerstocking on her head comes up and gives me good card and says, all her many eyelids fluttering, in ridiculous broked-up English, *Naked ladies dancing on tables without bras.* Dot dotty dot. I was being pimped up. I was being offered illegal things by sly kind of temptress."

"And what did you do?"

Krokoff blushed. "Was many years ago," he said.

"I *mean*," Poon leaned forward, "what did you do when *the student* offered you the USB stick with the bit-torrented TV series on it?"

"Well, it sat there for a moment, like some drug Krokoff had never had a try-out with. I don't even have TV." He looked guiltily aside. "They say *just say no*, but is not that easy when you're offered it blatant, right there, on top of your office desk, free, no questions asked, bam-wham."

"You took it?"

"Was persuaded."

"Then what?"

Reluctantly, Krokoff replied, "Gave it a go-try."

"I thought you didn't have a TV?"

Krokoff blushed anew. "I told her that. She made me stick it straight into USB slit of desktop PC right there in my office. Copied all the files onto hard drive. Showed me how to look into them. Took five bare minutes."

Poon contemplated him for a few seconds. "Is that it? You're worried about having illegal video files on your University PC hard drive?"

"God in heaven, no! I am Ukrainian! Breaking flimsy laws is not problem!"

"Then what, Sergei?"

"This is where you get to confession. Shamefulest part. But let me speak, I need to say. It all starts with Korean lady actress. Her name in *Lost* is Sun, which in English means centre of universe, probably means pretty orchid or some tritey sentimental nonsense in Korean, but soon this pretty orchid becomes centre of Krokoff's universe. They say Ukrainian girls are most beautiful in world, well, that's not true if you have go in Budapest, but really, in depth of soul, Krokoff has Asian persuasion and not caucasian orientation. I had cousin from Kazakhstan and she was first love of Krokoff at fourteen years of old, and this Korean lady, though eyes very different, and much more nicely breasted, she remind Krokoff very much of lovely Kazakh cousin, but more virtuous, less of tart, a devoted married lady. Her husband cannot speak English so he obviously cannot say nothing meaningful to anyone, excepting her. But worst shame of all, Korean lady Sun proves my wicked student name Jane right. She is biggest not-sayer of entire first two seasons. I mean, it goes without saying that nearly everybody in programme is choosing not to say important things they should be saying all the time if they had one quart common sense. Or they get prevented from saying them, like when Iraqi devil-angel Sayid gets struck on nut with log by someone (they don't say who) when he is trying to send radio SOS distress call. I mean, if he makes SOS message they all get rescued, righto, isn't it? So he's not allowed to say it. But Sun, silky desirable Korean lady, she actually secretly does speak English but she pretends she can't. And Krokoff knows this but other characters, even husband, do not, and this just doubles over and triples up her seductivity, because Krokoff shares her secret with her, and you get to watch her in long-lasting pictures of her pretty face, which you can make longer if you slow the motion up, when you know she is understanding what everyone else says but is deliberately not saying she understands, and so you get to imagine yourself on the island just with her, that's where Krokoff is in his head at those moments, everyone else has not got clue but she and Krokoff. But soon everyone has not said at least one important thing to everyone else, or they've said it to one and told them not to say it to others, and if everyone was only honest with everyone else and told them the complete truth they would have attained rescue by episode three of season one and it would be pointless village mini-series instead of sprawling metropolis maxi-epic. And some people are even not saying more than they are actually saying. But then Krokoff does not want them to achieve rescue anyways because he's staring with love and desire at the hot Sun. So Krokoff doesn't just notice that everyone is stupidly doing the not-said thing but soon he *wants* them to not say the sayable things because if they do say those things rescue plane will come and Sun will disappear over the horizon back to Seoul and sexy satin sheets with dumb fisherman husband. And sometimes Krokoff realises that he is feeling all this in his own University office at eight o'clock in the evening! And because he is doing all this naughty stuff on his University PC, between episodes it's easy to look up Wikipedia and other trashbags like, and so in no time at all Krokoff is rooting like a rat in the sewer internet looking for discarded bones for gnawing. And then the real horror movie in Krokoff's own head begins. He starts to cottonreel on to the intertexts, those repulsive postmodernist things. So when Sawyer says, 'I don't even wear cologne!' Krokoff finds himself laughing because he's been down in the sewer and seen there the advert for Davidoff Cool Water with the same male actor as the hunk model! Ho ho ho. But I might as well be laughing with a noose around my neck, because by the time I understand crap like that I too realise I am beyond rescue."

Krokoff stopped. Poon was staring at him, wide-eyed.

"You're not saying it," he said.

"I'm lost for words," she replied.

"Is no joke!" he exclaimed. "I am *Lost*! Is sewer juice running through Krokoff's veins. It gets worse!"

"Oh God!" Poon moaned.

"You have heard of Lostpedia?"

"No."

"Is garbage internet dustbin site for lost rats like Krokoff. There these rodents share their bubonic bones with one another. Like Wikipedia but more wicked, concentrated hydrochloric acid trivia just all about *Lost*. I have become dirty rat just like them. Diseased. Two days ago at midnight Krokoff made his first Lostpedia online contribution. Yesterday, high praise feedback from several other *Lost* vermin. I admit it. Am *Lost*aholic. Am addict. Avril, you need rescue me! You do TV shit in your department. Do it for me. Take this vile student name Jane and her potion from me!"

Poon adopted a pragmatic, sympathetic *mien*. "How deep are you in, Sergei?"

"Last quarter of season three."

"So three and a bit seasons to go?"

Krokoff nodded, sagging. "Will kill me. I swear, Krokoff will die if he does not get back to mainland soon."

"Are we talking full transfer of the student to this School? The entire student fee comes with her?"

"Anything! I am sure I can arrange."

"Have you spoken to the student?"

"Not yet. I've said nothing. For Krokoff, would be like waking up in bed with Hungarian whore. What does one say?"

"Best not to say anything, I suppose."

"You mean you will?"

"Is there something you're not telling me?"

"No! Unless you want Krokoff more humiliated than Krokoff is already."

"I mean anything important?"

"No. I swear on the life of student name Jane."

"Then send her an email and tell her to come and have a chat with me. But Krokoff, you're going to owe me one for this, once you've got your act together. "

"Ah, Avril, you are rock!"

Poon smiled drily. "Are we done?"


## Chapter Four (20 September)

Unlike the White House, the equally white Trump Building had a clock tower. Buckrack had disposed of his second histrionic cigarette while standing under it an hour before. And in this non-figurative, real ivory tower, an actual academic, almost mythically, had his office. It was a square cubicle just under the clock, accessed by a door off a winding staircase that led upward to the temporal machinery itself. The occupant's improbable name was Robert McNamara (no relation), and he was likewise strange. He had entirely lost the Galway accent of his childhood after his impoverished family moved to Glasgow on the day of his eighth birthday. Later, having decamped to Oxford for postgraduate study on the day of his twenty-first birthday, his acquired

Glasgow brogue went through various Fabian metamorphoses so that he could be more easily understood by the uncomprehending middle class English students he met there. It would now have sounded quite refined to a Kelvinside ear, despite the fact that McNamara's only connection with Kelvinside had been his attendance at the University of Glasgow as an undergraduate, whence he returned each term-time weekday evening to his parent's mean tower-block apartment in the north of the city. Indeed, he sounded these days just like all Caledonian BBC announcers, anglicised enough to be adored by the English, Scottish enough to be an object of pride to the Scots. When Irish students, or at least the Catholic ones, discovered he was actually Irish, they revered him also. Only the Welsh were not stirred somehow intimately by his person, and indeed the one individual in the University of Odium who hated him was a Welsh administrator to whom he had been in the habit of writing lacerating emails. Others, including his departmental colleagues, held him at a distance, thought him a troublemaker, were wary of the fact that he published about Marxism, sought to avoid his Irishy-Scottishy-unEnglishy habit of satirising those he considered fools and footlers with his council-house-*cum*-ivory-tower-vocabulary-boosted-tongue. But none disrespected him, because he had the reputation, in the nine years he had been President of the academics' trades Union, of being a man of unusual integrity and suitably socialistic moral virtue. Even senior managers, who had reason to find him and his fellow Union officers obnoxious in their stubborn resistance to their plans and stratagems, had a soft spot for him, the way a whore has for a virgin: he was what they had once been but knew they could never be again. Then suddenly, one day, to the astonishment of everyone, like someone in a Philip Larkin poem, and a bit like his more infamous namesake, McNamara had resigned his Union membership, reasons never given to anyone, and went into a kind of silent internal exile, even volunteering, when space was short in the School of Political Science, to take the only vacant room that remained in the Trump Building, a room far too confined, remote and lacking in ostentation for a full Professor such as him, which no one else wanted, because hardly anyone ever went there, and which he wanted for precisely that reason.

Unusually, however, today – which was McNamara's fifty-ninth birthday – James Redman was there. He was looking at McNamara's broad back and broader waist. McNamara was gazing through the window, his bulk almost hiding its frame. Outside in the distance the city of Odium shimmered to the east in the full light of the late morning hour, and McNamara said, "There must be something better than this."

Redman replied, after a pause, "I thought you asked for this office, no?"

"Oh no," said McNamara, turning around and sitting down in an armchair opposite Redman. "I did not mean the office. I love the office. It suits my increasingly isolationist bent. I meant this political torpidity, this nothingness of a polity we are in, even this cipher of an institution we work for, this empty vessel, this whited sepulchre. But then everywhere else is probably the same, or worse."

"Well," Redman ventured, "I thought the isolation was your way out."

McNamara smiled wryly. "Isolation is a way *in*, James, never a way out."

"That's gnomic of you, Robert," Redman said. "You know, you often strike me as being like some weird Celtic version of Aung San Suu Kyi."

"Oh no!" said McNamara, this time more sharply. "By comparison she's a paragon of unwavering Asian persistence, like some feminine pacifist General Giap or even Ho Chi fucking Minh himself. Nothing like western inner turmoil me. I am here because I hate myself even more than I hate what's outside me."

Redman felt the need to say something at this outburst. He wanted to ask, of course, after McNamara's inner turmoil, and why he would hate himself, a man only one Welshman was known to hate. But he said, instead, "I meant, it's like you're under some kind of self-imposed house arrest here."

McNamara did not acknowledge the comparison. "I met her, you know. She was married to a fellow don at Wolfson, my Oxford college. I was there when she left and returned to Burma. I often saw her in the Senior Common Room. A woman of astonishing grace and a curious beauty, so imbued with some kind of ineffable resolve and vigorous purpose, despite a seeming deep sadness, that I never knew what to say to her except hello. She had a beautiful, winsome, never quite full smile. I used to eavesdrop on the conversations she had with others. She never put a word wrong, and was unceasingly courteous and kind. I also met Benazir Bhutto, who was in Oxford at the same time and who, by comparison, though sexier, seemed to me a hound from hell. Do you want another coffee?"

29

"Er, no thanks."

"Then what is it you do want, James? I've been improvising conversation while you sit there looking shifty. I sense my counsel is being sought. If it's Union stuff, you can fuck off. *That* kind of politics I have left behind. It did nothing but cause me grief and it will cause you grief too."

Redman stirred. "Someone has to do it, Robert."

"Yes," McNamara agreed, "but it doesn't have to be you."

"True. But for now it's me."

McNamara sighed. "It *is* fucking Union stuff, isn't it?"

"In a way," Redman said. "But only indirectly, and you don't need to know the details. It's more a moral matter. You could think of it more in terms of the ethics of revenge, if that's easier for you. That's what I wanted to seek your opinion about."

McNamara grunted. "If you put it like that, I am in danger of being interested. I thought, however, that Jesus Christ had the last word on the ethics of revenge two millennia past."

"And you, Robert," Redman said sceptically, "are a turner of the cheek, are you?"

"You know I'm not," McNamara said. "But I sense, under the guise of seeking my advice, you are in fact trying to tempt me into complicity in something I probably want no part of. What is it the guy says in *The Sopranos*? 'Just when I thought I was out, they pull me back in.' Is it now you doing that? Why aren't you having this conversation with scissors-sister Poon?"

"Actually, he's quoting *The Godfather Part III*."

"Really?" said McNamara. "I haven't seen that. I don't watch movies these days. TV series seems altogether more cinematic, fuller, more epic."

Redman shrugged and said, "Anyway, you judge." He removed Miller's USB drive from his pocket and placed it on the low table between them. "I was given this by a dying man this morning, a man who has nothing to lose, a man who was wronged and, being in a position in which moral obliquity had little meaning, took an unusually radical step to right the wrong. He was also uncommonly successful, and his delight at the outcome is probably a little obscene. I feel a bit like I've been handed a murder weapon, having witnessed how effective it is, and invited to try it myself."

30

"For God's sake, stop talking like a Poe character. Who? Who was wronged? Who wronged him? How did he screw them over?"

"You don't, as I say, need the details. But he was wronged by Tweedledee and Tweedledum, and this drive contains recordings of all the telephone conversations between the twins since late July, which he obtained by … let's call it sheer cunning. One of them, the only one I've heard, is enough to get a member of the University's clinical staff disbarred from his profession tomorrow. There are a hundred and twenty three more."

McNamara's left forefinger was between his teeth and he was staring at Redman in some wonderment. "Jamesh, Jamesh, Jamesh." He shook his head slowly. "Thish ish impreshive." He laughed. "I must say, as the students used to say, *respect.*"

"It just dropped into my lap."

"And?"

"I wanted to know what you thought."

"What I thought you should do with it?"

"Yes."

"Well, I find it hard to imagine you will resist the temptation to listen to what's on it."

"It's true. I am tempted."

"Of course you are."

"So?"

"So what? You don't need my permission."

"But I want to know what you would think of my doing that."

"Christ. Is this really a moral dilemma you want me to debate with you? Or are you asking me to caution you about the obvious risks? Or do you, dear boy, *actually hope for my encouragement*? What if I *simply don't care*?"

"I think it's unlikely that you don't care, Robert."

McNamara looked over his glasses. "*Why* should I care?"

Redman shrugged. "Maybe you too are interested in revenge?"

McNamara stood up and walked to the coffee pot and poured himself another cup. "Ah, so it's not my better self you want to hear from, but a voice from my dark side? You've come, like Mephistopheles, to lure the soul of the good Dr Faustus into sin?"

Redman smiled. "I would merely like your spontaneous thoughts on the matter. My own, I admit, are confused. I'd like to test them against your touchstone. On the one hand, you know the people involved. You know the kinds of things they do. On the other hand, you've gone all Zen and seem rather detached these days from the kinds of passions these things stir up when you're still in the trenches, like me."

McNamara frowned. "I really do not know why you are issuing all these unlikely Asiatic analogies for my current choice of circumstances. I assure you there is nothing so profound or enigmatic to be puzzled over. But let's review the options anyway. I assume the recordings were acquired by criminal means, yes?"

"Apparently not. The person who acquired them is technically authorised to handle this kind of data."

"But you are not. So your possession of them is what is criminal."

"At first I thought so. But I soon realised that if the data contains evidence of malpractice or malfeasance then I think the case could be made that they were given to me with a potential Public Interest Disclosure in mind. I was given them in my capacity as a Union officer, in the course of Union business, and the Union has made PIDs in the past. I also know that at least one of the recordings – the one I heard before I knew of the others' existence, and which I got from another source – would easily merit a PID."

"So far so good. Then you can go ahead and listen, no?"

"I can plot the graph along the x-axis of the law. You're right. It's more the y-axis of morality I am having trouble with."

"Ethics?" McNamara snorted. "Honestly, James, you and your Cambridge notions. What is this, Industrial Conflict *versus* The Good Life?"

"There are more things in heaven and earth, Robert," Redman quoted. But still he eyed the USB stick on the table, matt black and self-contained, full of mystery and promise, like a miniaturised Kubrickian monolith.

"I see you," said McNamara, "looking at that thing the way one ogles a belly dancer in an Egyptian restaurant. One wants to reach out and – "

"Well, exactly," Redman agreed.

"Then," said McNamara, "take the advice you came to get. Let the sun go down on your curiosity. Sleep on it. That usually works for most people."

"It's a good idea," Redman said. "But can I leave it with you? If I don't – "

"Oh, I see. You fear you won't be able to resist the big trade union deputy president hard-on it's giving you?"

"I *know* I won't," Redman confessed.

"So your virtue is actually no more laudable than the gap between a nicotine addict's smokes?" McNamara smiled. "It's actually restraint you are asking me to impose, not a call to conscience and duty? A sort of *hide my fags from me, will you?*"

"If you like."

McNamara gave a sigh. "Well, I guess if you do take a belly dancer home with you at night only one thing is likely to happen. No skin off my nose, I suppose. Tomorrow, coffee, noon, in the *Stern am Rathaus* downstairs? You can have it back then."

"Okay."

There was a short pause.

"Is there something else?" McNamara enquired.

"No," said Redman. "But, what, you're kicking me out? You want me to leave? Doctor's appointment over?"

McNamara looked surprised. "No. But I thought you said you had to see Tweedledum and be the monstrous crow."

Redman took out his phone and checked the time. "I have ten minutes."

"So," McNamara continued, "let's say you do listen to the recordings. Is there something you are hoping to find?"

Redman pondered. "Not particularly. The calls were all made over the summer recess. I'm actually surprised there are so many of them, but then Covet seems to be a shark who never sleeps. The one I heard was a nugget of gold in the personal case I was dealing with, but there has been nothing else of any moment, in the last couple of months, that I've had any inkling of. And unfortunately the nugget is going to be buried from the light of day once more in a Compromise Agreement. I expect the calls to reveal the usual war of attrition stuff, mind you, chipping away at the coalface here and there, as ever, but I don't have my ear to the ground on any major skulduggery. They use codenames, apparently. They called the person I was representing *Loser*. Ironic, really, as he's turned out the winner in this case. Well, sort of."

"I do not hesitate to point out," McNamara said, "that *Tweedledum* and *Tweedledee* are also codenames."

"But less openly disparaging," Redman replied.

"I'm not sure about that," McNamara disagreed. "Just more literary, no? Pretty pejorative all the same."

"Then not used with an intent to conceal or deceive. I think that's the difference."

McNamara shrugged. "If you say so."

Redman sensed again that McNamara wanted to let the conversation fade, and decided to change the subject. "Did you know that Rachel Brace was retiring in a month?"

McNamara narrowed his eyes. "I did." Then, after a pause: "Given that she has been the belly dancer I've taken home most nights for the past year and a half."

Redman, after some seconds, gawped.

"You didn't know?" McNamara asked. "Then I am pleased. We have indeed been as discreet as we planned."

"But," Redman spluttered, "but – "

"Now, now, James, just because you think she's a granny, being the modest age you are, and seem to consider me some Zen monk, that's no reason to be so shocked. What lights my candle need not light yours."

"All I meant was," Redman recovered, "you've kept that close to your chest."

"I've kept myself close to Madam Brace's chest," McNamara winked lasciviously.

Redman blew out a breath of *gee-whizz* air, then ventured, "Has she been ... confidential?"

"You mean," said McNamara, "has she confided Tweedledum's secrets to me or has she kept his secrets? You want to know if she's been my cochlear implant in his inner ear?"

"Well, yes."

"No. I told her I wanted to know nothing. It was easier that way for both of us plus, after I resigned the Union presidency, I genuinely wanted to know nothing. I've been more interested in Rachel's gyrating navel, if you get my drift."

"Please," said Redman, "spare me the geriatric images. But, then, you don't know?"

"Know what?"

"That it was Rachel who gave me the recording from Asterisk's phone? What I mean is, she pretended to give me the recording from his phone, because ... Christ!" He gulped. "She must know! She must know about these recordings of Miller's! It was Miller who persuaded her to take the blame for divulging the recording that won the case I am going downstairs to see Asterisk about."

"Yes," said McNamara, "I did know about that. When Miller approached her she asked me what I thought she should do. Rachel has hated Asterisk pretty much forever. But Miller only talked to her about one recording, the one you've heard. No doubt he did not want her to know as much as you now do. After all, what would she do with knowledge that he had a total treasure trove of telephone tittle-tattle?"

"She never asked him where he got it from?"

"Of course she did. He told her he made it himself but that if he was known as the source his case would be potentially impossible to win because of the possible criminal dimension. Even though he's dying he *did* have something to lose: his case, the settlement, all that cash. But because she was retiring *she* had nothing much to lose *and* something to gain. And so we get back to revenge: her revenge on Tweedledum. Her chance to be the monstrous crow."

"But," Redman was still incredulous and a little hurt, "why didn't you tell me?"

"Well, firstly, she forbade me. But surely it's obvious, James? It was a tactic. You couldn't know 'til after you had won the case. You walked into your meeting with Asterisk yesterday believing the recording had been obtained by whistleblower Rachel – someone other than Miller. You thus acted with a clear conscience on his behalf and with her seeming permission. Had you known that Miller was the source, and that he'd pulled it out of his superabundant lucky bag of devious recordings, you might have baulked. Everyone knows how proper you are."

Redman looked appalled. "But I feel manipulated. Like I've got your hand stuffed up my arse."

"*My* hand? What did I do? I simply did not tell you something I had been forbidden to tell you. If anyone's hand was up your arse it was Miller's, while his other hand's been knock knock knockin' on heaven's door. What, you're going to hold a dying man to some supreme standard of verity, when he's trying to get compensation for what he's been diddled out of, a nest-egg to leave behind for his wife and kids, a reseizure of the plunder that's been illegally stolen from him by those two malevolent pirates? You expect a man drowning in the cancer tank to play by the rules of the game? You expect him to go down like the *Loser* they called him? Rachel did the right thing, a final favour to him. You did the right thing, you went into the ring for him when they knocked him down and you KO'd the bastards with the leaden gloves he gave you. You won. How often did we ever really beat them, James? And not only that, but now you have the spoils of war: the other recordings. You might be able to cause even merrier hell with them."

There was a substantial silence.

Redman eventually stirred. "So you knew about Miller and Rachel, but you didn't know about the other recordings?"

McNamara shook his head. "Not 'til you came in here today with them. Miller didn't tell Rachel about them. So she couldn't tell me about them. And she made me swear not to tell you about her and Miller's stratagem."

"But here am I," Redman said, "telling you about them."

McNamara nodded. "Yes. But you needn't have."

"But I did. I wanted your advice."

"I gave you my advice. Sleep on it. We'll talk about them more tomorrow."

Redman stood up. He was trying to contain his anger and failing. "But now," he said, "now I know the truth and I have to go downstairs and lie to Asterisk."

"You knew the truth before you came in here to see me this morning," McNamara replied. "You knew more than I did. A couple of pieces of the jigsaw had been withheld from you, that's all. You were still going to go into Asterisk's office, knowing what you did, and take him for all you can get. And I'm sure that is still what you will do. I can't imagine you will throw the case overboard in an epileptic spasm of probity just because you were kept a little in the dark."

"No." Redman walked to the door. "I won't." He relaxed a little as he stopped on the threshold, but seemed still dismayed. "Yet I feel like a pawn on a chess board."

"More a rook, I think," said McNamara, and then, after a moment, added: "A monstrous crow."

## PART TWO
### 24 OCTOBER – 25 OCTOBER

### Chapter Five (24 October)

Rachel Brace, the sheet of McNamara's double bed tucked under her armpits because an unexamined prejudice suggests that readers probably do not seek a visual description of naked sixty year-old breasts, looked longingly across at the man who had, half an hour before, given her a semi-vigorous seeing to. "But why did you not tell me all this before?" she chided.

McNamara turned from the computer screen with its list of files. "For the same reason we never talked about any of it. Until today you were an employee of the University of Odium and I did not want to mix business with *etcetera*."

"But," protested Rachel, "that pretty much ended that day, when Asterisk kicked me out, or rather told me to take my last month as a holiday."

"All the same," McNamara replied. "Best to do these things properly."

"I guess," Rachel said.

"The thing I can't figure out," McNamara went on, "is why he seemed to accept your fairy tale that he had made the recording when he hadn't?"

"Because he does make lots of recordings. He just couldn't remember. He was also fuming and baying for my blood, and he only got worse when I gave it to him straight between the eyes and said the bloody phone call was illegal and outrageous and he deserved to be hung, drawn and quartered for it. My fake confession seemed to convince him that he had done it after all. He would have loved to sack me, I'm sure, but he obviously knew that was impossible, given the hand grenade I was holding."

"Leaving me to *sack* you," McNamara quipped cheesily, his eyes glinting.

"Uh-huh," Rachel responded invitingly.

"Later," he said. "I have to go out for half an hour."

"Shame," she said, then, pensively, "What I can't figure out is why he called me in about it after his meeting with Buckrack. What did Buckrack have to do with it? He'd only just arrived. Do the calls tell you anything about Buckrack?"

"Nope," said McNamara. "He's mentioned only twice. In late July Tweedledee calls Tweedledum and says, 'I had a long talk with a guy called Buckrack on the plane from LA the other day. Remind me to talk to you about him when we next meet.' The day before Buckrack appears he calls him again and says, 'Buckrack will turn up tomorrow morning. Act as instructed.' That's it, nothing more."

"I called Alison. She says Buckrack has been in three times to her knowledge, and every time it seems to freak Asterisk out. The last time, she said, he was positively shaking afterwards."

"Well, right up to the eve of Buckrack's arrival they are not using a codename for him, which is what they usually do when something nefarious is being discussed, or when they want to be plain insulting."

"And you?" Rachel asked. "What's your codename?"

"Why," said McNamara, "I am the *Secretary of Defense*, of course. Which makes Covet LBJ and Asterisk Dean Rusk, or somebody. I think what they mean is that I should be on their side, being a Professor and all, but I have turned unexpectedly into some weird raving internal opposition. But they don't mention me much, and compared to the other codenames mine is pretty polite."

"E.g.?"

"Well," McNamara glanced at a written list on the desk. "Poon is known as *Bowling Ball*."

Rachel looked puzzled. "*Bowling Ball*?"

"Yeah, you know, the way you put your middle finger ... "

Rachel giggled. "That's pretty witty."

"Must be Covet's. Asterisk isn't clued up enough for that, though I wouldn't put it past him to find these things on the internet to try to impress Covet. She's also sometimes referred to as *Fajita Eater*. Miller, we know, was *Loser*."

"Which just seems even crueller now that he's dead. They should fry in hell."

"Agreed. It took me some time to figure out that Redman was *Dr Watson*, because we actually have two real Dr Watsons on the staff, one of them, believe it or not, in the actual Medical School, which is a hoot."

"It's not entirely insulting, is it?" Rachel mused. "I mean Watson is a good guy, no?"

"Perhaps the suggestion is that he is rather limited compared to Holmes. Needless to say, there's no *Sherlock*."

"No," Rachel said. "But then I suppose you've staked a claim to that name yourself now, no?"

"How'd you mean?"

"Well, destroying the USB stick he gave you, but copying it first and poring over its contents these last few weeks. James must have been furious."

"He was. Though I think I convinced him it was for his own protection."

"But Robert," said Rachel, moving her pillows and sitting up, though not enough to reveal presumably withered nipples, "what gave you the right? Were you not stealing his scoop as well?"

"Right?" McNamara grumbled. "There's no right in any of this. It's all precisely *wrong*. Every one of them – Miller, Covet, Asterisk, even you, perhaps, and ultimately James as well – all acted in the *wrong*. It's what this place has become. It's like a little city in which the only order possible is created by everyone committing crimes which cancel the others' crimes out. When James came to me with the recordings he was talking precisely about *revenge*."

"Yes, but you didn't *destroy* the files, Robert. You copied them and lied to him. That was a wrong too."

"Yes," McNamara admitted, "it was. Still, it's like my father always said: sometimes experience just needs to make the decision, without reasoning it out. You know about James's lack of *sangfroid*, how passionate he gets, how crusading, how all *Martin Luther-King* he can be. He'd have spent the last month being eaten up by these recordings, trying to decode them, planning a campaign around them, when what he really needs to do is write his book."

"So? Maybe that's what's needed. Maybe there's too much *sangfroid* in the veins of this place."

"But people exploit his goodness all the time, Rachel. It's exactly what Miller did, setting the whole thing up via you. And that turned it to wrongness."

"But the end was good, no?"

"It was good for Miller. Or good for his family, I mean. I don't see how it was good for James. All it did was make him even more the enemy of Tweedledum."

"I disagree," said Rachel. "Those recordings would have strengthened his arm, not weakened it. Yet you took them off him."

"Strength is not the same as right," McNamara sighed. "But let's not argue. I could give them back to him anytime. I just see no need to. From what I've heard it's all gossip and nastiness and effing and blinding. What's new? We could have guessed they did that anyway. It's exactly what *we* do." He stood up. "I have to go over to the Hall. A Hall Tutor wants to see me about something. You'll stay?"

"I was promised an *I am boss* night. I get to use you entirely for my selfish pleasure."

McNamara smiled wryly. "That's correct."

"I'll be here," Rachel said.

It had once been called Barraclough Hall of Residence, after a minor aristocratic family in a neighbouring county, in the days when such appellations were considered to lend weight and dignity to provincial institutions. But two years previously it had been renamed Coolwipe Hall, in honour of the sponsorship of the Coolwipe Toilet Hygiene Company, which had its world headquarters in Odium. A study had been done. With thirty-six thousand students and six thousand staff, the University consumed (including thefts) approximately fourteen hundred toilet rolls per day during term. The annual cost was estimated at over a hundred and fifty thousand pounds *per annum*. Coolwipe's offer to partner with its local University by supplying it, free for a five-year period, with its revolutionary Moisture Tissues (impregnated with aloe vera and camomile) resulted in an annual advantage of over two hundred and thirty thousand pounds, once the savings and price differential with ordinary toilet paper had been factored in. This seemed cheap at the price of merely a new sign over the door of the erstwhile Barraclough Hall and some relatively tasteful green floral logos in lavatory dispensers.

There had been a time when McNamara might have poked fun at such a decision in committee. He had been tempted to suggest that the new name be "Fresharse Hall", partly because a few like-minded critics round the table would have acknowledged and enjoyed the pun. But, to everyone's surprise, he had acquiesced without comment. It had become difficult to argue against such a move. While it meant that henceforth he would be the Warden of a Hall of Residence whose name ineluctably reminded one of clean-up operations subsequent to evacuation, it saved money and the new tissues were unarguably a luxury compared to the frictive industrial grade scrolls which had preceded them. The absorbency of the latter was questionable and their caustic effect on haemorrhoids was undoubted. Thefts rocketed, because even the staff now purloined Coolwipes, which was why the dispensers were hermetically sealed and only one tissue at a time was released. It was plain to everyone who Coolwiped (a new verb around campus) that there was no going back after doing so: parched recycled chemically bleached paper would not be allowed anywhere near the anuses of generations of Odium alumni again. The company had offered the University an advantageous deal at the expiry of the free five-year period. But by that time, McNamara had it on good authority, the University would be looking to trade up, at a new sponsor's even greater expense, to hi-tech Japanese hydro-toilets with integrated blow-dryers.

In any case, Coolwipe Hall of Residence was way down the pecking order of sponsorship, at the bottom in reality as well as figuratively. It was a squat cuboid of 1965 concrete slabbery built on reclaimed marshland near the campus's western perimeter. From the front it looked like an enormous grey and brown shoebox with a copper lid gone green from decades of rainfall. It was not the ugliest residence on campus. In 1966, when higher education in the United Kingdom was still organised along what one could tenably call a Soviet system (accepting only élite cadets and each year turning out cadres of well educated, market-unfriendly graduates) the University Grants Committee issued an edict that no further capital allocation would be made to subsidise University Halls of Residence after December of that year. Odium did not have time to commission plans for a new hall, so it took the recently completed blueprints for Barraclough, turned them through one hundred and eighty degrees, and built the virtually identical Wykenshawe (now Boxitgood) Hall down the hill at its rear. Thus

Coolwipe was the joint ugliest residence on campus and, with its near twin, could enjoy only modest expectations of patronage. At the top of the pyramid was Powell Hall, the only one of the fifteen Odium residences which retained a human designation, the University's one attempt to create something that looked architecturally like an Oxbridge College. It seemed forever immune to having its original name blown away by the cyclones of twenty-first century commerce, as it was already endowed by the estate of a dead Conservative Cabinet member of eld whose private largesse exceeded anything the world of trade might calculatedly muster. But all else was fair game, and those on slightly lower rungs even attracted titles which advertised multinational companies. Toyota Hall stood adjacent to the Toyota Engineering Building, which was why the Vice Chancellor's chauffeur-driven limousine was a Lexus. Adobe Hall, near the Adobe Computer Laboratory, had even had its façade renovated to make it look as if it were built from brown mud.

None of this was in McNamara's mind as he walked the hundred metres from his house to a door at the car park end of Coolwipe still marked "Trade Representatives' Entrance". Nor did he on this occasion reflect ironically, as he had often done in the past, that this sign might these days truthfully be posted on virtually every main entrance on the Odium campus, and not just those out of ordinary sight. Instead, as he paused before entering to pop half a Viagra in anticipation of his return to Rachel, he was thinking of the unusual pleasure of their etiolated love. He knew that the young, including himself when young, would have scoffed at overhearing their private dirty talk, perhaps even been repulsed by their overweight congress, their weak libidinal wheezes, clicking joints, and paltry moans and groans. But the young would never understand, unless they were lucky enough to meet someone in later life who accepted their own and their bedfellow's growing physical frailty, that accommodation to the relentless decline of the body could take on the form of renewed mutual experimentation. The truth was that the tongue and the mouth were not as prone to dystrophy as the penis was to dysfunction and the vagina to slackness. The clitoris remained a taut, responsive miracle, the frenulum as excitable a piece of small tissue as it ever had been. Once a couple abandoned the illusion that sexual success consisted mainly in simultaneous climaxes involving a glorious engorgement within tightly clutching labia, there was a whole new world of blissful pampering of each other to discover. If one added the fact that contraception was no longer a matter to regard, and the psychologically stimulating insight that you were both building an empire of the senses from which the rest of the world assumed you had been exiled long ago, the possibility of regular thrills seemed unlimited.

It was because of these thoughts, having walked along an internal corridor and down a set of steps to the bunker-like Senior Common Room and entered, that McNamara did not register what to any man less preoccupied would have been the blatantly powerful sexual radiation which constitutionally emanated from Jane Blake. To be sure, even he could not fail, at each sighting of her, to make a rapid venereal appraisal. There was the wonderful head of full-bodied brown hair tumbling to halfway down her back, the large brown Hispanic eyes, the plump but well shaped lips, the perfectly formed nose, the beautiful complexion unadorned by make-up, and below the neck the 115-pound figure, accentuated usually by tight-fitting clothes, which amply displayed a fine, round but not too big behind, and anti-gravitational 34B breasts, with legs that went three or four inches higher than his own before meeting slim bracket-shaped hips and a proportionately thin waist. She was undoubtedly neat whisky to Rachel Brace's diluted beer. McNamara thought, as he always thought the moment he saw her anew, that male undergraduates must pretty well instantly cream their pants when introduced to her as their Hall Tutor. But no such ripple broke within his own self, he did not feel a snapping pang of immediate regret that no part of his own anatomy would ever come nearer to Jane's than the hand with which he shook hers. Even had he possessed a wooden horse, he would not have wished to force it through her gates of Troy. For he had discovered, with Rachel, that libidinal weakness was also great source of moral strength. It allowed him to look at Jane almost entirely aesthetically, the way a proper father might look at his objectively gorgeous daughter. Rachel made him happy. She was not even the mast to which he tied himself to resist the sirens on the shore. With her, there simply was no shore, just open sea.

Jane seemed to McNamara entirely aware of the adrenalin-inducing tendencies of her being, and while she did not dress to mitigate them, her faultless propriety of conduct seemed calculated to deflect them. Thus the handshake in which she curiously indulged at the opening of nearly every meeting. To be sure, her east coast Sweet Valley High accent destroyed instantly any illusion that she might be some latterday exemplar of Jane Austenish containment and reserve. But she also used, without apology and despite regular discouragement, formal titles instead of first names: "Good evening, Professor McNamara." She never flirted. McNamara had seen others flirt with her, and she always responded to them with studied, even marked, emotional neutrality. Her consistent comportment seemed, over time, to be a polite notice to the excited male: please detumesce. But despite her faultless and chastening manners, women tended to hate her. On the whole, on balance, McNamara quite liked her, although he did not think of her much except when they met in person. It was perhaps because of this that she seemed more comfortable with him than she often was with others.

They indulged in the customary small talk about the start of the new academic year and the fresh intake of students, and McNamara enquired routinely about progress on her Ph.D. without listening much to the answer. Jane asked cordially after his family, his two sons, whom she had never met. She smoothed her mid-length black skirt under her thighs with the palms of her hands and sat down decorously on one of the sofas.

"What did you want to see me about?" McNamara asked, taking a seat opposite her, about six feet away.

She appeared nervous. "It's not easy to talk about. I hope you won't mind. It's not about the Hall."

"Okay," he said. He was impatient to return to Rachel but determined to try not to show it.

He was not expecting her to say, "Professor McNamara, are you a person of faith?" And it startled him when she did.

Although his eyebrows raised involuntarily, he shrugged his shoulders to relieve himself of the surprise. "No," he said, "but I was raised a Catholic."

She smiled. She had a symmetrical, natural smile, and flawless American teeth. "I guessed," she replied. "With a name like yours. Me too. But I am a believer."

McNamara smiled gently, crookedly back. "And?"

She hesitated. "I am having something of a crisis, I think."

McNamara felt he also ought to wait a second or two before replying, "A crisis of faith?"

"No," she blurted. "I have been ... sinful ... of late."

McNamara drew in a heavy breath. "Isn't that more the kind of thing you would talk to a priest about?" he said.

"Yes," she said. "I would. I mean, I shall. But it's more complicated."

"How?"

"It's embarrassing as well as ... spiritually compromising."

"Okay," he said patiently. "We are confidential here, obviously."

"Yes," she said. "Thank you."

There was another lull. McNamara broke it. "Tell me more only if you feel you need to," he cautioned, hoping privately that the caution might be acted upon.

"I want to tell someone," she replied. "It's got to that stage."

"Okay," he said.

"I've ..." He could see that she was biting her lower lip. She continued, "I've become involved with a member of staff."

"Ah." McNamara held up his hand, somewhat officiously, he thought. "Before you go on, whether or not this matters, can I just give you the low down on this kind of thing, from the University's point of view? Sin is not a category of offence the University concerns itself with. Relationships between students and staff are assumed to be private matters of adult consent unless there is a conflict of interest or you are under eighteen or deemed to be a vulnerable person. You are neither, I am sure, and the only avoidable conflict of interest would be with someone who assesses your work. Even then, all that needs to happen is that the conflict of interest is removed by ensuring the member of staff does not assess your work. If you are worried that you're doing something wrong, then you're not, unless the member of staff supervises you ... and, well, that's unlikely to be the case, right?"

Jane put her fingers to her teeth. She was too careful about her fingernails actually to bite them, but she worried at them for a moment or two. "Yes, I did look at the regulations," she said. "I am not so bothered about those. I'm more concerned with the sinfulness of it."

McNamara looked over his glasses at her. "Is this because you already have a boyfriend?"

"No," Jane said. "It's not a matter of infidelity. It's the nature of the ... new relationship."

McNamara pondered. "I understand. These things can become difficult. The member of staff, is he married?"

"No," she said. "And it's not a man."

There was yet another, this time longer, hiatus. McNamara took off his glasses and rubbed his brow with his fingers.

"Oh Lord, indeed," he said. "Okay. Can we leave the sin thing aside for a moment and just deal with the conflict of interest issue? There's no conflict of interest, right?"

Jane was silent. She remained so.

McNamara sat up. "Dr Poon?" he said, more loudly than he meant to. "You're having a sexual relationship with your supervisor?"

Jane hung her head and looked down at her shoes.

"Aw, Jesus!" he exclaimed.

Jane glanced up. "Please, Professor McNamara."

He caught himself. "Sorry," he said. He stood and walked to the window and thought for a moment. "Well, tell me what you feel like telling me." He turned and sat down again and listened.

She made to begin, but he cut her off. For some reason he found himself now instantly in listen-to-me-young-lady mode, as if she really were his daughter. "What are you thinking, Jane? You're not gay. Poon's been shacked up with another woman in Bigton going on ten years. She's old enough to be your mother. You manage well enough to dispose of the attentions of numerous young men around here, so what happened on this occasion? Oh, hell, don't start crying!"

"I'm sorry," she sniffed. "I know it's hard not to judge me. But I judge myself, believe me. I know it's wrong. I can deal with men. Maybe it's because she's not a man that it was different this time. I tried to break it off."

McNamara had always been unimpressed by student waterworks. They did not soften his heart, but hardened it.

"And?" he demanded.

"She said she missed me terribly. She pleaded with me and I went back to her. I don't know why, but this isn't like being with a man. She says she loves me. If I'm honest I missed her too."

"Jesus Christ!" he exclaimed, then he sighed, and subsided. He apologised again. "I'm sorry. Look, why tell me? What do you want from me?"

She said, half questioningly, "You seem to know how things work around here. And I know you know her personally."

"Advice, then?" he said. "First of all, let's be practical. Review the

46

options. You can continue, but she has to stop being your supervisor. You can end the relationship with her, and even then you cannot really go on being supervised by her. But she should already have told you that."

"She said if I stopped seeing her she'd be suicidal. It's like emotional blackmail. I've already changed supervisor once. How can I do it again? It begins to look suspicious."

"You mean Krokoff? Can't you go back to being supervised by him?"

"No," she shivered. "He's disgusting. To be honest, he was coming on strong. I changed my subject partly to get away from him. That's why I'm with Dr Poon now, which involved an entire transfer from one department to another in a different School. And that was only a month or so ago. What is it going to look like if I ask to change again?"

McNamara looked at her with some pity. "The only other option is to make a formal complaint against her, and the matter will be resolved by someone else, but I assume you don't feel that way."

"But how can I do that?" she said. "I don't want people to know about it. And I don't want to criticise her. She did harass me into it, it's true. But I did consent. I wasn't forced." Suddenly she looked frightened. "You said we were confidential, right? You're not going to tell anyone, are you? You're not going to talk to Dr Poon? She'd go crazy if she knew I had told you. She said we had to be very discreet."

McNamara considered. "No," he said. "But if you didn't want anyone to know perhaps you should not have told me either. I understand why you wanted to speak to someone, but you don't seem to want to entertain the only possible solutions. You could see a University Counsellor. It's free. You just call and make an appointment. It might do some good to talk it through with them, at least the, er, spiritual issues. Or your priest, of course, if that works for you. The practical issues are as I described them."

Jane dried her eyes. "Yes," she said. "Maybe that's a good idea. If I do that I might get some perspective on it."

"All right," he said. "Tell you what. You do that and then if you want to talk again we can. You're clearly in a bit of a pickle but I'm sure, if you give it some time, that it might work itself out in your mind."

Jane stood up and looked at him with gratitude. "Professor McNamara, please don't be angry with me," she appealed. "I'm glad I spoke to you, and I'm sorry if I've put you in an awkward position. I didn't mean to. It was just depressing me awfully."

"No," he said. "And I am sorry if I was short with you. That was wrong of me. These things do take time to resolve."

Jane extended her hand formally in a way that young twenty-first century women hardly ever do.

In difference, similarity. Jane Blake tottered through Coolwipe Hall to her small apartment on the third floor, genuinely nervous and emotionally overwhelmed by the enormity of the confession she had just made. McNamara, on the other hand, thought little as he departed the Hall of the interview that had taken place. After three decades of working in universities, he had become accustomed to thinking he had heard it all, only once again to hear something novel. But there really was a Zen part of him. In the way that he treated all confidential matters, he discarded almost immediately the details Jane had told him, like a letter thrown in a postbox and forgotten unless it was returned to him again at a later date. He was more concerned with Rachel and tonight's promised sexual excess. He stopped on the way and brought to mind an anticipatory mental image that might indicate if the Viagra was kicking in, a fantasy touchstone that would help his lower half obey a certain bidding: please tumesce. Satisfied, he proceeded. When he entered the house, it was entirely in darkness. This was a game he and Rachel often played, a kind of phallic hide-and-seek. He found her in the downstairs bedroom, on a product placement Eames leather swivel chair, her legs spread with wonderful obscenity across its arms, pelvis bared and appropriate organ gaping. To the reader's likely relief, he did not turn on the light before beginning his demonic work on his willing, vocally consenting subject.

Jane also entered her flat, likewise, but for different reasons, excitable. By contrast, however, after locking her door, she turned on the light. And sitting in her modest lounge, also on a swivel chair, but one without a brand name, she found, though fully clothed, with his legs crossed, Buckrack.

"Hello, Jane," he said. "Me Tarzan."

## Chapter Six (25 October)

Early the following morning, before his secretaries arrived for work, Nigel Asterisk was eyeing Buckrack tremblingly across the desk in his office. This was quite literally so, as in the last few weeks his right eyelid had developed a twitch, which he had experienced before, but on this occasion he attributed it to the stress and worry the American kept regularly bringing his way. Buckrack looked impatient and, as usual, slightly contemptuous.

"Another one?" Asterisk said.

Buckrack sighed demonstratively. "The first three were listening devices. This is a pinhead wireless camera and a miniature video recorder. I need them quick. They do next day delivery, so make the call now."

"But *why*?"

"Well, obviously," Buckrack persevered, "because we need to see something as well as hear it."

"*We*?"

"I'm sure you know Covet has approved it."

"Yes, yes. But this, and another request for a building master key, the illicit entry and the nefarious surveillance ... "

"Illicit? Nefarious? There's no law against an employer monitoring his employees. These are corporate offices, not private residences."

"But why? It's extremely irregular."

"You don't need to know why. I would venture that you don't even want to know why."

Asterisk scratched his head. "I don't have deniability. These orders are being made on my budget with my authority. The Vice Chancellor made it very clear that that's how it should be done. I'd like to know at least a little of what's going on."

"You can ask Covet if you want to know *why*," countered Buckrack. Then he seemed to turn conciliatory. "But, since you asked, I'll tell you *what*. Okay?"

Asterisk nodded in anything-is-better-than-nothing agreement.

"The first three bugs, the ones I requested in the first week, went into the offices of Redman and Poon and McNamara, all in this building. When I asked for the two master keys a fortnight later it was so that I could remove the one from McNamara's office. No conversation ever seems to take place there. As far as I can tell, McNamara receives no visitors at all. He has only postgraduate research students and seems to conduct all his business in the Senior Common Room of the Hall where he is Warden, and if I had a pad that nice I'd do that too. So I planted it there instead. I am not about to tell you what we have gleaned so far. That would be premature and it's for Covet's ears only. But matters have sufficiently developed for me to judge that we also need a video feed from Poon's office. That's where most of the Union information flows through and where the executive committee meetings take place. But we need to know who is present at the meetings and the audio alone doesn't give us that."

Asterisk looked troubled. "So we are essentially monitoring the executive officers of the Union?"

"McNamara is not an officer."

"Not anymore. But he is the ex-President."

"He's not even a member these days. Word is he resigned lock, stock and barrel over a year ago."

"That I didn't know," said Asterisk. "But they probably seek his advice all the same. Poon's not plugged in the way McNamara was."

"Nope," said Buckrack. "On the evidence of the last month he hasn't had a single conversation with anyone about Union matters, and certainly not Redman or Poon."

"That's hard to believe. The man's a Marxist, you know. A meddler in management business for years, unlikely to change."

"Well, I thought the way you do at first, and we'll continue to keep tabs on him, but the signs so far are that there are no longer spots on this leopard."

Asterisk picked up the order information on the camera which Buckrack had written down for him. "And how long do we think we will go on doing this?"

Buckrack was non-committal. "As long as it takes."

"As long as it takes to find out *what*?"

"That's really a *why* question disguised as a *what* question. But you can imagine how important it is for management to know what the Union is discussing."

"Yes," Asterisk agreed. As an afterthought he asked, "You plant these devices at night, I assume?"

Buckrack nodded.

"My worry is," Asterisk confided, "that they might be discovered."

"That's unlikely," said Buckrack. "They're so micro they can hardly be found without special detection equipment. That's one of the reasons they are so expensive."

"But how do we use any information we learn from using them without it becoming obvious that we have?"

"Oh, there are ways," Buckrack reassured. "Don't you worry about that. Now put the camera order through today. I'll be back first thing in the morning to pick it up."

Asterisk examined the peremptory Buckrack steadily for a moment, but he could feel his eyelid beginning to tremble uncontrollably again, and averted his look. "You can get the master key from the security office," he said. "Tell them to call me to confirm."

Once Buckrack had departed, Asterisk's mind drifted to episode four of season six of *The West Wing*, which dramatised C. J. Cregg's first day as White House Chief of Staff after Leo McGarry's heart attack. C. J. was being undermined by that son of a bitch Secretary Hutchinson, who was taking advantage of her inexperience in the role to circumvent her and go directly to the President about weapons grade uranium in the Republic of Georgia. C. J. sat down with Margaret, her PA, and asked her for advice. Margaret told her she should go through her policy wonks. "Right," said C. J. "How many policy wonks work for me?" Margaret replied, "A bunch." In the last ten minutes of the episode C. J. gathered her policy wonks and swiftly reasserted her authority over Hutchinson without having to approach the President directly.

The problem, Asterisk pondered, was not just that he had no policy wonks or equivalent. He did not even have a PA such as Margaret. Indeed, Rachel Brace, on whose experience he had long depended, had committed a decisive act of final betrayal, and Alison Stilt was little more than an obedient-to-command know-nothing. But the deeper difficulty was that Buckrack was not as evidently surmountable as Secretary Hutchinson. He was Jack Bauer, he had virtually said so. Asterisk had in the last month taken out a free trial subscription to Netflix to acquaint himself with *24*, and watched it compulsively with intensifying horror. What became very clear very quickly was that Bauer would go round anyone to get directly to an honourable President like David Palmer, and if the President was a bad egg like Charles Logan he would ignore even his authority. There was much to be learned from episode six of season five, for example, in which Chief of Staff Walt Cummings first persuaded President Logan to curb Bauer's seemingly irrepressible activities only to suffer the terrifying consequences, in front of the President himself. "The first thing I'm gonna do, I'm gonna take out your right eye," Bauer had then threatened, brandishing a knife in Cummings' face. "Then I'm gonna move over and I'm gonna take out your left." The President had stood by, powerless to prevent him, as the blade almost cut into Cummings, until at the last moment he confessed to his crimes and was subsequently found dead, hanging from a rafter. The entire series had sent regular shivers of recognition down Asterisk's pliable vertebrae. The Vice Chancellor was not David Palmer. He was much more like Charles Logan. Asterisk himself did not want to be Walt Cummings. He wanted to be Leo McGarry, minus the heart attack and his own currently flickering right eyelid.

At around the same time, Jack Russell decided to show his dogged discontent by lying flat out on his stomach with his chin on his paws staring reproachfully at his human companion. The morning had in fact begun well. He had roused Redman, who seemed likely to sleep eighty per cent of the time if left to his own devices, and managed to orientate his easily distractable intelligence into donning the necessary gear required for a vigorous run into campus. He had manoeuvred him out of the front door by carefully persuasive body language and a politic lack of overt vocal insistence, so skilfully, in fact, that Redman probably believed he was acting on his own frisky agency. They had reached the front garden gate and were about to start trotting when another human emerged from a car parked at the pavement and stood in Redman's way. This was a much fatter and altogether unhealthier breed than Redman's. The typical rituals involved in human standoffs ensued between the two: there was some baring of teeth and a few growls, Redman making clear with his feet movements (which Jack was well placed to observe) on just whose territory the encounter was taking place. But, while there were no amiable markers like a handshake there were also no hostile barks, and after a few minutes, Redman seemed to have given the other man behaviouristic permission, and the entire party, to Jack's dismay and renewed sense of frustration at the short attention spans of humans in general, re-entered through the porch of 111 Maryland Lane. Jack led them into the front room, where he intended to remain, visible and sighing every so often, like a bad conscience, eyes judgmentally piercing whenever Redman looked at him, until the latter, with his obviously limited brain power, eventually remembered the training Jack had given him.

Redman, although he had admitted McNamara to his home, nonetheless found it difficult not to show that he was cross. "We couldn't do this in my office?" he said testily.

"Well," said McNamara, "I figured you might throw me out of there, you being so angry with me and all. And I thought if you wouldn't let me in or talk to me here, I could always put this safely through your letter box." He offered Redman a manila envelope.

"What's this?" Redman asked.

"It's a second USB drive with a copy of the data from the first one, plus a paper summary of the content of all one hundred and twenty-four calls, including a table of codenames used by Tweedledee and Tweedledum and my deciphering of them. In short, it's the stuff Miller gave you, with my glosses."

Redman emptied the contents on to his lap, and quoted McNamara to himself. "'As you can see, I have taken a hammer to it, James. You really don't want to get involved in this surreptitious business. I thought it best to remove the temptation.' So what's changed in a month, Robert?"

McNamara replied uncomfortably, "Remove the temptation from you, yes. I succumbed to it myself, obviously. And you have been justifiably angry with me. I am sorry for the deception. I hope I'm not rubbing salt into the wounds, but I thought that we might get over it if I gave it back to you and showed that it was not worth bothering about in the first place. You must have been wondering, I imagine. So that's what the summaries and codename table are for – as you can see, there's not a lot there to bother about. The call about Miller is of course scandalous, but nothing equals it, and that matter is officially closed. They do speak contemptuously and disrespectfully of members of staff but it's hardly the stuff of public disclosure."

Redman was studying the papers.

McNamara added, "I do apologise again for not giving you a choice. But I was concerned that you might be getting yourself into deep hot water."

"Thanks, dad," Redman replied. Then he looked up. "Your table of codenames pretty much tallies with mine, except I have a few more, and

I haven't worked them all out. It took me a while to realise I was *Dr Watson*. But you haven't really answered my question, *Secretary of Defense*. Why did you change your mind?"

"Truly, genuine regret at the discord my action caused between us," said McNamara. "But what are you talking about, *your table of codenames*? How do you have a table of codenames? You gave me the impression you hadn't looked at the data."

Redman arose and stepped over the huffy, stewing Jack Russell. "Let's have some coffee," he said. "Then you can drive me into the office."

In the kitchen, over two cups of what McNamara found a stupendously bowel-moving brew dispensed from an expensive Italian coffee maker, Redman enlightened him thus: "I did not look at the data before you showed me the drive you destroyed. That's true. I was also incensed at what you had done. You removed my option. The deal was that you would keep the drive and I would sleep on the decision. In fact, I had on balance chosen to take your advice until the moment you told me you had decided for me by apparently shredding the data. Call me a contrarian, but from that point on I really wanted to have it. So, a few days later, when I took Miller's signed and finalised Compromise Agreement to his home, I asked him if he still had the recordings. He didn't. He had erased them. But he had something better – the original executable file. He went straight to a computer in his own house, logged on, installed the program on a random machine which runs twenty-four-seven in some University student computer room, and handed me the username and password for an untraceable email address. Whenever there's a call to or from Tweedledum or Tweedledee, an email gets sent to that address with a link I can go straight to and access the archived recording. The email server and the audio files are not even in the country – they're in North Korea or somewhere else that hasn't signed some treaty or other. It's apparently beyond all reasonable detection. So for the last few weeks, thanks to your patronising unilateral making up of my mind for me, I've had a live wiretap up on all their phone conversations."

McNamara felt a movement in his intestines like the shifting of tectonic plates. "I don't suppose I have any ground anymore to counsel against involving yourself in such a course of action. Can I at least ask what are the results?"

Redman made a puffing noise. "Mixed. Obviously when Covet is here in Odium the phone calls between him and Asterisk are reduced, on some days non-existent. I imagine any sensitive business they discuss in person when they can. But you do realise that what Miller gave me were *only* the conversations *between* the two? The program actually records *all* the phone conversations made to and from both their University mobiles and office landlines. It captures *everything.*"

McNamara's eyes widened as his lower bowel expanded. "I am going to have to use your toilet in a minute, but tell me, how much data is that?"

"Well, predictably, dozens and dozens of calls a day. Frankly, I am just about drowning trying to keep up to date with it all and make sense of it. Phone discourse is so lacking in context, often broken, incoherent, miscellaneous. It refers all the time to other conversations or written information or a sphere of action the speakers have knowledge of but the eavesdropper doesn't. It mixes the trivial and the potentially momentous, but you regularly cannot distinguish one from the other. It's often like symbolist poetry, it seems to gesture penumbrally to things way beyond itself, and when you concentrate for any length of time on specific enigmatic utterances – in which if $x = y$ then the meaning is $z$ but if $a = b$ the meaning must be $c$ instead – you soon realise that simply by virtue of spending so much time on it you may be according it a significance which it possibly does not have. Then, if the same subject comes up again, which it can appear to, even in the very next phone call, you have to operate on the basis that either trivial meaning $z$ or momentous meaning $c$ may be under discussion, even though $z$ or $c$ are contradictory outcomes of a previous indeterminate reading. Thus numerous possible interpretations branch out exponentially. When you add to this the knowledge that these two guys deliberately use codenames, and possibly even codewords, at least with each other, but perhaps with others too, you get undecidability of enormous magnitude. In short, you can get lost pretty quickly in the maze of language and reference. But that's just about what they say. It's the meaning of pregnant silences which are truly difficult to crack: the import of things they don't say. It's a labyrinth, in a word."

"I have a bad feeling in my gut about all of this," said McNamara, "but thankfully that is a labyrinth whose contents more easily yield themselves up. Excuse me for a few minutes."

In Redman's upstairs toilet, a place McNamara, like most men, found congenial to brief meditation, he tried to meditate. Buddhists might think his seated absorption a lavatorial form of *zazen*, but on this occasion, failed Zen master that McNamara had never intended to be, it led not to the highest perfect awakening of *anuttarā-samyak-sambodhi*, nor the full enlightenment of *samyak-sambodhi*, or even the basic awakedness and understanding of mere *bodhi*. In fact, as McNamara noticed with gratification the pack of one hundred Coolwipes on Redman's bathroom shelf, he realised that his closeted thought processes had led him only into an old familiar kind of craving and desire he had tried so hard to abandon.

"I was not expecting this," he said to Redman after he came downstairs, "but can I make it all up to you by offering my assistance in the task?"

"I could do with some help," Redman replied.

In the front room, far out of earshot, forgotten by both of them, a sleeping dog lay.

### Chapter Seven (25 October)

"Here we are, Jane," said Buckrack, "two Americans abroad. Far from home. Thrown, inadvertently it seems, into each other's company. You're an east coaster and I'm a west coaster, but despite our differences we have more in common with each other than we do with our temporary hosts."

He left the seat he had taken opposite her and approached her in relaxed manner as he held forth.

"You ever seen dungeon porno, Jane? A lot of it starts like this, with a young, beautiful, shapely woman tied up, gagged, a hood over her head. I bet you have. Girls your age and of your type are always less innocent than they make out. You can imagine how it develops, the super-slow removal of the cloaking garments, the hood second last, of course, the duct tape round her mouth last, if at all, once the woman has been subdued and understands the need not to cry out, the obscene groping during the process which the girl is powerless to prevent, the probing of nether orifices with alien objects, her leisurely induction into unwilling submission." He approached until his lips were close to her ear. "Thing is, Jane, that's not what this is, and you're going to wish it was as trouble-free as that by the time I'm done."

He walked around the back of her. "You probably share my American puzzlement at the lack of basements in English houses, although in fact they're not so common in California. But then I discovered this loft space in this place they let me have, which in many ways is even better. It has these readily available beams I have cuffed you to, it's just as dark, if not darker, than any cellar, it's further from ground level, which makes it less likely any noise you make can be heard outside. It has only that one little skylight it's impossible to reach even if you could get free, and that one little trap door with an eight-foot drop you need ladders to negotiate without peril, even if you could unlock it from the inside, which you can't. And it's an empty house, I'm its only resident, and I'm new here, I have no friends yet, so no one visits. I'm sorry I had to keep you here all last night, but I had some errands to run, and I needed to make a point, and I confess I wanted you to be a little weary. It must have been cold too, no? What was that?"

Jane was writhing in her upright position and making humming noises of protest. She had been hoisted by a rope linked under the cuff chain that connected her wrists, so that her body was vertically elongated, her arms stretched high above her head until she stood virtually on tiptoe. Her ankles were also bound with rope. Buckrack took off the black hood. Jane blinked painfully in the harsh electric light from the single naked bulb, tears pricking her eyes. She had already been weeping. She was much more dishevelled in appearance than when she had turned the light on and first seen Buckrack in her apartment the night before. Her long hair was in disarray and her face marked by lines of despair. Once her vision had adjusted, she looked at him with wide, supplicating eyes, murmuring through the silver-grey heavy duty tape he had wound tightly round her mouth and the back of her head several times. She breathed heavily through her nose.

"Oh, I'll give you a chance to talk when I think the time is right, Jane. I'll even let you have some water. But for the next few minutes you need just to listen to me." He sat down again. "I realise that words only achieve so much, and I'm near the end of getting you to cooperate by means of merely verbal persuasion. I didn't need even much of that to take possession of item one, your passport." He lifted Jane's bag off the folding table next to his seat and removed the small booklet from it, showing it to her then throwing it on the table top. Next he extracted a blue purse. "Item two, your bank and credit cards and ready cash." Then a mobile telephone. "Item three. And, item four, the keys to your apartment." These he jingled before his face, smiling all the while, finally tossing them on the table with the other things. "And, finally, your iPad with, yes, oh dear, most of the relevant passwords, particularly to your email and Facebook accounts, saved by default, so that I don't even have to extort them out of you." This too he placed on the table surface.

"You wouldn't make much of a spy, Jane. Too incautious. These were all just sitting on your desk or in drawers in your apartment when I went in there last night to wait for you, apart from the keys, which I easily took from your hands as you stood there frozen in fear and amazement. And now that I have all these, Jane, I can exercise a considerable measure of control over your conduct when I set you free, which I assure you is what I intend, as long as you promise to behave yourself and do as you're told. Do we have a deal?"

Jane nodded vehemently.

"Clever girl," he said. "Are you thirsty?"

She nodded again.

"Anything to get that gag off, eh?" he mused. "I understand. In a moment."

He reached down to a supermarket bag at his feet and produced a long black woollen sock and a red-netted plastic box containing four medium-sized oranges. He ripped the net and placed the box on the table. Slowly, he took three of the oranges and dropped them one after the other into the open neck of the sock. Then he twisted the neck closed and twirled the fruit-filled sock around by flicking his right wrist.

"I don't know if this is true, but I once heard the claim on some TV show that oranges in a sock, used to beat someone, leave no visible bruises. What do you think, Jane?"

Jane's eyes narrowed and she shook her head, moaning feebly and twisting her body the little she could.

"Can't remember the name of the show," he said. "But it wasn't *Lost*, I can tell you that." Then he smiled at her knowingly. "*Lost*. I only started watching once I learned that you were studying it, Jane. I can't say I'm as big a fan as you seem to be, but tell me, is there anything from season one that the present situation reminds you of?"

Jane was still for a moment, then nodded her agreement.

"Yes, that's right. Sayid and Nadia. So touching. There he is, a committed torturer, tasked with getting information from and then executing a young woman much less, I must say, much less lovely than you, Jane. And he helps her escape instead, improbably, then falls in love with her, very unlikely, and spends all his time, because it is fantasticated TV after all, searching the globe for her, her photo in his pocket."

Jane looked at him fearfully.

"But that's not quite what's going to happen here, Jane. Oh, I am going to let you go. But I won't be showing you the same sentimental empathy. And why is that? Well, to begin with, I already have photographs of you, and I have already been searching for you, and it wasn't that difficult to find you."

Buckrack took one step towards her, swinging the sock through the air at his waist. It thumped on her left rib cage and her body swayed to one side as she let out a muffled shriek of pain.

"The second reason is that, as you remember, Nadia manages to convince Sayid, with little more than some shared banal nostalgia for their childhood and a ladylike palm caressing the back of his hand, that he is not *really* – whatever that means – a torturer. Personally, I find those flashbacks very sketchy and unconvincing in plot terms. It's a weak-minded viewer who doesn't acknowledge that the irony of Sayid being tortured by the mad ugly Frenchwoman in the present, on the island, has distracted us into craven gullibility about his past, that and the fact we are learning some petty new detail that has previously been withheld from us, namely who's the chick in the pic, the kind of titbit we sit before the screen for much of an hour, our right paw raised, waiting to be tossed."

He swivelled his body and hit her on the right side as if he were playing a backhand at tennis. She crumpled in the opposite direction, with a cry that seemed to sound from under water, kept from falling only by the bonds which secured her to the beam.

"Well, I too am not by habit a torturer. But you are not going to persuade me to do anything other than what I am now doing. In fact, you are the one who has compelled me to this and a few other acts of moral inexcusability of late."

He struck her again on the left side, forehand, harder this time. And again on the right, backhand, even harder.

"I guess you might never have wanted to be a fat girl 'til now," Buckrack said. "A spare tyre might absorb some of that impact, no? Funny how everything depends on the circumstances. We might love being ourselves in one situation, but wish we were entirely someone else in another."

He put the sock down, reached into the supermarket bag and produced a plastic bottle of water. "Drink?" he suggested. "That might stop you playing dead."

Jane roused herself as he came towards her again. She looked at him with insipid affirmation. He reached up and placed the opened bottle on the horizontal beam behind her. Then he reached into his pocket. "Here, in my right hand, is a small pair of cosmetic scissors, with which I shall, carefully, and without harming a pore of your pretty cheek, cut through the tape. Here, in my left hand, as you might be able to sense, is a much heavier duty pair of scissors, which, if I tighten them a little – yeah, you feel that? – are at the moment acting like a nipple clamp calibrated a bit on the pinchy side. Now, when I remove the tape, you are going to remain silent unless spoken to unless you want your right nipple on the floor and a lot of blood staining that neat white blouse. There will certainly be no shouting or screaming. If there is, the gag goes back on and the nipple comes off. You got that? Once you've had your water we'll have a short conversation which, if it goes to plan, will also result in your body remaining consistently intact. Okay?"

Rigid with discomfort and fear, Jane nodded pitiably.

Buckrack cut through the tape carefully on the left side of her mouth and then, with care, without tugging at it, peeled it slowly off her skin until her lips were exposed. He left the flap of tape dangling. Jane was silent. He took the bottle and offered it to her. She drank slowly, their eyes meeting.

"I need," she said in a whisper, "to go to the bathroom."

He observed her calmly. "I understand," he said. "It's of no particular consequence to me if you do it in your pants, as I have a garden hose outside I can just reel in here and blast you with after making you strip down. But drink the rest of the water, then answer the couple of questions I have, and then you can go to the bathroom. As I say, if you can't wait, be my guest."

He held the bottle to her lips again and Jane gulped the water until it was empty.

"I repeat, Jane," said Buckrack, moving away and returning to his seat, "you're *so* incautious. I mean, that water could have had anything in it. Rohipnol, say, or something else to encourage you to acquiesce. But don't worry, it didn't. I think we already have an understanding, and before you leave here in a little while we shall have an even deeper compact that will ensure, if you value the skin on your back or the nipples on your front, that you do exactly as I say. That way you won't be punished again or worse. But I will come to that."

He picked up her iPad and opened the cover. "For now the one thing I need is the username of your bank account – the one "Daddy" pays into regularly – and your account password. If you hesitate to give me those, or you mess me around, like you pretend you don't remember them or give me the wrong ones, then I'll put the gag back on, let you shit or pee yourself, or both, then reel in my hose, get you naked, get you wetter but cleaner, and then some. I should explain why I want access to your bank account, in case you suspect I am a common thief. It simply makes it more easy for me to control what you do once I let you go, because without access to cash or credit, without a passport, without your email and Facebook accounts – oh, did I tell you I had changed the passwords on those already? – you are a little limited in your capabilities and correspondingly somewhat dependent on me. I only want this to be so for a short time, mind you. I have no wish to deprive you permanently, not of your liberty, certainly not of your charming bodily parts, not even of the money. So I am going to leave whatever I find in your account untouched. I am not here with the intention of confining you for long, or disfiguring you, or robbing you. But I am going to lock you out of your account for a little while. As long as you grant a few further requests, you will get out of this present situation before evening falls, with little more loss of joy than a few future nightmares. You will also stay out of prison. That is a promise."

Jane swallowed heavily. "Who are you?"

Buckrack sighed. "Actually, I intend to tell you that also before I let you go, because it will make all of this infinitely more comprehensible to you. But for the moment, and because you want to go to the bathroom, could you let me have the bank details, please?"

Somewhat timorously, she ventured, "If it *is* sex you want, there are easier ways."

Buckrack looked genuinely shocked. He shook his head. "Jane, Jane,

Jane. A nice try at being Nadia, if a tad more sassy. But I agree. If it were sex I wanted, there are easier ways. You should therefore conclude, as I've already intimated, that sex is not what I want. Now please stop playing for time. All you'll do is soil yourself. The bank details? I can see from your card that it's www.bostonsixthbank.com, and I am on their site already."

Somewhat in a whimper, Jane said, "The username is all one word, 'songsofinnocence', no upper case."

Buckrack entered the details into the iPad keyboard and waited. "A reference to your poetic namesake, huh? That's cute. And the password?"

"It's 'songsofexperience'."

Buckrack chuckled. "Real cute, real cute. Now, it's asking me for the second, third and seventh characters of what it calls your 'gateway code'."

"All capitals. H, E, A".

"Just give me the whole thing, for my records."

"Capitals T-H-E, numeral 4, capitals Z-O-A-S."

"Is that one of Blake's too? A lesser known one?"

"Yes."

"Well, I'm going to change that, then I'm going to change the other two as well to things much more recondite that an *aficionado* of any one subject couldn't guess. Really, Jane, you make identity theft so easy. But hey, I'm in! Good girl. Okay, Jane, just under fifteen hundred a month, converted from sterling: a University of Odium research scholarship, I see? But a balance of over thirty thousand dollars, now how did that happen? Oh, look, another round two thousand dollars a month from Daddy too? And he really is called William Blake? Yet he doesn't pay you from his bank account but via a *PayPal account*? Then in May this two thousand suddenly becomes a one-off five thousand dollars, and then exactly two thousand a month again, until the first of this month, and suddenly another five thousand. A bit strange and irregular, no? No doubt you have an explanation, but don't even try me: I know more than you think. And it's a lot of money for a postgrad student." He looked at her and smiled. "I see that you've been making regular transactions, right up till yesterday, small sums too, supermarket stuff, Amazon. So this really is your main account, huh? Well, that's what I wanted. I don't see a card for any British account in your purse, and this account tallies with the American card you have, so I am going to assume this is all there is right now. I'll let you have some cash for necessities when I let you go. If by chance you have another source of funds I think you are going to be very careful about how you use it once we've had our closing chat. Now be silent while I lock you out of this particular account. The bathroom is only moments away, I promise. I hope you can contain yourself."

After a few minutes, he closed the iPad. "Done!" he reported amiably. "Okay, Jane, you remember last night I played you a recording of the conversation you had in the Senior Common Room with Professor McNamara?"

She nodded dully.

"You can therefore logically conclude that there was recording equipment in that room and that Professor McNamara let me install it there. If I can put it this way, Jane, there are people in the University who are cooperating with my enquiries. They may have needed some convincing as to why, and from a properly recognised authority, but that clearly happened, so they know more than they seem to. So you mustn't be too trusting of anyone once I let you go. It should be obvious that you've been under investigation for some time. So here are a few rules to this game of ours. If you like, I'm releasing you on a kind of parole, and I need surety of your compliant behaviour. Professor McNamara is under instruction to do and say nothing else in respect of these matters. If you say anything to him about the recording, or about what has happened between us, you can expect him to react with studied incomprehension, as if you are an idiot or a lunatic. He does not, in any case, know that I abducted you, tied you up and slapped you about a bit. I admit he would find that a bit unorthodox. But he has played his small part in this matter, and it is at an end. Therefore, as you will inevitably encounter him, you should behave as if none of this took place at all, and as if he knows nothing of it. If you don't then you can expect to fail this probationary test of mine, and to experience predictable consequences. One thing I shall certainly do is remove all that cash from your account, before I do other stuff that's even nastier and more permanent. Are we on the same page?"

Weak with pain and fear, Jane agreed.

"You can also conclude," Buckrack continued, "that there was a microphone in your apartment and that it's still there. That will be monitored continuously, and not just by me. As I've tried to make clear, you should assume I am not working alone. Now I know it will be your instinct, when I let you go back there, to try to find the microphone and dispose of it. But let me advise that you will almost certainly not find it, but that even if you do, you had better leave it where it is. I will know if you destroy it or move it, obviously, and that will only lead me to come round and visit some further punishment on you. Therefore why bother looking? Until further notice, if you wish to leave your apartment for any reason you will call me at a number I will give you and I will assess the reasons for your request and either grant or deny it. If I call you and you fail to pick up within ten rings, day or night, you can expect me or others at your door or on your tail pretty quickly. I am now also going to give you some detailed advice on how to conduct yourself in the next few days and weeks when you are not in your apartment, and particularly about the thorny and unexpected problem that you have created in respect of Dr Poon. But before I do that, I want to show you a photograph."

Buckrack reached into his shirt pocket and took out a regular six-by-four of a man around thirty years old and a woman of roughly the same age, who both held a small baby. The adults in the photo were smiling broadly.

When Jane saw the picture her already pale face visibly blanched.

Buckrack looked down, then up again. "Well, if that didn't make you shit your pants, Jane, maybe you're not so desperate after all."

## Chapter Eight (25 October)

That evening, as Jane was in fact released by Buckrack, and went stumbling back to Coolwipe Hall, stunned and panicked by the enormity of her kidnapping, Buckrack's violence and the now hostile stamp which every object in the world seemed to possess, McNamara was sitting with Redman in 111 Maryland Lane. He had returned, not so much to help Redman with the task of understanding Asterisk's and Covet's calls, but to persuade him that the wiretap was a lost and dangerous cause. He knew that things were too far gone for mere moral persuasion, so had decided that the best course was to demonstrate that the practical returns from such surveillance were seriously outweighed by the risks in carrying it on. He was aware, while he listened to all the calls with Redman, that this approach created a risk of its own: Redman might think that he was permanently joining forces with him in his shady endeavour. But he felt confident that the exercise would demonstrate the truth without explicit exhortation. In this he was to prove quite mistaken.

"The problem is, James," he said as they sat drinking scotch afterwards, "you're going about it in the wrong way. I don't know what it is about postmodern literary people like you, but you are far too preoccupied with what you don't understand, with the slipperiness of meaning, than with what is so obviously graspable. These are phone calls made with generally practical purposes in mind, conducted on the hoof, not tissues of carefully crafted language, texts to be explicated. Most of the gaps in your understanding are caused by simple lack of context. Any call can refer to some other piece of information you don't have, or decision you don't know about, and so its full import evades you. What's your instinct? To worry over its meaning, to promote that worry into a paranoiac suspicion that if you could crack its code then you would have access to some startling, scandalous truth? There are so many calls like that, and the task of interpreting them would be endless. I say the best thing is to ignore all that. Pay no attention especially to the tatty, unprofessional way in which they talk about the staff, the insulting *noms de plume*, and so on. Focus on what you want to know, and don't be distracted by what you happen to find. I assume what you want to know is anything affecting the Union or its negotiations with management. Well, what have you found? Not much."

"Granted," Redman replied. "But I don't agree. For example, there's the call Asterisk had with Poon about the management proposal to link Annual Performance Review with salary increments. So, we have him calling Covet prior to that and Covet telling him that if the Union holds out against the proposal he should concede and they will try again in a year. But Covet tells him to try horse trading with a handful of minor morsels, things the Union has wanted for a long time, especially time off for the President for Union activities, and additional payment for Union officers invited onto union-management working groups. Asterisk then calls Poon immediately after, before the Union meeting which was planned to discuss the proposal, and he tells her that, although management has a legal duty to consult with the Union about the proposal, it is going to enforce it anyway, whatever the Union thinks. We know from his call with Covet that this is a lie: if the Union stands firm in its opposition, he's been instructed to back down. But he throws her the morsels he has been told to, which happen to include a personally tasty piece for her as President. He's even got this costed and presents it as a thirty-plus-thousand-pounds *per annum* subsidy that management is giving to the Union, even though they have a legal obligation to allow officers time off or payment *in lieu* for Union activities which they have simply never honoured. There's no mention that the proposal will save the University over a quarter of a million on the annual wage bill as well as put our members under the cosh of performance-related pay. Poon swallows this lie whole, no doubt because of the big sugared pill she personally sees it as. She then comes to the meeting – I was there – and informs us that management are going to enforce the proposal. She tells us nothing about the phone call with Asterisk. Instead, *she* argues that we should not resist the proposal but go back to management and bargain to the Union's advantage in return for our agreement. The net result is that the Union executive agrees, although I didn't personally, Poon goes off to Asterisk, gets what he's already offered her, and some individuals on the Union executive come out of it better off, her most of all, while the membership as a whole comes out of it very badly. The entire thing is perverse. All that seems to me pretty important to know."

McNamara had listened patiently. "But what's your point? So what, Covet and Asterisk outplayed Poon at poker. That's how the union-management game gets conducted up and down the land. They bluffed and won this hand. It's frustrating, perhaps, but hardly surprising. There's no point getting vexed when you find out your opponent had weaker cards than you thought. And it's exactly what you did to Asterisk in the Miller case. You beat him at poker."

"I beat him because I had a fucking royal flush, not because I bluffed!" Redman exclaimed. "And I had that hand because Miller was deliberately dealing me great cards. I'm not bemoaning the loss of this hand. I'm saying that if we can see what cards Asterisk and Covet have we can't be so easily bluffed. And this simple little computer program lets us see their cards."

"It lets *you* see their cards," McNamara corrected. "But it's hard to play poker with a big mirror behind your opponent and get away with it. Sooner or later they may look over their shoulder and figure out how you're doing it."

"It's a bad analogy, Robert. First of all, it's not a big mirror behind them they can just turn round and see. It's more like I'm telepathic. It's a tiny piece of code on an anonymous University workstation that sends recordings of their conversations to some godforsaken lawless outback, from where I anonymously retrieve them using an untraceable email address. Even if they discovered it, that's not going to lead them to me."

"In which case, what will draw attention to you will be the pre-emptive actions you may take based on information you gain by underhand means. And you do know this is criminal. What are you taking such a risk for?"

"Oh, listen to yourself, Robert. Covet and Asterisk have done criminal things under the radar for years, you and I both know it. Now when I employ the same methods you wax lyrical about the wrong."

"It's not about the wrong. It's about the risk. It's also about what it will do to you, how it will distract you, how it threatens to consume you, how it will perhaps damage you, never mind the fact that it may ruin you. Look at what it's done already: you suspect Poon of being corrupt, or at least weak-willed, so now you will be on the lookout for other such instances, on guard against her."

Redman scoffed. "*You* are going to lecture *me* about being suspicious of *Poon*? You've never trusted her."

"But I'm not acting on my mistrust. That's the difference. I've removed myself from any position where my mistrust of her has any relevance."

"Ah," Redman said. "Perhaps we should talk about that, Robert. You removing yourself from a position. Because it's what you have also wanted me to do for a long time, and I have never figured out why. I mean, like everybody else, I've never known why you resigned in the first place, much less why you think I should follow suit."

"I resigned for an obvious reason. It was doing me no good."

"It wasn't a position to be pursued for the benefits to yourself. There was a greater good you were meant to be pursuing."

McNamara grunted with indignation and seemed about to give vent to his feeling, but then he checked himself. "You know I know that, and you know that I did pursue that. I think it's obvious what I am saying, because you just gave an example of it yourself. We might as a Union have wished to pursue a greater good, but most of the time as officers we were frustrated from doing so, or at best put a finger in the dyke until the flood returned to wipe us out a year later. I did the work for nine years, James. I hardly gave up at the first discouragement. But after that period, when I did an accounting of my effort compared to the benefits, all I could truly point to were a half a dozen personal cases in which I had made a serious difference to individuals: an early retirement on health grounds here, an over-the-top disciplinary case there. Maybe I was not personally very effective, but no one else seemed to want to do it. Even Poon, as far as I understand it, had virtually to be press-ganged into it after I resigned. You might well condemn her compromises and subterfuges. But all the causes I would have considered worth making a principled stand for at the beginning of my period had been lost by the end of it, and not for lack of trying on the Union executive side. And I was a lot more experienced than Poon as far as politics goes, and I still carry pretty serious ideological baggage. But the problem is, I decided, that it's not really a Union at all, but a professional association, with a membership that is largely atomised and individualistic. The members are essentially greedy, self-centred, competitive careerists of the most stab-you-in-the-back kind, hardly heroes of solidarity. Academics are, on the whole, with a few exceptions, despicable human beings, driven by craven self-interest. The members to this day include a Dean of Faculty, Blandford, who tweets people every time he is cited in a journal, who is so stupid that he thinks an absence of real intellectual gravitas can be compensated for by advertised self-importance, which has developed into a real psychosis in which he thinks that Twitter has made him a public figure, and that anything he tweets, from having a cup of tea in the morning to getting extra booths in a toilet, is *de facto* noteworthy. But things can get worse than having members who happen to be idiots in high places. Even Pro-Vice Chancellors, sitting on the other side of the table from us at pay talks, were sometimes members. What kind of union permits its members to act expressly with the interests of management in mind in union-management negotiations or voting situations? Damn it, even Asterisk qualifies for membership, and you couldn't deny him it if he applied. But then, the rank-and-file, as it used to be called, is torpid and inactive. We had difficulty getting quorate ordinary meetings unless the issue of parking spaces was on the agenda.

68

In fact, back then, it *was* the *Association* of University Teachers, too timid even in name to wish to be tarred with the brush of being a trades union. It's only recently started calling itself the University and College Union, and that only after a merger."

Redman leaned over to top up McNamara's glass. He retorted, "In what way does any of that argue against what I am doing? All it amounts to saying is that conventional, time-honoured methods are bound to fail. I am proposing a departure from such methods. I am suggesting that the only way to make a difference is by adopting nefarious tactics similar to those deployed by Tweedledum and Tweedledee."

McNamara sighed. "Make a difference? Oh, the romance of it all! Have you noticed how much the language of the left tempts us into feeling that we can do something finite that will make a permanent change? But this is not an epoch of revolution, James. It won't bring forth an outlaw like Trotsky who can engineer a gear shift so profound, even on a small scale, that the vehicle can never again be thrown into reverse. And even if you could, at what cost to yourself? Before you dismiss what I'm saying, I don't just mean legal *risk*. I mean at what cost to yourself, to your being? Really, what impulse is being followed here, what is the determining aim of the access you now have to these private conversations? Was Miller looking for justice or revenge?"

"He expressed an interest in 'nailing' them. I guess it was either, or both."

"And you? Do you want to 'nail' them as well?"

"I want to outwit them. I know I'm finished negotiating with them, because they never have real negotiations anyway. When they can't use *force majeure*, they constantly try to move the goalposts, or if that fails they resort to strategies which are little short of corrupt or even illegal, and if they are found out in those attempts they pretty much use outright bribery. So I guess I feel it's time to fight fire with fire, and all Miller did was give me the means."

"But why not just walk away and do what you came to work in a university for?"

"Maybe, for one thing, because I am forty, not sixty, Robert. I have twenty-five plus years to go on surviving in an institution like this, whereas you could probably retire tomorrow if you had to. There is also the fight-the-good fight argument and to hell with whether you win or lose. Not to mention the fact that I wouldn't be surprised if I did manage to turn up some public scandal worth blowing the whistle on, given what I already know about Covet and Asterisk and how they operate. So I have reasons not to buy into your quietism. I'd rather not retreat into the study right now and write my own defeatism up. Look what happened to you."

McNamara was stultified in a near-muted way. "What do you mean?"

"Well, shortly after you resigned, off you went and wrote a book with the worst title in the world: *Actually Non-Existing Communism*. Curious, that at just that point you should write not a rallying cry to a new socialist politics, but an account of the God that failed."

"Oh, for Christ's sake, James, I'm a political scientist, not a manifesto writer. The book was about the substantial difference between Marx's conceptions of communism and what happened in the USSR, China, Cuba, *etcetera*. I think it said some things that still needed to be said, with some detailed contemporary case studies, namely about Marx's conception that communism would only take off in advanced capitalist countries, not the backward feudal ones that laid claim to it, and about the serious intellectual mistakes we make if we equate Marxism with what actually occurred under the name of 'real socialist' revolutions. I don't see what was defeatist about it."

"No, but it's how it was manipulated, the arguments it was used to support. Did you notice that every popular review basically made out that it supported the thesis that socialism had proved to be a dead-end, and Marxism therefore an historical aberration?"

"Yes, but the academic reviews didn't say that."

"Who reads them? And the TV interviews? That Discovery Channel history of the post-Cold War you appeared on, for example? You might as well have been Francis Fukuyama. Its general thesis was that liberal capitalism was the best we could hope for."

"I can't control how selectively I am read or edited. I know the book did not say that, and anyone who really reads it knows that. The book's the thing, not coverage of it. What I argue and what the media present me as arguing are not the same. And in the end, whatever misconceptions others have, in myself I am content with what I did."

"My point," Redman went on forcefully, "is precisely that you don't control these things, and you're being naïve if you think the book itself, however well it's done, with its relatively small readership, has the same influence as those accounts of it. That's why you shouldn't be content.

Sure, this is what the liberal media do with a book like yours: they process it according to some familiar ideological template. Just as I can't control Poon or Asterisk the ways things are. So I'll break the rules instead. I won't observe the template, because observing the template means we lose nearly all the time, or can hope for stalemate on a few select issues at best."

"*My point*," McNamara said, "is that it was *academic* work *about* politics and economics. It was an attempt to get people to think straight about a complex issue. It was not a *political* work that aimed to get people to act in a cause. I could argue with you that getting our thinking straight might *lead to* more rational actions but I'm not even bothered to justify it that way. It needs no such justification. I was doing what an academic is meant to do."

"And *my further point* is that right now I am not interested in doing what academics are meant to do when Tweedledum and Tweedledee are corrupting the very institution in which they are meant to do it. If they get their way academics a generation younger than you won't get to do what they are meant to do, you see? Damn it, we might already be at that stage, for all we know. And if we are, then me turning aside to finish – ah, who am I kidding? to start! – my bloody book on Raymond Williams is just folly. This way at least I get to find out what exactly it is they are doing. And it just happens to be me in this position. No one else is. So yes, as I said before, someone has to do it, and that someone, yes, in the present situation, has to be me. You can help, which would be welcome, or at least not hinder, which is pretty much all you have done."

They were silent for some time. Redman tilted his glass to suggest a refill. McNamara was thoughtful. "I am not intending to help you further with this beyond this evening," he said decisively. "But I will pitch in with my thoughts on what we have listened to, as we've already come that far. And of course I will say nothing to anyone about it."

Redman poured from the bottle dejectedly. "Okay. Well, then, as we seem to have settled that, I'm listening."

McNamara sipped. "I repeat, so far there isn't much that's Union-related, although I can accept the obvious point that there probably will be. I also repeat, focus on what you *can* understand without too much interpretative work: that might help you with what you don't get. It's tempting to think that things are in code when they are just discreetly expressed. The one thing we know is coded are the names of a number of members of staff, but we were able to work all of those out virtually independently. Your list and mine are the same."

Redman took up a piece of paper from the table between them. "All except one," he said. "*Avenger* does not appear in any of the calls Miller recorded and so isn't on your list. Yet it appears on numerous occasions in the ones I've eavesdropped on. I can't work out who it refers to. But it strikes me as one hell of a code name."

McNamara shrugged. "Perhaps we should listen to those calls again," he answered wearily.

## PART THREE
26 OCTOBER – 29 OCTOBER

## Chapter Nine (26 October – 27 October)

If it is in their thirties that men truly become aware that they are not indestructible, and in their forties that they generally experience the first serious twinges of mortality and loss of life force, then it is in their fifties that they begin to see signs of their future end on the horizon. In the case of Professor Sir Evan Covet, aged fifty-seven at the time of this narrative, this was so.

It had begun one morning ten years before when he awoke with a mysterious pain to the left of his solar plexus. At first he thought it might be a cracked rib or simply some muscular strain, but as months passed and the ache persisted without diminishing, he began to worry that it might be something more hostile. The area was not far from the heart, and when he looked up diagrams of that organ he considered the inferior vena cava the only passageway so positioned as to be the likely source of the problem. His fantasies of some impending aneurysm or possible sudden thrombosis (both things he had not at first fully understood but after meticulous research came to know the full intricacies of) were allayed by his private doctors, who pointed out that the posterior vena cava, as it is also called, derives its name from the fact that it enters the rear of the heart, carrying blood up alongside the spine from the abdominal region. It could not be the cause of a pain in the front of the body. For the same reason, his occasional nightmares of cancer of the spleen, which he knew could kill a person in weeks, were dismissed. They were also fairly sure it was not a problem with the lower oesophagal sphincter. After various tests, X-rays and a mid-body MRI scan, the doctors' best and vague guess was a "musculo-skeletal dysfunction" which was undetectable and probably nothing to worry overmuch about: just one of those things we can expect as we age, but unlikely to be debilitating or fatal. This had proved seemingly true over the years, but the problem remained chronic to this day, reminding him constantly that a small zone of his body was dully and recalcitrantly refusing to do its job efficiently and in cooperation with the rest. It was not the kind of thing that painkillers could combat. Infrequently there were small sharp needling pains in the area which felt like they were occurring just under the surface of the skin. If he made any abrupt upper body turns to the right the region tightened into a knot of inhibiting, though not excruciating, pain. But it was worst when he coughed or laughed. Either activity stimulated the muscles in the area to convulse, and with each contraction and expansion he experienced something like a stabbing sensation, which often sent his right hand groping towards it in alarm. He therefore trained himself to avoid situations in which he might cough or laugh much.

Two years or so after the unilluminating diagnosis, he woke up in the middle of the night in a five star Cape Town hotel (it is odd how often these things emerge during sleep: you can go to bed feeling perfectly fit but be aroused in a state of horrible mortal fear) because he had a throbbing in his left hip. He put his hand down there and could actually feel the muscles spasming and rippling. He had an ominous sense of something very bad about to happen, when what felt like a crack of lightning struck from the hip to the knee, as if a whip had been lashed inside his leg. He started up bodily and howled, or rather emitted a sound which was like a loud low moan and a high pitched squeal combined. He managed to get himself upright before the next attack came, and when it did it sent him crashing naked to the floor, gibbering in severe distress and, because it was so entirely unexpected, serious fear. He was too terrified and preoccupied by the shock to be able to formulate words. All that came out of him were unrepressed small shrieks and heaving sighs. His conduct so frightened the mediocre black prostitute who was with him that, instead of using the bedside phone at which he gestured to call for help, she hurriedly threw on her clothes and made a swift escape from the room, leaving him clutching his thigh with both hands and rocking his body on the carpet. The recurring pulses, burning, stinging like electricity with some excess voltage pangs added for good measure, did not stop for ten minutes, by which time he was in real tears, for the first time he could remember, certainly the first time since childhood. The attacks came again the next day while he was trying to relax in the jacuzzi, and his reaction half flooded the hotel bathroom. He checked himself into a private hospital nearby, where a far from mediocre white consultant instantly diagnosed sciatica, and told him, incredibly, "not to worry" because he had not slipped a disc.

"It first happened to me," the doctor said, "though in the other leg, when I was thirty-eight, so you can count yourself lucky at your age."

Covet wanted to know if it was likely to occur again.

"Maybe," the doctor replied.

"Did it happen again to you?" Covet asked.

"Sure," nodded the doctor laconically.

"What can I do to prevent it?"

"Well," said the doctor, perhaps with a certain sense of liberty from constraint because he was unlikely to see the patient again, "they say posture control, exercise, and stretching help. But I do all that and I still get it every so often. I recommend stoicism. It's the best medicine known to human kind."

And return it did, in the same leg, every two or three years. After the second episode, which occurred while he was driving his Mercedes on a rare family holiday and almost caused him to kill his wife and two teenage children as well as himself, Covet started to think there was something physically wrong with the left side of his body. More doctors told him there was little chance that the permanent crisis in his midriff was at all associated with the occasional attempted *coup d'état* in his sciatic nerve. But he could not help but think that the left wing nature of both was part of some constitutional eruption, perhaps even a sea change in the *zeitgeist* of his very brain. A CT scan of the latter revealed no relevant change in the structure of that organ. It was still pretty much the same thing that had got him his First Class Honours in Law from the University of Dundee. Nonetheless, his right side began to watch out for his left side as if it were some ailing Siamese twin. What his gold standard health package could not get him without personal cost – and it got him regular acupuncture, osteopathy, physiotherapy, angiograms, biopsies, urinalysis, sigmoidoscopy, and a gamut of other miscellaneous tests and procedures and treatments – he invested in: posture chairs, back braces, a car with no clutch, memory cushions, Scholl foot arch supports, regular swims, an infrared sauna, to name but a few.

Yet still the waves kept coming in Canute's direction. On the day of his divorce, as he finally and reluctantly removed his wedding ring, he noticed that his left hand trembled while his right remained still. His dental issues appeared to occur only on the left side of his mouth, as did his tongue ulcers. He had a bout of psoriasis on the left elbow, and a fungal infection on his inner left thigh which, upon investigation, drew his attention to what was adjacent: a retracted left testicle, significantly higher than his right. His left eyelid, by contrast, was the one which drooped a little lower. When he looked at himself naked in the mirror, as he often now did, he thought he saw a curious asymmetry in his limbs and curves. He even took a high resolution digital photograph of his nude self against a black backdrop, divided it vertically in half, and examined the contrasting halves mathematically insofar as Adobe Photoshop and his insecure knowledge of geometry would permit. The exercise did not reassure him.

And then, eventually, one evening, as he sat in front of his fifty-two inch LCD home cinema watching the last episode of the first season of *Breaking Bad*, which he had consumed in back-to-back fashion over four evenings at his minor mansion, alone, mainly in darkness and rural autumnal silence, all through which he had felt his mind slowly whirring and speeding up to the velocity required for an incipient realisation, a kind of epiphany in slow motion, he arrived at a conclusion which, while astonishing, he felt intuitively to be correct. His ailments were a punishment. They had been visited upon him as retribution for an adult life which, he knew, had in almost every regard lacked virtue. It was not that he thought there was anything divine or demonic actually at work within him. While he had been raised in the Reformed Presbyterian Church of Scotland, and was to every external witness of his public conduct a Calvinist to the very marrow of his being, he knew himself to be, privately and in truth, a quite Godless man. He did not believe in any metaphysical actuality in which everyone is born a sinner, and as such is subject to God's wrath and the punishment of death, which means eternal separation from God in Hell unless the sinner repents and turns in faith to accept Jesus Christ as the only means of salvation. The only part of this ridiculous proposition he subscribed to was that everyone is born a sinner, which was exactly why, he reflected, he had thoroughly revelled in duplicity, vice and hatred from the day of his first full academic appointment in Edinburgh: it was the natural state of Man and not something to be considered unusual, just something you should try to be better at than others.

But the developing story of Walter White, as he watched it fascinatedly, reached out to him over four nights some spiritual tentacle which seemed to proffer an hitherto untouched insight into his ongoing physical malaise. Walter, upon being diagnosed with cancer, could be seen descending abjectly from loving husband, father and dutiful Chemistry schoolteacher into crystal meth dealer, liar and murderer, in a way that could not conceivably end well for him at the far-off conclusion of season five. As Walter's physical integrity began to collapse, so too did his moral sense at the same rate abandon him. It hardly took a major leap of logic (or newly found spiritual wisdom) on Covet's part to understand that an ethical regeneration might also restore his own corporeal balance. The trick, he realised, was to be Walter White in reverse: to live Walter's life backwards, away from wickedness in the direction of the good.

Covet retired to bed, feeling peculiarly light-headed, although he had drunk no Drambuie, as was his regular evening habit. He experienced some sleepless hours, but not as an insomniac does, writhing in frustration at his failure to appease Morpheus. Rather, he conned and cast up to himself his lifetime of deceit and infidelity, his many backstairs manoeuvrings and masterful manipulations, his bullying, his loathing, his prejudices and superiority, his consuming avarice and addictive double dealing, his confidence tricks, his glorious blackmail gambits and mind-game victories. This was done not in a spirit of remorse, but as if they were so many sandbags he was now capable of throwing out of his rapidly ascending balloon: *ad astra*, as it were, but not *per ardua*. He was priest to his own confessor, forgiving himself without need of either benediction or penance. At last he fell into a peaceful sleep, and dreamed, joyfully, that he was Adam, alone in the Garden of Eden.

The dream ended with the sound of hammering. It took him some moments to realise that someone was banging heavily at his front door, many metres away downstairs. This was unusual: Homestead Park was no Eden, but it did have twenty-four hour perimeter security, and unannounced visitors were a virtual impossibility. He thought it must be his chauffeur, and that he had overslept, but when he looked at the clock he saw that it was not yet 6am. He got out of bed, put on a dressing gown and nimbly walked the long walk along the upstairs hallway, the rapping at the door increasing in volume but not yet having for him, as it might have by now for the reader, any suggestions of *Macbeth*, the primrose way or the everlasting bonfire. As he started to descend the staircase, indeed, he remarked on his sobriety and the fact that, despite his foreshortened sleep, he felt curiously alert and, well, *well*. Crossing the large drawing room to the front lobby, he strode across the vestibule and approached the outer door.

Parting the curtain, he saw the glaring face of Buckrack, and reacted with an internal alarm he only just managed to conceal.

"Open up," Buckrack said through the glass.

Covet unlocked the door and hissed, "What the hell?"

Buckrack pushed past him and he closed the door and locked it once more. He pursued Buckrack into the drawing room, where he found him standing beside a coffee table.

"How on earth did you get here?" Covet demanded. "How do you know where I live?"

Buckrack made a sound of exasperated disbelief. "You're surprised at *that*? I am ex-CIA, remember. These things are pretty easy to me."

"But how did you get past security?"

Buckrack winced in amusement. "British country residential park security? I may be sixty-two but you think I can't scale a wall and avoid cameras?"

"But we *agreed*," said Covet forcefully. "No personal contact. You're meant to use the mobile number I gave you."

"Yeah, well, something came up. No one is gonna know I came here, but I wanted to get you before you went in to work."

Covet eyed him with anxiety. "What do you mean?"

"I need some coffee," Buckrack said.

"You need coffee?" Covet repeated impatiently.

"Yeah, the news will keep."

"Christ!" Covet exclaimed, and turned towards the kitchen. Buckrack removed his coat and threw it on a sofa, then planted himself beside it.

Five minutes later, Covet was holding a breakfast mug in his hands and watching Buckrack remove a photo from his bag, printed on plain white copy paper.

"Do you know this girl?" Buckrack asked him. "Ever met her before?"

Covet picked up the photo and examined it. "No. Not that I can remember, at any rate. Who is she? And why?"

"Her name is Jane Blake. She's a postgraduate student at Odium."

"I know hardly any students. I meet them occasionally for photo opportunities, but mostly I avoid them."

"She's a beautiful girl. You'd remember her if you'd met her, right?"

"Not my type," Covet rejoined.

Buckrack laughed. "I think she's one of those girls who's pretty much any man's type. Maybe even any woman's type. She's sex on legs through any set of eyes. She's in the Department of Cultural Studies. Her supervisor is Poon."

Covet tried to look more interested. "I see. So?"

"She's also a pastoral tutor in McNamara's student residence. Does that ring any bells?"

Covet appeared faintly enlightened. "Ah," he said. "I am beginning to remember now. Yes, I asked McNamara to give her that role. She needed a place to stay. He was a bit reluctant to bypass the usual selection process, but he gave in. It's coming back to me. But I don't remember her being in Cultural Studies. I thought she was in the School of English."

"Why did you do that?"

"Why did I do what?"

"Why did you make a special effort to find a postgrad student somewhere to live? Don't you have an accommodation office for that? A bit beneath your level, no?"

"Normally I wouldn't concern myself with that kind of thing, but she was one of the students who got a Vice Chancellor's Research Scholarship. I sometimes help these students out, as my office is attached to their award, and there are very few of them. Yes, I remember now. That's how I might have met her. But that was nearly a year ago. And my memory may be defective, but I'm sure she wasn't in Cultural Studies. Anyway, stop beating about the bush. Why are you asking?"

Buckrack raised his hand. "In a moment," he said. "She *was* on the English programme, but at the beginning of this academic year she transferred into Cultural Studies. Change of direction in her Ph.D., apparently. But this Vice Chancellor's scholarship, who makes the decision on that?"

Covet sighed. "It's open to nominations from across the University. If you are a Head of School you can apply on behalf of any new post-graduate research student. I chair a small committee which looks at the nominations, I take their advice, and then I make the final decision. That's why it's called the Vice Chancellor's Research Scholarship: it's in my gift. I only ever normally meet the students when they arrive and take up their award, and even then it's usually just a five minute handshake job for a feature in the University *Newsletter*."

Buckrack put down his coffee and looked levelly across the table. "It seems a little weird to me that you hire me to monitor Poon and McNamara, the current President and the previous President of the Union, and here we have someone else with relatively regular one-to-one access to both of them, partly because of your efforts. I have bugged their offices, and she is often in both of their offices. Now, I thought what you wanted was inside information on the Union's activities. I didn't think conversations with students were likely to be interesting. But what I'm beginning to wonder is whether one of the things you actually want me to hear and report on is what she discusses with them?"

Covet smiled in the negative. "This is what I'm paying you for? You're way off. For a start, I hardly know this girl. The only thing I ever did was put her in McNamara's Hall. I didn't know she was going to end up being supervised by Poon. It's just a coincidence. And I agree with you. I can't see how what she discusses with them can conceivably be of any interest to us."

"But why McNamara's Hall? Why ask a guy you have very poor relations with? Why not lean on someone else, another Warden likely to be more unquestioningly obedient?"

"Okay," Covet shrugged, "I did it to irritate him. I knew he would protest about normal procedure, equal opportunities, that kind of thing, and I wanted to take some pleasure in reminding him who was boss. I didn't get much. He caved in pretty quickly."

"A coincidence, then," Buckrack echoed. "Well, it's turned into a pretty interesting coincidence. That's why I'm here."

Covet patiently clasped his hands under his chin. "Go on," he encouraged.

"Okay," said Buckrack. "As you know, I currently have three microphones up and running: one in McNamara's study in Coolwipe Hall, and one each in Poon's office and Redman's office in the Trump Building. They are high spec omnidirectional mics and they record in pretty good quality any sound or speech in the room, even at the furthest spatial extremes from the mic. That's why they were fairly expensive. They are noise activated and send a wireless audio signal after activation to a receiver in my house, to which recording equipment is attached. I can even record conversations happening simultaneously in any of the three rooms. The results so far have been what I have given you: not a lot, pretty much standard Union business in Poon's office, the odd phone call about Union business in Redman's office, and nothing at all in McNamara's study. Until the night before last, that is."

Covet opened his palms. "And what happened the night before last?"

"Listen for yourself," said Buckrack. "I came out here to let you hear this."

He placed a recorder on the table and played the discussion between McNamara and Jane Blake.

When it was over, Covet said, "It's not without interest. McNamara gave her reasonable advice. I think everyone knows Poon is gay, no news there. All it is, though, is she's doing the dirty deed with this girl and there's an undeclared conflict of interest. There's not a lot I can do with that, however."

"Not on its own," Buckrack agreed. "But now we know. It won't be difficult to get evidence in a form you can use. It's just a matter of setting it up, and I wanted to know if you'd like me to do that. I'm sure you can force her resignation or fire her based on that and, pretty much at a stroke, you've sabotaged the Union. That's the kind of thing you've been after, no?"

"Well, yes," Covet acknowledged in a judicious tone, "but she'd only be replaced by Redman. It's true that I wouldn't mind breaking them, but this wouldn't do it, it would only get rid of her. And in some ways Redman would be a bigger problem than she is as President. I was really more interested in finding out what they are planning and how they are responding to management proposals and initiatives. We've got a busy year of radical stuff ahead and I need to be able to stitch them up. We can keep this in our back pocket for now."

"So you don't want me to follow it up? This opportunity may not last. You heard yourself, the girl is trying to break it up."

"No," Covet said decisively. "I don't want this thing going too far afield, so we need to keep the student out of it, for now anyway."

"But I'll report any further conversations she has with McNamara or Poon?"

"Yes, do that."

At the door, Covet said, "You mustn't just arrive here like this again, no matter what comes up. Phone me on my personal mobile. We'll meet somewhere more out of the way if the need arises."

"Okay," said Buckrack.

"But there is one thing. Why did it take you two nights to tell me about this?"

"I didn't get to the recording 'til early this morning. I had been reviewing the others from Poon's and Redman's offices. Nearly all of it turned out to be dross, but nothing of any interest to us ever seems to occur in McNamara's study, so I tend to leave that stuff 'til last. I almost didn't listen to it at all when I realised she was just a student. But when I did I came over as soon as I could."

"Right," said Covet. "Thanks."

Covet shaved and showered. The encounter with Buckrack had come like a bitter aftertaste of everything bad he had been reckoning over in bed the night before, but he realised that it was unrealistic to expect that he could instantly follow his new path of virtue without clearing away the practical obstacles the past inevitably would leave in his way. In any case there was not much to tidy up. He would simply not pursue the matter of Poon and her new paramour. He would wind Buckrack's surveillance operation down by telling him to discontinue it in a day or two. There would be no need to give Buckrack a reason: he would hardly complain if he was allowed to run out the remainder of his one-year contract in salaried idleness. He would even let him return to LA if he wanted, and never the twain should meet again. As he dried himself off he remarked that his body felt firmer and suppler than usual, and when he looked in the mirror he appeared less anxious and haggard than he often did. He also felt younger, lighter limbed. There was very little troubling his mind. In fact what dominated it was a sense of relief, akin to that experienced when you have been at some brink beyond which there is an abyss of danger or the unknown, and you draw back and purposefully walk away. It was a good feeling, a safe feeling, and one he could not remember ever feeling before. Perhaps he had been living close to that gulf for a lot longer than he imagined?

He even decided to make himself some scrambled eggs while he waited for his driver to arrive. This was a new thing too, as he normally had breakfast meetings in his private dining room at the University, and hardly ever cooked. Stirring the wooden spoon in the saucepan, hearing it thud hollowly against the edges, with the light dairy smell wafting up into his face, gave him a sense of domesticity and comfort. Instead of more coffee he made himself warm milk, which he had not drunk since he was a small boy, and wondered at its neutral, calming, unstimulating effect. He heard the car draw up at 7.30, just as he was finishing it. He took his briefcase and coat and exited the house.

It was still dark, though the sky was lightening prettily and the driveway was illuminated by the portico lamps. His driver, Brian Blackfoot, got out of the car at the bottom of the entry steps. He was a large portly man with a kind face and a thick avuncular moustache. But Covet noticed something in his greeting and his expression that lacked the usual geniality. He was about to ask if anything was wrong when he saw the rear doors open, and out stepped two men even larger than the chauffeur. He recognised them as Harmwell and Wolfitt, the Chief of University Security and his Deputy. They were wearing their customary black *Reservoir Dogs* suits and white shirts whose chilling effect Covet had often approved of, but which he did not relish now. Harmwell was holding a large buff envelope. His expression seemed a combination of pain, awkwardness, and determination. There seemed nothing promising in any of the three.

"Vice Chancellor," Harmwell nodded, but did not wait to be invited to start ascending the steps, followed by Wolfitt. As they approached Covet saw Blackfoot turn with resignation and get back into the driver's seat and close the door. In an instant the two security men were towering in front of him, their blackness and broad shoulders actually blotting out nearly everything he could catch of the morning sky.

"I am sorry about the unannounced visit, Vice Chancellor," said Harmwell, "but we are under instructions from the President of University Council. You are not to go into work today. I am told the letter in this envelope explains everything."

Covet felt feeble. These men normally did his peremptory bidding without question, but there was a steeliness about them today which seemed unopposable. He felt his briefcase almost slip out of his moist hand, and bent his knees to put it on the ground. The slight crouch made him seem so physically powerless that he saw both Harmwell and Wolfitt look away on a kind of shared human impulse to spare him his dignity.

"Give me a moment," he said, and turned from them. He broke the seal on the envelope and pulled out a letter printed on official University notepaper, dated the day before, which read:

Dear Sir Evan,

The University has today received information submitted under the provisions of the Public Interest Disclosure Act 1998. As you know, the Registrar immediately informs me directly as President of Council of all such disclosures.

The University's Public Interest Disclosure Code is used to deal with information received from anyone which expresses a genuine concern that there are reasonable grounds for believing that:

1. a criminal offence has been, is being, or is likely to be committed; or
2. a person has failed, is failing, or is likely to fail to comply with their legal obligations; or
3. a miscarriage of justice has occurred, is occurring, or is likely to occur; or
4. the health and safety of any individual has been, is being, or is likely to be endangered; or
5. the environment has been, is being, or is likely to be damaged; or
6. any of the above are being, or are likely to be, deliberately concealed.

The Code also provides that the identity of the discloser shall not be revealed unless this is essential in any investigation.

The information received today gives rise to genuine concerns that possibilities indicated by (1), (2), (3), (4) and (6) above may have arisen as a result of actions taken by you in your official capacity as Vice Chancellor and/or personally in specific relation to University business.

Given the gravity of these concerns, I have asked the Registrar to establish an internal investigation team which shall report confidentially within 28 days. While this investigation is ongoing, and until further notice, you are suspended from duty on full salary, and should not attend the workplace or engage in any other University business.

You will be required to participate in the investigation in due course, and shall be given further appropriate details as to the nature of the disclosure as part of that participation. Should you feel that the matter requires legal representation, you should retain your own counsel, as the University lawyers cannot be made available to you for these purposes. While there can be no prohibition on your discussing this matter with colleagues, I assure you that it will be dealt with in the strictest confidentiality by the University. You are advised, however, to make no attempt to contact members of senior management likely to be dealing with the case or with members of the investigatory team unless approached.

You should immediately surrender to Mr Harmwell, in his capacity as Chief Security Officer of the University, your University mobile phone and the personal computer provided for your use at your residence at Homestead Park. These items are the property of the University, as is your residence, and Mr Harmwell is authorised hereby, consistent with the terms of your tenancy agreement, to enter your residence without any further warrant in order to retrieve them.

I shall write to you again formally at the earliest opportunity.

Yours sincerely,

Maximilian Knight

President of Council

## Chapter Ten (27 October)

Covet made three calls in rapid succession. The first was to Asterisk, the second to Buckrack, and the third to McNamara.

An hour and a quarter later, McNamara was sitting on the same couch Buckrack had occupied earlier in the morning, examining Covet with just a hint of curiosity.

"An unusual emergency, you said. But even so, your house in the country? I've never been here before. A call before eight in the morning? Why couldn't we do it in the University? And why me?"

Covet returned his look with an amiable smile. "I wasn't planning to go in today. I got called late last night and the more I thought about the situation the more it seemed necessary to address it instantly. I am sorry about the early call, but it's probably best that we get a head start on this issue. I am grateful that you agreed to come."

McNamara sighed. "Okay," he said, semi-expectantly.

"You remember that young woman I asked you to appoint to a pastoral tutorship in your Hall back at the beginning of this year?"

McNamara sat back on the sofa. "Jane Blake?"

"Yes. How is she doing?"

"As a tutor? She's okay."

"You see much of her? Does she talk to you?"

"Enough."

"How does she seem to you personally? Has she had any problems?"

"What kind of problems?"

Covet smiled again. "I know how you are about confidentiality, Robert, but we've been here before. Nothing is confidential from the Vice Chancellor."

McNamara eyed him sceptically. "If you know how I am about confidentiality, then you know that's not something I agree with. But maybe if you tell me what the concern is involving Jane Blake I might be able to help."

"Fair enough. What I am about to tell you *is* strictly confidential, of course, and needs to stay between us."

McNamara smiled wryly. "I see."

"We had a problem in the School of English over the summer. I don't know if you remember, but Miss Blake was originally registered for a Ph.D. in that School. She submitted a written complaint to the Registrar about a member of staff in the School with whom, apparently, she had become romantically – which is to say sexually – involved. She had broken off the relationship but the member of staff was hounding her, harassing her, becoming quite obnoxious about it."

McNamara felt Covet scanning his expression.

Covet said, "Do you know about that?"

"No," McNamara replied.

"She didn't say anything to you about it? Seek your advice?"

"She didn't discuss any sexual relationship with a member of staff in English with me," McNamara said.

"Did you hear about it from anyone else?"

McNamara shook his head.

"It wasn't on the bush telegraph?"

"No," said McNamara. "Was it true?"

"Well, we don't know, and we didn't want to find out," Covet went on. "I decided to try to resolve the problem unofficially. I managed that without too much difficulty. I spoke to Stokes about it, just before his term as Head of English came to an end in July, and we decided that the best way of avoiding embarrassment was to propose that the student transfer to another School. Stokes dealt with the member of staff. There seemed no problem in academic terms, and the student was agreeable to it. I spoke to Cooper in Cultural Studies, and we agreed that Avril Poon could take the student on, although we didn't tell her why, of course. Cooper tipped her off that she would be approached about an internal student transfer, that she should take on the student, and that was it. Miss Blake transferred to Cultural Studies, as you no doubt know, at the beginning of this academic year."

"I see," said McNamara. "So that problem was solved. Obviously something else has happened."

"Yes," said Covet. "Yesterday the student lodged another formal complaint."

"About the same member of staff?"

"No – about Avril Poon."

McNamara raised an eyebrow. "And what was the complaint?"

"Well, this is the thing," said Covet. "The complaint was pretty much identical. Except this time the student claims to have had a sexual relationship with Poon."

McNamara was silent.

"Did you know anything about it?" Covet asked directly.

"What? That she was having a relationship with Poon? Well, everyone knows Poon is a lesbian, but I didn't have Jane Blake down as gay."

"No, that's not what I was asking." Covet shifted in his seat. "Thing is, I don't believe it. I don't believe it for a second. What I meant was, did you know she was lodging the complaint?"

"No," McNamara replied. "But why don't you believe it?"

"Well, think about it. The student makes a complaint about getting burned over sexual involvement with a male member of staff in summer and then goes pretty much straight off and does the same thing again three months later with a female member? On the face of it, it's preposterous. I'm beginning to think neither of the complaints is true."

"You think she's lying? Why would she do that?"

"No, I think she must be off her bloody head. Nuts. Goo-goo. Loca."

"She doesn't appear to be mentally unbalanced. Not to me, at any rate. A little obsessively observant of decorum, perhaps, but not off her trolley."

Covet clasped his hands. "Look," he said, with seeming reason. "I could let this complaint run its course, have an investigation, and so on. Even if it's not true, that would be very embarrassing for Poon and the Union. The mud will fly."

"With respect," said McNamara, "what do you care about Poon and the Union? I would have thought something like this might make you somewhat gleeful."

"Robert!" Covet exclaimed indignantly. "That's low. I do have some care for the truth, whatever my past conflicts with the Union."

"Well, an investigation will establish the truth. I agree: that's something we all value."

"Yes, but if this got out to the media, the mud would also stick to the Union. And we could be opening any kind of Pandora's Box here. I am not particularly keen for it to be established that an Associate Professor in the University of Odium, who also happens to be the President of the academic trades Union, is having a lesbian affair with a student she supervises, even if it is true. Think of the effect it would have on applications."

"You might get lots more gay girls applying," McNamara joked.

"Yes, I can just see the headlines: 'University of Sapphodium'. But can you help me here, Robert?"

"*Me?*" said McNamara. "Help *you?*"

"I mean us, the University. Surely we have common cause here. You can't possibly wish to see a scandal whipped up around Poon?"

McNamara laughed. "I don't give a damn about Poon. Poon can go to hell for all I care. She's an unprincipled clown and not a very good academic. Books about *Star Trek* and *The Simpsons* and TV show fandom? In fact, I'm not sure I even share your disbelief. She's exactly the kind of person who might have sex with her supervisee. For all I care you can sack her and ship her back to Madras, the more public humiliation the better."

Covet was genuinely surprised. "But that's unfair, Robert. She's been working very cooperatively with us. I don't mean it as an insult to you, or to dredge up things from the past, but relations between the Union and senior management have never been better."

"Precisely," said McNamara. "That's another problem I have with her. When relations between a union and management are so wholesome one should be somewhat worried."

Covet shook his head. "But, Robert, what about partnership? We're all trying to work together for the same thing: a better university."

"Even if this University were made better, it would still be pretty awful, by any measure, because it has people like Poon in it, who have been permitted to carve careers out of their leisure pursuits. You can pretty much get a degree in her department by playing computer games and 'studying' Twitter. But it's not a union's primary role to work for a better university. It's a union's job to represent and further the interests of its members. The two things may coincide. But your idea of a 'better' university and a union's definition are likely to be rather different. Personally, I don't care anyway. I am not even a member of the Union anymore."

"I had heard that, Robert."

McNamara was surprised. "From whom?"

Covet waved his hand. "People talk, Robert. I can't say. But I didn't imagine you had undergone a sudden sea change of political values. From commitment to apathy?"

"I haven't. But then, if you get rid of Poon, who becomes President? Redman. He's way better than her, anyone can tell you that. He has much greater potential as a scholar too."

Each sat back, having reached a discursive stalemate.

Covet made a last effort. "Look, I was hoping you might intervene with this student. You know her. For her own benefit, try to persuade her to withdraw the complaint."

"Why?"

"Because she's mad!"

"That's not been established. And even if she is, mad people have a right to complain. Or there may be method in her madness. Or her madness might have some wonderfully carnivalesque consequences."

"But it could just as easily have been *you* she made such a complaint about."

McNamara laughed. "Then I would *know* that she *is* mad or lying, wouldn't I?"

Covet said, "I can't believe you're not prepared to help."

McNamara said, "Yes, you can."

As McNamara drove the twelve miles back to Odium in his Ford Mondeo, he was puzzled by his truly profound indifference. His not caring, he realised, did not have even the saving bitter edge of cynicism, the relish of *schadenfreude*, or the self-indulgent pleasure of apathy. The unprecedented call from Covet and the weirdly personal meeting at Homestead Park, in the man's own absurdly opulent paid-for home, hardly registered in his internal seismometers of motivation or involvement. He felt as one can feel when looking out of the windows of a plane, above the clouds, in a certain celestial-seeming zone in which everything below is obscured and its reality removed, the few glimpses of it one is afforded making it seem contourless and transient, something to be passed over, moved beyond. Covet, even in the lap of his own personal luxury, had seemed small and impotent, a kind of helplessness behind his eyes, although McNamara could not summon up the volition to speculate why.

The country roads subsided to the motorway, then there was a mile or two of dual carriageway through the humdrum industrial suburbs of Odium, until he reached University Drive, then the west entrance, with the coat of arms on the green wrought iron gate which read *Ipsa Scientia Potestas Est*. Then, as he drove towards the Trump Building, there were the students. The bells of the tower where he had his office were ringing ten and the young people were moving after the first classes of the day, meeting in gauche physical postures, chatting in painfully un-English rising intonations learned from American TV programmes, their light public embraces too self-conscious and stagey to convey true intimacy, the utterances of "Hi!" upon encountering one another using too elongated a vowel to sound convincingly familiar, their brave attempts to present faces which seemed confident failing to disguise the deep insecurities churning within. Whatever world they occupied, it was not his, or Covet's, or even Redman's. They no doubt naïvely believed that the University, to which these days they paid such high fees from their parents' pockets, was primarily organised around the need to teach them. But the truth was that students were little more than incidental to anyone involved in the managerial politics of a twenty-first century university, just as, with the one troublesome exception of Jane Blake, they hardly figure in any decisive way in the manifold twists and turns of this tale. Students may believe that they have at least bit parts in the show. In truth, they are merely extras.

It had been a long time since McNamara had learned the names of the students in any class he taught. The term "students" merely designated so many empty vessels filled anew each year by a different set of bodies. Their ignorance of virtually everything seemed to deepen as his own wisdom, through experience and scholarship, grew. It had consequently been many years since he had truly prepared for a single class. He knew everything one needed to know to deliver his subject at student level off the top of his head, had heard all the questions and repeated all the answers so many times that he often felt like a juke box merely playing various tunes at the pressing of corresponding buttons. He was a great actor at the lectern, could simulate a passion for knowledge and even spontaneous humour very well. But really, for a long time, it had all been happening on auto-pilot. One day a well programmed android would be able to do it. He was not careless about his teaching, but carefree: hardly any care was in fact required to do it. And perhaps this was also now what was happening in other dimensions of his life. Perhaps it was what the march of age always did, unless some new wholly unexpected challenge or drama arose to force you to rethink your ways and bring you back into a state of worldly engagement. And was it not good, this detachment? Was it not what many holy books described as the ultimate goal of existence?

He parked and entered the Trump Building, walking past Covet's and Asterisk's suite of offices in the west wing, on his way to the clocktower steps. As he entered his office he saw that an envelope had been slipped under the door, with his name written on it. He opened it and took from it a single folded sheet, on which he found a handwritten, anonymous note:

There are listening devices in the following rooms.
(1) Your study in Coolwipe Hall, in the bunch of fake roses between the two bookcases
(2) In Redman's office in this building, fixed to the underside of his desktop, near the front.
(3) In Poon's office in this building, on the right rear side of the signed picture of Patrick Stewart on the left wall.
These devices are all identical. They are half a centimeter in diameter, and look like a washer made of black rubber with a fine black mesh in the center of the ring. Remove them and keep them in a safe place. There are no other bugs. Further information will follow.

An hour or so later, McNamara caught up with Redman at his home in Maryland Lane.

"Was there one in Poon's office too?" Redman asked.

McNamara nodded. "I've got all three at my house now."

"How did Poon take it?"

"Gobsmacked, I think the word is. I showed her the note, told her I'd been to my study and your office, that we'd found the bugs there, and then we relieved Captain Jean-Luc Picard of his attachment. I didn't have much time to talk to her, she had a class at eleven. I said we'd meet later."

"It has to be Covet, right?"

"Unless there's some MI5 investigation we don't know about."

"I can't believe it. I can't believe they're bugging us."

"Why not? After all, *you're* bugging *them*, aren't you? Jesus, is this what it's come to? 'Odiumgate'? On that score, did you play any of those phone recordings in your office? Could they have heard them?"

"No," Redman reassured. "I only do that here. In fact, while I was waiting for you, I looked through the most recent stuff. Covet called Asterisk this morning before you went there. It showed up on Asterisk's work mobile. You ought to listen."

McNamara raised his hand with a grimace of distaste. "Oh, really? This stuff makes me feel contaminated."

Redman looked him in the eye. "You ought to listen."

He turned to his computer and played the audio file.

ASTERISK: Hello?

COVET: What the fuck, Nigel?

ASTERISK: Er, Vice Chancellor, I wouldn't have taken this call if your ID had shown up. I, I, I … we can't be talking, Vice Chancellor.

COVET: You listen to me, Nigel. What the fuck is going on? Why was I the last to know?

ASTERISK: I can't discuss this, sir.

COVET: You fucking bet you can, you fat prick. Why did you not let me know about this yesterday?

ASTERISK: I couldn't, it's a PID, you know –

COVET: So fucking what? Since when do I not see PIDs before you copy them to Knight?

ASTERISK: But it was a PID about you –

COVET: You miserable fucking fart, Nigel. Isn't that the *very reason* to show it to me?

ASTERISK: But the rules, the Code, I can't. You can't know who it's from.

COVET: The Code? The *rules*? The rules are there for us to apply to other people, you tit, you *arse*. Send me a fucking copy of this thing now!

ASTERISK: [*nervous, gulping*] I can't, sir.

COVET: You can't, Nigel? You *can't*?

ASTERISK: We shouldn't even be communicating.

COVET: You stupid cunt. You *fucking stupid cunt!* Have you any idea how much shit you're in if I'm in it? You imbecile! Tell me who it's from then.

ASTERISK: You know I can't do that. My hands are tied.

[*Silence. Heavy breathing on Covet's end of the conversation.*]

COVET: [*in a low voice*] Listen to me, Nigel, you ungrateful cocksucker. This isn't the end of this matter. You better think about all this carefully and consider what Niagara of piss is about to cascade on your head if you don't listen to me and do exactly what I tell you. But for now, make sure *Avenger* is on that fucking investigation team, do you hear me? Make sure.

ASTERISK: I can do that, yes.

COVET: You had fucking better. Soon. Today. *Now.* [*Conversation terminated.*]


McNamara was quiet for a moment. "When was that call?"

Redman checked his screen. "7.37am."

"That was before he called me. He called me about 7.45."

"He didn't use his work phone for that either. I don't have the call."

McNamara thought further. "He told me this morning that Jane Blake had lodged a complaint yesterday."

"About Poon? About them shagging, right? You did tell her when you met her that she could make a complaint."

"Yes, but I got no sense that she was going to do that, and not the very next day."

"Did you mention that to Poon when you saw her?"

"No, she hasn't got a clue. Covet wanted me to persuade Jane Blake to withdraw it. He says he doesn't believe it."

"But this isn't a regular complaint, it's a PID. And it's not about Poon, it's about him."

"But how could Jane Blake make a PID about *him*? She's just a postgrad student. She doesn't even know him."

"Maybe it's a coincidence. She *did* make a complaint, but the PID is from someone else?"

"You think? He calls Asterisk at 7.37 about a PID, is clearly apoplectic about it, then eight minutes later he calls me about something entirely unrelated and much less urgent and asks me to drive out instantly *to his house*? Surely the Blake complaint could have waited if it wasn't the same thing? It would explain why he was so keen to have it withdrawn. The PID must be from her. But how does he know that? Asterisk refused to tell him. Maybe he just guessed?"

"Maybe you can find out from her?"

McNamara shook his head. "We don't know enough. And did you notice the spelling in the note: 'centimeter', 'center'? It's American, not British. And Jane Blake is American."

"You think the note might be from *her*? Do you know her handwriting?"

"No. But she's been in my study, she's been in Poon's office. Whoever put those bugs in needed ready access. I can't explain how she could put one in yours, or why she would put them in any, but this whole thing has become so espionage-parodic I can imagine anything. It's like being in an episode of *Homeland* or something, except with none of the national security implications that make that seem profound. It's a fucking shitty little provincial English university, for God's sake!"

"There's one other thing," Redman said. "He told you he wasn't planning to come in to work today. That's a lie. I know from a couple of previous calls that he had several appointments this morning. Something happened that prevented him going in. That's why he had to get you to go there. My guess is, given the PID – "

"That he's been suspended?"

Redman nodded in agreement. "Which means the PID must be pretty grave."

At that moment, Redman's computer registered with the usual two tone sound that a new email had arrived. He looked at the screen, then back at McNamara. "Another call from Asterisk. Three minutes ago."

McNamara rolled his eyes. "Let's hear it," he said.

Redman pressed play.

BUCKRACK: Yeah?

ASTERISK: Ah, Professor Buckrack. I believe the Vice Chancellor has spoken to you?

BUCKRACK: Make this quick. Yes, so I know he wants me on the investigation. When's the meeting?

ASTERISK: 12.30 today. It's been my top priority. The paperwork is on a collect-and-sign only basis, from me personally, in my office.

BUCKRACK: Fine. I'll come in now. [*Conversation terminated.*]

Redman looked at McNamara. "So now we know for sure who *Avenger* is."

McNamara turned and gazed cogitatively through the window onto the street. A director would have made a fine cliffhanger of the moment (even though the actionless scene itself lacks all suspense), probably by shooting him in profile from inside the room, fading in a Sean Callery soundscape, then taking the next shot full-face-on from the other side of the glass, Redman out of focus behind McNamara, camera panning slowly away, the music volume reaching a crescendo as he paused before whispering the entirely unnecessary confirmation, "It's Buckrack!"

## Chapter Eleven (27 October)

"Gentlemen," said Professor Richard Helms, "good afternoon. You have now had time to read the papers. I am sorry that you will have to wait for lunch, but it was necessary, for obvious reasons, that we convene at only a few hours' notice. I am sorry that all we were able to let you have this morning was a copy of the letter of October 26 from the President of Council to the Vice Chancellor but, as you can see from the Public Interest Disclosure document, this is an ultra-sensitive matter on which we have to keep a very tight and highly confidential rein. That is why we are holding these investigatory meetings in camera, without a secretary. I shall be personally responsible for the minutes. I am sorry that you are

95

permitted only to read the paperwork while in this room, and that you cannot take any of the papers away with you, but I should imagine that the nature of their contents makes it obvious why that is so. We are intending to deal with this investigation with utmost despatch, and to make recommendations well in advance of the twenty-eight day deadline which we are obliged to meet. It is obviously a matter which requires a speedy resolution. We must also bear in mind our legal obligations under the 1998 Public Interest Disclosure Act, which is why, I presume, I as a Professor of Law have been asked to chair the investigatory meetings. You will find our terms of reference on the first page of your papers, and I would like to stress that we are charged only with making recommendations to the University on how it should deal procedurally with the Disclosure made by Ms Blake, not with deciding on the case itself: in short, we may recommend that the case be dismissed, pursued by means of another more appropriate procedure, or answered without legal prejudice, and so on. It is for the President of Council to consider our recommendations, although he is not obliged to accept them. This is not a court of law, and the standards of evidence required by a court of law do not apply. We shall weigh the evidence we are given in order to arrive at our recommendations, of course, and, although we shall not be hearing witnesses today, we do have the power to call witnesses and to question them. We can compel employees of the University to attend as witnesses. We can only request that non-employees attend, and they have a right to refuse."

He turned his head to the left and smiled gently at Buckrack. "Now, although most of us know one another, we have not all made the acquaintance of Professor Buckrack, and I am going to suggest some introductions before we get started. I am Professor Richard Helms, Professor Buckrack, but you can call me Dick. Officially I am here as the University Assessor, which is a fancy name for the campus legal bod the University calls in when it wants something dealt with that has a legal angle, but which they don't yet want to pay a practising cash-hungry lawyer to do."

Buckrack smiled back momentarily and then looked at the other four men seated around the table. "I am Cannon Buckrack. I retired from the US State Department last year, where I worked for most of my career, which also included a period of eight years on the National Security Council. I am finishing a book on intelligence-sharing between the major western powers and, I *also* presume, this was why I was hired on a one-year research contract: I think the intention is to attach my research to a certain School to help float it through next year's Research Excellence exercise." The others chuckled lightly at this. "I think I am a member of this investigatory team because I may be able to help with some of the, er, *trans-Atlantic* issues it raises."

"Thank, you, Cannon. I think there is one particular matter you were looking into with the Registrar just before the meeting, and we'll hear about that in due course." Helms looked expectantly at the others. "Mike, would you?"

The tall, thin, moustachio'd man to Buckrack's left, who had been twitching a pair of bicycle clips on the table in front of him, said affably in an Irish accent, "I am Professor Mike Mansfield, Pro-Vice Chancellor for Teaching and Learning. I can't claim anything as exalted as having been called to the bar like Dick, or having held high government office like you, but in my spare time I do help appoint Justices of the Peace."

At this there were further fond guffaws, of a kind that only university professors are capable of bestowing on one another in their own exclusive company.

The next man took his turn. "Well, as we are all saying a little something of ourselves, according to Google Scholar I am the fifteenth most cited metaphysician in the world! Professor Walt Rostow, Executive Dean of the Faculty of Arts. Pleased to meet you."

And the next: "Professor Pierre Salinger, Deputy Pro-Vice Chancellor for the Student Experience. I'm in the Business School. When I am not helping to forge the entrepreneurs of the future, I run the staff wine-tasting club. You're very welcome to come, if you'd like. Let's talk later."

There were chortles, but none from the last man, who had been unsmiling and unresponsive throughout, mordant, grey, a little hatchet-faced. He said, "I'm Harold K. Johnson, Deputy Vice Chancellor. I don't have any spare time. I help run this place."

This was followed by some shuffling of papers by a few, a polite pause from all, and the placing of Helms's elbows on the table.

"Thank you, gentlemen," he said. "Now to our task. I will begin by summarising the facts of Ms Blake's Disclosure, but let me first of all give a little detail about her, solely based on her administrative record. Ms Blake is twenty-three years old. She came to the University in January of this year, having graduated *summa cum laude* from Amherst College, Massachusetts, where she majored in English. She was originally registered in our School of English Studies, where she was supervised by Dr Sergei Krokoff, but transferred for academic reasons at the beginning of this academic year to the School of Cultural and Area Studies, where she is supervised by Dr Avril Poon. Her supervision records are all up to date and show nothing unusual. She was a recipient of a three-year Vice Chancellor's scholarship, and we happen to know for sure that she did meet the Vice Chancellor on at least one occasion, at a reception for beneficiaries of the VC awards in February: there is a group photograph of her with the VC and three other award holders in the March *University Newsletter.*

"Ms Blake claims, however, that she first met the VC almost a year before, in April of last year, in fact, in a hotel bar in Boston, while she was still in her final semester at Amherst, and this is where her own, er, disclosures about herself become, shall we say, *unusual.* She confesses to having financed her education at Amherst by means of regular prostitution. She says that she was essentially 'a call girl with mainly high finance clients' whom she procured in Boston, well away from Amherst, but she also admits to having slept with two of her male professors at Amherst in return for, er, 'academic assistance', by which I take it we mean that they artificially boosted her grades or in some other way ensured that her work was good enough to receive excellent marks. One may wonder why Ms Blake takes the risk of telling us these things. Perhaps she believes that the Public Interest Disclosure provisions prevent any repercussions from being visited upon her as a result of what she discloses, but that is a moot point in English law if the Disclosure itself constitutes a confession to criminal activity. I am looking into it. But let us leave that aside for the moment. We may have reason to come back to it later in the investigation, particularly if Ms Blake chooses to present herself as a witness.

"So, Ms Blake claims to have first met the VC in a hotel bar in Boston. She claims that he paid her for sexual services more than once during this visit. She further claims that he returned to Boston in the summer, in July, and resumed with her their illicit liaison on the same financial footing. She then pretty much asseverates that they decided to get their kicks on Route 66. The VC, she says, told her that he had three weeks' holiday, and they spent it together on a road trip across the USA, sharing hotel rooms all the way. In short, he hired her as a sexual companion, something she says she had done with clients several times before. It is not clear from her document whether this was her idea or his, but probably that is of no relevance. The only thing that matters is whether or not it is true.

"It was in Las Vegas, Ms Blake says, 'both of us smashed out on cocaine after a night at the tables', that the VC proposed to her a 'plan' to bring her to England as his, well, I am not sure that 'concubine' would be the precise term, but you've all read the document: the alleged 'plan' was for her to apply as a postgraduate research student to Odium and for him to 'set her up' with a VC scholarship, which was essentially in his gift, in return for ongoing sexual favours. Ms Blake says she accepted this offer, and that it all went smoothly. Thus she ended up as a student here last January, by her account. Their summer road trip ended in Los Angeles, where they went their separate ways. He bought her a ticket back to Boston and himself flew to London. They did not meet again until she came to England, though she claims they kept in touch regularly by phone.

"When she arrived, she says, the VC proposed a new 'plan' with a new tariff of reward. He would give her an additional two thousand US dollars a month in return for an undertaking 'to sleep with no one else he did not ask me to'. His payments to her had hitherto been in cash, but on account of the regularity of these new remittances, she tells us, he set up a pseudonymous PayPal account in US dollars under the name of William Blake (her favourite poet, she explains), so that it would look as if the payments came from her father. She encloses as evidence screen shots of her online US bank account purportedly showing these payments.

"It soon became clear, she wishes us to believe, that the VC wanted her to put her considerable skills as a courtesan to use in sexually seducing a member of staff, namely Professor McNamara in the School of Politics. The declared motive was revenge: Professor McNamara had recently retired from a long period as President of the local branch of the University and College Union, and the VC wanted payback for all the conflict and trouble Professor McNamara had caused him in the past, and possibly whatever useful information might be revealed in the course of pillow talk. To this end, apparently, the VC again 'set her up' with a residential tutorship in Coolwipe Hall, and gave her the direct mission of bedding Professor McNamara, to whom she would henceforth have regular daily access. Ms Blake expresses some surprise that she was unable to succeed in the planned seduction despite repeated attempts on her part. She goes into some peculiar details about the young woman's art of sexually ensnaring older men in this section of her document, I think to give us a sense of how hard she tried, egged on continually, she wishes us to know, by the VC. Apparently Professor McNamara did not respond to whatever erotic opportunities were being offered him, and after two months she concluded, and told the VC, that it was a lost cause. McNamara was, it seems, a fortress which could not be assailed with success. He survives this bizarre narrative with flying ethical colours, I must say.

"The VC, she goes on, finally accepted her failure, although it exasperated him beyond measure, we learn, 'that Professor McNamara could once more reject something he' – that is, the Vice Chancellor – 'found ineluctably desirable'. She has a way with words, does our Ms Blake, especially when referring to her own sexually charismatic qualities. But the VC then came up, her report has it, with yet another revision to his 'plan'. He wanted to find a way for Ms Blake to seduce the *current* President of the Union, Dr Poon. Ms Blake asserts that she objected vehemently to this idea, and states that this was the point in their relationship when it all began, for her at least, to turn sour. Apparently she did not 'do' women: her prostitutional bent had always been exclusively heterosexual, as it were. But the VC offered two large financial incentives, to be paid up front, which she found it difficult to resist: five thousand dollars to seduce her supervisor in English Studies, Dr Krokoff, an outcome which could then be used as a form of blackmail encouraging him to acquiesce in severing their supervisory relationship, and then another five thousand dollars to have sex with Dr Poon, after she had become the new supervisor. The Krokoff phase, it seems, succeeded almost instantly. Krokoff leapt into bed with her at the first gentle invitation in late April, we are told. The deal with 'Evan', as she calls the Vice Chancellor, was 'for no more than three sexual encounters with Dr Krokoff'. At the same time, Ms Blake proposed to Krokoff a change in her thesis topic which was more suited to Cultural Studies and less amenable to his expertise. Krokoff seemed bemused and discombobulated by this change, but had become almost immediately besotted by her, and so he seemed cooperative. She broke it off with him after the 'third encounter', how much of a strange kind we can only wonder. These three liaisons were apparently carefully spaced out in time to keep Krokoff in a lustfully compliant condition, and the last of them occurred in May. When she told him subsequently that he could expect no more, Krokoff seemed to go instantly mad with sexual deprivation. He pursued her 'like a rabid dog', she writes, 'and with a sexual hunger that threatened almost to make itself public' until the middle of June, when she departed again, she claims, as the VC's companion on another business trip to America. The VC paid for her ticket personally, she adds. She spent some time with her sister in Massachusetts, then joined him again for a re-run of their earlier road trip. She mentions that they laughed hysterically together in Chicago and Albuquerque at the pathetic emails she received from Krokoff during this time, and she attaches those emails to her Disclosure. They made me laugh hysterically too, whether or not they are genuine, but, if we can authenticate them, which may not be straightforward as they seem to come from a private email account, I suggest to you that Dr Krokoff's conduct may also be something we must make recommendations about. We shall see.

"After this, it was easy to make an end of Krokoff as supervisor. As he was a mere pawn in the game, and not the prime target of the latest 'plan', the VC apparently did it on the QT. He flew back to England again from Los Angeles, as did she, though separately. He had a bit of hush-hush parley with the two relevant Heads of School, he told her. Krokoff was given a severe talking to and reacted like a frightened rabbit, Dr Poon was softened up in the late summer to expect an approach from Krokoff, heard him out in September without being fully aware of the depths of his depravity, and agreed to what she had already been primed for, that is, she accepted Ms Blake as her transferred doctoral supervisee.

"According to Ms Blake, though innocent thus far, Dr Poon did not even have to be conquered. She started coming on strong at virtually their first meeting, and has been doing so for the last month. It appears that Professor McNamara is the only human being of either sex capable of resisting this young woman's excessive sensual charms. Virtue topples in immediate defeat and bows before them. Perhaps we need to consider carefully whether or not we call her as a witness, lest we too become numbered among the vanquished. But, if we are to believe Ms Blake, it is in her revulsion to Dr Poon that she came to realise the limitations, if not of her attractions, then of her professional capabilities. She simply could not bring herself to commit to an act of lesbian congress. She went back to the VC, she claims, and said she could not go through with it: Dr Poon was disgusting, revolting, a same sex conjunction was beyond her. She even asked him to take back the five thousand dollars she had been paid in advance for the mission. He refused, became overbearing. He purportedly said on one occasion two weeks ago, and I quote: 'You fuck that Chapati bitch now. I want her clitoris on a platter!' Ms Blake refused. There was a standoff between them. Eventually, last week, he relented. She could keep the money, but if she was not going to have sex with Poon, she had to agree to cooperate in framing her for the misdemeanour. Ms Blake would make a formal complaint that *Dr Poon* had seduced *her*: not far from the truth, the VC pointed out, as this was what Poon had been trying to do in any case. The mud which flew from the allegation would stick, and Poon would then, I suppose, be a 'Chapati bitch' in the disciplinary doghouse. The first step in this new manoeuvre was to confide in someone else that there really was a relationship with Poon, and the person the VC chose to receive this fictional confession from Ms Blake was Professor McNamara. Ms Blake reluctantly agreed. She saw McNamara four days ago and told him the lie, apparently under the guise of seeking his avuncular advice. The idea, it transpires, was for the VC then to inveigle McNamara as a witness in the fabricated case against Poon, knowing, as the VC did, that McNamara already had contempt for Poon and would willingly assist in her downfall. But before this could happen, Ms Blake had a sudden, it would seem her first ever, convulsion of conscience. She could not go on like this anymore. She spent a sleepless night, writhing with her demons, and eventually heard the voices of the angels. The next day, October 25, she made an appointment with the Vice Chancellor at noon on the morrow at what she calls their 'usual hotel'. Her intention was to try to persuade him again to give up on framing Poon, but this did not get off the ground, only her feet did: the meeting turned into a routine recreational romp. She went home in a state of some self-loathing, she wishes us to understand, and spent the remainder of the afternoon writing this colourful but literate three thousand word PID then emailed it late that afternoon with the evidence she had to hand, but she says with further evidence to follow, to the Registrar. And this, gentlemen, is how we come to be in possession of the explosive memoir, imagined, loosely based on a true story, or as apparently genuine as the *Confessions* of Rousseau, of Odium's very own Mata Hari."

There was a profound silence in the room, a sealed-off annexe to the Human Resources Department, which was housed in a building nearby. Professor Buckrack looked calmly contemplative. Professor Mansfield toyed anew with his bicycle clips. Professor Rostow puffed a small blast of air through his lips. Professor Salinger put his chin on his chest and opened his eyes wide, darting looks at the others in the room. Professor Johnson grimly twiddled his thumbs for a while and then said, "Do we have any inkling of what the 'other evidence' might be?"

Professor Helms raised his hands to signify the vanity of idle, legally suspect speculation.

Buckrack said, "It would have to be better than what we've got so far. The JPEGs of bank statements, the email correspondence from Krokoff, both could easily be faked. If there's to be anything else, I'd expect photographs, or videos, or the like. Something that shows them together. There's nothing here that definitively links the two."

Helms, who had just taken a drink of water, cleared his throat. "Not here, no. But we did take the liberty earlier this morning of checking the implied timeline, and the geography. The VC *was* in Boston on business in April last year. We have his hotel bill: the University paid it. It was the hotel she names, the one she said she met him in. We have no details of an American trip in the summer of last year, because that was a personal holiday. But his vacation in the summer just gone was tacked on to a business trip. We paid for the open jaw ticket to Boston, returning from Los Angeles, and again we paid the hotel bill for three nights in Boston: the same hotel, in fact. The bills are all in his name and specify only one guest. So some of the locations and dates she gives for April last year and summer this year tally with our records of his business travel. The question consequently arises, how does a postgraduate student know the VC was in those places at those times, if she was not with him? *Prima facie* there is no reason to consider that she could have been legitimately involved in the Boston business meetings. Of course, even if she did meet him, that does not in itself prove that there was any sexual relationship. We will, of course, ask him if he has an explanation. Cannon, I believe you looked into something with the Registrar just before the meeting?"

"I did," said Buckrack. "On her matriculation form she does list her next of kin as 'William Blake, father'."

"So," Johnson said, "the payments on the bank statement are actually from her father, then?"

Buckrack shook his head. "No. Her father's name is not William Blake." He passed around a photocopied sheet. "She lied. This is the last page of her old American passport, which was a five-year passport she surrendered at renewal two years ago. You can see that she has written the name 'James Arthur Blake' as the first person to contact in case of emergency and identified him as her father. I cross checked the given address in Quincy, Massachusetts, which is also the address stipulated on the matriculation form. A James Arthur Blake lived there until eighteen months ago. He was renting. He was not the owner. He died. Her father is dead. No one called Blake has lived there since."

There was general amazement.

"How on earth did we get this document?" Mansfield asked.

Buckrack shrugged. "As I said, I worked for the US State Department. It took a telephone call to Washington. That's the trans-Atlantic dimension I was referring to."

"Gosh," said Rostow. "I imagined old passports were destroyed."

"Destroyed?" Buckrack echoed. "They're far too important a source of data to be disposed of. In my country, at any rate."

Rostow sat back and whistled. "Can you check the PayPal account the same way?"

"Less easy," said Buckrack. "PayPal is based in San Jose, California, but it's not a US government department, so its records are not so susceptible to immediate examination. We'd need a court order. However, it is interesting that the PayPal payments on this statement seem to come from the European subsidiary in Luxembourg. That's a pretty strange way for an American citizen to make PayPal payments within the USA. It suggests that the account holder registered the account from within the EU, even though it is specified as a dollar account."

Salinger had been looking around, and as if realising that he was the only one who had not yet contributed to the discussion, took a breath and decided to say, "So those facts tell us?"

Helms said, "They do not tell us anything definite. Ms Blake does not mention the matriculation form in her document. Possibly she forgot. But it suggests, when looked at in the terms established by her other claims, that she wished it to be a matter of false record that she had a familial connection with a William Blake who, that same month, began making payments into her Boston bank account. In other words, it suggests a potentially conspiratorial agreement between her and the person who opened the PayPal account in the name of William Blake, and she claims that person was Sir Evan Covet. The fact that the originating PayPal account was registered in Europe rather than America is consistent with that claim."

Johnson glanced out of the window. "Christ," he whispered.

"But it's not conclusive of any such thing," Buckrack added.

"No, that is true." Helms rallied. "Now, before we go any further, let me describe the legal minefield we are negotiating here under the University's Public Interest Disclosure Code, which was adverted to in the President of Council's letter to the VC. It seems clear that the Disclosure before us from Ms Blake does seem to express, and I am quoting again, 'a genuine concern that there are reasonable grounds for believing' that the kind of nefarious things usually dealt with under the Code have taken place, are occurring, or are likely to eventualise. Do we have any alleged criminal offence? Yes, in fact we have several: engagement in prostitution, drug-taking, bribery, and potentially others. Is there any suspicion that a person has failed in his legal obligations? Well, if the VC has conducted himself towards the staff of this institution as Ms Blake says he has, there would seem to be multiple failures of duty of care, as well as favouritism in the award of a scholarship to her: if the latter is not in default of his legal duty, it may nonetheless be construed as yet one more criminal bribe. A miscarriage of justice was also allegedly plotted in respect of Dr Poon, if there was serious intent to 'frame' her for acts of professional misconduct or indiscretion which she did not actually commit. The health and safety of Ms Blake herself was inarguably endangered by the VC if he engaged with her in drug-taking and coerced her into having sex with others. All of the above, if they have been going on for as long as it is suggested they have, inevitably involve concealment, a concealment it is Ms Blake's avowed intention in making her Disclosure to end. In fact, the only thing stopping us from having a whole slam dunk across the entire six-item sweep of the PID Code is that no environmental damage, it would seem, has occurred."

"I agree there is a great deal of concern in the terms of the Code,"

Johnson said. "But as Cannon just noted, we're still in the realm of conjecture. There is nothing solidly associating these two people in what we've seen, other than her claims. She might be clinically insane, hallucinating, or just off on a bender, forgot to take her pills."

"She might," said Helms. "Dare I say we all, as it were, hope that is so? So you are correct, Harold. I suggest that the next step, therefore, is to agree to reconvene tomorrow and call some witnesses to attend, yes?"

## Chapter Twelve (27 October – 29 October)

The meeting did not take place the next day, because its necessity was overtaken by events which seemed to speed up time itself, and make the rendition of three days' happenings possible in brief compass only by a kind of verbal montage, whose televisual equivalent might be accompanied by a cheaply licensed song such as "Times of Trouble" by Temple of the Dog.

As the closeted meeting chaired by Helms was getting under way, McNamara, who had returned with Redman to the Trump Building just after noon, opened his office door and found another envelope, this time with only two words written on it:

Release this

Inside was a copy of the letter from the President of Council to the Vice Chancellor. It took only a few minutes for McNamara to find Redman and for them jointly to agree to obey the envelope's imperative. It took less than one more minute for them to decide to keep Poon in the dark and to dissociate the release to the press from the Union. They took fifteen further minutes to compile a list of daily and weekly newspaper education correspondents from the internet, and at lunch time McNamara wandered over to the School of Political Science and, while the School secretary was out to lunch, faxed the document, without any cover sheet or other explanatory gloss, to every one of them from the office's ageing fax machine. News spilling onto newsdesks using such an obsolete technology is a rarity today, and its form made sure it was paid peculiar attention to. By mid-afternoon the calls began to come in to the

University press office. By late afternoon Redman's wiretap started registering enquiries from the press office to the Registrar's mobile phone. By the time he arrived home that evening, Redman was able to listen to a series of increasingly manic and petrified calls from Asterisk to everyone, including the President of Council.

By the following morning, which was a Thursday, the campus had become infected with that unique bacillus, the British reporter. To begin with, these were members of the "quality" press, which had already run the story of Covet's suspension in their early editions. But by lunchtime they had produced endospores of the tabloid and TV kind, and all serious hope of holding a further meeting, with witnesses, had to be abandoned. Newsmen and women were crawling all over the campus grounds and, denied access to administrative officials, they were buttonholing anyone and everyone capable of giving a soundbite or a quote: students, librarians, secretaries, academic members of staff, even the benighted Poon, who seized the chance to be recorded for dinner-time news bulletins, on which she was singularly privileged above the various University of Odium *vox pops*, and said that she would be approaching the University as President of the Union to demand further information. McNamara and Redman at first managed to prevent her from mentioning the bugs they had found in their three offices, but by the afternoon, a couple of interviews already under her belt, fantasising ecstatically of potential celebrity and greater exposure, she offered an exclusive to the BBC and was swept down to London in a chauffeured car. In a state of self-important media intoxication which she considered would make her the envy of her departmental colleagues, ignoring repeated calls from Redman on her mobile, drafting a letter to the Registrar on her laptop, she appeared on *Newsnight* and brandished in front of Emily Maitlis's amused and mischievous eyes a photograph she had taken of the three listening devices. They put her up in the Grange Langham Court Hotel, two minutes from Broadcasting House, where she watched reruns of snippets from her interview on Sky News, and masturbated on the ample double bed in wild self-congratulation.

On the Friday morning, after a sumptuous breakfast but before leaving the hotel, she emailed her letter on Union headed notepaper to the Registrar, with a copy of the photograph, and, knowing well enough how the media works, copied it with unrestrained prodigality to the press. The letter made a formal request under the Freedom of

Information Act, asking if the University had purchased the three listening devices, a question the Registrar legally had twenty-one days to respond to, and named McNamara and Redman, without any attempt to gain their consent, as the two other Odiumgate victims besides herself. On the car-ride back to Odium she continued to ignore calls from Redman, but took every other, arranging *en route* an impromptu press conference in the courtyard of the Trump Building, a mere few yards from the Registrar's office. It turned into a gloriously triumphant affair, she thought, after which the media gaggle turned and invaded the building, thronging the corridor outside Asterisk's office, knocking over a security guard and gaining entry, in what, to the police called to eject them, seemed an ironic parody of a seventies-style student occupation. Asterisk decided that it was in his interest to faint, and was filmed leaving the building on an ambulance trolley, flanked by two paramedics and six members of Her Majesty's Constabulary, hounded by a semi-circular scrum of press persons, most holding up portable recorders and taking pictures with their phones.

Buckrack had acted in advance of everyone. On the afternoon of the Wednesday, before the press invasion, while the telephone lines were only mildly warm with the first preliminary enquiries, he returned to Homestead Park and persuaded Covet to leave. Covet had reason to thank him, from the safety of his alternative rural hideaway that Buckrack drove him to, when he saw on TV reporters and paparazzi stationed outside the main gates of Homestead Park the next day. From that moment on he depended on Buckrack entirely, not just for information, but for all feelings of security and protection, as well as advice and judgment. Buckrack felt like the only friend he had in the world. On the first night, over a dinner Buckrack brought in, but which tasted of nothing to Covet, and a similarly supplied bottle of scotch which tasted of something, he confessed what he thought he could no longer withhold and, from what Buckrack had to tell him of Jane Blake's Disclosure, he pretty much reckoned was now undeniable: that he had indeed slept with her in America, and twice taken her on holiday, and arranged for her scholarship, and all year had paid her a monthly retainer. He continued to disavow that getting her a tutorship in Coolwipe Hall was a stratagem to entrap McNamara, but three whiskies later he admitted to that too. Two more down the gullet, in a state of glass-smashing despair, he went the whole hog and confessed to the planned and paid-for entrapment of Krokoff and Poon as well. Eventually, in alcohol-fuelled tears, single malt virtually squirting from his eyes, he begged Buckrack to save him, any way, any how. Could he, would he? Buckrack said he'd done it before and could do it again, but it was going to cost. Anything, Covet promised, anything. Buckrack went back to Odium.

The next day, Thursday, Buckrack let himself in to Jane Blake's apartment, informed the moping miss that they had to talk, and removed her once more to his campus house. He did not brutalise her this time. She was too much in terror of him, as she had been for the past week while subject to his surveillance and random unannounced visits, to do anything but comply. He sat her down and also got her a takeaway meal and gave her free access to alcohol. He told her what had been happening. He then proposed a deal by means of which it could all be over, her torment dispelled, and access to her money and identity restored. She grasped at the offer like a saving straw and, in that state of strange intimacy which descends on the vanquished when they are enticed into a compact with a victorious foe, especially given the fact that he was the first person to whom she had ever been able to confess all the putrescent corruptions of her recent life, she felt an odd solidarity with him. As he walked her back to the hall he seemed to her a guardian by her side rather than her nemesis, and to her own amazement she found herself thanking him. She even looked at him, as he prepared to part from her, in a way that she could not but reflexively do, in a mode of invitation. He returned her gaze, voiced his rejection of her unspoken proposition, cursed at her, and turned his back. Instead of reacting with offence at his repulsion, she realised, as she returned to her flat, that she was beginning to admire him. She had come to like McNamara for the same reason. It was now only men who restrained themselves from the temptations she projected whom she could find it in her heart to respect.

The *Newsnight* revelations later that same evening came as a surprise to Buckrack. He was alerted to them by a call from Covet, who gibbered to him on the phone and seemed so convincingly to be having a seizure that Buckrack undertook to drive again the hundred miles or so to Covet's other country residence. By the time he got there Covet was in such a state of alcoholic disorder that there was little Buckrack could do other than take the bottle away from him and put him to bed, himself bunking on the couch near the recently refreshed liquor cabinet. In the late morning on Friday, a monumentally hungover Covet required more tender loving care than one ageing man usually finds it decent to extend to another, but Buckrack gave it. He told Covet that he had a plan for dealing with the Odiumgate situation, instructed him sternly to stay off the booze, and drove all the way back to Odium once more.

Arriving in the mid-afternoon, he discovered that Asterisk had collapsed and been taken to the University Hospital. He went there immediately, encountered the police cordon protecting Asterisk's private room from the press but persuaded one of the officers to tell Asterisk that he needed to see him, and went in upon Asterisk's invitation. Asterisk did not look particularly ill, but he did appear excessively vexed, and, as Buckrack was implicated in the bugging, Asterisk believed he had good reason to help him out of the jam he had been placed in by the Poon letter. This Buckrack promised to do. He spoke to the police again and arranged to have Asterisk transferred home, with the cordon to be relocated to his house. He told Asterisk to check himself out of the hospital, and travelled home with him after they had exited by a service door. On the way, he asked Asterisk where he would find the purchase orders for the listening devices and the pinhead camera and recorder. Asterisk told him his secretary, Alison Stilt, would have all the more recent records. Buckrack said he would remove the relevant documents and that Asterisk should stay home on sick leave until further notice and communicate with no one other than him. Asterisk agreed. Buckrack made him put in one call to Harold K. Johnson, informing him that, with both Covet and Asterisk *hors de combat*, Johnson as Deputy Vice Chancellor was now in charge, and that he could expect a visit from Buckrack.

Buckrack went back to the Trump Building and found Johnson already moving into Covet's grand office. Police and security were everywhere. Johnson badgered him for information about the latest developments, but Buckrack told him that the less he knew the better. He did divulge that he had spoken with Covet and Asterisk and that he was charged with solving the current public crisis. All he needed right then was to be taken to Alison Stilt's office, where Johnson would tell Ms Stilt to cooperate in providing whatever he required. It was better if he asked no questions. Johnson, impressed by Buckrack's decisiveness, concurred.

They went there, and Johnson said the few necessary managerial words to Alison Stilt. He then left, as Buckrack had instructed him to do. Buckrack asked Ms Stilt where recent purchase orders made by the Registrar's department and their associated invoices could be found. She produced two fat document wallets for him, which contained all the relevant paperwork. He asked her to open the Registrar's office and went in there alone with the wallets. Ten minutes later, he emerged and gave them back to her. Then he returned to Johnson once more. He told him to call a press conference later that day, in which he should acknowledge that the Vice Chancellor had been suspended. The important thing was to associate this, as the press were already doing, with Poon's revelations about the listening devices, and to make no mention of the Jane Blake Disclosure, of which no one but very senior University managers, the investigation team and Miss Blake had any knowledge. Johnson demurred for some minutes, but was persuaded by Buckrack's reminder of the legal force of the confidentiality with which the Disclosure had to be treated. He would hold the press conference. As Buckrack left he told Johnson not to try to contact Covet or Asterisk directly, but to go through him. Johnson said he would.

By this time Redman and McNamara were themselves on the run from the press. The day before, in advance of the media assault on both their unsecured homes which occurred as a consequence of the Poon letter, they had escaped (McNamara with the three listening devices, Redman with his home computer) to Rachel Brace's modest two-bedroomed Bigton abode in Annapolis Drive. McNamara willingly snored through the night with Rachel. Redman set himself up in the spare room, monitoring the activity on Asterisk's phone, although there was little traffic. He guessed that Asterisk was now cautiously conducting whatever conversations he needed to have in person. Then, in the late afternoon of the third day, he picked up Asterisk's call to Johnson warning of Buckrack's imminent visit. Redman discussed it with McNamara. For over an hour McNamara then chivvied Rachel, who was an initially reluctant but ultimately consenting accomplice, into calling Alison Stilt for any pertinent information. It did not take her long to find out from Alison what she thought Buckrack had come for. It had to be to purloin the purchase orders and invoices for the bugs.

The three watched together, with a sense of rising frustration and defeat, the evening television news, in which, after a seemingly impressive bout of *al fresco* grandstanding by Poon, it was reported that Professor Harold K. Johnson, assuming for the time being the helm of the University of Odium, had promised at a hastily convened press conference that a thorough investigation would begin next week into the Odiumgate charges and confirmed that, until its conclusion, the Vice Chancellor had indeed been suspended. He affirmed, however, that the University was at this stage entirely unaware of any listening devices being planted in its employees' offices and, beyond the claim by Dr Poon and the inconclusive photograph which she had released, it had yet to find any strong evidence which would verify her assertion.

Shortly after the news item ended, McNamara's mobile phone began ringing. He held it up and showed it to Redman. The call was from Poon. He let it ring without answering.

Then Redman's phone rang. He ignored it.

## PART FOUR
### 1 NOVEMBER – 5 NOVEMBER

## Chapter Thirteen (1 November – 3 November)

The weekend permitted a sense of calm and order to return to the verdant campus grounds of Odium, though McNamara and Redman made no attempt to witness it: both stayed away, as they knew the two-day absence of reporters was an illusion which was at any time likely to be broken. Both had run out of ideas as to how to break it themselves, and were trusting somewhat to their intuitive sense that media wheels, once in motion, take a while to stop. Redman found that a ceasefire descended also on his wiretap. Asterisk's phone was now as dead as Covet's. But the Sundays, tabloid and broadsheet alike, remained alive with rumour and speculation in their synoptic accounts of the drama unfolding in a provincial English university town. Sir Evan Covet was too much an establishment figure for them to leave off encircling the indignity that had befallen him, sniffing for blood, nuzzling in the entrails. The press would almost certainly be back on Monday.

One of the reasons for their return was Professor Drago Baum. He seemed an unlikely source of renewed coverage, but he made himself into one. Baum had been sent to the University's China campus in Chongqing three years before as an Associate Professor. He had managed to establish the germ of a School of Education there, which was as much if not more of a laughing stock among the academic staff of Odium than the home campus's much larger sister School. Educationists are viewed with contempt by the majority of those who like to style themselves scholars, perhaps because the latter hold pedagogy in similar low esteem. The former are besmirched by their association with the training of schoolteachers, an embarrassingly vocational task, and academics generally look down upon schoolteachers, whose ranks are filled, it must be acknowledged, mainly by mediocre graduates who have difficulty finding employment in any other respectable profession.

Baum in person radiated no prepossessing charms which might modify this stereotypical evaluation. He would not have made the needle on a charismometer twitch. He was considered a plodder by his few friends, a drone by the multitude who were indifferent to him, and a Quisling by the two persons he had surprisingly managed to inspire to the heights of bitter enmity. What was worse than all of these, he had grown up in a suburb of Birmingham, a regrettable personal failing to which his thick Brummie accent adverted everyone every time he opened his mouth. These middling qualities, however, were exactly what the senior management of Odium sought in the people it sent to China to make things happen there. And when Baum "delivered" on the Chongqing School of Education (that is, created an administrative edifice which could be given such a name, whatever it was in reality), he had been rewarded with a Chair in the previous November's round of promotions. Afforded the opportunity to label himself Professor of anything he wanted to be Professor of within his field, and after a convivial snifter with the Vice Chancellor in the lobby of the Banyan Tree Hotel in Shanghai, at which he was extremely gratified by the condescension Covet showed towards him, he settled on "Professor of International Education". It did not matter that all his hitherto published work had been on either National Curriculum revisions or the relationship between government education policy and School Examination Boards in England and Wales. It wasn't so much that it accurately described what you did, Covet told him, but what opportunities a title in tune with the *zeitgeist* could be used to generate, and "Professor of International Education" were four words any Vice Chancellor would be happy to see in sequence on his university's website in times like these.

Baum spent the next year trying to write his inaugural lecture, a task incumbent on all new Professors, which had to be delivered in Odium within a year of appointment with the "informed lay person" in mind, as inaugural lectures are by tradition always open to the public. This had proved an excruciating grind, an almost impossible ordeal, in fact, because he knew nothing at all of International Education, which was little more than a slogan used by Odium to euphemise its vaunting overseas ambitions, a term with no scholarly valency, or indeed any accepted real world referent. The lecture was to be delivered on 1 November, exactly three hundred and sixty-four days since his ascension to his Chair, and as late as the week before it he had managed to work up only a few scraps which he considered might be acceptable fare, even to an audience comprised mainly of know-nothings. And then he read on the website of *Times Higher Education* (to which these days he earnestly subscribed) that Professor Sir Evan Covet had been suspended as Vice Chancellor of the University of Odium. Rumour around campus said that there was a major scandal in the making, that Covet's days were over. Covet would not be there to introduce him at his inaugural, or to hear it. Other press sources and those who bore to speak with Baum seemed to confirm the gossip, and there was Avril Poon, on television, clearly throwing down the gauntlet, challenging her fellow academics to arise and build a new Jerusalem on the crumbling ruins of Odiumgate. Why should she get all the limelight? What was she, anyway? An Associate Professor in Cultural Studies? She was no Professor of International Education, that was for sure.

There is a tide in the affairs of men which, taken at the flood, leads on to fortune. Baum had read that in his school days in Dudley, and at this juncture fancied himself something of a Brutus to Covet's Caesar. Poon was merely Casca, the one who had struck the first blow: but he would deliver the fatal stab. It was, he knew, the case that he had nothing much of value to say to his audience as things stood anyway. What he had managed to cobble together was little more than a convenient confection, a panoply of anodyne insights, supported by no authentic knowledge or experience or commitment on his part. How much better to stab with *the truth*. He would – as many another Elizabethan tragedy than the single one he had read put it – seize occasion by the forelock, for she is bald behind. On the Friday before the lecture reporters were not difficult to find on campus, and his insinuation to them, as he put the flier in their hands, that his imminent inaugural lecture might be an event worth attending in the current climate, was winkingly understood.

All of which explains why Professor Harold K. Johnson, at the end of his first full day as Acting Vice Chancellor, was intimidated to see, as he burbled a laudatory three minute introduction to Professor Drago Baum (written by Baum), that members of the press seemed significantly to outnumber members of the University and of the public in the lecture theatre audience. He did not have time to ponder the unusualness of this, or the reasons why it might be so, because he had somewhere else to be and, in any case, this was a phase already passing strange. Once he had concluded his brief ghost-written encomium, Johnson slipped away. Baum had the floor. He stepped forward, smiled a little nervously, and began.

"Ladies, gentlemen, colleagues, er, members of the press, my lecture tonight is entitled 'International Higher Education in China: Challenges and Solutions'. I have recently returned from a three-year spell at the University of Odium's China campus in Chongqing, where it has been my job, on a practical daily level, as well as on a theoretical plane, informed by many years of experience and scholarship in the field of education, to encounter such challenges and to find solutions to them. I was initially intending to share with you this evening some of the actual challenges I faced and how I successfully solved them. But not only would I be doing you a disservice if I pursued that course, I would also be doing a disservice to *the truth*. And it is the truth about 'International Higher Education in China' – a phrase which in reality denotes the commercial invasion of British universities such as this one into the backward Chinese educational marketplace in pursuit of enlarged income from abroad and political clout at home – which I wish to avail you of tonight. So let me commence.

"British universities in China are running a racket. There is no other word for it. The imperatives are fundamentally monetary, not educational, and the satisfaction of these imperatives is ultimately at the root of every questionable decision taken, every amateur appointment made, every backstairs manoeuvre executed, every policy of the home institution flouted, every academic standard allowed to go by the board, and every corrupt genuflection given to a dictatorial, undemocratic, morally retrograde communist regime. When I say 'International Higher Education in China' I mean you to understand that all these accommodations, taken together, are really what the term denotes, but which it, with its seeming beneficent aura, disguises. You might have thought I was going to talk on this occasion about the problems and dilemmas involved in teaching non-British students. I am not. I am going to describe to you instead how we crucify our cherished educational aims at the altar of Mammon. That is what, under the auspices of 'International Higher Education', British universities are now doing in China.

"How do we do it? Well, let us start at the very beginning of the process. You have a meeting with ministers of the British Cabinet at which you talk their language, namely the language of business and trade. Education, in this parlance, is an exported good: it shows up positively on our balance of payments. While you are not the first British educational institution to float the idea of stepping foot in China (in fact, you are simply trying to jump on the bandwagon because of the seeming public *coup* performed by the first one which did), you are unambiguously reassured, by twinkling ministerial eyes in the cocktail reception which follows in Whitehall, that a knighthood is pretty much in the bag for you personally if you see it through. The Foreign Office finds you, with amazing speed, a highly placed Chinese businessman, whose English is rudimentary but whose pull in Beijing is considerable, and you make him your Chancellor for five years – an honorary position, to be sure, but one which allows you to assign him flunkies and considerable expenses on his frequent trips to the UK, whose prestige, moreover, he himself can use as a kind of personal currency back home. No matter how much this costs in merely financial terms, it pays off in manifold ways. He takes care of all the necessary preliminary machinery, and gratifyingly reports that, as far as Beijing is concerned, you are pushing on an open door. All you need to be prepared to do is follow the rules stipulated by the men who will be behind that door.

"The first thing these men tell you, with a huge portrait of Chairman Mao behind them, is that you will not choose the city in which your Chinese campus will be situated: they will. Nor will you own the land or have control over the buildings, the architecture, the student residences, or the on-site services: these will be the remit of an 'educational corporation'. That body will hold a seventy per cent stake in 'the venture'. You will have only thirty per cent, although you will be permitted to cream off one tenth of the operating profit from that thirty per cent and return it to the UK home institution.

"There will be no equal opportunities in student recruitment. You will be able to accept applications directly from international students, but not from Chinese nationals: applications from them will be accepted only from provinces the Chinese Ministry of Education deems from time to time eligible, the Ministry will determine whether or not the students meet the agreed criteria for entry, and will then allocate students, acting as your proxy, to you. In particular, although it is understood that you are an exclusively English language institution, you will not make the same demands of competence in English from Chinese nationals, at either undergraduate or postgraduate levels, that you impose on successful international entrants, but will provide a 'foundation year' in which Chinese students lacking in this regard shall be taught English by you to a presumably sufficient standard for them to be able to continue. Even then, you shall not, at this continuation stage or any other time, subject these Chinese students to objective English language proficiency testing of the IELTS or TOEFL kind. It is an assumption that no more than two per cent of students shall ever fail to proceed in any one annual cohort.

"Your institution will accept a Communist Party official on its Management Board, in reality a kind of ideological overlord whose officially described function will be 'Ministry of Education Liaison', and who may at times act as your institution's advocate, or smooth out any difficulties which may arise with Chinese state officialdom you cannot be expected to understand, but whose role need not be too explicitly stated: it is understood that his word is final on all matters. He will organise the Party members among the student body. You will also comply with Chinese government requirements that all Chinese (but not international) students shall be subject to compulsory extra-curricular physical and political education, that they shall be assessed in these two areas, and that they must perform adequately in them to survive in the institution. If they do not, they will be excluded.

"This last is the first matter you baulk at, and the officials no doubt smile that it has taken you this long, because it is in fact their penultimate demand (the final one is that you must agree to accept the censored Chinese internet and make no effort to circumvent its imposed constraints). You explain that personally you are made of the stuff of *realpolitik*, but your own staff back at home will find it difficult to approve these compulsions, particularly the one about 'political education'. It will be viewed by them as the forced instilling of dogmatic Marxist propaganda, and will never be accepted at curriculum planning stage. They explain that it is non-negotiable within the legal framework of the Chinese state, but experience has taught them that this has been an ideological stumbling block before, and they have therefore devised a method that means it requires no approval: the instruction in both physical and political education will take place off campus and need therefore appear in no curriculum presented to your home institution for endorsement. It is simply necessary that you know it will take place. At this you wave your hand and agree. In short, you signal no opposition to everything they formally require of you.

"What follows from this acquiescence is an institution which, almost from the get-go, resembles nothing like the British one, but bears its name and awards its degrees. Because you have relinquished any say in the running of on-site buildings and services, you discover that students are racially segregated by the 'educational corporation' which commandeers the infrastructure. The Chinese students are domiciled in single sex halls of residence in which each dormitory, a room with two sets of bunk beds and a single toilet and shower, is shared among four students. Communist Party student members are distributed evenly throughout these residential blocks to form a supervisory cadre. The Chinese halls are closed at 11pm each night, latecomers being refused entry, and there is a communal lights out at midnight, when the internet is also disconnected, until 7am. The international students reside in their own separate blocks, which are open twenty-four hours a day: they have single occupancy rooms with *en suite* bathrooms and uninterrupted (though still censored) internet access.

"You discover that most of the Chinese students at entry, including postgraduates, have little or no English. You are the most expensive university in the whole of mainland China and they feel privileged to be in a prestigious foreign institution, but hardly any of them can express such a statement, using such words, in anything but Chinese. The struggle to teach them, in one foundation year, enough English to be able to meet the demands of even a typical first-year British university curriculum in any subject is clearly doomed from the beginning. But you are not permitted to test their English proficiency by any objective means at the end of the year, and remember, nor are you permitted to fail more than two per cent of them. In actuality, nearly everyone passes, by a combination, during this foundation year, of turning a blind eye to their rampant plagiarism and teaching them that 'paraphrase' of an original is the replacement of every sixth word by a synonym. Not that they ever really get to know what a synonym is: in my three years in Chongqing I never saw a student with a half-decent English language dictionary, never mind a thesaurus. Once they discover that libertine approaches to the assessment of their entirely derivative (or more accurately duplicative) work are acceptable to you, these methods of cheating and charlatanry quickly become their engrained reflex habits.

"The better students in the foundation year tend to pass by copying high school essays written in Chinese from a site called Wenku Baidu, then running these through Google Translate. The results are outlandish gibberish in English, but they do not give the appearance of being plagiarised, even though they are, and the students manage to get marks averaging in the mid-fifties. The same essays submitted in Odium itself would be lucky to receive what we call a 'soft fail' – that is, they would get a mark between thirty and thirty-nine. The more mediocre students plagiarise English internet sources entirely and tend mechanically to replace occasional words or phrases with (usually incorrect or hilariously inept) English alternatives. Their mixture of cut-and-paste English with improvised Chinglish receives marks averaging in the high forties. In Odium this kind of work would be a 'hard fail', that is, the mark would be below thirty. The weakest students of all simply submit entirely plagiarised pap, which, though understandable as English, is often grossly nonsensical in a different way, as it is usually not material of any academic kind that is being plagiarised, but magazines, trashy websites, newspapers, general discursive detritus. You might wonder why work of this nature, which would receive a zero mark in Odium and potentially lead to removal of the student from the University on grounds that its submission is academic misconduct, can receive marks averaging in the low forties in Chongqing. Well, the line is obvious: you must hold to the *diktat* that no more than two per cent of students can be failed. You cannot with a clear conscience, however, reward outright plagiarism. The solution is ingenious, and it is in devising this solution that you truly demonstrate your ability to cultivate the Chinese way of doing things. You ensure that such work is *never categorised as plagiarism*. How do you do this? Firstly, you ensure that suspected cases of plagiarism must be referred for adjudication to Heads of School by individual tutors. Before the tutors are allowed to refer, however, you make the burden of forensic proof intensely demanding of detail and subject to a highly bureaucratic procedure which must be followed separately for each individual student. With classes of more than two hundred students, in which perhaps over fifty per cent have rather blatantly committed plagiarism, this is clearly impossible. The staff thus do not refer, because they cannot write one hundred or more such referrals within the twenty-one day time period inflexibly set for marking students' work. When the tutors complain about the injustice of this procedure, the Head of School has a word in their ear and tells them they can do anything they like with work strongly suspected of plagiarism as long as they don't fail it outright, because students are not permitted to appeal against their marks. The tutors thus give the lowest marks they can get away with: forty or slightly above.

"Some students' English does improve as they progress, but stumblingly, haltingly, and seldom gets beyond the basics, with only a few stories of heroic individual accomplishment. Over a period staff become inured, not simply to mediocrity (there is enough of that among students here in Odium itself) but to the downright inanity, stupidity and gormlessness of Chinglish. Virtually every teaching session at Chongqing, one colleague told me, is like taking a remedial class in any subject at an English comprehensive secondary school, minus the bad behaviour. Eventually, staff begin to disregard the fact that the work is mostly incoherent drivel and perform a rough translation (Chinglish to English) on the fly in their heads as they mark it, then give a mark based on what it would have looked like in some alternative non-existent Chinglish-is-English universe. I have seen Ph.D. degrees awarded in Chongqing for theses which seem to have been written by an average British thirteen-year-old (you will note that all of these theses have been excluded from the UK online repository of doctoral theses, and for good reason). How, you ask yourself, do staff put up with it? Well, it must be understood that only a handful of these staff would be able to hold down an academic job in Odium itself. For the most part they are the usual foreign legion desperados one finds on the English Language Teaching or International Schools circuit, or star-crossed Ph.D. graduates who have found themselves unemployable in the UK, Australia, Singapore, Canada or the USA. Some of them do not have English as a first language either. Hardly any have ever worked in a UK institution of higher education. Those who can find a job elsewhere get the earliest flight out. Those who cannot remain. They are easily whipped into compliant local shape by a small tier of (no more than a couple of dozen) senior managers seconded from Odium with very hard-nosed business purposes in mind. These managers also ensure that conscientious Heads of School in Odium who try to interfere are foiled in their attempts to rectify the shocking quality problems they witness there. The final results are almost cosmically staggering. The universal grade average of students in Chongqing, hardly any of whom can write a single fully grammatical sentence in English at graduation, is a mere nine percentage points below that of students in Odium.

"In brief, the typical UK university in China is like a decayed pineapple, entirely rotten from the inside, whose outer husk is nonetheless maintained to give the illusion that it is edible. A persuasive fruiterer is still able to sell such a pineapple. Perhaps, however, there is a better analogy. The University of Odium at Chongqing is not really the University of Odium at all, but is maybe best understood as a franchise operation, a local mutant zombie relation of the real thing, like the KFCs and McDonalds and Starbucks of the kind you see in the untrendy shopping malls now rising from the filthy streets of dilapidated Chongqing itself …"

He went on for much longer, but this was food and drink enough for the assembled press. The lecture ended with a few cheers and some applause, but not from the reporters or photographers, whose hands were too busy with their mobile phones or cameras. They surrounded a jubilantly smiling Drago Baum at the close, grasping copies of the text of his lecture which he had prepared in advance to thrust into their outreaching palms, a lecture reprinted entire in one daily newspaper the following day, in excerpts in many others, beside an inevitable picture of him in professorial lecturing posture, a caption running underneath like "Baum: 'British universities in China are running a racket'", or "Drago Baum explaining how the University of Odium is 'best understood as a franchise operation'".

Baum read all of this stunning and copious coverage the following day, surrounded by a small mountain of newsprint, with swelling heart and rising mojo. For the first time ever he felt an enormous sense of pride in his own courage and daring and achievement, at least in so far as they could be measured in front of his very eyes by sensational column inches. His gamble had paid off. Cometh the hour, cometh the man. He found it hard to imagine that he would ever feel this good again throughout the remainder of his life. He was right. It was while he was looking, with a golden afterglow still tingling in his veins, at his picture in the *The Independent* ("'We crucify our cherished educational aims at the altar of Mammon,' Professor Baum stated") that Harold K. Johnson called him and fired him, without notice, for bringing the University into disrepute.

"You stupid ass, Baum," he said. "Have you any idea what you've done? Do you really think the Chinese will take all that crap sitting down? Did you really think you were big enough to get away with it? Can you imagine what kind of shit storm is coming our way from out East? You witless bastard!"

The same newspapers reported on the morrow the suspected suicide of Drago Baum. It appeared that he had carbon monoxided himself in his own garage one or two hours after Johnson called, a year to the day since he had become a full professor, an academic made man. His death finally did it for Johnson too. That afternoon he was summarily relieved of his duties both as Acting Vice Chancellor and Deputy Vice Chancellor, and sent back in shame to his ordinary post in his academic School. The Foreign Office was kicking up a stink. The Chinese Ambassador had been to see them. The lecture Johnson had introduced had caused a diplomatic incident, and the member of staff who gave it had now gone and topped himself into the bargain.

"Jesus, Johnson," the President of Council expostulated in the Vice Chancellor's magnificent office. "Have you any notion what you've officiated over? What you've allowed to take place? Do you seriously think we can withstand yet another scandal? Why did you not stay and stop him giving the bloody talk as soon as it got out of order, which was about one minute in? But no, you buggered off and the idiot went on an insane bender anti-Chink monologue, in front of all the newspapers of the land and an ITN news crew. The University of Odium is on its way to hell in a public handcart, and you've given it a push!"


**Chapter Fourteen (3 November – 5 November)**

The University of Odium proved to be a Hydra with only three heads. Once those of Covet, Asterisk and Johnson had been lopped off and put into cold storage, no one else dared hazard his mazard. Maximilian Knight, as President of Council, convened an emergency meeting of what remained of the Management Board, but discovered that this simply precipitated among more than half of the Pro-Vice Chancellors a spree of instant resignations from their senior administrative roles in preparation for incipient flights back, *à la* Johnson, to the relative obscurity of their Schools and Departments. Even those who were not thrusting termination notices into his hands were unwilling to step any closer to the toxic spill which had resulted from the triple decapitation. Knight got the message, called the Secretary of State for Education, and told her that he too was tendering his resignation from his voluntary position, with immediate effect. The rat which remains on the sinking ship is a stupid rat.

In previous periods more carnival-inclined or more anarchistically minded than the twenty-first century has yet been able to emulate or imitate, students and staff of a modern university most probably would have revelled in the radical opportunities thrown up by even the briefest disorder of things. This did not turn out to be so at Odium. There were no teach-ins or flowerful staff-student assemblies of any other kind. Nothing was perceived as being up for grabs. Instead, the immediate reaction to media revelations of the power vacuum, as they rippled through the ranks of middle management, was to abdicate all assigned responsibility. If there was no pretender to the throne, there was no point in pretending there any longer was a throne. Many Heads of School simply stayed away to listen to how things unfolded on the Radio 4 news.

Poon, who had been feeling sidelined for days by the Baum affair, checked the Union records and, though he was predictably not a member, decided that it was a useful pretext for an emergency general meeting of the Union nonetheless. Redman did not attend, but hundreds of members of staff abandoned their lectures and seminars at three in the afternoon to do so. The meeting was a real humdinger, with a bigger turnout than anyone could remember, plus there were lots of TV cameras, which encouraged unprecedented displays of performative militancy throughout the proceedings. No one exceeded Poon, at the podium, in this mode. One had to admire her daring in calculating the chances that a motion in favour of an immediate *en masse* staff walkout would succeed. But her stock after Odiumgate was high, and she had turned off her mobile so that frantic calls from Union HQ, which wished to impress upon her that a walkout without a formal ballot would be entirely illegal, should be ignored. Her motion carried the day, and the entire nation witnessed on TV the consequent *débouchement* from campus of the loudest phalanx of Ph.D. holders ever seen in the recorded history of the world. Then they all went home, and left the stage even more bare. Poon's diary filled up quickly with new media engagements. No one was available to comment on the management side.

The Odium Students' Union, by comparison with the one represented by Poon, had it ever been a political entity, was never one under Covet. He had kept it well financed (which was not in institutional terms very expensive) in return for a "partnership" in which it stuck to organising social rather than political events. He mixed with its elected officers many more times a year than he had ever deigned to meet with McNamara or Poon or Redman, and if the SU President did not exactly have a seat at his table she was generally invited to lick up the crumbs which he let fall from it in her direction. The current SU President, Ivy Littletot, was, as a matter of genuine strong emotion, scandalised by the reported suspension of Covet, for it also eclipsed whatever of his reflected glory she could bedazzle others with. She had in fact quickly organised a student petition for his immediate reinstatement, and more attention would have been paid to it had Ivy's stats been better on ratemash.com. As things stood, that site did not have her down as one of the "hotter" female Odiumites. There was only one vote against her name, in fact, and she had put it there herself. But when Poon's walkout was announced a different light bulb sparked into life in Ivy's head which might galvanise the campaign for the return of the Vice Chancellor. She drew up a template email for students to send to the Office of the Independent Adjudicator, in which they could complain about every single class they missed. Students now slept gratefully late, and extended their gratitude to their University by an endeavour (in what remained of the day) consisting solely of filling out the blanks in this template and sending it to the OIA every time they heard from someone sent to recce that the convener or seminar tutor had failed to show. By the second morning following the Wednesday walkout, a large updatable display was already in the eyeline of anyone ascending the steps to the Students' Union, which multiplied the number of cancelled classes by a wild estimate of the number of students to whom they were intended to cater: "25,420 STUDENTS DENIED THEIR RIGHT TO TEACHING YESTERDAY". In short, the student body seemed to erupt into a spontaneous consumer-style revolt. On the same day, the national press let everyone know, the OIA's server crashed.

McNamara and Redman avoided reporters by taking self-certified sick leave on the Monday, Tuesday and Wednesday, during which they remained under voluntary house arrest at Rachel Brace's. But the walkout faced them with a dilemma. If they stayed away, they would be deemed to be participants in it. If they did not remain in their sanctuary, but ventured into the fray, there was no telling what might happen. McNamara, who had found the last few days quite sexually enchanting and was even considering asking Rachel to move in with him on the strength of how well they cohabited, was in perhaps too mellow a mood to judge the situation aright. He made the mistake, over evening drinks with Redman, of committing himself to a five-minute monologue about "dukkha" – the Buddhist concept of "suffering" or "unsatisfactoriness" caused by a discrepancy between the reality witnessed and one's expectations of it – in the service of an impromptu argument that they should sit tight. Before he could finish, Redman lost the rag and told him (in not so many words) that he could stay where he was and chant his sutras and mantras asking Buddha to turn the fucking Dharma wheel if he liked, but he'd be damned if he was not going to clutch and cling in a worldly way to a proper sense of truth and right, however imaginary these seemed from the shade of the Bodhi tree.

Redman thus went in to teach his classes on the Thursday morning, and in doing so almost lost the real rags from off his back. Reporters massed around him outside the entrance to the Trump Building, barking leading questions and inviting him to fellate their out-thrust microphones. It was several minutes before police and security could clear a passage for him to enter, and when he got to the seminar room, late, he was dumbfounded to find only one of the students in the class, Betsy Pankin, waiting for him. Betsy seemed equally surprised and a little disappointed. She had only come, she explained, so that she could report his absence to the others, and they could all send yet another batch of aggrieved emails to the OIA. She had not prepared. He wasn't going to subject her to an hour of one-to-one teaching, was he? No, he said, he wasn't, and she could do whatever she liked. Then he threw open the ground floor window and escaped into the service road at the rear of the building, leapt over the adjacent wall, and retreated on foot back to Rachel's. McNamara met him with a brahmavihāratic smile.

On the Friday morning McNamara retreated to Rachel's upstairs toilet with a newspaper the early-rising Redman had passed to him with a sour face and rolling eyes. There, with his boxer shorts around his ankles and his elbows on his knees, he reluctantly permitted his increasingly luminous mind to be defiled by a long feature entitled "The Odious University" by one "Melanie Oldtosh, Education Correspondent":

Whatever one may think of Professor Sir Evan Covet, the abrasive and outspoken Vice Chancellor of the University of Odium, it has to be acknowledged that, in less than two weeks without him, the institution he has led for thirteen years has plunged headlong into a spectacular meltdown, and one which may yet change the face of higher education in Britain as we know it.

Sir Evan, who once attracted the approbation of Margaret Thatcher and the ridicule of his colleagues for suggesting that UK universities ought to be privatised, was suspended on full pay by the University on October 27 after an anonymous whistleblower alerted it to legal and other concerns over his professional conduct.

The nature of these concerns remains officially unconfirmed, but they have been linked to his alleged role in the bugging of the offices of two officials and one ex-official of the University and College Union (UCU). Dr Avril Poon, President of the Odium branch of UCU, and one of the academics who claims her office was bugged, filed a Freedom of Information request last Friday on the part of UCU, seeking confirmation from the University as to whether it had purchased listening devices.

The two other purported victims of bugging are Professor Robert McNamara and Dr James Redman. Neither has been available for comment this week, although Dr Redman, who is the UCU Vice-President, reported for work yesterday in what is being seen as open disapproval of the unofficial action of the Union members he represents. He appeared so indignant and affronted by reporters, however, that he refused to answer any of their questions.

The University has two more weeks to respond to Dr Poon's FOI request, and has stated that an investigation is under way. Until that investigation makes its recommendations, it seems that the

University intends to remain tight-lipped over "Odiumgate", as it has inevitably been dubbed.

One problem may be that there are hardly any senior managers remaining at Odium who might make any public comment. Sir Evan has been in hiding since news of the Public Interest Disclosure hit the headlines. On the day Dr Poon filed UCU's FOI request, Odium's Registrar, Dr Nigel Asterisk, took official sick leave after collapsing in front of reporters who had invaded his office, and he has not yet returned to work.

The Deputy Vice Chancellor, Professor Harold K. Johnson, lasted just a few days before he and several members of the University Management Board resigned their administrative positions on Wednesday. The same day saw the voluntary departure of Maximilian Knight, President of the University of Odium Council, whose letter to Sir Evan in October first set the train of recent events in motion.

The reason for the spate of managerial resignations earlier this week was a blistering indictment in a public lecture on Monday evening – by its own Drago Baum, Professor of International Higher Education – of the University's operation in Chongqing, China, where it has one of its overseas campuses. Among many other accusations levelled by Professor Baum was the charge that Chinese students in Chongqing suffer compulsory indoctrination with Communist Party propaganda as part of their studies.

The Chinese Ambassador made a formal complaint to the Foreign Office about the "anti-Chinese" nature of the lecture. Professor Baum was fired on Tuesday, and his body was found later the same day in what appears to have been a suicide. Coming on top of the "Odiumgate" accusations, Professor Baum's death seems to have been the final catalyst for the University's vertiginous descent into turmoil.

On Wednesday afternoon, a mass meeting of local members of UCU, which considered the bugging allegations and the sacking and death of Professor Baum, ended in an unofficial walkout. Many non-unionised members of academic staff, seemingly in sympathy with the strikers, have also refused to attend work for the remainder of this week.

Lecture theatres and seminar rooms at Odium have, for the most part, stood empty since Wednesday afternoon, and there seems no end to the unofficial action in sight, despite the fact that the national office of UCU has dissociated itself from the walkout and urged its members to return.

Students yesterday were collectively appalled by the failure of academic staff to turn up for classes, and have begun filing mass complaints to the Office of the Independent Adjudicator, the higher education watchdog.

The Secretary of State for Education, Dr Shirley Tang, was asked questions about the Odium situation yesterday in the House of Commons. Her responses took everyone, apparently even the seemingly prepped questioners of her own party, by surprise.

She informed the House that matters would not be sufficiently righted simply by taking legal action to force Odium lecturers back to work, and that she had decided, in consultation with the Prime Minister, on "more radical measures". This led to disbelieving obstreperousness from the Opposition benches, including a speech by one backbencher which contained mock Mandarin phrases.

Dr Tang, who is British Chinese, ignored the raillery. She went on to announce that she had appointed Professor Norbert Conquest as interim Acting Vice Chancellor of Odium until the resolution of the crisis. Professor Conquest is currently Vice Chancellor of the University of Surleighwick, a mere thirty miles north of Odium, and is known in academic circles as an economist of the unfettered free market.

What the "radical measures" are that he might put in place became clearer yesterday afternoon when he arrived in Odium and issued a statement saying that his own University would be opening its doors to Odium students who wished to transfer permanently into comparable degree courses at Surleighwick from the beginning of next semester. Odium students who exercise the option will also be offered financial compensation in the form of reduced tuition fees at Surleighwick, his press release added.

The announcement was greeted with scorn, and rejected as a bluff by Dr Poon, architect of the unofficial walkout, during an interview with her on *Channel 4 News* yesterday evening. By contrast, the Odium Students' Union President, Ms Ivy Littletot, featured on the same programme, said it was great news for Odium students, who were being denied value for money and deserved to have such an alternative. She predicted that many Odium students would take up Professor Conquest's offer.

No one in senior management at Odium was available to comment on Professor Conquest's statement, although one Associate Professor, who wished not to be identified, wondered if he would be willing to take on members of Odium's academic staff as well.

Reaction from other university Vice Chancellors, however, has been immediately explosive. One, who also declined to be named, said that the entire affair was an example of cynical opportunism on the part of government to force the hand of the HE sector into dog-eat-dog competition for students. Another, similarly off the record, claimed that Professor Conquest's behaviour was not that of a caretaker, but more that of a corporate raider, a liquidator, or an asset stripper.

However, he agreed with other VCs, who said without hesitation that if the Surleighwick offer were to be confirmed then they too would consider making similar approaches to the discontented students of Odium, and put equivalent transfer systems in place in their own universities without delay.

There can little doubt that Professor Conquest's offer is serious. An email to all Odium students yesterday evening indicated that an application system for those wishing to transfer to Surleighwick would be up and running by the middle of next week.

In an unusual departure from typical BBC practice, two scheduled guests were dropped at the last minute from yesterday's live *Question Time* programme so that Drs Poon and Tang could face each other from either end of the debating table. Dr Poon rancorously repeated her charge that the Surleighwick initiative was a ploy to blackmail striking Odium staff back to work.

Rather more coolly, Dr Tang replied, "Students no longer care if you go back to work, now they know you can no longer treat them as a captive market. You are about to find out that student mobility means more than sending students for an exchange year to your campus in China."

At the end of a tumultuous fortnight, then, the University of Odium appears to be a dying animal eyeing a flock of expectant hungry buzzards gathering steadily overhead. Students are next week likely to initiate what has never been seen before in UK higher education, something like the equivalent of an academic run on the bank.

If Professor Sir Evan Covet wishes to save his University from the gathering gang of predators, he had better come out of hiding this weekend.

McNamara finished reading the article in something of a *dwalm*, a word he had first heard during his childhood in Scotland. His head was dazed, but so was his left leg. Pins and needles were radiating up and down its lower half, and his foot was so benumbed that the floor beneath it seemed to give and slip away beneath him. He rested his arm on the sink and tilted his weight to the right. He stamped his left sole lightly on the wooden planking, and a disorientating electrical charge seemed to go off in it, rising rapidly all the way to the knee. He winced. It was strange that such light contact with the world could produce such discomfort, and even stranger that something that could not actually be called pain seemed even less desirable than it. He hobbled downstairs, holding on to the banister, noting with relief that the nervous repercussions reduced to lesser and lesser tingles with each step. By the time he reached Rachel Brace's living room he was no longer limping.

Redman was holding a cup of coffee and staring out of the window. He turned and looked at McNamara.

"Poon's fifteen minutes of fame," McNamara shrugged, gesturing at the newspaper. "Nearly over, I suspect."

Redman did not answer at once. Then he said, "Whether we do something or nothing, things go against us."

"Poon's not exactly been doing nothing," said McNamara.

"I don't mean Poon. I mean you and me."

"We went public with Knight's letter to Covet, didn't we?"

"Yes," said Redman. "And all that did was bring vampires onto campus, to whom Poon offered herself as a willing human sacrifice. If we hadn't done that, the entire matter would have been dealt with internally."

"Maybe not. There was Baum, after all. No one could have predicted that."

"Baum? I knew him before he went to China. He was a worm, and not the sort that turns. I can't prove it, call it intuition, but I suspect he was playing to the press gallery. If that's true, it was also avoidable."

"Another fifteen minutes of fame, then, and more abruptly terminated. But don't you at least savour the fact that he blew the gaff on China?"

"Yes, but to what end? A decimated executive, a mass flight from the field? Half of Management Board vacated, and then the Union ran away too, and now the students are preparing to exit. It's like a boxing match where the two fighters leap over the ropes and go back to their dressing rooms, then the audience drifts home, leaving just the referee – Norbert Conquest – standing in the ring, declaring himself the winner. It's rich. I was meant to be defending the interests of Union members. We end up in a situation in which lots of them may be out of their jobs by February and the whole sector goes into government sponsored competitive freefall. What a victory!"

"Hardly your fault," McNamara consoled. "Things have a habit of snowballing."

"Maybe not," agreed Redman. "But what I actually *tried* to do, the monitoring of Tweedledum's and Tweedledee's phone calls, I had such hopes it would be revelatory, conclusive, and it came to nothing. It was a dry well."

"It helped us interpret things a little better. We know Buckrack probably filched the invoices for the bugs, for example."

"But what good is that? It's only knowledge of how we were defeated. It *changes* nothing. We can't use it."

McNamara sat down. "I've often found that succeeding in changing things for the political good leads to unanticipated consequences which are bad. Call me a pessimist, if you will."

"No," said Redman. "I don't think you're a pessimist. I'm beginning to think you're just *correct*. But I can't reconcile myself to ignoring what's wrong the way you do."

"Don't," said McNamara. "That's not it at all. I don't ignore what's wrong. These days I try to fix it the only way a person really can."

Redman sat down opposite him. "And how's that?" he said.

"In my self," McNamara answered. "In so far as I am able, I try to fix the wrong in my *self*."

## Chapter Fifteen (5 November)

As if in testament to the incendiary nature of events of the last two weeks, fireworks began to thunder and crackle over the University of Odium at 9pm. Watched by an awestruck gathering of upturned eighteen to twenty-one year-old faces, they boomed and blossomed over the University lake, like sketchy sparkling flowers filmed in time lapse against the darkened sky, each living and dying quickly in an ephemeral glistening gorgeousness, the report of each explosion quickening the heart and exciting the blood. The student body, insentient to the charms of political carousal to which the previous week had tempted it, did not remain immune to the alternative of gross physical arousal. Many of the minority of virginities which had somehow managed to remain intact for the first six weeks of term were finally lost that night. Ivy Littletot, who was no virgin, but was statistically much closer to virginity than she regarded right and proper, found herself in uncommon favour on account of her recent media exposure. Becoming increasingly drunk and convivial on tequila mixers, she enjoyed two straight offers and one queer flirtation, and before the night expired had rough sex with a male member of the SU Executive. She did not know if it was the beginning of something that would last, but she was nonetheless grateful for the intrusion.

Sex was not on the mind of Jane Blake. The iron laws of supply and demand, inevitably advantaging girls like her over the Littletots of this world, meant that it seldom needed to be thought about. It could easily be found with the right look or word, and wallet. Ivy would have been bemused to know that Jane did not even want it, and had not really wanted it, in the sense of a genuine need or desire, for a very long time. What she wanted, on the contrary, was to escape its ravening clutches, to be no longer dependent upon it, to live in something closer to a state of chastity. She yet could feel stirrings of desire, but these were now for men who showed unusual restraint, who were moved, whether it be because of age or rectitude or fidelity or a certain elevation of being, only by things more profound and of greater lasting value. She had first felt it with McNamara, although with him it had seemed to take the form of unconquerable indifference towards her. Buckrack, however, she had clearly placed in a state of powerful emotion, albeit negative, filled with loathing for her, hate and cruelty. But these she could understand, in the circumstances. They did not diminish her growing respect for him, even while she suffered their effects. Now that he was safeguarding a course of action that would relieve her of those effects, and one that would provide a substantial sum of money for no sexual exchange of any kind, she began to feel a kind of new hope for a better life for herself. In a way, Buckrack might turn out to have been her redeemer.

As she sped south with him along the motorway towards Covet's second country retreat, Buckrack at the wheel of the hired car, she wished he was more amenable to conversation. She had hoped she might be able to make him understand her better, but he resisted being drawn by her gambit of trying to explain to him, in some kind of mitigation, why she had become what she had become. He was not contemptuous, however, rather purely purposive, focused on what had to be done. He curtailed her by saying that it was too late for such exculpations. She tried anew, telling him that she was intending to turn over a new leaf. He said it didn't matter to him. After that there was silence. They drove on, fireworks displays flashing up silently in the distant sky on left and right as they passed villages and towns on their route.

Buckrack became more vocal when he drew into a service station near the end of the journey, and bought them both coffee. What he spoke about was essentially practical, but she was glad to hear the sound of his voice. He was not any longer the seeming madman who had first kidnapped her and tormented her, dispossessing her of her identity, then monitoring her movements and actions and communications. Instead, he appeared keen simply to ensure that the meeting with Covet would conclude without any hitches. His warm American tones even reminded her of the homeland he had said he would be taking her on a plane to afterwards. She wondered as he talked if she would ever see him again there. She imagined he would not want that, but she felt an odd dissatisfaction that this and the flight might be the last time she would have any contact with his reassuring strength and confidence.

"He will want to talk to you," Buckrack was saying. "That's why he insisted on a last meeting. In a situation like this, the guy always wants closure. We'll let him do that. I will leave you alone with him, but I'll be listening right outside the door in case anything goes wrong. The thing you need to remember is not to deviate from the script we agreed."

"Yes," Jane said earnestly.

"He's almost certainly going to ask you why you submitted the Public Interest Disclosure when you did. He doesn't understand that. To his eyes it will seem a betrayal for which there was no motive and, looking at it objectively, it is. What's your answer to that?"

"I had a change of heart," she recited from memory. "I couldn't go on any longer, especially after what he wanted me to do with Dr Poon. I was in over my head."

"Right," Buckrack said. "But then he is going to ask why you didn't talk to him first."

"I meant to," she reeled off, "and in fact I tried. That's why I asked to see him earlier on the day I finally sent the document in. I was intending to explain. But it just turned into what it always turned into, lunchtime sex. I wasn't able to bring myself to tell him I wanted it all to end. Afterwards I felt degraded and demeaned, and I submitted the complaint in a state of despair."

"That's right," said Buckrack. "That'll do. He still won't understand it, but it will be enough. You weren't thinking straight, you were emotional and irrational, to the extent that you didn't even calculate too much the consequences for yourself. You don't give him any more information than that. If he wants to talk about other things you can say what you like: your past, your affair, his feelings. It's all very likely, but I know you've heard that sort of thing and dealt with it before."

"Okay." Jane felt herself blushing slightly. "But when it's done, when we leave, you will give me everything back, right?"

"Yes," Buckrack confirmed. He reached into his pocket and handed her a slip of paper. "This is the changed password on your email account. Memorise it so that you can access it once you see him transfer the funds. You will then send an email to the Registrar withdrawing your Public Interest Disclosure: Covet will dictate the text. You can change the password to anything you want after that. Then we will drive off to the airport. The only reason I am getting on the plane with you is to make absolutely sure you leave as agreed. It departs at 6am. I have the tickets. I will give you your ticket and your passport at Heathrow."

"Can I see it?"

"The passport?"

"No, my ticket."

He looked at her disapprovingly, but put his hand into his inside pocket and brought out the tickets.

She looked at them both and said, "Did I have to pay for those? Did you buy them using my account?"

"No," he answered patiently. "I bought mine, and Covet paid for yours. I gave him your passport number and he had it sent to me."

"I see," she acknowledged. "Good."

He went on, "At the airport I will also give you the new password to your bank account. You can change the access codes again, so you will know you have sole control of the account before we are in the air. You can check at the same time that I have not touched your money, as I promised. I doubt if you'll be able to see the cleared funds for the international transaction by then, but you'll have witnessed him do it, and it's irreversible. You'll also get back your Facebook account – though you'll find that 'William Blake' is no longer in your list of friends, as he's deleted himself – and your cards and the rest. Once we clear customs at Boston, we'll part. And you'll never see me again. I have a return ticket."

Jane's heart sank slightly at this last piece of information, but she disguised it by expressing a more venal concern. "He will go through with it, right? He will transfer the money?"

Buckrack snorted gently. "It's taken him a week to make the necessary financial arrangements, but you'll get your fifty thousand dollars," he affirmed. "And so will I."

Covet had spent the last ten days viewing another three seasons of *Breaking Bad*. At first he had begun watching it when he was drunk, but he had had difficulty following the ins and outs of the plot, and twice he had fallen unconscious and woken up in the middle of the night with a nasty head to find the DVD looping its episodes mechanically, a situation he found degenerate, and which sharpened his sense of being out of control of things. He went back and started from season two again, watching in the afternoons, until he could stay away from the bottle no longer. Had he reached season five he would have felt some sympathy, as he paced his modest cottage, often talking to himself, flying into rages and unwitnessed outbursts, with Walter White stuck in the snow in a backwoods cabin in New Hampshire. As it was, however, in the lucid though depressed hours in which he had followed the narrative since, he found much to identify with in Walter's plight, especially his near-continuous state of heightened anxiousness and paranoia. Walter's ability to get out of impossible spots by means of his own ingenuity and daring, overcoming his natural fears, impressed Covet mightily, were in fact a fillip which lifted his spirits each day before he downed more each night. The end of the last episode of season four, in particular, he found talismanic, as Walter, with cuts on his face and a plaster over his nose, told Skyler, in marvellous two-word sentences, "It's over. We're safe. I won." Covet vowed then not to watch the final season, if ever, until the current crisis was likewise over, he was safe, and he had won. The victory would come at a price, but at least he would not have to find a way to blow half of Jane Blake's body in two, the way Walter had Gus Fring's. And he would at last be able to get out of the horrible game he had been playing with himself and with others.

He heard the car door slam on the isolated road outside the cottage some time after eleven o'clock, and he waited tensely for the last few moments. The week had passed as such, like treacle pouring from a jar, as he made the mechanical, bureaucratic arrangements to gather enough money together, over sixty five thousand pounds in all, into an appropriate account from which he could pay Jane and Buckrack the fifty thousand dollars each that would be the cost of his reprieve. He was unused to waiting for anything, could normally demand things in double quick time. This, the final day, had dragged by in even slower motion. He had tried not to drink, but a quarter bottle of scotch had already passed his lips. Still, he did not feel too incapacitated, and took heart that it would soon be over.

He opened the door, which gave straight onto the living room, as he heard the crunch of their footsteps on the tree-sheltered gravel path. Jane stopped as she saw him framed in the light under the lintel, and stayed arrested a pace behind Buckrack, who turned and looked at her. He saw her eyes meet Covet's momentarily and then she bowed her head.

"It's okay," Buckrack said gently. "Let's go in."

Once inside, Buckrack indicated the armchair nearest the door. "Sit there," he told her. "And Sir Evan, I suggest you sit over there." Covet complied and took a seat several feet away. Buckrack remained standing.

The situation demanded a decent silence. Jane's knees were placed together and the palms of her hands were on them. Covet crossed his legs. At last he said, "Does anyone want a drink? I know I do."

"Not right now," said Buckrack. "There is a matter we need to deal with first."

He reached into his coat pocket and pulled out a small padded envelope. He upended the envelope, thus emptying its contents – a miniature video player, a memory card, and a small black circular bead mounted at the end of a one-inch pin – onto the coffee table which was between Jane and Covet.

"Sir Evan, you might remember that Jane asked to meet with you at noon in your usual hotel on the twenty-sixth of October."

Covet looked at him with an expression that said this was not a good start. "Did I tell you that?"

"You did, though you maybe don't remember. You were not, shall we say, in the best state of mind."

Covet relaxed. "Okay," he said.

"Do you know what this is?" Buckrack asked, pointing to the small black device on the pin.

Covet said, "No."

Buckrack looked at Jane and then back to Covet. "It's a wireless camera which sends a combined video and audio signal to this, the recorder. The files are high definition, much better than any cell phone could capture, and are stored on this memory card. You wear it like a brooch. It's hard to notice, especially on a woman's coat lapel, which is where Jane was wearing it when she knocked on your hotel room door that day."

Covet stared at him, then transferred his stare to Jane, who was looking down at her hands.

"Yes," Buckrack said, "she was filming your tryst. She put her coat over a chair facing the bed."

Covet seemed about to gag. A vein on his temple was enlarging. He looked up at Buckrack again. "Have you seen it?"

"Some of it," said Buckrack. "Not all of it, but I had to check. It's clearly you and her. The duration is about ninety minutes."

Covet closed his eyes and sat forward, bowed, raising his right hand to his forehead.

"Don't worry," Buckrack continued. "The fact is, she told me about it voluntarily and gave it to me when I proposed the solution to your mutual predicament. She says she has not made any copies and I believe her. I did check her computer, her iPad and her phone, and there was no sign of a copy on any of them. Had she wished to hold onto it for any purpose she simply needn't have told me about it. Shocking as it is, I'd take it as a sign of her good faith."

Covet cried out incredulously, "*Her good* – ?"

Buckrack raised his hand. "Yes," he said. "However it may look, yes. But you have it now. I don't believe she does."

"It's true." Jane spoke softly for the first time. "I don't have a copy, and I'm very sorry."

Covet shook his head. "But *why* – ?"

"Sir Evan," Buckrack interrupted again, "perhaps you can discuss this in a few minutes. You simply needed to know about it first off. I don't think she would even use a copy if she had it. It hardly shows her in a good light either."

Covet relented. "Alright, but there are a few other things I need to get straight with her."

"Of course," said Buckrack. "We have some time if you two need to talk. But I think we should get the main business out of the way."

The pair sat silently with Buckrack standing over them. Neither moved. Covet continued to glare at Jane but she did not return the look.

"I understand," Buckrack cajoled, "that there is some justified bad feeling on one side, and some awkwardness on the other, but perhaps you two need to see this more as a simple business transaction. It's unpleasant, but these things happen. Sir Evan, you need to transfer the money to Jane's account. Then she will send the email."

Covet stirred himself resentfully and got out of the chair. "I've got it set up on the computer." He walked over to a desk on which sat a brightly lit laptop.

Jane did not get up but watched him from a distance. She was distracted by Buckrack gesturing with his hand for her to stand. "You need to see this," he said.

She walked with him over to the desk at which Covet was now seated. Both stood behind him.

"This is my current account balance," Covet said. "As you can see, it is over seventy thousand pounds. There is my name. This is your name, Jane, bank and account number."

Buckrack took Jane's bank card out of his wallet and handed it to her. She leaned over and checked the details against it.

"Okay," she said.

Buckrack held his hand out for the card and she returned it to him without question.

Covet continued, "You can see the sum to be transferred here – fifty thousand dollars. When I confirm the transaction you will see a message telling me that the transaction is final and that once I have confirmed again the funds will be instantly withdrawn and cannot be returned. You will then see my new balance, which will be about thirty-one thousand five hundred pounds less – whatever the exact sterling equivalent of fifty thousand dollars is at today's exchange rate." He looked over his shoulder at her. "I am going to confirm the transaction now and I want you to check the text of the popup message."

Jane nodded. Covet moved the mouse and clicked once. Jane read the screen.

"So when I click one more time you should see the transaction go through and you can check the new balance," Covet resumed. "Then you will write that email I need you to write. Agreed?"

Jane assented once more. Covet turned, sighed, and clicked again. The three watched the transaction complete. Covet then surrendered the chair so that Jane could log onto her email account.

Once she had done so, he said, "Let's make it short and sweet. 'Dear Dr Asterisk, I hereby wish to withdraw the Public Interest Disclosure I submitted to you by email on 26 October. I was not in a balanced state of mind when I sent it, having not taken my prescribed medication for several days, which had placed me in a profoundly delusional condition. I wish to make it clear that the document is in its entirety dishonest and untrue. I am ashamed to have written it and would like to offer my humblest apologies both to you and anyone else who has read it and, most of all, to the Vice Chancellor for the acute offence and distress which it must have caused him. Yours sincerely.'"

Although he was puzzled by the wholly unhesitant and unquestioning manner in which Jane quickly typed and despatched the missive, Covet felt a certain small resurgence welling within, which began to displace his previous resignation. It was good to be dictating again. As she logged off, he turned away, and with something approaching actual breeziness said, "Perhaps we can have that drink now?"

Buckrack declined. "No, thank you. I'm driving. My work is also pretty much done here. I think I should give you two some time to talk alone and say goodbye. Jane, I will be just outside the door on the porch. I'll wait for you to come out, then we'll go."

He left. Covet poured Jane some scotch and sat opposite her again. Some of his lost *bonhomie* was returning, although it was tinged with sardonicism.

"I suppose you missed your regular pay cheque at the start of the month," he said. "But what I just did more than makes up for it, I imagine."

Jane eyed him coolly. She felt feistier now that the transaction was completed and Buckrack was on guard at the door. "What do you get paid, Evan? Seven hundred thousand dollars a year? It's not even a month's salary to you. It's what you would have given me had I stayed another two years."

"That's true," said Covet, "minus what I would have paid it for, of course." He sipped his drink. "I suppose I do have the video. Remind me, what did we get up to that day at the hotel?"

Jane's eyelids flickered. "It was one of your 'do as I say' days."

He smiled. "That should be quite a memento. But why?"

"Why what?"

"Why the video? Was it your plan to blackmail me all along?"

She answered, "No. But things went awry after Poon. I wanted out. I didn't think you'd be agreeable. The video was meant to be for leverage rather than blackmail."

"I see," he said. "But then just a few hours later you submit a document to the University, recounting our history, but without the video? You go public? I don't get it."

She shrugged. "You might find it hard to believe, but I thought it was time for the truth. A man in your position? Doing the things you do?"

Covet guffawed in disgust. "A man in *my* position, Jane? What about your whole *Kama Sutra* of positions?"

"Yes," she said. "It's true. I have done very wrong things. But I don't hold much power over others, except for sex, which, believe me because I know, can only be used to control the already weak. I haven't ever deliberately set out to entrap men in ways I could use against them, to damage them in the eyes of others. I was selfish and uncaring, yes. I may have warped some of them, but not without their willing consent. What you were using me for was quite different. You made me a honeypot, a kind of snare. No one ever did that to me before. It's a step above the ordinary kind of lust. That's just bad, but you, well, you are wicked. I'm just a whore, no worse, no better."

He gazed at her. "And I thought ..."

"You thought *what*?" she sneered. "Are you going to give me that old line? You thought I had feelings for you? Look in the mirror. Better still, look in your soul."

"No," he replied mutedly. "I was going to say something about my feelings. I thought I loved you."

She leaned forward in her seat. "You thought you *loved* me? First you pay me to fuck you, then you pay me not to fuck other people, then you actually *pay me to fuck other people*. Is that your idea of love? Giving me cash to seduce Krokoff? You didn't even stop at the humans with cocks. You loved me so much you wanted my tongue in Poon's hairy axe-wound as well. It wasn't love, Evan. I'm used to being treated like a sex doll, but to you I was a different kind of instrument altogether. Well, it's over, and if you expect me to sit here feeling sorry for you or eating humble pie, it's not happening."

His eyebrows raised an inch up his forehead.

"Look," she said. "You had your fun. I got my money. That's all it was ever about. It got a little complicated, but you've wriggled out of it. I learned what my limits are, and how I have to change. I'm not sure you have. I see no conscience in your eyes at all. You're like some kind of lizard or snake."

She got up. On instinct he arose as well and, ensuring that he left a gap between them over which they would not make physical contact, he crossed and opened the front door.

They both saw bright yellow, but Covet saw it better than Jane in the second they both had to take it in. Buckrack was standing ready in the porch, dressed from head to foot in oilskins zipped up to the neck, with a hood around his head. There was something in his gloved right hand, but neither had time to make it out properly before he lunged forward with the full weight of his body, emitting a loud empowering roar, throwing out his left arm to push Covet bodily over, and making one swift, decisive, upward movement from his waist with his right.

Jane's vision became cloudy at the edges. The surface of her body tingled with racing endorphins and her hearing instantly disappeared, or was rather obliterated by a kind of white noise. She looked and saw a thin black object slanting downwards to the right from the area between her navel and her chest. Covet, sprawling on the floor, saw it more as it was, the butt of a heavy kitchen knife buried up to the hilt. Jane looked up at Buckrack's face. He was removing the hood and staring at her with fascinated determination. His expression seemed to speak of a certain foreknowledge that had been denied her, although it also appeared, now that his features were blurring, to be forgiving her for something because her penance had finally been done. There seemed even to be a little regret or sympathy in his look. Her hearing returned slowly as the ringing in her ears faded. She was not aware of herself breathing. Her lungs seemed too full or too empty of air – she was not sure which – to make speech possible either way. She was making sounds of a sort, or rather her body, which now seemed a kind of foreign object, was producing involuntary noises from the throat, guttural, catarrhal. It took a step back. Neither Covet nor Buckrack moved. Her vision was narrowing even further, and her eyes opened wider in automatic compensation. Buckrack's eyes, conversely, seemed to narrow the more unblinkingly he watched her. There were now thick black rings encircling what Jane could still see, and what she could see seemed to be receding down a lengthening tunnel. Her body took another step back. Her hands dangled uselessly in front of her stomach, unable to make the journey all the way to the knife handle, and there was the first feeling of something hot and gushing, travelling down her belly beneath her shirt, then coursing around the waistband of her skirt, slightly ticklish. It seemed damp down there, but her neck was locked in position and she could not bend it to look. She became aware that her mouth had opened wide and she was unable to close it. Her jaw seemed paralysed and she thought she might be dribbling. She staggered back one more step, and her calf made contact with the edge of the coffee table. Her thighs felt weak and had begun to shake, so it seemed natural to try to lean back and sit on the table. As she did so, she found herself losing balance, wobbling and falling completely, her waist rolling across the wooden surface and momentum carrying the top half of her body further back, over the far edge, where her skull struck the arm of the easy chair with an upholstered thud and she lost consciousness, her head and shoulders on the rug, the rest of her body propped up over the table top. Her lower limbs had splayed as they gave way beneath her and left the floor, forcing open her coat, so that all Buckrack could see when she finally went inert was her bottom half, sticking over the far table edge, her skirt hitched up, her legs gaping wide at an obtuse angle, as they had too frequently been in life.

It was a very televisual death.


## Chapter Sixteen (5 November)

"What the *fuck* have you *done*?" Covet screeched.

Buckrack, still in his full oilskins, had been standing over the table, watching blood seeping along the torso of the upturned Jane, emerging from under her clothes, dark at the white skin of her exposed throat, flowing sideways into the reaches of her long brown hair. Now he looked over at Covet, his eyes narrowing once more, and pointed to the chair near the computer, the furthest from the front door.

"Sit down," he hissed, "and don't you move!"

Covet did as he was told and inched towards the seat.

Buckrack noticed that Covet was shaking. "Have another drink," he said, picking up the whisky bottle and pouring a large one, which he passed to him. Buckrack poured another and put it and the glass on the half of the table that was not occupied by Jane's jutting lower legs. He stepped out of the front door and brought in a small green denim shoulder bag, which he placed on the floor near the exit. He sat down and took a drink.

"This is the time for me to ask some questions," Buckrack said. "Then I'll fix this."

Covet sat doggedly quiet.

Buckrack asked, "Do you remember when we first met?"

Covet swallowed. His upper lip trembled. "On the plane from LA to London last summer. We sat next to each other in first class."

"And that was the first time you ever saw me?"

"Yes."

Buckrack first nodded and then shook his head. "It wasn't the first time I saw you." He reached into the shoulder bag and brought out two envelopes, one large, one small. "Have a look," he said, throwing the larger on the table.

Covet picked it up and pulled out a sheaf of white papers on which were printed various colour photographs showing him and Jane.

"That's you and her in Boston," he said. "Not the first time or the second time you met, but the third: you went there to start your second road trip together. Then there's one of you having lunch in Chicago. Drinks in Colorado Springs. It was wise to avoid some of the 66, all those cattle towns in North Texas, for example. But Silverton, where you stopped, see, for gas, is even better in winter, when the passes are snowbound. There you are kissing in Santa Fe, and holding hands in Flagstaff. Happy memories? You can keep them."

Covet, in agitation, mumbled, "But this was before you and I met."

"True," said Buckrack, "but I took them. You've read *Lolita*, right? You know, when Humbert takes Lolita off for a year-long road trip?"

"I, I, " Covet stuttered, "I think I saw the movie."

"Too bad," said Buckrack. "Neither version can compare, although I actually think the remake was far superior. Anyway, Humbert starts to understand, but too late, that someone was following them most of the time, another guy. That other guy was me, in your case."

Covet was visibly startled.

"I know," Buckrack assured him. "I've seen this so many times. You considered you were alone and, when you realise someone else was watching you, you start to think of what you did in more moral terms than you did at the time, or rather you always knew it was immoral, all the time, but you get frightened about the consequences of having been found out. It's a contrastive shock, because the immorality itself was so hedonistically satisfying."

Covet put the photos back on the table and his hands went to his face. He tried to compose himself. "Am I in some kind of trouble?" he asked.

"Are you," Buckrack repeated, "*in some kind of trouble*? There's a dead woman on your floor and her blood is ruining your carpet. Does it feel like you're in *some kind of trouble*?"

"I mean, a CIA guy was following me all across America. Why?"

"Ex-CIA," Buckrack reminded him. "Though technically, you're right. At the time I was still with the Agency. But I wasn't following you. I was tailing her. You never saw me, because I was always a fair way behind you. I simply put a tracker above the rear wheel of the car. While I was about it, I put a listening device under the dash. All those long drives, all those long conversations ... "

Covet closed his eyes, then made an effort to open them again.

"Why? Was she ... was she some kind of *spy*?"

Buckrack laughed. "You've been watching too much television, Covet. She wasn't a spy."

"So ... so you put her up to this? The two of you were in on it? To blackmail me?"

Buckrack scratched his head. "More and more. No, I am not the bigger conspiracy behind her smaller conspiracy with you. We were not a pair of happy-go-lucky con-artists, her and me. She didn't know me either then. Where do you get these crazy notions? Real life is less dramatic than that. She was a whore, who knew her market well. You were her client, or perhaps her victim. If that's the right word, I was simply another one of her victims. Let me show you something else."

He took a single photograph from the smaller envelope and held it out in his hand, displaying it to Covet across the table. This was a regular-size developed print, a family photo, all smiles, of a relatively young man and woman with a small baby.

"You can't have this one," Buckrack said. "Because that's my only son, his wife and daughter. He was an Assistant Professor at Amherst, in the Literature Department."

"*Was*?" said Covet.

"Yes. He shot himself in his garage last May. You're figuring it out, right?"

Covet's brow furrowed. "He ... ?"

"That's correct," said Buckrack, returning the photo to the envelope and then the envelope to the bag. "Happily married as he seemed to be, indeed as I think he was, it was not enough to stop him succumbing to her, what shall we call them, admissible attractions? Of course he wasn't rich like you. But he paid her in kind. He wrote her essays for her. Hence her magnificent degree. It all blew up in his face, of course. She cut it off with him almost as soon as she had the scroll in her hand. By that time she was fucking you and God knows who else. From the note he left – I was the one who found him, you see – his good feeling for his wife seemed entirely to have evaporated, he was, it seems, genuinely in agonising love with Penelope Pussylips here, or thought he was, but he was about to be found out, there was an investigation ongoing at Amherst, all causes for despair, and no one to talk to, the usual kind of suicide stuff. His wife doesn't know. It's better for her and my granddaughter that she doesn't. I kept the note to myself. It named our

Cleopatra, though. I took it badly. The Agency gave me compassionate leave, but that only allowed me more time to think, perhaps not very well, perhaps morbidly, but then we're all human. You have two grown sons, Covet. You can imagine."

"I am sorry about your son," Covet said, as soberly as he could. "But revenge is – "

"They say many things about revenge," Buckrack interrupted. Then he jerked his thumb at Jane. "The dish on your floor is certainly getting colder by the minute."

Covet tried again. "Well, you've had your revenge, then, no?"

Buckrack pondered. "In a way. The problem with revenge, though, is that the revenger becomes engorged with a weird sense of justice. That's what revenge is, really: the pursuit of justice by irresponsible means. It gets conducted in a private, unaccountable manner, it becomes a law unto itself, a virtue that is at once a vice. You're a vengeful man yourself, Covet. McNamara – you wanted your revenge on him, for example. Then that impulse spread to others. You wanted your revenge on Poon, and to get that you put Krokoff, who as far as I know had done nothing you could personally feel even slighted by, in harm's way as well. Before you know it you start wanting the scalps of those who are even *associated* with the object of your revenge. I wonder where it leads if the revenger isn't stopped? Pehaps he even starts taking revenge on people *in advance* of any wrong they commit against him. Maybe I should better understand you by examining what's happened to myself."

Covet raised both hands defensively. "Look, you're not thinking straight. If you're talking about me, well, surely you've done enough to make me suffer? I think we've both been the victims here. I know what I did with her was wrong, and I've been almost ruined by it. You might not believe me, but I had come around to that understanding myself. Just before all this broke I had made a promise to myself not to go on with it, to try and make amends."

"Don't worry," said Buckrack. "I am not intending to prolong your suffering much beyond this conversation. But I do want to have it. It might help you comprehend things. As for you setting it all aright, what are we looking at here? In the last half hour what you've tried to do is extricate yourself. You haven't wanted to acknowledge the truth of what you did and live with the consequences of that truth. You've tried to cover it up so that you can continue. Oh, what, you're going to go on and build a new, more benign dispensation? On the basis of a massive falsehood? And what does that involve, more falsehood within falsehood? Getting rid of the dead body on your floor too, perhaps, so that it can't be connected with you? Suddenly, after a lifetime of slowly consuming corrosion, if you can get away with just one more deceit, the biggest of them all, you'll lead yourself by the hand into Damascus?"

Covet bit his lip. "I'd like the chance. Look, I was going to pay you fifty thousand. I'll double it."

"You'll pay me? You'll pay a man you think is called *Buckrack*? You still think that's my real name? Oh, what? You think an ex-Agency guy can't get a fake passport with any name he likes? The name I chose was even intended as a provocation but, oh no, you respond to it like one of Pavlov's dogs. The bell of *Buckrack* sounds and you throw money at it. I have often wondered, in the time I have known you, how a guy who was once a distinguished Professor of Law became such a Lord of Misrule. But then I realised, not that you're stupid, but if anyone can get your attention and press the right buttons in you that you do act pretty stupid pretty predictably. Your vanity, that's the key, especially your failure to understand that power over people and controlling them are not the same thing. It makes you so easy to play. All that talk in the car with her I heard as I drove five miles behind you, you never twigged that she was the one in control, not you. She just knew how to do it. She had a gift for adjusting the narrative. You didn't notice how she suddenly changed the theme one day and started saying, even though she'd already blown your mind with her skilled sexual antics, that even greater things could happen if you were open to it? She was several moves ahead of you. You were going back to Nevada, the cocaine was already in the bag again, but the second whore she got for you that night, oh, that was a new high altogether. You know, the one that wasn't mentioned in the document she sent to Asterisk, the one whose head she held by the ponytail and pushed down on your cock while she fed you with her own tits? The one who obeyed every sexual command voiced to her by Jane, upon whom Jane encouraged you to visit the most extreme fantasies your mind could concoct? You think Jane didn't know that girl already, that the entire episode wasn't deliberately staged? It didn't cross your mind that the porno sandwich stunt was designed to break you, to unman you? You thought that was *real life*? And didn't the stratagem work, like the drugs had worked the previous year, when the entire crazy plan for you

148

to bring her to England surfaced and was quickly consented to? As if that wasn't already a loss of judgment too many, didn't you now entertain delusions of potentially limitless power over others? Without stopping to think how Jane obviously knew that, unlike a wife, if you're going to stay with a whore, *it has to keep getting better*?"

Covet looked horrified. "How do you know about that night in Vegas?"

"You fool!" Buckrack spat. "You still don't know that she *told* me? You still think that *she* submitted the document to Asterisk, not *me* using her email account? It hasn't occurred to you that I *controlled* her? That I still control her bank account, for example, that you've already put fifty thousand dollars into, and which still has lots of the money you paid her this last year? That I know everything you did with her because I forced her to tell me? That the video camera she turned up to the hotel wearing in her lapel that day was given to her by me, and that her calling you to arrange the date was also her doing my bidding, while I recorded the whole liaison remotely? That she was acting under my instructions to make it as raunchy as possible?"

Covet glowered at him speechlessly. Buckrack got up and took the whisky bottle in his gloved hand. He poured two more measures and sat down again.

"You will appreciate," he went on, "how hard it was for me to keep my poker face that morning in Homestead Park when you denied virtually all knowledge of her, when I knew you had been playing sex games with her just the afternoon before. I'm not aware of the precise point at which I decided that you were probably worse than her. It's true that I was not in the best state of mind when I went to Boston to find her in the middle of June, after I used the resources available to me to discover she was coming back to the States. I was grieving badly over my son's death, I was not sure exactly what I intended, but I pretty much stalked her in Boston while I weighed up the possibilities, and then, something which made everything immeasurably more interesting, in walked the man who turns out to be the Don Draper of Odium, not quite my inexperienced son, but someone who ought to have acquired more balance of mind and soundness of judgment, and who can definitely do a lot more harm to others because he hasn't. I knew all about you I could find within twenty-four hours. By the time the three of us had crossed the country together in our trans-American caravan I knew a whole lot more about you than I could ever find out from archived records and internet pages. I wasn't sitting in that seat beside yours on the flight to London by accident. You're so utterly naïve, Covet, such a soft touch. What did it take to hook you in as you sat there in the afterdaze of three and a half weeks of constant jizzum-squirting and strumpet-playing? A few hints about my history in the intelligence services, a business card for a fake consultancy referring you to an improvised website promising discreet solutions to corporate problems, one, just one follow-up call from me, a further single lunchtime meeting in London where I proposed that straightforward bugging of offices would probably end your Union troubles, and that all I needed to be able to do it for you was simple cover within your organisation? I flew back to the States and handed in my notice. I even took the three months' pay without being required to do a single further day's work: it ran out just last month. They were glad to let me go. I was nothing but grief-stricken dead weight by then, so the story went, and it was probably true. Eight weeks later I was a pseudonymous Professor in an English university fitted up with a research profile you and I jointly invented. And it got me real close to Jane Blake, with the added convenience that anything I might decide to do to her would not even be on my own soil or under my own name. There is no Cannon Buckrack in the USA. The real me is believed to be living in painful retirement back east. And when I step on that plane to Boston in the morning, I won't be using my return ticket, and Buckrack will cease to be, except for an English bank account into which the University of Odium will continue to pay salary for the next ten months, and which I will empty, as I will empty Jane Blake's. Not that I need the money. I intend to give that to my daughter-in-law. It'll be some compensation for her, but of the thinnest kind."

Buckrack's revelations, mingled with alcohol, had put Covet into a deep mental stupor. He felt like a barrier upon which wave after wave of guilt, then anger, then remorse, and finally fear kept crashing. He looked at Jane's stabbed body. "What are we going to do with her? Surely you can make her disappear too? I mean, you know how to do that, don't you?"

Buckrack smiled. "What I was going to do next depended on you. It would follow from your reaction when I told you all of this. I guess you need a few minutes to think about it. Have another drink while you do."

He stood up and refilled Covet's glass, recorked the bottle, and remained standing. Covet took a gulp. "I don't need time to think. I want you to get rid of the body. I'll help you if I have to. I just want her erased, along with the evidence. As I said, I will even give you more money, if that's what you want. I can handle things administratively after that, as long as she's not easily discoverable. No one knows she's here except you and me, right? Even if they find her, nothing more than circumstantial evidence will point to me. I know the law. And I didn't kill her, after all, whatever else I did. But I swear I won't mention you if I am ever asked."

"No one would believe you anyway," Buckrack said. "It would seem a tall story."

"That's true," said Covet. "So let's dump her somewhere."

Buckrack surveyed him one last time and said, "That's your solution? Are you sure?"

"Yes," said Covet. "She was trash anyway. No one will miss her."

Buckrack nodded.

With a movement which Covet did not have time to see, the two-thirds empty whisky bottle was transferred from one of Buckrack's hands to the other and brought crashing down on the top of his forehead with such force that it cracked open. Whisky spray stung into Covet's eyes, broken glass lashed his face and he slumped rightwards like a cow shot with a captive bolt pistol. He did not pass out entirely, but could only flail a little on the floor, quite impotent. He really did seem to see stars, as he remembered from childhood cartoons, and hear bells, or at least one prolonged drone that resounded unceasingly. He had a sense of Buckrack moving for his bag near the door. When he opened his eyes they seemed to be on fire, but he caught a glimpse of white cord, like TV aerial wire. He struggled to get up. Buckrack seemed a little way off, doing something with the wire, but Covet could not find his feet or even prop himself up on his arms. He then felt himself dragged bodily, Buckrack's gloved hands under his armpits, his oilskins rustling, and something tight being wound around his neck. The blood in his head seemed constricted, adding to the awful concussive pain, and his chest heaved for air. The old pain to the left of his solar plexus flared, hideously sharper than usual, as if something inside was about to burst open there. Buckrack was grunting loudly and straining. Covet felt himself seemingly hoisted upright by the force at his throat, suffocatingly, until he almost lost purchase on the surface beneath him, feeling it only with the balls of his slippered feet, his heels unable to reach it. The periodic wrenching at his throat stopped, and he felt suspended, his toes twitching as his feet tried to find something solid beneath them. A few moments seemed to pass. His pounding heart slowed a little and he was able to open his wet eyes. Buckrack was below him, looking up. Covet found himself perched in a standing position at full stretch on the coffee table, with what he guessed was the wire, acting as a noose, slung over one of the ceiling beams and secured he knew not how. He could see Jane's legs from the knees downwards sticking out stiffly to his left, but not the rest of her.

Between Covet's flickering eyelids, Buckrack appeared to be breathless and savage-faced with exertion. He bent down to the floor and took hold of one of the table legs, looking up as he did so. "I wanted you to be conscious at the end," he said. With that, he pulled the table leg hard towards him. Covet felt the slightest of jolts. Air popped in his cheeks as his throat contracted, then escaped as his lips flew open despite clenched teeth, and his head was flicked back. There was a brief rushing sound in his ears, like a recording being played in reverse, and he heard nothing else.

Buckrack got up from the floor and sat back in a chair to recover himself. He watched Covet spasm stiffly for a moment, then averted his eyes. Seeing that there was still some scotch in his glass, he swallowed it. Looking back, but only at Covet's feet, he saw that they were at last still.

He was sweating. He got up and went outside to find colder air. Some moments later he walked to the car, took Jane's suitcase out of the boot, and brought it in to the living room, laying it down in a corner. He unzipped it, took her passport, phone, keys, iPad and purse from his bag, and placed them in an inside compartment of the suitcase. Then he closed it again. He checked around the coffee table, taking the pinhead camera but leaving the other items. He picked up the empty glass he had been drinking from and put it in his bag. Satisfied, he stepped over to Jane and, bending down, gripped the handle of the knife and pulled. It came out surprisingly easily. He stood a while over the body, to let most of the blood from the blade drip on her rather than leave spots on the carpet. When it stopped he went to the back of Covet and, placing the handle against his dangling right hand, pressed the fingers and thumb in a fist around it. Then he let go and the knife fell to the floor.

He turned off all the lights and went outside again, leaving the door half ajar. A late fireworks party seemed to be in progress in the nearby village. He could hear the distant bangs and fizzes, but they were coming from the rear side of the cottage, so he could see only their peripheral illumination rather than the explosions themselves. In the open porch he pulled off his gloves and oilskins and put them in a refuse sack he took from the bag. He tied it and walked along the path beneath the trees. He reached the car, and put the bag and refuse sack in the boot.

Turning one last time to look at the house, he was just in time to see a single rocket shoot up into the sky above its roof, bursting in a glittering shock of white, purple and red, which was seen a few seconds before the deafening bang of its detonation reached him. Then there was the shrill metallic rustle as he watched its many sparks shower and fall and finally wink out, silver smoke spreading in their wake across the inky night sky. In the distance the spectating village crowd roared and clapped in approval. Their shouts and echoes too, eventually, died away. Just as the last of them did so, he heard a faraway tolling. The village church bell was chiming midnight.

**EPILOGUE**
**8 NOVEMBER**

## Chapter Seventeen (8 November)

It was a rare sunny November noontime, without cloud cover, and therefore cold. Standing on the corner by the O2 shop in Bigton High Street, Redman, holding a large envelope under his arm, scanned the pedestrians walking towards him from the direction of the University. Even if Asterisk came by car and parked, his final approach was most likely to be made on foot this way. At last he picked him out by his rather wombling gait, portly, padded further in a large brown winter overcoat. Asterisk was casting cautious glances from left to right in some trepidation, evidently, of being recognised. Redman toyed with the idea of doing the whole thing in public, right there in the High Street opposite a charity shop, partly to increase the Registrar's discomfiture, partly to minimise the time he had to spend in his company. But when Asterisk finally came up to him, and suggested they get out of the public eye pronto, he concurred pragmatically. They turned a corner and went into a cavernous coffee bar and found a seat in a corner behind an abutting wall.

"I don't see why we had to meet out here," Asterisk said. "A bit cloak and dagger, no?"

"Neutral territory," Redman offered by way of an explanation. "And after all, we know that some offices at the University tend to have listening devices in them. What hasn't been cloak and dagger about the last few weeks?"

Asterisk tilted his head in sour recognition of an awkward truth. "You said on the phone that it was important, urgent even. I hope so. The place is in meltdown. This is my first day back and I can barely spare the time."

"It's not exactly Lehman Brothers," Redman countered. "But

nonetheless I may be able to help you with our current fiasco."

"You?" said Asterisk. "How?"

Redman took some papers from the envelope and placed them on the table.

"These, I believe, are yours," he said. "Invoices addressed to you for three microdevices. These three microdevices, to be exact." He reached into his jacket pocket and showed Asterisk the small black receivers in a plastic wrapper in his open palm. "I have made copies of the invoices, but these are the originals. I'll keep the microphones unless you want to get legal about them." So saying, he returned them whence they came.

Asterisk had started a little, but now had put his thumbnail between his teeth while he slowly calculated what might be about to happen.

"How did you get these?" he asked, placing one index finger on the invoices.

Redman turned over the envelope so that its address side was face up. It read:

STRICTLY CONFIDENTIAL
Professor Robert McNamara
Warden
Coolwipe Hall
University of Odium
Odium
OD2 3PF

"Postmarked Odium, last Friday, first class," Redman added. "He picked it up when he went in on Saturday morning. But he found the prospect of talking to you too distasteful, so he passed the task to me."

"So McNamara knows?"

"Yes. He also agrees with us having the conversation we're going to have. I wouldn't be having it if he didn't. In fact, it was more his idea than mine, but I am persuaded."

"And Poon? She was the one who submitted the FOI about the bugs."

"No. She doesn't know we have the invoices."

"Why not?"

"She's an idiot."

"That's true, but she's an idiot who's on your side."

Redman sipped his latte. "I think the distinction between a union side and a management side is a bit behind the curve, in the present circumstances. The management side is virtually, and in one case literally, dead. You are the last man standing, as far as I can see."

Asterisk grimaced at the directness of the reference to Covet. "And now what? You want to use this to knock me over as well?"

"We could, of course. But what would that achieve? An argument could be made that we are now on the same side."

Asterisk tinkered with a spoon. "How so?"

"Well," Redman explained, "let's speculate on the outcome if we decide to make it public that we have the invoices. The first thing that would be established beyond any reasonable doubt is that you personally were responsible for Odiumgate. I know Covet was probably the one who ordered it, but his head has already rolled, as it were, and your Nuremberg defence is not likely to succeed. The lesser guilt of mere complicity would not save you. Even if it did, you would then have to explain why you suppressed the invoices in the face of a legally binding FOI request. That alone would make your position untenable. So I think the second inevitable consequence is that you'd certainly be out on your arse in a jiffy, and that last stroke in the clean sweep of existing management would leave the field entirely clear for Sir Norbert Conquest and the pecking hordes to ransack the carcass. The third thing that would come to pass is that Poon's Hero of the People status, which is looking a little shaky without the material proof, would be consolidated beyond measure, when in fact her lack of discretion and forethought is one of the things which has brought us to the current state of emergency we're in. It might occur to her members who will be made redundant by the raiding of the tomb that they would not have lost their jobs had she shut up, but that insight will probably come too late, and one thing is for sure, Poon won't be among their number. Getting rid of her would look like managerial vindictiveness. If Poon had these invoices for a moment, she'd do an instant Statue of Liberty pose with them right outside your office window. In short, if they are revealed, one more member of management goes down, but hundreds of staff jobs are lost, and the University's reputation is comprehensively destroyed. Why would I want that? I'm not being personally generous to you in offering to give them back to you. It's just that your head on a pike has very low value these days. Sorry to say that, but it's true."

"Alright," said Asterisk, "but how does giving them back to me solve anything?"

"It doesn't," Redman replied, "on its own. It gives you the choice, though. Let's say the invoices were, er, *lost*, and I'm simply returning them to their rightful owner. I don't intend to make it my business what you choose to do with them. You might let your dog accidentally chew them, for example."

"Why don't *you* just destroy them?"

"No," Redman said brusquely. "I mentioned that to McNamara, but he insists that his hands must be clean, and I agree with him."

"But if I don't give them up I'm in default of FOI."

"Which is no different from where you are right now, without your pretence to yourself that the papers mysteriously disappeared. We both know that you agreed with Buckrack that he would remove them."

Asterisk said, "You *know* about Buckrack?"

"I know," Redman said, "that it's his handwriting on the envelope. Quite why he should remove them, seemingly for your benefit, and then hand them to us, patently not to your advantage, remains a question I was hoping you might answer. Did you guys fall out over something?"

Asterisk was wide-eyed. "It's complicated. It's best to leave Buckrack out of all this."

Redman considered. "Okay," he said, "to be continued."

Asterisk pulled the papers a bit closer and looked at them cursorily. "What you are saying is that you are giving me these documents back and yet you still want me to do nothing with them? So why have you kept copies? If I don't divulge them you could simply produce your copies later to expose the fact that they were suppressed by me."

"I could do that *now* with the originals," said Redman. "The copies are just a form of insurance."

"You mean for future twisting of my arm, that's it, isn't it?"

"No," Redman said. "Just personal insurance for me and McNamara. You won't be dealing with me in future. After this meeting I'll be resigning my membership of the Union. Recent events tell me that it's not something I want to be involved with any longer. This is the last act I'll perform in an official Union capacity. But I want to make it clear. All I'm doing is giving you the papers back. I am not telling you exactly what to do with them. I just hope you'll act swiftly on a choice to do the right thing with them, which is nothing."

"Which is to do the *wrong* thing?"

"But for the right reasons this time. And to do it quickly. If Poon's FOI request can be responded to soon, like today or tomorrow, and you confidently declare no knowledge of any bugs or any record of their purchase, then it will settle much of the present disorder. Poon will be out on a limb. The staff will come back to work. Baum's death has been eclipsed by Covet's, and the manner of his could be presented so that he seemed the one bad management apple. You can blame anything negative on him: dead men tell no tales. You can get the University lawyers on Conquest's case and force him to back off, even go for a judicial review of the Department for Education's decision to appoint him Acting Vice Chancellor. If you start fighting now it may limit the damage, and we probably won't lose too many students."

Asterisk stroked his jaw. "And what assurance do I have that you're not just setting me up for a fall later? I do what I can to fix all this now, then when we've recovered ground in a few months, you spill to the press about my true role?"

Redman sighed. "I guess you have to trust me when I say we won't. We really don't care that much anymore, McNamara and me, and we won't be talking to Poon. So trust us if you can. If you can't, so be it. But there is an opportunity to stop the rot. I think you should take it. You can, on the other hand, play straight and release the documents, but that would simply end your career in ignominy right now. So what have you to lose?"

After a time Asterisk nodded slowly, and prepared to leave. But Redman put his hand on his elbow. "Not yet," he said. "There was something else."

Asterisk remained at rest.

"It's about Covet," Redman continued. "Perhaps just to satisfy my curiosity, if nothing else. There was the weekend TV news, of course, and this morning's papers. But they were very thin on details. Nothing much other than the postman finding him hanging in his cottage with Jane Blake stabbed to death on the floor. What more can you tell me?"

Asterisk was initially hesitant. "It's a bit hush hush, as you can imagine. The police called me yesterday. That's why I'm in today. We had a Management Board meeting this morning. I say that, though it was only me and Conquest, really. But, hell, we are going public with everything later this afternoon, so it hardly matters anymore, the details will be in the public domain soon. I suppose Buckrack told you about the PID?"

"No," Redman said. "He didn't."

"No?" said Asterisk. "For the life of me, I can't work that man out. He's very unpredictable. I'm banking on him keeping his mouth shut. If I can

I'm going to give him a very wide berth in future."

"The PID?" Redman prompted.

"The PID was from Jane Blake," Asterisk said. "She and Covet had been having some sordid affair for over a year. The police already had it down from the crime scene as a straightforward murder plus suicide, and the PID pretty much supplied all the motive they needed on his part. They were not as flummoxed as I was by the fact that she withdrew her allegations by email on the same night they both died, because apparently he had just paid a whopping sum out of his bank account into hers before she did that. So it seemed to have got to the blackmailing stage. Something must have turned bad after that, on the night itself. They were drinking. It looks like she attacked him with a bottle and he stabbed her, or, well, it's hard to imagine he stabbed her then she managed to hit him with a bottle, but I suppose it could have been simultaneous, or she reached for the bottle when he threatened – doh, what's the difference? It hardly matters. Then he hanged himself. There were pictures of them together at the scene which corroborate the PID, even a video of them having sex, apparently. The blackmail materials, I imagine. It'll be in all the papers tomorrow once we release the full text. I have a press conference in the morning."

Redman thanked him for the information. "Did you know she told McNamara she was having an affair with Poon?"

"That's in the PID," Asterisk said. "Though apparently it wasn't true. The girl couldn't bring herself to sleep with the stupid bint. It's all very complicated. But rest assured Poon doesn't come out of it well. McNamara does, though."

Asterisk was opening his briefcase to put the invoices inside. "In fact," he said, fishing a document out, "why not read it for yourself? You'll soon be able to anyway. Here it is."

He handed the Public Interest Disclosure document over the table and picked up the invoices. Redman glanced through the pages but was interrupted by Asterisk asking, "Buckrack didn't send you an invoice for a camera and recording equipment?"

"No," said Redman.

"You don't know anything about that?"

Redman shook his head.

"Oh," said Asterisk. "Good! One less thing to worry over."

He was about to leave, but turned around before doing so, and said, "You know, Covet was an awful man. I can't say I'm sorry he's gone, even spectacularly gone. A terrible bully. A total shit. It's not nice to say, but I can't imagine there's anyone who loved him. I'm convinced even his family didn't. He made me do lots of things I'm not proud of. You're aware of the kind of stuff I mean. I wanted you to know that it often wasn't the real me you were often faced with. In the universities I was taught in and worked in before these things couldn't have happened. With him off the scene, I think I have a chance to do things right, to help run the place with a renewed sense of decency."

Redman looked at him with the most finely calibrated expression Asterisk had ever seen: the face registered twenty per cent approval, twenty-nine per cent scepticism, and fifty-one per cent dubiety.

"You can try," was the reply.

# RETURN TO ODIUM

**Chapter One**

When the moment came, it sounded more like the crack of a rifle shot than an explosion.

On the high crest of the hill that was Red Road, far from the milling crowd of hundreds strung out across the waste ground, down on the flatland on the other side of the high rises, Robert McNamara had been standing alone for fifteen minutes, in a silence he had never known here, which only the detonation finally broke. The roads all around had been closed to traffic on account of the planned demolition and he had had to make his way here on foot. He followed the countdown from a position on the pavement opposite the little store he had never gone into as a child because it was the shop next to the Protestant primary school on Red Road whose name he could not now remember. There was always a newsagent's near a Glasgow school, placed to tempt sweet-toothed kids each morning as they clutched their yellow threepenny bit or silver sixpence, not knowing until the last few moments, when inside the very emporium itself, if the large glass jar they would point to would contain pear drops or kop kops or liquorice string or, on cold days like this, dummy cigarettes which one could actually seem to be smoking. Most of his early walks to school, he recalled, were prefaced by this eager anticipation of confections, which were poured and weighed and folded in a little white bag which was then stuffed into pocket or satchel, provisions against the trial-by-boredom of the coming day, not to be savoured until morning playtime, a long fifteen minutes of sugar-fuelled relief and delight.

There had been a similar shop near St Martha's, his own Catholic primary school, which he could see now if he turned all the way around and looked north, its squat brown bulk extending across the ridge of a hill yet higher than Red Road, about half a mile distant as the crow flies. What was the name of that sweetshop? Gaffney's? McGaffney's?

He had never known the name of the store he now waited near. Catholic kids and Protestant kids did not mix in the days of his childhood. There was usually disorder if they did. The school on Red Road was eventually closed and became a community centre just after he had left Glasgow aged twenty-one, and the remaining McNamaras had been decanted from the high-rises to a house on the edge of the city after an asbestos scare and a fire which had killed a boy in the tower across from their own. They had transformed the block McNamara had lived in, first into a YMCA, then into accommodation for nurses at Stobhill Hospital, and then – irony of unbelievable ironies – into a hall of residence for students at Strathclyde University. The store had successively reinvented itself in parallel. On brief trips back home, McNamara had witnessed it as an Indian takeaway, then as a hairdresser's, and the last time he remembered it as an off-licence. Now it was a pizza shack.

He reflected that there must be others in the vast throng in the offing down below who had also once lived here and who had, like him, come to see the architectural execution. Did they think of themselves as victims of the condemned, or were they grieving family? He had no real wish to find out. The idea of intermingling with them, of trading brief details or anecdotes of a time past, in fragmentary exchanges which would have resurrected in him that also long-gone, more vulgar version of the Glasgow voice he still possessed, had never seriously arisen in his mind. He had no wish to pretend to share with people whom he knew were essentially strangers. They had no doubt mainly chosen their spot because it offered the best view of the occurrence as a spectacle. From where they stood, they could see the entire row of four nearly one-hundred-metre-high columns that would fall simultaneously that afternoon, and it would be thrilling, sensational, the nearest thing to the Blitz that any of them, most likely, would ever experience outside a movie.

These buildings had, for a while, been legendary, the highest residential blocks in the whole of Europe at the time of their construction. McNamara, however, was watching just one tower, and he had to be on this side of it, because it was on this north-facing façade, nearly two hundred feet in the air, that he had lived all those years. Imagining as all educated people do that he was somehow singular, thinking that for him the buildings' end would have a meaning whereas for the others it would be merely a happening, he felt he had come to confront the moment rather than consume it, in a kind of reckoning. He had even overstayed nearly a whole week since his father's cremation in order to do so.

He had suffered one shock already. When they had moved into the apartment almost exactly half a century before, in 1967, in the January, after his early years in a Springburn tenement with an outside toilet and a single metal bath which passed daily among six tenancies, he had been just tall enough, when he ventured onto the verandah, to look through the gap between the balcony's protective panel barrier and the metal banister which topped it. The view thrilled him. Any view would have thrilled him, because their previous abode had had no view at all, never mind any spot inside from which fresh air could be breathed or laundry windily dried. The verandah looked east along a straight treeless avenue. At hundred-yard intervals, on the right of this unadorned grey ribbon, stood the other three behemoths of Petershill Drive, and he took some pride in the fact that they were not quite as tall as his. Nonetheless, everything was still massive, gigantic, thrusting skyward greyly in defiance of all nature, and he loved it.

It was a view but no vista, however. At the end of the avenue, where it rose in a slight incline, extended a truly monstrous slab of three similar tower blocks facing him directly, all combined in one structure, like colossal dominoes glued together on their longer sides. It had the effect of a huge horizontal door, permanently closed and barring all sight of everything beyond it. It was so enormous and forbidding that it occluded the sun that rose behind it until well into every morning.

His grandparents, his father's mother and father, had lived in the centre section of this slab. Once McNamara had asked his father – a betting man, horses, who watched weekend racing on TV – what a furlong was. His father had taken him out onto the verandah, upended a plastic basin and perched him on it so that he was a few inches taller and could see further down. He gestured along the line of tarmac avenue by wiggling a finger to and fro. "That's a furlong," he had said. "From here tae granny and grandad's is a furlong." And then his father had said something else of the kind he often said in these brief moments together, smiling as he did. "They lived here before us, but no' *furlong*."

There was no furlong now. The momentous slab was already gone. Six months before, in phase one of the planned destruction of the entire housing complex, the planners had brought it and an identical structure not far from it crashing down into two small continents of rubble which spilled at ground level across the grassy areas and playgrounds and the furlong McNamara had frequented as a boy. He had watched the razing of his grandparents' erstwhile home from every angle YouTube had to offer, with a detached curiosity which had not prepared him for the actuality of standing on the spot and coming to terms with its real

165

absence. A week earlier, on the morning of his father's funeral, he had found himself staring east, from a distance at the end of Avenspark Street, along the line of what had once been the furlong, and seeing nothing. It was like looking at an old friend whose head had suddenly been cut off. The February sun was weak, but it was the first time he had seen that sun in this place at that hour of day in his entire life, and it was blinding.

The countdown ticked away. McNamara took out his phone and held it away from his body, his own old tower block captured in its vertical video frame. He would watch the decisive moment on screen, and felt oddly protected from the likely impact by the veil the phone seemed to provide. He counted up again from the bottom storey of the block, from one to seventeen, and kept his eyes grimly fixed on the four windows on the left of the seventeenth floor.

The detonation was precisely on time and, at this distance, he saw its effects a second before he heard its report. It took place in all four towers simultaneously. On the screen he saw sharp, violent horizontal exhalations of dust and smoke spume out at various levels on the lower half of the building before the short clap of the explosion reached him, and to the left of the phone he could see the other three blocks move and shift in a blur and begin to dislodge from their moorings. He could not but be distracted by them for a second, looking to the left of the phone to see them totter and begin to assume strange angles. He snapped his eyes back to the device, making an effort to hold his arm and hand still, and saw that his own block had started to move too, so that he could no longer locate floor seventeen. He watched the great skyscraper destabilise and begin to sag. It seemed to wilt and give up the ghost and now there was a slow upswirl of dust and debris climbing the screen, accompanied by an onrush of sound reaching his ears, like a slowly gathering wave before it crashes, and suddenly there was a patch of over-exposed light from the sky at the top of the screen as the roof of the building started to lower with its fall. He was aware, to the left of the phone, of the emergence of great patches of light as the other three pillars dropped cleanly away, like men before a firing squad, except for the noise they all made, which grew from a sibilant sigh to a voluminous rumble which extended and extended much longer in time than he had imagined it would, as if it were all happening in slow motion, or as if it were taking place on a planet where the hold of gravity was weaker, eventually becoming a deafening roar for a few seconds before the beginning of a truly terrifying cacophony of dissolution and collapse. But his ears told him one thing while his eyes, fixed to the screen, told him another. The building on the phone screen was still falling and crumpling, but it had not gone completely like the others, it seemed to be offering some stubborn resistance, like a living thing, like Orwell's elephant, crying out in pain, down on one knee, but refusing to die with just one shot. Then it disappeared from view on the screen as brown and grey dust billowed skyward from all directions, engulfing everything that could still be seen of it.

McNamara lowered the phone and stood silent and rigid. The surge of noise withdrew as quickly as it had come and he thought he heard cheers and whistles and claps reach him from the now hidden crowd below. But he could not be sure because his ears were ringing. The dust cloud rampaged up the hill towards him, fast and menacing, so that he feared it might swallow him up, and he even held his breath in anticipation. But it lost all its thrusting energy thirty feet inside the safety barriers and slowly, slowly, over many minutes, it gradually thinned out and receded.

As it cleared, a still vast shadow became discernible behind it, tilted at a weird, calamitous angle, about half its original size, seeming almost to be swaying slightly in the still, cold afternoon. His own tower block had not completely gone. For the first time in decades he felt again a tingling sense of pride in its superiority to the others. As the smoke thinned and dispersed and his thoughts cleared a little with it, he whimsically felt that his scenario was a little like Charlton Heston's at the end of *Planet of the Apes*, but instead of raging despair he felt a quiet triumph that not quite everything had yet gone down into oblivion and disintegration.

At last he could see the entire remains. His building seemed to teeter on some brink, daredevil, defiant, angled grotesquely leftwards, at maybe a twenty-degree tilt. He started to count the storeys, this time perforce starting from the top. On the right side of the building he counted sixteen surviving levels. On the left he counted thirteen – and a half.

He did not know how long he stayed rooted there. After a while he set off in something like a fugue state. Four streets intersected at the top of Red Road. The way downhill was obstructed by security barriers, but he tried the other three like a lost dog at any crossroads, making his way along them spontaneously, then stopping and retracing his steps and ending back where he started, staring hypnotically for moments on end at the teetering tower block. At last, as if inspired, he simply decided that he had nowhere specific to go and opted to wander.

There was a large recreational area to the north behind fences and chained gates. It had once been a vast expanse of three or four asphalt football pitches – they had called it simply "the red ash" – but many years ago it had been locked off with bright eye-catching notices on display speaking of danger and land subsidence. These were now grimy and faded. Apparently there was an old forgotten mine underneath the entire surface that young boys had happily played football on for years. But McNamara remembered from his youth that fences around here were simply barriers through which one sought entry via a hole, and it did not take long for him to find one. As the wintry day began to darken, a half moon already low in the clear cold sky, he found himself strolling aimlessly across the terrain of his childhood sporting adventures for the first time in fifty years. He had forgotten all about this place.

Eventually he arrived at what he remembered was a disused railway cutting. The line had been axed by Dr Beeching around the time McNamara had been born. It had been used in the First World War to bring wounded servicemen to Stobhill Hospital, but he remembered it as a curious untended scar on the landscape, with two foul-smelling and rubbish-strewn tunnels at either end. He went right and headed for the smaller tunnel, and would have gone through it had he not been distracted by the lights of All Saints Church, off to the left, which he had attended as an adolescent. He climbed the incline towards it and heard from afar the sounds of an organ and singing. It was a Sunday and this must be the beginning of five o'clock mass. The hymn sounded puny and ridiculous from a distance, so he skirted the church grounds and found himself on Broomfield Road and, giving in to an absurd whim, a few hundred yards later, he turned into the Broomfield Tavern, a grim council-estate pub which had been his father's local, but into which he had never ventured.

He emerged after two hours of silent drinking and observing younger men playing pool and watching football on the largest television he had ever seen and speaking to one another in coarse loud voices that sounded always just below the level of shouting. He carried in a bag by his side a half bottle of blended whisky, the best the place had had to offer by way of a carry-out. Though the worse for wear, he knew where he was going, and plodded off up the gentle slope of Rye Road, then right into Scotsburn Road with its refurbished but still mean tenements, then left into the gentle downward decline of Ryehill Road. This route took him past All Saints School, a secondary establishment for the baby-boomer generation that had succeeded his in the early sixties, and which he had therefore never attended, but which he had watched being built, brick-by-brick, or rather breeze-block-by-breeze-block, on his daily bus journeys to St Roch's in Townhead. All Saints too had vanished, at least in the incarnation in which he had known it, its population having shrunk from the seventeen hundred it housed in the mid-1970s to a mere six hundred today, the imposing main building that had once been there having disappeared and been substituted by a titchy little thing which sat meekly in the still expansive original grounds.

On he went, feeling like Gulliver in Lilliput. The two-room library at Rockfield Road, the terminus for the number 55 bus, simply wasn't there at all anymore, and nothing else was in its place. There were just green tufts and brown scrub. Right at the dual carriageway of Wallacewell Road, left at the similarly wide and steep Northgate Road, past the small Church of Scotland and jerry-built Sunday school at the bottom of his father's garden, and then huffingly, puffingly, left into Northgate Quadrant and, after a drunken fumbling for keys, he entered the house where his father had literally seen out his life. McNamara strode with urgency to the toilet to placate his disorderly prostate, and finally slumped into the bolstered armchair in which dad had had his only and final heart attack, not being found until four days later, the neighbours alerted by the smell, the TV still on, with many flies on his body already (as the woman from upstairs had felt the need to report).

McNamara sat in the darkness and drank the whisky dry, straight from the bottle. At nine o'clock he suddenly realised that he was too drunk to drive and that his intention to leave in the early evening had been overtaken by bibulous events. He stumbled into the nearest bedroom, his father's, crashed and seemed to wake one moment later, though it was now two in the morning and he had a headache. The bedroom still reeked of his father's cigarettes, but this was preferable to the still ineradicable stench of rotting flesh to be encountered in the living room. He went into the small bathroom, took one look at the still unwashed bath and decided, no, maybe not, in fact, definitely not. He turned off the electricity and gas at the mains, checked all the taps, was thankful that he had already packed and put his suitcase in the car, left the house, locked the door, stepped into his Ford Mondeo and turned the key in the ignition.

He was not yet fully sober and so, ten minutes later, it did not feel all that unusual to be standing in his old bedroom, panning the flashlight of his phone around the remaining three outlandishly angled walls, with hundreds of thousands of tons of concrete tottering directly above him, and the dark shard of an immense steel girder protruding through the roof above where his bed used to be. There were indeed always gaps in security fences around here, and he had readily found one close to the block. He gave little thought to night watchmen. If there even were any, he doubted that they would come within three hundred yards of the now-leaning tower of Petershill, and what would they do if they encountered him anyway? Prosecute for trespass? A fine? At his age, what did he care? He wouldn't even bother to talk his way out of it or feign the mad Professor. But, sure enough, there were no watchmen. There was nothing to protect anymore.

He was surprised he could get right into the skeleton of the base of the building. He had come only for a closer look, imagining that there would be a miniature Munro of wreckage barring any possible entry. But in fact the colossus had come apart in the huge iron-rod-reinforced segments of which it had been pieced together, like a scaled-up fallen Jenga puzzle or a disarranged Stonehenge. Some of these hunks had split into smaller pieces, but these were still so enormous that, now at rest against one another, they formed a crazy maze of awnings and jagged arches and lurching tunnels that even a fat man like McNamara could wend a way through by stooping and bending and being careful of foot.

The kitchen at the end was entirely gone. His parents' bedroom, to the right of it, was ground down almost entirely to the roof. Only a small angle of what had been his sister's bedroom remained, and when he shone the light inside all he saw was grey-white blank and broken stones. But about three quarters of his own bedroom, towards the building's central staircase, remained. He had had to stoop sharply to gain entry, but once inside he saw that the walls and roof sloped upward and away, and he was even able to stand upright in part of what remained.

The actual spot, he reflected, meant nothing, was all wrong. He had not lived at ground level. Now nearly forty years since he had left it, he could expect nothing here that spoke to him or of him. There was no floor at all, never mind a carpet. He assumed that the boulder-like forms which crowded the space were what remained of it. At the far end from where he had gained entry he saw a mangled white door that he knew instantly was not the same one he had handled all through his second decade of life. That left the walls and the roof. These were damaged and holed, but not so much that he could not imagine The Incredible Hulk pushing the building upright for a few moments, righting the angles, so that he could re-envision the room where he had grown as a youth in a succession of oft-repeated acts. Here he had done his homework, discovered masturbation, drawn a moustache on his upper lip with a black felt-tip pen and stood with a tennis racquet in front of a mirror while the radio played, read books, fumbled with the bra-hooks of two or three girls he sneaked home while everyone was out, often sat with one or two schoolmates playing records, put up posters, smoked secret cigarettes and even more secret dope, gazed out at the distant Campsie hills beyond the city. Here had been the bed, there the small desk and lamp, over there the paraffin heater that reeked, and later the Calor gas heater that caused so much condensation, the chipboard wardrobe, the chest of drawers with his Sanyo cassette player on top. Here he had repeatedly listened through the wall while his sister, aged fifteen, was willingly fucked senseless by her older boyfriend. Here, latterly, he had insisted on his privacy and imperiously excluded all three other members of the family. Here one morning he had opened the university letter, his back to the closed door and his heart pounding, which had proved to be his exit visa from this room, and eventually Glasgow, and Scotland altogether.

He sat on a piece of smashed concrete and bowed his head, his fingers to his temples, his back to the room. Great drunken tears welled up and splashed on his shoes. His mother, ten years dead. His father, ten days dead. His sister, who despised him and he her, not met with this century, except at two funerals. His ex-wife, on husband number three. His two sons, grown up, flown the nest. Rachel, abandoned by him just

171

weeks before. And now, this ruined fortress from which, when he raised his tired eyes, there was no longer that distant, hopeful view, but merely a mound of lopsided, broken stones, crowding together in the half moonlight, like relics in a vandalised cemetery.

He drove. West along Petershill Road, left onto the long drag of Springburn Road, where the National Carriers main depot had been, where his mother had worked as a secretary, now a Tesco. On down to Townhead, St Roch's miraculously still there at the end of Royston Road, and not far past it the Royal Infirmary, where both his mother and his grandfather had died, where he had last seen both of them alive. He was aiming for the M8 east but instead he chose to take it westbound to Charing Cross, where he came off and drove down past the Hilton Hotel, built on the very spot where his father had been born, then back and left along Woodlands Road, slowly up and over and down the hill of University Avenue, the reading room on the right where he'd spent so many hours, the mock-gothic spires on the left where he'd taken so many classes, the entire place spookily empty under moonlight, right at Byres Road, past Hillhead Library, where he'd worked one summer, delightedly finding himself the only lad alongside nineteen slightly older girls, up Queen Margaret Drive, into Ruchill, where his father had lived as a boy, now Bilsland Drive, what had his father's street been called? He struggled for the name but without it he would not find it on the GPS. He kept going on what proved to be a circular detour, left into Hawthorn Street, past the Cowlairs depot where his father had been a British Rail wages clerk, right again onto Springburn Road, down once more into Townhead, St Roch's, the Royal, crassly hiding the cathedral as always, the M8 east, signs for The South.

Motherwell flashed up, and he suddenly remembered Bruno. Bruno. Another Catholic, they'd been indivisible friends at Glasgow University for three years, Bruno studied languages, his father was also Irish, but Bruno had been born in England, Warrington, wasn't it? His family moved to Wishaw when Bruno was in his teens. Damn it, he even remembered Bruno's school, Our Lady's High, Motherwell, and yet he couldn't remember his own father's Ruchill street name. Bruno was the last person in life that McNamara had truly looked up to, a walking multilingual thesaurus even at twenty, a face like a movie star, everyone thought he was Hispanic. Unlike him, Bruno had not meekly assumed a

172

Scottish accent as a way of fitting in but maintained his suave, defiant Englishness, though he had a way with all kinds of voices and mimicry and could do all shades of Scottish and English and Irish and Welsh, leaving everyone around him with their sides splitting. They'd lost touch in McNamara's last year, when Bruno went off to Paris on his year abroad, because when he came back McNamara was gone, off to Oxford to do his D.Phil., and the next thing McNamara knew, it was ten years later, and Bruno was on TV and radio all the time, with a changed name, a bloody comedian, not a stand-up, an impersonator, doing The Establishment in different voices, satirising Neil Kinnock and Michael Heseltine and David Coleman and Paul McCartney and everyone else you could think of who was famous and male, and not just British but foreign too, given his languages, part of a popular sketch show, then he got a show of his own, and he was even more hilarious, gut-wrenchingly, lung-challengingly mirthful and politically biting all through the Thatcher decade. McNamara used to watch his Saturday night show with his young sons and they'd go into school and tell their friends their dad knew Bruno, though that wasn't his name anymore. Then, yet another decade on, no, no, more than that, fifteen years maybe, McNamara was coming off the set of *Channel 4 News*, he'd been doing a live interview about some political event, something they thought a Politics Professor was right for, when the studio manager thrust a mobile phone into his hand, said there was a call for him, and it was Bruno. Bruno had been watching and he knew the studio manager personally and he called her right there and then and asked her to catch McNamara as he came off set and McNamara was overwhelmed and they spoke briefly and Bruno wanted to meet again but he was leaving the country next day to do something in America, though he'd be back in a month or two, and three days later McNamara opened *The Guardian* and found out Bruno was dead in a Las Vegas hotel room with too much crack cocaine in his veins. He wasn't even brought back home. They scattered his ashes somewhere in Nevada.

Lesmahagow, Hangingshaw. Lockerbie, where the remnants of the Pan-Am plane came down. England now beckoning, silhouettes of hilltops becoming lower in the moonlight. Ecclefechan, birthplace of Carlyle, the sign said, but which McNamara remembered as the spot where he'd once passed a car ablaze, and a woman screaming by the side of it, bawling someone's name into the roaring white and yellow flames, and he'd stopped, and got out, and made to go back to the scene, but just then a fire engine and an ambulance screeched up, hoses were turned on, he saw that he was not needed, and he turned around, and drove off again, never knowing quite what had happened here.

He stopped at Gretna Green. There was a twenty-four-hour truck stop and he thought to venture in for some coffee, but he closed his eyes for a few moments and, an hour later, woke gasping and spluttering from a dream of his father burning in a Ford Mustang in the Nevada desert, Bruno standing beside the car, doing an impersonation of Ronald Reagan, with an atomic bomb going off in the distance behind him, and the ludicrous steeples and minarets of Las Vegas falling like ninepins through the heat haze. It took him some moments to realise where he was, so contrasting was it. It was freezing cold. It was dark. He was still just in Scotland. His head ached dully, but it was not so bad as before. He found himself suddenly sobbing and beating both his fists on the steering wheel of the Mondeo. He took out his phone and looked at the time. He lurched out of the car, pulling his overweight body with difficulty, unzipped his trousers, pissed in a ditch, and got back in.

He drove into England. Carlisle, Penrith. The M6 would be quicker, but that way Warrington lay. Bruno's family, McNamara realised, must just have got out of Warrington, turned left, driven straight up the M6 and A74, and turned right into Wishaw after two hundred miles, simple as that. But it did not seem a night for direct routes, whatever the time. He took the A66 east and kept his foot down, careless of speed cameras or ice. What did it matter? What did anything matter now?

Brough, Bowes, Scotch Corner, the A1 south. Racing towns that reminded him of his father: Catterick, Wetherby. Why did everything mean something, why did every place name bear associations now? McNamara had once hired a Toyota Hilux in Bangkok and driven for hours and hours with his elder son, north, through places no tourist went, tiny little towns and villages that looked not much different from what they probably looked like a century ago, the signs all in Thai, hard to tell a hotel from a big house, no English spoken anywhere, no pictures on wayside food menus, everyone they met staring at them with incomprehension, and he knew if he had been alone it would have been alienating, but with his son with him it felt like a hilarious adventure to both of them, all the way up to the Burmese border, and then along it, down the border with Laos, a crazy three-week road trip, a different, stranger place every night, the stranger the better. Yet now, when he was on his own, nothing was strange, everywhere was impregnated with significance or remembrance or familiarity of one kind or another, and he wished it would stop, he wished he knew little and had experienced less. It was as if he had exhausted the world and it had nothing left to give except repetition and dread recycled in bad and worsening dreams.

Pontefract, Wentbridge, Doncaster.

The moon was no longer visible.

Tickhill, Blyth, Ranby.

Tuxford, Newark, Claypole.

The sun was up when he reached the Bruntham turn-off, and saw the first sign for Odium.


**Chapter Two**

Two and a half hours later, James Redman found himself in a slightly awkward colloquy with Vice Chancellor Archibald Spooner. Redman had been in the commodious office of Odium's Vice Chancellor on the ground floor of the Trump Building only twice before, but the difference in the appearance of the room now could not be ignored. Gone was the sleek modern business-signifying furniture in black and grey that had marked the style of the late Sir Evan Covet. In its place were heavy burgundy drapes with rich golden tie-backs, baroque red leather chesterfield sofas and a rich, deep-pile scarlet carpet. Red seemed to alternate with green, despite the old maxim forbidding their admixture. There were numerous lime-shaded Emeralite desk lamps, and taller standard lamps with shades with the marbled hue of watermelon skins and further gilted hanging cords, all very rococo. Two Italianate statues of nude males, slightly smaller than life-size, stood on plinths in bright window recesses, their likewise slightly smaller-than-life-size penises facing all visitors over each shoulder of the Vice Chancellor, whose desk was so positioned that he always had his back to them.

The current incumbent of the office presented himself in similarly flamboyant and slightly antiquated style. He appeared to be in florid health and was not overweight. He wore a paisley cravat and an open-necked shirt, over it a navy blazer with bright gold buttons from whose breast pocket peaked a deep red handkerchief, sporting grey slacks pressed to a fine crease, with white socks and shiny black tassled loafers below. On his head was a resplendent mane of smooth hair, browny-blond, luxuriant for a man in his sixties, long but expensively cut, touching the right shoulder of his jacket, towards which it was swept over, so that his left ear was always visible. He was marked with a tan deeper than any which could reasonably have been sustained by the British climate. Below his mouth of full pinkish lips was a dark brown mole, on the right of his close-shaven chin, although the rest of the face was smooth, almost glistening, a little soft. He wore a bracelet on his left wrist and on both hands several rings, but none of them indicating marriage. His fingernails were roundedly manicured and very clean. As a polished assemblage he too was difficult to overlook.

They had proceeded past introductory small talk. The third person expected in their meeting was a few minutes late and, apparently to do no more than pass the time, Spooner had begun, in an affable drawl, to seem to try to tease out from Redman some details of the scandal surrounding his own predecessor's demise.

"But you were in the thick of it, no?" he nudged gently, in a deeper voice than his soft features suggested was likely. "You were one of the people whose offices the Union claimed he bugged."

"I was," Redman replied laconically. "But no bugs were ever found."

"You think Dr Poon made it all up? Surely not? She said Professor McNamara came into her office and found the very bug that had been planted there, and showed her the two others. She took a photograph of all three, she claimed."

"I wasn't there," said Redman, shifting a little in his seat. "Is this what you want to talk to both of us about?"

"Oh no, we have much bigger fish to fry!" Spooner reassured him enthusiastically. Then, more pointedly and worldly-wise, tapping his nose, he added, "I got the strong message that there are stones it is better to leave unturned, don't you agree? Nonetheless, this was a lot of rum stuff to take place in a British university, no? Sort of things, if they happened in a novel, you'd shake your head at in incredulity."

Redman smiled gently at what seemed a subtle reference to his own credentials as a Lecturer in English Literature. "Last term required a lot of suspension of disbelief, it's true."

Spooner sat back, beamed, and looked about to continue when, without a knock, the heavy door was opened and McNamara stood in the entrance, a slightly flustered young secretary a step behind him. Spooner at once arose and beckoned McNamara towards him while simultaneously waving the secretary away. "It's alright, Eloise, no need for formalities, we've been expecting Professor McNamara."

Spooner glided across the carpet and extended his hand as the door closed softly. McNamara took it briefly and said, "Excuse my slight lateness. I was travelling through the night."

"Not at all," said Spooner. "I'm glad you could make it."

Redman looked at McNamara with a silent internal shock. The older man seemed the opposite of the colourful surroundings. His thinning hair was greyer, except on his face, from which all traces of his beard and moustache had been removed. His face looked curiously younger, but also gaunter and weaker. Without its previously permanent hirsute surround his mouth appeared smaller, the lips thinner. He was dressed completely in black – suit, tie, belt, shoes, socks – except for a plain white shirt which stuck out at the belly. His eyes were tired and rheumy. He was a little stooped and his shoulders sagged. His movements towards the proffered chair were slow and deliberate. He seemed to take no interest in the novelties of the redecorated room.

Re-assuming his seat, which seemed more like a throne manqué, with a hint of Charles Rennie Mackintosh in its high back, Spooner said breezily, "Robert McNamara, a name to conjure with, eh?"

McNamara looked back through heavy eyelids. "I was born before the Kennedy administration. A mere coincidence."

"But I wasn't aware that you were Scottish, like me!"

McNamara again made a lugubrious reply. "It would appear that you have to be Scottish to be the Vice Chancellor of Odium, yes, but in fact that rules me out, as I am actually Irish. I grew up in Scotland, however, hence the accent."

Spooner smiled smoothly and said, "Glasgow?"

McNamara nodded slowly.

"Which part?" asked Spooner. "I'm from Giffnock myself."

There was a pause in which McNamara seemed to study the new Vice Chancellor for the first time. At last he said, "Balornock."

Spooner looked puzzled. "Balornock? I'm not sure I know –"

"If you grew up in Giffnock," McNamara interjected bluntly, "you wouldn't."

177

After the briefest of pauses, with the air of a man who knows how to restitch an unexpected hole in any conversation adroitly, Spooner said, "We must look at a map and you must show me sometime."

McNamara nodded expressionlessly again, his eyes closing and opening as his head was lowered and raised.

"Now," began Spooner, and then was distracted by a notification sounding from the smartphone on his desk. He looked at it briefly. "Excuse me, gentlemen, I can't really ever turn this thing off in case something urgent arises, and so it may beep and blip occasionally while we are talking, but the good news is that all the sounds are customised for certain types of message, and so I will only need to react to it if what we hear is a train whistle or, in the worst possible scenario, a foghorn. The twenty-first century, eh? Remember when things were simpler?" He nonetheless flipped open the cover of the phone so that he could see its screen.

"Okay," he resumed. "We have about twenty minutes for me to try to explain some new and exciting directions we are taking here at Odium and how I hope you two gentlemen may be able to play a significant part in them. Will you bear with me while I expatiate a little, leaving some time for your questions after I sketch out a few ideas?"

Redman looked uneasily sideways at McNamara, whose demeanour gave no cause for reassurance, as he simply continued to stare straight ahead at Spooner.

"Sure," Redman said. "Feel free."

Spooner smiled graciously, clasped his beringed fingers together in front of his face, tilted his head to one side so that it was no longer hidden behind his praying hands, and began.

"I am an historian by training, as you may know," he started. "But I do not intend to dig too deeply into the, er, *history* of what took place here last term, of which you know much more than me. I am assured, however, that you both played a major part in saving this institution from outright disaster, a disaster that would, had the present government gotten its way, have affected the whole HE sector very badly. Of that Dr Asterisk has convinced me in the most fulsome terms. In fact, he paints you both as the heroes of the piece.

"Now, I have been made aware also of your, er, *history* in the University, the trades union activities, your joint disaffection from all that, and for good reason, but also the unique knowledge you have of how a twenty-first century university like this one works, and not least your familiarity with the particular people here, by which I mean not just the academic staff but also the senior management team, as well as the administrative organisation, and so on. Not to put too fine a point on it, you know the ins-and-outs of things I have only begun to grasp in the mere month or so I have been here. But please note that I see myself as coming from the same neck of the woods as you. By that, I mean, my entire professional life in academia has been in the Arts, Humanities and Social Sciences, like you. Not only that but, politically, I see myself as a liberal. I am not sure if you would describe yourselves using that word, but I am certainly no right-wing conservative of the Sir Evan Covet kind.

"Now, we sit in an institution that is eighty-one per cent science if we go by research funding income, a little less than that if we go by student numbers. It has, in the past, under Covet, pretty much followed the money, in my view to the detriment of disciplines like ours, which have been relegated in the last twenty-five years to having little more than the status of icing on the cake, and a very thin icing at that, icing which has been forced even to pay for itself, against all enlightened common sense. We all know that Theology and Philosophy and the Classics cannot reasonably be expected to operate at break-even, never mind a profit. Indeed, from what I have gathered, many of the people down the hill in the sciences would gladly get rid of the icing altogether, were it not for the fact that they receive constant reminders, or maybe kicks under the table, to the effect that a cake is not really perceivable as a cake if it does not have icing to decorate it. These are the people who have largely been allowed to run this institution heretofore.

"But they shall be allowed to run it no longer. They all scrambled like cowards – the senior managers among their number, I mean – to escape the blast zone of the Evan Covet blow-up. Needless to say, since his suicide, though I shall name no names, many of them have crept back inside the circle, seeking reinstatement. But I have ignored all of them. They showed no loyalty to him or, worse, to the institution. They proved that, when the breach was agape, they were not prepared to leap into it. Whoever was going to close up the wall, it was not going to be them. They were fairweather friends to the University of Odium. Their loyalty was proven to be merely to themselves and nothing larger. Yet even your enemies do not say that of you. Even Dr Asterisk, who left me in no doubt at all how much you opposed Covet, made it clear to me that, when the chips were down and the government was making its opportunistic move to compromise the entire sector, you acted to save the day when you could easily have let the havoc be wreaked."

Spooner was interrupted by two short pips from his smartphone. Seeming slightly annoyed, he glanced at it, then pushed it slightly further away from him.

McNamara asked, "How much did he tell you?"

Spooner shook his head and gestured dismissively with his hand. "We agreed to keep it vague. It seemed best."

Redman said, "But none of this is about the future. You are talking about the past."

"Yes," said Spooner, "thank you for reminding me. It was intended as context merely. I will come to the main point. I intend to put an entirely new managerial team in place. I intend, over the next three years, to create a virtuous economy in the Arts, Humanities and Social Sciences which will raise the proportion of their activities in the University to forty per cent of the total instead of their current twenty per cent. And I would like your help."

"A virtuous economy?" said Redman sceptically. "That sounds like a euphemism."

"From twenty to forty per cent in three years?" whistled McNamara. "The only way you could possibly do that is to downsize the sciences. But you cannot divert science funding to other purposes. No one is going to support that, not even us."

"Oh no, please, gentlemen, let me be clear. I am not playing with statistics. There will be no diminution in the sciences. It is simply that I intend to focus on a programme that concentrates all new effort on doubling the activity – in student numbers, research grant income, staffing levels, and investment in other resources – outside the sciences, at least on this campus. I cannot promise it for the campuses in China or India."

Redman sighed. "A new focus, a new emphasis, new efforts? Well, of course, they would all be welcome. But doubling the activity is pie-in-the sky without a major, and I mean major, cash injection."

Spooner looked across the desk and let a broad smile cross his face. "Yes," he said.

McNamara looked for the first time at Redman. Redman eyed him back. They returned their gazes to Spooner.

McNamara said patiently, "When James uses the word *major*, Professor Spooner, he doesn't mean modest local pump-priming of the kind the University might be able to re-allocate from its own discretionary funds."

Spooner was still smiling beatifically. "I know," he said. "He means systemic, across-the-board investment of an absolute kind. He means totally new money. And lots of it."

His phone chirruped and he glanced at it, picked it up for a few seconds, read something on the screen, then put it down again. His eyes alighted once more on the other two men.

"How," he said, "does eighty million pounds over three years sound, forty in the first year, twenty in each of the two years to follow?"

Redman blinked several times.

McNamara frowned and raised his hand to his head. "But that's, that's …" He was doing some rapid calculations. "That's a hundred and fifty per cent of my own faculty budget in the same three-year period, and Social Sciences is the largest of the three non-science faculties. Across the three faculties that would be something like a sixty per cent increase in expenditure."

"If you include the administrators," Spooner rejoined. "Actually, if we can find a way to streamline the administration, to centralise it into one body to serve all three faculties, instead of each of them having an independent administration of its own, allowing that new administrative structure to grow in staffing modestly but not unduly, the estimates I have commissioned reckon on it as something more like a seventy-five percent increase. Most of the money could be spent on new academic staff, new programmes, two or three new buildings, and scholarships."

There was a pause, while Spooner looked slowly from one to the other, seeming to savour the moment, though not too vaingloriously.

McNamara scratched his head.

Redman sighed again, but his sigh was a little different from the one before. It had something more positive sounding in it. "Well, I have a couple of questions," he said.

"You bet," said McNamara. "Like what's it got to do with us?"

"And where's the money coming from?" added Redman.

Spooner nodded. "Okay. As I shall explain, the answers to both questions are linked. First of all, what has it to do with you? Well, I need people I can trust. I need people who might engage wholeheartedly with the opportunity to make this place a properly balanced University again, rather than the technocratic market-chasing machine it has become, the business-in-all-but-name that it's been reduced to, about which you have complained and protested for many years to no avail. You are not the only people who fit into this category of trustworthy individuals, but you seem to me among the few. For example, Professor McNamara, have you ever thought of being a Pro-Vice Chancellor?"

McNamara coughed a dry laugh. "There are some desks I won't cross to the other side of."

Spooner pursed his lips in seeming slight dismay, then relented and brightened a little. "Okay, I understand that. Then how about Dean of your own faculty?"

McNamara frowned. "My faculty already has a Dean."

"Yes," said Spooner, "but her term as Dean finishes at the end of this budgetary year. The new dispensation would not begin until the new budgetary year on August first. You could replace her then. And, Dr Redman, though you are not a Professor and I could not offer you such a senior managerial position, I could make you Vice Dean in the Faculty of Arts, and give you a leading role on the committee that would plan for the new growth and implement it. Moreover, I could relieve you both of teaching for the next three years in order that you may concentrate on this vital work."

He let these proposals hang in the air between them. The silence was broken by repeated *toot-toots* from his phone. Spooner breathed out sharply in exasperation. "Gentlemen, excuse me, it's the train whistle, second in seriousness only to the foghorn. But it happens more than you'd think. My colleagues have a more heightened sense of emergency than I do after the events of last term. I must take this, but I should be only a few seconds. Forgive me."

He got up, but he did not leave the room. Instead he crossed to one of the bay windows, speed-dialled and looked out over the lake, his hand on the head of one of the naked male statues. He held the conversation in discreet tones, but he made no attempt to prevent them from overhearing it. He spoke genially and professionally, as he had done throughout.

"Yes, Nigel. Your text. A situation, you say? Can you give me more detail? Okay. But I am in an important meeting right now. Yes, Professor McNamara and Dr Redman. We should conclude soon but I don't wish to interrupt it for something that will probably turn out to be a false alarm. Please gather as much detail as you can and ask Eloise to call you when we're done. Then you can come and see me directly after. Yes. And thank you, Nigel."

He hung up and returned to his seat behind his desk.

Redman said, "And the money?"

"Ah, yes," said Spooner, and the first hint of awkwardness crept into his expression. "Thereby hangs a tale. But it's a tale I am not responsible for starting. I can only write its conclusion. Its original author died before he could complete it. I mean, of course, Sir Evan Covet."

"Oh," said Redman.

"Oh oh," said McNamara.

Spooner smiled again and raised his hands, his palms facing him, in what at first looked like a gesture of supplication but then, as his arms went higher and his eyes also turned upwards, seemed to be taking in their entire surroundings, asking for them to be considered.

"This building," he said, "in fact, almost every building on campus, used to be called something else. We, or I should say Sir Evan, traded those old names for cold hard cash. He was very good at it. I saw the figures in the minutes of a University Council meeting. In total he raised about eleven million, just from renaming our real estate, virtually magicking money out of nowhere, from nothing, from companies and wealthy individuals who wanted their trade mark or moniker on concrete or, in the case of this one, limestone. Now, what I am about to tell you need not remain confidential, because we are officially going public with it at noon, in about an hour. This building, this was the jewel in the crown obviously, and for this Covet got a cool million from –"

"The Donald," said McNamara, rolling his eyes.

"Well, ahem, yes, but you know, it's hard to knock, I think, really. A million is about ten years of non-clinical professorial salary including superannuation, or fifty non-science scholarships for a year, and for what? For nothing? For simply redesignating a heap of lifeless stones? There's a certain amount of brilliance involved in a deal like that."

"If," replied McNamara, "you are happy to live with the ideological associations, which Covet clearly was. Not to mention remaining silent, and making your own science academics remain silent, when Trump built a golf course on a site of special scientific interest in Scotland."

"I agree," said Spooner, "but these are not problems, I'm afraid, which have died with Covet. You know that it was just a minor tax write-off, the renaming of this particular pile, just a marginal excess from Trump's British resort operations, little more than small change for public relations purposes? When was that, six, seven years ago?"

"Two thousand and nine," Redman said.

"Well, Covet kept on courting him once he'd got a foothold. Remember, Trump has Scottish ancestry. Covet didn't get into golf for nothing, apparently. It was all about Trump. And again, think, this is a man who has given his name to an entire university and not just buildings, even though Trump University is not a real university. And they genuinely got on, he and Covet. Now, this was long before anyone had any idea that Trump would run for President, never mind win. Covet was just hanging on in there for whatever he might get for us, for Odium, but when Trump won the Republican nomination Covet really ramped up his own woo-Trump campaign. I've seen the file. Covet was down there at Number Ten with David Cameron at least once, asking him to smooth out some of the wrinkles between HMRC and Trump's British companies, pointing out the kind of patronage that might arise for British education, or at least for Odium, from a less ruffled relation between them. Whether or not it worked with Cameron, who knows? It's hardly something that would be in writing. But it wasn't just Cameron. There was a whole host of lesser ministers and under-ministers Covet badgered too. Did you notice, after Cameron resigned, that Theresa May said nothing critical of Trump? Covet was among the people who wrote advising her to stay silent, just in case, *just on the outside chance* that Trump might win. And all through that time, Covet was talking to Trump, writing to him, even apparently meeting him quietly for half an hour when Trump came to Scotland during his election campaign. The burden of it seemed to be that Covet persuaded him, in order to win the votes of all those white supremacists and evangelicals back home in the US, that he would have to say things that would piss off the entire liberal world and damn near every foreign government that mattered, and that what he had to do if he was by chance successful was have a strategy in place to buy back favour with that same disgruntled world afterwards. And it seems to have worked. In fact, Trump liked the idea so much that he moved on it even before he won the presidency. His people talked to HMRC, they negotiated a future three-year deal on the taxes from his British operations, he threw in another few million on top, he already had a connection with Odium, after all. It's all a bit opaque but, I am assured, totally above legal challenge. The irony is that Covet died only a few days before Trump won the election. It was me who got the call, from The Donald personally, ten days after he was sworn in."

McNamara faltered, swallowing hard. "You ... you ..." His voice trailed off drily.

"I think what Robert is trying to say," piped up Redman, coming to his rescue, "is that ... you are seriously telling us that Odium is about to receive a donation of eighty million pounds from...", and he could not help but raise his voice somewhat for emphasis, "...the new President of the United States, *Donald fucking Trump*?"


## Chapter Three

They left Spooner's inner temple, and walked without speaking along the corridor. Nigel Asterisk appeared on cue from the door of his Registrar's office, almost as if he had planned deliberately to encounter them. As they drew near he nodded in acknowledgment. Redman returned the gesture and slowed, but McNamara kept walking.

"Amazing news, no?" Asterisk said to them both, looking askance as McNamara brushed past.

"Er, yes," said Redman, still moving, but more slowly. Caught between a wish to exchange words with Asterisk and a need to close the widening gap with McNamara, he found himself walking backwards. "Totally a cause for amazement."

Asterisk changed direction and moved towards him, following him with some urgency. "So what do you think? Are you in?"

Redman looked over his shoulder. McNamara was gone, already out in the Trump Building quadrangle. He jerked his head in that direction. "We have to talk."

"Okay," said Asterisk, halting. "Call me."

Redman nodded and turned around, hurrying through the exit, past the tub of flowers into which, though he did not know it, Cannon Buckrack had thrown his cigarette on the morning of his first meeting with Asterisk the previous September, and out into the middle of the quad, where McNamara stood waiting for him.

It was bright and chilly outside, but the air was still, with no breeze. On such days the sounds in the flagstoned quad were amplified and echoing. The centre of the Trump Building was not busy, though Redman could see a familiar figure striding purposefully through the east arch in their direction. This was Elfyn Dethbridge, the Deputy Registrar, whom McNamara called "Buttons" and told anti-Welsh jokes about. Dethbridge saw Redman from afar, over McNamara's shoulder, and nodded with strained courtesy as he approached.

"Well," Redman said to McNamara, "what did you think of that?"

"Pah," said McNamara without reserve, "he's a *fucking gaylord*."

At this resoundingly voiced condemnation the balding head of the passing Dethbridge, which had been nid-nodding towards the entrance from which they had just emerged, twisted around on its stalk, scowling. He caught Redman's eye.

"Oh," Redman called to him in attempted apology, "not you, Elfyn. Someone else."

This explanation did not seem to have the desired assuaging effect. It made Dethbridge simply glower more intensely, or as severely as it was possible for him to do. In truth his face mimed the behavioural contortions he thought might indicate reproach, but to the dual sources of his sudden offence these were read as the mere semblance, and no more, of the drooping retreat of a shrinking violet. It appeared that Dethbridge had no time to stop, whereas in fact all his instincts were telling him to move away faster, though he managed to put on a show of exaggerated stiffness caused by enhanced affront.

McNamara had noticed Dethbridge only when Redman hailed him, a few seconds before his stiffened form disappeared into the bowels of the building. "Ah, Buttons. He must be going to see Baron Hardon. You know, Buttons was once stranded on a desert island for three years –"

"You've told me that one, Robert."

"Ah. Pity. Well, it's just gone eleven, maybe it's the time of day for him to take a lovin' spoonful from Spooner."

Redman squinted at the older man in the cold late morning sunshine. "The Buttons routine I get, Robert. But the sudden homophobia? Where's that coming from? About one in twenty of our colleagues seems to be gay and about one in ten of our students. There's a lot of it about, haven't you noticed? You even get your LGB with T and an added letter every week these days. It's become entirely respectable. Isn't one of your own boys gay?"

"Ah, well," said McNamara. "That's different. He's a perfectly decent gaylord, not a *fucking gaylord*. Just as there are some hetero-women who are loveable sexy minxes and there are others who are just filthy poxy sluts. There're many shades of gay."

Redman smiled. "I wasn't asking what you thought of Spooner. I was asking what you thought of what he had to say."

"Ah, fuck him," said McNamara contemptuously. Then he tutted and started on the more rounded response that seemed required. "Tell me if I'm wrong. He wants to co-opt us into some quasi-managerial positions in order to help him make a hard sell. He needs us to endorse the Trump brand and he's prepared to bribe us each with three teaching-free years as a reward. But what he's really after, though it was all between the lines, is help in dealing with the anticipated Union backlash and maybe a battle from the scientists too. As soon as this becomes public knowledge, in an hour or so, Poon – hah! our other resident gaylady-in-chief – will be building barricades in the air and having visions of herself in the newspapers again, playing Dame Avril Scargill. She'll be calling emergency Union meetings by this afternoon and there'll be an unholy return to another odiousness-of-Odium phase of the kind we just got out of. The scientists will probably join forces with her out of their usual greed and massive sense of entitlement. Why would we want to get mixed up in that kind of thing again?"

"Granted," said Redman. "But he didn't seem so bad. It looks like he's insisted that, though he'll take the money – and how can he *not* take the money, *seriously*? – he won't have it dictated to him how he'll spend it. And he wants to use it to create a massive upswell in the human sciences, not the technocratic ones. Sure, he's caught in an absurd contradiction, given where the money is coming from, as well as what he says about his own moderate politics. But he's prepared to buck the obvious trend. There'd be fat on our slice of the land again. That seems worth compromising on a few principles for, no? There can hardly be another university in the country where they could even dream of such a thing."

"It depends," McNamara replied, "what those principles are. You perhaps forget, James, my near-terminal isolationism. I'm close to out-Crusoe-ing Crusoe. I'm not sure I even need a Man Friday these days.

How do you compromise on that? Or, to change the island analogy, while Prospero in there is about to conjure up a storm that will also inspire Sycorax-Poon, I don't fancy being Caliban to either of them. It sounds like you do."

"I'm just saying," Redman soothed, "we should think about it and maybe talk more when the dust of the announcement has settled. He's given us until the end of the week." He looked anew at the man before him, and gestured to his dark attire. "How are you, Robert?"

McNamara heaved a sigh. "I'm tired. I was driving all night. I need to go home and get some sleep."

"How was the funeral?"

"That seems a while ago now. It's already going down into … I got through it."

"And Rachel?"

There was a pointed pause while McNamara stared straight at him.

"Fuck Rachel," he said.

They parted, and Redman sauntered into the ground floor School of English by the opposite entrance. He strolled down to the middle of the corridor and turned left into the School Adminstrator's office, through an empty assistant's antechamber which buffered it from the traffic of the main thoroughfare. There he found Lorraine Quant, who was on the telephone at her desk by the window, but she extended her free hand, and he took it and squeezed it gently. Then she withdrew it and pointed to a seat. He watched her with her back to him, gazing over at Asterisk's office opposite, as she wound up the call.

"Yes," she was saying. "Again. That's the fourth working day in a row, only two of the absences notified. No call from him this morning. He just didn't show up, *again*. Professor Matthews had his meeting with the British Academy people at eleven and I had to log on to Yunus's computer to check that he'd organised the coffee at the start and the catering at twelve-thirty. That's where I found it. Right there on the desktop. I opened it and looked at it and it seemed to be what it said it was. Professor Matthews hadn't arrived yet and so I called you. I remembered that training session we did on this kind of thing and I followed the steps. I didn't know where else to go for advice. I hope I did the right thing. You have? And what did the VC say? I see. Elfyn? He's coming over now? Five minutes? Okay, I'll wait for him. Thank you.

Bye-bye."

When she hung up and turned to him she appeared troubled, but they both had got used to not prying into each other's professional business. It made for a simpler life.

"We still on for tonight?" he asked.

"Well, yes," she said, distractedly. "But I think it's going to be a rough day. I... I...".

"Trouble?" he prompted.

"It's Yunus."

"Not in again, I see?"

"Well, it's worse than that. Come and look. But we'd better be quick because Dethbridge is coming over soon."

"Yes, I saw him in the quad. He thought Robert had outed him and was a bit cross."

She led him out into the front office and closed the door and turned the lock.

"Robert's back?" she said. "How is he?"

"He seems in bad shape. Dented. Cynical."

She crossed to the computer on the assistant's desk and flicked the mouse to activate the screen. Then she pointed with one elongated finger at a particular icon.

Redman leaned in closer.

"Fark," he said, as was his wont with her. "And that is what it is, is it?"

She nodded. "It does appear to be an ISIS training manual, yes. Asterisk said no one else should open it, so don't, but I did when I first saw it. How to make explosive from fertiliser, how to pack it in a suicide jacket, how to choose targets, how to use an AK47, how to conceal knives on your person and the best way to use them to kill, how to conduct yourself under interrogation, and so on. A couple of hundred pages, with diagrams and photos. The kind of thing we are meant to call in immediately, and so that's what I did."

"Fark again," he said. "But it doesn't seem like him at all. We all have him down as a rather gentle soul, a bit of a New Age leftie, in fact, you know, the soft kind. Doesn't he run with a dance troupe or something? Hardly a jihad man. I mean, leotards?"

"Yes," Lorraine said. "You think you know someone, right? But actually that wasn't what shocked me most." She pointed to another icon next to the one for the ISIS training manual. "Open that and you'll see what I mean. I thought it meant 'US' as in 'USA' but I figure it just means 'us'. You'll see why when you look at it. I'll retreat while you do. I don't want to see it again."

She went back into her own office and Redman took the seat before the screen. He clicked on the video file, and recoiled almost instantly at seeing Yunus's close-cropped, well groomed beard and moustache wrapped around a dark, stiff penis in porno point-of-view perspective, with muffled sounds of excitement off-camera. A male voice was hissing, "Yeah! Thassit! Take big mouthfuls of cock! All the way down yer throat! Be a good little boy and lemme see me dick disappear inter yer face!" It did not take long for Redman to grasp that Yunus appeared to be a consenting, indeed enjoying, participant. A moment later he understood that the movie had been shot by the fellated cameraman, no doubt using his phone, from the very office chair he now occupied.

"Jesus Christ!" he exclaimed, and leapt up. "*What the fuck?*"

He turned around. Lorraine was at her desk again, both hands on either side of her head, over her ears, her eyes closed.

"Did you tell Asterisk about that too?" Redman wondered.

"Not yet, but they're going to find it. I can't delete it, can I?"

Redman pondered a moment, regarding her shock. "I suppose it's not that much different from what we –"

"It's altogether different," she snapped. "For one thing, I don't have a cock. For a second, I don't do it while you are sitting in this chair, in my workplace. Nor would I at all if … if you said such filthy things."

Redman grunted. "And, yes, and … he's a practising Muslim, no?"

"You think? I wonder. I'm beginning to see it as just an excuse to bunk off twice during the working day for a bit of extra me-time."

Redman laughed. "Or *he*-time."

"Those so-called prayers had a habit of taking up to an hour, not twenty minutes. It didn't seem to matter how many times I talked to him about it, he just disregarded me. But then I am a woman, aren't I? Oh, he was never unpleasant, quite the opposite. He had a sweet way with him, everyone agrees on that, even me. All this lot down the corridor, all your fellow academics, they all seem to love him, are forever chatting to him while the work waits and waits. Even the Head of School, oh yes, Matthews seems to think he's a little darling. So I hesitated a long time. But to tell you the truth, it had already got to the point when I was about to press the nuclear button on him, especially after his absences this last week. I've had nearly a year of this crap, tolerating him, expecting him to buck up. It got beyond a joke. I've been the one getting all the blame for his complete lack of care in his job. I didn't quite expect it would end this way though. It makes it easier."

Redman dawdled a little, as he often wanted to do in Lorraine's orbit. "Well, at least the man in the hot seat didn't seem to be Dethbridge," he laughed. "That wasn't a Welsh accent."

"Speaking of whom," she gathered herself, "you had better leave."

They kissed briefly.

Redman went out into the empty corridor and closed Lorraine's door, crossing to his own office directly opposite. As he fumbled in his pockets for his keys the double swing doors at the end of the corridor were thrown open and a tall, hatchet-faced man, powerfully built, wearing a long brown overcoat, strode briskly in his direction. Flanked as he was by two equally tall uniformed policemen, he might as well, Redman fancied, have had CID stamped on his forehead. It took a few seconds before Redman noticed Dethbridge scurrying to keep up behind this surging, triple-breasted human wave of law enforcement.

The detective stepped straight up to Redman. "The School Adminstrator's office?" he demanded.

Redman pointed silently across the way. The detective nodded and rapped forcefully on Lorraine's door. As he waited for it to be opened, he indicated wordlessly to both constables that they should assume a position on either side of it. Redman saw Lorraine's face briefly in the gap that opened up, at which point the plain clothes man turned and raised an open palm to halt the pursuant Dethbridge.

"No," he said decisively to the Welshman. "I need to talk to Ms Quant alone. I shall call you in when we have finished."

He disappeared inside, leaving Dethbridge stranded outside Lorraine's closed office, looking from one to the other of the constables.

"Do you know how long he will be?" he said to them.

One of them shook his head silently, with lower lip protruding, then took his eyes off him and stared straight ahead.

Dethbridge turned to see Redman standing in his open doorway. "Er, James, do you mind?"

"Do I mind what?"

Dethbridge raised a hand towards the interior of Redman's office.

"You want to come in?" Redman guessed.

"Yes, thanks," said Dethbridge, moving forward. "And can we leave the door open?"

"My door is always open, Elfyn," Redman grinned. "Would you like coffee? I have an Italian espresso machine. I even have biscuits. We runners need to maintain our calorie intake."

"I don't run," said Dethbridge.

"I can see that," said Redman. "I meant marathon men like me. My 'we' was not meant to include you. It was more royal."

Dethbridge frowned testily. "Since I'm here," he said, taking a seat, "since I'm waiting –"

Redman interrupted. "Why are you here, waiting, Elfyn? What's afoot? You came in on the jet stream of the Flying Squad and then got blown out of it."

"Oh that," Dethbridge fluttered. "I can't say, it's hopefully nothing. Dr Asterisk sent me over to keep tabs on these officers."

"You don't seem to be doing that. You could have insisted when he waved you away. You surely want to know what he's asking her, whatever the hopefully nothing is about?"

"I, I … I can't discuss it with you, James. But since I'm here I *would* like to discuss what happened earlier, in the quad. I won't take it, you know. I don't have to stand for it."

Redman finished spooning coffee grounds into the machine. "Stand for what?"

"For that kind of insult."

"What kind of insult?"

"Professor McNamara's. I am just doing my job, James, I should not be subjected to –"

"But I told you then and there," Redman replied, "it wasn't you he was referring to."

"Oh," said Dethbridge, "it just so happens, by sheer coincidence, that as I am passing –"

"But why would you think, automatically, that he must be referring to you?"

Dethbridge halted in his speech, seemingly a little caught out by the question.

"Milk, sugar?" said Redman, deliberately making it sound as if he were using a term of endearment.

"Just a little milk," Dethbridge replied.

"Ginger nuts or jammie dodgers?"

"No, just coffee will be fine."

Redman handed him a small cup and saucer and took a seat on the other side of his desk.

"As I was saying, there are University policies, you know. And it was in a public place."

Redman grimaced slightly in disagreement "Well, it was a private conversation going on in a public place which was entirely empty apart from me, him, and latterly you. Robert had his back to you. I can assure you that he did not know you were there. And as I said, he was not talking about you. So there was neither intent to offend you, nor should you be offended, as you were not the object of his comment."

"Well then, who was?"

Redman sighed. "Why don't you ask Robert?"

"If," said Dethbridge, "he was referring to the only other person it is likely he was referring to, then the disrespect is even worse."

"Really?" Redman sat up, a little interested now. "It's more disrespectful if said of one person than if said of another? How's that?"

"On account of his position."

"Whose position?"

"The position of the insulted person."

"But how could he be insulted if he couldn't hear it?"

"That's beside the point. A person of high standing should be able to demand respect."

"I see," said Redman. "So, it was more disrespectful to say it of that other person in his absence than it would have been to say it of you in your presence, because of that other person's, what, his *rank*?"

Dethbridge thought about his own logic for a moment and then, hesitantly, answered, "I think so."

"Well, that's an argument I'll have to consider for a bit, especially as we don't really have *rank*, as such, around here. It's a university, Elfyn, not the military or even your Odium police force out in the corridor there. Relations are meant to be collegiate."

"Collegiate?" Dethbridge snorted. "How collegiate was Professor McNamara's conduct?"

Redman groaned. "His conduct? Since when did two informal words spoken privately in an off-the-cuff exchange amount to something as formal as *conduct*? That's a bit officious, no? And I say again, why don't you take this up with Robert? He's the one who said it, not me."

"Because, because," Dethbridge stammered, "he's impossible to talk to. He has always been impossible to talk to. He is utterly uncompromising, even contemptuous."

"No, that's not true," said Redman. "I'll grant you he often gives the appearance of *impatience*, but not to those who know him. You do realise that he is something rather special in his field, and that with a research assessment coming up he's an asset to the University and his School? Other places have been trying to poach him, but he has stayed. People with his kind of *rank* often appear to be a little Olympian and forbidding."

"That gives him no special licence," Dethbridge insisted. "It gives him no right."

"But didn't you just say that men of higher rank demand, what did you mean exactly, greater regard?"

Dethbridge sat in frustration, as if feeling led into a conversational impasse.

"What you could do, as you seem so over-vexed by the matter," continued Redman, "is you could go and tell the person you think he was referring to what you heard him say, and let that person decide what to do."

"That's preposterous!" exclaimed Dethbridge. "How could I? How could I possibly?"

Redman smiled kindly. "Then maybe let it go," he suggested.

Dethbridge did not seem satisfied. Rather, he made as if to exercise his anguish yet further in speech, but the attention of both men was at that moment distracted by events in the corridor.

A young man, presumably a student, had appeared before the sentinel constables and was engaging them in conversation; or rather, he was interrogating them, and they were refusing to answer.

"What's goin' on 'ere, mate? Wotcha doin', uh? What's happenin'? Standin' there?" He spat questions at the two officers, turning his head from one to the other, so that Redman could see his face in profile. The policemen ignored him resolutely. He was olive-skinned, but his accent was unmistakably east-end Odium, and the voice seemed a little familiar to Redman. "Cat got yer tongue, what? Gonna stop me if I try ter go in?"

This last question seemed so pointlessly rhetorical that the officers' continued refusal to answer was a given. One of them tapped quietly on

Lorraine's office door. By this time Dethbridge was on his feet and moving agitatedly towards the corridor, but the young man had now disappeared, moving outside the field of view offered by Redman's framing doorway.

Redman got up and followed Dethbridge, stopping at the threshold and looking curiously along the corridor to the left. The student had not departed, but was loitering ten feet away. He had taken out his phone and was making a call. Dethbridge seemed to be trying to intervene with the constables, but was as neglected by them as the young man had been, because Lorraine's door had opened and the sizeable, grim-expressioned detective had emerged. One of the officers leaned in to him and spoke in his ear, nodding in the young man's direction. The CID man stepped a foot or two into the passageway and regarded the student stonily.

"'Ey, Yunus, 's'Faraj. Yeah, man, you not in? Am at yer office, bro'. Der's cops 'ere, so you stay away, man, they's guardin' yer office, outside it, two of 'em –"

He went on talking with ostentatious loudness, but the detective had obviously decided that he had heard enough. He turned to the uniformed officers and twitched his head in Faraj's direction.

"Take him," he said. "I'll have to call in and have the other one picked up."

The two constables instantly moved in unison like a pair of large guard dogs acting on instilled command. They swept either side of the nonplussed Dethbridge, one of them pushing away the weak barrier of his one outstretched arm so forcefully that Dethbridge was virtually spun round in a pirouette, then stood rooted to the spot as he watched the spectacle which unfolded.

So did Redman.

Within seconds one officer had taken Faraj by an elbow and the other had closed a fist around his phone, plucking it from the young man's hand before seizing his remaining arm.

"Oi, what da fuck?" cried Faraj. Entirely ignored, his voice began to rise to a shout. "*'Ey, ya fuckin' leave me alone, yeah? Who the fuck do ya fink ya is? Gerrof, ya cunt! Ow!*" He was struggling as they pinned his arms behind his back and one of the officers magicked a pair of cuffs from somewhere on his person.

Alerted by the noise, doors began to open along the corridor and some of Redman's fellow academics' familiar heads bobbed out. Students who had been beyond the double doors at the end of the corridor opened them cautiously and gazed wide-eyed at the arrest from afar.

Faraj began appealing to these witnesses. "*Hey, check it out, peepul! Nazi fuckin' state at work! I was doin' nuffin'. So why d'ya fink that is, yeah? An innocent Muslim? Look at these cunts doin' their shit right where ya work! In a fuckin' university!*"

He was writhing in the officers' grip, leaning his body forward and trying to drag them along behind him, but he was held back by their strength, pitched at an angle at which he would otherwise have naturally fallen, like a cartoon character running into the face of a powerful wind.

The two constables seemed practised at what they were doing and were not in the slightest flustered, though they gave the sense that they were becoming a little impatient.

One looked at the other and said, "Down?"

The second took an instant to nod and reply, "Down."

"*Fuck yer mothers! Fuck yer pets and yer daughters!*" Faraj was now upbraiding them in a high-pitched scream. "*Ow, yer breakin' my fuckin' arm, pig! Fuck yer auntie and yer uncle!*"

One of the policemen put a hand on Faraj's back and pushed him forcibly while the other flung an arm under his chest to ensure that his landing was not too heavy. The latter then applied pressure to his head, keeping his cheek against the floor, while the former put a knee in his back and expertly cuffed him. The only part of his body that could now move were his lower legs, his heels flailing helplessly a few inches off the ground.

"*Wotcha doin' now, eh? Ya see this, peepul? Ya see what they did! Do not turn away! Bear witness ter the totalitarian British state in action! Wotcha gonna do, boys? You gonna shove a truncheon up me arse? Is that it? Or ya need some dick down yer throats and this the only way ya can get it? Go on then. Turn me over, take down me pants and eat me meat! Swallow that shaft, ya Fascist cocksuckers!*"

It was at this obscene explosion of gay-baiting that Redman recognised in what context he had heard the voice so recently before.

## Chapter Four

There was no teaching at Odium on Wednesday afternoons, which were designated as a sports period for the students and a meetings period for the staff. Thus, two days later, Redman found himself in the School of English's staff common room, seated in an unobtrusive corner of a large improvised square of desks, regarding most of his colleagues with dispirit and dismay. He had positioned himself, as he always did, across the room from Lorraine, in part to maintain their habitual pretence of distance between them, in part so that they could exchange meaningful looks throughout the usually tiresome and sometimes absurd proceedings. But today Lorraine, her face framed by the neat lines of her short page-boy haircut, sat tensely upright, in a bright white blouse and navy skirt, by far the most pointedly dressed woman in the room, surrounded as she was by those of her kind scattered around in dowdy floral frocks or jeans worn with capacious, bosom-disguising t-shirts.

The six student representatives were shuffling out before the meeting's reserved business began. They had, in the ordinary business session just concluded, raised one or two tentative questions concerning events of the preceding forty-eight hours but, delicate millennials that they were, paragons of obedience to authority that they wished maturely to show that they aspired to be, they did not prickle, they instigated no further friction, when told by the Chair that these matters were still confidential and could for now be discussed only in their absence.

The Chair was Professor Bernard Matthews, the sixty-six-year old Head of School, a D. H. Lawrence specialist who refused to retire and who subscribed to the view that the purpose of Literature was to promote what he was happy to call "roundness of life", a term he glossed, when challenged about it, by saying no more than "it requires explication only to those for whom it is not already an apprehended experience manifested in concrete feeling". Redman eyed him with some foreboding at the manner in which he was likely to handle what was to follow.

Matthews was a small hunched creature, who since middle age had cultivated the weathered appearance of an outdoors man, largely by avoiding sunlight and patiently acquiring anxiety lines on his face, his main access to anxiety being immersion in the works of DHL, which, he earnestly believed, forced greater existential demands on their readers than anything else the world conceivably had to offer. He had published on no other writer in his thirty-five years at Odium, and the endless stream of Lawrenceana which he had steadily released into the gutters of low-status academic journals and paperback introductions and coffee-table biographies had made him a modest name in a contracting field. DHL donated much to his private as well as his professional life. He wrote pseudonymous poems based on Lawrencean tropes and motifs which suffered punishing rejections from small magazines, was passionately absorbed by videos of copulating animals that he found on YouTube, and was a member of a spiritual paganism sect whose headquarters, fittingly enough, was in Taos, New Mexico, and which he visited at least once a year. Despite the self-declared roundness of this life which harnessing himself to DHL had contoured for him, he nonetheless bore certain grudges heavily and sometimes without disguise. He resented his parents for not giving him a name like Rupert or Lilly or Oliver but instead provoking others to think of him, when first introduced, as the diminutive *doppelgänger* of a boorish one-time Norfolk turkey farmer. In order not to repeat this error he had named his one daughter Ursula, only to experience a depression which lasted for years when she unaccountably changed her name, on her eighteenth birthday, to Lucy. He owned one of DHL's jackets, which he had paid a lot for at auction, and draped it over the back of his seat whenever he wrote on Lawrence or, as now, when he chaired meetings. When Lorraine Quant had asked him within a few weeks of her appointment why he carried "that grubby old Oxfam thing" around with him, he had taken an instant and abiding dislike to her. He lived in permanent puzzlement as to why the several offers he had made to other men for a literal *blutsbrüderschaft* had never been taken up. He had, of course, married an older German woman who was twice his size.

With the students safely out of the room, Matthews *ahemmed* and began to intone reedily, peering through his bifocals at a spot on the floor before him and seldom looking up to make eye contact with the assembled staff.

"Well, now," he said, "I am sorry that we have to come to that part of the meeting in which the febrile outer world, the drab domain of politics and the state on this occasion, trespasses upon our scholarly insouciance. As I think you all know, our much liked School assistant administrator was arrested and incarcerated by the local constabulary on

Monday afternoon, and the whole of my time since then has been consumed, literally *consumed*, I assure you, with trying to find out what on earth this sorry debacle is all about. Indeed, I find it a matter of some regret that this matter went outside the School before I could be apprised of it, and could probably have hushed it up and spared us all the pain of this meeting, as well as whatever else is to come."

At this he lifted his head and gave a rare glance in Lorraine's direction over the top of his spectacles.

"Poor Yunus," said a female voice originating from somewhere inside a baggy t-shirt but outside his eye line. Matthews lifted a genial, pacifying hand in its direction.

"However," he continued, "Lorraine has revealed the official policy on this sort of thing to me and I accept that it was probably incumbent upon her to make a snap decision and we shall all just have to live with the consequences of that snap decision. It seems that Yunus did have what they call a 'terrorist document' on his office computer, and his story is that he was sent it by a student with whom he is friendly in the School of Politics, because that student had asked him to print it out for free on account of the fact that he, the Politics student, didn't want to pay for the printing himself. But it was apparently all *bona fide*, the document was genuinely for the student's research. We can probably all be generous enough to overlook the low-level dishonesty in the arrangement. I know I am minded to. No point in rocking the boat for a few quid's worth of paper and toner, slap on the wrist kind of thing for Yunus, eh, softly softly? Or so I thought. In fact, I went straight over to the Registrar's office first thing this morning with the intention, quite frankly, of giving him a kick in the wind and demanding that he put an end to all this palaver and stop playing it all so by-the-book, not least because we are missing the sterling services of our young administrator and are all having to do things ourselves that we don't know how to do but he did. We all know that he cannot exactly be replaced by a temp, now, can he? But I'm afraid that that's when things got a bit more complicated. What I am about to say should remain in this room, but the problem for us is not simply that our Yunus has been, I must say I think rather ludicrously, arrested under the Terrorism Act, but we have a much bigger problem in that there is now apparently some, er, confusion as to his immigration status. It seems, although Yunus has been with us for about eleven months, that no one has yet definitively checked his right to work in the country. So the much bigger problem that faces us now is that we are likely to be without an assistant School administrator for quite some time."

At this there were groans.

Matthews looked again at Lorraine.

"It's not my responsibility to check his immigration status," Lorraine said defensively but firmly. "That's an HR function. Indeed, I spent months reminding them of it and eventually gave up."

"Och, but wait a minute here!" exclaimed a Caledonian voice from the row of staff opposite, among whom Redman sat. Redman did not bother to pitch forward and look. He knew that the voice belonged to Dr Donald Doyle – the School's very own The Donald – who had succeeded him as Union secretary when Redman had resigned the previous term. This ascension to office, as well as the fact that this year of 2017 was the centenary of the event that he considered the high point of all history, had got Doyle's considerable dander up even more than usual. The Donald was an aggressive Trotskyite with Chinese teeth and a scar across his small hard slit of a mouth which he attempted to disguise with a ragged red beard and an unkempt moustache. McNamara had once told Redman that Doyle hailed from Shettleston, a much rougher part of Glasgow even than McNamara's, "lumpen-proletarian as compared to ordinary proletarian" was how McNamara had put it, and that this would largely explain Doyle's instinctive bluntness, his inflexible ideology-controlled thinking, and his simple-minded politics.

"Jist wait a minute," Doyle went on. "Noo look here, Bernie, yae huv tae be kiddin' us, right? The real issue here isnae the lad's papers. Ah think we aw know that's a complete red herrin'. If Ah've ever seen an *ex post facto*, that's wan. Thuv gone lookin' fur that oan purpose tae spare thur blushes. The polis, Ah mean, mebbe University management anaw. The cops know the kid's no' a terrorist an' that whit they did wis jist racial profilin', pure an' simple. Nae way, absolutely nae way, wid the boys ha' bin clapped in irons if they wur white, um Ah right?"

There were murmurs of assent from a few people around the table who had managed to understand fully what Doyle was saying in his broad uncompromising patois. Redman felt his eyes wander in irritated boredom around the room, eventually alighting on Sergei Krokoff, who was secretly reading a book, as he often did in staff meetings, especially during Doyle's dogmatic and hectoring monologues, of which the Ukrainian freely confessed he had never understood a word. Poor Krokoff, Redman reflected ruefully, the abject he of the Jane Blake Public Interest Disclosure document which Nigel Asterisk had given to Redman the previous November and which Redman had felt obliged, because the older man was mentioned in it, to pass to McNamara, as well as to force Asterisk to suppress. Krokoff, the sorry dupe. Krokoff was out of it, this was all happening in a different world to his, one that did not concern Krokoff in the remotest fashion. And yet Redman envied Krokoff a little in that moment. Nothing whatsoever trespassed on his insouciance, for sure.

Doyle had meanwhile been droning on. "Naw, whit we huv here is a wrangful arrest uv wan ae oor number, uv an ordinary worker, in fact, made under completely reactionary legislation, an' that's the real thing up fur discussion. An' whit we need noo is solidarity, no' jist blubberin' ower the fact thit we'll aw huv tae dae mair a' oor ain admin. Wuv goat tae stawn up an' be coontit, ev'ry wan ae us. Illegal immigrant ma erse. Naebiddy roon this table cared if he wis illegal or no' 'til noo. Kid's a total scapegoat. An' let's no' forget, there's another scapegoat tae, the other wee yin, the student fae Politics, whit's his name, Faraj? Ah wisnae in the buildin' it the time, but those a' ye that wur aw saw him wrangfully arrested right here in oor corridor oan Monday efternin. Thur hooses huv bin raided and thur bein' illegally detained. Noo, the Union executive's discussed this, it its lunchtime meetin' the day, an' there's a plan uv action developin', so Ah say we haud oan an' wait for their cue. It'll come soon enough. Untae then, let's make sure we don't keep quiet aboot it at aw, in fact, but *tell everbiddy* whit happened here and start drummin' up support fur these two innocent lads. This could be big. It's already aw oor the papers."

There was a brief silence, except for one or two indefinite *uh-huhs*. In the chair, Matthews, who also found Doyle tricky to understand and frankly rather intimidating, hesitated a considerable few seconds before summoning himself to respond, but as he did so he was spared by Redman, who said, with a great definiteness that Matthews found rather impressive, and again without moving forward to look at Doyle, "No."

Lorraine exchanged stares with him across the room.

"Whit?" Doyle roused himself and lurched forward to squint along the row of seats at Redman in the corner. "*Whit?*"

All eyes turned on Redman.

"No," he said. "Hardly any of that is true. It's not at all the case, for example, that his immigration status is irrelevant. It's extremely relevant and cannot be ignored. Granted, that was not why he was arrested but, if one potential offence comes to light in the investigation of another, it's hardly surprising or unusual. And we simply cannot say that we don't care about employment law. We all should care about employment law. It's there to protect us in our jobs. But most of all, neither of these arrests was wrongful and nobody is being illegally detained. I don't personally approve of the provisions of the Prevention of Terrorism Act, but if you've looked at it, you'll see that it provides for arrest on the grounds of mere possession of a so-called 'terrorist document', which it appears is incontrovertibly true in the case of both of these suspects. So the arrests were perfectly legal and not in the slightest wrongful. That is, they were in complete accordance with the law governing arrest and the law under which they were arrested. The Act permits detention for up to twenty-eight days without charge, but charges can be brought only if, in addition to possession, it appears that the possession was with a view actually to committing an act of terrorism. That does seem far too long a time to me, but that's the law, and only two days have so far passed. The police are entitled to take longer to establish the facts. There is no particular reason why we should accept the story given by the suspects, though it may turn out to be true. We simply don't know enough to rush to judgment or action. And lastly, this has absolutely nothing to do with the Union. Neither of these two men were UCU members or eligible for membership."

This was all said in a steady voice, but by half way through it Doyle's slightly demented eyes were already darting in their sockets and, by the end of it, his lower jaw was hanging in a satirical, somewhat malicious grin, as if he were enjoying in advance the put-down with which he intended to rebut.

"Ye done?" he jabbed at Redman. "Bugger the law. It's an unjust law. An' you urnae a UCU member either any mair, so don't tell those of us who ur whit's the Union's business and whit isnae."

Redman sighed deeply. He felt a blow-up coming on.

At the same moment, in the common room of the School of Politics, McNamara was likewise immured in a staff meeting, witnessing with almost complete detachment a now fully developed verbal blow-up in its violent, ongoing eruption. It was not simply that he refused to engage in the openly confrontational discourse that had come quickly to define the meeting. In fact, he was more akin to Sergei Krokoff than to Redman, at least in that, though he did understand what was actually being said, he did not appreciate why any of the participants seemed to care so passionately about it. In the scheme of things, in McNamara's mind, it all seemed piteously trivial. His mind was more occupied with what he considered truly important things.

By contrast with the ongoing exchange in the School of English, here the antlers currently locked were right-wing rather than left-wing. In the chair was Professor Frank Dashwood, a distinguished conservative political scientist who was currently a minor consultant to a Whitehall think-tank advising Theresa May's government on its Brexit plans. For ten minutes he had been parrying increasingly intense onrushes of censure, castigation and contumely from Bradley Gooltree, the doctoral supervisor of the arrested student, who had once been in the military and knew nothing at all about politics, yet had managed to secure a job at Odium to teach about the trendy grant-attracting topic of terrorism, of which he had certainly experienced something, but on which he now adopted a pragmatic liberal stance rather than the bellicose waterboard-all-jihadi-bastards line he knew he had advocated, and indeed put into practice a few times, while on active service as a sergeant in the Parachute Regiment.

Occasionally Dashwood would look over at McNamara as if soliciting his aid. The two men had, over the years, built a fairly solid bridge, of mutual respect if not friendship, that spanned the ideological gulf between them, at least on the purely personal level. McNamara found Dashwood to be competent, honest, hard-working, decent, well balanced, and of good humour, with admittedly the major personality *hamartia* of being a dreadful reactionary. Dashwood considered McNamara's politics to be other-planetary, but undogmatic, just as the man himself seemed well rounded, worldly-wise, tolerant, phlegmatic, knowledgeable and humane. He had met with McNamara before the meeting and asked him, without guile, if he would offer his assistance should things get as hot-under-the-collar as he expected them to. McNamara had seemed sincerely puzzled at the idea that there might be any trouble at all and mumbled words to the effect that he was sure

Dashwood could deal with it if it arose. Now that daggers were being openly drawn, Dashwood was hoping that McNamara would intervene, and was beginning to feel uncomfortably under pressure and isolated. No one seemed to be on his side or prepared to defend him in what he knew was his perfectly rational response to the situation, and moreover one which he had no other choice but to make, given the advice he had already sought from, or rather been given by, senior management. There was, Dashwood knew, a great deal of personal vindictiveness abroad in the room, because every member of the School's academic staff except him had voted for Britain to remain in the EU, and some of them, particularly a small trio of conspiratorial Germans whom he and McNamara privately called the Red Army Faction, feared for the long-term security of their jobs. Anything that might increase the heat below this already simmering pot of personal animus was likely to be fed into the fire.

"I tell you again," Gooltree was saying emphatically, "I spoke to the police for *three whole hours* yesterday and I told them Faraj was a genuine postgraduate student and that this document was a legitimate document for him to possess for the purposes of academic research and that they had absolutely no reason to hold him in custody. But they just wouldn't listen. They kept asking me all kinds of irrelevant stuff about his behaviour and his friends and his political views, things that are personally intrusive and impertinent and off the point. Even when I told them I used to be in the Paras and I was on their side and I was no radical, they just would not yield. I wrote to the Registrar and the Vice Chancellor yesterday evening expressing my outrage at the whole thing but I have yet to get a response. So what I want you to do as Head of School is stop stonewalling, stop thinking just about your own position, and get down there and give this new VC a good talking-to and make him exert his influence to get *this innocent student of ours* out of jail."

Dashwood had been struggling to get in a word. He now was permitted a reply. "I heard you the first time you said all that, Brad, but you didn't answer my question. Did you *know* he was going to download this document? Did he tell you he was? Because it might make a significant difference if he did and if you then advised him of the legal issues involved. But if he didn't, why didn't he? And it looks as if he didn't because there has been no prior communication from us notifying him that it was acceptable to do so."

Gooltree's entire upper body, and indeed his legs below the desk, shook in tremors of exasperation throughout Dashwood's speech, but still he did not answer.

"Vy? For vot reason?" This was from a member of the Red Army Faction, Griselda Rotfang, also known to Dashwood as Ulrike Meinhoff, a blubbery-jowled scowl atop a flak jacket at the back of the room. "Vy should he do zat, seek anyvone's permission? He is adult, is ziss not so? He is doing ze research. Vot does he need ze permission for? Zis is a democracy, zer is ze freedom, zer is no censorship, he is arrested for nussing."

"Well," said Dashwood patiently, "there is the very small obstruction of the Prevention of Terrorism Act. I believe they have a similar thing in Germany, Griselda, no? And there is the even tinier but still significant problem of the University's general and our own School's particular code governing the ethics of research procedures, the latter enforced by a standing committee in the School, on which Brad here *happens actually to sit*, and which approves or rejects detailed formal applications and otherwise advises students on the ethics of potentially controversial research actions with a view to compliance and record, one of which such actions rather obviously happens to be obtaining an ISIS training manual that gives instructions on and advocates murdering innocent people, but which this student seems to have just gone ahead and downloaded on a School computer off his own bat and then sent through the University email system to a member of staff in another School. If we could show that we approved this action in advance then the outlook would be rather rosier for the student. But from the police's point of view the fact that we knew damn all about it looks potentially incriminating for him, as if the student seems deliberately to have concealed the action from us in a manner *not entirely disconsonant* with what an actual terrorist might do in order to prevent detection."

Dashwood glanced again imploringly at McNamara. But McNamara was there in body only. His thoughts were in fact dwelling, as they still did every day, on the mystery that was Cannon Buckrack, a man he had never met or even seen, whose mere voice he had heard on a recording of just one short telephone call, someone of whom he knew nothing other than the four syllables of his name, but who had for some unaccountable reason chosen him, Robert McNamara, to be the recipient of communications which had led to and explained the

205

dramatic downfall of Sir Evan Covet, the seemingly irrepressible Vice Chancellor of the University of Odium until only three months before. Then he thought of Jane Blake's Public Interest Disclosure submission, a copy of which he had been given by Redman while both she and Covet were already freezing side-by-side in the same police mortuary, the one that had outlined Covet's plan to have her seduce McNamara, to entrap him into disgrace, for what? For his politics? According to Jane's document, her purpose as a tutor in the student hall of residence McNamara oversaw had really been to implement Covet's malicious design upon him. She was a sexual weapon in a proxy personal war that McNamara had not known was even being waged, and his sense of violation at the time this knowledge came to him had shaken him deeply. And yet he could not consciously recall a single occasion on which the young woman had said or done anything remotely suggestive or flirtatious or ambiguous in his presence. In his remembrance she had been entirely chaste. Had he simply not noticed? Was he really so enamoured of Rachel Brace at the time that he had entirely missed the erotic overtures of such a beautiful young woman? Jane herself had claimed in writing that she had made such attempts on his person. But she had later also sent a written withdrawal of that document. Had she made it up just to blackmail Covet, who seemed to have paid her off the very night she retracted it? Did anyone have the answers to these questions? Was he ever to have them settled?

He became eventually aware of loudening voices in the meeting and he looked up and saw Dashwood struggling, beleaguered, put through the wringer, perspiring, barely holding his own.

"Yes!" exclaimed someone loudly, emphatically, a note of zestful self-righteousness in the male voice. "Vot about ze *academic freedom*, huh?"

McNamara raised his hand to catch Dashwood's attention. Dashwood saw it as a benediction and returned a beseeching look, feeling that a silent prayer had at last been acknowledged.

"I shall speak now," McNamara said. He turned in the direction of the last utterance, knowing precisely whose it was. He faced the lanky, blond Dr Heinz Benz, the Andreas Baader of the Teutons, so tall his legs sprawled several feet out below the deskline, his entire body so sketchy and stick-like that it gave the appearance of a geometrician's teaching accessory, seeming to be capable of up to fifty-seven varieties of angle in any single posture.

"Do students," McNamara enquired, with apparent naïvety, "have academic freedom?"

Benz paused to think for a moment then nodded efficiently. "Yes, of course, zey should have ze academic freedom."

"No," said McNamara politely. "I was not asking for a normative, but rather a constative, answer."

Benz paused again for exactly the same amount of time and once more his head oscillated with the same precision engineering. "Yes, of course, zey should have ze academic freedom."

"I shall try once more, Heinz," McNamara persevered. "Are you expressing a *wish* that they *should* have academic freedom or do you think it a *fact* that they already *do* enjoy this freedom?"

Various algorithms ran rapidly within Benz's software and came up with a query which sounded, because speech has no question marks, like a paradox. "Zey have zis freedom, zey do not?"

McNamara sat back in order to draw his catechism to a close. "They do not. This is a plain matter of statute, both Parliamentary and University. The Parliamentary statute ensures academic freedom for the institution. That is, it guarantees the non-interference of the state in the University's freedom to teach and research on what it chooses. Anyone who knows, to take an example entirely at random, German history of the 'thirties and 'forties, will understand the supreme value of such formalised legal protection. The University statute guarantees a similar freedom to teach and research, even on controversial subjects, without threat to one's employment, as long as one's activity is within the law, *for its academic staff*. But not for its students. No question of academic freedom in the matter of these two arrests, therefore, can possibly arise."

Benz recovered quickly from the brief does-not-compute expression which flickered across his face. "Ah, no, ze usser arrested man, ze one ze student sent ze file to, he was a member of ze staff, so –"

"He was a member of the *administrative* staff," McNamara specified, "not of the *academic* staff. Thus neither of the two arrested men can claim that their academic freedom was breached, because neither of them has academic freedom. It is most important that you understand this, so that you do not go off at a misleading and quite untrue tangent. Now that you do know it, to argue that either of these men has academic freedom would be an act of wilful demagoguery."

A few swift internal sub-routines later, Benz, his CPU evidently a little under strain, mustered the fragile reply, "Zen I zink zat is outrageous. Ze students should have zis freedom."

"It's a matter of established law who has the freedom and who doesn't," said McNamara.

Griselda Rotfang, adopting a pose of ostentatious comradeship, like a Dorothy showing sympathy beside the suddenly dented Tin Man of Heinz Benz, summoned up a dark grimace of uglier-than-usual power. "Zen zis is a wrong law. Zis is an unequal law. I say *fick* and *scheiße* and *verpiss dich* to zis law!"

McNamara sighed deeply. He felt a meltdown coming on.


## Chapter Five

McNamara exited his father's house and turned right into Northgate Road. After a few minutes a road-sweeping vehicle approached on the far side and then suddenly stopped. He could see the driver, though in silhouette only, twisting round and looking deliberately towards him. He walked away, ignoringly.

The scene changed. He was now half a mile further on, striding purposefully past what had been his aunt's house on Wallacewell Road. A lorry was coming towards him. The road-sweeper appeared once more, this time on the wrong side of the road, driving towards the truck. Again it stopped, this time veering so that other vehicle had to brake and mount the pavement. As he drew level with it, McNamara looked into the cabin. There was a much younger man than him in there, with blond punky hair and a nose ring, looking out at him, clearly waiting for him.

The other truck was now suddenly not there at all. Looking through the window, McNamara had a sense of watching TV with the sound down. The younger man was talking to him, addressing questions to him which McNamara lip-read as, "You don't remember me?" and "You've decided to stop and talk at last?"

McNamara went up close to the side of the cabin and shielded his eyes from the sunlight in order to see better. With the window still closed, he asked to whom he was speaking. The young man simply sneered and mouthed, "Look at this." Then he turned his head all the way around. The bottom half of it was shaven clean, with the blond hair shooting out only above the earline. Below this line was a tattoo of a map of a somewhat misshapen England and Wales. There was no Scotland, or, if there were, it was hidden underneath the hair

McNamara pulled open the door, seized the stranger by the back of the collar and dragged him out onto the pavement, demanding to know who he was and what business he had with him. The young man repeated phrases which were still only lip movements with no sound and which, although the words varied, all had the same gist: "Oh, you still don't know..."

Again the scene dissolved and resolved. They were not any longer in the road, but in the dark shell of McNamara's bombed-out bedroom on Petershill Drive, yet another mile further down a familiar route. The heavier McNamara had the stranger pinned against the wall and was threatening him with violence if he did not explain himself. The other offered no resistance at all, seemed limp and acquiescent, and it now occurred to McNamara that maybe this was some kind of trap into which he had been cleverly lured. He had the sense that the young man's hands, which were clasped at the back of McNamara's waist, were moving, manipulating. Then he felt something plunge into the small of his back with a sharp sting. A needle, perhaps. The arms around him suddenly formed into a tighter grip, and McNamara surmised that he was being drugged. He felt himself slipping out of consciousness, and at that moment the stranger began to laugh obscenely, to roll his tongue around his lips, and then he leaned in close, and began to lick McNamara's face...

When McNamara reared up from the bed, Redman's diminutive Jack Russell was toppled back on his haunches and seemed alarmed for a moment, though by some gymnastic miracle he reached the floor on all fours and began energetically to chase his tail. With a start, and just managing to stifle a petrified moan, McNamara saw a slim figure in dark cameo in the frame of the bedroom doorway.

"Only me, Robert," said Redman.

McNamara felt the shock recede, then his heart began to race. "What the fuck, James?"

"You forget?" asked Redman. "I told you we were running in this morning and you agreed to dogsit. You said you'd leave the back door open."

McNamara groaned as he remembered. "Christ, I don't know what smells worse, your dog's breath or your BO."

"Never mind us," Redman replied. "What is the bloody stink *in here*?" He had crossed to the desk by the bed and was now pointing at the smoking paraphernalia strewn atop it – a pouch of light Golden Virginia, a nearly empty packet of Rizlas, a small and not empty baggie, an ashtray. "Jesus, Robert, I thought you handed all the dope you confiscate over to security?"

McNamara rubbed his eyes with his hands and grumbled, "Well, I have a new policy now. I destroy it myself. I burn it."

"Bit of a risk, no?" Redman cautioned.

"What risk? At my age? I'm nearly sixty. You think I need this job anymore? You think I care about any of it?"

"Still, there'd be the embarrassment, no?"

"Fuck embarrassment," McNamara growled. "Christ, it's legal in half of America these days. This country is beginning to feel like it's in its own Prohibition era."

"Eeeeew!" Redman suddenly exclaimed with disgust. "What the fuck is *this*?"

He was pointing at the iPad on the desk.

McNamara sagged and fell back on the pillow and let his eyelids flutter shut. "Did something happen to you in childhood, James? How did you never develop a sense of privacy? So what, I watched some porno and jacked off. It helps me sleep. Don't tell me you don't do that."

"Well, yeah," said Redman, "but I don't shoot my load *all over the screen!*"

"Don't worry, it's waterproof, wipe clean. Tell you what, why not offer it to that maniac pipsqueak hound of yours? He'll probably lap it up."

"Euch!" Redman exploded, and bent down to the dog and ruffled his ears and babytalked him. "Don't you listen to the nasty man! Don't you pay any heed to Professor McNamara! I won't let him poison you with his penis juice!" Then, still crouching, he laughed and said to McNamara, "Good to know your engine still goes, though, I suppose."

McNamara sighed.

"Will you, please," he said with exaggerated tolerance, "fuck off downstairs and make some coffee, and take that neurotic cur with you? When I said I'd leave the door open I was not imagining you would free-roam about my house like a Puritan prosecutor, feeling licensed to pass comment on my drug habits and levels of cock energy! Do you have a search warrant? No, thought not. So bugger off out of my bedroom. I will join you in five minutes once I have washed this sandpaper tongue-scum off my face."

Redman retreated to the kitchen and, in due course, McNamara padded downstairs to join him.

"So check this out," said Redman, pulling an iPad mini from his rucksack. He flipped it open and added jocularly, "You won't mind if we use my iPad rather than yours?"

McNamara reached for his glasses.

"They already have a Facebook group," Redman continued. "Links to newspaper and TV coverage, links to half-baked blogosphere coverage, they've even got a legal fund going this early, there are sweet mini-hagiographies of Yunus and Faraj. Apparently they are 'human rights activists' now. They've been leading a secret political life, it would seem. Faraj has had a little underground political mag going for the past year, apparently, some kind of insipid Chomsky-inspired libertarian left-leaning online thing, to which Yunus is a regular contributor. Needless to say, no mention of the other kinds of contributions Faraj squirts into his Yunus. Innocent and idealistic youngsters in every way, it would appear. The Odium Two, they're being called."

"What?" McNamara was incredulous. "By analogy with the Birmingham Six, say? That's laughable. The two of them haven't even been charged, never mind convicted. But who is 'they'? I mean, who has set up the Facebook groups? Yunus and Faraj are still in detention, it's only three days in, they'll get to speak with no one, so they can't have done it."

"Nominally," said Redman, "it's our very own Ivy Littleot, Students' Union president. She's the official Facebook group owner, at least. She'll be all fired up after her crusade last term, no doubt, except apparently she does not have the favour of the new VC the way she had with Covet, and so this time she's not defending senior management but attacking it. However, my suspicion is that the whole thing is the brainchild of Donald Doyle, probably with Avril Poon's connivance. They can't act formally as the two most senior Union officers because it's not strictly speaking a Union matter and hard to make into one, and they probably don't want to risk losing a vote at a Union general meeting so early, so my guess is that they're turning it into an unofficial campaign instead, looking to build a groundswell of popular support, which they'll then use as a fulcrum to get the Union formally involved. Just look at the press coverage – it's gone international in just three days. I mean, yesterday's *Le Monde*, for godsake? The media to Poon is like dung to a beetle. She's bound to be right at the centre of this."

McNamara held the small screen closer and intoned from the list of news outlets. "BBC, ITN, Channel 4, every broadsheet except the *Telegraph*, the *International Herald Tribune*, the – what? – the *Taipei Times*? Why is it being reported in Taiwan, of all places?"

"Reuters," Redman shrugged. "They syndicated it."

McNamara had clicked on one of the links. "Yes, I see. But this *Le Monde* piece, it's all wrong, it refers to them as 'un professeur et un étudiant'."

"Because that's what Reuters syndicated. When you refer to 'a member of staff' in a university the usual assumption is that you mean an academic. So keep it ambiguous, like that, in your press release, and watch the media make the assumption you hope they will, is my guess as to what they did."

"Christ!" McNamara burst out. "This local group has over a thousand members already! In three days?"

"All they have to do," said McNamara, "is click 'join group'. But what's more important is that it also has over four thousand shares."

"What does that mean?"

"Over four thousand members have posted it on their own Facebook timelines. That takes just two clicks. Remember, this group was set up only yesterday morning. Some of our students have hundreds and even thousands of Facebook friends. The group is going viral. The next thing we'll probably see is that that exponential sharing in itself becomes a media story. The whole trick, which Poon knows well, is to keep new things happening so that coverage can be ongoing."

"Look at all these comments," McNamara said. "They go on forever. Christ, academic freedom! Pffft. It's all rumour and gossip and assertion and exaggerated speculation. It's close to fantasy. These people know nothing at all."

Redman nodded. "But it's a snowball running downhill. Keep liking and sharing and commenting and it soon becomes unignorable. It signifies by its mere ubiquity. It must be true because so many people can't be wrong. McLuhan was a bit premature, but what he said is true now: the medium really is the message."

"Yes, but come on, it's a storm in a teacup. They'll be let out soon. I don't think these two are terrorists, do you?"

"Of course not," Redman agreed. "But if I were the police, I'm not so sure I'd let them go so quickly. For one thing, the police will see it differently from us. They'll want to comb through everything, and they'll want to throw up some mud to make the arrests seem reasonable. I assume that's what the kerfuffle about Yunus's immigration status is all about."

"What is he?" asked McNamara. "Moroccan?"

"Tunisian," said Redman. "So, remember the Tunisian beach attack two years back? Thirty of the thirty-eight murdered were British. There's a big fat flag in Tunisia on their terrorist maps."

"But Faraj is a Brit, right?"

"Yeah, he's an Odium kid, lives with his family in the east end. Apparently the cops have turned their house upside down. I think they'll keep the two of them a little while longer and then they'll release Faraj but hold on to Yunus on an illegal immigration charge."

"Then that should cripple the campaign, no? I mean, illegal immigration, that's peanuts compared to terrorism. You can't build a mass campaign around a single dodgy passport. And remember, this is Odium, hardly a centre of student protest. Stick him on a plane back to Tunis. End of."

"You think?" said Redman. "I'm not so sure. I have a feeling about Faraj. He's an expert needler, he likes to provoke, he's got sharp little chips on both shoulders. He's an attention-seeker. He was virtually asking to be arrested in the corridor the other day. I can't see him walking free and just settling back down into a seat in the University library to tap out the next chapter of his Ph.D., especially if his lover is still in detention. He likes the drama. He's an *activist*. He'll be intoxicated by the minor celebrity. He'll be the poster boy for what he will think of as a mass movement, inside this little goldfish bowl at any rate. Just imagine the next number of his webzine. All this material! And you haven't forgotten, have you, that Trump is coming? This is surely all going to be repackaged and delivered anew during his visit."

McNamara was surprised. "Trump? Coming here? Since when?"

"You didn't see Spooner's press statement on the news on Monday?"

"I don't follow all that shit. I mean, who cares? What's he coming for?"

"I'm putting your slow thinking down to the smokety-smokes you've been having, Robert," Redman replied. "Obviously, he's coming to hand over the cheque, in two weeks. He's apparently coming to Odium right off Airforce One, even before he goes down to Number Ten. It's just possible that Theresa May might have to show up here at the same time in order not to appear slighted. Now just imagine that, a mere three weeks after all this. Trump the pussy-grabbing racist, May the right-wing isolationist, both descending from the skies above Odium at the same time? You bet they are going to keep this campaign rolling and tie it into that."

McNamara shook his head in comic despair. "I see. That will provide a focus for all kinds of high jinks," he agreed.

Redman picked up his iPad and shook it. "If only this were all," he said, putting it in his bag and removing a couple of stapled sheets of paper. "But there are also suddenly very virulent and *engaged* collective emails, in my School anyway, flying in all directions from students whose idea until yesterday of a political novel was something like Ian McEwan's *Saturday*. And then there's this, which I got last evening."

He handed over the pages, and slowly drank his coffee while McNamara perused it.

PRESS RELEASE
22 February 2017

### Odium University Staff and Students Protest Against the Use of the Terrorism Act on Campus and Demand Academic Freedom

Two members of the University of Odium, one a student and one staff, were arrested on Monday, 20 February. Concerned students and staff wish to express concerns about the operation on a number of grounds.

#### 1. Academic freedom

The arrests purport to be in connection with "radical material", which the student did possess, but only for research purposes. Lecturers in his department, as well as academics elsewhere in the University, are deeply perturbed by the ramifications of his arrest for academia and political research. An academic who knows the arrested student well explained that his research focused on contemporary political issues which are highly pertinent to current foreign policy. The criminalisation of research of this nature undermines academic freedom, suggesting serious political constraints on what may be researched at a university.

## 2. Racism and Islamophobia

There is universal agreement that the arrests would not have occurred had the two men been white. The zealous nature of the operation, which caused great distress to the men, was encouraged by their ethnicity and religious backgrounds. Police conduct during the operation, including the targeting of other ethnic minority students for questioning, also suggests institutional racism. When the arrests are looked at in relation to heightened "security" measures, official harassment of Muslims, and widespread withdrawal of civil liberties, a picture of a damaging climate created by terrorism legislation becomes evident.

## 3. Use of Terrorism Act to attack political activists

While questioning members of the University who had not been arrested, the police have been collating information on student activism and peaceful campaigns. They asked many questions about the student peace magazine "Resolution", for which both arrested men write, and about other political student activities. The presence of the police on campus has fomented fear amongst some students. Many see the operation as a warning from the police that they are likely to arrest anyone engaged in peaceful political activities.

## 4. Behaviour of the University

The University's near-complete silence on the matter has upset students and academics. Its one short statement (published on Tuesday, 21 February) constituted nothing more than a request that students, however they react to the arrests, should not "unsettle the peace of the campus". Meanwhile, the University appears to have called the police onto campus in large numbers to ensure that students and academics initiate no organised political action. The University has ignored the fear caused by the large police presence and investigation into legitimate political activities, the concern of staff and students about the criminalisation of research, the racist and Islamophobic nature of the police's conduct, and the signs that the University provided information to the police on its own members, potentially racially profiling its staff and students.

Academics and students throughout the University of Odium, and members of the public from the wider community, are demanding:

215

a.   The right to academic freedom;
b.   An end to the criminalisation of political research;
c.   A stop to police and University racism and Islamophobia and the full enjoyment of civil rights and liberties.

We demand that the University of Odium publicly:

a.   Acknowledges the disturbing nature of the police response, and makes a formal complaint to the police;
b.   Admits the unreserved innocence of the student and staff members arrested;
c.   Apologises for the distress caused to them, their families, and their friends;
d.   Guarantees academic and political freedom;
e.   Commits itself to freedom of speech and freedom of expression on campus.

**[ENDS]**

Notes for editors:

The document above will be published in the form of a petition in the next week, to be signed by professors, lecturers, other University staff, students, and members of the wider community. An ongoing campaign will be organised against the improper use of terrorism legislation, along with lawyers, academics, students, and members of the public.

McNamara removed his spectacles. "I'd call it sub-hysterical. It almost constantly draws attention to its own tendentiousness. It jumps to conclusions like a lemming, wilfully interpreting simple facts in the most paranoid manner conceivable. It uses intemperate motivating adjectives in excess. It's amateur demagoguery of the most obvious kind, a discourse of smoke and mirrors aimed at producing the cheapest polemical effects. 'There is universal agreement that the arrests would not have occurred had the two men been white.' That's just transparent bunk, it's simply made up to incite, it's based on no evidence of general opinion at all. And the entire document deliberately omits to mention the key fact that the 'member of staff' was not an academic in order to disguise the bankruptcy of what it has to say about academic freedom. As for the demands, well, they're beyond preposterous. No one is stopping anyone doing any kind of political research. We can do whatever we damn well want. We can even download ISIS training manuals if we like, we just have to clear it first, obviously, and leave a paper trail of the approval, but that would be a formality. This fool of a student just decided to ignore that elementary procedure. Still, who'd have thought, eh, the University of Odium and politics? Oil and water can mix after all." He tossed the papers on the kitchen table with distaste. "But that! It's written with such political bombast, as if the authors had waited all their lives to pen something in the nature of a radical manifesto, and were gagging on their own narcissism all the while that they did so. Who would you say is responsible?"

Redman smiled wryly. "It's Doyle translated by Poon, for my money. Though it looks as if Gooltree gave them a quote."

"Gooltree!" McNamara's head flapped from side to side again. "The vile cunt used to shoot Muslims dead for a living. I wonder how many he helped to rendition or pack off to Guantanamo."

"Perhaps," Redman ventured, "he experienced a conversion on the road to Damascus."

McNamara laughed wearily. "James, are you laying these things before me the way the Devil offered Jesus all the kingdoms of the world while he was in the wilderness? Because I see no kingdoms of the world here. I do get the sense, however, that you want to *do* something."

Redman regarded him for a moment. "No," he said, "but I am intending to accept Spooner's offer of the Vice Deanship of Arts when we see him tomorrow. And that is going to inveigle me into the Trump scenario."

"You are?" McNamara could hardly disguise his astonishment. "Well, good luck with that."

"You see," Redman explained, "it will frankly give me some say, some power even. I can go on sitting where I am, seeing things from the perspective of a lowly frog, or I can accept the opportunity to help direct things. Why risk letting someone else get that kind of control? We know there are very few who won't bungle it. I also wouldn't mind three years away from teaching, to be candid. But if I am going to accept it, and my reading of the runes is correct, I am going to have to ride a big bucking contradiction. So how all this plays out is something that concerns me vitally."

McNamara nodded. "I understand. I really do."

"And you?" Redman rejoined. "You won't consider the Deanship of

Social Sciences?"

McNamara shook his head.

"So," Redman said, "you won't be coming to the meeting with Spooner tomorrow?"

McNamara seemed to consider gravely for a moment.

"Actually," he said with thought, "I think I shall."


**Chapter Six**

After showering and changing at McNamara's, Redman walked up the hill to the Trump Building. It was only nine-fifteen and the School of English was quiet. He tapped on Lorraine's office door and turned the handle and was surprised to find it locked. He took out his mobile and called hers and heard it ringing inside the office. She answered.

"It's me," he said. "I'm outside in the corridor."

"Oh," she said. "Wait."

A minute later the door was unlocked and she opened it. He could see that her eyes were red with tears.

"Come in," she said, and locked the door again behind him. She stepped towards him, asking for his arms to encircle her. He took her to him and held her warmly.

"What's wrong?" he asked into her ear.

"It's today's *Guardian*," she said. "It's on the table there. It names me as the person who reported on Yunus and even has a picture of me from the University website. It also has a quote from Matthews saying he knew nothing about it. But they didn't call me up for a quote. I got no chance to comment. And now other papers are ringing. *The Daily Mail*, for godsake, though they actually seemed sympathetic. *The Times*. I just said no comment and hung up. And now the hate mail has started arriving. Emails from anonymous addresses, things on Facebook from fake identities, even those two things there, I found them slipped under the door when I arrived. Don't read them, they're vile."

Disobeying her, Redman picked up the two notes, took them in, and blanched. Next he looked at *The Guardian*, already open at the appropriate page. By the time he had finished he was seething with repressed rage.

"When did this thing become such a snot rag?" he said rhetorically. Then, to her: "You should go home. This is just the beginning."

"But Matthews –"

"I'll go and talk to Matthews. But you shouldn't have to put up with this. This is a justifiable reason for absence. In fact, if you're not here, Matthews is likely to feel a greater sense of crisis – no you, no Yunus, he'll start to sense that things are falling apart in the School. So go. Let me have these."

He picked up the hate notes and *The Guardian*.

"Alright," she said. "Will you come over tonight?"

"I'll come over before tonight."

He put his hand behind her head and drew her to him for a short kiss.

She smiled. "I love you."

He kissed her again, longer this time, saying, "And I love you. Now let me go and talk to Matthews and don't be here when I come back."

When he knocked on Matthews' door he did not wait to be invited in, but entered without ceremony.

The top half of Matthews' face was visible above his computer screen, the back of which faced the door.

"Oh, hello, James," Matthews said. "Can it wait?"

"No, I'm afraid not." Redman brandished *The Guardian*. "Have you seen this?"

"Er, no, I don't –"

"Quote: 'Professor Matthews said that Ms Quant had reported the matter to senior management without either his permission or authority.' Unquote."

"Oh," said Matthews. "Good. I'm glad they quoted me correctly. Bothersome business, this."

"Bothersome? It's certainly bothering Lorraine. She's had hate mail, you want to see?"

He put the notes in front of Matthews, who peered at them silently.

"Blimey," said Matthews. "A bit harsh."

"A bit *harsh*? She's got emails and Facebook messages as well. Other newspapers are calling her up. She's had to go home. She's shocked and depressed and feels hurt and threatened."

"Oh, dear God, no!" Matthews expostulated. "She's gone off sick?

I've got to finish this Everyman edition of *England, My England* by the end of the month. Now's not the time."

"Has it occurred to you, Bernard, that you should be defending your staff, not hanging them out to dry?"

"But I don't know what you mean," said Matthews defensively. "I am defending the staff. I'm supporting Yunus. He's in jail, you know."

Redman heard his voice rising in volume. "He's in jail because he had an ISIS training manual on his PC! Lorraine has done nothing questionable at all. She followed procedure!"

"Yes, yes, of course, I know," Matthews said. "I didn't mean I was supporting Yunus *against* her."

"Well, that's what it looks like from this!"

"Really?" said Matthews. "Really? But what I said to them was true, no? And, actually, *actually*, what I'm really doing is trying my best not to get involved."

"How do you expect not to be involved when you are the Head of School in which it happened?"

"Yes, no, but, I mean, you were at the meeting yesterday, right? You saw that most of the staff were sympathetic to Yunus's plight? I know you aren't, but –"

"That's not in fact true," Redman said. "But I don't see why Lorraine should suffer collateral damage for just doing her job. Yunus seems to have put himself in the position he's in."

Matthews placed an agitated hand on his forehead. "There was a lot of collateral damaged at yesterday's staff meeting, James. It ended in a blood bath once you and Donald got at it. That's one reason I think it best not to get further involved."

"But you *have* to do something about *this*, Bernard," Redman insisted. "You can't stand by while your own School administrator is getting anonymous threats and obscenities. Go and see Asterisk."

"The Registrar?" Matthews grimaced. "I tried that yesterday morning. He virtually kicked me out of his office and told me it was nothing to do with me and that I should stay clear of it."

"What he meant was that you should stay clear of the Yunus business. But he'll be sympathetic about *this*."

Matthews pondered for a moment, glancing longingly at the text of D. H. Lawrence's "The Primrose Path" on his monitor. "No, really, it's all too complicated. What would I say to him? What could he do? I don't think he has a lot of time for me."

Redman's nostrils flared. "Alright, *I* will go and see him."

Matthews brightened. "Really? Would you? Well, that would be capital! Anything that might get Lorraine back to work sooner rather than later would be very welcome. And the Registrar speaks highly of you. Must be all that, er, union work you used to do."

Redman turned on his heel, but before he left he looked back at Matthews once more. "For what it's worth, if you get any more media calls, I suggest making no comment."

Matthews' face was already half-hidden behind his screen again, his hands poised above the keyboard. He looked up briefly, nodded agreeably and piped, "Wilco!"

Redman had no problem getting to talk to Asterisk these days, but on this occasion it was particularly easy. Within seconds of his calling the Registrar's secretary, Alison Stilt, he was put through directly. When Asterisk came on the line he was peculiarly warm.

"James," he said. "How opportune that you should call just at this moment. Something's come up on which I would value your thoughts. Can you come over right now, by any chance?"

Within sixty seconds he had crossed the quadrangle and was sitting in front of Asterisk's enormous desk, beside Drusilla Frost, the University's Director of Communications, who seemed a little miffed that he had been asked to join her meeting with Asterisk *in medias res*. They exchanged stiff hellos.

There are four things modern senior university managements look for in a Head of Public Relations: absolute loyalty (to management, that is, rather than to the staff below them or to the institution as a collective entity); unquestioning obedience; a flair for knowingly telling lies without compunction; and a decided photogenicity (because cameras are often involved). Any three of these qualities is sufficient for success in such a role, and only mendacity, strictly speaking, is unnegotiable. But woe betide the PR man or woman whose stock falls to possession of merely two of these characteristics: he or she is at that point on his or her way out.

Drusilla Frost had occupied her position for a very long time because, uniquely, for most of her incumbency under Covet, she had possessed all four. Now in her late forties, however, her looks were beginning to slide, and she had taken to disguising their deterioration with increasingly fetching forms of dress and coiffure. Today she was wearing a chastely seductive cashmere twin set and slacks, and her dark black hair was gathered at the back in an immaculate chignon designed to reveal hooped gold earrings. Upon Covet's death and throughout the several weeks of media fire-fighting which had ensued, Drusilla had become accustomed to operating without the usual checks on her from above. She now felt that she ran pretty much her own show, indeed on some days the entire show, and in this period of temporary independence her capacity for permanent obedience to her superiors had declined even more sharply than her erstwhile beauty. Asterisk had of necessity seen a lot of her in these three months, felt indebted to her for helping him hold the baby, and had become a little bewitched by the delicate and arousing scent of Chanel which surrounded her like a magnetic field, as well as the deep Anne Bancroft voice and her svelte, still gracious figure. Redman, by contrast, held her in a contempt which, over the years, had been more than reciprocated.

"James," Asterisk began, "I don't know if you are aware, but there was a press release yesterday –"

"Oh yes," said Redman. "I've read it." He held up the copy of *The Guardian*, which he had brought with him. "Lots of it is in here, word for word, this morning."

"Oh!" said Drusilla with dismay. "You've seen that."

"Yes," said Redman. "And of course, the members of staff named in it are now being called by the rest of the media. In fact, Nigel, that's what I wished to talk to you about."

"I see," said Asterisk, with a forced smile. "I should have guessed that I had no need to get you up to speed. It happened, after all, in your School."

"Yes," said Redman. "I even witnessed the first arrest with my own eyes, as did half of my School colleagues."

"Do you," Asterisk ventured, "have a view on the, er, affair so far?"

"Yes," Redman said. "I think the arrests were perfectly under-standable, and I wish to save my colleagues from being crucified in public for their association with them – especially the School administrator, Lorraine Quant, who reported the matter to you in the first place, as it was her duty to do, and is now receiving hate mail as a result of her good judgment, and thanks to *The Guardian* naming her, of course. She's just had to go home because of the shock and worry it has caused her."

Asterisk tutted and shook his head in sympathy. Then he looked at Drusilla. "You see? I did say we could rely on good sense and balance in some quarters."

Drusilla nodded and turned to Redman with a practised smile that suggested she was turning down the level of refrigeration she usually maintained in his presence.

"James," she said, her vocal chords suddenly producing the deep tones of cordiality she turned on only in moments when she recognised a potential ally, "this press release, do you have any idea of its source? It bears no contact information."

Redman was slightly on his guard, not least because he felt himself once more too close to a natural enemy for comfort.

"Not really," he answered, "though the 'academic who is familiar with the arrested student' is almost certainly his supervisor, Brad Gooltree. As you might expect, the arrests were discussed at length in the staff meetings yesterday of the two Schools involved. So I'd guess that the authors originate in one or both of those Schools. It's a document designed to recruit others to a cause, obviously, and by turning its demands into a petition it's essentially sounding a clarion call for an ongoing campaign around some very controversial terms which are like chimes of doom to all non-thinking liberals: Islamophobia, academic freedom and, dare I say, though he's not been mentioned yet, Donald Trump? No responsible newspaper should have reproduced it without any indication of source, but after last term Odium is a sitting duck it's deemed fair to fire at outside the normal rules of engagement. I'd say you can expect a lot more, and a lot worse."

Drusilla moved her head up and down, seemingly appreciative of the warning. "The press release says nothing about the School administrator or the Schools involved, yet the author of this *Guardian* article obviously got that information in addition somehow."

"Well," said Redman, "the release would have been sent with a covering email which possibly offered more information and probably a contact number for comment also. It's a hand-in-glove deal. The article says nothing about the source of the information because the reporter is hoping for more fuel for the fire later."

"So," said Drusilla, "if we looked at emails sent out from both of those Schools yesterday..."

Redman waved his hand in negation and disapproval. "No. Forgive me, but I think you are going along entirely the wrong track if what you are seeking to do is stifle this story at source, not least because a freedom-of-speech flag has now been stuck in it. Imagine what prying into people's emails will do to enflame that issue. In any case, it was probably sent from a private email address, not a University one. The story is out there now, for better or worse. It's now about managing it, keeping it in proportion."

Drusilla seemed a little piqued at Redman's dismissal of her suggestion, but Asterisk stepped in to rescue her.

"As you can tell, James, this has taken us a little unawares," he said. "We did not expect quite such a sudden and public overreaction and it's the last thing we want, of course, having just recovered from, er, what happened last term. Now these demands, which are going to be petitioned for, well, they are inflammatory and unreal and hopelessly undeliverable. We took the decision that we had to call the police, and the police are usually cooperative with us, but as soon as they arrived we lost all the influence over them that we seem to have over more minor matters. Terrorism, or suspected terrorism, seems to fling them into a different set of frenzied routines, and an entirely different set of people seem to have got involved – CID, Special Branch, not PC Plod and Sergeant Smith. All the police currently on campus are not here questioning people because we want them to be. They've just swarmed here of their own accord. We couldn't stop them if we tried."

"I know," said Redman. "I saw that during the first arrest. They paid no heed to Elfyn at all, even when he was just trying to talk to them."

Drusilla seemed to have recovered from her momentary annoyance. She perked up.

"So," she said, "and correct me if I am wrong, James, you seem to be agreeing with us that it would be good if we could find a way to take the wind out of this campaign's sails?"

"Well, of course," Redman answered, "but not by trying to identify and silence its orchestrators. They would simply use such a move as evidence of the very censoriousness the campaign is opposing."

"What if there were another way?"

"Like what?"

"Well," she said, "we have a video."

"Ah," said Redman, "you mean the video of Yunus giving oral sex to Faraj?"

Drusilla was genuinely startled.

"How do you know it's Faraj?" she demanded.

"Believe me," said Redman, "it's Faraj."

"Wow!" exclaimed Drusilla. "Even better!"

Redman narrowed his eyes at her in disbelief. "You can't be serious, Drusilla. You can't be suggesting going public with that video."

"Well, not directly, not ourselves," she explained. "More of having it 'leaked' and then having to react to it when prompted."

"But Drusilla," Redman protested, "that's a private matter between two consenting adults. It's not fair game."

"Huh!" Drusilla jerked her head back dismissively. "It wasn't very private, was it? It was stored on a University hard drive and, if I'm not mistaken, the Odium logos in the background and the office furniture rather conclusively prove that it was filmed in his own office in your School. I even went in there and checked the layout and the angles and everything. Now there's an instant sacking offence if ever I came across one."

"No, no," Redman persisted. "It's beyond all decency, Drusilla."

"Yes!" she agreed. "It *is* beyond all decency! And I imagine its revelation will create a massive withdrawal of sympathy for both of them. Don't you? Two gay Muslims, *in flagrante*? It's dynamite!"

"Please!" Redman turned to Asterisk. "Do not do this to him. It would destroy Yunus, maybe Faraj too. Think of their families, their friends."

"The thing is," Asterisk explained, "we have to sack him, and we have to sack him today. The police are absolutely categorical that the last stamp in his passport is faked. They told us this morning, and with that knowledge and no countervailing evidence, we can't continue to employ him beyond today. If we sack him because he is illegal, it looks bad for us. He's been with us almost a year and we failed to do due diligence. But if we sack him for gross misconduct –"

"But don't you see?" Redman pleaded. "The campaign will then be about homophobia as well as Islamophobia. You'll have the gays rights lobby down on you as well – as it were. How bad do you want this to get?"

"Bottom line," said Drusilla, "we want this campaign strangled at birth, or at least before Trump comes."

"That's never going to happen, Drusilla," Redman countered. "It's possible that Yunus and Faraj might not even be released before Trump comes, and the longer the police hold them, the more this campaign will build and build. Even if they are released, the campaign will then rally around them in person, making them into symbols for this soft-in-the-head 'humane' liberal consensus that the students and a lot of the staff mistake for real politics. There'll be a lot of carnival and drama because, basically, there are teenagers involved, middle-aged ones as well as actual ones. You can't extinguish this overnight. All you can do is counter it over time."

Drusilla shook her head. "I say we go for the jugular. It's the quickest way. It's efficient and direct, even if there is a lot of blood. Bang bang, they're dead."

Redman suddenly had a brainwave. He looked to Asterisk.

"Have you run this idea past the VC yet?"

"Not yet. Of course, I intend to."

"Have you given thought to how he might react to it? I mean, of how he might feel *personally* about a proposal to out and shame two gay men in this way?"

Asterisk looked instantly uneasy.

Redman rubbed the point home. "It might not be a good idea even to suggest it to him."

Asterisk sat back and thought new thoughts. "Actually, Drusilla, I think James may have a good point."

Drusilla sighed impatiently. "Then what? What's the immediate next step?" she implored.

"I suggest," Redman continued, "that if you have to sack him, you sack him on the immigration issue and simply take that on the chin. I don't have too much sympathy for him on the job front, to be sure. He was apparently pretty useless. This way it appears to be no more than incompetence on your part, a failure to check one person's paperwork in a large organisation with thousands of staff, but it's clearly deliberate deception on his. The police will get all the opprobrium for pursuing the immigration issue like the petty bureaucrats they are, not you: you can honestly say that your hands were tied. Quite what happens to Yunus after that I don't know, and honestly I don't think we should care. He might be deported pretty swiftly and then you won't have him to deal

226

with any longer. As to the campaign, you undermine it, but you won't be successful if all you deploy are officious managerial statements that are simply pious and don't engage with people's concerns. For a start, you can point to the hate speech that is being directed at your own members of staff and you can rally directly to their defence. These people are victimised individuals. Here are two examples, put under Lorraine Quant's door just this morning. These are the originals."

He passed the two notes to Asterisk, and went on.

"Then you get non-aligned members of staff, not the usual obvious stooges or yes-men, to make a public statement defending the University from the charges this press release and petition make. You *do not* – no offence, Drusilla – turn this into a routine, mechanical PR exercise. You have to form an opposition which can rally around your ideas and your discourse, not quite the way the other side are going to create events and spectacles for the media circus, but you have to get beyond simply issuing press statements *ex cathedra* and thinking they will have any effect. Don't expect to win. You'll take a big hit, you'll be defeated in the eyes of *Guardian*-reading liberal public opinion. But you can foil them, you can point to the excesses they will indulge in and the stupidities they will utter. But to do so, you have to engage, you have to abandon the cynical Olympian aloofness which is your default mode in these situations, you have to show that you are standing up for a set of positive values that it may be harder to have petitions and letter-writing campaigns about, that are less glamorous but actually more vital. You have to be prepared to articulate a positive idea of a university that isn't just the usual verbal slick and gloss. As far as I can tell, an approach like that should chime with the VC, no?"

Asterisk was looking more positive. "I do like the sound of this. But, you know, it's easier said than done, for us. To be blunt, James, with a few exceptions like yourself, well, and I'm sure Drusilla wouldn't even contradict me when I say it, the stooges and the yes-men are the ones we tend to deal with."

There was a silence. Redman stared at Asterisk with some accusation in the look.

"Nigel," he said, with the determined air of someone calling in a promise, "you and I had a meeting last November after Covet's death, and you told me things were going to be different. You told me you wanted to run this place with a renewed sense of decency."

Asterisk looked rather sheepish at this reminder being voiced in front of Drusilla, who did well to conceal any outward reaction. Nonetheless, he replied, "That's true. I did. And I do. It's just that, if we are to follow your advice on this issue, we could do with your knowledge of how things work on the ground here, which, there's no point pretending otherwise, is better than ours."

Redman held Asterisk's eye for a moment, until he was satisfied as to his good faith.

"Alright," he replied.


**Chapter Seven**

McNamara had not told Redman the entire truth about the contents of the last envelope he had received from Cannon Buckrack. He had deduced that it must be from Buckrack because it contained the invoices which proved that the three "Odiumgate" microdevices had been purchased on Asterisk's budget. Buckrack, he knew, had entered Asterisk's office to remove these invoices, though the assumption that he and Redman had made was that Buckrack had done so with a view to covering up their existence, whereas it now seemed that the American's intention had been, on the contrary, precisely to reveal it. But inside the package was also a copy of Jane Blake's Public Interest Disclosure. When Redman gave him this document a few days later, having received it from Asterisk, McNamara had deliberately feigned ignorance of it. Yet he had read and re-read it many times already, with near-total bafflement at the account it gave of her relations with him, which did not correspond to his perceptions in the slightest and seemed completely made up. And there was yet a third item in the package whose receipt he had hidden from everyone. It was a small black thumb drive which contained only one file – a video file.

When McNamara read Jane's document on that November Saturday morning, he had no idea that Jane and Covet were at that very moment beginning to decompose simultaneously in Covet's country cottage. He presumed that it had been sent, like the previous documents, as a revelation, a means by which Buckrack could blow the gaff on Covet as he had done before, by using McNamara as his conduit.

The video of Covet and Jane having sex in the hotel – which McNamara had watched, of course, open-mouthed and astonished – seemed to have been enclosed as verification that her Public Interest Disclosure was indeed truthful, and McNamara imagined that Jane had somehow contrived to make the video with a view to securing such proof. It was absolutely clear from the film itself that she had positioned the camera deliberately, that she was playing to it, and that Covet was not aware of its presence.

He found himself in a mental paralysis for several hours because, while he knew how Buckrack had come into possession of all the documents, he could think of no satisfactory explanation for how he had also acquired the video, unless he had somehow stolen it from her, which would be an act consistent with the little that McNamara already knew of Buckrack's behaviour. But if Buckrack had done so, did Jane know? Yet how could Buckrack be connected to her in so personal a way that he could have done such a thing? Buckrack's intentions now seemed clear enough: while acting as if he were an agent of Covet's, he had in fact been surreptitiously aiming to expose Covet's wrongdoing all along, although why he would wish to do so was a mystery. The delivery of the video to McNamara was presumably to be explained as the passing on of ultimate evidence of the Vice Chancellor's misdeeds for McNamara to use in order to destroy him. Beyond that knowledge, however, he knew nothing at all about Buckrack, who was a mere phantom without solid substance in McNamara's mind, a faceless, insubstantial ghost who had merely pushed incriminating documents his way. But this – this video – was an obscenity, and a divulgence too far. Any person who shared it would become enravelled in its salacious repugnance, and McNamara had virtually discounted the idea of telling anyone about it the moment he saw it. He was by nature a bottler-up rather than a pourer-forth.

Jane Blake may have been no saint, indeed it appeared she was more the opposite of a saint than McNamara had ever envisioned, and yet he had known her, he had spent time with her, he had had everyday conversations with her, and he had found her inoffensive, even sweet, and certainly seeming-chaste in her behaviour towards him, at least. Although Covet had increasingly appeared like the Devil come to earth in human form – an impression which her document and the video redoubled in force – he felt intuitively that using the film to expose

Covet would be to wrong her most cruelly, unless it were perversely her wish.

In the evening, after much thought, he decided to try to find out. He called her mobile number.

To his confusion, the call was answered up by a gravelly male English voice.

"Hello," McNamara said. "Could I talk to Jane?"

"May I ask to whom I am speaking?" replied the man, over-formal.

"It's Professor McNamara. Could you pass her to me, please?"

"That would be Jane Blake you're after, sir?"

"That's right," said McNamara, becoming slightly puzzled at the officiousness of the responses at the other end.

"Could you hold just a moment, sir?"

There was the muffled sound of a hand being placed over the mouthpiece and then a different man's voice came on the line.

"Hello, sir, this is Detective Superintendent Nesbit of the Buckinghamshire CID. Can I ask how you know Ms Blake?"

"CID?" McNamara was taken aback. "Is she in some kind of trouble? Why do you have her phone?"

"Well, sir, the most I can say at the moment is that she is part of an enquiry. You know the young woman, sir? You say your name is, er, McNamara?"

"Professor Robert McNamara." He was then asked to spell his name. "Yes, she's a postgraduate student at the University of Odium, where I work. She lives in a student residence I am responsible for. She's a Hall Tutor, which means she helps look after the undergraduates."

"Well, yes, that certainly tallies with the documentation we have. So you are her employer?"

"Not exactly," McNamara replied. "But sort of."

"And you were calling her why?"

McNamara improvised. "I just needed to speak to her about some business in the Hall," he said.

"I see, sir. Well, I am glad you called, because we have been trying to get hold of someone at the University who might help us but, it being a Saturday, we are not having much luck. We were really hoping to speak with a person who knows her."

"Well, I do know her, naturally."

"Then, sir, if it wouldn't be asking too much, is it at all possible that you could come down here now, I mean to Buckinghamshire? I cannot stress how urgent it is. It's a couple of hours' drive, but I can have a car sent to pick you up immediately. And they shall of course return you afterwards."

McNamara went. An hour later he was sweeping past Northampton and then Milton Keynes in a police car with two Odium police constables who knew nothing of the purpose of their drive and could not enlighten him. He was not even certain which Buckinghamshire town they arrived at, and failed to ask, so bewildered was he by the turn of events. He was delivered to the underground car park of a large grey police station, where the Detective Superintendent was waiting to meet him.

Nesbit was a polite man, circumspect, but routine, obviously experienced in dealings of this kind.

"To be honest with you, Professor McNamara, it's really no more than positive identification we require at the moment. We have two bodies here in our morgue, a middle-aged man and a young woman. We are pretty sure who the man is on account of the property at which the bodies were found, though if you can help us with either or both I would be grateful."

"You want me to identify dead bodies?" McNamara repeated, stunned into disbelief.

"Yes, sir, if you wouldn't mind? We need to try and resolve this matter quickly so that we can inform relatives. Could you come with me? The morgue is on this level, and I'll try not to keep you long. I do warn you, it may not be pleasant."

He was led to the cold mortuary, where an attendant un-ceremoniously slid Jane Blake's dead body out of a deep-freeze compartment. McNamara gazed upon her ashen-white face, which seemed like a poor half-finished waxwork facsimile of her, eyes closed, dark discoloured blood staining her neck and clotted in her long brown hair, as well as in what he could see of her clothes around the shoulders. The sight rendered him speechless for several moments. His bowels rumbled.

"Is this Jane Blake, sir?" Nesbit asked after a respectful pause.

"Yes," McNamara blurted out weakly.

Nesbit made to have the body put away again almost immediately.

"The man, sir, as I say, we are fairly confident of his identity, but I

231

wonder...?"

McNamara was beset by waves of adrenalin and shock. His legs felt weak. He managed to stutter, "Yes, yes, of course."

Covet's body, though bloodless, was even more disquietingly ghastly. The features were twisted in a caricature of pain, all asymmetrical, and there was a violent brown welt around his neck.

"Evan Covet?" Nesbit asked expectantly.

"Sir Evan Covet," McNamara replied. "He's the Vice Chancellor of the University."

"Oh, *Sir* Evan Covet?" Nesbit repeated. "I see. That's useful. Did you know him well?"

McNamara shook his head.

"And the young woman?" Nesbit went on. "When did you last see her?"

McNamara tried to cast his mind back. "Come to think of it, not for a while. Maybe two weeks? I can't be absolutely sure."

"That's alright," said Nesbit gently. "It's usually a bit of a shock, this kind of thing. We can always speak later. Tell me, did she ever give you any indication that she was in a relationship with this man, with, er, *Sir Evan*?"

McNamara shook his head, aware that his denial was technically true but that it concealed a great deal of knowledge that he had recently acquired.

"Was she?" he asked disingenuously.

Nesbit seemed indecisive about how much he should divulge, but finally confirmed, "It looks that way from evidence at the scene. It's a bit early in the proceedings and we're still piecing things together, but it appears, most likely, to be a crime of passion."

McNamara gestured with both hands in the direction of both bodies. "What happened?"

Nesbit's mouth twisted to the side as if he had already said too much. "There's not a lot I can say at this stage. It's an ongoing investigation."

"But," said McNamara, "all the blood?"

"Oh, the lady?" Nesbit tapped his solar plexus. "Single knife wound. And the, er, gentleman, well, as you probably could see, it looks like asphyxiation by hanging. Not an unusual combination when there are two bodies involved."

"Not unusual?" McNamara echoed incredulously. "Not unusual, you say?"

Nesbit smiled, but kept the smile small, decently contained. "Not unusual in my line of business, I meant, sir. Obviously a bit of a jolt for a civilian like yourself. Where there's a double death like this, it's often murder followed by a suicide."

"You're saying," murmured McNamara, his shock deepening still further, "that he *stabbed* her, then *hanged* himself?" He felt close to stupefaction now, hardly able to think straight at all. His upset evidently showed, because Nesbit put a steadying hand on his elbow.

"No, Professor McNamara, not for sure, it's more me just thinking aloud. There are further forensics for us to do, and there will have to be post-mortems. We'll know more then. But it's hardly the first time I have seen something like this."

"I don't understand," McNamara said. "Why here? Buckinghamshire?"

"The deceased gentleman owned a property nearby," said Nesbit. "That's where we found them."

It did not take much longer. McNamara was surprised how few questions the Detective Superintendent wanted to ask, but in fact Nesbit seemed more concerned to let him go, and expressed his gratitude sincerely more than once.

"Oh," said McNamara on the way out, remembering something through his turbulence of feeling and perplexity of mind. "It just occurred to me to say, I also saw him personally, Sir Evan, and more recently, a week or so ago. No, a little more than a week. It was very unusual. He called me early in the morning and asked me to drive out to his home near Odium. He wanted to speak with me about *her*, about Jane. He told me she had lodged some kind of formal complaint with the University. He wasn't clear, but he seemed to want my advice."

"A written complaint, sir? Do you know what it was about?"

"He said it was about sexual harassment, but he was rather vague on the details. These things are usually treated very confidentially. He wanted to know about her state of mind. I told him she seemed normal to me, although I found it very strange that he was involving himself in the matter. Then later that day, or perhaps it as the day after, it was made public that he had been suspended from work. You should contact the University Registrar. He will know more. His name is Dr Nigel Asterisk."

"That's very useful to know," said Nesbit, writing the name down.

"He can also help you with her contact details. She's American, by the way."

"Yes," Nesbit replied, "we have her passport."

"Can you," McNamara asked tentatively, "keep my name out of it? Dr Asterisk and I do not, how can I put it, get on. I'd rather not have to account to him. This is going to cause chaos, and I'd prefer not be dragged into it."

Nesbit considered this request for a moment and replied evenly, "Of course, sir. I see no reason why not. You've been extremely helpful to us."

The detective then accompanied him to the waiting police car. He asked McNamara to say nothing to anyone about the matter until a firmer conclusion had been reached, and expressed his thanks yet once more. Then, as a parting word, and with some genuine pathos, he added, "She was only twenty-three. She seemed a fine-looking girl. In life, I mean. Not so much in death."

Those were the last words Nesbit exchanged with him. The policeman never, in fact, called on him again.

On the journey back to Odium, McNamara found himself sliding into a deep depression for which he could not find a word. It was not grief, nor was it loss, but a profound sorrow at life wasted, of vitality despoiled, of a promising future annihilated. He was touched to the quick by the snuffing out of Jane's being, and by the time he reached home his resolve to say nothing to anyone about the video or her Disclosure had become an inflexible determination. He weirdly felt that he owed it to her that her name and her memory be no more damaged than they already were. She had already suffered the most extreme penalty possible for the follies she had committed. What point would there be in besmirching her further?

He locked and chained his doors, drank half a bottle of scotch, and went to bed.

It was that night that his bad dreams began.

He found himself in the Senior Common Room of Coolwipe Hall with Jane Blake sitting across from him, as she had been on the last evening he had seen her alive. He was appraising her sexually, she knew it, she was encouraging it, and he was liking it. She stood up, crossed the room to him with a few elegant steps, and got down on her knees before his half-reposing form.

Imperiously, in exactly the mode in which Covet had preferred to speak to her in the video, he began to order her to please him according to his whim.

"Bare your breasts," he said confidently.

Slowly, smiling like a votary, she undid the buttons of her shirt one-by-one, then parted the silky fabric to allow him to admire her dark, stiff nipples.

"Jiggle my junk," he ordered.

She compliantly unzipped him and eased his balls and cock out into view. She took his member in her right hand and gently stroked it, watching it grow with an admiration bordering on devotion.

"Tongue my titan," he commanded arrogantly.

She giggled and kissed his scrotum, allowing his enlarged bratwurst to rest on her face, where it balanced on her nose and was sandwiched between her eyes. Then she put out her tongue and allowed it to travel the length of his now stiffened meat stick, a manoeuvre she repeated several times for his delectation.

"Suck that sausage," he encouraged arrogantly.

As if he were granting her a great privilege, she bent forward a little and wrapped her lips around his swollen thundersword, stroking it moistly as she slid her lips back and forth along it. McNamara closed his eyes and put his hands behind his head in supreme delight, allowing the pleasure to course through his veins.

"That's it," he whispered. "Blow me!"

All at once she stopped, and withdrew his majesty from her mouth. He opened his eyes to look at her with the scornful disapproval of a short-changed customer. She was still hovering close to his exposed elephant. However, she appeared no longer as the perfectly primed sex bomb of the video. Without warning, the face on her slackening body had become that of the grotesque, cinereous, ugly heap on the mortuary slab, except that its eyes moved and its other features twitched, zombie-like.

Horror began to well up within him. Her expression was becoming more sour and minatory by the second.

With an inspiration whose origin he could not fathom, McNamara found himself now commanding, "Blow that babymaker!"

Jane's face quickly re-assumed, film-special-effects-like, its living lineaments. Vital colours rapidly resurged into her flesh. She began to smile flirtatiously once more, and leaned forward again to take his chopper in her chops.

"Fellate my phallus," he essayed.

She fellated.

"Flange that fleshtower!" he exclaimed, with renewed self-possession.

She flanged.

"Feast on my fuckmutton!" he cried triumphantly.

She feasted.

Intransitive verbs were apparently accepted coinage in this exchange, he concluded. Would it work, he wondered, if he cheated on the alliteration?

"Shmoke my shaft," he gambled experimentally.

She halted forthwith. He was looking at the brown crown of her stilled head and could already see the hair fading and becoming desiccated. He could feel in her lip-grip a new unwillingness which suggested that a second erection-chilling interruption was about to occur.

"Quaff from my quiverbone!" he ordered anew.

She readily resumed, with clear intent to quaff.

"Siphon that soldier!"

He started to sense the slow, satisfying semblance of incipient siphoning.

"Drain that drillhammer!" he bellowed in ecstasy.

As he ejaculated he heard the brassy booming of Wagner's "Ride of the Valkyries" surging from the distance, but this turned out to be no more than a deformation of his mobile ringtone, which eventually bounced him into consciousness.

It was Redman, telling him about the death of Covet being reported in the Sunday papers. McNamara held a brief discussion with him on the phone, during which he felt the warm wetness between his stomach and the sheets turn cold. Redman came round an hour later and the crapulent McNamara, with his head pounding, held another fitful, disjointed conversation with him. McNamara dissembled lack of interest. He likewise said nothing about his visit to Buckinghamshire the previous evening, partly in observance of Nesbit's injunction, but also because it was strongly associated in his hungover brain with the disturbance he felt at the dream he had just had. He gave Redman the invoices and they agreed how Redman would deal with Asterisk in respect of them. Redman left, and they did not see each other until several nights later.

During those several nights, McNamara kept the dead Jane alive in his dreams with the embalming fluid she extracted from his sappy cucumber in obedience to his very deliberately worded imperatives. In wildly mixed-metaphorical wet dreams, his nocturnal self plumbed the nether regions of the alliterative lexicon of love, while the drip-fed Jane Blake duly plumbed his nether regions. She tickled his tallywhacker, massaged his microphone, and frotted his firehose. When she had finished kindling his candle by rubbing his roger, she devoured his dragon, hoovered his heatseeker, and would even (phonetics regularly trumping orthography) keenly nosh on his knob yet capriciously decline to guzzle on his gigi. She fed at his fudgehole and, bungholing his banger, proceeded to poopchute his piston. Thereafter, she needed little persuasion to cockholster his cumgun or leather his longfellow, with the consequence that his joystick was inevitably jizzcreeked. The pampered Professor awoke each morning with a bishop like a badly bent boomerang.

He called in sick and spent the days alone. Rachel Brace, Asterisk's ex-secretary, the living woman of his own age with whom he had been falling in love a mere week or two before, called several times, but he put her off. He would go through these days feeling fits of crestfallen self-reproach at the Covetousness which had arisen within him, which mounted at times to the delusion that somehow Sir Evan's damaged soul had at death transmigrated into him, forcing his own out like an invading cuckoo. But as darkness approached he became more like a vampire in a coffin, looking forward leeringly to the orgy of the senses with Jane which each new witching hour promised.

Then one night, the night he next saw Redman, he could not get to sleep. Redman brought news from the outside, from a world that seemed to McNamara to have retreated to the horizon, news such as Redman having convinced Asterisk that Jane Blake's Disclosure could not be made public as it would most likely give rise to lawsuits from Sergei Krokoff and Avril Poon, and that such further scandals would destroy the modest opportunity there now was for Odium to rebuild after the shattering earthquake it had suffered. When Redman passed

237

him a copy of the Disclosure he already possessed, conscience awoke, and McNamara finally told him, swearing him to secrecy, about his trip to the morgue the previous weekend, and blamed that for his obviously poor state of mind and morale. Redman was touchingly sympathetic and promised to help keep the world yet longer at bay. He would, for example, have a discreet word with Rachel. He would tell Asterisk to call Frank Dashwood and let him know that McNamara would not be reporting for work for a few weeks. Asterisk seemed eager to comply, these days, with any recommendation Redman had to make.

When Redman departed, McNamara felt for a while that what he had said to the younger man might be true, and that all he might need in order to recover was the time and the relief that Redman would secure. He had suffered a trauma. Surely the dreamer was not morally responsible for the content of his dreams, however ignoble they were? Yet he was sensitive to his own deceit. He knew that his waking self had been altered too, indeed even now he was savouring the hypnotic feeling of libidinal corruption at the thought that, in only an hour or two, he might once more get to enjoy all kinds of cock-roguery with the succubus Jane.

Yet Jane would not come because sleep would not come, which meant that McNamara could not come. He tossed and turned for close to two hours, before a solution presented itself which was suitably unscrupulous. He pulled open a bedside drawer in which he had thrown a small baggie of marijuana he had confiscated from a student in Coolwipe Hall earlier that evening. He would normally have called Security and passed it to them, but his current hermit-like instincts had governed his choice, and he had decided to procrastinate. There was a generous amount of ganja in the baggie. A preliminary tryst with Mary Jane, he reflected wryly, might ease him in his passage to the faerie Jane.

He had to dress and make a trip to a local garage for tobacco and rolling papers. Back in his bedroom, he constructed a classic elongated doobie which, although double-wrapped, seemed to him makeshift and crooked, exhibiting none of the conical perfection routinely achieved in the past by his younger, nimbler fingers. Nonetheless, it burned well, and after a few hot inhalations he felt the old, light, paradisal excitement start gently to suffuse his limbs and permeate his brain. A few drags later, his found himself gently stroking the head of his little brother and smiling, not simply to himself, but beaming idiotically at the empty darkened room. By the end of the joint he had coaxed the Little Boy into being a Fat Man, standing up straight with the aid of the iPad, the dead Jane and the dead Covet, and disregard of the moral questions raised by virtual necrophilia. For much of the video Covet's face was not in shot, so it was not altogether impossible for McNamara to imagine himself in the then-enviable position of the then-VC, especially if he turned down the audio.

McNamara took his time. Two or three gigglesticks later, something occurred which he did not recall from his youth. As a teenager he had found the experience of spliffing largely valuable from a cerebral point of view, delightfully disarranging his thoughts and modes of thinking. But now it seemed more physical, in that it made him all arousal and goose-flesh and nipple-stiffened and irresistibly libidinal, to which a larger-than-usual, and indescribably intenser-than-usual jizzplosion eventually testified. It was an emission on a mission. And its objective was to splash itself onto the two-dimensional naked form of Jane Blake, conveniently miniaturised on the screen he held before his standing-to-attention lap-soldier. It was accompanied by his genuinely involuntary cry of surprised bliss brought on by its unmistakably elongated rapture. Drained of all energy in a moment, McNamara was barely able to discard the iPad on the bedside desk before collapsing back onto his pillows in a fuggy warm glow, which carried him, gently but euphorically, towards a deep and uninterrupted night-long sleep.

Superior orgasms followed by truly restorative and unbroken rest? What man in his sixtieth year would not embrace the medicinal plant which offered both, especially one following immediately upon the other? Within a week McNamara had doubled his on-hand supply of weed, courtesy of some rigorous sniffing-out of offenders in the Hall. At some point in the next month, a little despondent at the predictable downturn in sensation caused by his regular nightly toking and stroking, he discovered and purchased from Amazon a revolutionary masturbation gadget, made in Japan and called the Tenga Fliphole, a marvel of engineering which reproduced in latex the design of the human vagina (encased in a sturdy plastic-hand-holdable and warm-water-washable housing) and provided a leak-proof container for his testicular outpourings, as well as making McNamara newly grateful that he lived in the twenty-first century.

He soon grew tired of the repetitiveness of Jane's video as sole stimulus. But it did not take him long to find a porn actress, among the cast of thousands freely on offer, who approximated to Jane's looks and body morphology, if anything even improved upon them, and who flaunted herself in better light, was captured with much more varied camera work, and whose cinematic *oeuvre* was so plentiful it seemed, for his practical purposes, unending.

Nights passed in the company of the Jane surrogate, the lubricated Fliphole, his lop-sided joints and his straightened and pampered member, just as each day passed in anticipation of their all getting together again to party very soon. He had not reckoned, however, with the Christmas recess. By the middle of December the student body melted away, the Hall emptied, and there was an instantaneous famine of dope. McNamara soon ran out and spent a disconsolate, depressed, sleep-deprived night whose flattening, enervating effects he had almost forgotten. Chastened and craving, he idled for an entire morning, wondering how he was to cope for the whole of Christmas and New Year like this, when a fix for both his compromised sexual and psychotropic habits prompted itself salvationally from the depths of his inner travel agent.

Amsterdam was colder than Odium, but McNamara made things more comfortable for himself by not mucking about with budget options. He took a deluxe room for two weeks in the Grand Hotel Krasnapolsky, right on Dam Square. Cannabis cafés and weed-retailing establishments are a few hundred metres away, some of them with microscopes through which you can eye before you buy. Much the same is true of the red-light district, which is even closer: the girls stand in lingerie behind glass doors, in full view of the human traffic perambulating past on the canal sides. McNamara was excited to discover that there was an entire terrace of Hispanic harlotry, and when he had located a girl who approximated once more to the phenomenology of Jane Blake, he responded to her moues and shaken cleavage by opening the door and engaging her in conversation.

She said she was from Puerto Rico and that her name was Conchita Dentada. She was undeniably toothsome. She did not at first wish to leave her cramped cubicle, which he presumed was where she exercised most control over unpredictable customers. But it was a mere matter of money to persuade her. Once she saw his resplendent room and the thickness of his wallet, she had no trouble staying the night in his hotel bedroom. Likewise, she had no qualms about meeting any request for any manoeuvre, no matter the indignity of the position it put her in, of the language used to make it, or the fact that McNamara was often reposing with an enormous smouldering fatty between his lips while she complied likewise. He let his imagination run wild, and surprised himself by some of the obscenities he devised, though he noticed that the majority of them were linguistic rather than physical. By week two, McNamara was reflecting that he had never devoted himself so much to Eros in any one place and time; while Conchita was agog because she had never bagged so many Euros in any one place and time. She virtually moved to the Krasnapolsky and entered a state of temporary concubinage with him. McNamara determinedly treated her much worse than he had seen Covet treat Jane. Partly he was curious just to see how much sexual abjection money could buy. He even insisted that she respond to the dead girl's name, which she did. When the fortnight was over, neither of them, in truth, regretted it: McNamara on account of the experience of feeling like Caesar, Conchita on account of the experience of not feeling poor and, in the topsy-turvy system of values they had implicitly contracted should pertain, rather impressed with herself that she had managed to attract a repeat customer for two weeks, and moreover one who had remained "faithful" to her. They even laughingly agreed to do it all again sometime, and he took her phone number and email address.

McNamara returned a few days into the new year without a shred of moral reserve, but rather a feeling of triumph: he had seen, he had conquered, and he had repeatedly come. If anything he felt complacently satiated, and for a week he moved around the house, preparing for the resumption of his duties, with a feeling close to contentment which his penis and testicles did not complainingly interrupt. By the time they did rouse themselves again, the students had returned, and the Mary Jane and the faerie Jane were once more on tap. He continued his dalliance with both until, almost exactly one month later, he took a call one evening which informed him that his father had been dead for nearly a week.

He smoked even more than usual that night, and his iPad required a soapy damp cloth the next morning, all the same.

## Chapter Eight

When Redman arrived at the Vice Chancellor's office on the Friday morning, he was surprised to see that McNamara had got there before him, unusually early. McNamara was grateful at the advent of the younger man, for he had already wasted three minutes of life enjoined in idle small talk with the Vice Chancellor. Spooner's casual conversation, like that of all Vice Chancellors, was predictably dominated by the first person singular pronoun, and unremittingly sprinkled with the names of celebrities or otherwise famous people he had met. To divert himself from the droning of this drone, McNamara had taken to tilting his head so that the penises-and-scrota assemblages of the nude alabaster statuettes behind Spooner appeared to pop out of the Vice Chancellor's ears. He was excessively rewarded for this manoeuvring when Redman came through the door and Spooner turned to greet him and was thus to be seen in profile, one small parcel of genitalia seeming to sprout from the crown of his head, the other appearing to issue from his mouth.

Pleasantries were exchanged. A flurry of further chit-chat was summoned forth from Spooner to herald Redman's arrival, from which McNamara and Redman learned that Spooner had been a friend of "Theresa's" at Oxford in the mid-seventies, that he considered his friendship with the Prime Minister merely dormant rather than extinct, and that he intended (this was said in a way that might easily have been accompanied by a wink, but was not) to make it volcanically active in the near future. McNamara neglected to look impressed; Redman tried his best to look so; both surmised from Spooner's smirking reaction that he had convinced himself that he had in fact made them so.

Spooner deftly turned the talk to business. Would Redman accept the Vice Deanship? He would. Splendid. And if the offer to be Dean of his Faculty were offered again to McNamara, would he reconsider it? As usual, McNamara seemed to rain on everyone's parade. His answer was incontestably flat: he would not. Disappointment was registered and acknowledged, although this was what everyone had been expecting, so the gestures were not unduly laboured.

What no one (except him) expected was for McNamara to add, "But…"

Spooner and Redman turned their looks towards him simultaneously.

"But," McNamara repeated, "were the offer of Pro-Vice Chancellor to be renewed, I would accept that."

Redman's eyes widened. Spooner let out a delighted guffaw.

"I have given it a great deal of consideration in light of our circumstances," McNamara went on. "I now regret my impulsive refusal of the offer. I can see that we are in extremely unusual times and that I may be useful in the office."

"That," exclaimed Spooner, nodding and smiling, "is wonderful news! What a successful meeting!"

"There is just one condition," said McNamara, "which I hope will not seem unreasonable and which may also make a great deal of sense.'

After the briefest pause, Spooner said, "I'm all ears."

"Well," said McNamara, "as we know, each PVC is given responsibility for staffing matters in a faculty other than his or her own. I'd like to have that responsibility for James's faculty, Arts. The reason should not be disguised: it means that the Dean of Arts will be in a pincer, with me directly above him and James directly below. Why do we need or want that? Because I assure you that the Dean of Arts is a fatuous oaf and that most of the trouble we are going to experience over the association with President Trump will come from staff and students in the faculties of Arts and Social Sciences. I cannot have staffing responsibility in Social Sciences, as it is my own faculty. But don't waste me on any other. It has to be Arts."

Spooner mulled this over. "It would involve a bit of a reshuffle," he thought out loud. "But look, would you be prepared to be the International PVC, in your more general role? That's what I really need right now. There's stuff to do on China, and different from what you might imagine."

McNamara spread his hands genially. "I'm happy with any general role as long as the staffing responsibility is for the Arts."

"Done!" boomed Spooner, and looked at his desk as if mourning the lack of a gavel.

"Well," said Redman afterwards in the coffee bar, "here was I thinking that the socialist shocks of history could not be surpassed after Jeremy Corbyn became leader of the Labour Party, but now we have an openly Marxist Pro-Vice Chancellor (International) of the University of Odium, and he's already acting the part, saying, for example, not a single damn word about it before that meeting. What's going on, Robert?"

243

"The Arts thing was partly to support you," McNamara said laconically.

"I get that," replied Redman, "and thanks. But I still don't understand how you managed to flip over like this. You have always said you would never take a managerial role above Head of School. You've always been adamant that those above that tier lose touch with what academia is."

"I just decided that you were right. Why let someone else do it? If we want the show to be more our kind of show, we'd better start helping to direct the show, no? I'm in my sixtieth year. It hardly matters if I lose touch with academia now. I'm not planning to be in it much longer anyway. Last chance to do something different, perhaps. I assumed you'd be happy as you seem to have arrived at the same conclusion in respect of yourself."

"Well, yes, I am happy," Redman confirmed. "I just always imagined us forming a permanent opposition. I never saw us being part of *the government*."

"Speaking of which, in the ten minutes he spoke to me after asking you to leave, he told me he's got to go down to Whitehall late tomorrow afternoon for a meeting with the Minister for Higher Education and that he needs me on the China campus by Monday morning and for the rest of next week. I have to fly out tomorrow night. He made no bones about the fact that the meeting with the Minister is *about* China."

Redman took a breath. "What's afoot?"

"I'm not sure. I'm not even sure that he's sure. He said he won't be able to brief me until Sunday. The Chinese must definitely have been raising hell since last term. I mean, they were publicly denounced by a Professor of this institution. I'm assuming I am some kind of peace envoy."

"He said it would be different from what you might imagine."

McNamara grunted.

"You'll miss tomorrow's demonstration, then?" Redman added.

"What's that?" said McNamara.

Redman pulled out that morning's *Guardian* and pointed to a headline:

**Student researching ISIS tactics held for four days**
- Lecturers fear threat to academic freedom
- Manual downloaded from US government website

244

He made to hand it to McNamara but the other waved it away. "Summarise it for me," he said in disgust.

Redman warmed to the task once he had begun. "The article reveals that the student – Faraj – had sent an electronic copy of an ISIS training manual from a US government website for his research into terrorist tactics to the administrator – Yunus – so that the latter, a personal friend who had access to a printer, could print it out for him for free. Another member of staff – Lorraine – discovered the document on the administrator's computer and reported it upwards, which ultimately led to the police being called in. There's a quote from Dr Griselda Rotfang, of your School, who is Faraj's personal tutor: 'He's a serious student, who works very hard and is looking to have a career as an academic. This is of great concern for academic freedom but also for the climate on campus.' It further reports that students have begun a petition calling on the University to acknowledge 'the disproportionate nature of its response to the possession of legitimate research materials'. The reporting seems based largely on the anonymous press release I showed you the other day. The petition refers to 'radical material', of which the individuals were in possession 'for research purposes' – even though Yunus has no research remit of any kind – and calls for the University to show that it 'guarantees academic and political freedom on campus' and expresses the view that this incident constitutes 'a serious violation of academic freedom'. It ends by saying that there will be a march on campus tomorrow at 3pm in defence of academic freedom. 'Thousands are expected to attend.'"

He put the paper down. McNamara was silent. He blinked a few times, then said, "You ever been to China?"

Redman shook his head.

"It's an awful place," groaned McNamara.


"So, Drusilla," Redman found himself expounding in his office an hour later, "the defence of academic freedom is to be the rallying cry for the campaign. After all, who would *not* want to defend such a thing? It's not going to be about whether or not Yunus is legal or illegal. They are going to portray the University as a super-obedient drongo to the present illiberal state."

"But all we did," said Drusilla, "was call the police, as we are meant to do, and at that point the matter did not involve academics or students. It was only about an administrator."

"Which precisely shows your slavish, knee-jerk obedience to your political masters. The campaigners are not interested in the truth. They're interested in making politics out of nothing."

Drusilla acknowledged the circumstances with a nod. "So what should we say in this afternoon's press release?"

"Keep insisting on the truth. The reason this is a purely legal matter and not a political one is that academic freedom is exclusively the attribute and privilege of *academic staff*. It does not extend to students, not even postgraduate students, and it certainly does not extend to University administrators. The relevant University statute stipulates very clearly the categories of University members who do have academic freedom. It also specifies that the freedom it grants is for research conducted within the law."

"I'm not sure that's going to sound very *liberal*, is it?" Drusilla rejoined pointedly. "The bad spin on that is that students are second-rate citizens as far as academic freedom goes. It's never a good line, to tell people they don't have a freedom or are unequal. It makes them feel disempowered."

"It's the *truth*," said Redman exasperatedly. "That's what laws do! They define things like freedom to act and who has power to do what. But you may be right. We're probably on a hiding to nothing, especially as none of them or their student audience will pay attention to any of the media you send the press release to. The whole thing is being driven by Facebook, not by the truth."

"Nonetheless," she said, rising, "I shall have this written up and pass it by the Registrar and VC and get it out. We have to say something about this demonstration. As for what happens after the march, my office may be in touch with you for advice. Unfortunately I must be away all next week."

"Where to?" he asked.

"China," she said miserably. "There's going to be a lot of press, apparently, and they need me there. With Professor McNamara, I've just been given to understand."

Redman was gallantly helping her with her coat and made no comment.

She turned. "Forgive me," she groaned. "I know he's your colleague, but he's an awful man."

*

Redman and Lorraine slept late the next morning. She refused to accompany him to the campus demonstration, but Redman needed to see it with his own eyes. Despite its commencement at the late hour of three o'clock, the estimates of thousands of attendees turned out to be woefully optimistic. He calculated that there were about six hundred people at the assembly point opposite the University library. He kept aloof from both the gathering crowd and the security guards and local constables acting as marshals, watching the event from a distance. When the short serpent-like assembly set off on its winding, circuitous route around the main campus roads, he did not follow it but walked directly the four hundred yards to a small hill overlooking the march's finishing point at the Trump Building, where the University (acting under Redman's advice) had permitted a makeshift platform to be erected in the car park.

He awaited an absurdly ironic afternoon of loud unhindered public speeches condemning a lack of freedom. He did not expect, when the crowd came surging up University Drive, that each participant would have donned a tan-coloured adhesive gag, and that the mob would thus arrive in complete, melodramatic, orchestrated silence. He had been wrong. It was not simply academic freedom that would be the motivating theme but, ridiculously, grotesquely, freedom of very speech itself. The previously ideologically sleepy campus of Odium, an erstwhile playground for the offspring of the international bourgeoisie, had now, in the space of a mere term and a half, seemingly catapulted itself to the status of the British equivalent of UC Berkeley or Kent State, albeit on the basis of largely manufactured fictions rather than facts. There were press and television waiting everywhere, to the left and the right and the front of the six hundred, as they rode like a wave the final half a league of their noble charge for imagined justice.

While he was made to feel nothing like the professional in an Ian McEwan novel who smugly (and with obvious authorial approval) goes about his privileged daily life while a million people march in London to protest against their government's prosecution of an illegal war, Redman toyed with the comparison. He did so not just because it was a Saturday, but because he had an inkling that, had they been distractable from the poses they were striking, or from the incredible collective silent obedience to which they were paradoxically intent on submitting

247

themselves, many of the students before him, some of whom he had taught and who knew him personally, would have described him as exactly such a compromised figure. Had he and his politically minded colleagues not complained for years about the lack of student activism at Odium? And yet, when it now showed itself, it did so repellently, in the most delusional of guises, a demagogic concoction no serious, reflective political person could swallow.

Two young men had been incautious in how they handled a computer file; one of them had virtually invited arrest by his provocative behaviour in front of the police; the other had consequently been discovered to be an illegal immigrant. But rather than cope with this procedurally low-level affair in which both knew that they were at fault, the two had, in order to divert attention away from their own obvious indiscretions, cooperated in magnifying it to the proportions of a racial and political scandal and persuading thousands of others – about six hundred of whom now stood as gullible sentinels to the pair's abused human rights – that the dual roots of the problem were the reactionary British state and their own entirely blameless University. In fact, it was obvious to anyone with Redman's knowledge that the real stirrer was Faraj, who, as well as being unwilling to pay for his own printing, had strutted like a trouble-seeking turkey-cock before Redman's and the police officers' eyes, and as a result had got Yunus even deeper in the legal soup than himself. And now hundreds stood to defend them, or at least to go through the vocal and physical gestures associated with such an aim, as if both were martyrs for freedom rather than a brace of posturing, chaos-causing fools.

Redman did his best to inhibit his gag reflex as Donald Doyle mounted the platform and began on a salivary Shettlestonian rant. There were plentiful cheers (the mouths seemed quickly to have abandoned their obstructing Scotch Tapes because of the perceived demand for frequent spontaneous acclaim and applause) yet Redman doubted if more than half of what he said had been understood. He was succeeded by the local constituency Labour MP, a virulent anti-Corbynite whose extra-marital affair with her Parliamentary research assistant had a month before been revealed by the *Daily Express*, and who probably was there in order to get some better press coverage for herself. She received an uproarious welcome of which Rosa Luxemburg might have been envious. She prattled and got through five minutes with slogans and clichés.

But the best was yet to come, and caused pulses of euphoria in the crowd, which more and more seemed to have assumed the characteristics and demeanour of fans at a gig just before the main megastar act. Thanks to the wonders of modern technology, Donald Doyle explained, it was possible for Yunus to speak beyond the confines of the immigration detention facility to which he had been moved that morning and in which he was now a "political prisoner". And so saying, Doyle put the microphone to the speaker of his mobile phone, whence issued the reedy voice of Yunus: "Friends, students, members of staff, fellow members of the academic community…"

Redman could not bear the burlesque for much longer. Waves of incredulous, bitter gall swept over him, almost making him dizzy. He wondered whose enforced silence it was that the gagging had been meant to symbolise. All had certainly been free with their words today and, now, even Yunus found no impediment to addressing the crowd, nor had anyone been stopped from saying pretty much anything they liked for nearly a week. Within a few minutes he had turned on his heel and was heading away from this scene of parody politics. Yunus's populist drivel, punctuated frequently by mindless applause, slowly faded from his hearing: "The Home Office conducts itself like the Gestapo. They have no respect for dignity. They treat foreigners as things. The recklessness they show is becoming of a totalitarian state. I thank all for their support. It's been heartening. I'm grateful to everyone who has helped me and shown solidarity, from students to Members of Parliament. I think this is more like the Britain we know, and not the brutal tactics of the Home Office…"

When McNamara opened the door of the black chauffeur-driven Lexus which called at his house late that afternoon, its back seat contained an unpleasant surprise.

"Drusilla!" he exclaimed. "What a pleasant surprise."

He got in awkwardly.

"Have you been sent to brief me on the way to the airport?" he asked.

"I've been sent to accompany you to China, Pro-Vice Chancellor. Have they not put you on the senior management email list yet?"

"Oh, for goodness sake!" he erupted tetchily.

Drusilla bridled. "I know we have had our disagreements in the past, but I didn't expect you to be so instantly oppositional to me now."

"No, you misunderstand," said McNamara. "It's the title. 'Pro-Vice Chancellor'. You cannot call me that, I will not answer to it. Neither that nor 'Professor McNamara'. We spent many years on hostile first name terms, Drusilla, so let's keep it that way."

"But without the hostility?"

"Well, of course. We're not on opposite sides of the argument now, are we? In any case, I have always assumed that you were not necessarily personally committed to the positions you had to defend when I was President of the Union branch. I was doing my job and you were doing yours."

"Gosh," she broke out. "That's the nicest thing you've ever said to me." She picked up some papers she had on her lap. "Okay. Since you are not yet on the mailing list, let me fill you in on the other big news. Have you seen the VC's letter to *The Guardian*? We eventually decided to respond to today's demonstration in that form rather than a press release."

McNamara took the paper. "This is what James Redman has been helping you with?"

Drusilla nodded. McNamara scanned the letter, reading aloud a few choice phrases. "'The incident was triggered by the discovery of an ISIS training manual on the computer of an individual who was neither an academic member of staff nor a student and in a school where one would not expect to find such materials being used for research purposes. ... Our concerns were conveyed to the police as the appropriate body to investigate. No judgment was made by us. ... Much has been said on the matter of academic freedom, most of it careless, entirely false and bearing little relation to the facts.'"

He finished. "Not bad," he reacted. "Though if something is *entirely* false it bears *no* relation to the facts, not *little* relation to the facts. And it's perhaps somewhat legalistic, a tad lacking in acknowledgment that things have turned out a bit messy."

"Ah, criticism! Now I know where I am."

"No, no, it's accurate all the same. You will be aware that we – I mean Redman and me – are not used to a Vice Chancellor who takes good advice and tells the truth. I'm not sure the truth is going to do much good in these circumstances, but there's no other way."

"When I saw the VC yesterday he was more concerned to tie this thing up and conclude it and not allow it to survive until President Trump's visit."

"Good luck with that," said McNamara ruefully. "But was he able to tell you any more about China? What exactly are we doing there?"

"Well, everything is difficult and touchy with China now, after last term." Drusilla looked at her watch. "He'll still be with the Minister now, especially if it's something, which I gather it is, that the Minister is not going to like. All I know is that we'll be briefed on Sunday, that you – well, both of us actually, but you will obviously do the talking – have a meeting with Mr Ching on Monday, I shall issue a press release later that day, and we shall remain for the rest of the week dealing with the plentiful coverage that it is anticipated will be the consequence. It seems to be important that we speak from China rather than come back to the Odium immediately."

"Mr *Ching*?" he said.

"Ah, yes. Mr Ching is the person who essentially makes all the major decisions with respect to the China campus."

"But the Provost is someone from here, no? He's not Chinese."

"Professor Miles Dudd, yes. But he's not really in charge, of course. Mr Ching is the Chair of the Chongqing City Communist Party – CCCP for short, ha ha. It adds to the confusion that his other name is Chong and he is thus Chong Ching of Chongqing, but he seems to think this suggests that he was destined by fate for the position in the Party he now occupies. His office seemed impressed when we sent your CV yesterday afternoon. They have never done business with an actual Marxist from Odium. I'm not sure they even knew we had one."

"Oh," said McNamara, feeling a dim light starting to dawn. "Is that why I have been deemed suitable for this task, Drusilla? I might smooth over the enormous faultlines that have opened up between us and the Chinese by means of a little knowledgeable table talk about the materialist dialectic and surplus value?"

"Would one not send a Catholic to meet the Pope if one had a choice?"

"Let's hope he doesn't actually read any of my publications that mention China. They say it was not a Marxist economy or polity at any stage, even in 1949, never mind later."

"Oh, Mr Ching won't do that. He doesn't speak English, and as far as I can tell he's no intellectual, just a Party functionary. But he will want his picture in all the papers with a prestigious Western Communist."

"I'm not a Communist, Drusilla."

"I think that may get lost in translation," she replied wryly.

"Christ," he muttered. "I suppose I need to accustom myself to this grotesque pantomime."

"It sounds like pantomime," said Lorraine, pouring another gin and tonic for them both.

"That about sums it up," answered Redman. "Not helped by the police transferring Yunus to a detention centre in the morning, so that he could freely use his phone. They were wiser with Faraj. Apparently they didn't let him go 'til after the rally."

"He's out?"

"Well, of course. He didn't do anything criminal. But it's turned into something like an Ealing comedy. Two guys twatting about has become an internationally reported human rights incident, and now that Faraj is liberated you can bet the rhetoric will soar into stratospheric realms of nonsense about how truly oppressed he is. We'll be hearing all about wrongful arrests, despite the fact that both arrests were perfectly legal. We'll have speeches about racism, even though the one remaining issue is no less mundane than the fact that Yunus has committed a petty criminal offence by acquiring a fake stamp in his passport. There will be endless gnashing of teeth about academic freedom, despite the fact that neither of them has such a freedom because neither of them is an academic. Yunus's detention centre will be described as if it's something out of Solzhenitsyn. In short, prepare yourself for all sorts of fiction, poetry and drama, because the real story is too drably administrative and routine for anyone at the demo now to accept, given all the energy and effort they've put into believing the hype. Yunus and Faraj should really be in advertising, because in the last week they've convinced greater minds than theirs that a crock of shit is actually a pot of gold. And we are all going to pay the price."

"Not me," said Lorraine. "I'll stay away if it's going to get worse. In fact, I think I'll send an email to Matthews saying that right now, and ruin his weekend."

"What with the death threats and all," Redman grinned, "I think you could be looking at unchallenged weeks or months off."

"Maybe," said Lorraine. "But I might simply start looking for another job. I used to work in a primary school and, to be frank, it wasn't a place where I had to suffer such lies, cowardice and skulduggery."

Redman nodded.

"Or, to be even more honest," she added, "such stupidity."


## Chapter Nine

Enter a man in a white suit which never showed a stain. His name was William Stoner.

The fabric of his unvarying apparel did not remain pristine miraculously, as if in divine outward indication of his moral flawlessness (although he *was* flawless in many more dimensions than the merely ethical), or because it was made of a new synthetic chemical compound, but because he always had ten identical white suits, was (without seeming to be an untouchable) naturally careful what he stood near and where he sat and whom he brushed up against, and had an uncommonly conscientious dry cleaner. If, on private inspection, any of his all-silk ensembles bore a blemish that proved inerasable, he immediately gave the garments to Oxfam.

Stoner did not personally believe that one's outward phenomenon in the world indicated a great deal about one's inner being, but he knew that most other people resolutely did believe that, and that they generally seemed greatly impressed in their dealings with those who maintained high standards of dress. As such an insight demonstrates, he had an enviable understanding of the needs of others: indeed, his being quite free of egoism or vanity, it might plausibly be argued that he dressed selflessly, essentially *for* others, as a kind of impeccable example of *how to be*. Something about the whiteness of his clothes, he came to know, suggested that he was a flag or even a dove of peace. He considered himself nothing of the kind, but like most super-intelligent people was all too aware of being read like a Barthesian myth, and of the seeming advantage (to the world, not to himself) of his being so interpreted. Were he to meet himself as a character in a novel, he knew, his own disbelief would have difficulty in remaining suspended; but in the real world of Odium, where disbelief was a universally required ability for survival, he was taken seriously as a kind of human touchstone of the absolutely civilising qualities of learnedness.

What Stoner did believe in, it possibly goes without saying, were values just like those: for example, that knowledge was the Holy Grail, and that universities existed exclusively to seek it and pass it on. Quite how he ended up at the University of Odium, therefore, is a puzzle requiring explanation.

Stoner was born in north Africa sometime in the nineteen fifties. More than this he never vouchsafed and, oddly, few people asked. It was as if his issuing forth into the world were better comprehended as a continental, rather than a merely national, event. The lack of questions as to his nativity, we may infer, was partly explicable by the accompanying assumptions of a colonial inheritance, the dark details of which might have sullied the spotlessly favourable impression which nearly all his interlocutors had formed of Stoner by the time any mention of his origins may have arisen. Stoner was saved – though his ignorance of the fact actually prevented him in a more profound manner – from ever having to tell anyone that his white unmarried forty-year old father had conceived him upon the conquest of a native farm girl of fourteen, then abandoned her upon hearing of the pregnancy, only to take a renewed interest in him once he popped out of the womb pale white and showing no traces of the expected Moorishness. The father did not go so far as to appropriate the boy as his own son, but chose rather to oversee his fate from afar, and to provide for him, in excess if need be, like a conscience-stricken Dickensian criminal-turned-patron. Stoner never met him. He was packed off to boarding school in England from the age of five, but not before learning the most exquisite Arabic from his young mother, who was not yet twenty.

By the time he went to Oxford, he already spoke English in such a way and had a bearing of such maturity that he was often mistaken for a college fellow, not least because, as he did to this day, he constantly smoked a pipe and smelled permanently like an ashtray. But as he once quipped to McNamara, whom he first met there, he would have preferred to be the college Othello. He had as a youth intended, improbably, to study agriculture, from some feeling in his bones that it would honour his farming mother's increasingly distant memory (she having died in a not-deeply investigated hunting accident on his father's land a mere year after Stoner's departure to England). But in the Bodleian Library's Islamic manuscript collection he found many more compelling ways to keep her in mind.

Since 1602, when it opened, the library had possessed a manuscript of the Quran, which he first held with a kind of awe and then read with increasing understanding and pleasure. The Persian illuminated manuscripts beguiled him. Within a week he had switched to Arabic language and literature (having originally enrolled to study Spanish), which he did by barging into the college rooms of Britain's then greatest living Arabist, and convincing him that his days at pole position were inevitably numbered, and that it would therefore be wise to start training his replacement, who would be him, William Stoner. Like everyone else, the ageing Professor liked Stoner so much at first meeting that he readily agreed upon hearing the young man's fantastic spoken Arabic. When the old man died twenty years later, Stoner was among those who carried his coffin. Everyone present remembered the funeral well, for, while the rest of the congregation was bedecked in black, Stoner chose that moment to assume his evermore permanent public suit of white.

He was never able to replace his mentor at Oxford. While a postgraduate student there, writing the thesis that would prove on publication that there was a really cool new guy in the hot field of pre-Islamic Arabic poetry, Stoner fell in love with, spoke to, impregnated, then married (in that order) a high-born young American woman who had come over on a Fulbright scholarship. Within a year of the birth of their daughter, he found himself teaching in the University of Missouri at Columbia, and living in a splendid town house a few select streets away from his new wife's excessively affluent parents. Unfortunately, his wife turned out to be a manic depressive whose depressive mania had not shown itself in the refined environs of Oxford, where she had fled largely in order to escape the robotic Puritanism of her landowning parents, which had been her depression's primary cause. It displayed itself with a recurring vengeance, predictably, almost as soon as she re-entered their orbit, not least because, in addition to the already long list of things they disapproved of vocally, they disapproved extra-loudly of her ruptured hymen, for whose destruction they mistakenly blamed Stoner. This, in some senses, was a punishment she deserved, for she actively misled them (as she had misled Stoner) as to his culpability for this breach. Her hymen had in fact said hi (and goodbye) to a man long before she had left Missouri for Oxford.

Oxford was one of the few places on earth where someone like Stoner would not seem too unusual, and where to be married to him might feel like an advantage to a woman so emotionally constituted. But in Columbia his odd singularity (and the fact that her parents loathed him) came to feel like a social stigma. His daughter, moreover, looked like him, but not the mother, another fact her parents resented. They proved to be solicitous grandparents, spending much time with their new grand-daughter. The consequence was that, along with her grandparents and her mother, she became one of only five people in the world who ever found it in their hearts to despise Stoner. Stoner knew she had loved him as a little child, but her sensibilities, increasingly manipulated by his wife and her parents, were gradually turned against him. The other person who hated him was an unusually misanthropic colleague at Columbia called Lomax, who tried his best from early acquaintance to damage Stoner's career, only to be foiled once every two years or so when Stoner published the latest in his near-biennial, discipline-defining and promotion-bearing monographs. He was a full Professor at Missouri within a decade.

The handful of hatreds originated solely within the hearts of those who bore them rather than being prompted by anything Stoner actually did or was. He remained entirely innocent in his very adult way. Even his eventual – one might say inevitable – infidelity to his wife was conducted in a kind of innocence, or at least with a kind of purity, the purity of a deep and genuine love for a woman willing to requite it, but which Stoner, in a repetition that proved Einstein's definition of insanity wrong, felt once more even before speaking to her. She was English. She was a good deal younger than him. She was an Arabist. She had come over from Oxford on a Fulbright for the sole purpose of having him as her supervisor. Being a smoker herself, she did not mind his carbonised odour. To do justice in describing their candid relation as it burgeoned would demand an entire chapter of a novel, and a battery of Lawrencean literary techniques – from his unique cadences to his idiosyncratic lexis to his organicist tropes – which might draw the unwelcome quasi-critical attentions of Professor Bernard Matthews to any author who attempted it. To be succinct, suffice to say that, at the end of her period of study, Stoner eloped with her to England. He repatriated himself. As soon as she could, his wife divorced him, and he married the woman he loved and who loved him back. The remainder of life was generally once more beatific to him, because he had dealt with hatred in the best way it can be dealt with: he had walked away from it. He could have written a self-help book on achieving happiness through goodness and patience, had his vocabulary been down to it.

But Oxford was closed to him. He was simply too good. None of the incumbent Arabists wanted him queering their pitch. McNamara, who was now at Odium but not yet in the trough of his own alienation from it, persuaded the University to establish an Institute for Arabic Studies, and to offer Stoner the headship. For a time, Stoner ran the small unit in the time-honoured traditional way, as a research centre of some excellence. But when Sir Evan Covet arrived, he took a dim view of the teaching of an ancient literature largely about deserts, men and camels, and so reconfigured it to his and the contemporary market's pleasing that Stoner opted, without confronting Covet, to take a permanent back seat. Ten years further on, it had become the Department of Arabic Studies, but by far the greatest source of its income was the contribution it made to McNamara's School's popular postgraduate degrees in counter-terrorism, by means of which it provided linguistic training to young people avid for careers in various international security services, principally American and European.

Stoner was a familiar figure on the Odium campus in his twilight years, often walking with what seemed an exaggerated swagger, his right hand usually clutching the bowl of his pipe, smoke billowing from him as if he were a steam train moving at very slow speed. The distinctive gait people attributed to his presumed colonial privileges, or imagined was a sign of his Oxonian-bred self-confidence, but in fact he had picked it up by osmosis in Missouri, where most people were so fat that they had to adopt a swagger in order to be able to lug their hips around at all. Everyone found him charming and inoffensive, though not because he lacked bite or acidity. Once, at a dinner held to mark the presence of academic visitors from Barcelona, he had in the middle of an impromptu speech made a remark about bloody Catalans and their constant snivelling and whining for independence. It was not said in jest, yet everyone assumed that it was, and all laughed at the mischief-making of the mega-erudite rapscallion.

All of Stoner's attempts to make an opinionated mark on the world tended to end this way. No one took him seriously but, instead, concluded that he had a wickedly teasing sense of humour. Eventually, he abandoned these insidious intents to disturb the universe, and simply watched the smoke that rose from his pipe, realising that the greatness of his moment had already flickered, that he had settled into the status of something like an institutional treasure. Above all he decided never to force any moment to a crisis, but to be deferential, politic, cautious, even if at times it made him, with his famously vast and capacious mind, seem almost ridiculous. As he grew old, this calculated reserve made him appear to others even more monumentally Eliotic than he was. The permanent white suit seemed the perfect apparel for a man whom everybody loved and cherished, but hardly anyone listened to.

As Redman was walking away from the Saturday rally in disgust, he encountered Stoner. The older man had been standing a little further back up the hill, watching the event, just as Redman had been doing.

Stoner took his pipe out of his mouth and greeted him. "I didn't know it was you 'til you turned around, James. I'm not sure why I came here, but I felt I had to. It's a sorry spectacle."

"Yes," said Redman, "and one founded on conscious lying."

"I know," Stoner agreed. "The young man, Yunus, he gave me to believe, when he said he worked in your School, that he was a lecturer there. It's only as a result of this brouhaha and all the press coverage that I discover he's an administrator. Now, he never actually *said* that he was an academic, but the fact that he left the truth *unsaid* throughout all our discussions was, I have come to conclude, deliberately misleading. I never checked because, well, I just never thought it was a deception anyone would try to get away with. You'd know you'd be found out in the end. To his credit, he has enough encyclopaedic knowledge to be able to pass himself off."

"I didn't know you knew him personally."

"I've been meeting him about three times a week for the last year, in the afternoons. We speak Arabic together. He's very well informed about Arab current affairs, you know, and widely read. He teaches me things."

"Ah," said Redman. "That perhaps partly explains his absences during normal work hours. As for the lying about being a lecturer, he's going to keep trying to give that impression. You heard his speech there, yes? 'Fellow members of the academic community' were his actual words, I think."

258

"It's a shame," Stoner puffed, "that a young, intelligent, promising life should allow itself to drown in lies like that."

"It's a shame that he's causing so much trouble for everyone else by those lies."

"That's true too," said Stoner, "but you know, most of those people down there, the students and the staff, they are the stupidest arseholes of this place, its worst, not its best. There are twenty thousand students in the University altogether. The few hundred down there are just the brainless scum. That Scotsman, for example, Donald Doyle, is it? Have you ever seen such an obviously ignoble creature, someone so perceptibly to be avoided after just a single glance at him? Yet they applaud him. Someone or other would be using them, they'd be believing this arrant nonsense or that utter bilge. The puzzle is how Yunus can associate with them, even in this disembodied telephonic manner, or rather how he can cater to them with that ridiculous speech."

"It's been a verbally violent campaign," said Redman. "It so happens that it's the stupid, or the gullible, who are offering to ride to his rescue. He's persuaded himself to throw his lot in with them because, well, they seem his best chance. I wouldn't be surprised if he thinks that their campaign might actually succeed in freeing him, it's been so vocal and loud."

"But that's the basest of self-deception," said Stoner. "I consider him too intelligent for that. He's not thinking straight."

They heard distant roars and cheers from the assembly down below.

"And the reason he's not thinking straight," Stoner went on, "is that all he can hear these days is the noise of that rabble, drowning out all sense. He does not yet understand that all salvation is founded upon an eventual embrace of the truth, no matter how humbling. I don't think this is because of a defect in his own intelligence. I think it's inexperience."

"I disagree," said Redman. "I think it's vanity."

They stood for a moment in silence, watching the crowd, Stoner savouring his pipe. "Well," he said, "we shall find out."

Stoner went to visit Yunus in the detention centre the next afternoon. It was in Lincolnshire, near Spalding. He was expecting something rather prison-like, and there was a barbed wire fence marking a distant perimeter, and no other significant buildings around it. But the building itself and its innards more resembled a university Hall of Residence. Inmates (so said the brochure in the waiting room) had their own private en suite rooms. It had a common room, a games room, a TV room, a dining room, and a library. The visiting room had partitioned booths. It was clean. Stoner did not fear for the whiteness of his trousers as he sat and waited.

Yunus did not appear for a while and when he did he was smiling broadly. As he put his arms round Stoner he said, in Arabic, "Sorry, I was talking to CNN."

"Yes," said Stoner, returning his Arabic. "I heard you on the radio on *The World This Weekend* as I was driving across in the car. 'Kafkaesque'? You really think this place is Kafkaesque?"

"Oh yeah," said Yunus. "Worse."

"But," said Stoner, "they have told you what crime you have allegedly committed, no?"

"Well, yes," admitted Yunus.

"And it's all been dealt with, so far, within one week? And you have a preliminary court date in another week? So they are processing the case relatively quickly, keeping you informed of it, letting you see your lawyer and visitors, yes?"

"I don't think speed or efficiency has anything to do with it. It's more the manner in which they treat you."

"I see," said Stoner. "You know that in *The Trial* Joseph K. is kept dangling and never knows what he is being charged with and is eventually killed 'like a dog'?"

"I never got to the end of it, to be honest."

"I suppose what I am saying is that these analogies you imagine perhaps make it less rather than more easy for you to cope with the short period of detention, they perhaps encourage you to look at it less stoically and, in fact, to suffer more than is necessary. Take the idea that you have experienced something like Gestapo treatment from the immigration people. I mean, you have not been tortured at all, have you?"

"No, but, as I say, it's more their mentality."

"You mean they think like the Gestapo but don't act like the Gestapo? I presume this thinking of theirs reveals itself in some actions, though?"

"They mainly ignore you. They treat you as if you are not fully human."

"By leaving you alone most of the time? Is that all? But they have explained why you are being detained and why you are going to court. The stamp in the passport, right?"

"Yeah, right."

"And it is an illegal stamp, Yunus, is it not? You paid to have it forged, correct? You know that they are in the right?"

"I'll address that issue in court."

"No doubt. But we are private and confidential here. You and I have always spoken openly and freely. We have often spoken of the value of personal integrity. What will you say in court?"

"I'll say that the stamp is genuine."

"As I understand it, the problem is that that particular stamp was not in use by the immigration services on the date it bears. It had been discontinued a couple of years before. So you could not possibly have got it legitimately."

There was silence. Yunus had stopped smiling. "You come here, I agree to see you, I thought you were my friend. I thought you wanted to help."

"In what way?"

"With the campaign."

"Actually, I came simply to see you. I did not intend to discuss the campaign, which is a sideshow, but just to reassure myself that you were in reasonable spirits. I can see that you are actually in *high* spirits, the finest of fettles. But the campaign does not seem to be about your immigration status, Yunus, which is the one matter now outstanding, given that you and Faraj have been freed without charge on the terrorism counts. The only reason you are in here is that you have a forged stamp in your passport and are an illegal immigrant."

"It's a stitch-up," protested Yunus.

"Now, now, I don't think so," said Stoner. "After all, Yunus, it wouldn't be the first time, would it? You did deliberately give me the misleading impression that you were an academic staff member, and you have done nothing to disabuse me of that impression for the last year. In fact, you have only a second-class degree in Business Administration from the University of Jendouba. Not that this matters to me or says anything about your actual self. You are a deeply intelligent young man and I am sure, if you had had the luck to study something you love, like literature or philosophy, that you could have been an academic. But there is an element of deception in your behaviour, of wishing to be seen as something more exalted than what you are. And I worry that perhaps the excitement of being at the centre of a campaign is having the effect of an adulatory distraction from the fact that, if you go to court, you will be found guilty and probably deported or, worse, sent to prison then deported."

"I'm confident about my case."

Stoner shook his head. "That is impossible, Yunus. I think you are prepossessed with something else."

"What do you mean?"

"It may appear to you – you're on the BBC and in the newspapers every day – that you are the eye of some epoch-making storm, politically profound, heroic, even. The media have fallen for the 'academic freedom' blather because it makes for a good story. But the truth is, you are attempting to keep an issue alive which is procedurally dead. The only live issue is now your immigration status, and that has nothing to do with the University of Odium, indeed they were witless enough to take your word for it. But you seem to want to promote the idea to the world that you are blameless and that you ended up here because of a gutless University and an oppressive government. In fact, you are here because you bribed someone to forge a passport stamp, and that person didn't do it very well."

"With all these people behind me, I'll win my case."

"But they are not behind you in your case, Yunus. They are behind the straw monster of violated academic freedom, which never even happened. They hear you say that you are innocent of the illegal immigration charge, and so they are persuaded, because you precisely try so to persuade them, that it is a trumped-up police trick in order to punish you for something much more politically serious. But you and I and anyone who thinks knows that your case is in fact glamourless and dispiritingly everyday. If you are found guilty, and go to jail, I imagine you can delude yourself that you will be a political prisoner, but let's get real. You'll serve six months and then they will stick you on a plane back home to Tunisia, that great land of freedom, democracy and human rights. Who wants that?"

Yunus now seemed to be simmering with anger, but he contained himself. "And what do you suggest as an alternative?"

"Proceed from the truth. Call off this ridiculous academic freedom campaign you are waging against your ex-employer. If you do that, plenty of people in the University will offer themselves as character witnesses for you. Nobody in the University has any interest in seeing you behind bars, but you have done nothing but calumniate them for the last seven days, so no one who matters now feels like helping you. Admit to the illegal action. You might get a suspended sentence. It might help should you make an application to remain in the country thereafter. It might forestall a deportation. But the most important thing of all is to acknowledge the truth and not to perjure yourself."

Yunus stood up. He did not offer to embrace Stoner this time, but held out a hand, and took the older man's and shook it without much enthusiasm.

"I wish I could thank you for coming to see me," he said, with a formality which seemed now to be the only thing repressing his self-righteous indignation. "But we fundamentally disagree. You overrate the truth. It has only a small place in politics. Politics is all about opportunity, and a truly political person does not shirk an opportunity like this when it arises, because it is not just about him, but about all those on whose behalf he seizes it."

Stoner understood that he was something worse than no longer welcome: the main thing now was that he was no longer *useful*. "Then you really are in something like Kafka's *The Trial*," he said as he paused before finally leaving the place. "You're in a fiction of your own authorship."

Stoner had to drive into Spalding on the way home, looking for somewhere that sold pipe tobacco. It being late on a Sunday afternoon, this was not a straightforward task. Everywhere was closed on the approach to the town, which seemed sedgy and overgrown, as if the local council had no money to manicure the place with any regularity. House after house with off-white or brown porridgy rendering slid past. These finally gave way to a warren of tarmac and brick streets around the town square, which in fact appeared to be more of a town triangle, its ageing architecture not unpleasant, but dirty and crumbling, down at heel. The Lincolnshire landscape and the soulless small-town streets reminded him of Missouri, except Missouri was better looking.

He found an open petrol station near the centre and made his purchase. As he returned to his car, which he had parked in a side street, he saw that he had left it in the shadow of a great dark warehouse-type building. It was constructed of corrugated metal, which had turned mottled grey in years of weather. Along the top, to admit light, was an entire row of windows, every one of which had been shattered, presumably by stones thrown upward from the pavement with deliberate intent. The seemingly bombed-out structure was surrounded by cracked and weedy paving slabs, and lent a grim mood to the row of ragged houses at whose end it squatted.

He walked past his car to the end of the building and, looking up, saw that it had been a postal sorting office. He remembered that the Royal Mail had been privatised three or four years before. This must have been the consequence for Spalding, and no going concern had stepped in to give the unremarkable edifice a continued role in the economy of the town. A brief image of the alabaster-white Trump Building flared up in his imagination, as if to suggest a deliberate contrast. Its concerns, and his concerns with its concerns, seemed a sudden extravagance in a world in which "academic freedom" and even "freedom of speech" must be of trivial moment compared to the imperious need to work and earn. He was fleetingly disgusted by the rhetoric of his own comparatively pampered profession and class. Yet poor Spalding, in the fifth richest country on the globe, was still a haven compared to the townships of the north African land of his birth. What was talk of freedom or self-integrity worth in a world thoroughly governed still by need? He sat in the car morosely, smoking his pipe with the window open. He finally drove off with a sigh and a shake of the head.

He turned on CNN straight away when he got home. He then went into a bedroom to change.

After a few minutes the Yunus segment was played. Stoner came into the living room in his shirt, underwear and socks, and stood to watch it. It was a recording of a telephone interview, accompanied by a still photo of Yunus. Under it were given his name and, misleadingly, the words "University of Odium, UK". Stoner heard Yunus claim that his re-arrest most likely would not have happened were it not for the initial political context of the first arrests, that the authorities had been draconian in their actions and that this was clearly their attempt to try and "cover up the initial mistake". This was expressed with great media fluency, which only increased Stoner's sense of unease.

He called Redman. There was no answer, so he left a short message: "Hello, James. Stoner here. I saw Yunus. You were right and I was wrong. He is indeed a case of overreaching self-conceit. Ciao."

Afterwards, reflexively, he went into the bedroom and examined the suit he had been wearing that day, which he had spread out on the top of the bed.

He gave it very close scrutiny. But it bore no stain.

**Chapter Ten**

McNamara had never been to Chongqing before. But he had visited Ningbo, where the first ever British university campus had been set up twelve years before, and where he had witnessed, to his horror, an unimaginably miserable franchise operation with Nuremberg archit-ecture and students who could speak hardly any English. He had encountered a young female student there one day who was not Chinese but had come from Denmark on a one-semester exchange visit. She was a sociologist. But in Ningbo, which hardly had a Social Sciences faculty to speak of, she was forced to take modules from a degree course in a pseudo-subject called International Communications. He asked her what she thought of the course. She immediately erupted in a flood of tears. "It's terrible," she had said. "Everything here is terrible. It's the biggest mistake I ever made, coming here." He had agreed with her silently. Even after he left, he felt contaminated by the Chinese conception of a university and, most of all, the abject British willingness to cater to it.

Chongqing is a city much further west than the near-coastal Ningbo, which is usually a bad sign in China, the interior being generally less developed and much poorer. But in fact he had found little difference in his admittedly brief impressions so far. He was shocked, virtually before he had left the airport, to witness the dreadful local manners, which he realised he had noticed on his last trip but must quickly have forgotten. Drusilla, whom on the outward journey he had begun to appreciate as a woman with a decent sense of style, had been to China many more times than him, and did not, as he had thought she might, immediately curl up and die. In fact, she seemed to have learned a fair amount of transactional Chinese, and to be professionally inured to the host of indignities one regularly had to see, avoid, or actually suffer: people bumping into you and not murmuring even the slightest apology, failing also on every occasion to hold doors open for anyone following; if you arrived at a gate and there was someone on the other side, they just pushed through, and even if you held it open for them they did not say thank you; queue-jumping seemed universal; no matter what you said to a taxi driver, his first utterance was a very loud question that sounded like "Samah?", simply because they were white and he therefore assumed he could not possibly understand Drusilla's Chinese; even female taxi drivers, of which there were a few, did this and likewise sounded like snarling dogs, usually with two or three teeth missing. Everyone appeared to dress in cheap fabrics, like chiffon, with styles that had not been seen in the West since the nineteen-seventies. The men in particular often had a slack-jawed look, and almost all of them smoked, even in tiny elevators with signs which prohibited it; the women sported whacky hairdos and big ugly glasses and sat with their legs spread wide in public places, happily burping loud and long after eating. When they spoke into their mobile phones the Chinese often shouted (because the person they are talking to is far away, Drusilla explained, or, as she actually put it, "they think they are still in the paddy field"); men spat all the time, great gobs of grey-green everywhere, even sometimes on the floors of restaurants, most of which were insufferably noisy because they were full of sounds which simply did sound like high-pitched human squawking; an order to a waitress would result in her turning around and bellowing your wishes down the restaurant to the person at the counter; if you walked past this same restaurant at four in the afternoon, you would see the same waitress with her head on the table in an entire row of tables with similarly sleeping girls: they would all be getting some shut-eye until the evening shift began. Most restaurants were of dubious hygiene, which perhaps explained the rampant success of the many sprouting and comparatively antiseptic branches of McDonalds and KFC and Starbucks.

Drusilla had impressed him by pointing out that, despite much of it having been planned in the last decade, Chongqing was an utter disaster from the point of view of all modern design. For example, there were hardly any ramps anywhere, and pavements were sometimes as much as

266

nine inches or a foot above the road. Drains were often open; had it been summer, the streets would have stunk. Many public objects were placed at a height which guaranteed that human heads would crash into them. Every twenty yards or so a lamppost arose from the very middle of a pavement, making it impossible for pushchairs or wheelchairs to pass. It was as if the architecture had been demonically conceived deliberately to cause the maximum quantum of harm and inconvenience rather than the reverse.

In short, by the end even of their first shared meal on the Sunday evening they arrived, McNamara and Drusilla had begun to form a strong emotional bond founded on the shared racism and intolerance which seemed spontaneously to ignite within them when confronted with anything natively Chinese. Indeed, they began to enjoy the feeling of defending themselves and each other against the frequent assaults to their senses and sensibilities. When the empirical evidence presented directly to them seemed exhausted, they began to seek out less obvious cultural abominations and provocations to confirm them in their negative responses.

Although McNamara had heard that the Chongqing campus was owned by the same "educational company" as the Ningbo campus, and that it was in every architectural respect indistinguishable from it, he had considered this claim to be improbable, exaggerated. But in fact it was quite true. There was the same administration block with a clock tower, whose same chimes were in fact the same MP3 recording piped through a loudspeaker, with a road as wide as a motorway stretching out from it for a quarter of a mile, ending in three mammoth ugly white teaching blocks, behind which was exactly the same array of student residences as were to be found in Ningbo. The Ningbo campus had been *exactly* recreated in Chongqing, in the same way that urban planners reproduce the same tower blocks in different sectors of Chinese cities. The University Hotel, where he and Drusilla were put up, had the same number of floors, and rooms, and an identical internal layout.

The food in its foyer restaurant was tolerable; what it called coffee was inferior in taste to greasy dishwater. They opted for alcohol instead. While Drusilla was ordering, McNamara slipped away to his room to make a scheduled phone call to the Vice Chancellor. When he returned his face bore a rather different and startled expression, one that seemed a little prompted by a rush of adrenalin, as if he had opened the door on a room in which he expected to be welcomed by a puppy and instead had encountered a wolf. He sat once more opposite her and began to toy with his glass of red wine.

"Well?" said Drusilla.

"Not exactly what I was anticipating. Let me ask you, Drusilla, in what kind of detail were you briefed before coming out here?"

"As much or less than you," she replied. "The VC had a meeting with the Minister on Saturday; it was likely to be a difficult one, he said; he would instruct us on the actions to be taken as a consequence once we arrived here. I got the sense that he knew what he wanted to do but that quite how we would do it or whether we would be able to do it depended on that meeting."

"He didn't actually say what he wanted to do?"

"No. But I assume he has now told you?"

McNamara nodded. "You have a sealed letter, apparently? Spooner will entrust nothing to email about this. He reckons the authorities have access to all our China-based servers."

"Oh, yes," said Drusilla. "The VC gave me a letter. He said we would probably need it and he would tell me when to present it. It's for Mr Ching."

"You don't know its contents?" said McNamara.

"It's in Chinese," said Drusilla.

McNamara drank a little.

"Well," he said, "it's apparently a two-sentence letter telling Mr Ching that the University of Odium will be taking no more students and shall withdraw from China when the last cohort of its current students in Chongqing graduates. In other words, we're closing down the operation in four and a half years, little more than a decade after we opened it. I gather this is going to come as a shock to Mr Ching."

Drusilla's eyes had widened. "But not to you?" she said.

"Oh, yes," said McNamara, "I've just had time to get used to the idea as I was coming back downstairs. I wouldn't quite believe it unless the VC had told me himself. Apparently the Minister back in London is livid."

"I can imagine. She's ethnically Chinese herself. Educational cooperation is a likely plank of any independent trade agreement we make with China after Brexit. Anything that threatens such cooperation weakens the British hand."

"According to Spooner, he told her flatly that he held her personally to blame, that her attempts to shaft us last term over Odiumgate had been a deciding factor for him, and not just the grief the Chinese have given us ever since. If the Chongqing connection was going to be used to blackmail us, he informed her, the University Council would rather not maintain it."

"I'm surprised he managed to get the Council's backing, and, to think of it, to prevent anyone leaking the decision. I usually find out about such leaks quite quickly: it's me the media call."

"The Council is still a skeleton crew these days. After all the resignations of last term, it's down to half its normally operating numbers, and local worthies are more circumspect about signing up. Plus the VC deliberately didn't hold the Council meeting 'til Friday afternoon. So there's been little time for any leaking to be done."

"Should we be celebrating?" Drusilla lifted her glass. She was beginning to enjoy herself. "I hate this place and I hate coming here. If this is the last time ... "

McNamara reciprocated. "Yes, I think we should. We should never have been here. It was an appalling decision made for all the wrong reasons, principally so that Sir Evan Covet could get his knighthood, I understand. From the point of view of academic standards, it's been utterly ruinous. We've been dishing out Odium degrees like lollipops to Chinese students who simply wouldn't be admitted if they applied for entry in the UK. It's debased our coinage."

They clinked glasses and drank.

"The VC," McNamara continued, "gave some very specific instructions for the delivery of the letter and what we should do thereafter. One, there should be no parley or negotiation with Mr Ching. We refuse all offers of hospitality, deliver the letter, wait 'til he has read it, and leave immediately. Then we get out of town, go to Shanghai, and await the inevitable storm."

"More media outlets in Shanghai," she explained, "including Western ones. But why are we to be so rude when we deliver the letter?"

McNamara inclined his head in open acknowledgment of admiration. "I have to hand it to Spooner, he doesn't do things by halves. He is hoping that the Chinese will be so incensed that they won't accept the four-and-a-half-year wind-down period. If we can provoke them into being all macho and thoughtless, which is how they usually are, he's hoping they will take the huff and shut down the Chongqing operation *immediately*, at the end of this academic year. They'll transfer the students to other Chinese universities. Or they can simply take it over lock, stock and barrel. This being a totalitarian dictatorship, they can do that."

Drusilla asked, "But the non-Chinese students, what about them?"

"Transfer to Odium, all fees waived, for the remainder of their degree courses. It's like depriving them of a tent and replacing it with a villa. So not a big deal, or rather, a very good deal, for them. There are only slightly more than four hundred international students here. That problem can be solved in one stroke."

"So," Drusilla mused, "we are about to become public enemies numbers one and two in the Chinese press for the next few days."

"If we play our cards right," he said, offering another playful toast.

McNamara and Drusilla met Mr Ching the next morning in an opulent penthouse office accessed by a private elevator placed outside the somewhat more ordinary administrative quarters of the campus Provost, Professor Miles Dudd.

Dudd was a thin, silver-haired Dubliner, an art historian who had published one or two slim volumes on negligible Irish painting, which he considered reason sufficient to describe himself as a "writer" on his Wikipedia page. There was no Art History department on the Chongqing campus, of course: Dudd had been seconded to the job two months ago because no one else of professorial standing had been incautious enough to put themselves forward after the recall of his predecessor in the wake of the diplomatic rift which had erupted between Odium and the Chinese government. A contributory factor was that his departmental colleagues back in Odium were fervent in their encouragement that he should go.

McNamara knew Dudd as a beaming impostor, the kind of man who sees so little beyond his own diminutive ego that truly significant events pass him by without his noticing. He asked Dudd how things were going and the latter replied breezily, "Great! I see it as my role to let things happen!" At this smug and ridiculous statement, which Dudd emitted as if it were a *pensée* of Pascalian order, McNamara decided that he would accordingly make what was about to happen take place without giving Dudd any warning. He let the Irishman escort them to the

270

accompanying elevator in a practised staccato strut McNamara recognised as part of the simulacrum of flaunted power. Dudd had obviously fallen in love with the external trappings of the office: the chauffeur, the handful of flunkies, the house on the island in the artificial lake, the six-figure salary, the endless opportunities to speak in the imperative. When he had been at Odium, he had been a lolloper, head down and shoulders always sagging, slow of pace. Now he looked as if he were about to marshal squaddies on a parade ground.

Ching and Dudd appeared to be temperamentally suited to each other. The Chinese man had glossy cheeks, the stature of a Napoleon, was bow-legged, jaunty in his gait, bore a smile that was too broad to be anything but patronising, and he made disconcerting little grunts and gasps when he was not speaking, as if there were a tiny gremlin always busily at work in the olfactory bulb at the back of his nose. In other words, like nearly all local Chinese Communist Party bigwigs, he was a repellent little toad who listened to no one, or at least to no one in Chongqing. He greeted them with sweeping gestures of both arms and a booming, throaty, obviously prepared piece of rhetoric, in Chinese.

His P.A., a demure and rather cowed woman in her thirties whom Ching introduced as Meifeng,, bowed a little and translated instantly. Evidently she came from one of the parts of China where the phonemes represented by the letters *r* and *l* are not reversed in pronunciation, or she had been well educated. Her English was faultless. "Mr Ching welcomes the new Pro-Vice Chancellor of the University of Odium to Chongqing! He would like to convey the honour he feels to be meeting such a prestigious Marxist thinker!"

"Thank you," said McNamara.

Mr Ching beckoned for them to sit on a low couch and turned to make the short journey to the much higher seating position he wished to occupy on the far side of his desk. Dudd readily acquiesced and relaxed into the soft leather, but when Ching settled back into his chair he discovered that McNamara still loomed over him, his barrel shape somewhat intimidating, and that Drusilla had not accepted the invitation to sit either. She was standing at his side.

"I have a letter for you," said McNamara, "from Vice Chancellor Spooner. This is the only business we have to conduct today."

McNamara put the sealed envelope on the desk while the translator Chinesed his words uneasily. Ching's smile narrowed from four inches wide across his face to about three and a half, though it still remained imprinted there. He wafted a hand in the direction of the reclining Dudd.

"Mr Ching would be grateful if you would be seated," said Meifeng. It was clearly part of her role to verbalise physical gestures as well as translate articulated sounds, even when this was not strictly necessary. She appeared agitated.

"Thank you," said McNamara, "but no. We will stay for a few minutes if he wishes to read the letter."

While she explained to Ching, Drusilla looked at Dudd and advised in a low voice, "I'd get up if I were you. We're not staying, and believe me, you won't wish to either."

Dudd had got used to the language of command and instantly recognised it. Without thought or challenge, as if Drusilla were a senior member of the Odium Management Board rather than simply its most senior PR hack, he obeyed.

Ching now looked displeased. He reached for an ostentatious silver letter opener. He read the short missive with his lips moving slowly. When he looked up, his craniometry seemed to have changed. He looked more glabellous. His forehead had furrowed intensely and seemed now suddenly to be protuberant, forming a consternated shelf brooding above his eyes. These same eyes then turned up at McNamara, smaller, needling, narrowed, darker. He rose to his feet slowly, the page trembling in his hand, and said something in a low growl, the tone unmistakably menacing.

There was silence. After a second or two McNamara looked at the translator, who had her eyes aimed at her shoes, and was shaking her head slowly.

"I think," said Drusilla, "he just asked what the blazes, as it were, is going on."

"Okay," said McNamara, "he's got the gist." He held out his hand. "Goodbye, Mr Ching."

Ching ignored the proffered handshake. McNamara turned. Drusilla turned.

"But what the blazes *is* going on?" said Dudd, as he too turned.

"We're leaving," said Drusilla. "I'd come with us, if I were you. I can explain outside."

"I see," said Dudd. "Whatever you say."

They had taken only a few steps towards the door when Ching intercepted them, scurrying on short legs from around his desk and interposing himself between the exit and them. He was clearly in a rising fury, and his voice was still loud and rasping but, as he let off an entire paragraph of what sounded like scurrilous invective, the tone slowly changed, along with the expression on his face, and seemed to admit, towards the end, an element of pleading. At the cessation of his outpouring, McNamara looked to Meifeng. She had begun gazing downwards again halfway through his tirade. Now she slowly turned her face up.

"Cannot," she said to McNamara.

"I understand," he acknowledged. "It is obscene?"

She nodded.

Ching began to reproach the translator directly, jabbing his finger at her, clearly commanding her to translate his words.

"Let's pretend," McNamara suggested to her, "because it does not really matter what he says, not any more. Tell me, where did you study?"

"Thank you," Meifeng said very graciously. "I read English Literature at St Andrew's and then I took a Masters at Durham. I enjoyed my time in Britain very much. I miss my friends there. I hope to come again some time. It would be my dream to work there. This is most awkward."

McNamara smiled a little at her in sympathy. Then he looked at Ching severely and raised his voice and his hand, and to everyone's astonishment, especially Dudd's, he wagged his own index finger in front of Ching's snorting nose in an act of unambiguous physical provocation. "I did not come here to be insulted, Mr Ching!" he bellowed. "Now get out of the way, or I shall have to pick you up and move you aside personally. It's time to say *zàijiàn*."

They spent five minutes briefing Dudd, and then they both fled to the airport for the next flight to Shanghai. Drusilla fired off a pre-prepared press release to an enormous email list before they settled into their seats in the first class cabin. Things got even better in Shanghai, where they discovered that they each had been booked in for the rest of the week to their own private suites at the Ritz-Carlton at 8 Century Avenue in the Pudong district. ("Rucky Chinese number!" Drusilla exclaimed.) There was little time to relax that evening, however: the

273

calls started coming in from the UK media, eight hours behind China, almost as soon as they arrived, and McNamara was up all night because he agreed to do a live interview on *Newsnight*. Drusilla met him afterwards in the breakfast room, looking beady-eyed and slow-witted.

"How did it go?" she asked.

"Pretty well," he said. "The British media seem to think it's a good move. The hardest question I got was, why had we ever gone to China in the first place?"

"What did you say?"

"I said it was the vanity project of an ex-Vice Chancellor, part of a general overreaching on his part that ended in the ultimate catastrophe of last term. This seems at least partly true."

"And you can't libel the dead," said Drusilla cheerily.

"Can you believe they got a quote from Donald Trump? They played it just before my interview. He thought it was a great idea, getting the hell out of China. He praised Spooner personally. Said he himself would be looking to American universities to justify their presence in China too, now that NYU is here in Shanghai."

"Wow!" said Drusilla.

"Well, no, if Donald Trump endorses you, I think you should maybe start to get worried."

"It's a bit late for that!" laughed Drusilla. "In PR terms it's brilliant, especially given the Trump money deal. The story begins to look coherent."

"You mean it begins to look coherently right-wing," McNamara rejoined. "Still, I agree we did need to get out of China. It was a fiasco from the first. They asked me near the end of the interview about the other big Odium story of the moment, of course. That was not so good. I had perhaps said too much about the constraints placed on our operation by the Chinese. So they quizzed me about the 'similar lack of academic freedom' back in Odium itself. I think I may have been a bit too forthright. I said the allegations were contemptible and false. I repeated that neither Yunus or Faraj had academic freedom because only academics did."

"That's alright, then, isn't it?"

"I'm not sure. Everyone's up for a bit of China-baiting, they like it when sprats like the British throw a dart in China's whale blubber. But calling a pair of local Muslim boys liars goes down a lot less well. The David-Goliath dynamic seems to get reversed when we do that."

"I mean it's alright *in terms of discharging your functions*. It's alright in that you did not put a foot wrong or go off-message."

"Is that all it's about, Drusilla? Discharging your functions? Doing your little bit? Not questioning the overall wisdom of the direction of travel? Not taking issue with the morality of it all?"

"Yes," she said categorically. "That's what it's always been about at all levels in a modern university. I don't set the agenda. I present it."

"Yes, I understand that, in your case. But senior managers are meant to help set the agenda. Vice Chancellors ultimately fix the agenda. I had nothing to do with this decision, even though I approve of it in principle. I'm beginning to wonder how much it was approved – for just some accountability's sake, not a naïve belief in institutional democracy – by the hardly functioning University Council. From where I am standing it looks as if Spooner largely gerrymandered the decision himself and sent me out to execute it. That's pretty close to the moral equivalent of Covet bringing us out here in the first place. And so part of me wonders how deep he is in with similarly anti-China Trump. The British government didn't want us out of China; the American President was happy about it. Should a British university not pause for serious thought at facts like that?"

"What, even if the American President is giving you money that the British government isn't? Doesn't he who pays the piper call the tune?"

McNamara mulled this over. Drusilla was again correct in a purely technical sense. One of the reasons Whitehall had been unable to stop Spooner withdrawing from China was that it had largely washed its hands of universities' funding years ago and no longer paid for their teaching. As a consequence, it had little to blackmail or bribe Spooner with and little other means of traction with him. It did not fund the meagre research that had been conducted at the Chongqing campus.

"The fundamental moral problem, Drusilla, is that we work in an apparently public sector in which it should not be possible or necessary for the American President to have his thumbs in the scales of a British university."

"I don't see why not," she said feistily. "He can buy Scottish land and turn it into golf courses. It's just the logical outcome of globalisation. The key difference would seem to be that he can't actually *buy* the University of Odium but only donate to it. The only compromise we have to make is be polite and friendly to him while we bank his cash. It doesn't *determine* anything, which is why we are able to devote those funds to an expansion of non-commercial subjects. In fact, if you put what we have just done here in China into the narrative, we ourselves seem to be drawing a line under globalisation. There are limits to what we are prepared to accept in its name. And we are no longer prepared to accept giving away University of Odium degrees for a mess of Chinese pottage."

"It must have crossed your mind," he said, "that the only reason this is so is that we may have traded China for a similar mess of Trump pottage."

"Well, yes," she admitted. "But I repeat, ours is not to reason why."

McNamara went to bed and slept heavily, leaving Drusilla to deal with any daytime press. At around three in the afternoon he was awoken by a loud rapping on the door of his suite. He got up and answered it in his hotel dressing gown.

It was Drusilla. She looked jubilant. She raised both of her arms in the air and shook them in triumph. "Job done!" she exclaimed.

"What do you mean?" he asked blearily.

"The Chinese! They took the bait! They've pulled the plug! They're not prepared to put up with us for another four and a half years. We have to be out by the first of September. They're taking over the Chongqing campus, virtually nationalising it! It's to become a Chinese university! They're triggering the clause that allows them to buy back our holding. We're even making money on the deal!"

McNamara did not know what to think, but was rather swept up in Drusilla's infectious enthusiasm.

"I need a drink!" she whooped, and strolled into his room, heading for the mini-bar.

He did not remember exactly how or when they ended up in bed, though he could not deny that he enjoyed every moment they spent there. Drusilla was in a bewitchingly buoyant mood, she was dressed and made-up to the nines because she had been in front of cameras, she was full of praise for the way he had handled himself in public, all traces of their previous enmity seemed to have been wiped from her memory cells, and drink must have done the rest. The foreplay was long. Congress itself was not brief, but only because it was slow, a bit like sliding gently from a wet mud bank into slimy water, except that Drusilla

276

was warm, warm, and soft, and welcoming, and seemingly as desirous as she was desirable. The afterplay was gentle and drawn-out, peppered by much talking of a personal kind, and more alcohol.

For the rest of the week nothing outside the framing rectangle of their shared bed seemed to have any serious purchase on his existence, even as he dealt with the chores each day threw up. He got to know much about her which he could never have guessed, and to touch her in ways that he had never touched Rachel Brace, the last woman who had surrendered herself to him of her entirely free will. He felt nothing of the sordidness he had experienced in his dreams with the necrotic Jane Blake or her substitute pornographic diva or the ultra-compliant harlot who had superseded both in Amsterdam. What he did feel was perfectly figured in Drusilla's words late in the night before they left, as he came out of the bathroom, and the room was dark, and he heard her softly call his first name.

"Yes?" he said.

"Please make love to me again," she implored.


**Chapter Eleven**

"I'm sorry I didn't reply to your emails last week," McNamara said to Redman. "To be honest, we were so busy I didn't have time to catch up on them until we were in the departure lounge. The Odium Two seemed a little less urgent than the China Syndrome. But now I understand the two have been connected."

They were sitting in McNamara's kitchen. It was Monday morning, barely thirty-six hours since his return from China. He had just finished describing the Chongqing drama to Redman.

"It's a very clever campaign," Redman agreed. "Of course, it was Trump who sparked the flame. The students appear to be opposed to the withdrawal from China: you know, fling a few feel-good words at them, like *internationalism*, stir the slightest brotherhood-of-man feeling into their sensitive brain mush, say nothing at all about the abiding horrors of the Chinese Commie Party, especially its repression of free speech, and they're all yours. So when Trump opens his mouth and approves of the decision publicly, *and he's coming here on Thursday of this week*, well, he's suddenly in the eye of the campaign's souped-up storm. Never mind the grotesque contradictions. The political logic now is, Odium has become a right-wing University because it does not protect freedom of speech, and what other signs are there of this, or why is it so?"

"Become?" said McNamara. "This *is* a right-wing University, always has been in my time here."

"True, but in this caricature its recent financial association with Trump is offered as both confirmation and cause. It's a clever way of ensuring the campaigners have new things to do, stay active. The next protest has been called against Trump's visit, and we can expect that it will be an *invasion*, because thousands will pour in from far and wide to deride The Donald. The Odium Two will massively enhance their fanbase because their lieutenants, including large numbers of deluded staff, will be canvassing it, petitioning their supporters, all day long. And Trump will almost certainly say something inane to assist them."

"But the China decision had nothing to do with Trump."

"You sure?"

McNamara grimaced with incredulity. "You cannot possibly think Spooner was *doing Trump's bidding* in pulling out of China," he snorted. "Why would the President of the United States give a damn?"

"No, of course not," Redman replied. "But it's not about the truth or otherwise of specific claims. It's about smearing things together into a political Pollock canvas that students are persuaded they should like. First of all we have a building given Trump's name. Second, we accept a massive and possibly tax-dodging Trump donation. Third, we become the biggest institution of any note except Google to get out of China, something Trump said he would make American companies do. So you can see why we are now being read as rather Trumpish in our ideological complexion, surely? A mere ten years after promulgating our global expansion, we shrink back to our little home island. It fits right in with the Brexit mood, and let's not forget that Trump approves of Brexit too."

"Ha! Google!" McNamara exclaimed. "They threw in the China towel over censorship issues. How ironic!"

Redman noted the attempt at digression, and ignored it. He decided to make a more personal attempt to elicit an engaged response.

"For example," he said, "when they played the Trump tape on

*Newsnight*, and asked you if you agreed with him..."

"What was I meant to say?" McNamara interrupted. "That I think he is an idiot? Trump is about to hand over a truckload of gold. No serious person in my position would put that at risk."

"I agree," Redman relented. "It must have been difficult for you."

"No, in fact!" McNamara expostulated. "As Pro-Vice Chancellor of the University, I stand in for the Vice Chancellor. I don't speak on my own behalf. It's an office. Also, it so happens that *on this matter* Trump finds himself in agreement *with me*. It was me, after all, who delivered the letter. He was the one who was asked if *he* agreed with what *we'd* done. This then gets reverse-mangled by the fucking BBC and I am asked if *I agree with him*! It was the nearly dawn in Shanghai. I wasn't at my most alert."

"You simply said yes," Redman laughed. "Clever interviewer, that Evan Davies. So the University of Odium agrees with Donald Trump."

"That's preposterous!" McNamara scoffed. "What does that even *mean*? The statement simply turns a concrete particular into an abstract universal. It makes it sound as if we agree with all that is Trump, rather than our coincidentally sharing with him the same opinion on a single, small decision."

"And that's exactly how it is playing, as a universal, not a particular" said Redman conclusively. He reached for his iPad. "Let me show you something. It's called a mash-up."

McNamara groaned with disrelish as Redman logged on to the Facebook page of the Odium Two campaign. The two-minute video he showed McNamara consisted largely of a series of loathsome Donald Trump quotations, spoken by the man himself in interviews or speeches, interspliced with the repeated, identical scene from *Newsnight* in which Evan Davies asked McNamara if he agreed with Trump. Various written words and phrases had been edited in and bounced and shuttled across the screen for the duration, in subliminal transparent fonts, like "snake oil" and "misogynist" and "liar". There was also a low, slightly comic jingle sounding in the background. But the verbal soundtrack, with its constructed juxtapositions, created the primary effect:

TRUMP: When Mexico sends its people, they're not sending the best. They're sending people that have lots of problems. They're bringing drugs. They bring crime. They're rapists.

DAVIES: Professor McNamara, do you agree with Donald Trump?

McNAMARA: Yes.

TRUMP: The beauty of me is that I'm very rich.

DAVIES: Professor McNamara, do you agree with Donald Trump?

McNAMARA: Yes.

TRUMP: It's freezing and snowing in New York – we need global warming!

DAVIES: Professor McNamara, do you agree with Donald Trump?

McNAMARA: Yes.

TRUMP: You know, it really doesn't matter what the media write as long as you've got a young, and beautiful, piece of ass.

DAVIES: Professor McNamara, do you agree with Donald Trump?

McNAMARA: Yes.

TRUMP: I'm pleased that the University of Odium is getting out of China. American universities ought to follow their example.

DAVIES: Professor McNamara, do you agree with Donald Trump?

McNAMARA: Yes.

McNamara smiled with faint bemusement. "It's just so childish," he remarked.

"Facebook is where today's youth gets its news," said Redman. "The only thing they know about *Newsnight* is what they see on Facebook or Twitter or YouTube about *Newsnight*. They don't see satire as making fun of politics: they think it is a legitimate way of *conducting* politics. Look how many likes this has."

McNamara squinted at the screen. "Does that say what I think it says? Is that six figures?"

"In one week, yes. If you click through to YouTube, where the video is hosted, the number of watches is in seven figures. This is the biggest audience you've ever had, Robert. This is what you are to them. Trump's yes-man. Just read the comments."

McNamara gestured helplessly at the unaccountable juvenility of it all. What he really wanted to retort was that it really didn't matter what Facebook or Twitter or YouTube said, because he had a middle-aged but still desirable piece of ass. But he did not think that anyone in the University would want to hear about him and Drusilla just yet, least of all Redman.

*

Fifteen minutes later they walked together up to the Trump Building. There was an awkward moment as they stopped in the corridor of the west wing, McNamara intending to go right into the Vice Chancellor's suite, Redman hovering before turning left into the Registrar's office opposite. They looked briefly towards each other and their expressions glinted in the humour of the moment, its bejewelled ironies. McNamara nodded with half a smile and made his entrance. Redman went through his appointed door, said hello to Alison Stilt, and proceeded to the inner sanctum. There he found Nigel Asterisk and Drusilla Frost.

"Hello. Have you recovered from China?" he asked Drusilla.

Drusilla replied, "Not quite."

"I spoke to Robert," Redman said.

Drusilla gave a small, studied smile. "He was very firm," she said. "With the Chinese, I mean."

"You got on?" Redman appeared interested.

"Well, what did he say?" she rejoined brightly.

"He was extremely complimentary about you. Despite the task you both had, he seemed to enjoy it."

"Me too," she said. "And Professor McNamara was charming."

Asterisk interrupted. "We were just saying, it's like we're having a streak of good luck. Actually to be making money on the China deal is nothing short of a miracle. It's played well in the press, if not with the home students. To be shot of the entire thing by the first of September is just Dreamsville. But as one door closes a different trap door might open, if we don't manage Thursday with some deftness."

"I expect," Redman said, "that Thursday will be a political nightmare, not to say a massive security risk. Deftness has never been our stock-in-trade. We might try to find out what the Union is up to."

"How?" asked Asterisk.

"Robert is with the VC now. He's going to suggest that we drop in on Avril Poon."

"You and PVC McNamara? Before Thursday?"

"Right now, today," Redman confirmed.

"But why would the Union president share any information? The Union is against us on this. It's anti-Trump and pro-Odium Two."

"Not to mention being suddenly pro-China," Drusilla sighed. She

281

was making to leave.

Redman smiled wryly. "You never know. We might be able to persuade her by, er, leaning on old loyalties. In any case, the VC will decide. You're not staying, Drusilla?"

"Oh, Drusilla has another appointment," Asterisk explained. "We were just playing catch-up as she's been away. It actually wasn't Thursday I wanted to talk to you about. It was something else."

Collegial farewells were exchanged. Asterisk waved gallantly at Drusilla as she departed.

"I wanted to talk with you about a formal complaint in my possession," Asterisk began once the door had been closed. "It's about PVC McNamara and it's from Elfyn Dethbridge."

Redman guffawed and rolled his eyes at the same time. "Is this about what I think it's about? Nigel, you know as well as I do that you can stamp on this. The PVCs have a virtual forcefield around them, Short of embezzlement, or gross negligence, or doing the kinds of things Sir Evan Covet did, grievances about senior managers are never allowed to become formal. They get strangled, or otherwise silenced, at birth. And I bet this one isn't even alive to begin with. And he's your deputy. You can surely silence him."

"That was the case in the previous dispensation, yes, but this VC is keen to have things like this handled more by the book."

"Can I see it?"

"Unfortunately no, because it's confidential, of course. By the very book it must be, you see. Besides, I'm not technically involved. Formal complaints must be directed to the manager of the person accused, which in this case is the VC. Elfyn was naturally a little nervous about the form of words he should use to the VC and thus he discussed it with me and showed me his draft. I did all I could to discourage him, but on this matter he is displaying an unusual amount of nerve. I am seeing him later this morning. He is quite determined to force the issue. He's like a little volcano, to be honest. It's as if he's blown his top after years of grumbling."

"He has always detested Robert. They've never got on. But this is all over nothing. There's no case."

"Well, I don't know," Asterisk dissented. "He claims Robert called him *a fucking gaylord* in a public place on the employer's premises during normal working hours. And what with the recent silent LGBT revolution, that has perforce to be treated with all the same seeming seriousness as calling a black man a nigger to his face. These debacles can turn into employment tribunals if you're not careful. And he says he has a witness: *you.*"

"Me?" Redman scoffed. "I don't think so. It was out there in the quadrangle, on the morning of the arrests. Robert did refer to someone using those words. But it wasn't Elfyn. He didn't even know Elfyn was there. He had his back to him and he was talking to me. But I told Elfyn all this already."

"How do you mean?"

"I told him on the spot, at the very moment, as well as later that morning, over in the School of English, when he buttonholed me about it in a little hissy fit."

"He hasn't said anything about talking it over with you, not in the statement of grievance or in our conversations."

Redman digested this information uncomfortably. "Ah, I see."

"Do you think he's relying on the VC's likely, er, sympathies about, er, offence of this kind?"

"It's more cunning," said Redman. "Robert was referring *to the VC* and Elfyn knows it. We had both just met him for the first time. I didn't explicitly tell Elfyn that the VC was the *fucking gaylord* alluded to but he had worked it out. What he wants to do is call me as a witness to a grievance committee chaired by the VC and have it revealed that Robert, who is now in a direct working relationship with Spooner, because he has been gifted Vice Chancellorian preferment, said such a vile thing about him in public hearing just a few weeks ago. The intention isn't for Elfyn's offence to be acknowledged. He wants to engineer circumstances so that the VC and Robert are at personal loggerheads. What a nasty little plan!"

Asterisk pondered for a moment. "It's not in anyone's interests for this to happen."

"No," agreed Redman. "But I can think of a simple solution."

Asterisk's brows rose. "Which is?"

"I could lie. I could simply deny that Robert said any such thing."

Asterisk cleared his throat. "I foresee a problem. I mean, need I say, there is obviously an ethical problem, and so to solve that let's both agree right now that this conversation we're having never happened. But I really mean there is the practical problem of PVC McNamara agreeing to lie also. And I must say, I've become uneasy about lies when they are made a matter of record. They're more readily discoverable when they are in writing."

"It won't get that far. Neither me nor Robert will have to lie."

"How come?"

"Because you will indeed tell Elfyn that we had this conversation. And you will tell him that I denied that Robert said any such thing. He must have been misheard. It's an echoey box, the quadrangle. Elfyn won't even file the grievance if he knows I won't play ball. His entire case rests on my confirmation or Robert's admission. He is probably expecting Robert to deny it. But if he thinks I will also deny it, he'll know his case will be empty."

"So," said Asterisk, "you won't have to lie, if I am prepared to lie? I mean, you did not deny it. You did confirm it."

"I did," said Redman. "But *that part* of the discussion, let's agree, did not happen. The conversation which did happen was the one I just imagined. Or do you have moral reservations about lying to Elfyn to ruin this pathetic stratagem of his?"

Asterisk's expression brightened. "Oh no," he answered. "Not at all."

When Redman left Asterisk some minutes later, he was surprised to see Drusilla loitering at the end of the corridor with McNamara, giggling like a girl while he boomed out hearty laughter like Santa Claus, his hand on his stomach. He reflected that McNamara's jolliness quotient was spiking. There had been the half smile just fifteen minutes before. Now, as he walked with him towards the elevator, Drusilla having once more made her excuses to Redman and taken her leave, he saw from the corner of his eye that the older man was broadly beaming, standing more erectly, and altogether cutting a figure of recently enhanced gravity.

"So Spooner agreed, about Poon?" Redman asked.

"Yes," smiled McNamara. "He was over the moon about everything. He didn't even advert to the Trump dimension. I did. I expressed some regret at having not elaborated on my single-word affirmation re The Donald. But Spooner dismissed this as a bagatelle. What he did say was that he thought I should now be on the platform when Trump speaks on Thursday. He wants me to meet him."

"Oh, hell."

They stepped into the elevator and began their whirring ascent.

"It's not a problem," replied McNamara with some levity. "It should be entertaining. Also, don't forget, the Trump money is going to my Faculty and to the Faculty for which I bear staffing responsibility. So it's quite fitting."

Redman pulled a face. "The Faculty *for which I bear staffing responsibility*? Listen to yourself. You're talking like a senior management memo already. Atlas with the world on his shoulders."

McNamara laughed self-deprecatingly as they debouched. Again, Redman thought, behold the waves of amused light-heartedness emanating most untypically from the man. "I apologise. And what did Asterisk have to say?"

"Nothing to report," Redman lied.

They had arrived at their destination: room D4(b). McNamara rapped vigorously on the door. He did not wait for an invitation to enter, and stepped into the room ahead of Redman.

Avril Poon looked up from behind her desk. She remained seated. "PVC McNamara!" she hailed him. "But you're wearing fine silk, not PVC at all! I don't believe we have an appointment. And, wow, Vice Dean Redman too! And you are wearing a suit as well! What smart gentlemen you both are!"

"I regret the unheralded intrusion, Avril," McNamara said. "It's a somewhat urgent matter, and should not take very long. May we sit?"

All of them gathered around the teaching table in the middle of the room.

"We are hoping that you can assist us in a matter of security," commenced McNamara, "and the reason it is we who are speaking to you rather than the Vice Chancellor or the Registrar is that it concerns the activities of the Union. In short, we would be grateful to know what the intentions of the Union are with regard to its involvement in the demonstration planned for Thursday, and to offer some guidance from the University which we trust you will observe."

An ironic smile was twitching at the corners of Poon's mouth long before this mini-speech had concluded. At its end she shook her head ruefully but gently. "You two," she said witheringly. "You come in here like the Kray twins, but why should I be surprised? After all, I know you are both arrant liars. It was in this very room, not four months ago, PVC McNamara, that you took a hidden microphone from behind that picture of Patrick Stewart over there, and showed me another two microphones, and then both of you implied that I was a lunatic by ever-after denying the existence of those bugs, planted by a Vice Chancellor to spy on the elected representatives of his staff. Forgive me, but I don't trust liars. You have no right to any information about the Union's activities. Neither of you is even a UCU member."

McNamara, now glowering, took a breath. "That's not all we covered up, Avril. You want to talk about Odiumgate? You really want to talk about what was concealed that could still do damage to the living rather than just the dead? You remember Jane Blake? I never did tell you, did I, that she told me all about you and her? Or that we have a document in her hand that confirms, with details, claims about the sexual advances you made on her?"

Redman was sure he saw Poon blush, despite the Indian darkness of her face. He chipped in. "You see, we think the lid should be kept on private stuff like that unless there is some overwhelming benefit in exposing it."

"If, for example," added McNamara, "the Union were to withdraw from its involvement in the demonstration on Thursday, that would be an irresistible argument for ensuring that your predation towards Jane Blake remained discreetly concealed."

Poon looked acidly from one to the other. Seconds passed before she replied. "So, bullies, blackmailers, as well as liars, is what you are. Look at you. It's like *Animal Farm* without the revolution: you two pigs haven't overthrown Farmer Jones, you've simply moved out of your sty into the farmhouse with him and are walking around on two legs, or rather in two suits. You, Napoleon, you have the gall to use the word *predation*. You have just thrown into doubt the employment of hundreds of staff in China in the blink of an eye, given them summary notice and abandoned them to the *depredations* of the Chinese government. Just like that! You gave no thought to the consequences for them, did you? I thought not. And now, in the kind of backstairs manoeuvre that so typifies people of your nature, you both emerge from the disguises you have worn all your lives."

"People of our nature?" exclaimed Redman. "Said the Brahmin."

"Oh, cut it, Snowball. By the way, which public school did you go to? You think I didn't know? I saw you once in the coffee bar, reading Wodehouse and laughing. Dead giveaway. The answer to your request is an unnegotiable no. I'm no angel, but I'm not going to have my arm twisted because you have some embarrassing private details about me that you could spill to the world. Do what you like. Now fuck off out of my office, you cock-in-an-asshole combo."

It hadn't gone well, Redman reflected as he and McNamara retreated to the elevator.

"Did I hear her right?" McNamara said.

"Yes."

"She called us a cock-in-an-asshole combo."

"I don't think there was any actual suggestion that we are co-members of her gay entourage. I think she was just being super-rude."

"I was wondering which of us was the cock and which the asshole."

"My money is on me being the asshole. Shall we make a formal complaint?"

McNamara grinned at the playfully proposed idea. Still happy, Redman noted.

They parted. McNamara had a Management Board meeting to attend. Redman dawdled over to his office in the School of English. Despite the *contretemps* with Poon, he was beginning to feel some of the thrills of intrigue, the tiny shots of adrenalin that seemed to be a reward for scheming, bluffing, and threatening, even when, as on this occasion, they failed to secure their end. The failure merely made one's mind race in order to devise a more successful means of entrapping the enemy.

He picked up the phone and called Lorraine at home.

"I was thinking I might leave early and come straight to yours," he said. "I could be there in half an hour."

"There's early and there's *early*," Lorraine replied. "Forgive me, as someone with fixed hours of work, for thinking that ten on a Monday morning is mighty soon to be knocking off work. In any case, I'm going out for a few hours."

"Later, then. I was thinking we could do something a bit different."

"Different from what?"

"Different from usual. I mean, I could come straight in the door, we could agree that there would be no talk, I could push you up against the wall, right there in your hallway."

"I see."

"I could pull up your skirt and give it to you, standing up –"

287

"I'm not wearing a skirt," protested Lorraine. "I'm wearing an old pair of jeans."

"You could change."

"I don't want to change."

Undeterred by her lack of cooperation, Redman continued suavely. "Alright, then, jeans it is. I shall just have to throw you on the bed and peel them off."

"Have to?" repeated Lorraine. "No, you don't *have to*."

"I mean, I'd like to."

"Clearly."

"I could give it to you all afternoon."

"You could."

"You know, not so much romance as a good hard dirty fucking."

"I get the picture."

"Is that a yes?"

There was a brief but heavy silence.

"What do you think, James?"

The lack of affirmation finally stopped Redman in his tracks. "It doesn't sound like a yes," he acknowledged.

"No," said Lorraine, "it's not. Stay at work, James. Don't come to mine at all today. I will speak to you again when your need for a whore has passed."

The line went dead.

It hadn't, Redman reflected, gone well.

"Now, ladies and gentlemen," Spooner was saying in the splendour of his office to his seven Pro-Vice Chancellors and his Registrar, "now that we have welcomed Professor McNamara to his first Management Board meeting, and heard his summary report on China, it's time for my update on the visit of President Trump this coming Thursday. You can expect, from tomorrow, a great deal of Secret Service activity in this building and the routes to it, because the cheque-handover ceremony will take place in the Great Hall. Be aware that Secret Service agents are permitted to, and do, carry firearms, though they will not be armed when they interview every individual, including yourselves, who is likely to come into contact or close proximity to the President. They will brief you on decorum and other matters of conduct. Please follow their advice. Your individual appointments with the Secret Service are scheduled for tomorrow and you can find the times and venue in the briefing pack before you. Please ensure that you read everything in there before Thursday.

"I should say that, if Whitehall was already hopping mad with us – or more specifically, with me – over China, it's absolutely incandescent about the Trump visit. I can confirm with some pleasure that the Prime Minister, though she was, I know, sorely tempted, will not be paying us a visit in order to be the most prominent person to shake the President's hand on his first visit to the country since his electoral victory. Nothing has been or will be said in public, but I got a personal roasting from another woman in Number 10 on the phone over the weekend. That's how I know she's not coming. President Trump is diffident about meeting her now in any case: he told me he wasn't very impressed with her when she came to the White House the other month, and he prefers to wait for the full pomp and ceremony of a state visit, when she'll be eclipsed in the American press by his meeting the Queen. Her absence makes the security issues a little less vexing.

"We do, however, still have the problem of the planned demonstration to contend with. We have had meetings with the police, and the police have had meetings with those responsible for organising the protest. But we do not know exactly what shape the event is likely to take. The advice we initially received was that we should shut out anyone not officially involved from all three access routes entered from the north, east and west entrances to the campus. We can do this, as inside the gates, legally speaking, they are all private roads. In effect, this would have meant that the protest could take place only outside the campus perimeter, very far from this building. However, the projected numbers expected to attend occupy a range from the enormous to the colossal, something between fifty and one hundred thousand people. If all of them are kept outside the perimeter, they will choke every arterial road around us and the entire city will soon be gridlocked for hours. There are concerns about the effects on residents in properties nearby. We have therefore taken the decision to turn this building, and this building alone, into Fort Knox. The President will arrive in a chopper and land right out there in the quadrangle of what he calls 'my own British Trump Tower'. The ceremony is expected to last merely minutes. The invited guests in the Great Hall, as well as the media, using biometric security passes issued for the occasion, will have to check in

289

an hour before its commencement. When it's over, he will be helicoptered off again, and we shall be forty million pounds richer, with more on the way. Pray, please, for yet a further fall in the international value of sterling between now and Thursday. I worked out last night that every cent the pound goes down is worth about ten new academic posts to us.

"We intend to be cooperative with the demonstrators, as long as they stay outside this bunker, of course. We do intend to advertise the fact of those Secret Service guns as a deterrent to any idea of their trying to gain entry to this building. We have plenty of open spaces on campus and they will generally be as free as any member of the public is to enter and ramble. There will be massive security on all buildings, of course, particularly science buildings. We are pulling out all the stops on the catering front, and jacking up the prices. Indeed, the feeding of the fifty-plus thousand is expected to net us something between a quarter and half a million on a single day. That might just cover the cost of the extra security. There will, moreover, be large stages erected about fifty metres from this building, on which the protesters, or their spokespersons, will be at liberty to orate. This should give the lie to the idea that we frown on freedom of speech. We are, quite literally, providing them with the platform on which to speak. In reality, the two stages will act as an outer shield for us, as the crowds shall be corralled on the far side of them. Are there any questions?"

McNamara surveyed the array of professorial heads around the table, then ended the short hiatus.

"Not so much a question," he said, "as a probe, a seeking-out of views. It concerns the press. I've already been approached, directly, for comment on the Trump visit. Perhaps others have or will be too."

"Ah," Spooner piped up. "Yes, thank you. No need for a seeking-out of views, in fact. Only two people henceforth will talk to the media, myself and our Communications Officer, Drusilla Frost. If you are contacted by any reporters, refer them in the first instance to Drusilla. Say nothing, offer no comment or opinion, keep shtum."

He looked at McNamara. McNamara nodded. "I concur," he concurred. "I think it's easier for each of us that way, as well as promising to guarantee consistency in the University's reported pronouncements."

*

"No, you listen to me, Elfyn," Redman heard himself growling down his office phone in an unusually menacing voice. "There's not that much difference between a lie and a deliberate failure to tell the whole truth. And that's what you're doing. Take it from me, I've seen people not that dissimilar to you try to play similar doggy tricks in front of a Vice Chancellor. It didn't turn out well for them. They didn't think it through." He allowed his throat to relax, and the force in his voice eased. "Say you brought your complaint before a grievance committee, and called me as a witness, and I came in and agreed, yes, Professor McNamara did say those words, but he was most definitely not referring to Mr Dethbridge, and I told Mr Dethbridge so, twice. In your wish-fulfilment fantasy of what happens after that, you think the next question is going to be, well, to whom *was* he referring? But it isn't. The obvious next question is, is this true, Mr Dethbridge? Did Dr Redman indeed apprise you, not once but twice, of the fact that Professor McNamara was referring to someone else? And if so, if you knew that, why are you wasting our time with this misleading complaint? Do you think we care that Professor McNamara let rip an unguarded, politically incorrect accusation in a private conversation, if no offence was caused to the object of his insult? Do you imagine that we are more concerned about that than about an attempt by an administrator to undermine a senior officer of the University less than a fortnight after he has assumed his post? Aware as you are of recent scandals in the management of the University, Mr Dethbridge, is it your objective to drag the University down further into the mire? And so on. And what if you even got past these shockwaves of negative reaction and managed, somehow, to elicit a statement to the fact that Professor McNamara was actually referring to the Vice Chancellor. What? You are going to out Spooner officially in a grievance committee at which he is present, *which he is personally chairing*, in front of others, and on record? It will be you, then, won't it, who is drawing attention to the Vice Chancellor's gaylordiness? How can you ever have thought that such a situation could end anything but badly for you?"

He could hear Dethbridge's shallow breathing in the earpiece.

"In a way," Redman added with a small air of munificence, "I'm kind of doing you a favour in stopping you."

The line went dead.

## Chapter Twelve

Two days later, Redman found himself stepping, with a kind of resentment and dread, into the University Staff Club. A few years before, an internal survey had come round whose last question had been, "What single change would make you come to the Staff Club more frequently?" He had answered, "Its conversion to a teaching building." Soon afterwards the Club had abandoned its membership fee and structure and anyone in an eligible "job family" (as the current contracts so wholesomely put it) was free to wander in. It made its money by jacking up the food and drink prices and renting out rooms to other parts of the University in need of a cosy central location where catering could readily be laid on. So much in demand were its wood-panelled nooks that an extra such room had been created by throwing out the snooker table. The only times Redman had found himself within ten metres of the Club's cracked brown leather sofas and nineteenth-century newspaper rack were when attendance at some or other University meeting required him to be there. He had never gone through its mock country-house portal voluntarily or in response to some sociable invitation.

But now he had come to meet McNamara there. McNamara had once had a similar distaste for the Club – or was it for the staff? – but since his ascension to the status of equerry, he had rapidly been converted to the idea (and, even worse, the reality) that the Club was the best place on campus for senior managers to do all of the informal cajoling and gladhanding and threatening that was a necessary part of their success in the role. These were activities, everyone seemed silently to agree, that it would be too unseemly to perform in an official, not to say minuted, meeting.

McNamara had let it be known to Redman that he had been spending a lot of time in the Club this week. With the Trump money about to create the most magnificent sunrise the Arts and Humanities and Social Science Faculties had ever witnessed, lots of Heads of School, especially in the Arts Faculty for which he now had control of staffing, wanted McNamara to know how much they had enjoyed his last book, that they remembered the name of his ex-wife and two sons, and, incidental to the personally flattering courtliness which governed most of their speech, that he would be very impressed to visit their

Departments to see the "world class" academic initiatives suddenly taking root in every single one of them.

Redman half-expected that McNamara might by now be pulsing with the slight glow of a provincial Brando. He found him in the bar, smiling, as was his wont these days, with the particular kind of geniality that comes only after a substantial period spent exercising patronage. A fat black diary – a first for McNamara, that – lay on the table before him, a Mont Blanc Meisterstück LeGrand pen inserted between its pages. His attire was as sable as the pen's resin, but he was matt to its scintillating surface. Redman judged that he had none of the anticipated charisma that might parallel its gold-coated details or the white star emblem which surmounted it. He looked tired without, unpolished. Drinking beside him was not a Head of School but Stoner, in blinding all-white, looking as ever like man who could command a fee in a detergent commercial.

"Christ, it's ebony and ivory," said Redman, reaching out to shake Stoner's hand. "Last time I heard from you, you had just visited Yunus at his country retreat."

McNamara looked at Stoner. "I didn't know that," he said. "Isn't that like, what, Graham Greene visiting Kim Philby?"

Stoner put his filled pipe in his mouth, recalled that he was not allowed to smoke it indoors, sighed, and let it fall to his knee. He looked as if he were about to say what he indeed considered saying, which was no more contestatory than, "I have adopted a rule to be neither flattered or ruffled by personal comparisons." But as he conned these words over hypercritically – which he did very rapidly, because Stoner was a kind of computer which by default processed diplomatic outputs and only infrequently went haywire – he considered that they might suggest he was too much the Asimovian law-bound robot. What he said instead was, "Did Graham Greene visit Kim Philby? I didn't know *that*."

"He means in Moscow, after Philby defected," Redman chipped in. "Of course, he knew Philby before. Philby was his boss at MI6."

"Was Graham Greene in MI6?" said Stoner. "I didn't know that either. I assure you I have nothing to do with MI6."

"Come to think of it," McNamara went on, pursuing the tangent, "I can't get my head around Greene's favourability towards the USSR. I mean, it was long after Hungary. Everyone else was running away from the Soviet Communist Party. He went sprinting towards it with open

293

arms."

"Maybe he just wanted to visit an old mate," said Stoner. "You know, damn what anyone thinks, the man's a close personal friend, that kind of thing. Personal loyalty that refuses to be contaminated by societal condemnation. Quite a good impulse. An indissoluble bond based on human fellow feeling."

"No," said McNamara dismissively. "He was all over Eastern Europe through two decades, hardly just Russia, hardly just once, and hardly just to meet Philby."

"He thought Catholicism and Communism were reconcilable," Redman explained.

"He did?" said Stoner quizzically. "Well, they're not. Any fool could have told him that. Stupid man."

"But," said McNamara, "it was more complicated than that. He knew that meeting Philby in particular would cause a furore in the press and upset the Establishment apple cart. They were also probably worried what Philby might tell him which he might later reveal. No such things would motivate you to visit Yunus, of course, William. You are more the simple personal loyalty type, right?"

Stoner acknowledged that his attempt to deflect the conversation had been defeated. "You want to know about the meeting with Yunus? Fair enough. It was depressing. You should understand that I have in my mind an intellectually orientated, articulate, sophisticated young man I have come to know, I thought well, over a decent interval. I consider him rational and reasonable. I am not really too attentive to his political side. That showed itself only occasionally in any case. I had him down as passionate, perhaps a little idealistic and romantic about such matters, as people of his age tend to be, but not in any way extreme or rigidly programmatic. Mostly we talked about books and north Africa and, of course, the wonderful thing was that we spoke in Arabic. His Arabic is beautiful, by the way. In fact, the ironic thing is, I don't think he could say in Arabic the things he said to me in English. His inauthenticity would have rung hollow in his mother tongue. As this suggests, the person I met at the meeting seemed an entirely different creature. Would I say we quarreled? No. But I told him what I thought about his opportunism, the lack of any foundation for his public crusade, the harm he was likely doing himself. He was subdued, but his eyes were quickly flashing betrayal. A little bit dramatic. I sometimes thought I heard a stirring soundtrack filling the silences. He told me nothing that would be of any use to you two, though, if that's why you're interested. If he had, I'd let you in on it. Now I must step outside for a smoke. Excuse me, chaps."

As Stoner had left, McNamara went to the bar and ordered Redman a drink.

"You already have a tab?" said Redman.

McNamara rolled his eyes. "Thank you for coming. I've had so little time, and I have to go to a dinner this evening. How is Lorraine?"

"I don't know," said Redman wearily, sipping at his pint. "I haven't seen her since Sunday, three days now. I have spoken to her on the phone, of course, but she seems to be in a very discontented state of mind. I'm not sure if her discontent is with me as well as this place. She certainly wants me to stay away. But on the other score she appears to have arrived at the conclusion that universities constitute one of the circles of hell. She's been applying for jobs elsewhere, even in secondary schools, would you believe. Maybe she's right. Maybe it would be better if we didn't work in the same corridor."

McNamara looked sympathetic. "Well, of course, the death threats, the awful media coverage, the slapdash way we overlooked her distress, these will all have affected her deeply."

Redman looked confused. "We?" he said.

"University management," McNamara explained.

"Oh. That's who *we* is now. I see. Not you and me."

McNamara gave a short laugh. "I apologise. I have been talking in this corporate academic officialese all day."

"If you're accepting collective responsibility, you could always persuade them to do something to help her," Redman suggested.

McNamara's head tilted to one side. "That's more something you'd have to take to the Registrar, given that she's an administrator."

"I've already pulled one favour with him recently," Redman said. "I don't think I can push my luck."

McNamara nodded, "I'm sorry. I've been trying to observe the rather delicate separation of powers around here. I'd rather promised myself not to meddle in domains which are not my own."

Redman shrugged. "Okay. But you didn't ask me here to talk about Lorraine."

"No," McNamara acknowledged. "I was hoping to sound you out

about tomorrow."

"What about it? I know nothing more about what's planned. People seem much more suspicious of me now that I am Vice Dean. The usually loud rumour mill has stopped grinding in my vicinity. The gossip waterfall which seemed to follow me and rain on me continuously for years has dried up overnight."

"I know the feeling," McNamara agreed. "Actually, it was something specific I was going to ask you. As you know, I will be immured in the Great Hall tomorrow from an hour before Trump arrives. I understand that Spooner will be all wired up with a comms unit in his ear to give him real time updates on Trump's approach. That's mainly a line to the Secret Service. Someone else is doing the same thing with respect to our own security. But no one seems to be keeping a trained gaze on the demonstration itself. You know, what's happening, who's there ... "

"What are you asking?"

"I was wondering if you would be my eyes and ears outside the Trump Building. You know, talk to me on the phone, tell me what's going on, maybe film it."

"Film it?"

"Yes."

"Why?"

"Who can tell? Might be evidence if anything goes wrong. Would allow me to identify those in attendance."

"Why do you want to know who's in attendance? I mean, it sounds like you want to mark their cards."

McNamara harrumphed. "Oh, come on, James, let's not be naïve. We both know it's part of winning any struggle that you need to know who's up against you. There will be numerous University security cameras filming the event, so I don't see what's so strange about making a video. But I won't have personal access to the security footage. I need to know, when I encounter these members of staff at a later date, that if they feel strongly enough in their views about the Trump money and the Odium Two, views which they know are diametrically opposed to my own, that they'll go so far as to attend the first political demonstration of any substance in all my years at Odium. Why should I have to second guess their position when they already know mine?"

"*Go so far as to attend*? That's not dreadfully far, is it? I mean, it's hardly the last word in political activism, more the first, no? And the difference between you and them is that you are officially a publicly accountable figure while they are private individuals. You also happen to have a degree of power over them, which makes monitoring their extra-employment activities seem a little menacing."

"Extra-employment activities!" McNamara spluttered. "They will be attending in normal working hours! They'll be being paid – by *us*! – while they attend. What's not public about a political demonstration? And as for being publicly accountable, that's exactly what attending a protest event is: showing that you are prepared to account for your beliefs *in public*. They don't have rights of privacy in public because of the entirely antithetical meanings of the words *private* and *public*."

Redman was shaking his head. "I don't believe you. You, a senior manager, are asking me to spy on the members of staff attending a political event, so that you can personally identify them in a way that, by your own admission, might influence your later treatment of them, or the decisions you take about them, in the workplace. How did we get here? Where exactly did we take the wrong turning? Was it a long time ago or was it just recently? Why do I hear nothing about Buddha from you these days?"

All through Redman's questioning McNamara had been pulling his oh-don't-be-so-bloody-ridiculous face. But now it dropped into a more congenial mask, as all further colloquy between the two was inhibited by the entrance of Nigel Asterisk. He looked nervous. He approached them directly and sat with them.

"I was told you were here," he said to McNamara. "And James, how convenient, because this concerns you too. Tell me, Robert, you must have had your security interview by now, yes?"

"With the Secret Service?" said McNamara.

"Yes," said Asterisk.

McNamara nodded.

"But was there another man there, a different man from the one who interviewed you?"

"There were a couple of other guys."

"I mean a tall, hefty guy, about forty, red hair."

"Yes, there was."

"Did he speak to you?"

"At the end, yes. He showed me a photograph and asked me if I'd ever seen the man in it."

297

"Did you ask him why?"

"Why he was asking me?"

"Yes."

"No. I said no, I'd never seen the guy."

"I see," said Asterisk. "Let me get a scotch." He was away for a moment at the bar. When he returned to his seat, he said, "I asked why."

McNamara allowed a second to pass. "And what did he answer?"

Asterisk swilled a mouthful of whisky. "Do you think that makes me sound suspicious?"

Redman intervened. "Why would it make you sound suspicious?"

Asterisk leaned in to them, lowering his voice. "It was a photograph of Professor Buckrack," he breathed.

This information caused a prolonged three-way triangular exchange of glances so expressive that *The Good, the Bad and the Ugly* seemed momentarily to have a real-life rival. However, the mood quickly descended into soap opera or, at best, police procedural.

"He didn't explain why," said Asterisk. "He just maintained a long silence and repeated the question. I mean, where's the decency? How come he gets to ask me questions and I have to answer them, but he doesn't have to answer a single question I put to him?"

"Maybe," said Redman, "that was your mistake. You assumed without questioning that he had the power to do so."

"Or," said Asterisk, "I correctly inferred that he had a lot more power than I do."

"So," asked McNamara, "did you tell him no?"

"I told him yes!" exclaimed Asterisk. "I'm not going to lie to the CIA or the FBI or whatever he was."

"They have no jurisdiction," Redman said.

"It all happened rather fast, too fast to think. It seemed to be part of the Security Service interview at first, just another question. So I told the truth. Unlike you, Robert, I know what Professor Cannon Buckrack looks like. I said yes, and I gave his name."

The trio indulged in a further spaghetti-westernish moment.

"You'd have done better to lie," said Redman.

"How could I possibly lie," protested Asterisk, "about one of the Professors on my own staff? For god's sake, he's still on the books. The last phone call I got from Covet said Buckrack would be disappearing off the scene but to let his contract run its course. I didn't pay much

298

attention there and then, not least because Covet had been suspended from office at the time. But later, when I came to reflect on it, I agreed it best to leave our employment of Buckrack in place until the end of this academic year. If he kept getting the salary, he'd be more likely stay away. And none of us wants him back."

Redman and McNamara exchanged glances shiftily. "That we didn't know," said Redman. "But you could have corrected the lie later if it ever bounced back to you, said you hadn't looked at the photo carefully enough."

"There were other people who met Buckrack," said Asterisk, "like those at the Disclosure Committee. They would have identified him anyway when they were interviewed. Whatever, the main reason I am telling you both this is that I need to know you've got my back."

He was not made comfortable by the mystified expressions on the faces of Redman and McNamara. He became more persuasive. "Listen, we're all in this together. Why is anyone asking questions about Buckrack? How much do they know? What if they know about the bugs? We all participated in their concealment. How is that going to play out for us if it ever becomes open knowledge? A University senior management secretly recording the conversations of elected trades union officers? And then a deliberate cover-up by three people, fiddling with evidence?"

"I think it will play out rather more badly for you than for us, Nigel," Redman said. "After all, we were two of the people whose rooms were bugged. It was *you* who made the arrangements for Buckrack to steal the evidence. Our reasons for concealing the existence of the bugs were not morally equivalent to yours."

"No, he's right, James," said McNamara. "This is something we must try to keep the lid on. We can't confide in the current VC, he wasn't here then, and he knows nothing, and moreover wants to know nothing. If this got out it would be just another scandal, a revivified corpse of a dead scandal. We've got enough on our plate."

Redman cleared his throat and looked at Asterisk. "Why would the CIA or the FBI be interested in the internal shenanigans of an English university? It's obvious: it's Buckrack they're interested in. Look for the American."

"There is that," said McNamara. "Mind you, there's more than one American."

"How do you mean?" said Asterisk warily.

"Jane Blake," said McNamara. "She was an American, moreover one murdered, so the verdict read, by a British subject. That would seem to me to be the obvious crime we know about that would legitimise the intervention of the US authorities."

"Of course," said Redman. "And she planted the bugs. And if they are looking into her death then there's the whole issue of her Public Disclosure document, which Buckrack was involved in assessing, her affair with Covet... that's a lot of dirty linen."

"*Did* she plant the bugs?" asked McNamara.

"Didn't she?" said Asterisk, and coughed.

"Neither of us really got to the bottom of it," said McNamara. "It was obvious that she had access to my study and to Poon's office, but we could never figure out how she got into James's."

"Well," said Asterisk, "she *was sleeping* with Covet. He could have conjured up a master key from his back pocket. Job done."

"I see," McNamara nodded. "That's the obvious explanation. I am always forgetful about just how slippery the man was."

"I'm not allowed to be slippery," said Asterisk. "I managed to excuse myself pronto on a made-up pretext, but he wants to talk to me tomorrow morning about Buckrack."

"You didn't say no?" said Redman, and then watched Asterisk shaking his head. "It would have been better had you said no. I repeat: these people have no jurisdiction."

While Redman was repeating himself Asterisk had been getting up his how-could-I-possibly-say-no face. But now it morphed perforce into a merely melancholy mug, and he simply said, "To be continued." The reason was that all further conspiracy among the three had been inhibited by the re-entrance of William Stoner.


## Chapter Thirteen

McNamara was awoken on Trump Thursday by what sounded like a military convoy passing through the west entrance of campus, near his Warden's house. Heavy vehicles, their engines growling in low gear, clunked over grates, bounced across sleeping policemen, their

300

hydraulics hissing, occasional electronic bleeps sounding off as one or other of them made some necessary reversing manoeuvre. His attempts to go back to sleep failed. He lay for a while, looking with some satisfaction at the rumpled sheets in the half of the bed Drusilla had vacated last night: she had gone home in order to prepare for her busy day ahead.

At last he got up, and, looking at the clock, decided to do something he had often done, but not for some time. He made a pot of tea and four slices of buttered toast. He put them on a tray with two cups and a small jug of milk and a little bowl of sugar, left the house still in his pyjamas, dressing gown and slippers, and walked slowly towards the gatehouse that stood in the centre of the entrance road. Arriving there, he found the area to be in a great deal more of a hubbub than was customary at this time on a normal weekday morning. As well as the merely one security guard sitting sentry in the gatehouse, a further dozen were strung out along the pavements on the far side of the gate, between the two sets of iron railings on either side. They were guiding and gesticulating at the drivers of vans, cars, buses, mobile homes and motorcycles that formed a long chain tailing back well onto the perimeter road outside the campus. The larger vehicles were being turned into a subsidiary gate that opened into an enormous area of grassy land on the other side of the road from McNamara's house. The land had escaped University buildings expansion by being a little too marshy for architectural construction. Traditionally, it was used, as it was being used now, as a massive car park on University open days or for conference guests. When otherwise vacant, students could sometimes be found playing impromptu games of football or cricket on it. It was already a quarter full.

He crossed to the small upright gatehouse that sat between the electrified exit and entrance barriers. The sentry saw him coming and slid open the cubicle's window.

"Hello, Mr McNamara!"

"I'm sorry, Bill," McNamara said as he stepped onto the small kerb by the gatehouse and passed the tray inside. "This used to be a weekly fixture, but I've been remiss. I can't remember how long it is since we've done it."

"That's alright, Mr McNamara," said the grey-haired Bill, now pouring. "From what I hear, you've been busy."

"That's true." McNamara laughed and took the cup of tea Bill offered.

"We can breakfast at our ease today," said Bill, nodding towards the other security guards. "They're taking care of most of it so far, filtering it off before it gets to me."

McNamara looked all around. "Did you expect it so early?" he said. "Trump doesn't get here 'til four."

"Oh, it's been all hands on deck since six this morning," Bill replied.

"But this area they're filtering the vehicles into, behind Hooters Hall, won't it get full?"

"For sure," said Bill. "We expect it to be at capacity by ten."

"And they're – am I seeing this right without my glasses? – some of them seem to be pitching tents. Why?"

"Looks like they're intending to stay."

"This was the danger in opening the campus up, that it would become more than a demonstration: an occupation."

"I called it in when we first saw them making camp. But the word back was to let them do what they like as long as it's peaceful. I suppose we'll have to deal with any squatters tomorrow. The vital thing seems to be to keep them a certain distance from the Trump Building but otherwise allow them free rein. One of us went over and talked to a few of the campers, but they said the tents were just covering in case of rain. They weren't too polite."

Much of this was said through mouthfuls of heartily consumed toast. McNamara became aware of two familiar blurred figures becoming larger on the right pavement. It was Redman, in shorts and a singlet, running in to work with his dog, both of them slaloming between the chain of security guards.

"Welcome to Haight Ashbury!" Redman greeted them as he came into focus.

McNamara said his goodbyes to Bill and promised to return for the tray. He had learned what he wanted to know: something larger than a one-off protest seemed to have been planned.

"Would you like to come inside?" McNamara said to Redman, looking with some ironic distaste at the dog. "I'm sure I could find him a soft toy to rape."

Redman acquiesced. On the short walk to McNamara's house, he said, "I thought more about your request. I'll watch and report on the

302

demonstration outside the Trump Building, but I won't video it. I'll note the presence of anyone we mutually detest. How's that?"

"That's good enough," said McNamara. "Thank you."

Once inside, he made coffee and reported on his conversation with Bill.

"I've also been thinking a lot," he began when they were seated, "about the discussion we had last night after William returned and Asterisk left. I find his idea of the university to be intellectually indefensible these days, indeed on any day for the last hundred years, at least in Britain, but I think also anywhere else. He's almost Kantian, is William, what with the belief he has in the power of the university, properly managed, to deliver truth by means of reason. It's nearly a comic-book notion now, the kind of thing believed by people who have never been to university, or have had only a passing acquaintance with one. They think it's full of pulsating superior brains and boffins and is run on a model of the contemplative life, some kind of philosophical hothouse shot through with the rays of enlightened humanism."

"Whereas you and I know it," said Redman, "as an institution for the reproduction and maintenance of the technician class of the nation state. Or at least, that's how we knew it as students, with free tuition and maintenance grants for the small minority permitted entry. It stopped being that while I was a postgrad student, though I didn't notice that so much until I started teaching here. It got postmodernised some time in the early nineties."

"It started to get postmodernised, more precisely, in 1992, because of the Maastricht Treaty and its creation of the EU," McNamara explained. "The need for integration with other EU education systems led to the creation of interchangeable units of assessment and credit, so that students could move freely, on transfer or exchange, between European universities. This was shortly before your time. From that moment on students were no longer our great future natural resource in need of careful harnessing. They became little more than a market to be selling to, and all caps were instantly taken off international recruitment. We did well because, frankly, most continental European universities are so crap that even Odium looks decent beside them. Students were no longer viewed as a restricted reservoir of talent to be trained up at the state's cost to occupy pre-designated roles in the national economy, as we could just as well have a German doing a job in Britain as a Brit. The change was pretty instant as far as the economic dimension went, but it takes far longer for such a change to be accepted or even processed ideologically."

"We never accepted it," Redman agreed. "It's not that we were particularly enamoured of being at the service of the state, but it assured us of an institutional existence that wasn't based on commerce, and consequently we discharged a well defined public function. When the state washed its hands of economic responsibility for us, and turned us loose, we became little different from national or multinational companies, except that we were not permitted to have shareholders or turn a profit. Instead, what we had to turn were the equivalent of circus tricks in order to get customers, the most spectacular of which were our forays into China and India."

"Which," said McNamara, "are now at an end. Or at least China, the bigger of the two enterprises, is. And now, with Brexit, the EU is also soon to be at an end, at least for us. So we would appear to be at another turning point."

"A reversal?" Redman thought aloud. "You think we are going to spend the next twenty-five years getting back to where we were in 1991? That seems doubtful."

"I agree," said McNamara. "I don't see us returning to anything as civic-minded either. So much else has changed. Of course it is tempting to explain the whole thing as the idea of a university simply being subjected to zigzags and U-turns according to whatever way the trade winds of contemporary capitalism are blowing. There are some signs that a reversal of sorts will happen in parts of the economy where there is a deficiency of supply. Apparently foreign doctors are already in decline in the NHS even though we are at least two years out from the Brexit axe falling. They are abandoning the ship long before she sinks, not least because the British pound is now worth close to jack shit. I was told the other day that the government is already stumping up money for increased quotas in next year's intake in the Nursing and Medical schools, despite all economic plans for the next eighteen months having been already irrevocably signed and triple sealed. But in our neck of the woods that will hardly matter. Englishness or Britishness was the bottle our genie escaped from, so I see no mass return to Eng. Lit., your subject, as the precious purveyor of national identity it was once imagined to be. Nor do I see any likelihood that my School will go back to teaching Politics on the assumption that half our graduates will be doing British civil service exams at the end of it. Not a lot is clear. We may be wrong to overestimate the power of the current anti-globalisation wave. The era of the dominance of transnational capital won't end simply because the British and American governments seek greater isolation. This might just be a blip."

"Nonetheless," guessed Redman, "you feel in your gut that the Trump-Odium marriage signifies something new, a departure? It's a wave to be followed by other similar waves?"

"I do," said McNamara. "But we're going to be so preoccupied just keeping our heads above water that we won't be able to pay much attention to what the weather is like around us. We're swimming blind."

"*You're* swimming blind," Redman corrected him. "You have a say in what's going to happen. Me, I'm not swimming at all. I'm well under the surface, thrashing about."

*Civic.* It was a word, Redman pondered as he left McNamara's house, dog in tow on a lead, that had gone the way of *public service* and *collegiate*. Quaint terms now. They belonged to an irrecoverable age in which noble institutions were defined by being outside the usual nexus of commercial exchange and described using honourable, untainted words. The University certainly maintained a topographical and architectural facade which *civic* described well, having been erected on an old country estate, the Trump Building assuming a variety of roles as needed, now a kind of manor house, now a town hall, now a church, albeit with a mere clock tower rather than a steeple, but, aptly, with an enormous organ in its Great Hall. The entire campus, brooding with seeming benevolence over the town on the highest hill for miles around, appeared detached and above any imaginable fray, though this was a merely phenomenal deception. It was in reality now more like the wartime abbey of Monte Cassino, having long given up the purpose for which its founders had created it, squatted in and contested by rival factions, none of which seemed able or prepared to restore it to its proper function, but all of whom seemed very interested in it for other, more power-driven purposes. No one, least of all he or McNamara, was likely to come with a scourge to drive out the moneymen, overturn their tables, and declare to the hawk-eyed sellers of doves, *take these things hence; make not my Father's house an house of merchandise*. Not in a month of Sundays.

But hardly anything, now, at even this hour of nine on Trump Thursday morning, could be seen of the campus's civic remnants, its splendour of cultivated lawn and well cut masonry. What met the eyes and assaulted the ears seemed more indicative of a caravanserai. Trailers and vans and pickups and cars and bikes barricaded both sides of the tarmac snaking inwards from the west entrance, the majority of them having mounted the pavements on either side, so that other vehicles could still pass on the road, while pedestrians, hundreds of them, *thousands* of them, squeezed and shuffled among the tight spaces remaining along the very edges. Normally open vistas were blocked by high-sided metal transports of all kinds. There was booming noise, not just of massed chattering voices, but also, inevitably, of blaring music and distorted loudhailers, all of which seemed to make the air crackle and buzz like a that of a fairground. Every twenty metres or so the nose was teased by some new strong savoury smell, now hot dogs, now burgers and onions, now chips. All that was missing was the aroma of candy floss and toffee apples, no doubt absent because there were few children around. There was occasionally, however, even this early, the unmistakable scent of ganja.

The University of Odium may, these days, have had its fate inextricably associated with that of the global market, but one thing was immediately evident: the markets it gambled in did not typically contain the kinds of human specimen cavorting here today. One look at the crowds brought to Redman's mind the now little-heard descriptor *the great unwashed*. Truly, you could indeed tell who lived on the campus and who didn't from tide marks on necks and filth stains behind ears, the general grubbiness of many clothes and the greasiness of many heads of hair. He felt a little like George Orwell in Lancashire. It was no doubt probable that lots of these grey-fleshed creatures were students also, but if so they obviously came from establishments approved (or merely found affordable) by not-well-heeled parents. Redman had not particularly noticed how clean and attractive Odium students were until he was faced with these alternatives. If Odium was a freshwater ornamental pond replete with cichlids and pufferfish, this other lot were so much haddock and cod hoiked directly out of the cold, briny Irish Sea. By their numbers, their natures, and their noisomeness they made the whole campus appear irredeemably ugly, all the while comporting themselves with such casual entitlement that they gave the impression that they owned the place. This was, Redman concluded, because they were not here to study, or do anything otherwise cognitively challenging, but merely to piss about for a day playing politics.

He decided to walk the long way round to the Trump Building, encircling the campus in a loop that would take in most of it. He discovered that it seemed to be sectorised, by accident rather than design. Put bluntly, only about half of it seemed inspired by Roma caravan culture, with its anthem of the diesel generator and signature whiffs of frying meat. Some few hundred metres on, a vast tract of ground on either side of a long curve of road seemed dominated by spontaneous scratch team games, possibly because it was near the sports centre, where the land was flattened and superbly grassed. For reasons which he could not fathom, national flags had been hung out of bedroom windows in halls of residence, as if the day were an international competitive gathering in which patriotism had some role. But he saw no stars and stripes. Lines of protesters shuffled constantly in and out of these residential buildings, whose dining rooms were the mess halls for the day to their army of temporary occupation.

An incline gradually rose in this part of the campus, but it was not before one was atop it that one lost the feeling of being behind the front lines and entered what felt like the political sector. Again, this bore the outward stamp of spectatorial leisure, thousands stamping their feet and rubbing their hands in the chill morning in areas defined by huge batteries of flat-screen televisions, hooked up to each other in arrays which collectively bodied forth images easily ten metres wide by five high. They were all at the moment showing pictures of the empty main stage near the Trump Building, whose barricaded environs had been thronged early on and to which proximity for most was now impossible. Only the really early birds would be able to get within two hundred metres of Trump, who nonetheless would be entirely invisible to all of them, other than what might be seen of him on such screens.

Because Redman worked in the Trump Building, he had been issued with a special pass permitting him limited entry. The instructions that came with it told him to report to a desk in the main library, whence he was taken by a member of staff to a distant door which had to be manually unlocked, then there was another, nearer door, which he was ushered through on his own, and which was duly closed behind him. He found himself in a short corridor, in which four security guards, two men and two women, stood around a full-body backscatter scanner machine that looked as if it had been borrowed from an airport for the day. Once he had submitted to the scan, he was told to descend a set of nearby steps all the way to the bottom. He soon twigged that these steps must give access to the library's underground store of books, but was surprised after several floors to be confronted by a well lit corridor, guarded at its entry by a further ten security officers, who smilingly permitted him unhindered passage along it. It headed due south, and he soon gathered that this was the beaver's entrance to the Trump Building. Nor was it new. Painting flaked on the walls and some of the strip lighting started to flicker halfway along. There was a right-bearing dog leg at the end, where he encountered yet another security post. A door was opened and closed behind him. He recognised the door on the other side. It was next to an elevator in the basement on the north-facing edge of the building. He had seen it several times before. He had assumed it was a broom cupboard.

He walked upstairs. Mostly the building was deserted, and when it filled up later in the day the permitted hordes of press and media would be in its southernmost wing opposite, where the Great Hall was situated. The School of English was entirely desolate. But Redman had decided to make a regular working day of it for as long as he could, and so entered his office, sat down, turned on his computer, and tried to ignore the perceptible hiss and hum of the massed protestors outside, audible still across distance, over barriers and through closed windows.

Within ten minutes, he received an email from Lorraine. It read, "I thought I'd better tell you that I have an interview for a job at the University of Surleighwick next Tuesday. As you know, my parents live in Yorkshire. I will talk with you further after that." He digested this communication for a few seconds, decided he was not going to reply to it, and found himself assuredly comforted by a response that seemed to well up from somewhere deep within him and made everything seem so much more immediately bearable: *fuck Lorraine.*

## Chapter Fourteen

Had anyone been present, several hours later, to see McNamara emerge into the Trump Building from the subterranean tunnel, they would have witnessed the expression of a man who had realised that something seemed very wrong with current circumstances, but who was not sure exactly what.

In other words he was suddenly on edge, on guard. In fact, he had entered the tunnel in a much different, more routine mood. It is hard to imagine, he had consciously thought, that anyone with a reasonable level of education would not dread a day which promised to bring him physically close to Donald Trump, never mind one that was likely to be depicted as demonstrating complicity with him. But he had steeled himself to go through with it as a necessary performance directed towards a more desired end. Moreover, his actual role was planned to be minimal, little more than a momentary pressing of politically disgusting flesh.

It was the tunnel itself which freaked him out. There was nothing particularly scary about it, to the senses at least, but thinking made it so. As he walked along it he recalled that near the apartment blocks in Glasgow where he had grown up there was truly terrifying old railway tunnel, little more than a tube of corrugated metal screwed horizontally into a small hill adjacent to his local church, which had been the furtive location for successive generations of delinquents to pursue nefarious pleasures: shaggers in the sixties, glue sniffers in the seventies, shooters-up in the eighties, pissers and shitters at all times. Local adolescent lore had it that if you walked through that tunnel you came out the other end with at least one infection, if not several. By comparison, the present tunnel was antiseptic, reasonably lit, its walls professionally finished for the most part, urine- and faeces-free. The problem was its very existence, its being part of a plan precisely to undermine the exercise of public will going on above ground, its deliberate yet furtive facilitation of the institution's continued smooth running in the face of such an obstacle. Governments legitimately required secret passages in the eventuality of enemy attack, owed it to their millions of citizens to keep things going. But to discover that such a construction was being used effectively to ignore mass political protest, in what McNamara still thought of as a publicly accountable institution, appeared to him more than an unsettling development. It was closer to an obscenity in which he was a senior collaborator.

When he walked upstairs through empty corridors and entered Redman's office and began to express some of these reservations, the younger man experienced a little surprise, though he did not evince it. In part Redman was touched to see signs that McNamara's conscience was still alive, though perhaps pulsing only feebly, deep in the cave of office-bearing propriety in which the man seemed recently to have taken abode. But he thought it a bit late in the day for these anxieties, and said so. It would, in any case, he added, all be over soon.

McNamara was listening to Redman with one ear and attending with the other to the constant cataract of crowd noise, like that produced in a football stadium at capacity, seeming to surround the building, pushing through all its gaps and cracks, making its windows periodically vibrate.

Redman continued breezily. "Sit rep. According to the TV news Airforce One will touch down at Birmingham in the next fifteen minutes. Trump will be in the chopper soon enough. Outside on the local barricades the order of play in the next hour, I have discovered, is, firstly, a rousing demagogic performance from Donald Doyle, but it's not close captioned, so hardly anyone will understand it; two, Poon is then going to strut her stuff; three, our local Labour MP is taking a short break from her recently publicised affair with her assistant to contribute her tuppence worth of a speech; but pride of place goes to Yunus and Faraj, who are scheduled to Skype us all from Yunus's detention centre, projected onto massive screens, while Trump is in the building. I think this may deliberately give the false impression that Faraj is somehow also weirdly in custody. I will go outside in time to catch it all. Are you bluetoothed up so I can talk to you freely? We're keeping the line open for the entire hour?"

McNamara nodded. "If it's okay with you."

"Then call me when you're ready," said Redman. He watched as McNamara moved towards the corridor. "Oh," he suddenly remembered, "Lorraine has an interview for a job at Surleighwick."

McNamara halted. He closed the door and turned around. "Fark," he said. "You've known this for a while?"

Redman shook his head. "Email from her this morning."

McNamara took a few steps forward and, somewhat again to Redman's surprise, resumed his seat. "Hard to blame her feeling that way after what's happened here. Maybe it's not so bad. Surleighwick's only an hour or so away."

Redman returned his look steadily. "There was no consultation. Out of the blue. No invitation to discuss. Moratorium on even talking to her 'til afterwards."

"She might not get the job. It's hardly make or break."

"I'd consult with this *dog* before I applied for a job elsewhere," Redman asserted conclusively.

"The Eagle is in the sky," Spooner smiled at McNamara, tapping his right ear with his index finger. "Forty minutes out."

They were in a robing room behind the stage in the Great Hall, a space devised for the donning of antiquated garments during graduation ceremonies, long abandoned to other purposes since surging student populations had required that such occasions be transferred to the aircraft-hangarish sports centre on the fringes of the campus. Neither of them was dressed in any kind of robe. Both sported recently purchased suits. McNamara, in charcoal black, looked, as he nearly always looked, as though he were attending a funeral. Spooner was in a dapper, eye-catching, tan three-piece number and bow tie, and seemed ready at any moment for a constitutional on a promenade. He was perceptibly relaxed. McNamara, tense, wondered how he managed it.

"We are to begin our proceedings when Trump is five minutes out," Spooner continued. "Apparently my introductory speech is not important enough for him actually to be subjected to it. He just arrives, when I see him in the wings I announce him and give way, he assumes the podium, says something formal and prepared, then adlibs some fol-de-rol, you know, the irritating way he does, presents a giant cheque for the sake of the paparazzi, turns on his heel, shakes half a dozen hands in a line, including yours, then pisses off back to the airport. Personally, I think it's all deliberately choreographed at high speed to create the illusion that giving away forty million pounds is a trivial ninety-second job for him."

McNamara was eyeing the part of the Great Hall he could see beyond the door frame to which Spooner had his back. It was jammed with reporters, microphones, the bright lights of innumerable camera crews, colourful and familiar transnational media logos, University security guards forming a forward cordon on the main floor while Secret

311

Service agents thronged on the stage. It was the biggest show he had ever seen in town. He noted with some irony that not a single student or academic appeared to be among the massed bodies.

"The quicker the better," he said.

Spooner nodded in agreement. "The other PVCs should be here soon. Can you repeat the drill to them, decide on the order of the handshaking line? I have some TV and radio stuff to see to before we start."

As Spooner moved off through the door, Redman's voice sounded in McNamara's earpiece. "Doyle is up."

"He's started?"

"About to. I doubt if there's any real reason to listen, though. I can already paraphrase what he's going to say. *Och, Trump, away ye go back tae America, ya fat cunt. Long live the Odiumgrad militia!*"

McNamara smiled at Redman's half-decent parody. "The Glasgow nyaff's approach to international affairs," he said.

"Nyaff?" Redman repeated.

"A yelper, a complainer," McNamara glossed. "Keep talking to me."

Redman proceeded to maintain a more-than-passable monologue, hardly flagging for half an hour, painting a word picture for his visually deprived audience of one, like a radio commentator at a sporting event. It was more inventive and entertaining than the slightly hysterical and clichéd rants McNamara heard behind Redman's voice, the first in Doyle's rasping vernacular, the second in Poon's downbeat sing-songy, Diane-Abbott-soundalike cadences. Features of the demonstration to which Redman adverted included ethnic diversity, fashion sense, the ratio of women to men and of anarchists to less deluded people, the universal average mental age of the participants (finally estimated, after considerable thought, to be fourteen), coiffure, the banality of mindless chanting, degrees of physical ugliness, and the immoral pressganging of pet dogs (Redman having left his own safely in his office) into a political cause. At the end Redman was actually giving a running commentary on Poon's departure from the stage to preposterously exaggerated roars of acclamation. "And as she climbs gingerly down the makeshift stairs, her ever-fattening arse wobbling like a Chivers jelly, her gait grotesquely deformed by decades-long abuse of Ben Wa balls –"

"Hang on a minute," McNamara interrupted. "Something going on in here."

"Uh-huh. What?"

"Spooner. There's some disagreement between him and the Secret Service *gruppenführer*. It looks like he's starting his address five minutes earlier than planned."

Redman, outside beyond the barricades, was watching the adulterous local Labour MP ascending the steps of the stage and crossing it to the podium when the massive screens behind her, which had shown her head and shoulders momentarily in shot, went entirely dark. She began speaking with her lips to the microphone, but nothing of what she said was amplified. She tapped the mic's windshield, but again the percussion was not heard. She had begun to look around for technical assistance when the vast acreage of flat screen LEDs flickered into life again behind her, but this time unexpectedly showing the head and shoulders of a mightily salubrious-looking Spooner. For a second his face hovered there, smiling, like the good dream version of Big Brother. When he spoke his geniality did not fade, despite the incredible loudness of volume experienced if, like Redman, one was close to the stage.

What he said was, simply, "Good afternoon, ladies and gentlemen."

Crowd noises were sucked away into silence within a second. The intervention seemed to take everyone unawares. The Labour MP turned and leaned backwards and stared up at Spooner's monumentally large face, which loomed over her, the thwarted speaker's head barely reaching the bottom of the on-screen nose.

"Is this part of the plan?" Redman asked, raising a finger to push his bluetooth device further into his ear to counteract the increasing ambient noise. "Spooner is on all the screens. They seem to have been commandeered."

McNamara's reply could not be heard because a sudden explosion of booing and hissing and swearing and name-calling rose up in a deafening crescendo from the crowd and extended itself for ten or fifteen seconds before it began to abate. All the while Spooner's benevolent smile beamed out over the assembly. After one or two further interrupted attempts to begin his speech, and further generous patience on his part, there was a flurry of shushing that eventually permitted him to be heard.

Just before Spooner resumed, Redman heard McNamara say, "It isn't part of any plan I was privy to. He said nothing about broadcasting a speech to the crowd. I thought the speech was for the press in here only."

"When I say good afternoon, ladies and gentlemen," Spooner had begun again, "I mean the ladies and gentlemen outside this building, who I understand can now see and hear me, rather than the invited guests here in the Great Hall where I am speaking. I know that many of you are Odium students and it seems right that I should address you directly. I am aware also that there are many more of you who have come from far and wide and, let's not beat about the bush, you have done so to let it be known how strongly you oppose and wish to protest at today's event. Nonetheless, you are welcome. I should say that, although I cannot see you, I can hear you. You are making an impressively loud noise. Can I just check with you all, though, that you can hear me? If you can hear me will you give me a yes?"

"Lots of puzzlement in the crowd," Redman reported. "Even some amusement, if I'm not mistaken."

The hairs on the back of his neck suddenly stood on end at a ferocious boom of collective affirmation that issued from the crowd: "YES!"

"Fark!" he heard McNamara hiss.

Redman was retreating a few yards for the sake of his eardrums. "You heard that?" He looked at the screen. Spooner's white teeth showed in an amused grin.

"Too right I heard it," said McNamara. "We all heard it."

"Okay, good." Spooner gathered himself. "Now, let me get one thing clear at the beginning. Do you want me to accept this very large sum of money from President Trump?"

"What the fuck is this?" Redman wondered aloud to McNamara. "What's he playing at? This isn't how these things go down."

"NO!" bellowed the crowd in unison.

"I have no idea," replied McNamara.

On the screen, Spooner could be seen nodding with pursed lips. "Let me ensure there is no misunderstanding. You do not want the University of Odium to benefit from eighty million pounds of new investment?"

After the briefest of pauses, "NO!"

In the slight second of silence that followed an individual male voice somewhere in the mob screamed, "Blood money!"

"Twat," said Redman.

"What?" said McNamara.

"Not you," Redman replied.

"I understand," Spooner was saying. "But I want you to be very firm in your thinking here. It may be that you believe this money comes with conditions. It does not. This University has in the past, before my time, done questionable deals with some donors, I will admit. Many of the staff will remember the scandal around tobacco research three years ago…"

Redman, on a sudden inspiration, pulled his phone out of his pocket. "Robert, is there a BBC camera crew on this? Can you see them in the Hall?"

"Yes," said McNamara in the discreet undertone he had adopted throughout. "They're right at the front. But there are lots of others too."

Redman was tapping quickly on his phone screen. Spooner continued to drone in the background. Redman stamped the sole of his shoe on the ground with impatience as he waited for the 4G connection to buffer. "Shit, yes," he said at last, "it's running live on BBC World. I guess they think Trump is going to walk on any minute. I can see you. Does Spooner think he can persuade this lot to agree with him? Is he mad? Is it a stunt?"

"I really don't know," McNamara responded. "By the way, do I look as if I am talking to someone? Is it obvious?"

"No," said Redman. "You are pretty far in the background and your bluetooth earpiece is not in shot. You could straighten up your shoulders though. You look like a bit of a slouch."

"Our intention," Spooner was saying, "is to use this money, over the next three years, to double investment in the arts, humanities and social sciences. This will mean smaller classes, more staff, and a much larger range of scholarships for students who would otherwise have to pay full fees. We are looking to improve existing facilities and construct entirely new teaching buildings. Mr Trump is making the largest single private donation this University has ever been promised, indeed the largest ever in Britain, with no strings attached. He is not seeking endorsement of his political views or any other kind of influence. Are you really saying that you wish the University of Odium to turn down this offer?"

"YES!" came from the throats of many thousands, but this time the affirmation seemed a tad less fulsome than before.

Redman heard McNamara ask, "That sounded quieter in here. Did it seem quieter to you?"

315

"Quieter," said Redman, "but not quiet."

"Then you put me in a terrible dilemma," Spooner went on. "Imagine what the consequences of refusing such generosity would be. We live in difficult enough financial times. But you say we should still reject open-handed generosity. That is what you are all telling me? That we should reject it, yes?"

"Yes!"

"Quieter still," said McNamara.

"Yes," said Redman. "Is he trying to play them?"

On the screen, Spooner had paused and was looking curious. "Ladies and gentlemen, I'm not sure I heard that this time. Could you just say that again? You want me to reject Mr Trump's money?"

"Yes!"

"Now that *was* loud," said McNamara.

"What the fuck?" cursed Redman. "He's, he's –"

Spooner ploughed on. "We live in increasingly isolationist times, and face an uncertain future. Brexit will alter higher education in this country in ways we cannot yet anticipate, but nonetheless you wish the University of Odium to turn its back on a chance to secure its future for the next generation? Is that what you are saying?"

"Yes!" came the deafening, concussive response, and then suddenly the word was taken up by the mass as a chant, ever loudening, in quick repetitions, the Yesses bouncing off the walls and the stage and the barricades around, echoing, uttered perhaps in all thirty times until, before it subsided into a general roar of dissolute mass sound, it resembled the regular crack of jackboots on concrete, visually reinforced by thousands of arms punching fists into the air.

Redman's eyes were glued to the screen as the electrifying sonic wave of Trump rejection cascaded over everything and everyone. He watched as Spooner's face altered from its performance of quizzical scepticism to a kind of resigned, yet at the same time slightly amused, acceptance.

"My God," said Redman, "his face."

"I can't see his face," McNamara reminded him.

"He *is* trying to play them," Redman explained. "But I don't think he's trying to play them into agreeing with him. It's like he's playing the ball *to* them, letting it run *with* them, giving it away –"

"I see," said Spooner, and cleared his throat. The look on his face suggested that he was done with any kind of persuasion he may have seemed to have been attempting. "Alright then. The people have spoken. They have effectively said that Mr Trump is not welcome here. I do not believe his helicopter has landed yet and it shall not be allowed to land. Accordingly, henceforth, this building shall not be known as the Trump Building, for it would be an act of gross hypocrisy still to embrace his reviled name. And it behoves me, I believe, to conclude by rendering explicit in words the message which you, the people, clearly wish me to send to the President." His fingers gripped the lectern more tightly and he leaned a little further forward, looking straight into the lens of the camera. "*Mr Trump, you can shove your money up your ass.*"


## Chapter Fifteen

"What just happened? What the fuck just happened?"

McNamara heard no answer to his question, as Redman was trotting away from the suddenly surging, ecstatic, celebrating mob.

Around McNamara, on the stage and floor of the Great Hall, there had been a short pantomime for several seconds as hundreds of astonished glances were exchanged and palms of hands turned questioningly upwards. He himself was immobile, rooted to the spot, lacking any intuition or instinct as to what to do. The first person he saw act decisively was the American whom Spooner had been talking to earnestly just before he began his speech, one of the President's forward party. The man stalked vigorously towards the exit, passing directly in front of McNamara, his finger on his earpiece, declaring loudly, "Abort! Abort! Do not land The Eagle. I repeat, The Eagle must not land. *Abort!*" Then he was gone.

McNamara felt his elbow gripped tightly. He turned and saw Spooner's face, hot and animated, near his.

"Come with me, now," Spooner demanded. "We have to get out of here. I need to talk to you."

"But –" McNamara began. Then, "What –"

"Go with him," advised Redman telephonically, still in McNamara's ear. "I can still see you both on TV. Go. Find out what you can. Keep this line open. I want to hear what the fucker has to say."

A few moments later McNamara was riding upwards in a nearby elevator with Spooner, with what sounded like an ongoing riot happening in the distance, or hopefully just the orgy of mass celebration. Both men were breathing heavily, and neither had spoken since the doors had closed, but McNamara was amazed that Spooner still seemed less flustered than himself.

"Well," Redman whispered to McNamara, "aren't you going to ask him anything?"

McNamara turned to Spooner, but assuagingly the Vice Chancellor raised his hand. "We'll go up to the top floor, across the building, down in the other elevator to the basement, then into the tunnel," he said. "There we should have uninterrupted privacy. That's where we'll talk. It won't take long."

"Whatever," said Redman, already in his own privacy with McNamara. "Unbefuckinglievable."

McNamara said nothing. The two men walked purposefully along the straights of corridors and around their angles, into another claustrophobic elevator, down, out, through the tunnel entrance door, which was now locked but which Spooner had a key for, which he used, and then used again to lock it on the other side. Then he rested his back against the wall, let out a great sigh of relief, and began to laugh gently.

"I'm sorry about the guilty getaway," he said.

"Getaway?" McNamara repeated. "I didn't see any robbery to get away from. You didn't get any money."

"More a giveaway," Redman said secretly to McNamara.

"More a giveaway," McNamara repeated to Spooner. "You just turned down eighty million pounds."

Spooner was still chuckling. "Yes, you're right." He reached into his inside jacket pocket and took out a white envelope. A name was written on it in blue ink. "As my Pro-Vice Chancellor of choice, I would be grateful if you would contact the President of the University Council in order to deliver this to him personally. My last request of you."

McNamara looked blankly at the letter, and then again at Spooner.

"Obviously," said Spooner, "it's my resignation."

McNamara heard Redman whistle softly in his earpiece. "It was all planned."

"Why?" said McNamara.

"Why do I want you to give him my resignation letter?" Spooner asked.

"No. Why did you do all this? You prepared the resignation in advance because you intended this to happen, obviously. Everything in the Great Hall was a burlesque, performed for the cameras. You were always intending to refuse the money. Why not just say no all those months ago when the approach was first made? Why put everyone through this? Why drag the University through it, in public? Why make it look as if your decision was spontaneous?"

Spooner's smile seemed ineradicable. "I could give lots of reasons for that, but I can't hang about here for too long if I am going to evade the press. For one thing, it's not every day you find yourself in a position in which you can humiliate the President of the United States, live on global television. Ordinarily the thought of doing so would also not occur to one, but it is *this* President of the United States I humiliated, this particularly stupid fuckwit. I even refused him landing rights in the building bearing his own name. And I made thousands of people happy by putting his nose out of joint in public. In short, I made a massive point."

"That's it? *You made a point*? You engineered a situation involving thousands and thousands of people, you deceived your staff and students, to lure Trump into an ambush, just to embarrass him?"

"Oh no," Spooner said. "That's not how it looks at all. What everyone saw was me spontaneously obeying the will of the people, and normally disenfranchised people at that, students and youths, whom power-crazed bastards like me and Trump usually ignore completely. What people saw was a Vice Chancellor who's more in the Jeremy Corbyn mould, acting for the many, not the few. What people saw was an example of principled opposition, refusing to allow money to dictate to morality."

"But that's just an illusion. It was none of those things. It was plain suicidal recklessness. Where is the morality in using the entire institution as a dog to be wagged by your tail? Where is the morality in lying to everyone and whipping up this frenzy of political activism?"

"Well, that's easy. I just gave everyone a very good example of the effectiveness of political activism. I just made the myth of the people's will look like a reality. I do, of course, regret the necessary deceptions, and I can see that you object to being lied to yourself, though I find it a bit laughable that you are getting on your high horse about a very predictable thing, a mendacious Vice Chancellor. Mendacity would seem to me almost a requirement of the job in most cases. My predecessor was certainly no truth-teller, but note how I have helped additionally to erase his obscene legacy, his abject prostration to the market. As for suicide, I am fifty-six and have a pretty full pension pot and an already invested inheritance from a millionaire father. I hardly need to work, haven't *had* to work for a long time. But I did just make myself the best-known University Vice Chancellor on the planet. I just fucked over *Donald fucking Trump*, seen by many as the most hateful *person* on the planet, almost certainly the most loathed man with significant power. I just harpooned that power. I wouldn't be surprised to be installed as the President of an American Liberal Arts College at twice the salary within a couple of months. I'm surprised my phone isn't ringing already, frankly."

"Robert," Redman said, "there's no point in arguing with him. Nothing can be gained by remonstrating. He's exalted himself in his own head. He thinks he's fulfilled some personal destiny. And it's too late now anyway."

"I even got you out of China," Spooner said. "With profit. Christ, that alone was an achievement."

"I," McNamara said gravely, "am less morally cavalier about deceit than you are."

"Good!" Spooner nodded. "I'm glad to hear it. Because I would think it ninety-nine per cent certain that, ten minutes after this letter is opened, they will ask you to be the Acting Vice Chancellor of the University of Odium while they search for a permanent replacement. The reason I say that is that my letter itself strongly recommends you as the only possible immediate successor. You showed your leadership abilities in China. Play your cards right and you will be the permanent replacement also. I don't see them risking the position again on an unknown quantity, another outsider. And so, I give you that amazing opportunity too. Even if you do consider me immoral, you have the remedy. You *are* the remedy. I have *made* you the remedy. Now will you take the letter, please, because I really have to scram?"

McNamara examined the envelope, the neat cursive script, the polished and rounded thumbnail which rested on top of it, the smooth skin of the hand and wrist disappearing into the outstretched arm of the light brown jacket. He felt a jolt of nausea.

"Robert," said Redman's cool voice in his ear, "take the letter."

McNamara realised he was looking at tarmac, very close up. It was grey, it was hard, it was scarred and ridged, and it was a mere few inches from his eyes. It was also Scottish, though he could not imagine what test would be required to prove this obvious truth. He could feel great pain somewhere, in his lower body, below the waist, a drilling agony that pulsed, came and went, giving momentary relief before it bore into him again. Eventually he localised it in his left hip. Then he felt it in his right hip. He could hear someone talking, standing on the road above him, a gabble of indeterminate language to begin with, but he could not move his neck to see who it was. All he could do was roll his eyeballs, an act which brought into view a pair of black boots which he instantly recognised as his elder son's. This too gave some relief, until the words began to resolve themselves into comprehensible forms, and he heard one side of a conversation he assumed his son must be conducting on a mobile phone.

"Yeah, well," his son was saying, "the car's okay, but dad's a complete write-off. I'm just waiting for someone to come and scrape him off the road, then I'll be on my way again. I should be there in an hour."

The callousness of these expressions stimulated a degree of consternation in McNamara which his body seemed unable to express. He writhed, but all the writhing felt merely internal. No amount of struggle rewarded him with the movement or linguistic articulation which might signify life to any observer. Helplessly, he heard his son say, "Hmm, severed at the thighs, both legs, I doubt if he suffered, but whether or not he did, it's over now, so nothing to fuss about."

A car horn had gone off, blaring repetitively, and getting louder. The toe of one of the boots before his eyes made contact with his shoulder, at first prodding and then more strongly attempting to lever his body over. McNamara had by now got used to the fact that he was dreaming even in advance of awaking, and began to feel relief before the gently rocking hand of Drusilla in the bed next to him and the ringing of his phone had together lured him back into a world where his real son might in fact give a damn about his violent death.

The screen of the phone, which Drusilla held out to him still ringing insistently, read simply, "Unknown number". McNamara took it with a groan.

"Pwoah!" exclaimed a gruff male voice on the other end. "Professor

Candelabra, what a long time it's been, such a long time! It's more than thirty years since I listened patiently to all that Marxist guff of yours at Balliol, what?"

McNamara emitted a deliberate snort of indignation before reciprocating. "Boorish, you didn't take any of my classes. I made no contribution to the moderateness of your academic success. I vaguely remembered you from Oxford but I honestly didn't notice you much before you started popping up on telly years later. I do remember the nickname 'Candelabra', devoid of all wit and edge as it was, though I did not associate it with you. Now to what do I owe the displeasure, so early on a Saturday morning? What wrong so grave must I have committed to be punished by a call from you?"

There had been good-hearted chuckling on the line all through this raillery. The reply came, upbeat. "I too have heard 'Boorish' before, but I think I favour 'Bearish' as being more accurate, no? Haw haw. But I hear that congratulations are in order. You are the new Vice Chancellor of one of our Great British Universities. Bravo!"

"Not quite," said McNamara. "I'm *Acting* Vice Chancellor."

"Ah yes, I know, and there's many a slip 'twixt cup and lip, and all that, but still –"

"If I can look forward to calls from you," McNamara interrupted, "no cup will touch my lips at all. I did expect to be contacted by the Higher Education Minister, and so I was, yesterday, which was a work day, not the weekend, and from that point on I expect government intervention in the running of a university to be minimal, occasional, certainly not daily, and never on a Saturday."

"But but but," countered a voice reminiscent of The Goons, "things nonetheless have a tendency to go on happening even on the weekends, do they not? And although I am the Foreign Secretary, and nothing to do, thank the ancient gods, with our wonderful, world-class institutions of higher learning, I did not think it too much to lean upon a personal acquaintance as the basis for a useful discussion of the peculiar, shall we say, geopolitical circumstances in which we find the one you now lead. You're lucky the PM herself isn't on the blower, but she's probably having an early morning fruit tea admixed with her own tears. She considered Spooner an old friend and is probably aghast at his personal betrayal. So playing Atlas to this small world of ours falls to me."

"What," said McNamara, ignoring most of this, "would, in your view, constitute a *useful* discussion?"

"May I be blunt? Well, I shall anyway. A *useful* discussion would be a *fruitful* one. It would bear fruit. It would be one in which you agreed to offer a grovelling public apology to the President of the United States."

McNamara swallowed but did not reply. Seconds passed.

"I mean to say," the Foreign Secretary began again, "on top of the China debacle, in which I understand that you personally dealt the fatal blow, and which, oh, you have no idea, has caused not only damage to the interests of every one of our universities in Asia, but also untold, unimaginable harm to our broader economic relations with that continent, now, only a week later, you blow a huge public rasper at the unbounded generosity of the new President on his first touchdown on our soil since his election. You tell him to shove it, *a posteriori*, as it were."

"Spooner, not me."

"The prior occupant of your office nonetheless."

McNamara sighed. "And if I don't?"

"Well, we shall have to replace you with someone who will. There does have to be an apology, you do understand that?"

"Maybe," said McNamara. "But not a grovelling one. In any case, you'll be lucky to find anyone to replace me. I'm pretty much the last man standing. I will give an explanation and I will use the word *sorry* in respect of the bad manners Spooner exhibited. But there's a small favour I'd like in return."

"Pwah, I don't really think Odium is in a position to bargain!"

"It's really a trivial matter in the scheme of things. It concerns an ex-employee of ours. He's Tunisian."

"Oh, the one arrested on terrorism charges?"

"There were no terrorism charges. He's guilty of nothing except a dodgy passport, and he's about to go to trial for it. This has caused only division and conflict on this campus since it happened. I wondered what might be done short of a trial. A trial will only enflame everything further."

"You'd rather we administratively remove him?"

McNamara sighed once more. "I was rather hoping for something more humane than deportation. Like you finagle him a work permit so that we can reinstate him, and somehow make the illegal immigration charge disappear."

"Pfffffff," exhaled the Foreign Secretary. "Not my department, that. Bit irregular. Damned preferential treatment too, what?"

"Yes," said McNamara. "He's young, impulsive, yet his intentions were not ill: he does not need his life to be ruined by one or two minor acts of folly. And I could do without a local civil war."

"Hmm, hmm," murmured the voice in the speaker. "Okay, possible, but the apology..."

"I won't," McNamara repeated, "apologise for the refusal of the donation. I will apologise for the manner of the refusal."

"But will you ... grovel?"

McNamara raised fingers to his brow wearily. "If it does the trick, if that's what you really want, then alright."

The bargain was finally concluded and McNamara put the phone aside. He sat back on the pillows and admired Drusilla's naked back as it moved gently with her breathing. He pulled a lock of her hair to the rear of her neck so that he could see something of her face. He felt his loins stir lyrically. He shimmied down and brought the front of his body close to the back of hers, spooning, breathing in her scent, extending his arms to encircle her.

"I bet," he teased, beginning to kiss her shoulder, "you never thought you'd be in bed with the Vice Chancellor of Odium."

He felt her squirm suddenly in his arms. Mistakenly imagining that the reflexive movement was one of desire or pleasure, he did not wait for Drusilla to voice her agreement, and continued without paying attention to the fact that she did not.

# THE END OF ODIUM

This is a fiction. The events it depicts are entirely
imaginary. The commentary (by Dr Enos
Liddell of Booleshire University)
which appears in the occasional
footnotes is completely
factual.

## Chapter One

Odiumshire appeared doomed from the start. Writings from the times of the Roman occupation compared it unfavourably with the adjacent coastal region to the east and the hilly inland territory to the west. The former was tall and wide and almost entirely flat, perfect for arable agriculture and straight road-building to this day, if a little dull and Netherlandish to look at. The latter consisted of exquisitely lovely, medium-high mountains, the kind which, because they can be walked across rather than clambered up, have ever been the more frequented by humankind.

What was later to be called Odiumshire offered little meat to this richly breaded sandwich. It was characterised by low-lying turf interrupted by mere bulges or mini-hills or the odd rocky outcrop. Its soil was rippled here, mounded there, uneven and misshapen every-where, but entirely lacking in serious topographical drama. County-wide it was little better than marsh, porridgy under the thin firm topsoil, secreting numberless cavities of mephitic and often noxious gases, many of them deadly to all organic life. The Romans called it *terra invidia*; the term "Odious landes" is first found in the Middle English monastical manuscript now popularly known as *Travells in Drab Wastes*, thought to be of early thirteenth-century authorship.

For almost a millennium and a half after the Romans' departure, the denizens of Odiumshire struggled to extract a living from the barely encrusted sludge beneath them. The cleverer among them learned early to make for slightly high ground, which the mildly undulating terrain infrequently offered, as this provided the most secure and driest foundation on which to build permanent shelter. The landscape was so gently graduated that such heights were merely crests of hardly notable slopes, few of them more than a hundred feet above sea level, within easy reach of the river valleys which provided the best prospect of cultivation. Over the centuries these folks on the hills came to lord it over the inhabitants of the flats. They enjoyed a less polluted air and thus more vigorous bodily constitutions, reinforced by countless generations of separate genealogy, than the poor fume-breathing peasants below, pale and wracked throughout their shorter lives by the particles of toxic gas which the land exhaled whenever they ploughed or dug. By medieval times both your social standing and life expectancy in

Odiumshire could be read off from the (never high) vertical distance between your abode and cultivable land.

Then came the discovery that made modern Odiumshire. Large parts of the county were found to be densely packed with coal, seemingly limitless stores of it which gave a very different reason to dig, and to dig deeper. Perhaps it was their very hatred for their malevolent, poisonous soil that turned the people of Odiumshire into such redoubtable miners. They excavated fabulous caverns and tunnels into the earth with the zest and ingenuity (but also the butchery) of men bent on a sophisticated yet atavistically satisfying revenge, and extracted from them a black gold whose value was far in excess of that which potatoes and turnips in the shallower earth modestly yielded them after much tending. Odiumshire was not the only source of coal in England, but it was the richest, and the one mined with most zealotry. There eventually was so much Odiumshire coal that the surplus could be traded widely outside the county, where it fuelled the developing British industrial revolution.

The way forward for Odiumshire must then have seemed obvious. Scarce of fertile land, deprived of any natural beauty, marsh-gassed daily into chronic sickness, impotence, debility and idiocy, the county folk gloried now in the notion of cobbling and later cementing the soil over, forgetting it had ever been there, and starting anew with factories, warehouses, mills and canals. It was all paid for by coal, including the establishment of a new capital, the city of Odium, its location chosen on the grounds that it had the highest (or least low) elevation in all the county. It was unsuitable for mining or anything other than rudimentary farming but these deficits made its stony transformation into something productive, the modern manufacturing centre, seem all the more miraculous and desirable. Inured to hardship and ugliness for nearly fifteen hundred years, the people predictably did not pause to build a place of beauty. And so, for two centuries, this long episode of unusual affluence fell into a discernible social pattern: out in the county, men toiled to haul coal from the ground; this coal was sent, among other places, to the city of Odium, where it fed the engines of factories in which mainly women and children were employed.

The city's population boomed and its area sprawled as it came to specialise in plastics, tobacco and steel. But, like the mining of coal, all of these manufacturing endeavours had effectively ceased by the end of the nineteen-eighties. At the time, it was not clear how the rapid deterioriation of its industries could be followed by anything other than a correspondingly inglorious collapse in the city's fortunes. Yet thirty years later, this catastrophe had not taken place, and the reason should always have been patent, as it stood in the full light of day on the greatest of Odium's low but highly treasured hills, out on the very western edge of the city. Since the late nineteenth century this somewhat oversized hummock, thrusting up above all the flat boredom in its vicinity, had been the ostentatious parkland demesne of a cigarette baron. In the early twentieth it became by means of his posthumous charity the site of the University of Odium, which by the early twenty-first brought over twenty thousand students annually to the city and had become the largest single local employer.

The hill was itself overlooked by a turreted house built at the very apex of its slope, each of the four turrets commanding a 360-degree view of the dismal conurbation, the entire construction thrusting up like an excited flinty nipple on a single rocky breast. In it lived the University's Vice Chancellor – a man, in short, in a not very high castle.

Vice Chancellor Professor Robert McNamara was doing one of the few things he could choose to do himself these days. He was swilling out his jacuzzi. He might, naturally, have left it to the domestic cleaning staff to absolve the sins his body left behind on the white stone resin (this was no budget-observing moulded synthetic tub) but on surveying these sins he always found them too numerous for personal comfort, despite the fact that he took at least one long soak a day and was outwardly very clean. One could not say today that the water was dirty. There was the usual light scum of bodily greases, the odd fleck of cotton or wool clothing fabric, but the most multitudinous floaters were his own shed hairs, whose variegated colours bespoke their different points of origin on his person, and it was the behaviour of these assorted filaments in the draining water which often caught his attention. Most, of course, drifted languidly on the surface, only gaining speed rapidly as they entered the swirling eddy above the plughole to be sucked dizzyingly down, like helpless characters in a tale by Poe, into the unimaginable wet darkness below. But a few, and several more than one would expect, seemed resistant to entering that nether world, and gave the appearance that they were, in a battle against the tide, riding the thermal currents in the water as it receded with relentless regularity at almost one third of a litre per second (McNamara had carefully read the manual which accompanied the new jacuzzi) in order to reach the white wall of the bath where, miraculously, they clung and held on and were rewarded for their efforts, the waterline's tug power not equal to the traction potential between oily hair and stone resin.

McNamara knew that they researched such things in the Department of Materials Engineering. Only the other day he had been speaking to someone in that department who had explained a multi-million pound project to study the flow of dust in narrow pipes which, she claimed, had enormous importance for the future design of, oh, nearly everything. It followed that much work must also have been done by many persons on the behaviour of flotsam and jetsam, which surely had enormous importance for the present design of, to state the most immediately obvious, sewerage.

McNamara found himself curious, as he manhandled the showerhead in order to blast his remaining clinging hairs from the surface of the jacuzzi into a watery grave, not so much at the phenomenon of them seeming to swim to shore, but at the recondite vocabulary a materials engineer might use to describe it. He imagined that words like "thermal currents", "tug power" and "traction" might not be technically adequate. He experienced a temptation to call up the researcher in Materials Engineering and ask her if she could enlighten him, and felt sure she would oblige, but the impulse to treat one's staff as if they were a human Wikipedia, to which all Vice Chancellors are prey and to which too many regularly give way, did not last long. [1]

---

[1] One reason for his discontinuation of this line of thought was an academic's reflex: he knew that there were books even for engineering simpletons like him (such as Merle Potter, *Fluid Mechanics Demystified* [McGraw-Hill 2009]), which would answer his question if it ever became one that kept him awake at night, and like most academics he preferred handling books to dealing with people.

This is the first of several occasional footnotes to this novel, which have been commissioned by the publisher in order to give the literary reader the assurance that this is a volume above the common run, worthy of ponderous study and explication because its surface belies its depth. However, they shall generally (if not totally) refrain from eruditely explaining trivial matter such as the passing allusions to fictions by Edgar Allan Poe and Philip K. Dick in the last few pages.

It was replaced by a more fundamental urge to eat breakfast. He crossed to the adjoining bedroom, and dressed slowly and particularly, enjoying the view of the four-poster in the full length mirror which was also the sliding door of the capacious walk-in wardrobe. There still showed the impression left by the slender frame of Drusilla – a much earlier riser than him – in the Vispring Large Emperor mattress, a surprise given its seven-inch depth, faux suede mocha material, and medium tension (he had read the manual for the bed too).

The pain in his back was dull this morning, but not disabling. With waistcoat buttoned and tie affixed, he ambled into the upstairs hallway, a gait which became more straight-legged the moment his shoe made contact with the first step on the large wooden staircase, and which became a positive stride as the same shoe left the last step and he turned sharply into the kitchen to encounter Chivers.

Chivers was at the sink in his usual penguin-suit uniform. He was a local man, in his forties, to the eyes proletarian and to the ears uneducated, though in over twenty years in waitering he had acquired a silver service argot which, rather like his uniform, gave to his being a surface gloss of refinement. He was not as glorified as a butler or as debased as a dogsbody. McNamara knew that Chivers' job description specified his role, with studied neutrality, as "domestic personal assistant", but that was simply because the more accurate "footman" had been deleted from modern bureaucratic language.

"Morning, Chivers," said McNamara.

Chivers turned, the small stippled hammer of a meat tenderizer in his hand over some bacon, beamed ingenuously, and replied, "Good morning, Vice Chancellor. Coffee and eggs benedict? You had the florentine yesterday."

"Yes, that'll do nicely," said McNamara.

"Muffins warmed on both sides? Hollandaise drizzled on the whites only?"

McNamara answered in the affirmative with widened appetitive

---

Rather, they are likely to fill in many of the coy gaps all narrators are prone to leave in their stories, whether by accident or design, as well as ask questions and offer reflections with which leisurely readers are generally too lazy to engage. In short, they complete the novel and do not merely supplement it.

eyes. "Oh, and some black pepper on the yolks."

Chivers nodded approvingly. "Chives?"

"Why not?" said McNamara. "Is Dr Redman already here?"

"He is, sir. I offered him breakfast but he was content with coffee. He is waiting for you in the large dining room. I was unsure about his companion."

McNamara caught the cautious note. "His companion?"

"Yes, Vice Chancellor," said Chivers. "A dog, sir. Did I do the right thing in permitting it entry along with him? I also provided a bowl of water."

"Oh, yes," McNamara replied, "that's alright."

"Thank you, sir. Do go through and I shall follow presently."

Redman's usually excitable terrier was surprisingly dozing, stretched at length (though, being a short dog, his length was not very long) on the seat in the dining room's bay window, occasionally gazing monocularly into the large, resplendent garden, but not leaving the single flicked-up eyelid open for very long. Upon McNamara's entry his head raised an inch or two and his tail throbbed a little, though he did not bestir himself further and seemed rather merely to be going through the motions of welcome, soon resuming repose. McNamara divined that the explanation for this unusual lethargy might be found in the reek of human body odour that pervaded the room. He contemplated James Redman, who sat in yellow running vest and black shorts and a gleaming skein of sweat, at the end of the twelve-person Regency dining table.

"You stink," McNamara said.

"We ran in, and it's been a warm May," Redman smiled. "If I'd known you were going to be late I'd have taken a shower. So this is the pad Spooner chose for himself? Christ, it's enormous. Didn't it used to be the PR building?"

McNamara snorted. "Drusilla's one-time office is now her bedroom."

"And this this is where you eat?" Redman went on. "Shades of that famous William Orchardson painting, no, just you, Drusilla and Chivers?"

"I don't know it."

"You do. You just don't know it's by Orchardson."[2]

---

[2] In fact, McNamara did not at all know *The Marriage of Convenience* (1883).

McNamara shook his head. "There's a separate private dining room, more *intime*, on the other side of the kitchen, family size. I'll give you the full tour some other time. This room is for entertaining."

"You do much of that? Chez McNamara was seldom party central."

"More than I expected. But then it's easy when you have staff."

As if on cue, the approaching footsteps of Chivers could be heard. McNamara joined Redman at the end of the table. The conversation dwindled to pleasantries while Chivers served McNamara breakfast and then departed.

"I'm sorry it's taken so long," McNamara said.

Redman shrugged off the apology. "It's only been a month since you were confirmed as permanently in post and took up residence. And of course Spooner must have left an almighty mess for you to clean up. In the University, I mean, not the house."

"Yes and no. Yes to the mess, obviously, but no to me having to clean it up. Again, things are easier *when you have staff*. There was China, predictably, loose ends to tie. But I have put someone else on to that. After all, what did Spooner do whenever he wanted something decisive to happen there? He put me on to it. That's what Pro-Vice Chancellors are for. Of course, the Foreign Office twisted my arm and I had to issue an apology to Trump, but I only spoke it: I got someone else to write it. And doing that effectively solved the academic freedom protests, in that Yunus was not tried or deported, and is now on a citizenship track, and we have re-employed him."

"Yeah, I meant to thank you for that." Redman's sarcasm was detectable but light. "It was the last straw for Lorraine. She jumped ship

---

Being a modern political scientist, he found contemporary enthusiasm for an art as antiquated as painting an enigma. Being much more partial to occasional internet pornography, he would have seen more point in a video in which husband and servant laid the wife prone on the dining table and gave her a libidinous tag-team seeing-to. But he did not need pornography for that kind of thing these days. Only a few nights before he had laid Drusilla on her back on the very dining table at which he and Redman were now sitting, stripped her naked from the waist down and banged out on her a triumphal copulation for their presumed mutual benefit. On that single occasion he had polished the table himself afterwards rather than leave this task to his potentially gossipy servants.

for Surleighwick, moved there lock, stock and barrel."

"Things have ended between you?"

Redman nodded ruefully.

"That's a pity," said McNamara. "I am sorry."

"But you have better news on that front. How public is it, you and Drusilla?"

"No announcements. It's more obvious than public, I should say, given that she has virtually moved in and put her own house up for rent. She reports a twofold increase in the respect shown to her by senior managers."

"No wonder. It must be like having your proxy across the desk from them, and they are a fearful lot."

"A number of them made a rush for the door immediately after Spooner's resignation. We got rid of some dead wood, but also lost some major research grants. Of course, it is true that I know a lot more about what's going on now, thanks to her. She does report back to me and I presume the managers all assume that. So far this fact seems to have increased their competence and decreased their hubris. The downside is that she has, er, ideas."

"Ideas?"

"Yes, ideas," McNamara repeated. "Notions as to the direction the University should henceforth take, let us say."

"Care to share?"

McNamara grunted. "I don't pay too much attention to what Lady Macbeth whispers in my ear, even if we do live in a castle.[3] Not on University matters anyway. I seek more serious counsel for that." Then he added, "Like yours."

Redman looked surprised. "Is that why I am here?"

"Partly."

---

[3] A private joke which Redman does not possess sufficient knowledge to appreciate: McNamara is aware that Drusilla had once been married to a man whose surname actually was Macbeth. The unappreciated joke also contains an undetected lie: McNamara in fact paid a great deal of notice to Drusilla's ideas for the future of the University of Odium, largely because it saved him having to think things up himself. The very project he is about to explain was Drusilla's brainchild.

"You know that I have basically sunk back into the quicksand of the English Department? Yes, Spooner giving me a more senior role for a few weeks did make me think more at an elevated institutional level, but that bubble burst when he told Trump to shove the money that was going to pay for my thinking up his rear end. Afterwards I seemed to remember you advising me in the first term of the year to get back to writing books, doing what an academic does, which is what I am now trying to do. I've given up on higher causes. Pursuing them has done me no good."

McNamara waved his hand in the air dismissively. "I said that before the shit really hit the fan. It's been an extremely unusual year. Our long-standing corrupt Vice Chancellor commits suicide after, it would seem, murdering a postgraduate student with whom he has been having a prostitutional affair. His irresponsible, scheming replacement insults the President of the United States on live global television and summarily kills off our operation in China before resigning. In both the first and second terms this obscure provincial campus becomes a focus for the world's press on account of internal scandals and its future is held seriously in question. Yet we've survived, and while we don't have the Trump money the proceeds from the China sale will wipe out our deficit and make our administrative burdens simpler. In fiscal terms we will start next academic year better than the last, with balanced books, although our name is mud and applications are seriously down. Still, we do not have a future of annual income from China to look forward to, and as we were running a deficit even despite that, the finances have to be so planned that they don't slide again. We need to be able to manufacture a brighter, sunnier, less controversial future."

"'We'?" Redman grimaced. "You're invoking a collective I don't feel any part of. We both used to do that a lot, but the pronoun we used then was *they*. I can see that the new *you* needs these things, and I can understand that you want to form a group of people to help you achieve them, but then, as you say, that's what Pro-Vice Chancellors are for, no? I don't see any part I have in it."

McNamara sipped his coffee while listening. He put it down. "I seem to remember us both criticising *them* from the assumed standpoint of knowing better how to manage a university without allowing it to run out of control and into the calamitous accidents we've witnessed this year. But let me try another tack. It's true that a management structure is in place, but all the experienced Pro-Vice Chancellors from Covet's time have gone. Those put in post by Spooner and inherited by me are newbies looking to be told what to do. They're not planning the New Jerusalem. Real continuity comes only from the senior administrators, the Nigel Asterisks and Elfyn Dethbridges of this world, and if anything their erstwhile marginal hold on power has been strengthened by the disasters which have lately befallen the senior academics. Who's currently managing the place? They are. My *we* was more a rhetorical means of distinguishing *them* from *us*, the academics who are the only people who can run it in the proper spirit and with the correct priorities."

"*You*," said Redman emphatically, "are now paid to manage *them* and everyone else; *I* am paid to be managed, and no one is judging me on my contribution to the positive destiny of the institution. I'm not in the charmed circle which regards the fate of the University as within its circumference. The fact that you and I once joined in common cause doesn't make us a permanent double act."

"Yes," McNamara said patiently. "But it appears, contrary to all expectations, that in significant respects it is *they* who manage *us*. No doubt we always assumed that the boring routines of the academic calendar, the endless churning of student intake and outflow and grant application deadlines and legal compliance and all the like, were to a large degree in the able hands of this cadre, to use an old word: they were our civil-service-to-the-government kind of thing. We took these matters entrusted to them as secondary because predictable, the boilerplate stuff required annually of any university that wished to retain the name, as opposed to the strategies that might be pursued in order to make Odium distinctive, the primary thrust determined upon by academic as opposed to administrative concerns, or so we thought. Perhaps I should have been less astonished to discover that my predecessors had let this traditional sense of priorities rot on the vine. Spooner can probably be exonerated, he was here for so little time, and got to grips with nothing except China. His grand plan was merely the public embarrassment of a questionable benefactor. But the last decade of Covet's rule was no rule at all, or at best a pragmatic shifting and moving, almost entirely in the direction of money. This is what the files tell me, to which one's knowledge of the man lends credence. It also explains why we were running a deficit despite a prolonged period of increasing student numbers and higher fee income: research grants

336

decreased by sixteen per cent in that decade, and patent income flatlined. We were still pouring money into China until five years ago and there's been no net cash from India except modest returns in the last two. But Covet appears to have spent so much time in those two places and everywhere else in the world, chasing his golden fleece but also taking personal advantage to fashion something of a playboy lifestyle, that at some point he appears to have reduced all educational strategies to that one financial ploy, and delegated virtually the entire day-to-day running of the place to the Registrar. The long-term results should have been predictable: the place now runs like clockwork, but without alarm. Everything functions at the basic level, but there are no shrill blasts that alert you to the true nature and vigour of the engine. The administrative machine has grown to be almost as large as the academic one. It now costs just over thirty per cent per cent of the wage bill, but it is dedicated solely to replicating minimum conditions of existence – survival, if you like. It is risk-averse and has no conception of anything higher."

Redman still appeared diffident, though he did remark, "Thirty per cent is an awful lot."

"But there's more to it than that. In order to run the place in Covet's regular absence, Asterisk seems to have been allowed to specify and codify the roles of the academics notionally above him in the pecking order, like the Pro-Vice Chancellors. He simply wrote most of them into administrative policy, vast reams of trifling micro-managerial clauses: a designated Pro-Vice Chancellor will chair all committees tasked to oversee Professorial appointments, for example, or will personally introduce all Inaugural Professorial lectures, tedious nonsense several rungs below their pay grade which any Dean or Head of School is better placed to do. Needless to say, Asterisk is entirely blind to the contribution these PVCs should be making to academic strategy. Now that we are so far along the line in this habit, the working lives of the PVCs have become a welter of trivia, and they are pretty much used to looking to Asterisk for instruction when they have not already received a memo from him telling them at which research council meeting or airport or working dinner they should ensure their bodies, with or without their minds, should be present at a given time. Spooner did nothing to reform this corrosion in the hierarchy, if he ever even took note of it. When I was handed the reins I found that the practical job of the Vice Chancellor had effectively been parcelled out to these half-dozen or so other amateurs, who predictably run in fear of their professional lives when thunder is even distantly heard. In the first week or two I did almost nothing except ceremonial signings and handshakes and photo opportunities and corporate speeches, which were of course composed for me by an administrative flunky. I've only just begun to tackle this problem because, as I say, it's now encountered consistently in dozens of collectively agreed policy documents, which effectively write the Vice Chancellor out of the running of the University, and leave him almost entirely to the negligible blandishments of his footman, house cleaners and driver. I can't tell you how many times a day I hear the words, 'You don't do that, Vice Chancellor, we take care of it', or variants thereof, from the nice young underlings in my office."

Redman shrugged. "So change the policies, and redefine the roles."

"Yes, but it will take time," McNamara replied. "I have established a confidential strategic working group to do just that."

Redman nodded. "Good idea."

"It will need someone to oversee its reporting process, which will commence soon," McNamara said with a twinkle in his eye. "Someone who is not an administrator and has been made fully aware of the circumstances, will not blather abroad sensitive information, and preferably has a good grasp of redundancy procedures."

Redman's eyes did not glint in response.

"Advertise," he answered bluntly.

"I wish I could," McNamara complained. "But I am not minded to do so, as the report effectively needs to prepare the way for over five hundred people to lose their jobs. It won't just be administrators. It will be a sizeable number of academics too. And it's that side of it in particular that I was hoping you would help me with."


## Chapter Two

"I do apologise sincerely for the long interval," lamented Detective Superintendent Nesbit, plopping two sugar cubes into his complimentary milky coffee and stirring slowly. "But the cogs in my line of work often turn slowly."

Nigel Asterisk, weighing up the Buckinghamshire CID officer who had introduced himself after entering the Registrar's office five minutes before and now sat across the desk with his nose dipped into his cup, forced a smile which he hoped suggested that he was perfectly relaxed. "We did talk on the phone six months ago. I got the impression it was a formality, and released the student and personnel records you requested. I don't think we spoke again."

"You are quite correct, yes," replied Nesbit genially. "It did indeed appear to be a formality and, to be candid, I will be surprised if this visit and its inconvenient consequences do not prove to be mere formalities also. But I'm afraid we now have an Interpol request to seek some further information."

Asterisk allowed a look of mild puzzlement to steal across his features. "Why Interpol?"

"Oh, the victim being a U.S. citizen, it would appear that the Americans have requested further details in order to reassure themselves about our investigation."

"The Americans? You mean the U.S. government?"

"Oh, I doubt if it's gone any higher than the lower rungs of their Department of State. But who knows, maybe Mr Trump is making things deliberately difficult after, well, the unusual scenes which took place to prevent his visit here recently? In any case, I think we shall be able to reassure them, even if we have to go to a little more trouble to do so. I don't expect to learn anything that will lead to a different conclusion from that of the original investigation."

Asterisk felt a small pulse of relief within him, but outwardly turned on an expression of mild solicitude. "That is earnestly to be hoped for. You know, we have endeavoured to put it behind us, moved on. It would be difficult for us here in the University if this sordid affair were to be dragged out into the light of day again."

"That seems unlikely," Nesbit agreed. "There are just a few things I need to go over, and then I have to file a report. I am not at this moment expecting to speak to any staff other than you."

Asterisk made a gracious gesture of the hands which invited the policeman to proceed.

"As you know," Nesbit began, "the two deaths last November at the Buckinghamshire home of the ex-Vice Chancellor, Sir Evan Covet, are considered to be the murder by him of Miss Jane Blake, followed immediately by his suicide. The documents you provided after we met enlightened us as to her claim that they had been having a sexual relationship. Evidence found at the scene rather definitively confirmed this to be true."

"Yes, you were kind enough to tell me that. You mean the video of them together?"

"Yes," said Nesbit, with a slightly pained half-smile. "Proof ultra-positive, one might say, but luckily few will ever have to see it. It – the video file, I mean – was found on a memory card in Sir Evan's home. The metadata in that file – the invisible stuff that records when files are created, their encoding, and all of that – tells us that it was streamed from a live feed and gives hardware details of the feed camera. We know the camera model and manufacture. It's one of those miniaturised Japanese jobs, and this particular model is often sold mounted in jewellery, or in the frames of spectacles, or in the eye of a soft toy. In this case the video she made itself tells us that it was probably secured to the lapel of Miss Blake's coat, so we tend towards thinking the disguise to be something like a badge or a brooch. But we did not discover it in her possessions. Nor did we find anything that indicated purchase of it in her financial records."

Asterisk shifted in his seat. "Does it matter? Maybe she paid cash? Maybe she borrowed it?"

"Well, yes," Nesbit agreed. "But if she did either then there was some kind of interaction and exchange with another person we have not yet been able to trace, and which we'd like to know about. The more we know of a victim's movements and meetings in a murder case the clearer things tend to become. If we can tie down the source of the camera then we might be able to establish that she took willing possession of it."

"Willing possession? As opposed to ... unwilling possession?"

"Yes, I know," Nesbit smiled. "It sounds far-fetched, but in the most serious cases – especially the ones that bounce back to us from Interpol, I may say – we sometimes have to look at the possibilities from the strangest of angles, if only to rule them out as likelihoods. It's remotely possible, for example, that she was forced to wear the camera."

"Forced?"

"Or bribed. By someone else. We know she was fairly bribable. She appeared to receive a rather large bribe from Sir Evan on the fateful evening."

"But why would someone else – ?"

"Force her or bribe her to compromise Sir Evan on camera, in a hotel room? Oh, well, we now know he led a rather morally and financially compromised life, but he had managed to keep that well hidden until the last days. What if someone who knew about some of that dubious secret conduct of his wished to expose him? An enemy? I never knew him, but what I have come to know of him suggests a man likely to have had a lot of enemies."

Asterisk gazed across the desk, glassy-eyed in non-commitment. "It does seem a little far-fetched," he said evenly.

"Yes, of course," Nesbit resumed. "These are mere speculations, hypotheses thrown out for consideration in the expectation of their being swiftly discredited. To that end, it would help if you would allow me access to the University purchase records from, say, September to November last year."

Asterisk's silence was the first moment of observable awkwardness in the meeting. From a dry mouth he eventually said, "Why would you want those?"

"Well," Nesbit explained, "actually finding the camera itself is not very important. It's whose hands it passed through we are more interested in. I'd expect to rule out the possibility that it was the property of the University. The use to which the camera was put was itself a crime, you see, and establishing its ownership is important to assessing culpability, and when you add that to the fact that this may aid in more fully explaining the related crime of murder, it has become something of a priority. On the off-chance that Miss Blake did borrow the camera from someone, for example, we'd like to check if that person was a member of the University. I could get a warrant to inspect your transactions, but I was assuming that would be unnecessary."

"Well, of course," said Asterisk after a couple of heartbeats, "you may look into the paperwork of any department for what you need, but that may prove a Herculean task, scattered as it is all over the campus in filing cabinets and, I don't mind telling you, off the record, probably in doubtful order in some places."

"Oh no," Nesbit smiled. "It's much more simple. All I need for you is to consent for me to look into your account with each of your approved suppliers of electrical items. How many are you likely to have? Three, four? I know what I am looking for, so if you would speak with them and let me have a liaison person in each one with whom to make contact, I can probably get that concluded in a couple of days. I'll let you know when I am finished."

"I see," said Asterisk. "Yes, I never thought of that. I can't see any problem myself, but would you mind if I cleared that with the Vice Chancellor first? I am not expecting to see him today but I can probably get his permission quite soon and confirm it to you."

"There's no real rush," said Nesbit affably, "so, yes."

"Thank you. Incidentally – should the Vice Chancellor ask – why September to November? I mean, I understand November, when the murder took place, but why go back two months before?"

Nesbit was off-handed as he took his leave. "To be honest, it's about the minimum reasonable period I can get away with for my report. Anything shorter would look lazy of me, but I have other things to do than spend overlong on already shut cases."[4]

James Redman was very conscious of his testicles these days. Had he not been clad in his tight running gear this morning, he knew that he would have felt them slapping heavily against his inner thighs like mini-zeppelins as he walked briskly with his dog down to the soon-to-be-renamed Trump Building. As it was, the lycra of his shorts had clingingly marshalled them into a glistening black dyadic bulge so prominent that it had already made one female student who approached him from the

---

[4] Immediately after these words, once Nesbit had closed the door, Asterisk hauled open a drawer in his desk and pulled out a bubble pack of anti-anxiety pills. He had tried to stop taking these a month before, self-persuaded that McNamara's confirmation as Vice Chancellor heralded a period of much desired stability, and because the Jane Blake murder case, as well as horrid memories of Sir Evan Covet and Professor Cannon Buckrack, had seemed to have gone dormant for a comfortable period of time. But this interview with Nesbit made him crave them anew. His benzodiazepines will not, however, have kicked in by the time we overhear the beginning of his next conversation. Quite why narrators omit to include salient facts like these is any reader's guess (the obvious speculative answers are authorial incompetence, the deviousness inherent in being a teller of tales, and/or lack of interest in creating three-dimensional characters motivated by realistic impulses) but, not for the first time, literary scholarship hereby comes to the rescue.

front unambiguously aware of them, each of her eyeballs involuntarily transfixed on one of his imposing crotch-potatoes, her pupils conducting themselves in parallel, seemingly hypnotised, until she reached a distance from him at which some parallax point kicked in and her peepers seemed instantly to swoon and betray each other in a wild, cock-eyed swirl.

Redman had no particular wish to thrust his sub-pelvic humps in the face of the world in such a manner, but he did miss dangling those parts of his anatomy before the visage of Lorraine Quant, who had turned her pretty kisser away from both his nether and his upper being, gone testily to Surleighwick and left him with a surly dick. And yet, there was McNamara, that fat ugly fuck, whenever he felt like it, able to give his driller to Drusilla 'til she felt full of his filler. Redman had always disliked Drusilla Frost as a person, but this was a trifling detail when you wandered in a desert of sexual scarcity. His gonads, which now ached and groaned most of the time, would easily have persuaded him to drop worshipfully before her oasis, no matter how murky its waters. Indeed, so pleasant did even the remote prospect of being lost in Frost seem that he could almost picture it now, like a mirage in the parched wilderness, though the one thing wrong with the picture was that McNamara had somehow got there before him and was drinking the brackish pool dry. Down below, as he walked and thought in this vein, his twin eggs seemed to become even more hard boiled than usual.

Drusilla was not the only thing of McNamara's whose call evoked an unexpected response in him. A Vice Chancellorial proposal that half a thousand people should lose their jobs – in the unlikely event that it had been made by Sir Evan Covet a year ago – would instinctively have raised the hackles of both Redman and McNamara. But as McNamara had laid out this radical plan, both he and it took on something of a Stalinesque glamour which it was difficult for Redman not to find seductive. The cosmic justice one could mete out in a single vast purge! The joy with which one might help wield the scythe of redundancy and watch one's workplace nemeses felled in one blow! In his own School alone, to see Donald Doyle's head severed from its body and the rest of his Trotskyite self jittering brainlessly for a few moments thereafter! To add weights to the upturned back of Bernard Matthews as he was repeatedly strappado'd! To pull out the fingernails of Sergei Krokoff and hear him squeal like a little pig! And, naturally, by agreeing to help steer

McNamara's decimatory design, Redman had virtually assured his own immunity from the show trials which the redundancy committees would become. He knew that there was something morally amiss in his positive reaction, but reason is regularly outwitted by lust, whether it be for sex or blood.

His phone spasmed and chirped in his pocket. It was a text from Asterisk (another who might pleasurably and with justice be put to the sword) which read, "URGENT. Please come to see me ASAP." He replied that he would be there in fifteen minutes, entered the Trump Building from the rear, locked his terrier in his office, took a shower in the gents' bathroom, dressed in day clothes, and was actually there in twelve.

Asterisk appeared agitated.

"Remind me, who is Nesbit?" Redman asked in response to the Registrar's repetition of the name.

"The CID guy. The one investigating the murder. He came all the way here this time! He didn't just phone."

"Why?"

"It seems to be the Americans exerting pressure. I had a feeling it was all going to rebound on me when I spoke to that CIA guy just before Trump's visit."

"Rebound?" said Redman. "How?"

"He wants to look at our purchasing records. He's trying to find out where the video camera came from. The one used by Jane Blake to film her sexual liaison with Covet."

"So?"

"It came from me!"

"You?"

"I mean, it was bought on my budget. By Covet."

"Covet bought a video camera and gave it to Jane Blake to film him covertly? That makes no sense."

"No, I mean, it was ordered by Buckrack on Covet's instruction. Like the microphones he used to bug your offices. Or so I thought. I wasn't in a position to refuse. His story was he needed eyes as well as ears in Poon's office, that the listening device on its own wasn't enough."

Redman turned this new information over in his mind. "You have always made out that it must have been Jane Blake who planted the bugs. Are you saying that it was Buckrack? And that Covet in fact knew nothing about the camera?"

"I didn't follow it up. But it never got put into Poon's office. It ended up with Jane Blake, who seems to have used it to make a blackmail video. The invoice for the camera and recording equipment wasn't included in the ones Buckrack sent to McNamara. You may remember I asked you about it when we met a few days after Covet's death. But Buckrack did remove it from my files along with those others. And yes, it was Buckrack who planted the bugs, not Jane Blake. Jane Blake had nothing at all to do with the bugging. It was all Buckrack. I lied to you. I'm sorry."

"But how did a camera ordered by Buckrack get into Jane Blake's hands? We know that Buckrack betrayed Covet, but we never made any connection between him and Jane. Are you saying he set Covet up, using Jane? That's a reach, no?"

Asterisk waved a hand dismissively. "I don't know. That's not my concern right now. What I am in a flap about is that information about a camera bought on my budget ends up being an item of wanted evidence in a murder enquiry, and this is about to be found out by the police. How am I meant to explain that?"

"I thought you said Buckrack removed the invoice?"

"That makes no difference. Nesbit wants to look at our suppliers' records, not ours, and we can't erase them. He'll spot it in no time at all – they'll even have the unique serial number of the camera. Then the heat will be on me. Christ, I thought this was all over!"

Redman was slightly puzzled. "Then just tell the truth. You didn't know the camera was the same one. It never occurred to you. You were acting under instruction from Covet to supply Buckrack with what he demanded. You're not responsible for what he subsequently did with it. Let the police work it out from there."

"But I already lied to the CIA guy! I said I knew who Buckrack was when first shown his photo, but at the follow-up meeting I stonewalled and told them nothing. What if Nesbit knows that? If I bring Buckrack into it, it looks like I've been covering something up."

"Well," Redman shrugged, "you have. But so what? The CIA guy had no jurisdiction. You weren't obliged to tell him anything about an employee. He wasn't investigating the crime, only asking about Buckrack. He ambushed you."

"But, but – if this murder enquiry takes on a new life then we are right back in the shit again! We just clambered out of it. Imagine the press coverage. And, and – what will the Vice Chancellor think? He'll blame it on me."

"Then," said Redman, "best to tell him in advance. Not that blaming you would be wide of the mark, you understand."

Asterisk's hearing, or his attention, or both, were by now fading in and out. At his own evocation of McNamara's office, his distress seemed to reach its highest peak. "Oh God! Nesbit will find the invoices for the listening devices! He'll know they were ordered with my knowledge. He'll know they exist and that our denial of them was all a bluff. If that gets into the public domain, I'm toast. But if it's discovered that the new Vice Chancellor also knew and concealed it, then – oh fuck, oh fuck." The last four words were mumbled in diminishing volume rather than exclaimed. He slumped back in his chair and wilted there, pupils beginning to dilate, gazing towards the window with more than a hint of the self-dramatising.

"Then I guess," Redman consoled, "it would be better if I am the one to speak to McNamara."

"No," responded Asterisk effortfully. "Or at least not now. Give me some time. As soon as he knows he is bound to intervene, or to confess publicly in order to wash his own hands, and either way I am the fall guy."

"The fall guy?" Redman guffawed. "You were an active conspirator in Odiumgate! You facilitated the bugging of our offices! You've been serially lying about the gravest of matters. We simply agreed to help you cover one thing up. That's not much for McNamara to confess to, that he didn't go public with your guilty secret."

Asterisk's facial expressions were now taking place in pronounced slow motion. His flesh felt heavy. He tried to summon his jowls to perform the minimal elastic gestures of regret, and failed. "Yes, I know, that's true, but it's been good for the University! Imagine the kerfuffle if it had come out on top of the murder, or the Trump affair. We are both aware of that. Give me a little more time to paper over the cracks. I'll think of something. A week."

Redman did not appear agreeable, but after a moment of unflinching facial blankness from Asterisk,[5] he blinked. "It's Monday. I will tell him

[5] A sure sign, not that Asterisk was good at poker, but that, unknown to Redman, the Valium had now taken hold.

by the end of the week. You have until then, but make sure you keep me posted on what you are doing. Recent history suggests that skulduggery is a field in which you have meagre talent."

Asterisk, now almost incapable of talking, waved a hand in benign gratitude. A moment later, Redman appeared to have faded and vanished from his room.

Redman sauntered, testicle-sensitive, across the quadrangle to the School of English, where he fell into the seat at his office desk and set to processing the flood of students' extenuating circumstances forms which, it now being exam time, had fallen to his lot. Students as a collective – seeking mitigation for their disastrous performance, or no performance at all, in examinations or coursework – appeared to have grasped that a hidden illness which could not objectively be diagnosed but could be deduced only from the sufferer's personal testimony, was a much surer bet than any sickness with traditional physical manifestations. The most egregious case piled one phantom DSM symptom upon another into a veritable psychiatric Everest whose summit enjoyed such thin air that it seemed unlikely that anyone could stand upon it and breathe:

> since last year I have been formerly diagnosed with borderline personality dissorder, major depressive dissorder, post-traumatic stress dissorder, panick dissorder and currantly I have an active diagnosis of type-2 bipolar dissorder (tho I personally consider myself type-1 and hope 2 convince my doctors of this in the near future), on account of all these illneses, I have often found it difficult 2 concentrate on university work and worrying about not doing my work at times creates further anxiety illness as before I was diagnosed I know that I was hospitalised while at school for active suicidal ideation and mania, and that things could turn out very badly if I am not able as I was at school 2 convert academic failure into success on account of illnes, in fact last year, in my first year at Odium, I was again hospitalised after an actual suicide attempt caused by a manic episode (which I blame on the lack of a trigger warning before being forced 2 read Sylvia Plath's *The Bell Jar*, which I understandably did not finish, and in fact barely started, but also because my counsellor convinced me that I had been sexually assaulted when in fact I thought I had fallen in love), as for the 3 exams I missed, as well as all the others in which I did not do as well as I would of done in conditions of mental balance that I have not known since I was 11, I have recently been experiencing severe temptation 2 self-harm as well as suicidal

347

ideation, I did seek advice from the city Mental Health Crysis Team, but the person there "sham-shamed" me (i.e. shamed me for suppozed shamming), an accusation which of course predictably redoubled my paranoyd symptoms and led 2 a mild drug overdoze (for which I was seperately hospitalised), more recently still I have had visual and hearing hallucinations, in one of the exams I sat, I saw no words on the page, only wriggling worms, for example, and the clock on the wall did not tick but made the sound of jackboots on tarmac, needles 2 say, such fantasies make my anxiety intense and worsen my depression, also the medication I take for anxiety attacks and mania sedates me, which makes me 2 sleepy 2 read, study, write or revise much, on most days impossible in fact, so on the grounds of these documented mental health problems (documents attached in 2 ring binders) I seek **MITIGATION** for all my module assessments this academic year as I successfully did last year on similar grounds

Zani Fabula

Redman did not even look into the grey binders. He ticked a vacant square on the form which read "Refer to EC Board for determination", and passed on, with a deep sigh, to the next student.

This one, however, proved to be a contrary revelation:

Throughout the academic year problems caused by British Sign Language interpreters failing to translate key concepts explained verbally by my lecturers have caused me some local difficulties. This was especially so in modules which covered French literary theory (there is, to give just one example, no BSL sign for "jouissance" or anything like it) though I was largely able to resolve the ambiguities of these failed translations by turning to the originals in written French, in which I am fluent.

However, for the first week of semester 2 my latest interpretation company forgot to book any support at all (see attached email dated 7 January). I have been trying to offset the weakness of communication and support in lectures by doing more individual study, but on 29 April I developed a sore throat which I assumed would clear up quickly. However, it gradually became more painful and I developed a fever which inhibited me in the revision for my remaining four examinations. My GP diagnosed it as acute tonsillitis on 9 May and I was prescribed a course of antibiotics. (Please see attached GP letter dated 9 May.)

In fact, it turned out to be glandular fever, which worsened as the exam period went on, and resulted in serious pains in the throat and stomach area during my penultimate exam ("Metafiction and Metacriticism Part 1"). I went to the doctor's immediately afterwards and was referred almost instantly to A&E. I was hospitalised that evening with glandular fever and liver tenderness (my pain during the exam in fact originated in the liver rather than the stomach) and treated with a course of stronger antibiotics. I therefore perforce missed the final examination ("Early Eighteenth Century Satire") the following day. I was kept in for two nights and discharged on 17 May. (Please see attached letter from the hospital.)

Although I have been quite severely ill throughout the examination period, I feel I honestly did my best in the examinations I sat, and am confident that I have passed them all. I therefore seek only the opportunity to sit my last exam for the first time during the August resit period, if necessary, and if possible. It represents 50% of the module mark.

Alice Dean

Christ, thought Redman, tears almost pricking his eyes in cosmic surprise: a genuine case, accompanied with such a monstrously modest request, when so much more could have been made of it. He glanced at the supporting documentation, three single sheets of terse, unsentimental *dicta*: tonsillitis, glandular fever, swollen liver, antibiotics, failure of sign language interpretation agency to reserve a translator, student bodily incapacitated. Solid medical fact, undisputed institutional failure, unquestionable corporeal collapse of student, whose revival was then indubitably effected with proper hard drugs.

And so he pulled his keyboard towards him to write Alice Dean an email to say that she could take a first sit of the exam at the beginning of September. Before doing so, he pushed the paper form aside without marking it, and checked the student's run of provisional marks for her six modules: 86, 74, 72, 78, 38 (the coursework component of the module for whose other half, the exam, she had been absent) and 94 (a French Language option, the student having been exempted from oral examinations on grounds of disability). Everything was first class, much of it extremely so. No one with marks like that even required mitigation. It was already a first-class degree profile. Alice was an academic in the making if ever he had seen one, and probably a better one than him; indeed, a Dean already.

Shaking his head in sustained private bewilderment, but with a small yet positive sensation effervescing at the core of him, like someone who has plunged accidentally into a cold dank pond only hearteningly to witness a single large diamond gleaming warmly upon its sedimented vegetable bed, he started tapping the keys.

## Chapter Three

McNamara's favourite joke about the Deputy Registrar, Elfyn Dethbridge, presupposed his being shipwrecked alone on a desert island. Rescued many years later, the joke ran, Dethbridge proudly showed his rescuers two separate wooden structures he had erected with his own hands in the jungle. When asked what their purpose was, Dethbridge replied in his broad Welsh accent, "Well, that one's the chapel I go to, and that one's the chapel I don't go to."

There was something which Dethbridge had moral reservations about erecting with his own hands, however, and that was his penis, for he belonged to a dwindling, pathetic and, in the twenty-first century, wholly superannuated subculture: he was a guilty gay. [6]

He had watched with incredulity and horror, after twenty-eight sexually mature yet disappointing years of a generally unfulfilled forty-year old life, as the LGBT revolution swept miraculously across campus between the end of one academic year and the beginning of the next, like the shockwave from a silent bomb, raising like associated monoliths four letters symbolising some instant USSR-type revolution in the sexuality sphere, reducing all the complex, conflicted history of his own gay conscience, his immense agon, his *Elfyn in Fairyland*, to four characters which, as far as he could tell, stood for four things which had hardly anything in common. In his private life, Elfyn avoided Ls and Bs like a bad cold and the 'flu respectively, and most certainly ran from Ts

---

[6] One is tempted to draw adverse attention to the unremitting and unfashionable homophobia of C(l)ockman's narration. It rears up in every volume of the trilogy, centred on Avril Poon in volume one, dispersed among Dethbridge, Spooner and the two Islamic characters who figuratively read from the Queeran rather than the Quran in volume two, and is refocused through the lens of Dethbridge in this volume *passim*, but one should refuse to take umbrage. After all, apart from the likely postmodernist irony which may be adduced in defence of this irreverent gay-bashing, we can hardly claim that heterosexuality comes away from these fictions unmolested. Rather, it would appear that an understandable kind of Swiftian disgust at *all* sexual conduct and motivations is being relentlessly exercised. This anti-copulation motif should commend itself to asexual readers, such as the present commentator, who are too little catered for by literature in general.

like the plague. He had perforce a little more to do with Gs, out of a certain compelling bodily necessity which assailed him every so often, but he was generally wise enough to take excursions far from Odium in order to indulge this nefarious habit, putting much wander into his lust. He attended many weekend events (and often took longer, physically strenuous vacations) in Brighton, and dreamed of being Registrar of one of the universities there.

He was unaware that many heterosexual male students shared his disappointment at the trending LGBT monopoly being enforced in discourse on sexual matters among modern western youth, to the extent that to admit to being heterosexual or to live out the consequences of such an outmoded sexuality was now (they thought) seen by the young as a kind of death-in-life or, at least, a dreadful bore. But he was doubly appalled when (as he believed) these uncomplicated heterosexuals cleverly crafted two letters onto the end of the loathed abbreviation (LGBT + IQ) in order to enhance their own sexual credibility as "intersex" or "questioning", vague terms which were obviously invented in order to maximise their opportunities in being made to feel welcome in the bedrooms of dimwitted female undergraduates, who might in such loci then answer their many questions by allowing sex to pass between them.

Elfyn's fortunes in vagina-free penisandbumland were not enhanced by a pustular complexion, prematurely greying and thinning hair, more-than-incipient flabbiness of the gut, an awkward demeanour in social situations and, of course, his irremediable Welshness. But he had discovered over the years that physical abjection served him well. Men of his type of less-than-average personal attractiveness could more often than not compensate for their mediocrity if they presented a sexually servile aspect to their conquering knight with his super-extended lance. In just the last few days, indeed, he had been congratulating himself on his recent supine congress in an unusually local hotel with a significantly younger man from Spain who had, without money having to change hands for phallic favours to be dispensed, scorched Elfyn's lips with the frictional effects of his shuttling dude piston, and also turned his bowels into a split bag of mince by playing the aforementioned organ to diapason intensity inside the Cymric ring of his clutching anus, a virtuosity which had elicited loud Welsh solo vocal accompaniment.

That is, he congratulated himself on the encounter until the photographs and video (and almost simultaneously, the guilt) arrived in the mail. In a form which preserved them for posterity,[7] Elfyn did not find the ululations forced out of his mouth by a stiff yoghurt gun being forced into his anus quite so euphonous as he had imagined them at the time. He thought he had cried aloud with cinematic fervour; on the video, by contrast, it appeared to be a mixture of repeated grunts and squeaks, too porcine for personal dignity. Moving pictures of his rear attendant chasing him up Bournville Boulevard were unflattering to watch, but one particular still photograph on the USB stick, cropped and zoomed, showed something thick and sinewy like the end of a gym rope disappearing into his mouth to such a depth that his nostrils flared in the search for air and his eyes were crossed on account of maximised headspace pressure or nascent hypoxia. Visually, at least, it did not present the appearance of a dignified or even pleasurable pursuit. In fact, Dethbridge had enjoyed this free movement of the Spanish people so much that he had been forced to nurse some post-coital regrets at having voted for Brexit.

His mobile phone rang soon after he received the indecent package, the caller's number withheld. He answered somewhat absent-mindedly, his reactions still hobbled by the shock in that morning's post, and heard what sounded like an American voice say, "My, what a big mouth you have."

Dethbridge felt his eyes widen involuntarily and a certain chill creep up the back of his neck. "Who is this?"

"Oh," said the voice, American, now most definitely American. "I'm a friend of Tomás. You remember Tomás, the guy I paid to pick you up and fuck you a few nights ago after I'd installed the camera, with his consent, in the ceiling corner of his hotel room? Amazingly high resolution, these modern mini-cameras, as you can see. And Tomás wasn't cheap, so I am expecting more than a little gratitude for my investment in your pleasure."

"Gratitude?" Dethbridge echoed hoarsely, incredulous and scared.

---

[7] It seems more probable that Dethbridge was concerned with a less remote possibility than "posterity" suggests, unless that word's relation to "posterior" is consciously kept in mind: he did not want film of him receiving a load up his rear tube to be uploaded to YouTube.

"But, but, but you are trying to blackmail me, obviously. This video, these photographs! It won't work if you are trying to out me. My colleagues already know I am gay."

The person on the other end of the call did not laugh, but made a short sound of satisfaction which felt, to Dethbridge, that it must be accompanied by at least a smile. "Oh no, I'm not trying to do that. There is, of course, a difference between people knowing about your lifestyle in the abstract and getting to see it in all its real cock-gagging glory with you writhing naked beneath a stiff Iberian prong, and one almost half your age, incidentally. But no, it is not my intention to publicise the vigorous packing of your fudge. I am hoping that will not be necessary. All I really wanted to do was grab your attention so that you listen to me well."

At the amazing two sentences which followed, Elfyn Dethbridge – ever one to be seduced by dramatic prospects offered by individuals he sensed to be excitingly bolder than he was – pricked up his ears.

"I can help you become the next Registrar of the University of Odium," said the voice. "This will almost certainly happen if you follow my instructions."

A couple of hours later, McNamara, in his sumptuous office, was listening respectfully to the Head of the School of Earth Sciences, Professor Adrian Plumb. Plumb was more eccentric than McNamara remembered from having met him a couple of times in the previous decades. He was due to retire at the end of this academic year, and what McNamara recalled of the man's notable, earlier middle-aged vigour seemed to have withered away in his sixties. He was bald on top, had rheumy eyes, and displayed a slight but uncontrollable muscular tic on the right side of a mottled face centred on a now-swollen red nose. Gone was the smart suit he was always wont to sport on his then athletic, mid-forties body. He was now corpulent, wearing ill-fitting jeans and a grubby thin sweater, its sleeve-ends visibly abraded, the surface of it pock-marked with tiny pills of extruded, tangled fibres. McNamara wondered silently what had happened to diminish the man's physical condition (forgetting that his own outward appearance had only recently been effortfully raised from something rather worse than it), and thought, probably the usual: drink, divorce, the sedentary life, and creeping impotence.

353

Plumb had for a long time enjoyed considerable local celebrity on campus because he had, thirty years before, written a detailed geological history of the unusual promontory on which the University of Odium had been constructed, a tome which had proved revolutionary (or so it was bruited, by Plumb) in the teaching of his subject to first-year undergraduates. In their first semester of study these students now did not need to go on expensive, short-lived field trips to distant sites of earthly note, but instead to buy his thus ever-in-print expensive volume, by means of which they were taught to understand geology by reading the evidence of the immediate environment they saw daily all around them in the University grounds. Plumb's research for the book had also made him a terrific (if limited) raconteur in a way earth scientists seldom are: as long as you met him on campus and nowhere else, he could tell you virtually anything about the specific square metre of clay or silt or bog on which you were standing, or the building you were sitting in, when it went up, and the kind of foundations upon which it relied to remain fixed in the soil. He was, in this rather confined sense, monarch of all he surveyed, and his right there was none to dispute.

"I mean the caves directly under this building, the ones at the very bottom of the rock," Plumb was explaining in a slightly excited, nervous, high-pitched, etiolated chatter. "You know, you go down the concrete steps on the west side of this building to the parkland path, turn left and walk along the trail for a hundred metres or so, and they abut the shore of the lake, or rather the artificially created pond we call the lake. There are three large cavities in the rock, at least twenty feet high and thirty feet across, leading into the rockface, below the overhang."

"I know them," McNamara said. "But they are not in our purview. They're on the far side of the fence separating the park from the University. It's city council land."

"And that's the problem! No one at the city council planning department will take me seriously! This building was built on this rock ninety years ago, but we don't control the cliff wall on the park side, have never needed to. After all, it's just a cliff wall, isn't it? But this entire crag, whose sheer side it is, is ultimately nothing but soft limestone. And it's giving way! In the first cave, as you come along the path from here, there's now an enormous four-foot-wide fracture on the floor inside, extending inwards from the last fifteen feet of the cave and tapering laterally, getting wider as it recedes, possibly under and beyond its back wall too, deep into the structure. I don't know when it first developed, but it wasn't there a year ago. And the other two caves have now developed similar fault lines in their interiors. There's no saying when they will give. If these cracks are originating beneath the base of the rock, we're literally standing on shaky ground."[8]

Though they seemed to have been scooped into the yielding escarpment by three giant spoons, the caves had been naturally formed by ancient subsidence, Plumb specified (not failing to specify that the cause was not erosion, as no river had ever flowed in the seeming valley below): this is what made him suspect that collapse was possible at any time. McNamara let him prattle on, screening out most of his technical jabber, looking with feigned attentiveness as Plumb pulled-out drawings, photographs and a contour map from a box file he had placed self-importantly on the desk. He was privately more concerned with the pain in his back, which seemed to be flaring up once more.

The gaping cave mouths were magnets even to the least curious, especially passing youth, he reflected while half-listening to Plumb. The

---

[8] See, obviously, Matthew 7, 24-7: "Therefore whosoever heareth these sayings of mine, and doeth them, I will liken him unto a wise man, which built his house upon a rock: And the rain descended, and the floods came, and the winds blew, and beat upon that house; and it fell not: for it was founded upon a rock. And every one that heareth these sayings of mine, and doeth them not, shall be likened unto a foolish man, which built his house upon the sand. And the rain descended, and the floods came, and the winds blew, and beat upon that house; and it fell: and great was the fall of it." And so, I must issue a spoiler alert (I here speculate). While not as fully realised as their ancestral literary correspondents at Marabar, one intuits that the paragraphs introducing these hitherto unmentioned caves appear to constitute a passage to end things. I cannot be alone in predicting that they are an obviously contrived premise, slotted in here excrescently in order to forestall later accusations of irresponsible reliance on a *deus ex machina*, for the sudden cessation of odiousness promised in the novel's title. Just as the plot chaos will predictably arrive at an irresolvable complexity, expect this suddenly invented gash in the crust of things to erupt yet further so that the now Elsinore-like summit on which the University is arrayed is swallowed entire into the depthless chasms of the earth. Hence the novel's incongruous geological prologue, I now also suspect. This is the sort of thing that has to be made to happen when you attempt to represent the complexities of real academic life by means of the simplicities of thrillerdom.

first time he had encountered them himself, many years ago, he had not been able to resist the temptation to enter and explore. They were not considered dangerous, as they penetrated to a depth of perhaps only forty or fifty feet. And he knew that none of them had had any pits in their floors to catch the unwary, as Plumb was now saying one or all of them did. They had thus become a haunt of underage drinkers, drug users and roomless lovers. The last time McNamara had gone there, which he had to admit to Plumb was a good few years ago, there was graffiti on the walls at each cave entrance, broken bottles, condoms, and even the odd discarded syringe.

He eventually despatched Plumb with a promise to contact the city council above the lowly level of its planning department. The additional assurance that he would escalate the issue all the way to dizzy mayoral heights if necessary (insincere because the Vice Chancellor had already decided that Plumb was immeasurably more cracked than the cave floors over which he expressed such exaggerated concern) meant that the geologist left with a tight little smile on his face, exhibiting a slightly masonic smugness he had not often enjoyed but did perennially desire, appearing to be gratified by the fleeting arseprint he had left on the seat of power.[9]

McNamara sat in silence for a few moments, decidedly enjoying a brief fantasy, which had recurred ever since he had assumed his novel position and which he liked to indulge in brief moments of respite, of being a beleaguered captain of industry with whom many now sought an

---

[9] Indeed, Plumb dreamed that night of being an astronaut atop a gargantuan meteorite falling towards Earth's surface with what would be unignorable consequences, woke in an extremely enlivened mood, went out for a bracing five kilometre morning run which Redman would have considered a breeze, but felt the beginnings of pains in his chest upon his panting return. At his funeral ten days later his estranged wife (for McNamara had almost been right about that: divorce proceedings had already been initiated) felt extremely pleased, beneath her wholly simulated grief, that she – not he – would receive a handsome sum from his pension fund upon his convenient death in service, as well as not have to continue all the legal bother she had recently set in train in order to rid herself of him. McNamara too was thankful, for it meant that he need never honour his promise to pursue the matter of the putatively crumbling caves Plumb foresaw as a threat to the University's existence.

audience. The quiet hiatus was ended by the sound of his desk phone. It was his newly appointed, quiet, efficient Chinese personal assistant, Meifeng, whom he had personally rescued from the redundancy he had almost brought upon her in Chongqing, an act of patronage for which she was insanely grateful and fantastically loyal, and in respect of which he was endlessly self-congratulatory.

"Vice Chancellor," she said crisply, "we have lunch in five minutes with the group visiting from Taiwan. But there is a member of staff on the phone who is asking to see you urgently. Shall I schedule an appointment for later this afternoon?"

McNamara groaned operatically, putting a hand to his troubled brow. "Who is it?" he asked irritably.

The reply came, again with Meifeng's ever-notable, entirely un-Chinese trademark, the flawlessly pronounced *r*: "Professor Buckrack."

"I'd describe it as skeletal," Drusilla Frost found herself saying on the phone twenty minutes afterwards, "as personnel records go."

"Skeletal, how?" McNamara asked in reply.

Drusilla flipped through the manila folder on her desk as she summarised its meagre contents, which she had just printed off from the University HR database. "There's a letter of appointment, standard. The salary is on the high end, I'd say. It's for one year only, research only, no teaching, ending in the coming September."

"Appointment to which department?"

"To your department, the Vice Chancellor's. That and the wording and the short fixed term suggests it's what HR would call a consultancy research post."

"And what's that exactly?"

"As opposed to an academic research contract. The research output would be expected to be for internal consumption, in other words, not external publication."

There was a pause. Then McNamara asked, "So he's paid from my budget?"

"We'd have to check with payroll," said Drusilla, "but almost certainly, yes. It's not entirely unusual. What I mean is, it's not the only appointment HR ever made like that under Covet."

"What's the address?"

"Unusually," said Drusilla, with a first hint of the disreputable

357

creeping into her voice, "a hotel in London."

"Who wrote the letter?"

"Well," Drusilla said, more languidly, "I don't know. They have templates which they adapt according to the circumstances. No one writes them as such. They are form letters."

"Who signed it?"

"The Head of Human Remains, of course. But then she signs all professorial letters of appointment."

"She signed it? Did she meet the guy?"

"I rather doubt it. You can imagine how many appointments we make in an academic year, especially before the start of the year. She probably just scrawls her signature on an immense pile, one after the other. I don't expect she meets these people, or certainly not most of them. And knowing Evan Covet as I did, it was probably an appointment he made directly."

"Okay, so Covet would have interviewed him?"

"There's no record of any formal interview. We have a photocopy of his American passport, of course, a letter of employment clearance from immigration, but then they pretty much just do that if you let them see a valid passport, and a campus housing contract agreed after he arrived. He lives in one of those redbrick cottages on University Drive. You know, the ones opposite Carillion Hall. By the way, it's rent-free. That's in the letter."

"Is that also usual with such an appointment?"

"I'd say not. Free rent? We milk campus residents dry, when we can, usually."

"No application form?"

"No."

"Is there a job description?"

"No."

"A CV?"

"No."

"References?"

"No."

"So that's it?"

"Yes. Your own office may hold more records, though. But I found it odd too. And so I just thought to look at the data access record for the file. And what did I find? Weirdly, someone accessed that file this morning, about an hour or so before I did. Yet no one had done so in the entire six months previous."

Drusilla heard the sound of McNamara's fingernails drumming. "Who?" he finally asked.

"Can't say. Maybe someone in IT can tell you, if you ask. It was accessed at 11.33am."

After another short harrumphing pause, McNamara concluded, "Okay, can you send me the copies? Like, right now, send someone up with it?"

"Sure," she said. "I am seeing Dr Redman in a moment, you know, to discuss the redundancies, as you asked. Is it okay if I ask him to drop it in to your secretaries if he is going back to the same building? It would save me finding one of my own staff to do it. Difficult, at lunchtime."

"Sure, but seal it and mark it confidential. I don't want anyone in this office opening it. And don't speak with HR yet either. They don't need to know."

"Naturally," Drusilla concluded, and hung up.

In the few minutes before Redman arrived, she reluctantly allowed her mind to circulate around the discomfort she now felt whenever Covet's name came up between her and McNamara. In the first few weeks of their relationship she had expended many words to her new-found paramour in bad-mouthing the dead Covet without ever, of course, alluding to the fact that her mouth had been carnally good to him many years before his death, when she was Deputy Director of Communications, eager for the promotion which had, after several months of concupiscence on his part and studied marital infidelity on hers, followed. Covet had then moved on (with a precipitate punctiliousness which he had portrayed as proper) to batten on greener and less potentially thistly pastures. Indeed, she came to feel that he had promoted her, not as an ample reward for the sexual bounty she had profligately made available on loan from her then sex-deductible spouse, Mr Macbeth,[10] but rather as interest on the principal when Covet efficiently returned it. Things had at first felt non-mercenary with

[10] Told you so. One notes, *en passant*, that almost exactly halfway through volume one of the trilogy the reader has already been urged to think of Covet himself as echoing the protagonist of the Scottish play.

McNamara, their genuine attachment being pursued in a spirit of mutual freedom and not with thought of gain on either side. They had even consciously disliked each other before, but their feelings had seemed to undergo some alchemical transformation as they had bonded in China, and that slight feeling of magic had persisted for a while between them. The fact was that she had never expected McNamara to step into Covet's death-vacated Vice Chancellorial shoes – who had? – and thus to find herself the serial occupant of two Vice Chancellorial beds. But this unlikely event had soured her spirit, as it had coincided with McNamara's sexual demands becoming unexpectedly more tyrannical. Once he had accepted the managerial position he seemed to wish her to assume all kinds of new erotic positions. Covet, to be sure, had been Emperor-like in his lecherousness, but his conceited smiles had always hinted at the promise of rich patronage to follow. McNamara, on the contrary, had begun to bang her like a whore he had already paid in advance. With the one, it was fornication with a view to improving her job prospects; with the other, it now felt like pornification in order to retain it.

The great complicators in these thoughts were Drusilla's lack of comforting delusions in her now appreciably post-menopausal phase of life. She tended not to harbour romantic fantasies, possessed no flatteringly deformed self-image, and was childlessly untroubled by maternal obligations. She knew, for example, that physically she was an overripe fruit, but calculated that, to older men especially, this did not render her inedible. Her mental abilities she subjected to the same ruthless, delusionless appraisal: no intellectual she, she knew that performative competence in dealing with the press and public on the glossy superficialities of institutional life demonstrated her intrinsic and acquired talents to their fullest extent. Sexually, she considered herself open-minded enough to adopt the traditional role, happy to be a pleaser without being pleased, aware that a deficit in her own bodily enjoyment was bonus-balanced, usually, by some compensatory benefit in another dimension of life. This was why she had never felt any reservation in welcoming older, uglier men into her bed, when they were status-enhancingly wealthy or powerful. Allowing them to feel they lorded it over her was what permitted her to lord it over others. She was skilled at identifying such men and deliberately flying into their regularly welcoming webs.

Younger men, she found herself instantly thinking once James Redman stepped into the room, were an entirely different matter. The impression he made was not the one she had expected. Redman, she was aware, had despised her for a long time – she, the ever-spinning weathervane in the constantly shifting corporate winds – although their cooperation during the tumultuous events of last term had perhaps softened the edge of his dislike. She had hoped this was so, not least because of the erstwhile (and presumably still existing) friendly association between him and McNamara. But what she had never seen in him before was *vulnerability*, as in his slightly off-balance demeanour today, the tinge of emotional flush in the cheek, the perceptible sign of dilation in the pupils and the hint of pheromones in the air around him. It did not take her very long to twig (recalling dimly something McNamara had privately said about the departing Lorraine Quant) what was the likely, girlfriendless cause. Drusilla was something of a heat-seeking missile, and Redman was in heat. The younger man was unable to keep the rut out of his strut. His need for coition could not be hidden by volition. Within moments of his arrival, before the small talk was even over, Drusilla had concluded that right now this Redman would probably make do with even a scarlet woman. The other surprise she felt was that her curiosity at this intuition was not indifferent. It gave her a mental itch she felt an impulsive need to scratch.

"I presume," she said, "you got the attention you usually do when you pass through this office?"

Redman looked at her over the coffee she had given him, with what he thought was an innocent expression on his face, simultaneously wondering if she was mono- or multi-orgasmic. "I beg your pardon?" he said.

"Oh, the young things out there," Drusilla ingenuously smiled, gesturing through the wall, all the while picturing his topless form sliding down a similarly nudified female midriff, hovering over the navel with a hint of tongue (she was not yet sure if this was her own omphalos or someone else's). "It's no secret they consider you a looker."

This was an absolute lie. No one on Drusilla's staff trusted or liked her enough personally to divulge such perceptions to her, but she always found that a man's response to unverifiable but gratifying falsehoods revealed a great deal about his narcissism or his prurience, usually both.

"But there's no one in your outer office," Redman rejoined,

confident that his expression was inscrutable, as in his mind's eye he casually reached across the desk and began to fondle Drusilla's pleasantly plump left hooter with his right hand, pumping it like an old-fashioned motor horn, without complaint from her.

"Ah, it's lunchtime," she said smoothly. She had now decided that the carefully groomed pelvis which she imagined him kissing was definitely hers, and surprised and a little enchanted to envisage a full head of male hair down there in that spot, where she normally saw only the monkishly bald or balding. "Otherwise I'm sure you would have been the object of many coy smiles and sidelong looks. It must be all that exercise you do."

Redman coughed. He was already visualising three of her blouse buttons undone and his fingers confidently stroking her revealed cleavage. Reality impinged for a moment as he fancied he glimpsed a push-up bra whose purpose could only be dishearteningly anti-gravitational, but he dismissed this impediment to his wholly subjective pleasure deftly, as in his fantasy he arose, unzipped, and yearningly pulled out his banana and coconuts, and presented them to her invitingly on the desktop with a resounding scrotum-slap. [11] "Shall we talk about the redundancies?"

Drusilla readily agreed, while privately speculating, with a disguised but unforeseen internal frisson, that a younger fitter bull like Redman might even make her something she had always wanted to be: orgasmic.

Elfyn Dethbridge had been contemplating all day something even more enticing, he was perplexed to discover, than male sexual organs. Ever since his blackmailer had that morning introduced the prospect of the Registrarship of the University of Odium to his distressed wits, he had been like a cat who suddenly notices a bright shining light on the floor. He had quite put aside the extortionate circumstances in which the hope had been planted. Now he wished simply to pounce, and secure it as a reality.

"That's all there is?" rasped his consternated American blackmailer down the phone. "An appointment letter, a passport photocopy, an

[11] The important function Redman performs in this novel is, quite literally, to be a load of balls.

immigration clearance, and a housing contract? Have you left anything out? Are you fucking with me?"

"No, of course not," said Dethbridge, who was already feeling, without knowing it, something of the peculiar romance of Stockholm syndrome. "Why would I do that? But how does this help me become the next Registrar of the University of Odium?"

"It doesn't," came the reply. "Not on its own. This doesn't get you very far. There are a few more simple steps you'll need to take to unseat Asterisk."

Dethbridge started a little in his soul, as the cat does when the light on which it leaps just as quickly vanishes. "Who is this Buckrack guy anyway? Why did you want his employment info?"

"Never mind that," was the blunt response. "I need you to tell Asterisk. Send him an email after close of business today saying that Buckrack is back in town. Then report to me on any reaction tomorrow morning. I'll call you again later this evening with further instructions."

Dethbridge's inner feline suddenly spotted the light aglow elsewhere on the carpet, and was excited that it had not disappeared altogether. Nonetheless, he allowed this peremptorily issued order to whirr gently through his pleasingly abused cat-mind. "But how would I know that?"

"Easy," said the cold-blooded voice. "Tell him Buckrack called you up and asked you to pass on the message."

**Chapter Four**

McNamara had (wisely, he thought) deflected Buckrack's telephone request for a meeting. He told Meifeng to take Buckrack's number and say she would call him back. He wanted to be better prepared and not taken by surprise. With the little further information he had gleaned from Drusilla he decided to ponder the matter throughout the rest of the day's activities.

The visit of the Taiwanese delegation – members of the board of their scholarship awards body for postgraduate research in the arts – was not McNamara's idea. It had been organised by Professor Alexander Whipsaw, the Head of American and Pacific Rim Studies (a position which dictated that its incumbent was popularly called, unknown to

Whipsaw, "Chief Rimmer"). But as it was something the University could not have entertained while it was hand-in-glove with the Chinese government, McNamara now welcomed it, and had decided to push the boat out in order to woo the delegates into parting with some of the three million U.S. dollars they controlled.

Having met the delegates formally at a brief lunch in his oak-panelled private dining room, he retired to his office while Whipsaw rimmed them on a conducted tour around the campus to make whistle-stop visits to the departments that concerned them. Everyone, including most of the heads of those departments, would convene again for a grand, gold-prospecting, tongue-convoluting dinner in the evening. Chivers had come from the Vice Chancellorial house to organise the numberless flunkies, ensuring that they whizzed around the dining room all afternoon.

Redman delivered the confidential data from Drusilla to Meifeng a while later. When she brought it to him, McNamara saw a post-it note on the flap which read, "Too busy to drop in, but met with D. and will talk to you soon. Am working on the details today. James."

He scolded himself at having largely ignored Buckrack and all the historical drama associated with him since becoming Vice Chancellor. Scrutiny of the few documents inside the envelope told him no more about the man than he had already learned verbally from Drusilla. He called Meifeng back into his office and asked her to look in the departmental files for any further information on Professor Buckrack. She returned within fifteen minutes and told him she could find nothing.

The remainder of his work day passed without unexpected event. Mostly he had Buckrack at the back of his mind, but the thoughts went nowhere, merely whirling around and around in an inconclusive loop. He searched for him on the internet and found nothing.

The ache in his back had not gone away. It was an unignorable button of misery just below his rear ribs. He took two codeine tablets to dull it.

Meifeng popped in and out at intervals, in her efficient way, bringing documents for signature, materials to read, proposals for meetings. Each time she did so she never failed to give him a smile which radiated gratitude and authenticity. The last couple of times she did so he found himself admiring her pointy breasts under her neatly ironed pink blouse.

At 5.15pm, with everyone else in the outer office gone, he invited her back in.

"Sit with me and have a drink before we go to the dinner," he said. He had come to enjoy this benefit of his office, the unquestioned ability to frame requests as imperatives. It made him feel like the demanding Richard Burton in *Where Eagles Dare*. He liked the way it made some people seem uneasy. It was a clever method of ascertaining how comfortable they were with him. And Meifeng (just like the women cast in *Where Eagles Dare* for this seemingly same sole purpose) looked genuinely pleased, as if being permitted a rare privilege. "This is what is called an … apéritif?"

"Yes," he said. "Dry rather than sweet, usually. Mine's a gin and vermouth. What can I give you? The same? Or white wine?"

She deliberated briefly, and smiled again. "I would like to try what you are having."

"Two Martinis it is." He began to scoop ice cubes from a concealed fridge into two funneled glasses, and completed the concoctions at a similarly hidden liquor cabinet. "President Franklin D. Roosevelt did this every day for an hour with his staff around this time. There was one rule: no one present could talk about work. So let's follow his rule."

Actually, he wanted the slightly improper feeling of seeming intimacy with a woman whom he had at a disadvantage, moreover one who accepted the inequality between them, who regarded him with nothing but a sense of appreciative indebtedness. He felt unperturbed, therefore, at his desire to watch her sitting on his couch in a more reclining pose than usual, her stockinged legs angled and her breasts jutting towards him conically.

They talked, mostly about her. Meifeng seemed to acknowledge entirely his right to ask her about her family, how she was settling in Britain, her past as a student in St Andrews and Durham, how she spent her free time, and so on, without seeming to assume that she could ask similar questions in reply. She seemed, indeed, delighted by the attention. She accepted a second drink with alacrity, apparently amazed that he was prepared to spend any personal time with her.

McNamara continued to enjoy looking at her legs, and her breasts, and her jet-black hair, and her eyes, and her mouth. And she smelled good too.

At 6pm they bestirred themselves and walked along the corridor to the pre-dinner drinks reception. At the dinner itself, with considerable experience of these formal events under his belt, McNamara had himself buffered from the obsequies of the Taiwanese by ensuring that he had Meifeng on his right (for translation needs as required but, he noted, with additionally pleasurable benefits of the scented kind) and Whipsaw on his left, with the English-speaking head of the Taiwanese delegation, Professor Lin, opposite him, flanked by two other Odium heads of department.

The Taiwanese proved (contrary to McNamara's experience of the Chinese) to be unexpectedly relaxed and exponentially bibulous. In the lull between the main course and dessert, with much drink already having been taken by all, several of the delegates and their hosts were actually on their feet singing Beatles' songs, acapella, to tables full of smiles. It was proving to be a successful event. In the middle of "Yesterday" Professor Lin announced that he liked scotch. McNamara instantly called Chivers over and instructed him to bring them a bottle of eighteen-year-old Inchmurrin. It was liberally passed around. Twenty minutes later, seeing the popular demand, he asked for another.

Even though he was approaching full-on (real-life, not in character) Richard Burton now, he turned to Meifeng with the idea of impersonating someone even more famous, and said, "Let's do the old JFK and Jackie thing." After he had explained what this meant, they slowly toured the table like the presidential couple, shaking hands with everyone and spending a few moments exchanging pleasantries with each Taiwanese individual. They returned to their seats and McNamara beamingly drank more whisky, occasionally inclining to whisper confidentially into Meifeng's ear. As he was close to finishing his third or fourth large tumblerful, he realised with a sudden drunken intensity that he had forgotten entirely about Buckrack. An impulse to address this long-lingering problem assailed him. He looked at his watch. It was not yet 9pm.

"Meifeng," he said, "I need to borrow you for a moment." She looked surprised, in the way that a piece of property might raise a baffled eyebrow (if a piece of property possessed eyebrows) when its owner asked to borrow it, and followed him closely and obediently out of the room. They walked side-by-side along the corridor to the Vice Chancellor's suite of offices. McNamara had only a few minutes before been fantasising about doing just this in order to take Meifeng there and lay hands proprietorially upon her slim, cuspate body, but was now scolding himself inwardly at having entertained an indecent reverie for several hours about this mere underling and her sheer underthings.

Nonetheless, he still stole sidelong covetous glances at her shuttling stockinged legs, her wiggling rear end and her bountifully bobbing bicameral bosomy bulges.

"So funny," Meifeng remarked. "I have never met so many Taiwanese people together in one place. I liked them."

"Ah, yes," said McNamara, "of course, the three tees one is told never to mention in China: Taiwan, Tibet, Titshandlingmen Square…"

They had reached the door of the outer office. Meifeng had her key in the door and hand on the knob. She looked at him quizzically. Was it his boozy imagination, or had she just bodaciously boosted bra-braced Beijing-bred boobies towards him? [12]

He smiled playfully and, to cover his fatigue-fuelled Freudian faux pas, improvised. "Forgive me, it's a vulgar old man's joke."

She seemed, thankfully, unoffended. He blustered his way into her office and asked her to call Buckrack and tell him that he was too busy to meet with him the next day, but that, as it was urgent, he should come to the Vice Chancellor's house that night at ten o'clock.

Meifeng did as she was told. Buckrack did not answer her call. She left a voicemail.

They went back to the winding-down dinner and McNamara, pleading graciously the onerous duties of a British university Vice Chancellor, made his exit. He would leave the Taiwanese in the capable hands of Meifeng, thinking as he said so that he would have preferred to have had her left in his own incapable hands.

It was still light as he went out of the rear entrance of the Trump building, dusky, overwarm. He shambled up the hill in his unventilated, now tight-seeming three-piece suit, sweaty from the drink and his lustful orientation, pissant-concupiscent, thinking not of the lack of an air conditioner in the dining room but the absence of Meifeng's hair conditioner in his olfactory bulb, in the growing bad mood which impossible-to-satisfy sexual urges inevitably create when cocktailed with too much whisky. But at least, he reflected, the plentiful alcohol seemed to have kept at bay the inveterate throbbing in his back.

He was thankful in his knowledge that the house would be empty.

---

[12] The answer is no: Meifeng was born and raised in Nanjing.

367

Drusilla was visiting her ailing mother in her care home in London overnight and would not return until tomorrow afternoon; Chivers had been given the next morning off on account of his having done a back shift at the dinner. The prospect of a late-morning lie-in was gratifying: he had, in fact, no appointments at all the following forenoon. But the wish at last to encounter Buckrack, to confront him if necessary, was now an intoxicating imperative he lacked the judiciousness to delay.

He got out of his suit and had a quick shower, changed into comfortable clothes, went downstairs and treated himself to another large scotch. It was 9.40pm. It was dark now. Nothing happened at 10 o'clock except the pouring of another whisky. No one arrived. Perhaps Buckrack had not listened to the voicemail?

It was not for another quarter hour, as he was contemplating yet more stiff drinks, that the doorbell rang.

Redman was still sitting in his narrow office. It was dingy and confining, so dark indeed that even on a bright early summer day like this one he had to turn the main light on at 5.30pm. Despite the fact that it was on the ground floor at the rear of the building facing a blank, peeling grey wall, and had bars on the windows to deter burglars, it was nonetheless a room a Party apparatchik on the level above the execution chambers in the Lubyanka would have been jealous to occupy.

As McNamara sat with his Martini on his grey office Davenport, his penis mildly tumefied by his surreptitious eyeing of Meifeng's beshirted but discernibly acuminate chesticles, Redman had been periodically adjusting the hang of his hyper-ballic scrotum as it balanced on the edge of his swivel chair. He continued to toil, sometimes standing to ease his distressed cullions, through the entire period of the Taiwanese-honouring banquet taking place in another wing of the building, above a desk littered with spreadsheets and budget reports and personnel lists, an angled reading lamp washing their printed data in an extra-stark white light. He had a prized fountain pen which he used on special occasions, and could not think how it could be more fittingly deployed than in its sharp tungsten nib helping bureaucratically to slit the throats of known enemies and identifiable wasters and to score other dead wood which choked the congested and stagnating industrial canal of the University of Odium.

Time was short. The general letter announcing the redundancy procedure would go out to all staff the following day, and collective hysteria and paranoia could therefore be expected instantly the following afternoon. Recommendations for redundancy would be sought from heads of departments, but in reality this is not how human decimation works in a twenty-first century British university. Those to be executed would be chosen in advance by a trusted functionary like himself, and his reward would be not only that his own skin was saved, but that he got to enjoy the power over professional life and death that he now wielded on paper, a pleasure whose psychological importance has been little studied but is much understood by those who partake of it.

Before him he had up-to-date information on departmental incomes and expenditure as well as dreadful forecasts for the same for the coming academic year, listings of individuals' salaries and research monies they each had generated, and estimates of the cost of making individuals redundant based on their years of service. His official remit was almost entirely arithmetical: he was to target deficit-budget departments, theoretically to rebalance their budgets until they were prospectively ten percent in the black by recommending individual redundancies (because this surplus would in a short time pay for the anticipated redundancy costs), and forward this list to McNamara, who would then instruct the Head of HR to organise show trials for the pre-condemned individuals and arrange simultaneously for rifles to be loaded (in the form of prepared dismissal letters) for the firing squads which would follow on a date already specified at the end of June, namely the earliest date redundancy law permitted, so that the decks would be cleared and the blood hosed away before the beginning the of the new academic year in late September.

But Redman was not by nature inclined to arithmetical procedures: he was more geographically minded, and decided to slay his closest enemies first. He walked (in his mind) coolly down the corridor and lacerated the jugular of his own Quisling Head of Department, Bernard Matthews, and that of the dentally challenged Glaswegian Trotskyite troll, Donald Dooley. Next he sought out Sergei Krokoff, engaged him in seemingly innocent conversation, but stuck a rag in his mouth as soon as he started ejaculating malapropistic sentences, so that the Ukrainian soon choked on his own bad English as it gathered in his windpipe, eventually leading to a greater-than-usual laryngeal prominence which, as Redman turned his back and left the room, blew a hole in the front of

Krokoff's neck and sent a gelatinous spray of ill-chosen lexis onto the wall. He proceeded upstairs and summarily put to death Professor Gallstone and (sweet to witness her dark artery ripping) Associate Professor Poon. He crossed to the south side of the building and stalked the corridor in search of Reinhardt McGuile, the smooth-talking saurian Chair of Romance Languages; but McGuile's years of service were vast (almost three decades in post!) and the Department of Spanish, Portuguese and Latin American Studies was one of the few in the Arts to boast of a handsome financial surplus. It would be impolitic from a pecuniary point of view to dispose of him, no matter how much personal delight would be yielded by the offing of this learned goon who spoke five languages and of whom it was said that every time he farted an academic paper came out.

Redman eased his frustration by crossing to the Department of Russian and Slavonic Studies and leaving two carcasses in his wake. As he emerged from this scene of carnage he randomly encountered Dr Simeon Stylites, a ginger-headed balding bumbler who ran a pitiable postgraduate research outfit in Critical Theory, and cut him down gratuitously (Stylites was cheap to dispose of, with only five years' service), crushing his Adam's apple underfoot as he pulled out the blade. He took the elevator to the top floor and ran amok in Philosophy, [13] slipping on the resultant slime and viscera in the corridor as he subsequently traversed the same level to the French department, where he administered the *coup de grâce* to three (or four: he lost count) *autres*.

Gored to excitement in his imagination, he galloped down the stairs and left the building, sprinted down the hill, and went on a serial bloodletting in Art History, ending the barely interesting academic existence of, among others, Professor Miles Dudd, currently on recall

---

[13] One of the trio of here summarily noted liquidations in Philosophy was in fact savagely, synchronously ironic: at the very moment Dr Moynahan Pissant was struck down by Redman he was completing the "Working with Business" section of his personal University page with the following words: "I like working with business. I have with colleagues instituted a series of one-day training sessions for small companies in the Odium area centred on the theme of 'Making Ethical Decisions'. These draw upon existing philosophical research to help organisations make morally good hiring decisions and develop other principled employment practices."

from China, with minimal mercy and maximal pain. Exiting, he glanced across at the Department of History and noticed Professor Wilf Hindsight and his jolly Mexican wife, Dr Inés Retrospectiva, chatting amiably over cigarettes in the courtyard. He put an instant end to their smoking habit.

He jogged back up the hill (again, in his mind) to the Social Sciences building. There were three German leftists from the Department of Politics on his list. Ten minutes later, he was able to cross them off. When he emerged from the sliding doors of the building he noticed that his hands were trembling. He decided to take a brief break, returned to his office in the Trump building, and switched on his Italian coffee machine. He ate a couple of biscuits to replenish his sugar levels. He noted with medical interest that his vexatious arxidia now felt vastly more relaxed in their hot pouch than they had for several weeks. Fantasy slaughter was evidently therapeutic for them.

This had been merely the work of the afternoon hours. But Redman had by now no intention of stopping. He pressed on through the evening into the much less familiar territory of the science departments, where the research income was immeasurably more plentiful and deserving victims correspondingly much more tricky to identify. What was one to do, for instance, with someone like Professor Benjamin Fowle, who was in receipt of a grant of six million from the Engineering and Science Research Council to investigate the physical tolerances of various kinds of railway sleepers, but had not published one single-authored academic paper in five years, yet had had his name appended to over thirty articles written by members of his research team in the same period, the obvious bloody little sleeper that he was himself? [14]

---

[14] I have decided largely to allow the crazed academiphobia of this regularly cynical text to speak for itself, but I must confess that I am also (as a distinguished academic myself) rendered rather speechless by the virulence of the hatred towards workers in the intellectual sphere we can witness in this discourse. On the one hand, I consider most readers too enlightened to be swayed by the infantile wish-fulfilment impulses to which such satirical treatment of the academy panders (who, for example, would find even slightly credible the idea that men with considerable power and acting in accord with a grave public duty would expend so much libidinal energy in futile lust directed towards their female subordinates?). On the other, I know that there are

371

Redman slashed his way through or appropriately avoided such thickets as they came at him, and by the wane of the long May day his one-man genocide in the University of Odium was at last at a satisfying end.

He looked at his watch. It was almost 10.30pm. How time flew when you were determining fates!

He picked up his phone and called McNamara. McNamara did not answer. Redman left a voicemail.

The message was: "Hi, Robert. James here. I've just finished the redundancy recommendations. I'll drop by on my way home and slip it through your letterbox. I know you tend to stay up late, so if you fancy a drink, I'd quite like one after all this work. So I'll ring your doorbell in hope. But if you are not there, or don't want to be disturbed, I'll talk to you tomorrow."

**Chapter Five**

McNamara at first wondered if Buckrack's failure to appear promptly at ten o'clock was deliberately intended to indicate a certain coolness on the American's part. But the breathless Buckrack's panting excuse (he had not listened to the voicemail from Meifeng until close to the appointed time and had rushed as fast as he could, briefcase in hand, up the hill from his campus house) suggested a satisfying sense of urgency. Good, McNamara thought: he really does need a meeting, he's

---

ignoramuses and populist right-wing government ministers into whose laps it will readily be invited to dance. I vacillate, therefore, as to the degree to which I should intervene to correct this irresponsible text's obvious demerits and excesses in its parodic treatment of a serious and elevated institution. I state here that, after due ethical consideration, I reserve the right henceforth in these notes to set this frequently wayward novel on a proper moral course where I deem such action necessary. But one must not be too heavy-handed. I will only note for the moment (as a frequent railway traveller) that *someone* surely has to be in receipt of £6m (or perhaps more, who knows?) to investigate the physical tolerances of railway sleepers. If Professor Benjamin Fowle or his like has been given the boot (which is regrettably unclear from this passage), I worry for my personal safety while in transit, and so should you.

apologetic, and I have the upper hand.

Buckrack was physically unimpressive. He was visibly around the same age as McNamara, and though somewhat less corpulent, his stomach in its white shirt nonetheless depended flaccidly over the waistband of his jeans. He was flushed and sweaty-faced from his exertions in the warm night, a little bug-eyed, even.

McNamara invited him in, let him sit on the couch, and asked him if he wanted a drink. Buckrack, seeing McNamara's already well drained bottle of single malt, elected to join him. Annoyingly, however, he asked for ice. McNamara went into the kitchen and got some, then returned and sat opposite, by now rather inebriated, yet feeling composed, determined to control his drunkenness by not saying very much but listening closely and attempting to be inscrutable. He said he was sorry that he had not been able to see Buckrack in the afternoon, and gestured at him invitingly to come to his business.

Buckrack took a breath and began. "We may have a problem. In fact, I think we do have a problem. It seems that, after what took place here in the University, you know, the Trump fiasco, that the American authorities have been asked to look into the death of the American student earlier in the year, the one your predecessor murdered. Of course they cannot investigate it directly or officially, although there are unofficial things they can do. In fact, I think you'll find that the case has already been re-opened and that the CID, a guy called Nesbit, spoke to the Registrar this morning."

McNamara paused. In some ways he thought his drunkenness was aiding his abilities in deciphering the man, slightly alienating him from his speech, enhancing his abilities to read between the lines. And McNamara was accustomed by now not to giving direct answers, or giving non-committal ones, or asking lots of questions of his own before he answered a single one himself. Most people who spoke to him wanted something, and he consequently was used to controlling the discourse he had with them.

"Let's come to the so-called problem in a moment," he said levelly. "You say that *we* have a problem. But right now, I am wondering who *we* even are. You know who I am, it's a matter of public record. But I hardly know who you are at all. I know that your salary is paid from my budget. I have your personnel record. It's extraordinarily thin as these things go. I know that you were hired last September as a research fellow. But I don't know what you've been doing. You don't seem even to have been here in the last six months. Your campus house appears to have been empty most of that time despite a free tenancy agreement. And, oddly for an academic, I can't find a single trace of you on the internet: no publications, no conference papers, no previous university posts. I'm frankly puzzled. Would you care to enlighten me?"

It was Buckrack's turn to hesitate. "There's a limited amount I can say," he prevaricated.

"I don't know why that should be," McNamara replied. "But try me with the limited amount."

"You know," said Buckrack after a time, "that it was me who told you about the bugs in the offices? That it was me who sent you those notes? That it was me who blew the gaff on Covet?"

"I did work that out eventually, yes," rejoined McNamara. "I knew you were on the committee looking into Jane Blake's complaint against Covet, and I worked backwards from there and surmised a little. Only a small number of people had access to those documents. But I can't figure out why. How did you even know there were bugs in our rooms?"

"Because," said Buckrack, "it was me who put them there."

McNamara let his eyes widen a little. "It was you who did that? Not Jane Blake?"

"It was one of the things Covet hired me to do. I wasn't really a research professor, and I have no academic background at all. That's why I wasn't attached to any academic department. It was just a cover. I was more of a … consultant. I was paid to gather intelligence."

"You mean you were a spy, right?"

"If you like."

"Is that what you do?"

"I used to," said Buckrack. "I had a previous career in security services, let's say."

"Which one?"

"As I say, I can't tell you everything."

McNamara rubbed his nose and looked at Buckrack with narrowed eyes. "Alright, but why then tell us about the bugs? Why defeat your own purpose?"

"Look, that's irrelevant. It was good for you that I did, no? But if all of this is looked into again, it's going to be bad for all of us."

"For all of us? Why would it be bad for me? I didn't do anything."

"You knew. You lied. You covered it up."

"I didn't do anything. I denied nothing. No one asked me. I simply chose to remain silent about the fact that my privacy had been violated."

"Okay, sure, but if it all comes out now, that the bugs were real, that they really were put into private offices in this University by the ex-Vice Chancellor, think of the new public scandal you'll have to manage."

McNamara shrugged. "Then we'll manage it. It was a dead guy who did it. And you, of course, which is what I think you are more worried about. Your name will come up."

"Yes," Buckrack admitted. "And I can't let that happen."

"Tell me, why should it? You said they had re-opened the Jane Blake case. So they are looking again into her murder. What's that got to do with the bugs?"

Buckrack gave off the air of a man trying to be patient when he had very little time. "The CID spoke to Asterisk this morning. It was Asterisk who bought the bugs on his budget. Hardly anyone knows that. They were most likely asking him about the video camera, the one used to make the film of Covet and Blake having sex, but which wasn't found at the murder scene. They want to trace it, I am guessing."

"Wait a minute, wait a minute," McNamara interrupted. "Asterisk didn't only *know* about the bugs, he also *bought* them on his account?"

"Covet was covering his ass. If the bugs were ever found, he'd have blamed Asterisk. The paperwork would have been consistent with that claim. But we know they never were officially found. Everyone's forgotten about them. If Asterisk now tells the CID he bought the bugs on his account, he'll also tell them about me. And then you'll have to explain why this University hired an American spy to compromise its own staff."

"I see," said McNamara, still somewhat insouciant. "Yes, it'll be embarrassing, but not unmanageable."

Buckrack shook his head in exasperation. "You don't get it! I'm recently ex-CIA, okay! The story won't be that Covet hired a private snooper, it will be that a CIA guy – because no one will believe the 'ex' thing for a moment – planted bugs in an English university, that America is spying on its ally. Of course, this is total nonsense. Not even the Americans really know that this happened or that I was involved. Trump just thinks he's causing trouble for the University of Odium because you snubbed him publicly. He wants to teach you and the

British government a lesson by dragging out the Jane Blake enquiry and casting aspersions against the British and whipping up patriotism at home while it goes on. The British know that's exactly what he's doing. They can't be too happy that this University put them in this fix. But they have to play along. Now, if the CID find out that a one-time American intelligence officer did the bugging, then the shit really hits the fan. It won't be CID on the case after that but MI5. I don't want to be in the centre of that tornado. Nor do you."

McNamara sat back and sighed. "Let me fix us another drink," he said.

He went into the kitchen once more for ice for Buckrack's scotch and returned, resuming his seat.

His phone suddenly rang. He looked at it briefly, saw that it was Redman, then let it go to voicemail.

"Explain to me," McNamara said, "because I am puzzled about it. This video camera, the one Jane Blake used, how come it's the one Asterisk bought? How did Jane Blake get hold of that?"

Buckrack bit his lip impatiently, then relented. "Let's say I became aware of Covet's exploitative relationship with Jane Blake. It was that that turned me against him, made me decide to destroy him rather than assist him. There are some moral lines I don't cross, even in my business. So I made contact with her and helped give her a way out of her predicament."

"A way out?" McNamara replied, with some heat. "She got herself killed!"

"That's true," Buckrack admitted. "But who could have predicted that?"

"It's the kind of shit that sometimes happens when you fuck about with people's private lives," McNamara said venomously.

Buckrack tilted his head in acknowledgment of a truth. "Unforeseen consequences. But as I was saying, in my line of work we have to make it a habit of getting to know exactly who we are dealing with. The same way I know, for example, about your holiday last Christmas in Amsterdam, your whore, your dope-smoking."

There was a long silence. McNamara stared at his interlocutor. The atmosphere in the room had entirely changed. He felt a throbbing in his temples and an ache beginning to creep into the back of his head.

"What are you talking about?" he finally said, quietly.

Buckrack grimaced. "I was there," he said.

He unsnapped his briefcase and put an envelope on the table between them, next to McNamara's tumbler of whisky. McNamara opened it slowly and shuffled out half a dozen photographs: him in the Amsterdam red light district, him hand in hand with the prostitute he had extracted from her windowed street-side room, him going in and out of cannabis shops to make his purchases.

He looked up at Buckrack, his nostrils flaring. "You cunt!" he hissed.

Buckrack blinked and gave a slight gesture of seeming regret. "As I say, it's just one of the things we habitually do. I admit it's not pretty. I could say I am sorry, but you were the guy I told about the bugs. I had no direct contact with Redman or Poon, only with Asterisk in person and you, anonymously, in writing. Asterisk had many of his own self-interested reasons to keep shtum about all this. But I needed to know more about you. I needed to cover my own ass. Of course, I had no idea at all that you were going to become the Vice Chancellor here. That makes this information more powerful now, of course."

"So, what," said McNamara, suddenly flustered, "you're fucking blackmailing me now?"

Buckrack shook his head. "You could look at it another way. What I did with Covet he deserved, and it indirectly led to you now having the position you have. I don't consider you fucking around in Amsterdam and indulging a soft drug habit to be major moral failings. They're even perfectly legal, where you did them. They don't raise you to anything near Covet's level of selfish wickedness. I don't have any beef with you, I have no wish to upset your apple cart the way I did his. All I want to do is protect myself. I don't want anyone connecting me with the buggings, or what did they call it – Odiumgate? I just want your help in keeping my name out of it all."

There was yet another long hiatus. McNamara flushed, inwardly stewing. "And how do I do that?" he said in a defeated tone.

"The problem is Asterisk. He's a coward. He scares easily. He's the one likely to cave in and blab everything he knows. I'd like you to find out what information he may have given to the CID guy, either at their meeting yesterday or since. If he hasn't given them any information, I'd like you to find a way of stopping him doing so. Hopefully he stalled, but he has a habit of trying that at first and then collapsing under pressure."

McNamara considered for a moment. "I suppose I can look into that," he said. He leaned back in his chair and put his hands briefly over his face. He remained in that pose for a moment before revealing his features once more and taking a large breath of air.

To Buckrack's surprise, McNamara gave him a relaxed grin.

"You're good," McNamara said grudgingly.

Buckrack's mouth twisted a little, seeming to acknowledge the perverse irony of this statement.

"But don't you have other problems?" McNamara continued. "Bigger problems than this?"

"Like what?" asked Buckrack.

"Well, for one, the money transaction between Covet and Jane Blake on the night they both died. What was it, fifty thousand dollars?"

"I don't know. I read the news reports, of course," said Buckrack. "There was nothing in them about that."

"Really? You didn't follow the money?"

"Why should I?"

"Didn't you say you made a habit of knowing who you were dealing with?"

"Yeah, but Covet was dead by then. So was she."

"And where were you then? The day they died?"

"What does that matter?"

"I'm curious."

"I was here, in Odium."

"But not for long, seemingly."

"Meaning what?"

"Well, you completely disappeared right about then. The last thing you sent me was, it's true, postmarked the Friday, the same day, or the day after, they died. And yes, it was posted in Odium. But then, all of a sudden, *pouf!*, you're gone. You instantly vanish off the face of the Odium earth, the very same day they died. Where did you go? Where have you been all this time? I have often wondered."

"You don't have to know that."

McNamara gave a slight laugh. "Actually, as your employer, I think I have a right to know." Buckrack said nothing. "Thing is," McNamara continued, "I knew Sir Evan Covet better than you, certainly for much longer than you. I knew Jane Blake also for a fair duration. Not as well as I thought, obviously. Clearly she was ballsier and less seeming-innocent than I could possibly have imagined. She had an exploitative streak in her herself, to be sure, as events have proven. But she was no match for Sir Evan Covet in that respect. No, you're more of a rival to him in the black arts than she was. But of course, before you told me what you just told me, I didn't have you linked with Jane Blake at all in my mind. I just can't see her blackmailing him like that so easily, can you? I can contemplate her doing it with the assistance of someone with a greater genius for blackmail, though."

Buckrack looked calm. "I have no idea where you are going with this. It's a dead end."

"Well, bear with me," said McNamara. "As you know, I didn't take over directly from Covet. There was another guy before me. I certainly witnessed him showing some interest in the events of the previous term. Who wouldn't, right? But I didn't know how much until I succeeded him. And you know what he did? He managed to procure the final police report. It wouldn't have occurred to me that he could even get that, but he was better connected than me, he had friends in higher places. I found it sitting in one of the files in the Vice Chancellor's office. And one of the appendices in that report was a single sheet from Interpol on the bank transaction received a couple of weeks after the deaths. It shows the transfer from Covet's account, made on the Friday night, being cleared in her Boston bank account the following Tuesday, the same account she told us about in her Public Interest Disclosure. But it also shows that this account was virtually emptied the following day, the Wednesday. There was a couple of thousand left in it, but nearly all of it, the fifty grand and quite a lot more, was wired to an investment account in the Cayman Islands."

Buckrack maintained his silence.

"Now how," McNamara asked, "does a young woman, four or five days dead, transfer money out of her account?"

Buckrack gave what appeared to be a humorous chuckle. "The obvious answer is that it was pre-authorised."

"Maybe," said McNamara. "But who pre-authorises such a large transfer before they even have the money? At any rate, the British police didn't like it. Their report noted the oddity. At the time the report was written they recorded that they had made further enquiries and were waiting for a response."

"They closed the case nonetheless."

"Well, yes and no. They agreed with the coroner's verdict of a double suicide on the evidence available but recommended that the case be revised in the light of requested evidence yet to be received. Maybe that new evidence has now been received."

"Or," said Buckrack, "knowing how these things work, maybe the Americans looked into the bank transfer further and that's what piqued their interest. The result's the same. We both agree the case is now being looked at again. I'm not too bothered by the banking issues, and it's the first I have heard of them. I just don't want to get caught up in the new investigation."

"Yes, but I am not entirely convinced by your assumption that this is just Trump causing trouble to vent his bad mood at the University of Odium, because we injured his pride. In fact, I'm not entirely convinced that you yourself believe this. And the reason I am not convinced is that when Trump was on the way here his security detail, the ones who do the clearance in advance of his visit, before we pissed him off, had one guy – CIA, as it turned out – casually asking for information, precisely, about *you*."

For the first time Buckrack's eyelids lowered. "And what did you tell them?" he said.

McNamara smiled gently, and replied, "You don't have to know that. And it wasn't just me they asked. They asked everybody who was going to be anywhere near Trump on the day."

Buckrack cleared his throat. He took a final gulp from his glass. The two stared at each other.

"And how much do you actually know about me, apart from the fact that I went to Amsterdam for recreational drugs and sex?" McNamara went on. "For instance, what exactly is the state of your knowledge as concerns my health?"

Buckrack examined his interlocutor judgmentally for a few moments. "Well, you don't exactly seem in good shape."

"But do I look, for example, jaundiced to you?" McNamara continued.

"No," replied Buckrack.

"Must be the drugs."

"Drugs?" said Buckrack. "For what?"

"Well," McNamara went on, "it's odd, but it'll be good to tell someone at last. Funny, the things you'll say to a stranger. I have pancreatic cancer."

Buckrack was predictably silent.

"You have presumably never tried to blackmail someone before," McNamara said, "and discovered a minute later that they were terminally ill."

Buckrack saw the need at last to say something. "You don't seem to need sentiment, so I'll ask: how long do you have?"

"Weeks, probably," McNamara replied. "Months if I am lucky."

"And the drugs?" Buckrack resumed. "What are the drugs?"

"I can't even pronounce them," McNamara answered. "I just take them. I don't read the label."

"Show me them. Show me the bottle."

"You can eat shit!" McNamara fulminated, looking over the top of his glass. "I don't need to show you anything. It's yet another thing you don't need to know. What you do need to know is that, while I would in a perfect world wish not to go down in dishonour and scandal, my world these days is very far from perfect, as I am going down pretty soon anyway. So I don't really give two tuppenny-ha'penny fucks what you do. There's the door. Blackmail away. Unless you wish to tell me the truth."

Buckrack cocked his head to one side. "The truth?"

"Oh, come on," said McNamara. "I'm not prepared to buy your alleged fear of being roped into an international espionage debacle as sufficient motivation for you following me all the way to Amsterdam six weeks after you disappeared. Sure, I was the guy you sent the bugs to and whom you tipped off, but the whole Trump-CIA thing didn't happen for months after that."

"You forget," countered Buckrack, "that I may have learned about official American interest in the situation long before you did."

"Sure, it's possible," McNamara admitted, "and I can see why anyone wouldn't want to get sucked into the whirlpool. And spooked as I am by being under your surveillance in Amsterdam, common sense tells me you had more personal reasons for keeping tabs on me and supplying yourself with material for blackmail. You had something to hide, something much nastier than planting bugs at the behest of Covet. After all, there was the camera. The one she used to film their sexual assignation, that video you sent me. You gave it to her, right? You got Asterisk to buy it and you gave it to her? It was your idea for her to get evidence with which she could blackmail Covet? It is, after all, we know, don't we, what you do?"

Buckrack remained silent.

McNamara continued. "So, you are in possession of an unsavoury truth about me. You are offering to keep that truth concealed if I take certain steps to hold the police investigation at bay. And yes, I concede that I am not particularly minded to have the case re-examined and all this dirt dragged out into the light of day. But I really don't have to care that much, given that I am dying. And I certainly don't like being blackmailed. So now, why don't you admit to me the unsavoury truth about you? I won't be able to prove it anyway. It'll be your word against mine. You encouraged her to blackmail him, right? You even set the whole thing up?"

Buckrack said nothing.

"You know," said McNamara, "I don't give a damn about Covet or what happened to his money. And once he had killed Jane Blake the money was no good to her anyway. Things went awry for both of them and you somehow, I think, stole the money, right, and that's why you vamoosed? Isn't that the nasty secret you really wish to keep hidden?"

He let a longer silence prevail between them.

After some time, still without saying anything, Buckrack slowly nodded.

McNamara smiled gently. "There, that wasn't so bad, was it? As I said, it's sometimes good to tell someone." He looked at his empty glass. "So, now that we've traded personal secrets, and know each other better, let's drop all the attempts to cajole by means of threats." He sounded almost jovial. "After all, you're right, I probably wouldn't even be the Vice Chancellor if it hadn't been for you. I didn't exactly not benefit. The pension bump itself is probably more than the sum you stole."

Buckrack sighed a small sigh and said, with seeming sincerity, "Shame you won't get to enjoy it."

"No," said McNamara, "but my beneficiaries will when I die in service. Now, would you like a refill before we discuss further details?"

Buckrack proffered his tumbler. McNamara ambled into the kitchen with it. He stood drunkenly still for a moment, but swaying slightly, only half-remembering why he was there, caught emotionally off-guard by the sudden incongruous domestic quiet of the opulently furnished and gadgeted room. In the end he did not go to the tall, silver-surfaced Fisher and Paykel RF540ADUSX4 Goliath three-door fridge freezer, whose sixty-page user guide had, to his intense irritation, split one of many infinitives while lauding its smart ice maker. [15] Instead, seeing on a rack on the wall Chivers' WNTHBJ 304 stainless steel meat tenderizer – a gleaming hollow-structured device which weighed just over 700 grams and had both a shallow-nail surface and a deep-nail surface as well as gradual curved handles for a comfortable non-slip grip, and came with a heavy-duty mallet head but no annoyingly American English brochure – he took it firmly in his hand, strode a little lopsidedly back into the living room, and brought it down with full force on the top of Buckrack's skull.

## Chapter Six

Perhaps the most unaccountable thing about sudden inexplicable violence is that, while objectively it happens very rapidly (booze-befuddled burly McNamara was to batter bamboozled Buckrack a second and final time with his big-budget beef hammer within barely a blink of the first brawny brain-bash), it seems to take place, in subjective perception, at 600 frames per second. McNamara was thus able to view in wondrous slow-mo hi-def as, with the first blow to the crown of Buckrack's noggin, the American's neck compressed and shot down-down-downwards, while both his shoulders seemed to jerk upwards, then all four limbs jittered reflexively out at once so that the only part of him in contact with the sofa was, for an instant, his pile-driven tailbone. Then, as if it were on a pogo-stick, the head thrust up-up-up again elastically, and conveniently for the now whack-a-mole instincts which had overtaken McNamara, whose twirling right arm was already swinging the top-heavy meat mallet towards it side-on. Its grade 304 stainless steel surface thudded into the top of Buckrack's right ear and his entire body capsized clean over the low armrest of the couch and landed on the carpet, where it commenced silently to twitch then

[15] This is astonishingly accurate. See *ActiveSmart™ refrigerator: Ice & Water and Non-Ice & Water, E372B, E402B, E406B, E442B, E522B, RF522W, RF522A, RF610A & RF540A models* (Fisher and Paykel, 2013), p. 31: "Your ice maker is designed to automatically dispense ice until it senses that the bin is full. So the more ice you use, the more it makes."

tremble then shiver then convulse like that of a sledgehammered pig McNamara had once seen in a European film, though he could not remember, in his blotto and now incipiently endorphin-influenced state, if it had been directed by Jean-Luc Godard or Bernardo Bertolucci.[16] Fortuitously for the furniture, McNamara had led with the shallow-nail side of the tenderizer. Had he used the deep-nail edge there would most probably have been head pulp on the David Rockwell cream fireside rug and lopped-off fragments of earlobe and antihelix down the back of the white Casa Padrino cushions.

While the ghosts of Leon Trotsky and Joe Orton, wherever they were, no doubt froze in momentary supernatural empathy, McNamara steadied himself with one hand on the back of the sofa and peered curiously over its edge, as one might at a fly one has just swatted with a newspaper and which now lies helplessly quivering on the windowsill.

"You criminal spunkhead," he growled in a low voice. "I'm from fucking Glasgow."

Fortified by this occult, atavistic and neologistic declaration, he turned and went into the hallway and unlocked the cellar door. He returned and, grasping the prone Buckrack by the ankles, dragged him across the carpet.

"Fucking blackmail, eh?" McNamara continued in a monologue directed at the slumped American frame as his feet retreated out into the hallway, his arms stretched straight and pulling it laboriously after him. Buckrack's recently bombarded head bumped up and down on the metal base plate of the door at the threshold to the lobby. "You fucking led her right into the lion's den, you cunt. You dickass! You might as well have fucking killed her yourself, you tic-tac shit! You ball-less drosh!" He was running out of breath and cogent insults and had simply begun, unwittingly, to make up pejorative words which fitted in with his faltering respiration. Fricatives and plosives abounded. "You ... frope! You ... brasharse. You ... fucking ... drim!"

At last he got the body to the top of the basement steps. He stepped over it, knelt down, put his arms under the oxters, and heaved the

---

[16] McNamara is thinking of Godard's *Weekend* (1967). A live pig is also slaughtered in Bertolucci's *Novecento* (1976) but it is unceremoniously disembowelled, not charitably stunned in advance by being poleaxed.

unconscious Buckrack into a sitting position.

"You … shitfangle!"

Holding Buckrack bent at the waist with a knee propped behind him, McNamara hauled himself up enough to reach the light switch just beyond the door, and waited until the fluorescent tube below flickered into life, casting its stark glare into the white-bricked room. He eased himself further upright, panting with exertion, and as carefully as he could put the sole of his foot in the middle of Buckrack's spine, then pushed.

As the American folded forward and went tumbling, bonce over brogues, like a bowling ball rolled down the alley of the wooden staircase into the depths of the basement, McNamara himself lost balance backwards, staggered woozily, and careered Newtonianly into a thin-legged credenza, hurting his already irksome back.

"Faaaaaaark!" he spat out in pain.

He slumped over the top of the sideboard and got his breath back. Adrenalin jetted along his veins and whooshed in his arteries, banging at the gates of his heart and making him giddy. Pinpricks of light erupted at the edge of his vision like small exploding stars.

He gathered himself and clambered down the staircase after Buckrack, whom he found hunched up in a crumpled immobile ball, his face on the floor and his arse in the air above the bottom two steps. He pushed the body again with his foot to straighten it out. He leaned down, on all fours, close to Buckrack's face. The biff-costarded man was still breathing.

He found a length of flex in a cupboard and searched for a Stanley knife and cut it in two. One length he wrapped wrist-crushingly tight and tied around Buckrack's joined arms. Then he looped the other length through it and secured it to a wooden support pillar in the middle of the floor, with the double knot on the far side from the now shackled Buckrack. He finally hoisted himself up the stairs breathlessly, holding on to the banister at each step, turned out the light and locked the cellar door from the outside.

He crossed the hallway to the coat stand and had just dug his mobile phone from his jacket pocket when, through the frosted glass of the front door, only a foot away, he saw a flesh-coloured oval shape loom up at face height, then a hand extend to the glass and give three hearty raps.

"Hey, Robert!" he heard Redman exclaim happily, and could even see his smile and his blinks through the blurry window. "Glad you're still up! I'd love a beer! Lots to discuss!"

The sun always rises, on the odious as well as the good. The next morning it peeked above the horizon, clear and bright and promising more great heat, a minute or two earlier than it had the day before. Midway through his fatal morning jog, Professor Adrian Plumb noted (his last professional satisfaction) how its low half-disk cast short shadows down the long sloping field – which most people mistakenly thought of as a manicured lawn – that stretched up towards the Trump Building on the west side, revealing the wave-like shapes of the ancient agricultural furrows made by those who had once had to seek a much simpler existence than his, whose geological exertions he had adverted to in his locally famed topographic tome, and whose once-tilled earth his corpse would enrich within a fortnight. [17]

At a few minutes past nine, about half an hour after Plumb's body had begun to rigidify, unwept for by anyone, in a curtained cubicle in the University Hospital less than half a mile away, McNamara was brought into consciousness with a head non-verbally howling the Book of Ecclesiastes at him and the rest of his body echoing it with a translation in cellular terms of the Book of Lamentations. The cause of his crapulent awakening was his phone trilling at him from the coffee table, and the circumstances of the resurrection, he noted with puzzlement, involved his being fully clothed and covered with a blanket on the couch in his living room. He stretched for the phone and answered it groaningly without checking who was calling.

To his significant displeasure, it was Elfyn Dethbridge.

"I'm very sorry to disturb you, Vice Chancellor," Dethbridge started saying in his unreformed and hesitant Celtic lilt that made him sound

---

[17] His gratifyingly bereaved widow, taking some words from An Order for the Burial of the Dead quite literally, put his body to good horticultural use, getting local authority and University permission to bury it intact at the base of her beloved rose bush in the rear garden of their campus home. So Plumb fittingly became part of the very object he had so assiduously researched, so did he flourish as a flower of the field. He thereby joined that small group of the academic elect who not only interpreted the world he studied, but changed it.

permanently like someone with a low IQ. "But I am in receipt of a document I need to show you immediately. I called your office but you were not there yet."

A few grunted attempts to get Dethbridge to paraphrase the document were met by portentously expressed Welsh negatives and grave claims from deep in the valleys that it could not be discussed on the phone. McNamara reluctantly agreed to let Dethbridge come to his office in an hour. On no account was he going to allow the guttersnipe near his house. He hung up.

He then found himself looking at a box file on the table bearing a sticker on which was printed in bold the word "REDUNDANCIES". Next to it was a pile of photographs, the top one showing him holding the hand of a hesitant Hispanic whore in hallucinatory hash-habit Hamsterdam. Beside that, on top of a closed briefcase, was a note written in pen which read, "Call me when you wake up. James." Before he could reflect on any of these unwanted things, however, the phone painfully went off again.

This time it was an agitated Nigel Asterisk.

"Vice Chancellor, Vice Chancellor, good morning."

"Morning, Nigel."

"Vice Chancellor, I have some disturbing news."

McNamara closed his eyes and put a hand to his biblically discontented head. "And what's that?" he asked.

"It's Professor Buckrack," Asterisk answered, hardly able to disguise the sense of drama in his voice. "You know who I mean? He's here, he's back in Odium. He called Elfyn Dethbridge yesterday. I don't yet know why."

McNamara was not physically capable of sitting bolt upright but he felt some vague command within his slurrily operating brain stem that suggested he should do so.

"I'll have to call you back, Nigel," he said. "Excuse me. It'll have to wait."

He tossed the phone on the table and struggled to his feet. He walked stiffly out into the hall and turned the key in the lock of the cellar door. The first sign of something amiss was that he did not need to flick on the light. It was already on.

He could see in an instant that Buckrack was no longer in the relatively cramped basement. As he descended the steps slowly his bloodshot eyes took in the obvious signs of an escape. There was a plain, handle-less windowpane above head height, but also just above ground level, which permitted some natural light into the room during the day. It had been smashed from the inside and cleared of splinters so that Buckrack could get through it. As he neared the bottom of the steps McNamara could see that the wire flex with which he had secured Buckrack to the upright pillar had been roughly torn through. As he reached the very last step he smelled urine and saw, contrasting with the floor close to his feet, in a dark bloody puddle, two broken teeth.

Our American murderer and blackmailer and avenger and now dentally deprived and incontinent ex-CIA agent has, dear reader, believe it or not, an internal existence just the way you and I have. We would not wish, I am sure, actually to experience his subjective feelings on life (or possible death) just at this moment, but it is perhaps time to do what this triple-decker narrative has so far generally resisted: to explore his unique perspective a little, get behind his eyes and have a look around, and then (as he was to do from the temporarily imprisoning cellar) get the hell out these distressing surroundings after the briefest sojourn.

When those eyes that we are now imagining ourselves behind had opened, they saw nothing at all. Indeed, there was only a glimmer of consciousness, the merest thread of difference, for the first moment, between his couple of hours of violently enforced comatose paralysis and this faint sense that he was still alive. He was incapable of any immediate movement, although he became aware that there was some going on, a shallow rise and fall, in his chest. He was breathing. As moments passed the blackness of his vision commuted into a more graduated greyscale. It was, in fact, a moonlit night, and there was a little illumination in the room from some window somewhere. Then he thought he could hear something. But it was not external sound. It came from two sources in his own body. There was a droning that seemed to originate deep within his skull, which had slowly faded into awareness and then remained at a fixed volume, like an unvarying electric hum, as if a key on an old-fashioned synthesizer had been depressed in there and not released. On the right side of his head, moreover, it sounded as if a conch shell had been placed permanently against his ear, which seemed encased and insulated, and the nerves in his neck just below it seemed constantly to be fluttering, contracting and expanding uncomfortably, producing an unnatural flanging vibration deep within the cochlea, as if an unreal wind were passing to and fro across it. These two aural sensations seemed to act as a screen, making it impossible to discern anything sonic that may be taking place outside them in the room.

He was soon able to reflect on his pitiable plight, both physically and spiritually. To the natural demand for an explanation his affected brain struggled sluggishly but at last successfully to deliver him up a recent memory. He had not been without suffering in his life – he had, after all, once found his own son with a bullet-hole in the back of his throat and a Glock 17 on the floor beside him, in a garage not entirely unreminiscent of this dingy basement (and he had himself, as we know from his dealings with Jane Blake, not been slow to tie people to domestic stanchions when it served his own purposes) – but he had never quite suffered the specific personal shock of being improbably dual-slugged on the nut by a distinguished Professor of Politics. Such sophisticated men did not usually resort instantly to batonic blows to resolve testy disputes the way McNamara had.

Buckrack was feebly knowledgeable that he had enjoyed professional training and lifelong experience which should theoretically have conferred on him an advantage over ordinary mortals in just such a duressful situation. Yet when he tried to remember any particular taught or learned routine, he could summon up nothing useful. He did not know it, but as we have the brief privilege of being behind his eyes we may sweep a narrative light along the top of his concussed brain for an instant and confidently surmise that the bang-bang of McNamara's silver hammer, as it came down upon his head, probably impaired some specific cognitive abilities, perhaps temporarily, perhaps not.

Buckrack fell back on a more primordial propensity: murderous animal instinct. As he took to biting the tough plastic sheath of white flex which shackled him to the pillar, it was his visceral intention, upon releasing himself, to march upstairs and beat McNamara to death where he found him. Even when, after much worrying at the wire, he felt most of his right upper middle tooth crackle, snap and pop out with an accompanying spurt of saliva but no gum blood, he did not find his mind retreating to more sober consequential thinking. Indeed, his immediate reaction was to see it as a fortuitous plus: he would be able to bite a gouge in McNamara's throat much more deeply and painfully with a snaggled toothline than an even one. It was only with the second dental sacrifice that he became more pessimistic as to his chances even of slipping his fetter. This despair began with a premonitory cuspid creaking that seemed to last much longer than it really did in measurable time – as does the discrete instant when one decidedly loses balance and knows one is going to fall – before the canine seemed to fling itself out of his mouth like a fighter pilot ejecting from a doomed plane. Its point of fracture was much deeper than the first. It broke off nearer the root with a disgusting tearing of tissue, sending a hot needle of searing agony up through the nerve into the jawbone that seemed to reach high and lance the bottom of his right eye and make it wriggle and convulse in its socket. The psychic effect was like living a Freudian castration dream. A wave of debilitating impotence crashed over him and he fell prostrate, sobbing and mewling, flat on the floor, with a dim mindfulness that blood was now dripping from his mouth in quantity. As if in sympathy for this liquid loss, his bladder chose that moment to give up the ghost, and he pissed the processed product of McNamara's single malt into his pants.

Minutes passed. He flitted in and out of wakefulness. Impulse told him that time may be in short supply, and he made yet another compulsive effort, taking to gnawing and munching more cautiously, but doggedly, on the now pierced and frayed wire, slavering over it copiously, until, after what seemed an age, he felt the welcome tang of copper coalesce with the iron already in his mouth and, with one last horrible metallic bite, cut through the brittle strands.

From the same wire, wound and tied tightly round his wrists, it was easier to free himself. McNamara had secured it well, but in his sottish state, in which he had never contemplated Buckrack doing a Houdini, he had carelessly left several sharp implements in the basement. Buckrack lumbered to his feet and groped and pawed around the room. He found a light switch on the wall and turned it blindingly on. By this means he found an open toolbox and was able to hold a knife with the handle between his knees and saw slowly through enough of the flex that he could slip his hands from the unsevered, loosened remainder.

He sat for a moment in exhaustion and transient relief, then got back on to his feet. He made for the stairs but discovered within a step that this was to be no triumphal march. He lunged forward, with no control of his centre of gravity, and his left knee gave way under him and came down on the very edge of the first step with a grim crunch, exactly on the reflex point. The pain made him gasp and clutch at the stair rail. He got up and tried to put weight on the leg. The knee answered with injured protest. It did not want to go on any stair-climbing journey after being treated so badly. It turned instantaneously sullen and uncooperative.

Buckrack looked up the steps at the cellar door. It had a mortice lock and opened inwards. Even had his leg been willing, he could not kick it open. If he could find an axe or a hatchet somewhere he might be able to batter a hole in it, but this action would take too much time and he did not know what or who was now on the other side. It would be better to try to get out of the window and take stock from there.

He hobbled back across the room. There was a table beneath the window and, using a chair on which he placed his good leg, he was able to ease himself onto it, despite his tormented knee. He stood gingerly on one foot. His eyeline was now actually a little above the window, his head bowing a little under the roof. The window was recessed a few inches, with a border of masonry above it. It was in two panes, each about twenty inches high and thirty inches across, with a metal frame. He felt confident that his body could fit through it head first. About six inches beyond, across a gravel border, were what looked like shin-high bushes, their tops visible against the ghostly haze of the moonlit night sky.

He looked down for a tool with which he might smash the window, and then sighed with fatigue and futility. He should have picked up something before he had climbed up here, he now realised. The damaged knee was so weak that struggling back down and up presented a prospect of immense, time-consuming agony. Instead, he bent over twingefully and managed to get a hand on the chair and lifted it up onto the table. He put the back of the chair close to the wall under the window and placed his weak knee onto it for support, keeping his other leg straight. He looked at the window and saw his dishevelled, distressed face for a moment palely outlined in reflection, a dark stain of blood all down his chin. Then he braced himself with his hands on the chair back and, using most of the weight of his upper body, dived forward and head butted the right pane of glass in its centre.

He was not sure at first if the crack he heard was the glass or his forehead giving way. In his already concussed state, the bolt of renewed cranial and neck pain was only bearable because it had been anticipated. The humming noise that had been constantly in his skull seemed to leap up in volume for several seconds, but he managed to hold on to the chair and ride the trauma through.

When he looked up again there was a spider-webby shatter pattern radiating out from the middle of the window pane. He was heartened and slightly amazed that, in his present condition, he had calibrated the required impact so accurately. He reached out a flat palm and, still holding the back of the seat with his other hand, while finding that he had to wobble precariously for balance on trembling limbs, applied gently increasing pressure. The glass began to creak and yield until, with the gradually greater stress, it gave way and spilled outward, leaving a jagged hole. He felt slightly cooler air drift in and breathed more hopefully.

He slowly began repeating the procedure nearer the edges of the window, so that bit by bit he was able to clear most of the glass and leave a fairly complete opening. He thought, as he went through, he could most likely avoid the small spars at the top and sides which remained. It was the ones at the bottom of the frame that still concerned him. He could not dislodge these with the ball of his hand. If they were not removed they promised to add stabbing insults to multiple McNamara- and self-inflicted injuries. But he found that if he crooked his arm and used his bony elbow instead of his hand the most prominent of these too could be broken away.

He was relieved, when he now placed both feet on the chair, to discover that with his upper body at right angles to his legs, he could stretch his arms through the aperture he had created and support himself on them while he edged his head, shoulders, chest then stomach guardedly all the way through, keeping them from touching the small, sharp glassy fragments that still clung to the frame. Having gone as far as he could by this method, he rested his hips warily on the inside of the frame, wincing at the barbs he could feel on his front thighs and pelvis. With one hand he stretched and grasped at the root of one of the miniature bushes and tugged at it. It seemed to offer ample resistance. With one fist around it, pulling, and the other hand flat on the soil, alternately levering, he was able to scrape his way laboriously through the escape hatch he had created, with only a few cuts and lacerations to his upper legs.

The katzenjammered Vice Chancellor of the University of Odium was not able to process much by means of sensory data available to him in his now naturally air-conditioned cellar. He decided to return to his living room to call Redman.

"How are you feeling?" Redman asked him.

McNamara searched his memory banks for a phrase that might be meet. "Learish at his worst," he answered, and in the pause that followed found that he was mildly congratulating himself on this erudite, indirect riposte. Perhaps he was regaining his mind. "I mean King, of course, not Edward."

"Do you remember?" Redman asked.

"No," said McNamara. "Total blackout, I'm afraid."

"You fainted," Redman said.

"I fainted?" McNamara repeated.

"Yeah," said Redman. "You opened the door to me, looked in my direction like a wild animal, then just fell in a heap on the floor."

"I did?" said McNamara superfluously.

"You did."

"I was very drunk."

"I gathered."

"Did I say anything?"

"Well, not right then, obviously. And not much later either. I dragged you into the living room. You did resuscitate after a few moments, before I could call an ambulance. What happened?"

"As, I say … it was just drink."

"Then you were incoherent, for the most part. Jabbering, havering."

"What was I saying?"

"Expletives mainly. *Cunt, fuckhead, wanker,* that kind of thing. I presumed these terms were being used to describe someone other than me. And there were some things that sounded like words but weren't."

"Too much whisky can do that," McNamara said.

"Except for one complete sentence. You started giggling and then said, 'You know what I told him, you know what I told him? I told him I had cancer!' Then you chuckled some more and conked out again. I threw a blanket over you and left the box of redundancy stuff on the table next to the, er, photographs."

McNamara knew that the facts just recited implied questions. But as they were not explicitly stated, he chose to ignore them. "Yes, thanks. Clearly I was talking absolute nonsense. Havering, as you say."

There was no immediate response. Then Redman said, "Okay…"

McNamara filled the gap by answering cordially, "Thank you again. I'll get back to you on the redundancy matters soon."

There was another expectant pause. Nothing rushed in to break it.

Redman finally added, "There was something I meant to tell you. In fact, I would have told you last night. Asterisk had a visit yesterday from the police, asking questions about the Jane Blake murder. He asked me not to say anything to you but I had second thoughts."

"Oh, that," said McNamara. "It's true, then."

"You already knew?"

"Yes," McNamara said. "Asterisk is worried about the fact that the bugs and the camera were procured on his budget by Buckrack."

"So you did know that it was Buckrack who planted the bugs?"

"Not until yesterday, not for sure," McNamara replied.

Redman said, "Oh."

"I'll talk to Asterisk. Do me a favour. Don't tell him you told me."

Thus their conversation faltered to an end.

Buckrack was quick to discover that his life had been divided into two parts. There was the life he had had before McNamara repetitively clattered his capitulum, and now a kind of parody of that life afterwards.

Once he exited the cellar, all thoughts of returning to the scene of the warningless assault evaporated. Instant revenge was not now the priority: base survival was. He could hardly stand upright. His body kept tilting naturally to the left, putting the weight on his damaged knee, and he could stay erect only by deliberately counter-leaning to the right, which felt entirely abnormal and made his first few experimental steps freakishly teetering and uncertain.

At the back of his mind, behind the continuing humming in his brain, was now another constant buzz of unanswered speculation. He could not fathom why McNamara had set about him so viciously and forcefully. Confining him in the cellar afterwards and tethering him there had been done, presumably, with the intent of calling the police, and while there was as yet no sign of their having been summoned, the very prospect meant that he needed to quit the environs of McNamara's house as rapidly as his malfunctioning body would allow.

As he hobbled away, with each short step the vast extent of his distressful vulnerability was borne in upon him. He was entirely alone and seriously injured. His own outlaw actions meant that he himself could hardly solicit aid. He was not CIA now, and no extraction team would be swooping in on a Black Hawk to carry him away from the theatre of operations. He could hardly go to an emergency ward for treatment and care; if McNamara did summon the authorities and inform them of what had happened, such a place would be the first they would look.

The one bolthole he had within immediate reach was his campus home, though it was unlikely that he could stay there safely for very long. But it was the middle of the night and he could perhaps risk sheltering there for an hour or two, enough time to grab some personal things, clean himself up and make away in slightly better shape. But he had lost all sense of orientation. He was not sure in which direction his house was from here.

He halted, propping himself against a tree trunk, and managed to ease his phone out of his trouser pocket. He could use GPS to find the way. A moment later he was looking at the screen indecisively. The oddest thing was that it did not seem to be in colour. It looked flatly monochrome, its usually vibrant hues absent. This could hardly be a trick of the light. He was standing in a dark, sheltered arbour. Perhaps it had been damaged when McNamara manhandled him. But he had little time to consider the anomaly.

The first attempt to enter his passcode failed. He saw that the fingers of his right hand were trembling. He switched to his left but found this even less nimble. It was numb in all the digits, which were difficult to control. When he held it up and shone the faint pearly light of the phone screen upon it, it appeared to be fixed in an inflexible semi-claw shape. He cradled the phone back into his left hand and, with more deliberation, poked at the numbers on the screen with the extended index finger of his right. At the third digit his mind went vacant and he stood for several seconds in a forgetful mental miasma. He searched for the desired four-number series in his head, and then began to doubt the accuracy of even the first two. He nonetheless stabbed hopefully twice more at the screen and completed the sequence, but it failed. He tried again and was still incorrect. Halfway through the third bid he prodded hard enough to unmoor the phone and send it slipping out of his weak left hand to fall on the tree roots at his feet. Bending down to retrieve it was a painful trial.

And then some welcome vestige of his professional training seemed to ping in his impaired thought processes. The phone now was nothing but a liability. It could be tracked. He prised the back off with less than cooperative fingers, removed the SIM and the memory card and battery, and put them in his pocket.

He staggered forth, dumping the phone in a nearby litter bin, seeking in the distance for some landmark which might give a clue to the route home. Something told him that he should head over the brow of the hill he was on, where there was a large sloping grassy area with student halls of residence at the bottom of it. He was relieved to discover that he was right. Once he gained a vantage point from which he could overlook the downland, he was able to see a paved path which bisected it, because its line was traced out by a string of lampposts shining above it on either side.

He stepped gratefully forward and his foot immediately caught in stout rushes, and he bundled over headlong into a thicket of nettles. His chest heaved and wheezed with the smarts these imparted to his face and the bone-shuddering effect of the tumble. He lay quiescent for a few minutes, not only stung and aching, but now knowingly scared at his unaccustomed helplessness and fragility. He thought of simply remaining there and receding into a welcome sleep. But his frightened impulses would not let him. He dragged himself to his feet and stumbled on.

In this way he made the slow journey of about half a mile, sometimes veering somnambulistically off course to the right for twenty or thirty yards at a time before correcting himself, tripping and falling three times on the way, eventually getting close to his house after pursuing a bearing which was whatever the opposite of a bee-line is.

Twenty yards away from the front door, he saw through one of the windows the distinctive arcing beam of a torch moving inside the house. He stopped short and lumbered to the side of the brick building, edging around the sturdy bushes which sheltered the back garden to a point at which he could take in the entire rear of the building. He saw the torch flash again several times behind the curtains of the upper floor rooms. Finding standing dreadfully uncomfortable, he crouched down in the darkness. But this too proved impossible to suffer for long, and so he lay down on his side on the narrow pebbly ditch which bordered the garden, keeping watch on the house through the railings.

And in that position, a few minutes later, he fell asleep. He had his one painless ear to the ground, but he did not hear what was coming.

## Chapter Seven

McNamara could not have supplied anyone with a suasive explanation for his unbidden binate blitzkrieg on Buckrack's bodily belfry. He could not adequately account for it to himself, as he downed an entire carton of orange juice, took two multivitamins, a couple of Panadols and one five-hour energy capsule, but no pancreatic cancer medication.

His drastic action of the night before had not been premeditated. McNamara had discovered himself in his kitchen, excessively drunk and mountingly irate, ostensibly fetching ice for Buckrack's nightcap one minute, but delivering something a bit more like an icepick to Buckrack's skullcap the next. He remembered bellowing something absurd at Buckrack's unconscious carpeted form about having grown up in Glasgow. There was in fact some essential truth in this utterance, but only insofar as it was a kind of shorthand vindication of a primal reaction. Buckrack's blackmailing habits, which were usually no doubt the castings of a skilled angler into ponds of deep personal insecurity, had on this occasion been incautiously exercised near sulphuric waters, toxified by whisky and McNamara's complicated feelings about Jane Blake. The confidently fishing Buckrack had not drawn forth the merely modest catch he sought, but instead had provoked a teratoid Moby-Dick of fury and ferocity, which had surged clean up out of the depths and landed on the bank, crushing the unprepared piscator mercilessly.

It was this demonic spontaneity, issuing in bestial force, which most troubled McNamara, as he trudged into the Trump Building after having showered and dressed. Not for the first time, he was forced to reckon on something within himself which he had previously considered to be the very seed of evil at work in Sir Evan Covet. Had not his predecessor suffered the same lack of civilised restraint when he plunged a blade into Jane Blake's belly? Did the office of Vice Chancellor of the University of Odium now carry some primeval curse with it which ensured that it was nasty, brutish and short? Was the Trump Building really a veiled House of Usher whose master was condemned to a foreseeable doom? [18]

---

[18] Not for the first time, our narrator is Poe-faced. In the Gothic tale, Roderick Usher is withering away spiritually and physically in his "mansion of gloom",

Elfyn Dethbridge was waiting for him in Meifeng's outer office. Meifeng smiled broadly and without reproach at McNamara's arrival: she did not, then, appear to be in a mood of censure on account of anything in his behaviour the previous evening. Dethbridge, he knew, lived in a permanent state of private animus towards him, yet seemed more than ever today his usual cowed and deferential self. McNamara had discovered that it was not easy, as Vice Chancellor, to know if staff thought ill of you or not. Many of them did a little performance when in his presence rather than conducting themselves according to nature. Some seemed to find it difficult even to meet his eye, as if he were a Japanese Emperor or they would thereby be doing something akin to looking directly at the sun. So he never could quite tell what they were genuinely thinking.

He gestured Dethbridge into his inner sanctum and the Welshman, he reflected with apparent prejudice, obeyed with all the seeming pleasure of something entering his inner rectum. Then he waited, standing like a schoolboy in the headmaster's office before accepting McNamara's express invitation to sit.

McNamara was not in daily life a genuine homophobe, not a regular gay- hater or baiter or slater. His younger son was gay, and McNamara loved him without gayness ever being a detrimental feature in their emotional equation. No, with Dethbridge his revulsion was decidedly *a posteriori* rather than *a priori*. It was some obsequious, crawling, creeping, servile factor in Dethbridge's very being, he thought, which seemed to bring his otherwise incidental homosexuality into associative disrepute. And so, unsurprisingly, in their present encounter McNamara found distasteful what he always found distasteful about Dethbridge, namely every single thing, each nuance of behaviour, from his

---

grieving at the death of his "lady Madeline". The romance of Ethelred ("who was now mighty withal, on account of the powerfulness of the wine which he had drunken ... uplifted his mace, and struck upon the head of the dragon, which fell before him") seems to hover prophetically over Usher and the house, and both eventually fall "victim to the terrors he had anticipated". The house eventually disintegrates into the earth, with Usher's dead body inside it. The reader interested in how the presaged end of Odium is to occur need hardly read on. Take ye heed: behold, I have foretold all things.

mannerisms to his tones, from his facial expressions to his word choices, from the way he held himself awkwardly in his body to his false fawning before authority. This sour, rotten soup of detestable personal attributes, served up in an earthen bowl of bland Welshness bearing a floral pattern of awkward queerness, as McNamara saw it, did not activate pre-existing Taffy-bashing tendencies or inbuilt faggot-rancour but, instead, seemed to call these responses forth with all the naturalness one would expect in any person whose appetite, gustation and palate operated within the standard, well-adjusted human range.

Dethbridge, always vainly trying to charm, seemed to radiate harm; his constant attempts to insinuate himself led you to wish to exterminate his self; if he tried to nurse you he would curse you; he was more hex than sex; a poisonous infiltrator posing as a poised administrator; a mortal gallstone, not a moral lodestone; more cellular spatter than well-formed molecular matter. For the terms that adequately pinned down his essence you would have to consult an expansive historical dictionary – one with words in it like *varlet*, *caitiff* and *scofflaw*. His soul was a small dark blob made of an as-yet undiscovered, highly unstable element: odiumite. [19]

"This document was delivered to me in my office by hand just after nine this morning," Dethbridge was saying as he pulled a sheaf of papers out of an envelope he held. "But although it was addressed to me, it's not for me. It appears to be directed at the University."

McNamara reached over and took the document, looked at it briefly, and felt his neck hairs stand on end.

"Why was it delivered to *you*?" he asked with undisguised distrust, looking up at Dethbridge piercingly.

---

[19] I ask the typically unreflective reader to make an unusual effort and speculate where we are positioned narratologically by these prolonged, digressive, very unprosy sentences: presumably inside McNamara's hungover sensibility? One likewise wonders, on the other regular occasions when the text excurses into obtrusive alliteration and childish rhyming, if we are not hearing a kind of demented babble, short holidays taken away from good sense, the uncontrollable upfrothing of senile language onto a surface customarily smooth and well managed, caused by perturbations in the invisible depths below, fractures in the supportive crust, which as they multiply and extend surely point ahead to an almighty eschatological crack-up and collapse?

Dethbridge was wide-eyed innocence in adult human form. "That I don't know. But as it *was* addressed to me, I'm afraid I did read it. It's a writ, yes? And all I can guess about why it was served on me is that it mentions both you and the Registrar by name, though I don't understand what difference that should make. But this is why I called and asked to see you urgently."

McNamara blinked at Dethbridge for a few seconds. Then he said, as coolly as he could, "I don't think it's called a writ these days. It's merely a claim form submitted as part of a civil action. We get these from time to time, you know, damaged property, personal injuries, students suing us for their academic failure, mostly trumped-up stuff. But obviously it's confidential, and you should speak to no one else about it. Thank you for bringing it to me so quickly."

Dethbridge got to his feet. The meeting had lasted barely a minute. "If there's anything else I can do..."

McNamara nodded. "I'll let you know."

But then, as Dethbridge was making to leave, McNamara called him back.

"There was, now it occurs to me, one other thing," McNamara said.

"Yes?" replied Dethbridge expectantly.

"I understand you had a call yesterday from Professor Buckrack."

Dethbridge's reaction was nonchalant. "Yes, I did."

"What did he want?"

Dethbridge shrugged. "He wanted to talk to the Registrar. But it was late in the day, about 6pm. I assumed the Registrar had left and he was put through to me by, er, default."

"But what did he say?"

Dethbridge looked puzzled. He found himself shifting his weight a little from foot to foot. "He didn't say anything. When he realised it was not the Registrar he was speaking to, he simply asked me to tell Nigel he had called, which I did."

"Funny," remarked McNamara, unblinkingly.

"Funny?" Dethbridge repeated.

McNamara looked at him levelly, with a straight stare. "Funny that within such a short space of time you should be the conduit for two communications to those above you in the hierarchy." Then he scanned Dethbridge's face for signs of reaction, for any tinge of confessed guilt in the cheek or twinge of acknowledged nefariousness in the muscles.

But there were none. Instead Dethbridge simply pouted a little thoughtfully and shook his head. "I couldn't have spoken to him for more than twenty seconds. Who is Professor Buckrack anyway? I don't even know of him. He didn't say what his business was."

McNamara relented, then decided, with great effort, to try to sound emollient. "It's okay. Sorry. Listen, Elfyn. We have had our differences, I know. I'd like to be able to put those behind us. We are about to enter a difficult period. I am going to have to rely on the discretion and good sense of people like you in senior management. You'll see why soon enough. So I don't want there to be any hard feelings between us about things in the past."

The Welshman looked pleased. He smiled a little, constrained smile. "Of course, Vice Chancellor," he said. "I will do whatever is needed."

Once Dethbridge had gone, Meifeng came with yet another document, ensuring that his daily treadmill of bureaucratic reading continued to grind without let-up.

"This is Mrs Scheep's final version of the redundancies letter, Vice Chancellor, incorporating your amendments. She has already signed it. If you would like to check it over and sign it if you approve, I will have it emailed to all staff within the hour."

"Okay," said McNamara. "Thank you. I will read it now." Then, with a glance at the papers Dethbridge had delivered, he added, "Would you please contact the Registrar and ask him to come and see me as soon as he can after ten-thirty?"

Meifeng left, and McNamara turned his gruff attention and his migrainous morning-after mind to the six-page letter which was to spell out occupational catastrophe later that day for over five hundred employees. He finally added his signature to that of Surya Scheep, the Chief Financial Officer, and called Meifeng to fetch it.

"The Registrar is coming in a few moments," she said as she was leaving. "Shall I send him straight in?"

"No, give me ten minutes. Ask him to wait. I'll call you when I am ready."

McNamara spent the ten minutes reading the papers Dethbridge had brought. Then he called Meifeng back in a mood worse than his headache.

Asterisk blustered in, and started speaking instantly, and a little dramatically, as if the meeting were being held at his request.

"Bad news, I'm afraid," he began.

"You don't say," McNamara rejoined.

"It's Professor Plumb. He's dead."

"Adrian Plumb?"

"Yes."

"But I was just talking to him here in this office yesterday. He seemed to be under the impression that this building was going to fall into the lake."

"What?"

"Never mind."

"I got a call from his department. He didn't turn up to his nine o'clock lecture this morning. They called his private number. Someone told them he'd been taken to the University Hospital suddenly. Heart attack, apparently, at home."

"Jesus," said McNamara in a low voice.

"You will want me, of course, to make arrangements, contact his wife – "

"No. I'll deal with that. There was something else."

"Yes." Asterisk's judgment was again wayward. He seemed to think he had just been asked a question. "It's Professor Stoner. He's also in hospital, but he's not dead."

"What? William Stoner?"

"Appears he was mugged early this morning, cracked over the head, assailant stole his wallet. One of the campus residents found him, luckily knew who he was. He's still unconscious, in intensive care."

McNamara scratched his head. "Fuck. I'll contact the hospital."

"I can do that, if you like."

"No, Nigel, William's a close friend of mine. In any case, we need to talk, you and I."

"Oh."

"About yesterday."

"Ah yes, Professor Buckrack."

"No, not about Professor Buckrack. Well, indirectly. Did you try to call him back yet?"

"No. He didn't leave a number. I don't have a working number for him."

"Well, don't try. But on the subject of Buckrack, you have never really been candid with me, Nigel, have you?"

"What do you mean? I did tell you about him stealing the evidence of the bugs."

"Oh yes, you did that. You just didn't tell me that he planted them in the first place, and that he also gave Jane Blake the video camera she made the sex video with. Oh, I'm not stupid, Nigel. I wondered for a long time how Buckrack knew all about the bugs in my office, Redman's and Poon's. And over time I clicked that he – not Jane Blake – must have put them there. But now I also know what I didn't know, what you didn't care to tell me: that they were bought on your budget with your knowledge. You remember that night in the University club? The night you came in worried about the guy in the Secret Service entourage, the one you thought might be CIA, who showed you a picture of Buckrack and wanted to know if you knew him? I asked you directly if it was Jane Blake who planted the bugs. Your answer was, 'Didn't she?' You made out that she did it in collusion with Covet. And yet you knew fine well she didn't."

Had it not been for the Valium he had popped an hour before, Asterisk would now have been edgy, his eyes darting nervously around in their sockets. Instead he seemed to sag. "I, I …"

"You *what*?" McNamara spat. "You *lied*, right? You lied to my face."

Asterisk gulped. "But you weren't Vice Chancellor then."

"I am now. And you have lied by omission since I became so. You kept me in the fucking dark."

"But … but … it had all blown over. It was history."

"Well, it's not history now. I've got a bloody notice of a private prosecution in my hands. We – the University – are being prosecuted by the family of Jane Blake. By her mother, to be precise. She is attempting to prove our culpability for actions leading to the homicide of her daughter. Count one, our employee, namely Sir Evan Covet, murdered her. But count two, a named person allegedly colluded with Covet in conduct which assisted him in doing so: you, by purchasing listening devices that recorded her conversations when she was in Poon's office and my study, as well as the now missing video camera used to film their sexual encounter. And count three, two other named persons cooperated with you in concealing the existence of the bugs: me and James Redman. There's an affidavit from Avril Poon in here swearing that we did so. Now, I don't know, Nigel. I suppose Ms Blake's own written confession of her prostitutional activities and getting herself into mortal danger by such means may count against her reputationally in court. I guess Poon's sexual proclivities, especially as they manifested themselves towards Ms Blake, if they have to come out, may discredit Poon also, although we both know that what Poon says in her affidavit is essentially true. We gave you back the original invoices for the supposedly non-existent bugs. We kept copies and the very much existent bugs themselves. We never mentioned any of this to anyone. I'm not sure what your defence is going to be for buying them on your budget, though. And worst of all, this either costs us a packet to settle out of court – and to do that we'd need the approval of University Council, from whom we can hardly conceal this private prosecution the way you did the original Odiumgate affair – or the entire institution, and its two most senior officers, you and me, as well as Redman, get dragged through the mud in a courtroom trial. And yet you sit here and still don't tell me the whole truth."

"But I ... I can't believe this."

"You were visited by the CID yesterday! You weren't going to let me know, were you?"

"I ... I see ... James must have told you."

"I didn't learn about it from Redman. But you informed him and not me?"

"I was asking for his advice. It was only yesterday. I didn't see you."

"Oh, you were going to tell me today, were you? Now, don't fucking lie to me any more, Nigel."

"I was taking a period to think. I needed a little time. I was trying to find a way round the problem. But wait. If James didn't tell you, how do you know?"

"That's irrelevant."

Asterisk thought he had caught on to something. "Wait. Wait ... are you bugging *my* office now? I didn't tell anyone except Redman. You couldn't possibly know if he didn't tell you."

"Don't be absurd. I am not bugging your office. What the fuck is wrong with you? You were the one who conspired in a bugging scandal, not me."

Asterisk's eyes were like small wide pools. He seemed half way to paranoia already. "But you must be. It's the only explanation. It's impossible otherwise. No one but Redman knew about Nesbit coming to see me yesterday."

"It doesn't matter how I know. I know. I'm the Vice Chancellor, for god's sake. I know things. But I don't know because I bugged your office. The idea is insane. And it's not the main thing anyway. You didn't tell me about it, that's what matters. Why didn't you?"

Asterisk's mind was slowly burrowing its way into the desperateness of his position. "I needed time to figure out a solution."

"A solution to what?"

"The CID guy, Nesbit, he wanted to look at our purchasing records. I said he could, knowing he wouldn't find anything. The paper invoices for the bugs and the video camera are no longer in my departmental files. But no, he wanted permission to look at the electronic records of our suppliers. If he did that, well, he'd find the invoices on my budget for the video camera and the three listening devices, and then he'd come back at me and know I had been lying, and the whole affair would be blown wide open again. So I said I would need to run the request past you and get back to him."

"And why didn't you?"

"Why didn't I get back to him?"

"No, why didn't you run the request past me?"

Asterisk looked awkward. "Well, I told him I wouldn't see you 'til today. And I suppose I am now running it past you."

McNamara slapped an intemperate hand on his desk and Asterisk jumped a little in startlement in his seat. "But you *weren't going to run it past me*, were you? You didn't come here now to *run it past* me. You came to talk about Buckrack. Just like when you called me this morning it was to tell me about Buckrack. You had *no fucking intention* of telling me about this. You were looking for what you call a solution. What did you have in mind?"

Asterisk hesitated, then said timidly, "I was trying to get round the difficulty he posed. We couldn't stop him doing the search, he could get a warrant, but I wondered if there was some way of … "

His words petered out.

"Some way of *what*?"

"Some method of putting him off the scent … of frustrating his search … "

McNamara banged the desk even harder and Asterisk jumped a little higher.

"Some way," hissed McNamara through clenched teeth, "of not cooperating, of covering up the truth with a lie, or a deception, or a distraction! Exactly. Your whole fucking *modus operandi*! Conceal the truth to save your own neck!"

"But, but ... I was thinking about the position it would put the University in, not just myself."

"Oh, you fucking lying, short-sighted, pathetic little *cunt*!" McNamara snarled. "You half-created the position the University is in yourself with all your earlier lies! And now you want not only to keep me in the dark but to deceive the police when they are investigating a murder committed by the man who was at the head of this organisation! You think that is a solution! How much of a witless imbecile are you?"

Asterisk sat sheepish and silent. He could hold McNamara's enraged accusatory stare for less than a second or two.

With flaring nostrils, McNamara leafed through a few pages on his desk before him, and his tone turned judicial. "And now I have to clean up the shambles of your making. So let me tell you, and for once I hope you can face reality: you're finished, unless I can find some means of making this prosecution go away quietly. If I can't, I shall have to take the matter to University Council, either to approve an out-of-court settlement or make a decision to contest it. I have lost all confidence in you. I cannot trust you to be honest, not to conceal vital matter, or even to exercise the basic duty of care your office demands. You appear to have lost all proper professional judgment. And while that is the case, I will not have you where you can do any further damage. You are therefore suspended on full pay, pending potential disciplinary action. I will consider your case further in the next few days. You will hear from me at home by letter. You will leave this building immediately. You will talk to no one before you do so. You will not contact Detective Superintendent Nesbit on the matter of our purchasing records. I will do that. If he contacts you, you will cooperate with him truthfully. You will not be allowed on University property until further notice. If you disobey any of these injunctions, you will be summarily dismissed. Your suspension will be treated in the strictest confidence. Do you understand all I have said to you?"

Asterisk had sat through this monologue of simmering wrath in an increasingly cowed manner, his face gradually adopting the lineaments of chastened meekness, his Adam's apple moving up and down, his eyes becoming moist. Now he said, deferentially, "Yes, Vice Chancellor. Do you want his card?"

406

"Whose?" said McNamara.

"The policeman's. Nesbit."

"I don't need it," McNamara said dismissively. Then, to rub it in, he went on. "As you are aware, I already met him when I identified the bodies, something I told you about long ago while you still went on withholding material information from me. I know where to contact him."

Asterisk swallowed. "Okay, Vice Chancellor."

"But before you go," said McNamara, "you came here to talk to me about Professor Buckrack. So you will tell me, right now, everything you know about him, what you are aware that he did, your interactions with him, your conversations about him with Covet, every last whole goddamn jot and tittle, that's what I want, every particle of information you have on the man. And you will answer every question I ask you about these things. You got that?"

"Yes," Asterisk croaked, "Vice Chancellor."

McNamara sat back in his chair.

"Then begin," he commanded.

## Chapter Eight

The grilling took an hour, by the end of which McNamara was convinced he had bled Asterisk dry, and despatched him. He then noticed that his headache had blissfully disappeared, the performance of power and enforcement of fear on his detested Registrar seeming to act like a welcome analgesic.

But the new things he learned about Buckrack did not seem terribly useful, in the present situation, in helping decide what to do about him. Asterisk knew little about Buckrack's dealings with Covet and nothing about his interactions with Jane Blake. Buckrack's behaviour towards Asterisk, as told – his bullying and intimidation, his entirely minatory bearing – sounded convincing and familiar. Hearing of the mechanics of how Buckrack had come to Asterisk's assistance and removed the purchase invoices from his office files did not substantially enlarge McNamara's already first-hand knowledge of the American's ruthless skill in cover-up and deception.

He sat for some minutes doing something he did frequently: making a list of people he needed to see to address efficiently the list of issues that daily arose, which he would then pass to Meifeng, who would summon them to an instant meeting or get them on the phone.

Today's problems had rapidly grown to look like vexatious trials, intractable enormities. He had thought it would be tricky enough with just the redundancy missive going out. It was no doubt already causing startle-eyed reactions as the PDF attachment it came in was being scrolled incredulously down screens across campus. But now there was the additional problem of having received formal notice of an imminent private prosecution of the University. And he had just had to suspend his untrustworthy Registrar, whose multifarious functions, including dealing with the hot telephone calls that would start flooding in about the redundancy letter that very afternoon, needed quickly to be assigned to someone else. On top of that, he must decide without delay what to do about the renewed CID investigation. And to cap it all, the common denominator in these cumulatively avalanching and tormentingly beknotting difficulties was Buckrack, the unpredictable Buckrack, whom he had unthinkingly beaten up and held captive the night before, but who had escaped, was now a loose Cannon, and would do what unaccountable crazy shit next?

Something began to nag at the back of his mind as he made the list. Asterisk had wondered how McNamara had known about the visit of the CID officer. McNamara had not known until Buckrack told him the previous night. He had had it confirmed by Redman in their phone call that morning, but Redman had heard it directly from Asterisk. This left an unanswered question: how had Buckrack known? And how had he found out so quickly, so instantly, on the very day?

And then a horrible suspicion began to form in his mind. He picked up the phone. "Meifeng, would you get me the Head of Security, Jagger Harmwell? I need to speak with him immediately. Then please contact Elfyn Dethbridge. I need to see him now, or as soon as possible, and definitely before lunchtime. I also need you to call the University Hospital intensive care department and ask them about the condition of Professor William Stoner and let me know what they say. If he is conscious, please book a car to take me there around one o'clock. Then I need to see, as early as possible from two o'clock onwards, Dr Avril Poon in Cultural Studies. And, oh yes, could you also please let me have the next-of-kin contact details for Professor Adrian Plumb in the School of Earth Sciences..."

Nigel Asterisk, as he slunk out of McNamara's office, had decided to reassume a path he knew well and had strayed from only to his peril, that of obedience: not simply his chronic, habitual adherence to the edicts of whatever Vice Chancellor happened to be in place in the University of Odium that term (the position by now having become an alarmingly fast-rotating kaleidoscope of the shifting obsessions and arbitrary whims of its various post-holders) but to the much larger dictates of fate also. For against the cruelties of that capricious force he had at least made provision.

Stopping in his office only to pick up his jacket and his briefcase and his bubble pack of Valium from his desk drawer, he glid past his secretary in her outer office without word of explanation as to his leaving, as McNamara had specified he should, and went straight to the car park. He sat behind the wheel for a few moments, and experienced a small positive impulse he could not have bargained on, something one could not quite call relief, but an easement all the same, a kind of consolation, a feeling that the very worst was over and that whatever else was to come could not possibly be as bad. It had something to do with the expiation of the confessional. He had at last been able, even if under compulsion, to unburden himself of his secrets to McNamara. The current Vice Chancellor was in a state of unruly apoplexy towards him, and there was no blaming him for that. But it might pass in a little time if Asterisk remained compliant and untroublesome: give way enough, perhaps, for McNamara to accept his resignation rather than put him through the ordeal of a disciplinary procedure and ignominious dismissal.

As he reversed his car carefully out of its space and set off down University Drive, steering it carefully and with now accustomed sensitivity to being under the influence of a powerful tranquilliser, he awarded himself a gold star for being fifty-seven years old. While he acknowledged that no one deserves praise for this fact, because it involves little more effort than managing to stay alive, being above fifty-five meant that he could take a reduced occupational pension on early retirement any time he liked. He also considered that he deserved top marks for not being married, even though the faintest flicker of an opportunity to attain such a condition had never arisen in his entire span of existence.[20] But his enforced bachelorhood (which had in the past been a source of great personal insecurity and anxiety) now spared him the necessity of divulging his present disgrace to a spouse awaiting him at home, or of concerning himself with the financial repercussions that it might otherwise have visited on the dependants which would probably have been the fruit of his and a wife's conjoined loins. For years, now, he had been maxing-out on advance voluntary contributions to his pension fund. There had still been plenty left over from his six-figure salary to plough with uninterrupted regularity into a now formidably obese unit trust.

After ten minutes, he drew up in the drive of his three-bedroom detached home in a posh suburban cul-de-sac, the mortgage repaid in full a couple of years ago, now owned by him outright, the final badge of honour in his totally successful private pursuit of pecuniary prudence. Celibacy, property, pension: the legs of a redoubtable tripod which the vagaries of even the baddest karma would be unlikely to rock.

It was with this mollifying meditation that he pressed the remote on his keypad and watched the electric garage door tilt up smoothly so that he could roll the car into the empty space. With the added prospect of kicking back with more Valium whenever he felt like it, he unlocked the door in the garage wall that gave access to his hallway, stepped inside, cast his briefcase on the floor, and began to take off his jacket.

The door swung to and closed softly, pneumatically. For a few seconds he breathed in reassuring domestic air and savoured comforting household scents.

Then an American voice sounded from his rear, a voice he had heard before, from the blind spot which had been behind the door when he opened it. "Hey there, fatso."

He twisted around, his hands still holding the lapels of his jacket at the shoulders, and managed to cry out only "Oh my – !" before the flattened fist of Buckrack's right arm crashed into the middle of his face.

*

---

[20] Had it done so, we might with little doubt have expected – given Clockman's tendency towards broad farce in names – his wife to be called Hyphen, his son Colon, and his daughter Ampersand.

McNamara got through some of his to-do list. He managed to speak to Adrian Plumb's widow and briefly conveyed his condolences. He had in Elfyn Dethbridge, and to the visibly dilating pupils of the Deputy Registrar, informed him that Asterisk was unwell and would be absent for a spell, and that he needed him to act in his senior's place. Dethbridge's alacrity was fulsome, though he expressed a seemingly conditional keenness to take up residence in Asterisk's actual office. McNamara was not in a mood to cavil but, with an eye to what he wished to consult Jagger Harmwell about before then, put him off until four that afternoon. This was good enough for Dethbridge, who had to resist the urge to skip out of the room. Then McNamara called Harmwell and set up a meeting for 1.45pm.

By 1.07pm he was being swooshed into the University Hospital VIP car park by his driver, Brian Blackfoot, in the University Lexus, and by 1.14pm he was stepping through the doors of William Stoner's room in intensive care.

Stoner was awake but dazed, feebly irritable but grateful to be visited. His head was vastly bandaged: the fabric had been rolled under his chin and around both his ears as well as all over the top of his head, leaving only a U-shaped portion of his face visible. He was sitting upright, aided by a stout white neck brace, which, along with the cream hospital gown, enhanced the illusion that he had adopted a medical variant of a hijab.

"Still dressing all in white, I see," McNamara quipped. "What happened?"

Stoner grumbled. "It's what I get for playing the Good Samaritan. I was walking in, early, as I do, on that path near the Sports Centre. There are two cottages just there, you know, they back on to it. I thought I saw something in the kind of sloping ditch by the fence that surrounds them and I walked over, and sure enough, there's this poor chap, lying on his side, unconscious, seemingly, with a great welt on his ear, massive blue and black bruising and purple swelling on the side of his head, the front of his trousers all torn and bloody. I thought at first he might be dead. He'd clearly been in some sort of fracas. So I got down and spoke to him but there was no response. I put my hand on his shoulder and gave him a gentle shake. His eyes opened. He was a little bewildered, scared maybe. Then, all in a second, he lurched up, with a stone in his hand, and he thumped me on the skull with it. Didn't say a word. Next thing I

411

know I'm in here four hours later with a police constable sitting where you are. Bastard stole my wallet and my trousers, apparently. Left me in my damned underwear."

"Good grief," McNamara extemporised. "We might have some cameras there, you know. I can ask security. Do you have the policeman's number?"

His friend gestured at a card on the bedside cabinet. "Won't do my bloody head any good," he lamented. "Stoner stoned, you might say." [21]

McNamara remained another ten minutes to give sympathy and consolation.

Asterisk did not quite become the second person Buckrack rendered unconscious that day. The punch to the middle of his face did not lay him out, but sent him flailing backwards, as a consequence of which his head bounced against the lobby wall and his awareness and vision went immediately all fuzzy and dissociated. He had a sense of being bundled to the floor then dragged by the ankles, his mouth and chin wet with blood from his nose that got into his mouth and made him splutter and heave.

This activity soon stopped and he was left still. He eventually gathered that he was on the tiled floor of the small windowless utility room off his kitchen, with his head near the tiny doorstep at its entrance, the open door to his right, a washing machine and tumble drier on his left, and a large blue plastic laundry basket at his feet. When he arched his neck backwards to look, he saw the upside-down form of Buckrack, looming over him just outside the door frame, holding one hand to the side of his head, a large kitchen knife in the other.

"Just you stay there," Buckrack instructed, pointing the tip of the knife in his direction. "Don't you move. If you behave yourself I'll get a cushion for your head. If you don't I'll cut your fucking throat."

Asterisk had already resolved that obedience was best in all things.

---

[21] Indeed, he has ironically become the very man the Good Samaritan helped, whose thieving assailants "stripped him of his raiment, and wounded him, and departed, leaving him half dead" (Luke 10, 30). One is tempted to see this entire campus trilogy as a similar parody of the parable, in which a nobly intentioned institution is assaulted, destroyed and impoverished, and in which too many characters are divested of their garments.

Besides, he didn't feel like moving, far less resisting. But he was nonetheless a little curious.

"How did you know I'd be home?" he asked.

"I didn't," Buckrack replied. "I wasn't looking for you. I needed somewhere to shelter and I remembered your place from the last time we met, when I came and got you out of the hospital then brought you back here. You turning up in the middle of the morning is inconvenient. Now shut up. I need to get something to eat."

Buckrack retreated into the kitchen, and Asterisk began to hear the clatter of utensils. He realised he still had his jacket on, and carefully slipped his hand into various pockets to see if he could find his phone. But Buckrack must have taken it from him. He did find, with a little pulse of joy, the bubble pack of Valium. He popped a tablet out with his thumb and decided, in the circumstances, that two would be preferable, and so snapped out a second. He extricated them and snaffled them surreptitiously between his lips.

There now arose the smell of frying bacon and roasting coffee, the sound of sausages sizzling and eggs spitting. A plate or a cup also seemed to smash on the floor. After about ten minutes Buckrack returned with a small stool and a tray on which there was a large fry-up. He went away again and returned. This time he got down slowly to the floor, grunting, and in a kneeling position eased a cushion under Asterisk's head. He got up again with heavy breaths, and fell onto the seat, parking himself at a table just outside the door where he could watch Asterisk as he ate. The latter observed the American, flipped through 180 degrees, and thought he consumed the food in a slovenly way, like a baby, but slowly, tiredly. Asterisk woozily reflected that this may just be an illusion created by the unusual perspective and the oddity of the situation. Then he fancied he saw a great swelling on the side of Buckrack's head. But he could not make Buckrack's features out too well. It was dim in this corner of the kitchen. It became tiring on his eyes to keep straining to look, and eventually he let them flutter shut.

He began to feel incongruously calm and relaxed. Then he re-membered something.

"Why did you call me yesterday?" he asked Buckrack, his eyes still closed.

There was a long silence. He assumed Buckrack was still eating. He forced his eyelids open.

"You called yesterday evening. What did you want?"

The expression on Buckrack's face appeared grave. His quiet now took on the air of a thoughtful hush. He had finished eating. He was looking directly at Asterisk.

"You got put through to my deputy. Told him to tell me you called."

Buckrack continued to stare, immobile.

Asterisk closed his eyes again. He heard himself say snoozily, "Why?" Then he conked out.

As the man on the floor fell into a sleep, Buckrack was gazing at him stonily, a sliver of egg-whitey drool trickling an inch from the corner of his lips, reaching the curve of his chin and dripping pendulously onto the leg of William Stoner's trousers.

It did occur once or twice to McNamara, on the car journey back to the Trump Building, that he should have been making decisions based on the likelihood that the butterfly effect was in operation, especially when the evidence of consequences was so immediately observable and their magnitude not yet exponential. His walloping Buckrack instinctively on the head had created the circumstances in which Buckrack had thwacked Stoner defensively on the head. If this head-bashing (which he was not aware had already been replicated in classic non-linear dynamic fashion by his suspension of Asterisk, which had led just as directly to the latter's domestic nose-biffing at the end of Buckrack's remaining good arm) was stepped up, deterministic-chaos style, it was bound to lead to much more extreme outcomes than a few personal concussions.[22]

But in truth, although his own self-inflicted headache had gone, his

---

[22] The reader of the trilogy knows, unlike McNamara, that his violent action is not the *primum mobile* he thinks it is: Buckrack at the end of volume one, after all, smashes a whisky bottle over Sir Evan Covet's noddle before stringing him up with aerial wire. The American has a demonstrated predilection for the baton on the cephalon. Given this fact, McNamara's failure to find adequate motivation for clubbing Buckrack and restraining him with flex (other than being randomly drunk and redoubtably schooled in Glaswegian methods for resolving disagreements) is somewhat beside the point. It is, rather, an obvious narratological symmetry, a result of a different kind of determinism, the artistic kind that novelists get to impose upon their characters.

thinking was still hangover-jittery. He could not yet decide with any surety what to do about Buckrack. His thoughts refused to gather and cluster around the problem and quarantine it with a likely solution. They kept zinging toward it and bouncing off at tangents. So he procrastinated, in the hope that there may be a particular Muse[23] which eventually descends to aid beleaguered University Vice Chancellors who caused wounded and dangerous ex-CIA officers to run amok on campus and assault their staff.

Jagger Harmwell was waiting, with another besuited man, when he got back to his office.

"This is Phileas Foremost," said Harmwell, doing the honours, "from Security Solutions. I think he has what we need."

McNamara blinked once at the ridiculous literariness of modern names (this one surely had been made up, he dispiritedly reflected),[24]

---

[23] Or a *deus ex machina*, more likely. Just you wait and see.

[24] One could compose a small disquisition on the matter of names and the idiosyncratic way they are dealt with in this trilogy of novels. We can be sure that Robert McNamara's is not "made up": like almost everyone in the meeting of persons who considered Jane Blake's Public Interest Disclosure in volume one, his name is inexplicably filched from those of the real Cabinet members of John F. Kennedy's U.S. government. "William Stoner" has similarly leaked into the second and third of these campus novels from an earlier (but opposite of comic) example of the genre by the unsensationally named American author, John Williams. We know that "Cannon Buckrack" is a self-confessed sobriquet in which violence and extortion seem consciously united. "Sir Evan Covet" is little more than an obvious political-party anagram, although it does additionally typify the character's vices in the transparent manner of Renaissance and Restoration comedy (indeed, there is a Lady Covet in Thomas May's *The Old Couple*, a long-forgotten play published posthumously in 1658); "Redman" is likewise a patently ideological charactonym; while "Asterisk", suggesting a mere glyph which acts only to blank out a meaningful character notionally existing underneath it, aptronymically signifies the Registrar's obvious lack of spiritual distinction. Other examples could be copiously cited. On the occasions on which we (and McNamara) meet absurdities like "Phileas Foremost", however, we (and McNamara) may legitimately be thinking that we have simply wandered into a light vernal fog of randomly associative personal designations generated by a lazily time-serving author who is beginning to make even his own protagonist impatient.

but said nothing.

"How does it work?" he asked briskly, gesturing at the technical box of tricks Foremost was removing from a dark vinyl bag.

Foremost seemed rather proud of the machine – which looked exactly like a black-framed Etch A Sketch with a single knob – as if he had invented it himself. "Nothing escapes detection with this. Japanese. Used by Mossad. It's called The Tapfinder. Its range is thirty metres in diameter, so significantly larger than this room. Look, I'll show you."

He took a small button-shaped black flat rectangle from a recess in the back of The Tapfinder.

"This little thing is a typical modern wireless consumer listening device. It has a SIM in it, it and calls the person who put it there, or they can also call it and listen in, in real time. There are more advanced ones which, once switched on, also record and transmit audio data on the fly on a pre-set frequency to whoever wants to listen in to it later. Now, if I put this on the desk, here, and step away a few feet, all I have to do is turn the dial slowly on The Tapfinder, and it scours the entire frequency range throughout the room."

While this was going on, Harmwell looked sidelong at McNamara. "When I come to think of it," he said, "we should maybe have done this long ago, given everything that happened in the first term, though I was told no evidence of bugs had been found."

McNamara did not reply.

The Tapfinder gave a small chirrup of alarm.

"And there we are!" exclaimed Foremost triumphantly. He took a few steps back towards McNamara. "Not only does it detect it, but it shows here on the screen exactly where it is, and how far away on the x and y axes."

He picked up the model listening device, switched it off and replaced it in its plastic cavity.

"Now I'll do two entire passes," Foremost explained, "once up the entire frequency range, and once back down it. If there's anything else in the room it will find it."

McNamara and Harmwell watched and waited.

After forty seconds Foremost looked up and said, "Nothing. No bugs here."

"Good," said McNamara. "Now come with me."

He took them along the corridor to repeat the exercise in Asterisk's office.

It took a mere five seconds for The Tapfinder to locate an eavesdropping device on the undersurface of the desk. Foremost put his index finger to his lips. He crawled into the kneehole of the desk with his phone light on and found it magnetically attached to one of the metal brace plates on the left. He found its power switch and turned it off.

When he brought it out, he put on the top of the desk a small grey box about the width and thickness of a 9-volt battery, which was much larger than the button devices McNamara had found before.

McNamara made to ask a question, but Foremost waved a hand at him to be silent.

Foremost continued to turn the dial on The Tapfinder cautiously. After fifteen seconds or so, when he was close to the top of the frequency range on the first pass, the machine pipped again. Foremost looked at its screen, then glanced askew at McNamara and Harmwell. Then he inclined forward, pulled the top left drawer all the way out, bent over, looked into the drawer slot, put his hand in, fumbled for a moment, and removed an identical small box (but this time black rather than grey). It had been attached with an adhesive pad to the underside of the desktop within the drawer slot.

After completing the upward pass and another downward pass on The Tapfinder with no further result, Foremost said, "We can speak now. I have switched both of them off."

He bent over and looked at two devices. "Oh, wow," he whispered.

"I thought these things were meant to be small and inconspicuous?" McNamara said. "These seem pretty large."

"Yeah, they're not your usual consumer devices. Those tend to be smaller because the assumption is that you have access to them and can replace the battery every now and again. Like this one here in the back of The Tapfinder, they tend to run out of charge after a few days or, with power saving, a couple of weeks at most. It's the kind of thing a husband puts in his home to catch a cheating wife, or to monitor conversations you know are going to happen soon. But not these."

"What do you mean?" said McNamara.

"These are bespoke. The reason they are so relatively large, well, let's see, shall we?"

He opened the battery compartment of both devices. Inside each was a double stack of chunky silver button cells.

"Oh my God," said Foremost.

"What?" said McNamara.

"That," said Foremost, pointing, "is an array of eight LR1154 cells. When one fails, the next kicks in. It's the kind of arrangement you deploy when you want longevity in a small device. One of these cells is commonly used as a CMOS battery in a computer to power the real-time clock and retain BIOS settings, and lasts for years. If you put them in an array like this you can power a small device continuously for, well, months, probably longer as these things pretty much go to sleep until noise activates them. You can put these somewhere and leave them and not have to go back to them."

"You mean it's for, what, continuous long-term surveillance?"

"Yes. I mean, this is ... MI5-level stuff. Also, look, no markings, no serial numbers on the device itself. You can't buy these for thirty quid on Amazon."

The three men stood looking at the two little boxes.

"Is there anything we can do that would tell us where they came from?" Harmwell suggested.

"I doubt it," said Foremost. "Concealment is the objective. The best you could do is test the voltage in the batteries, and that would be a good indication of which was placed earlier and which later. I can do that now. I have a multimeter with me in my car. I mention this because there's something altogether weird about this."

"What's that?" McNamara asked.

"Well," said Foremost, "it's not uncommon to find several bugs in a largish room. This is the obvious place to put one, on the work desk, on the side where the phone is. A lot of talking gets done at an office desk. So you'd expect that. But you'd put the second bug somewhere else, like over there, across the room near that chaise-longue, armchair and coffee table arrangement. You wouldn't place it a few inches away from the first, like these two, would you? You'd simply be duplicating data that way. You see what I'm saying?"

McNamara said, "Please spell it out for me so that I am certain."

"I'm saying it's my guess that two different people bugged the room," Foremost clarified. "Whoever put the second bug in did not know the first one was already here."

## Chapter Nine

McNamara decided it was time to speak to Detective Superintendent Nesbit. He could not find his own card with the CID man's number and asked Meifeng to call Buckinghamshire Police.

At last he felt that he was beginning to piece together what had been happening. Foremost had tested the batteries in the two devices. Six of the eight in the black box were discharged, and three in the grey box. An arithmetical relation between these two facts led him to conclude that both devices were CIA issue. Buckrack had last been seen over six months ago, and had been in Asterisk's office alone, where he had placed the black bug in the Registrar's desk drawer; a CIA officer had interviewed Asterisk in his office three months ago, reached under the desk and placed the grey one on the metal bracing plate. Buckrack had been listening in to Asterisk's conversations since early November, the CIA since late February. This was obviously how Buckrack knew that Asterisk had been visited by Nesbit. And now the CIA presumably knew that their powered-down bug had been discovered.

Meifeng called to tell him that Dr Poon had arrived for their meeting. He put the two listening devices in his desk drawer, staring at them thoughtfully before he closed it. He marvelled at his own lack of any sense of drama. Odium had these days come to seem a place where almost anything was possible. Being bugged by the CIA at the whim of Donald Trump and having to deal with a rogue ex-Agency employee were not experiences he had expected on assuming the role of Vice Chancellor of an English university, but he was beginning to take them in his stride. It made other things – like the thing he was about to do – appear comparatively simple.

Avril Poon entered serious-faced and haughty, with something of a strut, sat down without ceremony, and glared at McNamara across the desk.

"Thank you for coming to see me," he began. "I thought we should talk."

"It would have been nice to have been spoken to, as the Union President, before you issued the letter about the redundancies."

McNamara replied, "It's not actually about the redundancies that I wished to speak with you. The letter that went out today announces the beginning of a consultation to which all the campus unions will, of

419

course, be invited. The information had to be kept confidential until we were sure about the way forward. No, what I wanted to discuss with you is this." He tapped a forefinger on some papers on the surface of his desk. "This is a notice of a private prosecution against the University by the family of Jane Blake," he continued. "It contains an affidavit from you swearing that the University, including me and James Redman as named parties, concealed the existence of a listening device in your office last autumn."

Poon harrumphed. "So what? It's true, isn't it?"

"It's arguable. Our saying nothing in order to protect the University from bad publicity is not necessarily active concealment. Redman and I were also bugged. We weren't under any obligation to comment publicly on the affair. It's true that we agreed not to participate in the internal investigation that sought to confirm if the bugs existed. We did not consider that such a revelation would do the institution any good, to wit the probable planting of those bugs by a student our ex-Vice Chancellor murdered, especially given the stormy waters we were then sailing in, to wit the fact that we were in the middle of a hostile takeover bid by another university. But your affidavit rather glosses over this context, and the fact that it was me who actually *revealed* to you that there was a bug in your office in the first place. Whatever I did, I did not conceal it from *you*. But I was wondering what you hoped to gain from involving yourself as a witness in this prosecution against your employer?"

"To gain?" Poon scoffed. "What makes you think it's about gain? It's about justice."

"Justice?" said McNamara. "Are you sure? Is there no admixture of motives of revenge? Or of wishing to justify your own less than temperate actions?"

"Think what you like."

"Okay, but have you considered also how much you have to lose? I mean, personally? Imagine this case goes to court and you are subject to cross-examination. Jane Blake's accusations about your sexual harassment of her were also concealed from public knowledge for the same reason the existence of the bugs was concealed, so you yourself were spared the indignity of being asked about them by the press. You won't be so well treated in an open trial."

Poon glowered back at him archly. "We've had something like this conversation before. Do your worst. But maybe you now understand why I am cooperating with her family. Sure, I misbehaved. Or rather, as I would put it, I was misled by a beautiful young woman bent on seduction. You may not have noticed that that is common and permissible between women these days. But nothing actually happened. It was just words. I temporarily lost my sense of professional judgment. And now she's dead. I didn't cause her death, but assisting her family is one way of making restitution for my weakness in respect of her. In any case, I'd say the chances of this case going to court are near to zero. You'll settle, if you're wise."

"You are doing this to *atone*?" McNamara said with more than a hint of incredulity. "That would demonstrate a nobility of moral conduct which, forgive me, I find it difficult to associate with your person."

"Sneer all you like," Poon replied.

"Okay," McNamara sighed. "I take it, then, that you intend to offer your resignation?"

For the first time Poon looked startled. "Why would I do that?"

McNamara stared back evenly. "Your employer protected your reputation by keeping confidential details of your actions which, surely, in the eyes of public opinion, you must agree, would have damaged it beyond repair. You don't seem minded to reciprocate. You cannot expect your employer to continue to have confidence in you if you participate in a prosecution of them concerning the very same matter. And you patently have no confidence in your employer. It would therefore be logical for you to part company with us at this juncture, no? Or do you expect us to still keep paying your salary while you collaborate in an action against us?"

"You can't fire me over this!" Poon exclaimed. "I'd take you to an employment tribunal and win, and then all the dirty laundry you are trying to conceal would be publicly aired."

"Oh," said McNamara, "I think we could. All an employer has to demonstrate for legal dismissal is their justifiable loss of confidence in the employee, and I think we can persuasively do that. But I didn't say anything about firing you. I said I assumed you would wish to resign if you intend to remain on your present course. We currently have two positions earmarked for redundancy in your department in any case, and your resignation would spare us one."

"What?" Poon lurched forward in disgust. "You're threatening to engineer my redundancy?"

"Oh, Avril," McNamara said, shaking his head, "you of all people know how redundancy works. It's never 'engineered'. It's a professionally conducted consultation. Everyone is looked at carefully, each person is assessed, their relative academic merits and demerits are weighed in the balance, their value and cost to the institution compared. Your predatory sexual advances towards a murdered female student, your demagogic coordination of an illegal strike, your public support for the academic freedom of a student and a junior administrator who were both entirely in the wrong and did not, in any case, enjoy the legally protected rights to academic freedom in the first place, no, these would of course be disregarded. We're much more likely to examine your research record. And what do we have? A book on *Star Trek*, an edited volume on *The Simpsons*, and a forthcoming treatise about fans of TV adaptations of Sherlock Holmes stories? Your work shows a tendency towards exploring, what shall we call it, the very obviously popular? We'd compare it to your colleagues' work. For example, how does it stand up against Professor Crumpington's recently published landmark 600-page history of American documentary film? Of course, we'd consider your relative years of service also, because the longer the service the greater the severance we would have to pay. Professor Crumpington has twenty-two years' service. You have nine."

Poon appeared on the verge of fulminating aloud, but seemed to think twice, and rested back in her seat.

"On the other hand," McNamara proposed, "we don't always calculate these things so crudely. For example, while we disregard matters of misconduct if they have not been subject to formal disciplinary procedures, we would place a high premium on actions which unambiguously show great loyalty to the University. Research profile and money are not the only currencies around here."

Poon stewed for a moment. "You mean," she said, "actions like withdrawing my participation in the Blake family prosecution?"

McNamara gave her a very gentle smile.

"For example," he said.

James Redman had called Drusilla Frost shortly after noon. She was just about to board a train returning from London. Her mother's dementia was getting worse and she had not even recognised her only daughter. Redman updated her on the redundancy situation and she braced herself to deal with the media cascade which would inevitably begin its first trickle later that afternoon. She had taken the day off and told her office to issue no comment in order to postpone the coming ordeal until the following day.

But Redman did not wish to talk only about the redundancies. He wanted to discuss McNamara.

"Does Robert seem himself to you?" he asked.

"I don't know what you mean," Drusilla replied.

"I'm worried about him. His health. I saw him late last night and he collapsed."

"Collapsed?"

"Well, he was pretty drunk, but he seemed, you know, beyond just normal levels of dissipation. Then he went completely comatose."

"I see."

"Then I called him at lunchtime to see how he was. His assistant said he had gone to the hospital."

Redman heard her say that she could not go into it properly right now, but as it sounded serious she would drop by his office straight off the train in a couple of hours.

Now he was waiting for her to arrive from the station when he got a call from McNamara. He was standing in his office. He preferred not to sit because his ungovernable inter-thigh area, in his mental imaginings at least, seemed more cantaloupes than jingle bells. Perhaps it was himself he should be worried about? If things continued in this growing fashion he would soon probably be able to bounce all the way home on his own two permanently attached spacehoppers.

"James," McNamara said, "I'm going to have to take Poon's name off the redundancy list."

"You're joking!" Redman exclaimed. "This is your chance. You shouldn't pass it up. Why would you? What happened?"

"Of course, I share your disappointment," McNamara said. "I'll explain when I have more time. But I need a replacement from her department. I was wondering about that endlessly annoying little Italian *sfigato*, the one who is always boasting about having met George Lucas. What's his name?"

"Oh, you mean Finocchio Piscialetto?"

"That's it. Let's ditch him instead."

"Oh, well. Agreed, but he's not much of a trophy."

"I know. But needs must. Gotta go. Talk to you soon."

Redman did not have a chance to ask how he had got on at the hospital.

Ten minutes later Drusilla arrived, looking stressed and tired from her journey. Redman insisted she sit down while he made her a reviving brew with his De'Longhi Magnifica automatic bean-to-cup coffee maker, which he told her laughingly he considered superior to McNamara's Gaggia Cadorna Plus in both beverage quality and outer styling, despite the fact that his own was about half the price at a mere three hundred pounds. [25]

When Asterisk woke up he found himself a prisoner in his utility room. He got slowly to his feet and tried the door. He must have been dragged or pushed a little further inside so that it could be swung clear of his head and secured with the key permanently lodged in it on the other side. It did not take long, however, before this key was turned and the door opened. Buckrack stood on the threshold, holding Asterisk's phone.

"What's your passcode?" Buckrack asked.

Asterisk told him. Buckrack tried it.

"You got a charging cable?" the American demanded.

"Yes, it should be on the kitchen top near the cooker."

Buckrack looked over his shoulder. "Okay," he said, "let's get moving. Pack an overnight bag. We're going for a drive."

Fifteen minutes later Buckrack, after inspecting with thoroughness the items Asterisk had put into a small valise, with the keys to Asterisk's car in his hand, told him to get into the driver's seat. He went to the boot and put the suitcase in it, then circled round to the passenger door and eased himself in. He handed Asterisk the keys.

"Open the garage door and start the car when I tell you," Buckrack said. "I'll direct you. But first, note this."

So saying, he flashed a six-inch kitchen knife in his hand, which Asterisk recognised as one of his own, whose sharp pointed end he placed a few inches from Asterisk's waist.

[25] A duel *ex machina*?

"Don't try to fuck around or do anything brave while you are on the road," Buckrack warned. "If you do the slightest thing wrong I'll get you to pull over and throw you in the trunk and drive myself. Keep to the speed limit. Don't contemplate any funny business around a police car. I will use this knife if I have to."

Asterisk gave as harmless a sidelong look as he could muster and nodded. It was only now that he was sitting in proximity to the American that he could smell soap and shampoo. Buckrack had had a shower and cleaned himself up. But he hadn't been able to disguise the ugly bruising and swelling on the side of his head.

"What happened to you?" Asterisk asked. "Did you have an accident?"

"Shut up," said Buckrack. "Now, before we set off, tell me a bit more about this phone call I was meant to have made to you yesterday. When was that?"

"It was apparently around 6pm. It got put through to my Deputy Registrar because I wasn't there."

"Your Deputy?" What's his name?"

"Elfyn Dethbridge."

Buckrack examined him closely. "Elfyn Dethbridge? What the fuck kind of a name is that?[26] His name has the word death in it?"

Asterisk spelled it out. "D-E-T-H. He's Welsh. In fact, there is a Scottish name spelled D-E-A-T-H, but it's pronounced –"

"Cut the small talk. I'm not interested. What did he tell you about this call?"

"He said it came through to him and when you realised you weren't talking to me you just left a message to tell me you had called. That's all."

"What's he like, this guy, Dethbridge? How long has he worked for you?"

---

[26] Even Buckrack is getting impatient about the unlikely names of his fellow characters, despite having chosen an utterly outlandish one for himself. As a matter of fact, however, Welsh boys are called "Elfyn" to this day, and although "Dethbridge" is now rare, modern variants of it (which were mainly deliberate distortions aimed at disguising the mordant sound of its first syllable) include "Deedridge", a name hardly ever found outside of Glamorgan.

"Well, gosh, he's been my Deputy for about five years. I don't know him too well. We don't socialise."

"You trust him?"

"I'm not sure," Asterisk said with deliberation, "that I trust anyone around here these days. Not after everything that's happened."

"Would he lie?"

"Elfyn?" Asterisk considered. "Oh yes, he would lie. But then, everyone in university senior management lies all the time."

"Does he like you?"

Again, Asterisk pondered for a few seconds and answered, "I doubt it."

"So he'd happily do you harm?"

Asterisk's head bobbed from side to side. "I expect so."

Buckrack looked thoughtful for a couple of moments. At last he said, "Okay. Drive."

As they reversed out of the garage Buckrack plugged Asterisk's phone into the USB charging socket on the dashboard.

"I'm gonna send your boss a text," he told Asterisk. "When he calls back I'll tell you to pull off the road. Now head for the freeway and drive south."

Asterisk's eyes flickered nervously. He did not say it, but he considered Buckrack his boss right now and was going to do whatever he said.

McNamara soon got a call back from Detective Superintendent Nesbit, who started the conversation by congratulating him on stepping into a dead man's gap.

"I heard it on the news," Nesbit said. "Someone should base a soap opera on your University. I mean, you couldn't make it up, could you? Usually all you get is universities boasting to the public about their marvellous achievements. With Odium you get the craziest stuff you normally only see on Netflix. Murder and suicide, terrorist suspects, a showdown with the American President. What next, I wonder?"

"Nothing, I hope," said McNamara. "I was simply calling about your request to view our purchasing records."

"Purchasing records?" he heard Nesbit say quizzically. "My request?"

"Yes, you know, yesterday."

"Yesterday?"

"When you spoke to our Registrar."

"I spoke to your Registrar?"

McNamara began to feel uneasy at Nesbit's echo questions, so asked one of his own.

"You didn't speak to our Registrar yesterday?"

"Did I? Not that I recall. I'm getting old, but I do tend to remember what happened yesterday. Has someone been impersonating me? That's a serious offence, you know. You can get six months for that. Police Act, 1996."

This was said in a chipper, humorous tone. Nesbit clearly thought there had been nothing more than a mix-up.

"Oh," said McNamara. "Obviously there must be some crossed wires at our end. I do apologise."

"Oh, that's alright," said Nesbit. "It happens."

"So, can I ask, since we are speaking, you're not still looking into the Jane Blake murder? It's just that I noticed my predecessor had received the police report a few months back, and I thought I might get asked questions about it by the University Council."

"Oh, no, case closed," said Nesbit.

"And the money that disappeared from her American bank account?"

"Ah, well, that, now that's a loose end which annoyed us for a while, but what can I say? The Americans didn't play ball when we asked for more information. Not that it's so important, mind you. We're pretty confident about our conclusion. Murder followed by suicide of the murderer. Happens all the time in our business."

After the call was over McNamara ate a sandwich he had brought back from the hospital, and cogitated. He found himself oddly enjoying his attempts to put the enigmatic pieces of this new puzzle together, and noticed that nearly all traces of his hangover, other than a besetting weariness, had now disappeared.

Buckrack had bugged Asterisk's office. He had heard Asterisk speaking with someone claiming to be Nesbit. This had alarmed him and prompted him to act. But that person had not been Nesbit. Now, who would have the daring to impersonate a CID officer, and for what purpose?

His thoughts were interrupted by a text from Asterisk. It read, simply, "I have news about Buckrack."

*

When McNamara called back on his own mobile, Buckrack ignored it. They had just joined the motorway a few miles before, and he instructed Asterisk to take the next exit ramp. He scanned the surroundings and indicated a service area with a large empty car park. When Asterisk parked up, far from any building or other vehicle, he took the keys from him and told him to stay in the car with the windows closed. He stepped out, locked the doors, put the knife in his pocket with his good hand around it, and walked some yards away on the driver's side of the car where he could keep an eye on Asterisk. He noted with some despair that he was still seeing everything in monochrome. Fumbling a little with the phone in his weaker hand, he returned McNamara's call and heard him say, "Hello, Nigel."

"No, it's me, asshole," Buckrack hissed. "Now just fucking listen. First of all, I have Asterisk. If you do anything to try to track me down, I'll kill him. If you don't do what I need you to do, I'll kill him. If you involve the police, I'll kill him."

He heard the long pause as McNamara's brain-clockwork presumably whirred and managed to get its cogs entoothed in this new machinery.

"Let me speak to him," McNamara said.

"Hold on," said Buckrack.

He walked to the car and gestured for Asterisk to open the driver's window.

"You're on speaker. Nothing about location," Buckrack instructed.

"Hello?" McNamara said. "Nigel?"

"Yes, Vice Chancellor," said Asterisk.

"You okay?"

"Yes, Vice Chancellor."

"Are you hurt?"

"Not really."

"Okay. Just cooperate with him. Do as he says. I'll talk to him and sort this out."

"Yes, Vice Chancellor. Thank you."

"That's enough," Buckrack interrupted and took the phone away. He walked some distance away once more. Then he asked, "Why the fuck did you club me on the head and tie me up in your basement?"

To his surprise, he heard McNamara scoff in a manner suggestive of someone who considered that he had the upper hand. "No, you listen to me, *asshole*. You can keep on doing your batshit crazy stuff like you're doing now but you're obviously desperate. If all you wanted was to avoid being associated with a minor bugging scandal you wouldn't go to the extreme of keeping people under surveillance and blackmailing them. You've got much bigger secrets to hide. And while we're about it, apart from now kidnapping one of my senior staff, whose safety I am naturally concerned about, why did you assault and rob another and hospitalise him this morning? And why did you steal his trousers and leave him half naked?"

"That wasn't intentional. But I needed money for a cab. I needed his pants because my own were torn and bloody."

"You hit him with a rock! You knocked him out cold. You could have killed him."

"He came upon me while I was asleep. It was an instant reaction. In any case, I was only there because you fucking decked me. And who the fuck was in my house in the middle of the night? Who did you call? Was that the cops?"

"I didn't call anybody. What are you talking about?"

"When I got to my house there was someone inside with a flashlight. That's why I couldn't go in."

"I fell asleep. I haven't told anyone about you. Not yet."

"Are you for real? I don't know whether to believe you or not."

There was a soft, slow laugh from McNamara down the line. "*You* don't know whether or not to believe *me*? Listen to Mr Sincerity."

"That's why I need some leverage in the form of your guy Asterisk."

"Christ," said McNamara. "All you've done is dig a hole deeper. But I'll tell you what. You want to hear of recent developments that'll make you realise how wrong you are?"

"What developments?"

"Okay, for one, I found your bug in Asterisk's office. It's now in my desk drawer. Your little black box. But you know what? There was a second one, very similar, only grey. Now I'm guessing you didn't put that one there, right? And if that's true, it's obvious who did. And they put it there after yours."

It was Buckrack's turn to pause and process. He stood blinking in the car park. He glanced over at the car and saw Asterisk with his head on the steering wheel. "Let me get this right," he said. "The second box was identical?"

"Pretty much," said McNamara. "So it was CIA, right?"

Buckrack did not answer.

McNamara went on. "And here's another funny thing. The police did not visit Asterisk yesterday morning. Whoever it was, it wasn't Detective Superintendent Nesbit of Buckinghamshire CID."

"How do you know?"

"Because I just called Detective Superintendent Nesbit of Buckinghamshire CID. He was never looking further into the case. As far as he's concerned it's practically closed."

"Fuck! You did call the cops. Did you tell him about me?"

"No. As I said, I've told no one about you. He's never shown the slightest interest in you. I don't think he knows you even exist. But someone does. So let me tell you what I think has happened here and you tell me if I'm wrong. How about that?"

Buckrack grunted, "Go on."

"Alright," said McNamara. "Obviously you got wind of the fact that Asterisk had been questioned by the CIA about you. After all, you had bugged his office in November before you left to keep tabs on his conversations. This is why you came back to Europe and started to watch those who had been involved in your original bugging, the ones you did for Covet, in other words people like me. But it wasn't the bugging that bothered you, rather the fact that you had done much worse things – the money, for one, maybe more – that you had to conceal. As it turned out, Asterisk played dumb about you when the CIA visited him in his office, but unknowns to him they also placed a bug there, because they knew he knew something and they were hoping to find out what it was. But it was you they were interested in. Agent gone rogue kind of thing, is it? Need to get a hold of this criminal ex-CIA guy before what he's done blows up all in public and causes major international embarrassment? I'm speculating. Quite how they realised you were the problem you are I don't know, but I am guessing it's something to do with that transfer of money to the Cayman Islands the British police asked but never got an answer about. Still, they – your old friends at the CIA – needed some concrete evidence of your involvement with Jane Blake and Covet. Obviously they weren't getting this evidence from their bug in Asterisk's office, so they tried to stimulate the situation by sending some guy in to Asterisk yesterday morning, pretending to be Detective Superintendent Nesbit of

430

Buckinghamshire CID, hoping to scare him after they had left into babbling about you in connection with the bugs – and they succeeded. He told Redman about you and they heard him do so. But you, clever guy you, unknowns to anyone at all, even to them, you had your *own* bug in Asterisk's office and heard all of it too, or thought you did. But what you were hearing was that the British police were looking further into the case. You fell for their trick too, even though it wasn't intended for you. And that's what brought you instantly out of whatever woodwork you were hiding in, to me, threatening to blackmail me in order to close down something that, it turns out, wasn't even happening. You didn't just get banged on the head. You got scammed into exposing yourself. Now they know you're here, somehow: you would know how. So, shall we take an informed guess who was in your house with a torch last night, looking for you?"

Buckrack did not reply but his breathing was heavy.

"It really is quite a plot," McNamara continued. "If I saw this in a movie I'd be scoffing with incredulity, myself. Unless it was a spy movie, of course, in which case this would all seem a little underwhelming and petty and simply not thrilling enough." [27]

At last Buckrack exploded, "Damn it!"

"Yeah," McNamara assented laconically. "The only thing I can't figure out is why you called Asterisk last night before you saw me. What were you trying to do, scare him?"

Buckrack answered, "I didn't. It was them."

---

[27] McNamara has clearly not twigged that he is in fact trapped in the genre of anti-climactic farce. Clockman presumably does not entitle his closing volume *Carry On Le Carré* (which would approximately sum up its content) because readers these days increasingly do not know what the *Carry On* movies were all about, or Le Carré's espionage novels for that matter (most of them written in the inspiration-destroying knowledge that ponderous and overrated movies or TV mini-series would be based on their ponderous and overrated content). Admittedly it is difficult to envisage Sid James as McNamara or Jim Dale as Redman, though a blacked-up Barbara Windsor as Poon or a Welsh-inflected Charles Hawtrey as Dethbridge are not entirely beyond a wild imagination. One can, however, now easily agree with McNamara's intuitive hint that Buckrack's revealed incompetence would entirely justify calling this novel *The Spy Who Crept Out of the Mould*.

"Them?"

"The Agency. It's an old baiting tactic. They wanted to frighten Asterisk into blabbering or acting on impulse. They can't get me to call the guy they want to frighten. So they call someone else and pretend to be me and get that someone else to tell him it was me and so he gets frightened because he's scared of me. Check the phone logs. I bet they didn't call Asterisk at all. I bet they called the other guy direct. What was his name, Deadhead?"

"Dethbridge."

"Yeah, him."

McNamara started in his seat. "Wait a minute!" he exclaimed. "You mean they might be using Dethbridge as some kind of misleading information channel?"

"Exactly."

"But he also appeared here today with a lawsuit."

"A lawsuit?"

"Well, a legal claim for damages. Jane Blake's mother is suing the University."

"She hasn't got a mother. Her mother is dead. There's no mother."

"Alison Blake. Here's her U.S. address and everything. The papers are from a London law firm."

"Her mother was called Alison Blake but that's bullshit. Alison Blake died in a car accident when Jane Blake was a child. You're being played. It's another piece of bait."

"I don't understand."

"Christ, you haven't got it yet? They want *me*. This stuff is done to rattle you and Asterisk into giving me up to them, getting you to help them locate me. All of it, the pretend cop, the call to Dethbridge, the lawsuit – all of them are ploys. None of them are real. They are all deceptions."

"Are you saying there's no lawsuit?"

McNamara heard Buckrack sigh. "It will all look official. There will be a real London law firm and it will have lodged real court papers. They'll have forged documents purporting to prove that Alison Blake is alive. But when you contact them to discuss the case it will be a CIA agent who visits you and they'll be seeking information about me and if you give it they'll promise to make the lawsuit go away. They may even have co-opted Dethbridge to do their work for them. Using him once might be an accident. Using him twice sounds like he's in on it."

"What? How would they do that?"

Buckrack scoffed. "How do you think? Blackmail. Bribery. Is this guy Dethbridge a saint? Does he have reason to dislike you or Asterisk? Does he have something to gain? As I say, check the phone logs. Was there really a call to him or Asterisk last night? Either way, he's bringing you chickenshit. Call the lawyer and see what happens. Call them today and set up a meeting as soon as possible and watch how quickly they come running. The person they send will be an Agency operative. They might have legal qualifications but that won't be their function."

"I see," said McNamara. "I'll do that. And so now you've kidnapped Asterisk as your insurance policy, is that it? You think I won't give you away as long as you've got him? How do you know they're not all up on his phone or mine too and listening in right now?"

"I doubt it. If they were on your phone in real time they would have known I was at your house last night instead of trying to find me at mine. There are methods of capturing phone data but since Edward Snowden the Agency pretty much has to go through GCHQ to get British call information, and they don't want the British to know about me. They want to seize me and get me out without the British being aware. As for Asterisk's phone, I'll be disposing of it after this call and buying a different one to contact you on, and that'll be just text messages from a spoofing service and you won't be able to locate the source. We've already left Odium. Expect no more voice calls."

"And what do you want?"

"It's simple," Buckrack said. "I need your help to get away. You give me that, Asterisk will be fine. You give any sign of cooperating with them or calling in the police, he won't be. I'm figuring you might not care too much personally about Asterisk, and you don't seem too susceptible to personal blackmail. But I think you might just not be prepared to let him die. So all you have to do is stall at your end. I need time. One of the reasons I need time is that you fucking brained me and I am injured and I need two or three days to recover and make a plan. So just do nothing. It's really that simple. Can we agree to that?"

McNamara said, "But I'll need to be able to speak to Asterisk frequently to check that he's okay."

"That's not going to happen," Buckrack replied. "But I may send you the odd photo as proof. You call that lawyer and I'll text you later this evening."

"Okay," said McNamara, becoming habituated now to the relentless skulduggery. Then a suitably cunning thought occurred to him. "By the way, do you still have access to what your listening device picks up if I turn it on again?"

"I do," said Buckrack.


## Chapter Ten

At around this time, Redman was withdrawing his post-climax penis from Drusilla Frost's still quivering vagina.

Their afternoon had seemingly proceeded seamlessly (but not semenlessly or without steaminess and seaminess and lubricating creaminess) from conversation to consolation to concern to conviviality to condominium to concoctions to concupiscence to condom to congress, but their consummation was not about to be consolidated by consanguinity; rather (on one side at least) it was to result in concealed conscientious contrition.

In other words, they had talked; Drusilla had expressed her sadness at her mother's worsening dementia; she had appeared worried by what Redman had to say about McNamara's possibly terminal condition and his sudden visit to the hospital at lunch time; they had indulged in the alleviation of mental distress which tends to be dispensed by gallows humour; Drusilla said she really wanted a drink and Redman had suggested going back to his place; he had mixed them some early cocktails; mutual lust was now strong enough to be acknowledged actively; a prophylactic was unspokenly considered advisable for obvious reasons even if pregnancy was out of the question; they fucked; both of them had orgasms, Drusilla first (and for the first time ever); she ostensibly found it all exhilarating; he, after enjoying the long-wished-for relief it afforded, rapidly became horrified at their impulsive perfidy, and did his best to hide it.

As he lay back on his pillow and felt his post-coital testes re-assume the comfortable size and consistency of pitted olives, he was aware of Drusilla's face hovering beside him, bearing a lascivious, shameless, satisfied smirk. He could not reciprocate it fully so gave back a tight little smile and tried to calculate how long he would have to spend in reassuring after-talk before he could put some distance between himself and what he had failed to consider beforehand: Drusilla's flabby breasts, greying hair, cellulitic buttocks and limited intelligence, as well as the now once more impinging facts of her being the partner of his long-time friend and possibly dying boss and of having personally detested her for nearly all the years he had known her.

Drusilla, on the other hand, did not appear to be afflicted with parallel neurotic seizures. She had clearly enjoyed the athletic pounding she had received, and all the edges of her previous anxiety seemed to have been blurred into comfort by it. She stretched languidly for five minutes and gave the impression of being at ease in her naked body. Nor did she seem too bothered by a need to talk. She made some dreamily intoned, flattering remark about the powers of a younger man; said that she'd have liked another drink but had better not, as she had to drive home; got up and got dressed; but left him in no doubt, as she let herself out, still simpering with deliberate archness as she left his bedroom, that she was looking forward to more sometime soon. Redman could only hope privately that when she saw McNamara again she would reconsider.

He mooned around his house for an hour. He tried to drink another cocktail but this only intensified his guilt and his sense of being the careless one in a classic mess-of-pottage scenario. He went for a shower but discovered that no matter how much he scrubbed himself he was also now trapped in a dismayingly clichéd all-the-perfumes-of-Arabia situation.[28] When the thought came into his mind that going for a run might help him flee his despair, he abandoned the idea almost immediately in the knowledge now that which way he fled was hell, his self was hell, and in the lowest deep a lower deep, still threatening to devour him, opened wide, to which the hell he suffered now would seem a heaven.

*

[28] Lady Macbeth has, paradoxically, reduced Redman to a haunted conscience. This and the blatant Miltonic allusion in the following sentence would seem to provide the warning that everyone should be given before they choose to study it – that knowledge of English Literature serves mainly to rub aggravating salt into the moral wounds of those who acquire it.

Dethbridge was still enjoying the feeling of settling into Asterisk's office when McNamara arrived unannounced. The Vice Chancellor seemed to be unusually breezy, certainly much more pleasant in manner than Dethbridge had ever experienced before. He was carrying the envelope that Dethbridge had handed him earlier that day.

"So, this lawsuit which was delivered to you this morning," McNamara said. "I'd like you to deal with it. Call the lawyer and ask for a meeting here in person, would you? Make the call today before close of business. Tell them you'd like to see them at their earliest convenience. Say nothing about my having read it. In fact, give them to understand that you have not even passed it on but that you'd like to have a preliminary discussion with them about it."

"Er, really?" Dethbridge said. "But why? I am not sure I understand. What would I say at a meeting with them? I can't imagine you would wish me to speak for the University on this matter, surely?"

"Oh no, of course not. I just want you to listen to what they have to say and then let me know while they are here. Depending on what they say, I may also meet with them. Just keep it simple. Call them, request a meeting here as soon as possible, and let me know when it is. And, as I say, do it now. I suspect they will want to meet pretty soon."

Dethbridge nodded obediently despite his puzzlement, and McNamara left.

He took out his mobile phone and tapped twice on its screen. He heard the soft feminine intonations of his American blackmailer as she answered. [29]

"So," she said, "You have news for me?"

"Yes," said Dethbridge cautiously.

"Where are you?" she asked.

---

[29] But, ah, the cunning power of literature to deceive! Until almost this point in the narrative we have been misled into assuming, have we not, that Dethbridge's blackmailer was first of all Buckrack himself but, even after that illusion was potentially dispelled, that the minatory voice at the end of the phone belonged to a man? Now it is suddenly revealed (in a manner simple to contrive in a novel but very difficult to pull off in a movie) that this previously coarse-talking CIA arm-twister is in fact a dulcetly enunciating woman. Shame on us for our sexist prejudices. What next? Are we to discover that J. D. Clock*man* is a deliberately deceptive name also?

"I'm in Asterisk's office."

"You are? And Asterisk?"

"He's, well … gone. Off sick, apparently, and will be for some time."

"I see. And what else?"

"I gave him the document a couple of hours ago. He came back to me and said he wants me to organise a meeting."

"As expected."

"But no. He wants a meeting between me and you, not you and him. He told me to give you the impression that he hadn't seen the document, like it was simply me calling you in response to receiving it."

"Right," came the reply. "Well, you go back and tell him no. Say we'll be happy to meet with him, but with no one else."

"I can do that," Dethbridge said. "But why do you think he wanted me to pretend?"

"Don't ask questions," said his interlocutor, and then she hung up.

Dethbridge picked up the desk phone, called internally to McNamara and relayed to him the bare bones of this conversation. McNamara told him to call the lawyer back and make an appointment for her to meet as she requested with him as soon as possible. Much to McNamara's surprise, Dethbridge called him back a few moments later and said that the lawyer was prepared to meet with him later this evening at, say, around 9pm? This sounded satisfyingly unusual to McNamara: what real lawyer would travel from London at the drop of a hat outside normal business hours when the appointment was not urgent and could easily be made for the morning after? Buckrack had been right. The "lawyer" was probably not in London at all, but already in Odium. The delay of several hours in the proposed meeting was most likely a contrivance to make it appear that a journey was necessary. The suggestion, however, also fitted with McNamara's own sense of urgency.

He looked at his watch. It was now 4.25pm. He called Dethbridge back and told him to instruct the lawyer to report to the security office when she arrived, where she would be escorted to their meeting.

Asterisk had spent an uncomfortable two hours at the wheel. He did not know where they were going and kept obsessively guessing as they passed junction after junction on the M1, until Buckrack instructed him laconically to travel east at Milton Keynes. His Valium had worn off and he was becoming more anxious, and with good reason. All the while

437

there was the tip of Buckrack's sharp blade in the rolls of fat that cascaded over the waistband of his trousers. He drove cautiously to the side of road bumps and slowed down at approaching small waves and troughs in the otherwise monotonous motorway surface (of which he was becoming hypersensitively aware), but even so, still he felt the near-piercing pinch of the point of the poignard become more intercostally acute every so often. It took him a while to work out that this was because Buckrack was, every few minutes, involuntarily twitching. Occasionally he was able to steal a furtive sideways glance at his kidnapper and see with mounting alarm that white saliva was slowly oozing from the corner of his mouth where his missing canine tooth had been, and sliding greyly down his chin and dripping off, unnoticed, onto the front of his shirt.

"There should be a pack of tissues in the glove compartment," Asterisk said once, hoping to ingratiate himself.

"What?" Buckrack replied, with what seemed like absent-mindedness.

"Your chin," Asterisk gestured.

Buckrack put his left hand up to his face. He did not feel any wetness because his fingers were tingling and numb, but he saw it blurrily on their tips when he withdrew them. After an over-lengthy pause he became unpredictably concerned of a sudden with comparative dialects. "Glovebox. It's called a glove*box*." He clumsily pulled at the small door (which he did not close but left open for the rest of the journey) and fished out a pack of Handy Andies.

Asterisk could observe fitfully only the phenomenal consequences of an act of which he was not aware, namely McNamara's dual hammer blow to Buckrack's cranium. The reason Buckrack was having difficulty saying things off the top of his head was that there no longer was a top to his head: the summit of his pate was visibly depressed like a sandhill after a moderate subsidence in its centre; the side of his skull around the ear was radically stoved in and brownly-blackly-redly-yellowly stained, the material displaced from the crater having rearranged itself in an alarming bulge that now swelled forward across his right temple, even pushing his brow out on that side so that a protuberant ledge had now formed over his right eye.

Fiction, fortunately, allows us to enter the heads of our characters more fully. McNamara's first blow had, in fact, not merely concussed

Buckrack, but fractured the skull at the coronal suture, the joint of tissue on either side of which the frontal bone and parietal bones align. The damage had gone as deep as the upper cerebrum, and caused significant damage to both the somatomotor and somatosensory cortices. His optic nerve had been none too happy at this vandalism in its neighbourhood, which was the reason it had gone on work-to-rule, as it were, and imposed a state of achromatopsia. The canalicular segment of his facial nerve on the right side had joined it in sympathy after being mildly mangled by the second strike, which had caused a large dent around the frontal angle of the parietal bone. This was the cause of the buzzing tinnitus in his right ear but, more seriously, the seemingly craniosynostotic effect which had resulted on the front right of the head was having slowly repercussive consequences across virtually all aspects of his brain geography. Imagine the mainland of Britain being thrust into the coasts of France, Belgium and Holland: the effects will be felt in Bulgaria. And so it was that, even on the unmolested left hemisphere, the posterior inferior frontal gyrus had begun to act up under the pressure, as Asterisk was soon to witness in Buckrack's increasingly evident misperformances in speech.

Not that there was much speech in the remainder of the trip. Buckrack guided mainly by cursory gestures with his stiff left hand accompanied by nasal grunting. Eventually they trundled into a small village, travelled its length, went past a weeping-willowy pond with two islets, turned right, then left into a gravel drive with a FOR SALE sign, and pulled up before a double garage next to a charming cottage in ample, isolated grounds.

"Oh my God," said Asterisk, at last recognising the place. "Why here?"

"Gimme keys," said Buckrack, ignoring his question. "Grout."

"I beg your pardon?" said Asterisk, offering the keys but not understanding the last syllable.

"Out!" spat Buckrack, waving the knife.

Asterisk exited the car and stood looking at the building. In the early summer heat the front lawn had become markedly overgrown.

"But what on earth are we doing here?" Asterisk protested.

Buckrack was impatient. "Grin!"

"I'm sorry?"

Buckrack grasped him by the arm and pulled him. "In!"

They approached a blue front door. Buckrack fumbled in his pocket and produced a set of keys, which he failed to apply accurately to the lock and dropped. He made to bend over to pick them up but the blood rushing painfully to his head dissuaded him and he quickly rose upright again. He pointed at the keys on the gravel. "Grem!"

"Get them?" Asterisk guessed.

Buckrack nodded minimally. Asterisk bent down and retrieved the keys, holding them up before the door. "Shall I?" he offered.

Buckrack motioned his assent and Asterisk unlocked the door. He turned and handed the keys back to Buckrack. "I hope you don't mind me asking, but how is it that you have keys to Sir Evan Covet's home?"

Buckrack did not answer but pushed him in a bundling manner through the opened door. Knowing the house well from his several visits to it, and the new-buyer-inhibiting fact that he had murdered two people in it only six months' before, he quickly located the windowless cellar, half-shepherded, half-intimidated Asterisk into it, and made the door fast behind him. A few minutes later he located a bucket and some toilet roll upstairs, opened the cellar door again, and brought the two items limpingly down the steps, still holding the knife in one hand. He put the bucket down and took a debit card from Asterisk's wallet, which he had earlier confiscated, and now extricated from a shirt pocket.

"PIN nummah," he said.

"I beg your pardon?" said Asterisk, looking with grim disappointment at the bucket.

"Gimme."

Asterisk had by now, curiously, got used to the idea that his life was in danger, but not his bank balance. "I say," he protested meekly, "are you going to steal from me too?" He suddenly wanted to Google to discover whether or not kidnap victims might be eligible for court compensation and was aggrieved that Buckrack had destroyed his phone. This line of thought was cut short as Buckrack raised the knife and displayed a manic expression on his now decidedly asymmetrical face. Asterisk uttered the PIN number aloud.

As Buckrack retreated up the steps, Asterisk heard him say, "Bringya foo soo." He translated this in his head and reflected that he was, indeed, rather hungry.

McNamara asked Meifeng to order the phone logs for the last two days on Asterisk's and Dethbridge's lines. Like almost all Vice Chancellorial requests, this one was met with the toadying rapidity with which his subjects supply an emperor's expressed needs. Meifeng received the logs from the communications centre by email within fifteen minutes, printed them out and brought them to McNamara in his office.

There had been no phone calls to Asterisk's or Dethbridge's University phones after 5pm on the previous day, as Dethbridge had claimed. Moreover, the only calls Dethbridge had made from Asterisk's office that afternoon were the ones he had made internally to McNamara about the meeting with the lawyer. The three calls he must have made to the lawyer were not logged, which could only mean that he had made them on his own mobile, and why would he do that? Once more, McNamara was forced to acknowledge to himself that Buckrack seemed to have assembled the puzzling pieces of the jigsaw accurately. Having put Buckrack's bug back into Asterisk's office before Dethbridge appropriated it, he hoped for further confirmation after Buckrack listened to the exchanges.

At 5pm he went home, where he found Drusilla, slightly tipsy and seemingly very happy, with a drink already in her hand, watching TV. She said that she had sent Chivers home and was planning (a rare occurrence) to make dinner for them both.

"How was your mother?" he asked, embracing her and kissing her on the cheek.

"Much the same," she replied.

"When did you get back?"

"A couple of hours ago," she said. "What has your day been like? I see the redundancy email went out."

"You'll have a busy day with the press tomorrow."

"Well, that's tomorrow," she said breezily. "For tonight, let's kick back and relax."

"I can't," he said. "Well, not in the gin and tonic way you mean. I drank too much last night. I have to go back in for a meeting at nine. I'm going to try to snatch some sleep before then. It's been an exhausting day. I'll forego dinner. Leave me some for later."

Drusilla did not object. Her mind was rather more enamoured with the warm sexual glow which persisted in her flesh than in conversing with the known (and now rather negligible) quantity which was Robert McNamara. This warmth was so insulating that it slipped her mind to probe him about the possibility that he had terminal cancer.

441

It was when Buckrack took the wheel of Asterisk's car to drive into Aylesbury (having taken a flat cap he found in the bottom of Covet's wardrobe which partly concealed his head wounds) that the extent of his visual problems truly struck home. The colourimetrics of his eyesight could not now have been measured in the 256 greyscale intensities of even a standard computer monitor. It was nowhere near as good as watching a black-and-white movie. It was much more degraded than that. It was not simply the colour-detecting cones of his retina which had been affected, but the light and shade-discerning rods as well. His vision was now capable only of something that fell roughly between the qualities of 2-bit and 4-bit greyscale, allowing him to make out perhaps eight shades, often stained or mottled, with no extremes of pure white (the brightest things were a murky cream) or deep black (the darkest appeared as a smoky, onyx-like grey). He now saw in distinct geometric chunks rather than in a smooth continuum, and when in serious motion, like in charge of a vehicle, this sensory deficit proved to be quite terrifying. It meant navigating a suburban architecture rendered Cubist and drained of nearly all tint.

Traffic lights were not the worst problem, although they were a significant one. He was relieved when he was able to trundle up behind a car already stationary at them and simply follow its lead, for otherwise he had no means of discerning when the lights changed. On the two occasions he found himself the lead car at a red light he waited until someone behind hooted for him to move on its turning green. But there were greater hazards. When luminosity abruptly altered, as when he drove under an overpass and was plunged into artificial darkness, he was incapable of seeing anything at all in the black void immediately before him, and then when he hit the large canvas of beckoning daylight beyond, everything became blindingly, contrastingly over-exposed and washed out for a second or two. Shadows of trees and telegraph poles cast over the road at first made him think he was about to clatter disastrously into an earthquaky, Californian fissure in the surface of the world that had instantaneously cracked open before him, and took getting used to. As he pootled through the outskirts like a paranoiac pensioner, his peripheral perception was too poor to notice other drivers casting sidelong, judgmental stares at him. Luckily he found a retail park off the main road into town, and stationed the car as close to the outlets as he could.[30]

The first thing he bought was a cheap mobile phone from a small electrical store, using Asterisk's name, address and debit card. Asterisk had not lied about the PIN number. Buckrack was even pathetically gratified that he could still manage to decipher digits and writing, but he became aware that interactions with others now seemed excruciatingly, inordinately laborious and anxiety-inducing. He could understand what the woman behind the counter was saying to him in her unusual accent, but it sounded like an interminable drone, and he negotiated her seemingly endless, upbeat questions and comments largely by means of repeated nods, grunts and affirmative ums, expecting that in disability-aware England she would simply assume, with personable charity, that he had learning difficulties or some such (which he technically now did). Then he went into a nearby supermarket and threw some ready-made sandwiches into a basket and got out as quickly as he could. Finally, he entered a DIY superstore, which was what he had really been looking for. He perambulated around it with a large trolley for twenty minutes and emerged with the following items:

> two heavy fibre glass panels, about two feet by three feet, of the kind used for internal dropped ceilings;

> twelve sturdy kitchen knives, all of the same type and length, with a one-foot blade and a four-inch handle;

> twelve packets of builder's putty, each about three inches square, sealed in plastic;

> a fifty-metre length of blue (though it looked grey to him) three-strand polypropylene rope, eight millimetres in thickness;

---

[30] This must be the Vale Hundreds Retail Park, just off the A418 at Aylesbury, which I can confirm in May 2017 possessed a mobile phone outlet called Matrix Communications, an Aldi supermarket, and a sizeable B&Q DIY centre. The description of his journey suggests that Buckrack drove towards the town on this same road. Given that his trip, though an existential challenge, was not of long duration, one is tempted to guess that the village in which Covet's cottage is located is Aston Abbotts, approximately four miles to the north of Aylesbury, not least because it has the requisite twin-islanded pond of the hamlet's earlier description (at the southernmost bend of Moat Lane).

a pair of heavy-duty scissors;

a roll of duct tape;

a hammer;

a packet of nails;

a six-pack of ultra-thin rubber gloves;

a bag of hooks of the kind used to secure curtain tiebacks.

These he tipped into the boot of the car before making the nervous but eventless drive back to Covet's cottage. He had been gone just over an hour. It was 4.45pm. He wasted no time in unloading his purchases and spreading them on the living room floor, with the exception of the sandwiches. These he threw without ceremony down into the basement for Asterisk to eat. He had no appetite himself. While he waited for the phone SIM to become network-active (the woman in the store had told him this should happen quite rapidly), he occupied himself with constructing the two simple homemade contraptions he had envisaged in his mind's eye, and which his shopping expedition had now made possible.

It perhaps goes without saying that his mind's eye was now as much, if not more, impaired in natural function than either of his non-metaphorical eyes. There is no need to keep the reader in a state of suspense over Buckrack's mental disorder when we are actually able, beyond what any neurologist might theorise or MRI scan display about his damaged brain, to make ourselves privy to his very thought processes. But still, language lets us down. One wishes that twenty-first century prose could do more poetic justice to his derangement – could describe it more gothically, let us say [31] – than is actually possible in an age in which terms like *paraphrenia, encephalotrigeminal angiomatosis* and *micropsia* comprise the appropriate vocabulary. Let us simply acknowledge that, with his pre-frontal cortex increasingly going to porridge, Buckrack was rapidly descending into what modern-day

---

[31] One suspects that the many and purple descriptions of insanity in Poe are once more being wistfully invoked (indeed, Frederick Usher is likewise described as having a "mental disorder" before his author's habitually lush language gets the better of him).

psychiatrists have (unwittingly wittily) called *intermittent explosive disorder*.[32]

He had, as we can appreciate, plenty of cogent reasons to be full of rage. It is no fun at all to have your braincase banjaxed and then be thrown immediately into a merciless, lonely drama of mere survival: it's madman-on-the-heath stuff, leads to a pointed sense of injustice, and makes mindless revenge appear a sober desideratum. There is a stage at which rage, arising as it may out of a certain emotional logic, becomes a besetting apoplexy, a caution-eradicating possession of the man by maniacal drives, convulsions of his normal sensibilities which convince him that unregulated destruction will set everything to rights, or at least equalise the wrongs. So thought Buckrack now.

All of which explains what he did shortly afterwards, when his newly acquired mobile phone pinged to signify that it was connected to the network. He called up a web page, entered a code, and listened to the recordings of Dethbridge talking to his CIA handler, made by the bug McNamara had earlier reinstalled in Asterisk's office. He sent these by anonymous FTP to McNamara's email address. Then, phone in hand, he unlocked the door of the basement and walked down the stairs.

"Havva photogra ya. Send to McNama," he told Asterisk in his slurring speech.

Asterisk stood up, relieved to have something to do.

Buckrack seemed to have decided that the artificial light in the basement was sufficient. "No," he sighed tersely, holding aside the phone, disapproving of Asterisk's instinctive attempt to smile. "Loo misable."

Asterisk complied by affecting a frown. The photo was taken. He was puzzled by the fact that Buckrack was wearing rubber gloves, but

---

[32] One should point out, on the other hand, that Buckrack was hardly free of vindictive, nay, murderous intent even before his brain was tenderized by McNamara's arcing meat-softener (whose parabola through the air, itself the cause of Buckrack's cerebral dysfunction, is a neatly symmetrical manifestation of a less recurrent ultraviolent syndrome in McNamara). But then, there's a lot of this about in the world of Odium, so much that it appears to be one of its organising principles: we have witnessed even Redman taking pleasure in a brutal, albeit imaginary, massacre of persons. Clockman can surely be indicted on moral grounds for potentially raising in prospective students the fear that they will not so much enjoy life at university as risk a savage death there.

even more surprised, as he turned to leave, to be invited to follow him upstairs for a change of scenery for an hour. "Bu behay yassel."

He climbed the stairs gratefully after the American, who stood at the top, waiting for him. He was hoping that he might be able to engage Buckrack in some humanising conversation. But as Asterisk's shoe was on the top step, the other man unexpectedly lunged at him with the side of his body foremost, barging into him with force and sending him reeling backwards. Asterisk lost his footing and rattled down the staircase on his back, his head thumping several times on the serried steps. The fall did not knock him entirely unconscious, but immobilised and disorientated him as he lay, half on the cellar floor.

He heard the ungainly clumping of footsteps coming back down the stairs, accompanied by solid grunts of strenuous effort, saw a quick flash of thin blue rope and minatory shadows, and then his trachea was painfully constricted, there were lights flashing in his stressed vision, he was gasping for air and not finding it, and his last thoughts before he departed this earth were that he was never going to enjoy a single day of his pension and would die intestate, even though he did not have a loved one to leave anything to.


**Chapter Eleven**

McNamara slept deeply for about three hours and was awoken only by the alarm he had set on his phone. Picking it up, bleary-eyed, he saw a text message on the screen which he was able to read after reaching for his glasses: "Photo. Also check email." He tapped through and noted the picture of a grim-looking Asterisk, in an unidentifiable location, time-stamped at 5.51pm. He opened his email and followed the generic instructions to download the three short audio files, to which he listened with a certain mordant satisfaction at the evidence they provided of Dethbridge's complicity with his CIA interlocutor.

He got up and took a shower and was downstairs by 8.30pm. From the kitchen came the smell of lightly burned food. From Drusilla, when he found her looking bemused and happy in the lounge, came the tangy smell of alcohol. At first he thought she was still merely merry, but after a few sentences of conversation he discovered that she was quite far gone. She seemed, nonetheless, to be in a very self-satisfied mood.

"Maybe let up on the botanicals," he said, indicating the drink in her hand. "Tomorrow may be a gruelling day."

She snickered. "Izzat what you did last night when you got so plastered you blacked out?"

"Up to you," he replied. "But how did you know about that?"

She smiled sardonically. "Redman."

"You spoke to James?"

"Yeah," she affirmed, and then added, "he called me about the redundancies."

"Oh," he remarked, "yes."

There was the silence that often intervenes in the discourse between a drunk and a sober person.

"Didn't you say," Drusilla garbled, "that you had a meeting?"

"I did." He bestirred himself, put on his jacket, and made to leave. "I'll see you later."

"I'll sleep in one of the spare rooms," she said. "Probably go to bed soon. Have to get up at six. Do not disturb."

"Okay," he agreed, and left.

He took the path round the side of the house through the long private garden that led down to the rear of the Trump Building. His sleep had been hugely restorative, and a sense of command was back in place. It was night, the sun having dipped below the horizon but its light still hanging like a bright sheet in the May sky, and warm, the many carefully tended flowers that lined his walk giving off honeyed scents and a feeling of abundant pleasure which had been missing in his recent days.

The "lawyer" who appeared in his office at the appointed time, escorted by security, was exactly what he expected from the narrative genre in which he now reluctantly accepted that he was an actor. McNamara enjoyed binge-watching contemporary television spy series, especially the ones which emphasised the bureaucratic dimensions of espionage agencies more than their sensational aspects, because these reminded him so much of life in a modern university. His appetite for them was sufficiently great that he had even graduated from the more obvious ongoing English-language specimens like *The Americans* and *Homeland* to obscurer subtitled examples like *Deutschland 83* and *Fauda*. It was often a struggle to tolerate the many ludicrous plot holes

447

and incredible twists of events that took place in the dramatically simplified reality of these imagined worlds, but they were nonetheless far more believable creations than the childishly exaggerative forerunners he had seen on the TV of his youth. He found that their wish-fulfilling shortcomings could be negotiated tolerably if they were counterbalanced by a sufficient quantity of humdrum human incompetence, error and inadequacy, as in *Le Bureau des Légendes*, whose second season he had recently finished watching. And so it was with some gratification that he noted that the woman now sitting across the desk from him – who had introduced herself as Ava Blunt – looked rather like the character Marie-Jeanne in the French drama: [33] fortyish, hair dyed because probably greying, plain, neatly but unremarkably dressed in a dark skirt and jacket, with an air of professionalism (and also, no doubt, an active microphone in her pocket and a knowing attitude when it came to civilian suckers like him). He determined to make it clear early on that he was no sucker.

"I won't ask you to get your phone and turn it off," he said. "I know they can listen in even when that is so."

"I beg your pardon?" she replied.

McNamara smiled weakly. "Whoever it is, wherever they are – London, Langley, both?"

Ava Blunt gave a slight inclination of the head and narrowing of the eyes that, he thought, might have been convincing in amateur theatre. McNamara said, "There is no need to keep up the pretence of being a lawyer."

"But I am a lawyer," she replied.

"Where did you study?" he asked.

She replied, "Cornell, then the LSE."

"What year did you graduate?"

"From Cornell?"

"From both."

"1997, then 2001."

"You did a Ph.D.?"

"Yes."

---

[33] The trilogy seems to be getting high on its own obsession with marijuana in these two slang-infused female names.

448

"Who was your supervisor?"

"Professor Arnold goddamn Schwarzenegger," she laughed, drily and humourlessly. "You'll be asking me next what my thesis was about. But you can find all that out by Googling me. I am not here to prove my *bona fides*, sir. I am here to discuss the case before us."

McNamara sighed and reached for his own phone on the desk. He pressed a button on the audio app and, on speaker, let Elfyn Dethbridge's side of the recorded conversations between him and Ava Blunt play out loud. As they did so he put a hand into a desk drawer and picked out the bug he had retrieved from Asterisk's office on his way into the building. He put it on the desk and stopped the playback. "Your property, I believe," he said, pushing the listening device an inch or two forward. "Standard CIA issue, I am informed."

Ava Blunt said nothing. She looked intently at the little grey box sitting on the desktop.

"You know I once taught the current UK Foreign Secretary?" McNamara went on. "You probably do. He phones me up occasionally. I have his number in my contacts. I wonder what he'd be forced to say or do if I revealed to him that the CIA had bugged my Registrar's office and was dealing duplicitously with my Deputy Registrar, as well as lodging confected lawsuits in the names of people who no longer exist, with ulterior motives, against a public institution, not to speak of impersonating a British policeman."

The lawyer still resisted comment.

McNamara leaned in towards the listening device. "Hello, Langley. Perhaps you could tell Ms Blunt in her earpiece what to say, as she seems lost for words? It's not quite going to script here." Then he sat back and folded his arms and stared.

Blunt put out her hand and turned the switch on the bug off, taking it and placing it in her handbag. Then she delved into her jacket pocket, took out her phone and did something on its screen. Finally, she reached into her ear and removed a small dark capsule, showed it to McNamara, and then put it also in her purse.

"Jesus," he said. "I was joking. You actually do have an earpiece and they really are listening in. Luckily, I don't care."

"You don't care?" Blunt repeated.

"Not about the lawsuit or the fact that you are CIA," he said. "But the ulterior motives, in those I may be interested. Are you going to tell me what they are, or do I have to guess? I may have ulterior motives of my own, although I assure you they are trivial in comparison to what I think yours are. Or I guess now that I have let you retrieve your property you could simply leave, and disappear, hopefully to intrude no more."

"I see no problem," she replied, "in hearing your guess."

"You want Buckrack, or the guy who goes by that name," McNamara stated flatly. "You've wanted him ever since you planted that device on our premises. I can't tell you exactly where he is, but I can give you the new mobile phone number he used to contact me in the last few hours. That should be enough to make your trail go warm. He said he'd be contacting me on a spoof number but it looks pretty much like a regular one to me. He told me he's injured and laid up and wants to buy time to make his plans. Unfortunately he has kidnapped Nigel Asterisk, my Registrar, and has been holding him hostage since earlier today. So either I let you try to deal with it or, if you don't, I call the police right after you leave here. I am guessing you don't want me doing the latter because you'd have involved them long before if you were comfortable with that, instead of pretending actually to be them instead. You presumably want to deal with Buckrack yourselves rather than let him fall into the hands of the British authorities."

Blunt considered and finally said, "When did he contact you?"

"Just before 6pm. He sent me an image of Asterisk by text."

"So," Blunt said, "why haven't you called the police already?"

"I was waiting to meet with you," McNamara answered. "If I involve the police then the whole thing goes public and this University suffers another massive reputational nosedive. You might be able to be more discreet, and probably more direct and effective."

"I see," Blunt said. "I understand. So, you wanna give me the number?"

"I'd be happy to," said McNamara. "But I need a formal letter withdrawing this spurious lawsuit, so that I don't have to report on it. I'd also like some elucidation on a couple of things. Like, why do you want him so badly? What did he do?"

"I can get a letter emailed to you almost instantly, certainly by morning." Blunt then took a breath and spoke in a way that seemed to commit herself much further. "We believe that Buckrack, as he likes you to think of him, murdered your predecessor, Sir Evan Covet, as well as an American citizen, Jane Blake. Buckrack's son had an extra-marital affair with Blake and killed himself when this fact was about to be made public. Buckrack found the son's body. He thus had strong motive to revenge himself on Jane Blake and he deliberately put himself in a position where he had ample opportunity. We couldn't prove any of this in a court of law but, yes, we can't risk someone with his detailed knowledge of our work falling into British hands. We need to secure him and get him off the scene. We've been trying to do so for months."

McNamara grunted softly in an attempt to disguise the internal impact these revelations had on him. They were of greater magnitude than he had expected.

"If we manage to do that, it solves your problem also," Blunt continued. "As for your kidnapped colleague, I'd agree with you that he has a better chance of survival if you let us deal with it quickly, in our way."

McNamara lifted his phone and toyed with it. "There's one other thing, also minor in comparison. Your involvement with Elfyn Dethbridge, the way you used him, how you got him to act on your behalf. Did you bribe him? I need to know."

Blunt shook her head. "We *persuaded* him."

"How?"

After the briefest of pauses Blunt answered, "I can airdrop you the video."

Buckrack did not play chess, but at his Great Game he had been no patzer: he had initiated espionage combinations which would have earned the respect of a Capablanca, if not a Botvinnik.[34] He had

---

[34] The suggestion seems to be that Buckrack is a world-beating grand master spy, among the most talented ever. The posthumous José Raúl Capablanca (whom we must assume is looking down on these actions between moves in a chess tournament in the heavens) may hold a certain sympathy with him because his own life ended with a catastrophic cerebral haemorrhage; the deceased Mikhail Botvinnik, a hard-line Communist who regularly acted as if his participation in international competitions was an extension of Soviet foreign policy, is unlikely to share this admiration for the ex-CIA man, though he may have a certain feeling for what we have hitherto heard from McNamara, given that he died of pancreatic cancer. But perhaps the deprecatory view of chess to be found in Edgar Allan Poe (a man whose deranged death's cause may forever lack precise

skewered and pinned and epauletted his opponents with practised precision. A novelisation of his mid-career would render him more heroic than this ending tale of its tail-end. But now that his real world itself was beginning actually to look like the chequered board, all blocky black and white, he was rapidly losing his acquired abilities in strategy, either attacking or defensive.

The sequencing of his moves was now more determined by desperate impulse than consequential thinking. Since the contents of his brainbox had been rearranged, revenge for wrongs done was henceforth at the front of his mind, or what was left of it, in his decision to return from initially unintended murder scene one to now fully intended murder scene two. To be sure, he had not lost entirely the spy's ingrained tendency to pursue the course of ruthless action which secures his aim most effectively: getting rid of McNamara as well as Asterisk would eliminate the two sources of first-hand information about him, as they were the only two people to whom he had recently made himself known. Once that was accomplished, it would afford him greater latitude to fade away undetected, to be the wandering ghost he had played surpassingly well until his current remedial revisitation to Odium had appeared, alas mistakenly, to have become necessary. Nonetheless, the blood that pumped his energies in this direction was not as cold as it should have been. His neurovascular coupling was too impaired for this any longer to be possible.

The journey back in Asterisk's car was ordeal enough in the fading evening light. In the dark of actual night it would have been entirely unmanageable. For the most part it was like playing a driving video game on a widescreen black-and-white TV monitor that was itself on the

---

specification) is really what lies behind the *mutatis mutandis* analogy: in "The Murders in the Rue Morgue" he calls chess an "elaborate frivolity" involving mere calculation as opposed to genuine intellectual analysis. Buckrack's judgment and foresight have certainly been lacking since his very first appearance in this third volume (we can now see that his forced re-emergence was like the movement of a pawn), to the degree that a couple of lost pieces of brain tissue appear now to have sent them over the edge into their opposite, unpredictable irrationality. He is no longer playing, but being played. That said, even pawns can continue to cause damage until the very moment they are sacrificed.

fritz, its screen flickering and jumping and its sound all muffled bass. Other vehicles hurtled past or towards him, or welled up into his vision as he approached them from the rear, like tall grey polygonal boxes (if they were vans or lorries) or streaking, low-lying slits of dim light (if they were cars). It was at times like running as a jackal at dusk in the middle of one vast pack, with a different pack coming the other way, in both of which giant and very speedy buffalo had got mixed up. Luckily most of it was motorway and he was able to settle in the slow lane and devote all his fraught concentration to obeying its gentle curves and cambers without the need to negotiate turns, traffic lights or urban multi-directionality. Even so, a journey that would usually last two hours took him almost three and a half, including two unscheduled breaks forced upon him by heart palpitations that arose from near accidents. By the time he parked on the road to the north of McNamara's campus home there was only a fading glow across the sky.

His plan had been to search for a ground-floor window left open against the early summer heat, or at least unlocked. He found none, but on the last explored wall of the house he saw, at ankle level, the cellar skylight from which he had escaped in the early hours of that morning. The broken glass had been cleaned out from the edges of the frame but the pane had not yet been replaced. The gap had simply been temporarily boarded up. On a chance that the cellar door inside had been left unlocked, he tried the board with his foot. It certainly seemed to give with moderate pressure. Getting onto the floor on his side, he jackknifed his legs and plunged the soles of both feet against the flimsy planking and satisfyingly felt it collapse. It did not spring away entirely and fall back into the subterranean room, but the tacks securing its top had burst loose along the edge and the wood had bowed inwards in a way that required him only to push at it firmly on both sides and lever it away. With the light board still in his hand he leaned in and was able to place it quietly inside. Then, with some grunts and stiff-limbed awkwardness, he got his body in after it.

There was now a bare modicum of late evening light coming in from his entrance, but as far as Buckrack was concerned, with his scrambled vision, it was almost total blackout in the cellar. The two things he could just make out were the faint luminosity from the gutted window whence he had come and, more hearteningly, a faint sliver of domestic light glimmering under the door at the top of the staircase where he wanted to go. These orientated him and allowed him to fumble and feel his way towards the bottom of the steps, which he then ascended laboriously on all fours, like a dog. He uprighted himself at the top and let the palm of his hand drift about the surface of the wall around the door, but could find no light switch. He then groped around the door itself at waist height and eventually identified its rounded handle. He turned it anti-clockwise, experimentally, and felt its sprung-action mechanism twist without hindrance. This suggested that it had not been re-locked on the other side. With the handle turned fully to the left, he applied some gentle inward force. But the door did not budge. He released the handle carefully and pressed an ear against the surface of the door. He could hear nothing from the house beyond. To be surer, because his hearing had been increasingly defective, he turned his face and pressed the other ear to it, with the same reassuring non-result. He took hold of the door handle and turned it once more and pulled again. He felt the faintest of shudders in its length. It seemed that the door had fallen a little on its hinges and that its bottom edge was in contact with the floor at the handle end. It was a sticky door, not a locked one. Buckrack took a deep breath, reached into his jacket pocket and fetched out the length of rope he had concealed there. Then he gave the door the kind of firm, positive tug he felt it would require to open it.

The unexpected events which occurred immediately thereafter took all of thirty seconds but had the slow-motion, lumbering qualities of a frantic dream. The door overcame the resistant force of the floor and opened with a noisy scrape, then jammed again when only six inches ajar. Buckrack momentarily saw in the hallway a black silhouette in motion, framed against bright white light from the kitchen beyond. He could not make out who it was, but the darkened human form could clearly see him, for he felt the light fully on his face. The other person froze and let fall to the floor a tumbler: there was the short, soft, gurgling sound of decanting liquid. The door was not yet open wide enough for Buckrack to pass through, so instinctively he began to struggle with it. Just as he did so the body in the interior lobby launched itself towards him with the seeming intention of crashing against the door and sending him flying backwards down the cellar staircase. At the last moment he managed to wrench the barricade fully open, but not soon enough to avoid the full bodily collision that ensued. For a split second in a freeze-frame world the open-armed Buckrack seemed to receive human contact in what looked like a passionate embrace. In the very next an anatomical chaos of interpersonally concatenated limbs and clanging heads and convulsing lungs and cracking ribs and kicking legs was cascading down the wooden companionway into the penumbrous bowels of the basement.

Miraculously, Buckrack found that he landed on top, and from the depths of his physical being found the wherewithal to overcome the concussions of the descent and reach down towards the barely visible face he knew was beneath him. He then howled in pain as he felt teeth clamp shut on two of his fingers, which he had to unplug with rubber-glove-finger-shredding agony from the mouth which had taken them prisoner. He felt blood rising to his face and adrenalin surging at his heart, giving him a new rush of strength with which he looped the length of cord in his hand around his antagonist's collar, flipped one end under the other to form a half knot and, ignoring the trauma inflicted on his bitten fingers, pulled both ends savagely away from each other as tightly as he could.

Drusilla Frost, her system awash with alcoholic spirits, did not experience much in the way of discernible pain. It was all over too quickly for that. Her head seemed to swell with liquid pressure, which is the predictable consequence of garroted carotids. As her windpipe collapsed with a faint cracking wheeze, she was preoccupied with two final reflections that vied for her attention. The first occasioned outraged surprise: she was, ridiculously, going to die before her elderly, senile, terminally ill mother. The second plunged her, in the single instant she countenanced it, into an infinite-seeming despair whose actual hold upon her living soul proved at least mercifully brief: never again would she feel the thunderous thwack of James Redman's dyadic ivory snooker balls against the wide-open pocket of her perinaeum. No one's life deserved to end like this, in a mere one-one draw between *la petite mort* and *la grande mort*, she might have vowed to argue with God or the Devil, had she not been regrettably ignorant of those expressive French idioms.[35]

---

[35] I do not belong (it should be clear by now) to that astringent, ascetic, slavish school of critics which demands that we accept a text as it is. I rather prefer to point out where an author could have done better. At first reading I immediately

Drusilla could have learned some things from Ava Blunt. A woman who routinely slings a .38 calibre pistol in a holster against her left breast can be expected to have meditated on the relation between sex and death. At the very least she knew that she wanted, Jim Morrison-like, to have her kicks before the whole shithouse went up in flames. And so her CIA-governed life was actually very like that delineated in similar characters in some TV series: in order to balance out the discipline and patience required by serious professional espionage, her personal life was a catastrophic disorder of short-term gratification and thoughtless excess, particularly in the sexual sphere. She was discovering that the forties was a good age, or at least good for her, because she was now senior enough to be mentoring relatively new entrants to the profession, most of whom were male and did not seem to know quite how to repel her usually very direct sexual harassment of them, or gave in to it for invidious reasons, or accepted it because for some the mere availability of sex will do even if genuine attraction is absent, or because they were just horny.

Which of these applied to Bradley Drumm, the twenty-nine-year old ex-Harvard frat boy on whose crotch she sometimes stroked the palm of her right hand as he drove them to Buckinghamshire, she neither knew nor cared. But she knew that Brad just adored the idea of a woman being so coquettish as to fool around with his cock and balls while he was driving a car (or undo her shirt buttons and flash a naked tit in his

---

considered how this callously erudite speculation might have been more cynically multi-layered by some additional authorial and well cadenced observation that Drusilla passed into death as mono-linguistically as she had experienced life only mono-orgasmically, until I remembered that we are told (in the second volume) that she is at least transactionally competent in Chinese. Still, if one is going to lather on the comedy in the midst of morbidity, which is the unruly tendency this novel relentlessly pursues, one might have added in a subordinate clause, "despite the French lesson given to her by Redman that afternoon". This would fittingly have transformed a mono-witticism, as it were, into a multi-witticism. But one senses that our author, unlike the sensuous, epicurean, Redmanish lover, is somewhat rushing to get to the end of the matter. The textual multiplicity we are offered is mere narratological repetition: not a mono-murder in a cellar, but multi-murders in cellars.

direction) and couldn't wait to boast to his friends. He pretended to blush, but she was sure he loved her iterating aloud what she was going to do with him, or rather to his genitals, when they got back to London after tonight's operation. And who among us, on the way to commit an extra-judicial murder, could say that they would not welcome such blatant, forthright distractions from everyday conduct? Given how events panned out in the rest of the night, no one would reasonably begrudge Blunt or Drumm such death-deferring lascivious foreplay.

The fact that the phone number McNamara had provided had led, when Blunt ran it through Langley, to a live connection at the actual address where the dead bodies of Sir Evan Covet and Jane Blake had been discovered six months before, was entirely convincing to her and her handlers back at HQ. Consent for her to proceed there immediately with Drumm and put an end to this vexing matter was given without demur, despite the lateness of the hour or indeed perhaps because of it: the target might arise and disappear by daybreak. It was perhaps the fact, the relief, the achievement of having at last actually fixed Buckrack's location in real time, after so many months of trying, that led the entire team handling the case to suppress their doubts about the ease with which they had been allowed to do so. Unaccountably, there was no conversation with Blunt as to why Buckrack, one of their own, had been so lax with his phone number or left the mobile switched on and so readily discoverable that Langley was able to hack its mic and listen in as Blunt and Drumm approached the house at around quarter-past midnight, she taking the front, he the rear, each giving whispered running commentary to HQ using bluetooth headsets connected to their own phones.

The listeners back at Langley had only the multiple audio to go on. But it was in the end lack of audio, an uninterrupted rustic nocturnal silence from every device, that finally told them that something must have gone terribly wrong. When they later replayed the recordings they thought they detected a similar pattern of sounds just after the two agents had tried to enter the property: front and rear doors were opened within seconds of each other, there was at both then a gentle noise like a creak, then a whoosh as of something travelling fast through air, which ended abruptly with a muffled thud which had also a bit of a flesh-and-blood squelch to it.

Thereafter there was absolutely nothing. Neither agent replied to the increasingly fretful entreaties that crossed the Atlantic and were transmitted, seemingly unheard, into their ears.

Langley roused someone in London (the very agent who had impersonated Detective Superintendent Nesbit in Asterisk's office two days before), got him into a car speeding towards Buckinghamshire to find out what disaster had befallen. But it was too late. HQ cut the connection with the agents' phones and remote wiped them as soon as they detected sounds of activity near them, about half an hour later, leaving live only the hacked mic on the phone Buckrack had left switched on inside the house. It told them little more than their man up from the capital was able to confirm from what he could see upon his arrival: the local police in the form of Detective Superintendent Nesbit and his assistants were already present on the scene.

**Chapter Twelve**

After the departure from his office of Ava Blunt, McNamara found himself slowly filling with a certain kind of joy. It was, to be sure, mainly the negative contentment of absent pains rather than the positive pleasure of present achievements, but that is what most men of his age are content to aspire to. He had just acquired information that would allow him to punish Elfyn Dethbridge, that obnoxious mosquito who had buzzed infuriatingly around his life beyond endurance; he had helped set in train events which might save Nigel Asterisk's life, a virtuous act which he did not consider undermined by the fact that he felt no particular responsibility for it and did not personally care one way or the other if it were to be snuffed out in the crossfire of an imagined shooting match (such an outcome would spare McNamara a degree of testy administrative bother, but on balance he hoped against Asterisk's death on account of the woeful press coverage that would inevitably follow it). He presumed there was a strong chance that the CIA might now rid the world of its and his Buckrack problem without noise or fuss, and he also considered himself not to have lost face in his direct dealings with them; above all, he could just about envisage the prospect that the University of Odium and his stewardship of it might not be mentioned in any further adverse public discussion, that the chain of troubles unleashed by the unruly American first invited onto campus by Sir Evan Covet may well now run out to an unremarkable end. He did not dwell on the objective truth that he was the Vice Chancellor of the University of Odium largely as an accident borne of Buckrack's many pestilential deeds; he preferred to consider how his position would be quietly consolidated if no more such deeds were possible.

He was the opposite of tired, close to chipper; he would have to wait until the next morning to exult in firing Dethbridge; Drusilla, drunk, had said she would be sleeping in a guest room; yet the warm early summer evening had a slightly magical feel to it which he wanted to prolong in company, and it was not very late. So he called Redman and proposed a nightcap and a catch-up. The younger man tried to cry off the proposed meeting, said he was exhausted. But McNamara was insistent and used to applying the moral pressure that often worked on subordinates, saying he needed some advice and that it couldn't wait, that he was prepared to come over to his place, and hinting that a confidential preview of the next instalment of the Odium soap opera (particularly as it affected the Registrar's department) was also on offer. Redman acceded. McNamara called the Security Office and asked them to order him a taxi.

But Redman was no fun. He did not even take a drink and seemed ill-at-ease. Perhaps he was weary after all, but it seemed to McNamara more that his mind was preoccupied with something else, so much so that even the dangled mention of the likely upcoming dismissals of Asterisk and Dethbridge did not appear to pique his interest. Finding him a wet blanket, McNamara returned home after a couple of hours, idly watched TV for a while to catch up with the news, took a sleeping pill and went to bed.

He was not actually woken by the unusual early morning knocking at the door: he had his dawn porter, Chivers, to see to such unpredictable occurrences.[36] Evidently this was not someone Chivers could turn away, however, for it was the batman's subsequent assertive

[36] And so the Covet-Frost-McNamara circle is closed by their explicit Shakespearian inter-association: they all come, so to speak, to feel their titles hang loose about them, like a giant's robe upon a dwarfish thief.

banging on his bedroom door that tugged McNamara out of his Zopiclone-induced mini-coma. The groggy laird of the manor did not quite catch the explanation which he thought was uttered by Chivers from the upstairs hallway before retreating once his unwelcome alarum call had been acknowledged. McNamara glanced blearily at his phone and saw that it was only some minutes after seven o'clock. Given the earliness of the hour he decided that a dressing gown over his pyjamas would be sufficient.

Downstairs, in the large dining room, he encountered a familiar face floating above the surface of the table. It smiled at him.

"Well, hello," McNamara said, barely concealing his puzzlement.

"Remember me?" came the reply. The man stood up to shake hands.

"Yes. Yes, of course. Mr Nesbit, right? We spoke on the phone yesterday."

"Detective Superintendent Nesbit, Buckinghamshire CID, yes. I am sorry to trouble you at home so early."

McNamara mumbled an offer of coffee, but Nesbit indicated that Chivers was already taking care of that.

"Is it something to do with the Evan Covet case?" McNamara thought aloud, his mind beginning to race.

Nesbit grimaced. "If only it were," he lamented. "No, no, it's rather more recent than that, though perhaps, we might find out, related."

McNamara noticed with some discomfort that Nesbit was regarding him in a studious manner. He ran a hand through his hair and sat down. "How can I help?" he asked.

"Your Registrar," Nesbit began. "Nigel Asterisk."

McNamara was waiting for a question but this toneless utterance was all Nesbit vouchsafed for the moment. Eventually he mustered what he hoped sounded like a reply ignorant of all data that could possibly have brought Nesbit here to talk to him in connection with Nigel Asterisk. "Yes, what about him?"

Laconically Nesbit answered, "He's dead."

McNamara did not need to perform his reaction. He felt the blood drain naturally from his face. Fortunately Chivers punctured the silence by bringing in the coffee, which allowed the hiatus to pass in an awkward domestic ceremony of pouring and clinking.

McNamara found himself staring down into his coffee cup with a hand on his forehead. "Good God. But I saw him only yesterday," he said slowly, then looked up. "Oh what, are you asking me to identify another body, like the last time?"

"No, no, that won't be necessary, not now at any rate," Nesbit reassured him. "We're fairly certain of the ID, he had plenty on his person, enough to leave it in little doubt. I will fill you in on the details in a moment, if you can be patient with me. You say you last saw him yesterday. May I ask when yesterday?"

"Late morning. I sent him home."

"Oh, was he ill?"

"Er, no, that's not quite it. How can I explain? We're in the midst of a major restructuring and Nigel's, er, well, his recent performance of his duties has been problematic. He was suspended pending disciplinary investigation."

"I see," said Nesbit, making a note in his notepad. "So, what, that would be around 11am, or after?"

"Maybe nearer noon."

"So that was quite some time before you called and left me a message?"

"Yes, but my calling you turned out to be an error."

"You thought I had spoken with Dr Asterisk and had made a request of him to see your purchasing records."

"Yes, well, no, what I mean is ... Nigel has – *had* – been in a very stressed condition of late, I believe, and we were uncovering many instances in which his judgment had become extremely confused. This turned out to be yet another one. I am not at all sure how he got the idea in his head that you had made any such request. I was simply acting on the facts as they had been relayed to me. They turned out not to be true."

"I see. And did you speak to him later in the day?"

McNamara gave the impression of considering this carefully. "I did, yes. He texted me and asked me to call him. Do you mind if I check my phone?"

"Go ahead. I think you'll find that he texted you shortly after you and I spoke. You then called him back and he did not answer. Then he called you back and you spoke for about ten minutes."

McNamara's eyes widened. "You've already done a check on my phone logs?" He looked at his call list. The policeman was accurate in his knowledge.

Nesbit shrugged apologetically. "It's part of the routine these days, sir. And it's why I'm here now. We find a dead man and yours is the last number he called. We're bound to check it out. But we only know that calls were made and the time they were made and how long they lasted. We don't know the content of those calls. Do you mind telling me what you discussed? And did he say where he was?"

McNamara exhaled, then stopped and looked at Nesbit quizzically. "Hang on, where did you find him? Why on earth was he in Buckinghamshire?"

"I'll come to that in a moment. It's one of the things we need to try to understand. Can you tell me what passed between you in your last conversation?"

"Nothing of any moment. He was upset about being suspended, wanted reassurance about the disciplinary procedure, or to see if he could avoid it, felt the need to apologise, said he would try and make amends. But mostly he just seemed in a state of understandable nervous anxiety."

"And did you have any contact from him after that?"

"I did. It was rather strange." McNamara checked on his phone, as there was no getting around the data it contained. "It was sent to me shortly before 6pm and was just a texted photo of him, but it came from an unrecognised number."

Nesbit dug out a phone and fiddled with it then showed the screen to McNamara. An undead Asterisk looked sombrely back at him.

"Was this the photo?" Nesbit asked.

"Yes," said McNamara.

"To be honest, if you say that's him, we've pretty much positively confirmed the ID. Can I ask, how did you react when you received this photo?"

"Well, I didn't see it 'til around eight-thirty, when I woke up. I had taken an early evening sleep."

"And?"

McNamara shrugged. "I didn't know what to make of it. As I say, he'd been behaving unpredictably."

"You didn't call the number back to ask?"

"No," McNamara said. "By that time at night I tend to leave things until the following morning, to be honest, and I suppose I just thought it was, well, a bit weird, but then, as I say, he's been a bit weird of late."

"When you say *weird*," Nesbit probed, "what kind of conduct do you mean?"

"Several things," McNamara said. "Poor judgments, stressed-out behaviour, paranoia. But, you know, these are not altogether unusual in a senior manager in a university, periodically, anyway."

"I see," said Nesbit. "And can you think of any recent reason why he may have been this way?"

"Well, not particularly, but between you and me, we are at the start of a major redundancy process, so tensions are, er, higher than usual. And that has been brought about partly as a result of the reputational hit we took from the bad press about the deaths you investigated at the end of last year. Nigel had to deal with the aftermath of all that. I haven't talked to him about it in detail – it's a subject we all try to avoid, to be honest – but I imagine it took its toll."

Nesbit nodded. He seemed to be accepting the repetitive clichéd generalities he was receiving amiably enough. "Do you know if he was taking Valium?" he threw in.

McNamara shook his head. "I'll admit that Nigel and I were not the closest of colleagues."

"Still," Nesbit sighed, "it fits what you say. We found some on him."

There was a lull.

"You were going to give me some more details?" McNamara reminded him. "It would be helpful to know what happened. I may have to prepare some kind of statement. I mean, was it an accident?"

"Oh, well, this is the thing, no. He was violently killed. Strangled."

McNamara went doubly ashen.

"I know it's a shock," said Nesbit, "but there's a more shocking thing. Do you recognise the place in the photo at all?"

"No," said McNamara truthfully.

"It's Sir Evan Covet's house. The same one where he and Jane Blake were found dead."

McNamara's head sank slowly into his hands, half in bewilderment, half in meditation. Nesbit concluded that the Vice Chancellor was momentarily speechless, and went on. "Now, quite what that means I currently have no idea. It could very possibly be some outlandish copy-cat thing, someone knows the house where two deaths took place is empty, decides for some bizarre reason to create another death there, but then, how did they gain entry without breaking in, and why would Dr Asterisk be there? And it's too much to believe it's a mere coincidence that Dr Asterisk works at your University too. Is it possible he had a key?"

McNamara looked back at the detective. "I'm sorry, I just don't know."

"I am waiting," Nesbit went on, "for a pathology report later this morning, but first indications are that he was killed maybe six, seven hours before his body was found. That's about the same time that someone sent you a photo of him. You have no idea who that could have been?"

McNamara looked blank. "When I saw the photo I simply assumed he had taken it himself," he lied.

"The phone it was taken with is registered in his name, and was bought with his debit card just a few hours before in Aylesbury. It was found in the clothes he was wearing, switched on." Nesbit seemed to be pursuing a line of thought aloud. "Now, my working assumption has to be that someone else was applying duress to him, not least because obviously another person murdered him, but that the phone itself had been wiped clean of fingerprints and presumably placed there deliberately. No calls were made on it, just the one text sent to you, as if the phone had been bought just to make that single communication. That suggests that whoever sent the photo had thrown away or destroyed Dr Asterisk's own phone, probably to prevent its location being traceable. They knew they would not be remaining at the house after they made the call, so they left the phone there. You saw him here around noon. You call me around two-twenty to talk about something he had mentioned about me. I call you back around two-thirty and we discover it seems to be a misunderstanding. He texts you on his own phone at approximately two-forty. He seems to be on the move by then. The call is from near the Odium ring-road. You call him back immediately but he does not pick up. About seven minutes later he returns the call in some agitation about his employment circumstances. We can place that call as having been made from a motorway service station on the southbound side of the M1. Almost three hours later you are sent, out of the blue, a photo of him from an unknown number, taken in a rural cottage in Buckinghamshire, the very one in which his previous boss and your predecessor in your post died. Dr Asterisk may already have been killed by the time it was sent. This is a very odd sequence of events that calls out for explanation."

464

He left this suggestion hanging ponderously between them, but McNamara said nothing in response.

"Would you be prepared," Nesbit tried another tack, "to show me the text he sent you at 2.39?"

"Yes, of course." McNamara located the message and passed his phone to Nesbit, who read it aloud.

"'I have news about Buckrack.' What does that mean? Who is Buckrack?"

McNamara's mind had been racing to get up to lying-mode speed since uttering his first explicit untruth a few moments before. "He's one of our research professors. His name had come up in the redundancy nomination process but I had told Nigel I was sure this was a mistake as he was on a fixed-term contract that ends this year and so was irrelevant. He had forgotten to tell me that he had checked on it and so was simply tying up that loose end. In other words, it was simply routine business. In fact, that's the only reason I called him back, for that information."

"Hmm." Nesbit was not entirely convinced. "You think he'd just say, 'You were right about Buckrack.' This message seems to be an express invitation to call him back."

"I agree," McNamara nodded. "But, as I discovered, he did want to talk about other things, and looked at in that light, maybe that's why he phrased it that way: so that I would reply to his text." He was becoming a little flustered. "You know, Detective Superintendent, this is a lot to take in, and it's very disturbing. It's hard for me to give the most thoughtful answers to your questions when this news is just hitting me like this."

"I understand," Nesbit nodded, a little benignly, "and I do apologise. Unfortunately, in these matters it's usually imperative that we talk to people who may be able to assist us quickly, before, in fact, they get too reflective. Their instant reactions are rather important. We can always clarify them with further talks later. But I'm afraid I cannot make this any easier, because there's more. Dr Asterisk was not the only person murdered at the scene."

"Good God almighty," McNamara reacted. "When will it end?"

"When will it end?" Nesbit repeated.

"I'm a university Vice Chancellor," McNamara explained. "But I feel that I've fallen into an episode of *Inspector Morse*."

"I see what you mean," Nesbit smiled wryly, "except it's not exactly

Oxford. I tend to hear more comparisons made with DCI Barnaby, myself."

"DCI Barnaby?"

"Yes, sir. *Midsomer Murders*. Set in Bucks, you see."

McNamara shook his head and blinked to indicate total ignorance of whatever was being alluded to in these references.

Nesbit pushed his phone across the table. "Brace yourself. I would not show you what follows unless I had to."

McNamara drew the phone gingerly towards him, reluctant to touch it, and put it in his field of view. He saw a photo in three-quarters profile of a woman he thought might be Ava Blunt, although he could hardly see the face because it was multiply impaled on four long-bladed kitchen knives, two in the eyes, two in the jaws. Further down, there were another two in the neck.

"What the hell is this?" McNamara demanded with genuine revulsion.

Nesbit winced in sympathy. "Last night a local villager was taking his dog for a very late stroll. When he passed the house and saw this woman standing in the front doorway in the moonlight he did not think too much of it. It was when he walked back the same way and she was still there in exactly the same posture ten minutes later that he started to sense something amiss. That's how we got called to the scene. To put it bluntly, the house was booby-trapped. When the door was opened a simple rope attached to a heavy board pulled back against the ceiling was released: a homemade hooks and wires and nails arrangement. These knives were cemented and also taped solidly into the board. It swung towards the door at head height and must pretty much instantly have killed whoever opened it. And not a single fingerprint to be discovered on the contraption. Do you have any idea who this woman is? The body was still warm when we found her, so we know that she died quite some time after Dr Asterisk."

"I can't even make out her features," McNamara answered. "There's too much blood. You haven't been able to identify her?"

Nesbit shook his head. "No personal ID on her at all. And, most oddly, her phone was entirely clean, not a single piece of data on it, which was true also of the young man who suffered the same fate at the back door. Our villager didn't know about him. We came across that extra corpse ourselves. By the time we reached your colleague in the basement we were prepared for almost anything. If you scroll a few images forward you will see the unfortunate young man."

"Do I have to? This is disgusting."

"I would be grateful if you would, on the off-chance that you can help us at all."

Bradley Drumm being somewhat taller than Ava Blunt, his eyes were at least undefiled in his deathly mugshot. They were open and seemed brimful of frozen startlement. The two top knives had stabbed him lower in the face. The two middle ones were in his throat. The lowest pair had lodged in his upper chest.

This time McNamara did not have to prevaricate. "I don't know who this guy is." He was relieved at being able to look away. "But this front-door-back-door thing, isn't that the kind of way police would enter a house?"

"Or criminals after a person," Nesbit said, reaching a hand forward to take the phone. "But, you see, whoever left these traps was obviously fearful that someone would come or at least expected them. You would think a person in that situation, or *people* if we are not to rule out the possibility that there may have been more than one, who had, I mean, gone to the lengths of purchasing a brand new phone and ensuring there were no fingerprints to evade detection, you would expect them, as I say, to be careful enough not to leave the phone so easily locatable, which is precisely what whoever bought it did. They even messaged you, which meant that someone knew the number. But you were the only person contacted on it. Only you had the number. No one else was in possession of it."

"But I didn't even speak to them," McNamara protested. "They just sent me a photo of Nigel. I had no idea why, then or now. Maybe they just did it to muddy the waters, cause confusion. They could have got my number from Nigel. Or maybe the people who sent the photo just aren't the same people who did these terrible things."

"Yes," Nesbit said, seemingly parried away by these speculations. "You are quite right there. I have of course considered that last possibility but unfortunately it is not one I can yet pursue. You can only work with the data you've got."

"I'm sorry I can't help," McNamara said. "But if you know where the phone was bought, maybe they can."

"Oh, yes, I have to get back to Aylesbury after the store opens and make those enquiries," Nesbit said, looking at his watch and getting to his feet. "There's usually CCTV footage. And we'll no doubt find out who these two sad souls are from their car registration. As for any announcement, I have to ask you to wait until we have contacted Dr Asterisk's family."

"He didn't have a family," McNamara said. "He wasn't married."

"Brothers, sisters, parents?"

"I'm fairly sure there's nobody."

"Oh dear," sighed Nesbit. "Though, looking on the bright side, that spares a lot of grief. I will check up on it and let you know when you can say something formal."

"Thank you."

"I'd be grateful if you remain contactable, you know, leave your phone on, that sort of thing, in case we have any further questions."

"Yes, of course."

Detective Superintendent Nesbit let the front door be closed behind him and stood there quietly for a moment or two. He had double-digit years in homicide cases and was too experienced to allow their usually gruesome features to disturb his *modus operandi*, which had evolved into a rough combination of logical enquiry based on a merciless suspicion of everyone, informed by the intuitive glory of instinctual hunches, all strongly tempered by what was possible within operational limits and budgets and his own variable sense of dedication. Like many professionals, Nesbit did not consider himself more than satisfactory at his job, nor did he aim to be anything higher.[37] He was not entirely content with the way in which McNamara had conducted himself in the interview. It was not that he could catch him out in any obvious lie or consciously thought that he had put on an act. It was, more surprisingly, that he had seemed too cold-blooded, not quite disgusted enough and far from sufficiently emotional at the horrific revelations. He had accepted them too readily, had not appeared amply stupefied and

---

[37] You don't say! After all, he readily wrote off the twin murders of Covet and Blake as a double suicide and failed ultimately to chase up Buckrack's siphoning of relevant money to an offshore account! He somewhat flatters himself, the reader must surely conclude, by daring even to cite comparisons with faultlessly successful TV-land sleuths.

incredulous. The words he had said in their talk were fitting enough; but his deportment and his tone while he said them had seemed all wrong. He was not adequately shocked. People told of the murder of someone they know do not as a rule display the wits required to hypothesize about the sensational event's details: they tend more towards speechless, numbed disbelief. They are seldom as coherent as McNamara had been. He should have been stultified, but was little more than dejected.

Nesbit began to walk across the crunching gravel towards the squad car that had brought him here. He had left the uniformed driver on the nearby road in order not to draw attention or concern. He turned around and walked backwards, looking at the grand house largely to appreciate how the other half lived. In doing so his eye was drawn to the smashed window at foot level along the side wall. He stopped and then, his enquiry still being at the stage at which everyone and everything was to be suspected, walked over to it. By the bright morning light he saw the kicked-in board on an interior surface beneath the opening. He got onto his knees, and then gently lay horizontally on his stomach. He fished in his jacket pocket, brought out his phone and turned on its light. His head disappeared inside the frame of the broken window. Then it was gently withdrawn and he got slowly to his feet, brushing down the front of his jacket and trousers, and strode away from the house.

When he got to the roadway he did not enter the car but leaned in at the lowered passenger window and spoke to the driver.

"Get someone from Odium city homicide up here, would you?" he said. "I'm going to have to go back to get this fellow to come into the local station, but when I bring him to the car say nothing. Just keep him here until the locals arrive."

He returned to the house and knocked again with the doorclapper. This time it was McNamara who opened up, still in his dressing gown.

"I'm sorry, sir," Nesbit said. "I have just learned of some developments. I am going to have to ask you to come with us to the station here."

McNamara examined him through narrowed eyes. "Are you arresting me, Detective Superintendent?"

"I hardly think that is necessary, sir," answered Nesbit. "I was rather hoping you would come of your own free will."

McNamara sighed with seeming exasperation. "May I get dressed?"

"Of course."

"Please come in and wait for me."

"Thank you." Nesbit stepped into the hallway while McNamara headed for the stairs. When he was turning on the landing, Nesbit said, "Do you live alone, sir?"

McNamara halted. "No. I live here with my partner."

"Is, er, she at home?"

"No, she's at work. She had an early start this morning."

"I see. Please don't let me keep you."

McNamara disappeared into the upper floor. Nesbit examined the closed door that must have led to the cellar and tried the handle, but it was locked and there was no key in it. He heard Chivers clunking away in the kitchen nearby.

And then there was a loud, horrified masculine yell from the top floor and a shuddering concussion on the roof above Nesbit's head which was surely, he intuited an instant later, caused by the heavy fall of an overweight human.


## Chapter Thirteen

Half an hour or so later, after McNamara's prone body had been removed and whisked away in an ambulance, Nesbit stood roughly where he had found McNamara's upended feet, near one of the legs of the four-poster bed, so that he could study what the Vice Chancellor had seen when he had slid open the door of his mirrored walk-in wardrobe.

He was interrupted by the return from downstairs of his Odium equivalent, a detective named Slim, who seemed to see himself as anything but equivalent. It was Nesbit's Received Pronunciation (and the fact that he probably knew what Received Pronunciation was, which Slim did not) as well as his precedence on the scene that had thrown Slim immediately into the subordinate role in a Padawan-Master relationship he considered reassuring and untaxing on the brain: it seemed to establish order in outlandish circumstances which a mid-landish brogue was ill-suited to bring under control. Slim had thus taken to speaking in nothing but questions he hoped would be answered, although he disguised his deficiency of initative by using the first person plural rather than the second person singular (which he was able to do despite his total ignorance, which Nesbit probably did not share, of the classification of grammatical persons).

"So we're sure that's the wife downstairs?" Slim said.

"Not the wife," Nesbit replied. He was not an enemy of the phatic but he disliked the redundant use of "so" at the beginning of sentences. "I don't believe they were married. He called her his partner."

"So do we have a name?"

"Drusilla Frost. Chivers told me." At Slim's look of puzzlement, Nesbit explained further. "The butler."

"Ah," Slim nodded, taking a note. "So are we taking him in for questioning?"

"Up to you," Nesbit shrugged. "It's your jurisdiction. But you don't seriously think *the butler did it*?"

Slim did not get the joke. He was not at all well versed in even the common-knowledge tropes of detective fiction. "But we don't suspect it was the husband, er, I mean, partner, is that right?"

"Professor McNamara? Well, it's true that there's something a bit fishy about his story which, if I were you, I'd probe," Nesbit said. "But you don't strangle someone in your own basement and leave them in full view and just go off to bed when you know a servant will be round first thing in the morning, do you? And though there may be the odd exception somewhere in history, affluent buggers like heads of universities don't appear to stoop to murder with repetitive regularity. Also, our man in the wardrobe here, he has an appropriate length of rope in his pocket which will probably have his and her DNA all over it, and I'm pretty sure we'll find that his DNA is all over her too, not to mention that he might have used that same rope on another victim just yesterday. And then there's the pieces of rubber in her mouth, which are obviously from the damaged glove he's still wearing. It looks to me like he broke in, killed the woman, and then concealed himself in here to await our Vice Chancellor. But he gently faded away before his intentions could be realised. Perhaps he was peckish and found something barely edible in the wardrobe that was actually rat poison. As usual, the post-mortem and forensics will probably tell us everything. Can't do much more with him until they arrive. But I'd certainly put money on him being your murderer, and probably mine as well. Which makes it a nice closed case for both of us, the perp having joined the choir invisible."[38]

"And do we know who he is?"

Nesbit suppressed a sigh. Superfluous "ands" at the beginning of sentences he also found an irritant. "Not yet," he said. "Clean as a whistle in the ID department. But that's part of the pattern in this particular wallpaper, isn't it?"

Slim looked around the room. He could not see any wallpaper. The walls were entirely painted in magnolia. But he said nothing.

"The interesting question," Nesbit went on, "is how he got into the state he's in. He's not a pretty sight, is he? He's been through the wringer. What was his motive? Still, can't complain. This is a day for the memoirs. Five stiffs in two separate locations within an eight-hour period. My previous record was three in two days. And the visuals, well, what can one say? Stunning."

Both spent a solemn moment admiring the grotesque spectacle of the dead man in the wardrobe. He was sitting against the dim back wall with his legs outstretched in stained trousers. At some point, most likely when his body had given up the ghost, his upper half had slumped

[38] The literary reader may consider the last comment a deliberate piece of learned condescension on Nesbit's part (Slim is most unlikely to recognise an allusion to a poem by George Eliot) were it not for the fact that Nesbit, despite his private linguistic pedantry, is not himself much of a reader but just sounds to the plebeian Slim like he might be one: actually, Nesbit thinks "joined the choir invisible" was first coined in the *Monty Python* "dead parrot" sketch. He is a kind of parrot himself, for he often repeats the unexamined popular opinion that *Monty Python* is the pinnacle of modern humour. This is why he possesses the complete DVD box set, which he repeatedly watches whenever he wishes to contemplate the heights to which he thinks comedic genius can, at its utmost, reach. His knowledge of the literary classics, likewise, is based entirely on watching film and TV adaptations. As if all of this were not worrying enough, he here confirms his penchant for "solving" – rather, *dis*solving – murders by attributing them to already dead people (Covet, Buckrack) and thus avoiding all the bureaucratic and footleather-destroying effort usually incurred in bringing them to trial. These people have often themselves been murdered, yet their murders he neglects even to posit, never mind pursue. His completion rate on high profile homicide cases consequently made him a living legend in the Buckinghamshire force. He is renowned for having proven more dead people to have been murderers than he has apprehended living ones.

forward a little and his jaw had thus dropped open, giving him a doltish, drooling, gap-toothed look. The black-rimmed eyeballs, still open, were no longer vitreous but clouding over, like two egg whites just at the moment heat starts to affect them. The skull was badly dented on the top and the side, the hair matted and tangled with caked blood, the skin on one half of the head yellowed and purpled, its surface at points having shredded off to form stringy, extruding lengths around the right ear. The face looked twisted and rickety, as if one plate of a vice had been secured on the crest of the brow and the other tightened on the bottom of the chin and the two plates had then been wrenched horizontally an inch in opposite directions, rendering the bone symmetry all skew-whiff, about ten degrees out of true. The shoulders also bowed and sloped at an ungainly angle. His right hand had fallen open with a kitchen knife still resting in its fingers, two of which were visibly sticking out of a damaged white synthetic glove.

Slim broke the silence in the most ponderous tone of meditation of which he was capable, apostrophising the corpse directly in what Nesbit may perhaps have been able to diagnose as a stab at Shakespearean tragedy, Act V, final scene.

"What are we going to do with you, eh?"[39]

When McNamara came to with the sounds and smells of a hospital around him, it was in the ambit of overheard voices. He recognised Nesbit's and did not open his eyes. The other speaker was a woman.

"When?" Nesbit said.

"Not before I have been able to examine him once he is conscious," the woman said. "There is evidence of a stroke whose severity we don't yet know. Until I see what condition he is in, you'll have to wait. The time window for reversing the damage in many kinds of stroke is hours.

[39] Despite the typical Clockmaniac snideness here, this is a suitably pentameter, if only half iambic, line. Moreover, the inclusive or royal "we" is often deployed in the closing declamation by whatever minor character has been shuffled onto Shakespeare's stage to wind things up with windy banalities (cf. "We shall not spend a large expense of time/Before we reckon with your several loves" etc. etc. These particular two lines are nothing but uncontrolled afflatus elongating a tragic play which is exiguously on the short side. They could easily be rendered as one: "It won't be long until I thank you all.")

And it's not as if he is going anywhere."

The two interlocutors seemed to melt away and McNamara drifted off again. Later in the day he woke once more and the welcome, still bandaged and braced head of William Stoner was regarding him from the side of the bed.

"You came to see me for a longer visit this time, old boy?" Stoner said with a little artificial glee.

McNamara made to respond but his tongue and lips did not move. All that came out was a throaty grunt.

It became clear to both of them after a few more remarks of Stoner's that speech from McNamara was not on the current agenda. He tried to move his right arm but it hung limply on top of the bed sheet. So he called his left arm into life while pinching its thumb and forefinger together and wiggling them in the air. Stoner went to get a paper and pen. When he returned with a nurse he laid them gently on McNamara's midriff while the patient's bed was raised to a reclining position.

McNamara stared at the little lined notepad in his lap. It slid to the side and fell off the bed. His reflexive attempt to stop it doing so with his right hand had entirely failed.

The nurse scrabbled for the paper and placed it again before McNamara, who nodded feebly and put the nib of the pen towards the white surface. Then he stopped. What were they, those shapes one drew to represent sounds? He could not find the word for them but he knew it began with a … and then he could not remember the letter it began with. There were a couple of dozen of those shapes but every child learned them young. He sort of remembered remembering them in a certain kind of order. How did it begin again? But that he could not at this moment recall.

He could, however, hear and understand Stoner and everyone else perfectly well. Eventually Stoner twigged and proposed a one-grunt-for-yes, two-grunts-for-no, three-grunts-for-don't-know system.

"You can't speak?" Stoner asked.

McNamara gave a double grunt.

"Can you write?"

The same response came. Stoner picked up the paper and scribbled something and put it before him. When McNamara looked at it, it said, "Can you read?" This made him excited and he grunted once and nodded his head and waggled his left index finger enthusiastically at the page. There were those shapes he remembered...

When Nesbit arrived again the doctor continued to make things difficult for him.

"Dysphasia?" Nesbit repeated querulously.

"In the case of Professor McNamara, inability to speak or write, but we have discovered that he can listen and read perfectly well. In other words, he is passively receptive to language but cannot actively produce it. I have him booked in for a CT scan in an hour, which will tell us the full extent of his trauma, but it will almost certainly be a haemorrhage in the left hemisphere of the brain. In most cases like this the patient improves, if at all, only after some weeks or months of therapy. It all depends on the severity."

"If at all?" Nesbit complained. "Weeks or months?"

"Well," the doctor went on, "as I said before, he's not going anywhere soon. So I suggest you check in again in a while and I'll let you know how he's doing."

Nesbit retreated and disappeared back to the depths of Buckinghamshire, emanating a trail of disgruntled bad feeling.

As they wheeled him through the corridors to the CT scan room, McNamara reflected that it was his long-term memory that was foggy. He remembered recent events very well. He knew that Buckrack was dead. He remembered pulling aside the sliding door of the wardrobe and seeing the American's slumped, discoloured, misshapen body. And he knew that it was almost certainly the double hammer blow to the American's head which had, if only eventually, finished him off. As the scanning machine slowly took multiple images of his own altered brain, he had time rather to congratulate himself. He had despatched a serial murderer. McNamara did not at this moment conceive of himself as a murderer. Nor did it occur to him that the deaths of Asterisk and two CIA agents, not to speak of fellow hospital inmate Stoner's being bodily assaulted with half a brick, had any consequential connection with his having whacked Buckrack into the middle of the next life with that handy meat tenderizer.

On the gurney-journey back to the ward it occurred to him that there was absolutely none of the customary pain in his back. To think that he had once hypochondriacally fantasised this as potential cancer of the pancreas!

Stoner returned to his bedside towards nightfall, this time with

Redman. They sat on either side of him and played a jolly game of twenty closed-ended questions. They managed to keep it so light-hearted and natural-seeming that all three of them almost convinced themselves for the time being that everything was totally normal and nothing ultimately devastating had taken place.

McNamara wondered once or twice where Drusilla was but none of the questions mentioned her, so he received no enlightenment, and was unable to ask. But he had a nagging intuition that he might never see her again.

Of course, the University of Odium died too. It was so fatally weakened that it could not ride the third colossal wave of public opprobrium and infamy to tower over it in a single year.

The Minister of State for Universities, Science, Research and Innovation stepped in to throw a spanner in the works of the always fired-up media circus as soon as it began erecting its tent.[40] She established what was termed an "inquiry". This sounded official and pukka to everyone who heard the word used to describe it on Radio 4 (which announced it with all the authority of a ringmaster introducing the next act), but it actually consisted of the Minister sending one unidentified but governmentally authorised man or woman or person of indeterminate sex to Odium, who met briefly with Elfyn Dethbridge and said, "You are in charge now. Sort it out." This anonymous person then left Odium and immediately travelled north to the city of Surleighwick, where s/he/them/it/ze met the Vice Chancellor of its University and informed him, "You have permission fully to incorporate the University of Odium. Our guy there is Elfyn Dethbridge. Tell him what to do." Having issued this ordinance, the said official returned to Whitehall and wrote an unsigned thirty-five-page document which was forwarded for formal approval to a Parliamentary committee, and approved.

Elfyn Dethbridge, who was about as knowledgeable of how the real world worked as the Elfyn Dethbridge on the desert island of Robert McNamara's favourite joke about him, did as he was told. He enlarged and completed the already launched redundancy process with the

[40] "OVERWHELMING DEATHS IMMOBILISE USELESS MASTERMINDS" spelled out *The Sun* in its first ever acrostic headline.

merciless thoroughness of a driver stopping and reversing to make sure a hedgehog is dead. By September the University of Odium existed no more. New entrants there would be welcomed to the University of Surleighwick, Odium Campus (USOC).[41] The expectation was that a change of nomenclature would make everything terrible that had taken place somehow rapidly be forgotten. And largely, in the way that a reader concludes one novel rather speedily in order to launch immediately into another, it was.

But not by James Redman. He bore the burden of the history of the University of Odium, but also transmitted it to future ages, in a very personal way. His employment was (like Avril Poon's) terminated as part of Dethbridge's massacre. When, a few weeks later, the Welshman was appointed as the new Registrar of USOC, Redman leaked to the media the video of him having kinky sex with a macho young Spaniard which had somehow found its way onto McNamara's mobile phone. This made the University of Surleighwick think twice, and it quietly erased Dethbridge from its payroll. He was never heard of again. Even in Brighton.

Over the summer, Redman moved McNamara out of the hospital into his house at 111 Maryland Lane, where he tended to him selflessly throughout a long recovery that resulted in the stricken man regaining the power of writing but not of speech. They came to form an odd

---

[41] Those of us in present-day institutions of higher learning (so high that we exist exclusively in The Cloud, like my own Booleshire University) often struggle with this antiquated, geographically situated notion of the university as a physical entity with buildings, land, a postcode, and academics and students who actually once met in contiguous spaces and temporalities. The entire Odium trilogy, indeed, is largely an object of contemporary interest because it is the very last gasp in the genre of the "campus novel" of the analogue epoch in which learning was conducted by means of discursive exchange between actual physical bodies in real time. No one now, in 2084, could cobble such an eventful narrative out of higher education, which these days is effected entirely by remote communicational means, which relies (in our inventive marketing language) on "no campus other than the hippocampus", and which in the precise sciences is entirely robotised; all of which renders impossible the gross interpersonal shenanigans which we witness in Clockman's historically notable (if artistically and morally deprecable) epic.

couple, the joined-at-the-hip double act he had once denied they were, surviving amply on Redman's carer's allowance and McNamara's disability living allowance and pension, sharing the reading of books and the gluttonous consumption of American TV series like a pair of companionable male spinsters. Both secretly considered these the finest, most peaceful years of their conflict-ridden lives. They also came to agree that a womanless existence tends to minimise the pains of men growing towards agedness.

William Stoner died attached to a ventilator in the same hospital a month into the Covid pandemic of 2020. So did McNamara a few weeks later. His last thought was, "Who the hell did Drusilla have sex with on her final day?" (He had read and re-read the post-mortem report more times than he could count.) But by then, using his own and McNamara's personal knowledge, and the copious electronic records they had both preserved from their employment, Redman had written and secured an agent for his first ever book, a five-hundred-page doorstopper called *The Fall of the University of Odium: the Inside Story*. A bidding war among publishers ensued; it was serialised in *The Sunday Times* and *The Washington Post*, its revelations of CIA involvement in serial murder on British soil making it a sensational bestseller on both sides of the pond and giving the newly elected President Biden yet another stick with which to beat Donald Trump. The two salient facts it did not reveal were the two things Redman and McNamara had never confessed to each other, namely that the former had cuckolded the latter and that the latter had murdered Cannon Buckrack. Amazon adapted it as a highly successful mini-series in 2022. Redman's bank account filled to overflowing with much wanted liquidity from many tributary streams.

Unfortunately for everyone, three years later, so did the North Sea. The Arctic ice pack lost its long patience with world governments not taking it seriously and decided to teach humanity a cold hard lesson. It cleaved in twain and pushed a fifth of its mass gently south into the Norwegian Sea. This warmed it up sufficiently to render it into vast icebergs which were then funneled into the North Sea, which heated the gargantuan masses of ice even more, especially just south of Aberdeen, resulting in the flatlands of east-coastal Britain and west-coastal Europe being entirely engulfed in ice-cold tsunamis which permanently raised the sea level by over a hundred feet. Most of Holland, Belgium and Northern France were entirely submerged. From just south of

Edinburgh to the south coast of England, the largely flat eastern seaboard of Britain became an archipelago of rare peaks which had been turned into marooned islands.

Detective Superintendent Nesbit, who lived in a pleasant four-bedroomed detached house in the Chiltern Hills, survived. He had been promoted to Chief Superintendent a few weeks before. But his work dried up in direct proportion to how very wet and thus empty of criminals his county generally became. Those who did not perish in the Great Flood fled to what remained of Britain, and so did he, outcome unrecorded.

Likewise, no one knows what fate befell Chivers.

It is well known, on the other hand, that Alice Dean became the first ever signing deaf person to assume a senior position in government (she was to be a long-serving Minister of State for Education), and is double-handedly responsible for ensuring that British Sign Language is now taught in all state schools and that no video is permitted to be circulated without subtitles. When she appeared on *Desert Island Discs* (largely guided by an impulse to self-demonstrate that Radio 4 needed to clean up its act and be more inclusive towards deaf people) she named James Redman as her personal role model of the decent human being.

Continuous British mainland now started only west of a wiggly line drawn from Newcastle through Leeds and Bristol to Exeter: essentially the ancient Celtic territories and a jagged remnant of the north of England. Redman was spared the need to join the exodus because he had earlier purchased an opulent six-bedroomed retreat in mid-Wales on the back of his authorial bounty, and was at last tasting the joys of domestic luxury which he had privately envied in McNamara as Vice Chancellor. But this did not save him. In late 2025 he was immolated in a calamitously destructive arson attack on his property carried out by Welsh nationalists who had risen up against the hordes of English refugees who had invaded their homeland. His bodily ashes were scattered in the Cambrian Mountains by natural, breezy means.

With London and Birmingham literally wiped off the map, and Edinburgh too close to the North Sea for comfort, the British Parliament removed to Glasgow. The West Country, now an island, declared political autonomy in 2026, and was not opposed, its move rather spurring the Scots and the Welsh subsequently to render themselves independent of each other also (the near-extinction of the

Conservative Party in consecutive general elections made this a mere Parliamentary formality). What remained of England was accorded intermediate principality status by the two larger nations, which eventually made a treaty absorbing its contiguous territories into theirs, so that by 2035 what had been Britain was now a massively enlarged Scotland (slightly bigger than the size of old England), an appreciably extended Wales (now almost as large as Ireland), and the Independent People's Republic of Wessex (basically Cornwall, Devon and what was left of Somerset and Dorset).

All three of these polities became mountingly, radically socialistic. They were thus viewed very warily from the now much more distant European continent, somewhat in the way that the United States viewed Castro's Cuba, and in Berlin and Rome and Madrid people consoled themselves that the divide first created by Brexit had in these latter days been made absolutely unbridgeable by the enormous stretch of dismal water now known as The Gulf of Europa.

In Odium, all that remained was the hill on which the University had grown, peaked by what had hitherto been McNamara's house and what had once been called the Trump Building. To get to it you had to take a boat from a city fourteen miles to the west on the coastal edge of the Bay of East Wales, yet many thousands of people did so every year. Because Redman's book and the resultant Amazon series had made it so globally famous, the state-owned National Trust bought the functionless island from the rapidly virtualising University of Surleighwick and turned it into a profitable visitor attraction. It was often compared to Alcatraz, but was generally considered to be much more edifying. As a spectacle it was dramatically enlivened by an inert population of five thousand life-sized human figures representing past students and staff. Tourists could lodge in the halls of residence and imaginatively relive the quaint experience of a campus-based education, wander through lecture halls thronged with stationary undergraduates cast in wax in roped-off tiered seating, or see them bent over scientific experiments in the original laboratories, or leafing through actual paper books in the lovingly preserved library stacks. Most popular of all was the Vice Chancellor's abode, where people flocked as they still do in the Palace of Holyroodhouse to the very spot where David Rizzio was murdered by trespassing rebels in 1566, to see the grisly cellar in which Drusilla Frost had the life choked out of her, before proceeding upstairs to the bedroom, where had been installed a waxwork tableau vivant showing Vice Chancellor Robert McNamara staring in terror and alarm at the incipiently putrefying carcass of the notorious American serial killer, Cannon Buckrack, revealed in the walk-in wardrobe, thence up a tiny spiral passageway to any of the four turrets that castellated the house, to gaze south-east across the sea and marvel that the nearest piece of continuous dry land in a straight line was Germany.

But even the tasteful theme park or still-life theatre or static fiction that the one-time University of Odium had become could not endure. Entropy stalks the universe. Decay ultimately infects all. Erosion gnaws until its destructive urge is consummated. Even earth does not abide. The salt sea, ever washing into the caves at the base of the stranded Holm of Odium (as it had come to be called), with each relentless stroke insinuating itself deeper inside the weak chalky foundations, turning them gradually to pulp, then to paste, then into a perilous puree, contrived for it a last, memorable fall.

No one died when its 693,940,207,425 tons of ancient geological matter collapsed on Michaelmas Day, 2047 (a date ironically close to that on which students used to arrive there for the beginning of their academic year) and left a vast smear of earth drifting on the waves, which the sea slowly absorbed into itself in the weeks that followed. The Holm had been declared unsafe and abandoned for over a year by then. It was considered so dangerous that the National Trust had not dared even to venture there to recover all its installed touristic paraphernalia. Five thousand waxwork students and academics, and one serial murderer in effigy, along with an estimated 150,000 yellowed library books, therefore floated pollutingly out into the grey liquid expanse. A single male human skeleton was also discovered during the salvage operation, its limbs intertwined somewhat obscenely with a staring waxen simulacrum of a female Indian student it seemed to be using as a kind of raft, which discovery fuelled social media speculation that perhaps there had once been yet another unsolved murder at the University of Odium. These rumours did not cease with the eventual identification of the bones as those of the prophetic Professor Adrian Plumb.

THE END

www.ingramcontent.com/pod-product-compliance
Lightning Source LLC
Chambersburg PA
CBHW020825030726
47496CB00001B/95

* 9 7 8 1 9 1 0 8 5 8 1 8 9 *